PRETEND: THE COMPLETE SERIES

A FAKE MARRIAGE ROMANCE COLLECTION

ELLA MILES

PRETEND I'M YOURS

BOOK 1

1

LARKYN

"I can't do this," I say, as Serena and I walk toward the front door of Sebastian's party.

Serena cuts her eyes to me. "You can totally do this."

I'm a twenty-two-year-old virgin. Tonight that changes.

I spent all afternoon scrolling through the ridiculously small number of men on my phone. Danny, Alan, Gavin, and Pat. None of them are great options to accomplish the deed. Danny is too short. Alan is too nice, and I think has a girlfriend. Gavin is hung up on Serena, and I don't want to sleep with him so that he can make Serena jealous. And Pat is not an option for so many reasons. But I need to find someone. Hence, why I'm attempting to get into the most exclusive party of the year. To find Mr. Perfect. I will not graduate from college next month still a virgin.

Who am I kidding? I once thought it mattered who the guy was. I wanted the ideal guy, to be in love. I wanted flowers and a sunset, followed by wine, candles, and a man who adored me and wanted my first time to be special. After four years of dating and no guy coming close to the picture I painted in my head, I'm desperate.

I want sex.

Maybe my first time won't be fantastic, but then I can experience a second or third time. And eventually, I'll meet a guy to give me the toe-curling moment I only dream about now.

I stumble again in my heels, and Serena takes my hand and rests it on her arm. "Well, you can as long as you don't fall flat on your face first." She chuckles. "Although, if you fell and showed the bouncer you aren't wearing any underwear, we wouldn't have any trouble getting in either. So, it doesn't matter what you do."

I glare at her. "Well, that wouldn't work because I'm wearing underwear. And I would like the school to not think of me as a laughing stock."

"Who cares if they do? We graduate in less than a month, and you won't have to see any of these people ever again."

I take a deep breath, letting the air fill my lungs before slowly exhaling. Serena's right. I can do this.

We strut, arm in arm, up the long driveway to the door. We get behind a group of loud girls chatting excitedly. I recognize them. They are in a sorority, and no doubt were invited. They are all in short, expensive dresses that accentuate their bodies and show how much money they are from. They don't flirt their way in. They are invited in.

We are next, and my stomach is doing flips. My legs are shaky, and not just because of the heels my feet aren't used to being shoved in. My heart is fluttering a million miles a minute in my chest. I should have taken a shot with Serena before we came.

"Name?" the tall man asks.

"Serena Toomer and Larkyn Day."

He scans his list, not bothering to glance at us. Our plan isn't going to work.

"Your names aren't listed," he says.

"Let's go," I whisper to Serena.

She ignores me, looking past the bouncer, who won't be seduced since he won't stop staring at his clipboard.

"Sebastian!" she shouts.

My eyes widen in fear. "What are you doing?" I hiss.

"Getting you in so you can get laid."

Sebastian turns in our direction and grins at us goofily. He doesn't know either of us, but Serena smiles at him and his eyes drag over my low-cut dress, and suddenly he's walking our way.

"Hey!" Sebastian says, and my heart sinks. I bite my bottom lip to keep from drooling. He's hot in his dark jeans and buttoned down shirt, which is open at the top, revealing his muscular chest. All he said was 'hey,' and my body reacts like he said the most charming pickup line. I need to get laid, so I stop fawning over every guy like this.

"Hey, we aren't on the list. A mixup, I'm sure. Any possibility you can change that?" Serena asks, shoving me forward, so my body brushes against his.

I'm going to kill her for this later.

But it does the trick. Sebastian's eyes glue to the cleavage the dress makes me appear to have, and then down to my abs, defined beneath the material.

"Absolutely!" Sebastian holds out his arm to me, and I nervously take it. I cut my eyes to Serena who winks at me as Sebastian leads me into his house.

"I'm sorry you weren't on the list. I don't know how I missed a beautiful woman like you. I wish we had classes together so I could have noticed you earlier."

I bite my lip and blush. "We do take a class together. You are in my marketing class." I don't add we did a group project together last year in finance, and he has been in almost every single one of my classes starting freshman year since we are both on the same business track.

He doesn't blush or show signs of embarrassment. I wish he would have noticed me before or realize who I am. I know his name and who he is.

"What's your name?" he asks.

"Larkyn Day."

He grins. "I love that name. I'm Sebastian King."

His smoldering blue eyes look at me, and my heart is his. I don't know how I ended on the arm of Sebastian, basically the king of the popular crowd, and I know that soon, he'll be leaving me alone to enjoy his other guests, but I'll remember this moment forever.

"Can I get you a drink?" he asks.

I nod, knowing this is when he dismisses me. I look hot, but I'm not hot enough. I'm wearing a nude colored sparkly dress, but it's not slutty enough to compare with the women skirting around us in dresses that are so short they can't wear underwear. Their dresses leave no curve on their bodies to the imagination. While I, I just hope this dress is enough to snag one decent looking guy that isn't already too drunk to fuck me.

Sebastian leads me over to one of the bars and gets me a white wine without asking what I want. He gets himself a beer. I start peering around for where Serena is so she can help me find a guy for the night.

I feel a hand on my waist and glance down to see Sebastian's hand wrapped around my waist, pulling me closer to him.

"Do you have a date for tonight?" he asks, leaning down to my ear so he can talk to me over the loud music blasting through the house. The band is out back, and we are in the front of the house so I can only imagine how loud it is out back.

"No," I say, taking a sip of my wine, so I have something to do with my hands, and I can stop blushing. The wine tastes overly sweet. I don't often drink, caring too much about staying healthy, but when I do, I rarely choose wine.

"Good, I needed someone to hang out with tonight."

Yep, now I'm blushing again like an idiot. I need to stop getting so affected by this man. I've had a crush on him since forever, but that doesn't mean anything. He's just being nice. He won't be the guy that pops my cherry. Even though I should be searching for that guy, I can't pass up an opportunity to spend some time with Sebastian first.

"You don't have a date either?" I ask, finally getting my voice back.

He looks down at me, his eyes lingering on my cleavage. "Now, I do."

My heart stops. Sebastian did not just say that. I must have misheard him. He's the most popular guy at our school. He can date any woman he wants. He's fucked most of the popular women. He doesn't want me to be his date.

But the way his hand grips my waist, as he starts leading me outside, it seems I heard him right.

Eyes. That's all I see when we walk outside, where the band is playing by the infinity pool. Everyone's eyes are on me. The guy's eyes rake over my cleavage and smirk at Sebastian approvingly. While the women alternate being glaring at me and giving Sebastian a sweet, come-here look.

I swallow, trying to get the lump in my throat to go down, but it's no use. I'm not in my element. I don't do parties. I don't hang out in crowds. I don't like attention. I prefer running down the road by myself with nothing but my playlist to keep me company.

Sebastian ignores the stares and leads me over to where a group of his friends is hanging out drinking their beer and wine around a cocktail table.

He greets them, but never takes his hand off my waist.

"And you are?" one of the women to my right asks. Her voice is much too high. And she chugs her wine in one motion, before she looks at me again, as she makes a noise in her throat that sounds like a threatening growl.

"I'm—"

"This is Larkyn. She's my date for tonight," Sebastian says, pulling me tighter into his body, so I get a whiff of his cologne. It's a strong scent, and it seems he used too much, but it doesn't matter. He's still appealing no matter how much of the stuff he uses. Especially, when he keeps calling me his date.

The woman scuffs and signals the waiter for another drink. The three men standing around the table all chuckle in unison like they know a secret I'm not in on.

Sebastian glances behind us. "Dance with me."

"Um..." I don't get a chance to say I don't dance. That I've *never* danced. He takes the last swig of his beer before taking my almost full glass of wine from my hands and sets it down on the cocktail table.

His hand moves to the small of my back as he leads me to the dance floor. My body feels hot as I gaze around at all the other people on the floor grinding their bodies together. It doesn't look like dancing. It looks like sex.

My eyes stare up at Sebastian's as he stands in front of me and starts moving to the music. While I stand frozen. I don't know how to dance to this music. He doesn't seem to notice. Instead, he grabs my hand and gently pulls me to his body. He twirls me around and grabs my hips, pulling me to his body, so my back presses against his front.

His hands guide me, as his body sways to the music, and I do the same. Our bodies glide together to the beat of the music. I don't know what to do with my hands, but I find them running over his, which glue to my hips.

I spot Serena out of the corner of my eye. She's dancing with her boyfriend. She must have snuck him in.

I smile.

Tonight is going to be a good night, even if nothing else happens. Dancing in Sebastian's arms, I can pretend I'm his. Pretend I live in a world of popular kids with fancy cars. I can pretend this is what I want. And who I am.

"You smell incredible," Sebastian says, grinding harder until I can feel the strain of his erection against my ass.

I blush. I can't take a compliment.

I want to turn and look at him, but I don't dare. My knees are already weak enough. If I turn and see his blue eyes staring at me like he wants to devour me, I'll lose my mind. I'd probably melt right here. Merely disappear into a puddle on the floor. Or worse yet, he might kiss me, and I'm afraid the act of him sweeping his tongue into my mouth might be enough for my body to orgasm. Here, in front of everyone.

He needs to stop the public displays of affection before I lose it.

He doesn't listen to my inner turmoil though. Instead, he makes it worse, by nuzzling my neck. And then, yep, I'm going to lose it, he kisses my neck, running his slick tongue across my sensitive skin.

My knees buckle, and he catches me in his arms, tightening his grip around my waist.

He chuckles. "Don't worry; I got you. I'm used to women getting a little weak around me."

My cheeks are bright red now. He's cocky, but I don't care. Usually, I would hate guys who say shit like that. But not guys who are as hot as Sebastian is. Not when he's holding me tightly against his hard body. I'm especially intrigued by the hardness, which continues to push roughly into my ass. Every time I move, it grows larger until I'm terrified, but also desperate, to feel the slick beast inside me.

Sebastian King could be my first. And that petrifies me. He could ruin me for all other men. Because it's not like he will stick around after the first night. Not when he realizes how inexperienced I am in bed.

He starts kissing my neck again, and my eyes close, enjoying his touch and trying to forget about everything else. Who cares that this won't last? I didn't set out tonight to get into a relationship. I set out to find a guy who wants to fuck me. And Sebastian King wants to fuck me.

"Want to get another drink?" he says suddenly against my neck.

I moan.

He chuckles again.

Shit, I need to stop moaning and getting weak in the knees every time he speaks, or he's going to realize I've never had a man touch me like he's groping me now.

"Drink?" he asks again, reminding me of the question.

Drink? He wants to get a drink now?

I sigh. I guess Sebastian isn't as into dancing as I am with him. Drinking means he won't have his hands all over my body as he does now. But I don't have a choice. If I say no, he might stop hanging out with me altogether.

"Sure."

I open my eyes as his hand slides down to my ass. I squeak when he pinches it, and I chance a glance.

He's smirking at me, his hands guiding me off the dance floor back to where his friends are still drinking. I glance over at them as we approach with his hand still on my ass. They are all staring, and then the woman who asked who I was before is no longer blinking her eyelashes as she glares, trying to make me disappear with her eyes.

I swallow hard and turn my glance away from them, trying to keep my confidence to continue letting Sebastian touch me like he is.

My eyes lock with a pair of dark eyes. The eyes of a man sitting by himself. He's holding a full whiskey glass, wearing a dark suit, which makes him blend in with the darkness around him. I can't get a good look at his features, except for his eyes. Intensely would be an understatement. This man has already undressed me with his eyes, peeled off a few layers of skin, and reached my soul.

I don't know who he is or why he's staring. He glances away a second later, and I'm not even sure if he was staring at me.

I turn my attention back to the table as we stop at the edge of it.

A waiter appears the second she sees Sebastian off the dance floor and without a drink.

"Wine again or something stronger?" he asks me.

My stomach churns and my heart races.

"Stronger."

He grins, liking my answer. He speaks to the waiter, but I don't hear what he says, and a few minutes later I've taken three shots of tequila. I feel good. Amazing. And I no longer give a shit what Avril and Naomi think of me. That's what the bitches' names are, I've learned.

I've also learned drinking with Sebastian is just as enjoyable as dancing. He's spent the entire time with his arms wrapped around my body while he presses against me from behind. The only time he ever stops is when he has to speak with the waiter to get us another round of drinks.

"Hell yes!" Blake says. This is the third time I've heard him say, 'hell yes' to anything anyone suggests, so it's not surprising he says it now.

"Fuck yea. It's finally warm enough to use the pool without you women complaining it's cold," Duncan says, eyeing Naomi.

Naomi doesn't look at Duncan's hungry eyes. She's only interested in Sebastian's. I try not to let any jealousy in. But I know Naomi and Sebastian have hooked up before. And if I don't hold Sebastian's attention, he could easily decide Naomi is the better option for tonight.

Sebastian holds a shot of tequila out to me, and I grab the glass, although I'm not sure if my stomach can handle another.

I suck in a sharp breath when I feel him place the salt on my neck. I've seen several of the men do it to some of the other girls here before. But he's never done it to me.

I feel lightheaded, like I'm floating out of my body. Even though he's had his mouth on my neck several times now, this feels more intimate.

"Shots!" Duncan yells.

Then, Sebastian's mouth is on my neck, sucking, as he licks the salt off, and then we both do the shot. I shake my head, hating the taste since I forgot the salt first. I need to try this game in reverse, so I get to lick the salt of one of his body parts. But I'm not brazen enough to try it, not without his suggestion.

He grabs for a lime and expertly drops it, so it buries in my cleavage. I go to snatch it, but he spins me around and leans down, retrieving it with his teeth as his lips brush over my cleavage.

My body warms, and my thoughts shatter. That was…hot.

He sucks on the lime a minute and removes it, smirking at me as usual.

I'm frozen. I can't move. I'm pretty sure I just dreamed that, because there is no way Sebastian had his face buried between my breasts.

But I get an evil glare again from Naomi, and I know it happened.

Sebastian interlocks his hand with mine, and he tugs me toward the pool, which has been mostly empty the entire night, except for the occasional drunk guy who decides to toss a girl into the pool fully clothed. *Why do guys think that's a good idea?* Women *hate* it. There is no way they are persuading any woman to sleep with them after that.

I glance around, looking for the pool house or someplace where people are changing clothes. I don't see one, but this house is large enough I'm sure there is one.

My eyes pop open when I see Naomi grab the hem of her dress and jerk it over her head until she's left in nothing but her black lacy thong underwear. Her dress was low cut, so she isn't wearing a bra, and she has no problem with the stares she's getting. I'm pretty sure every man in the area's erection grew at the sight of her.

Shit.

I can't strip. I'm not wearing a bra either, and there is no way any guy here is going to be impressed by my much smaller chest.

Women all around me continue stripping down to their bras and underwear, while the men remove their dress pants and jackets down to their underwear.

"Oh!" I squeal unexpectedly, when one of the guys strips until he's butt naked.

Sebastian laughs.

"Don't worry. I won't let Duncan touch you or come near you. You're mine, for tonight," Sebastian says.

I grin like an idiot. I love hearing him call me *his*.

But my grin falters the second I see Sebastian begin to strip next to me. His shirt is gone, revealing the muscles I've been feeling all night, and then his pants are gone, making his erection much more noticeable beneath his boxer briefs.

I gulp as my eyes rake over his body and become glued to his straining cock. I need to stop staring, but I can't. I want to know what that glorious erection would feel like rocking in my body. But it also terrifies me because I'm not sure my body is ready for such a massive intrusion.

"Like what you see?" he chuckles in my ear.

I force my eyes to drag up to his eyes instead of his cock. But my heart hates me a little for it.

"Sorry."

He lifts my chin up and then his lips are on mine. Exploring, tasting, devouring.

He stops and kisses me a moment later. "Don't be sorry," he says like the kiss was nothing.

Kisses mean nothing to a guy like Sebastian, but to me, kisses like that are rare. No, kisses like that never happen in my world.

I'm frozen as I watch Sebastian walk to the pool's diving board.

"Come on, baby," he says, doing a flip before diving in, in a perfect arch. His body gracefully hits the water and people cheer, holding up their hands, giving him a score of a ten for his incredible dive.

My mouth drops open, and I know I'm drooling. I snap my mouth shut, but it doesn't stop my erratic breathing.

I start taking a step forward, needing to be in Sebastian's arms. I realize I'm supposed to strip, so I hesitate at the edge of the pool while a dozen or so eyes stare up at me.

My hands tremble. I can't do this. I can't strip in front of these people. I'm not ashamed of my body, in fact, I love my body. But these people come from money. They have perfect bodies to go with their flashy dresses and expensive houses. Their parents have provided them with an incredible start to life with substantial trust funds waiting for them when they graduate to turn into billion-dollar businesses.

They are elite, while I'm ordinary. I may have abs of steel, but I don't come from money. I didn't get a boob-job like half the women in the pool to add curves. I'm flat, yet strong. And I have no intention of showing them just how ordinary I am.

Sebastian stares up at me expectedly, but even his gorgeous body isn't enough to convince me to strip naked.

Then, I see Naomi swimming toward him planning on taking

advantage of my hesitation. If I don't jump in, she'll be the one in Sebastian's bed tonight. Not me.

My hand goes to my back, pulling on the zipper without thinking. The zipper slides halfway down and then stops. No matter how hard I pull the zipper, it won't budge.

Naomi swims faster, and I jerk my body, trying to get the damn zipper to go down far enough that I can rip the dress over my head. The jerking makes me lose my balance though, and before I realize what's happening, I feel the warm water consuming me as I crash into the pool.

I pop my head back up hoping people won't care, but of course, they care. Laughter, hysterical laughter is breaking out all around me. Even Sebastian is laughing at me.

Dammit.

I give up. I can't fit in with these people even for one night. Not long enough to get laid, that's for sure. I should have stuck with someone in my own league.

Sebastian swims toward me.

"Here, let me help you," he says.

"No, that's ok—"

I stop when his hands touch my back. In the few moments of embarrassment, I forgot how electrifying it feels to have his hands on my skin.

He unzips the dress and reaches for the hem, pulling the dress off my wet body. No one can see my body under the water. This might actually work out for me. Then I move and realize my stupid heels are still on.

Before I realize what's happening, Sebastian has lifted me to the edge of the pool so that he can work on removing my shoes.

Silence.

I glance around, as the stares burn into my body. No one is laughing. And the men are wide-eyed as they stare at my body. My cheeks flush and my heart races, but I soon realize they are looking at me like they ogled at Naomi. Even some of the women are gazing at me appreciatively.

"Wow," Sebastian says, as he removes my second shoe. Somehow he already removed the first one without me noticing.

My eyes fall to his, as he stares at my boobs, and then my abs, like I did his cock earlier.

"Like what you see?" I ask, boldly repeating his words.

He smirks and grabs my waist, pulling me back into the pool and to his body.

"Fuck yea. Incredible."

I smile.

"How did you get abs like this?" he asks, raking his fingers over my stomach. "I might need some tips." He winks.

I laugh. "I don't think you need help getting abs." I glance down at his eight-pack.

He shrugs. "I guess we have something in common."

He kisses my lips again without warning, while my legs wrap around his waist and my arms wrap around his neck. I've never been this naked with a man before. But I'm not sure I want to wear clothes ever again.

His kisses trail down my neck, and I shiver.

"You cold?" he asks.

I shake my head no, as I shudder again when he licks my neck.

He smirks. "We are getting out. Larkyn's cold."

I pout. "I'm not—"

His lips slam into mine again, shutting me up. I moan as his tongue brushes against mine. I kiss him back hungrily, knowing at least my kissing skills are on par. But if he wants sex or a blow job, he's going to have to take the lead, because I have no clue what I'm doing.

He finally forces me to stop kissing when I realize the others are protesting us leaving the pool.

"I'm sorry, but Larkyn's cold. I'm going to get her some clothes from upstairs to change into. You guys enjoy the pool. We will see you later." He winks at me to play along with being cold.

"Yes, I'm so cold," I say, faking trembling again to keep up the ruse.

Sebastian chuckles as he carries me up the steps of the pool. I keep my legs wrapped around his waist, and my front pressed firmly against his chest, so no one gets a view of my breasts again.

"Let's get you into some dry clothes, but first you need to get naked and have a hot shower to warm you up."

I bite my lip to keep from smiling too brightly because I know what he's not saying. He wants to fuck me. And I'm more than happy to let him.

2

LARKYN

SEBASTIAN PUSHES the door open to his bedroom and kicks it shut behind him.

"Should you lock that?" I ask, between kisses, but I realize I don't care if the door is locked or not. If locking the door means having to stop kissing for a second, then I prefer unlocked.

He doesn't answer me. He kisses me until I'm moaning and purring like a kitten without an off switch.

He pushes me back against the bed, as his rocklike body stays cemented to mine, our smooth wet skin slick against each other.

"Fuck, why didn't I find you earlier?" he growls, as he leans back to earn a view of my body again.

My instinct is to cover my body, but then I notice the way his nostrils flare every time he takes a breath. The way his lips part a little more and his breathing is erratic with every gaze of my body. He wants my body. Just as I want his.

His fingers move down my body and hook into my white cotton panties. Most women wear lace thongs or nothing at all. I didn't want to lose my virginity while feeling like someone else. But now, in this moment, I wish I'd borrowed something of Serena's as she offered. At least I shaved.

My heart pounds in my chest as his fingers start lowering my panties. Fluttering creeps up from deep in my belly. And an unfamiliar ache throbs between my legs, begging for relief.

This is it. I'm going to be completely naked in front of a man. And he's going to fuck me.

This is my last chance to back out. His eyes stare at mine, give me one final warning to back out now, because once he starts, there is no stopping him. But I don't want him to stop.

My friends told me their first times were horrible. The guy was inexperienced and didn't know what he was doing. But my first time is going to be incredible. Because I'm doing it with Sebastian fucking King. The king of experience, and the epitome of sexiness.

I swallow, trying to find my voice to tell him this is precisely what I want. But swallowing doesn't do enough to give me a voice. I have none. Sebastian stole it. It's his now, like every other part of my body. I hope I can retrieve it when he's done with me. Because otherwise, this is going to hurt like a motherfucker when he leaves.

He leers like he knows exactly what he's doing. Ruining me. Making my body experience things I didn't think I could feel for a man I just met. Then shred my heart.

It's still worth it.

He starts lowering my panties, and my hips buck, impatiently needing him to move faster. Not because I'm afraid one of us will back out, but because my body literally can't handle another second of being a virgin. I need his cock inside me, the ache between my legs is building, and I can't hold it off any longer.

I need him rocking back and forth in an exquisite way, making me scream his name and want him forever. I'm not stupid; I know I only get him for tonight. My name doesn't have enough pull in this town for him to want me for more than one night. And I'm not experienced enough to make sex worth him coming back for more.

"You need to get your ass back downstairs now. Duncan got in a fight with James over Naomi," a beaming voice makes me jump.

Sebastian curses under his breath, but doesn't move as he

frowns, straddling my body on the bed, like he's going to regret his next move.

I can't see who entered Sebastian's bedroom, Sebastian's body is still covering me. Which means the intruder can't see my naked body either. It should bring me some comfort, but it doesn't.

"Go to hell Kade! Can't you tell I'm busy?" Sebastian says.

Kade? I try to figure out where I know that name, but I can't place it. It's familiar, but isn't. I don't think I've had any classes with a Kade, and I don't think Sebastian has any close friends named Kade. I don't know what the hell he is doing here.

"I don't give a shit. I'm not here to clean up your messes."

Sebastian rolls his eyes and turns his head abruptly toward the intruder as his still hard cock presses deeper between my legs. So close, yet so far.

"Then, why are you here? I thought you were here to look out for your little brother and to celebrate me graduating next month. I thought you grew a heart and gave a shit about me?"

Kade growls. "I am here for you. You're an adult now, though. I'm not dealing with this shit anymore. You do what you want, just thought you should know Duncan and James are fighting. Last I checked, they broke two bar stools and were getting close to the big screen TV of yours. And I'm pretty sure Mrs. Plitt called the cops."

"Shit," Sebastian curses, as his body springs off of me and races out of the room.

I don't rank as high as his TV. My eyes water, but I blink once, and the threat of tears is gone. I won't cry over a guy. No way. That won't happen. *Ever.*

I shiver, my body cold now Sebastian's warm body is no longer pressed against me. Suddenly, I'm acutely aware I'm naked except for my panties. And Kade still hasn't left.

My hand reaches out instinctively for the blanket lying on the edge of the bed. I need to cover my mostly naked body as fast as possible. Before I yell at this asshole for ruining my night.

Maybe if I stay here naked in Sebastian's bed, he will find me when he returns and pick up right where he left off?

Who am I kidding? I have the worst luck when it comes to guys. This isn't the first time I've tried to lose my virginity. I've had guys throw up on me, fall asleep, or get a text from an ex all seconds before we were about to fuck. This is just my luck. The universe really doesn't want me to have sex.

I jerk the blanket to my body, attempting to cover myself, as I get the nerve to glance up at the man standing over me.

He's gaping at me. His eyes take their time as he lazily explores my body with his, like my body is his to peer at.

My body warms under his gaze, and I forget why I wanted to cover up with the blanket in the first place. He's a complete stranger to me, but I let him stare at my body that is barely covered with a blanket. I want him to gape. Need him to.

It's a different stare than how Sebastian looked at me. But then, this man looks nothing like Sebastian. Sebastian has light shady hair and a fit body with a little stubble on his chin. This man is much taller than Sebastian. His hair is dark, and there is stubble on his chin and neck, although from the business suit he is wearing, I'm sure he shaved this morning, but it grew back by the end of the day.

Sebastian is still a boy. A college guy who lives for fun. Kade is a man. I'm not sure he even knows what fun is from how he's standing, like something serious is happening.

I thought I wanted Sebastian, but maybe Kade would do. He might not be as light-hearted as Sebastian is, but he oozes maturity. Kade knows how to handle a woman in bed, and the glimmer in his eyes says he would be happy to help me out.

I stare a moment longer, realizing the familiarity in his gaze. He was the pair of dark eyes I saw staring at me earlier. But his eyes aren't dark, not now that I've looked at them closer. They are auburn. Brightly glowing as he continues staring.

"You're staring," I say, pointing out the obvious. My voice is snarky, but I don't cover up or tell him to get the fuck out. Because I'd gladly swap one brother for the other.

What's wrong with me? I've become one of those women. The kind who only sees guys like a piece of meat, who are here to fuck me.

The kind who doesn't require any standards. No date. No conversation. No romance. I'm *that* desperate for sex.

He grins, and I see the little dimple form on his rough cheek. Yep, I'm one of those women who will give up my body to a sex god without thinking about the consequences. I've become the women I hate, and I won't apologize for it. I may not be able to convince a man like this to date me or take me seriously. But right now, dripping wet and practically naked, I know I can get him to fuck me. No man can resist a naked woman.

Kade closes the door Sebastian left cracked open when he dashed out. I hear the sharp lock of the door as he turns the lock, preventing Sebastian or anyone from entering.

My eyes widen, and I bite my lip to keep from smiling too wide.

I'm going to taste two *King's* in one night. My luck has changed.

He turns, and his eyes sink into my body again, making me squirm.

I want him.

He wants me.

Regret can form in the morning, now all I feel is lust.

My eyes cut to the bulge in his pants, confirming what his eyes are telling me. He wants me. There is no doubt about it.

He walks toward me, but I can't keep my eyes off the damn bulge. My cheeks flush the longer I stare, but I don't think there is any way I can be more embarrassed than I've already been tonight.

His hands press on either side of my head, but I can't focus on anything except his face that hovers over mine. He's going to kiss me.

I wet my lips in anticipation. Not sure how Kade's lips will be able to top Sebastian's, but as his lips lower and my toes curl before he touches me, I think he might be able to kiss better.

My heart pounds, my breathing stops, and my eyes close waiting for the kiss.

No kiss happens.

My eyes fly open, and he's smirking over me.

"Get dressed Larkyn, and I'll call you a car."

My mouth falls open, and my eyes widen. *How does he know my name? And why does he want me to get dressed and leave?* I thought...*shit.* He's not into me at all. His night, with his own date, was probably interrupted to deal with Sebastian's problems. But I don't remember a women sitting next to him when he was staring.

"What?" That's what comes out of my mouth. I'm a genius.

Kade pulls away. And I'm cold. And pissed.

I jump out of the bed letting the blanket fall to the bed. I'm still naked except for my panties as I watch Kade dig through Sebastian's drawers.

My anger pulses through me, but I don't know what to do with it. I'm not confrontational. I can't even stand up for basic things I want in my life. I have no idea how to stand up to a complete stranger. But if I don't do something, my anger is going to explode out of me.

"You don't get to tell me what to do! Sebastian invited me up here. I'll wait for him to return." I cross my arms over my chest as I glare at him. *There.* I did it. I told someone what I was thinking when I was feeling it. Mission accomplished.

Except Kade either didn't hear me or is completely ignoring me as he pulls some clothes out of the drawer and slams it shut, making me jump.

He gradually turns to face me.

"You don't want to lose your virginity to an ass like Sebastian."

My cheeks turn a brighter shade of red. "How do you..." I can't finish the sentence. It's not like 'virgin' is etched across my chest. The only person who knows is Serena, and she wouldn't tell a soul. He doesn't know I'm a virgin. It's a guess to get me riled up.

"I'm not a vir—"

He laughs. "Yes, you are. Now, get dressed." He thrusts the clothes into my hands. I take them because I'm too shocked to think through any of my actions.

"I don't know what my brother was doing with someone like you," he says, under his breath.

But I hear his words. And they sting like hell. *Someone like me.* Of course, I'm not good enough for his brother. I don't have a name worthy of this town. I don't have a business waiting for me to be able to take over when I graduate. My parents didn't donate thousands of dollars to the school. I'm a nothing. A nobody. And apparently, I'm not even worthy to fuck Sebastian for one night.

I want to yell. I want to scream. Tell Kade he's wrong. That Sebastian doesn't deserve me. But I've lost my voice. I can't whisper, let alone scream.

I grab the white T-shirt and jerk it over my head as a pair of shorts falls to the floor. I march toward him, hoping I'm daring enough to speak when I'm right in his face. I open my mouth and nothing.

He raises an eyebrow and crosses his arms over his chest while he waits.

I hate his smug expression. I may not be able to find the words, but my anger has focused elsewhere.

I knee him hard in the balls and turn, unlock the door, and storm out. I hear him groaning in pain as I exit, and now it's my turn to smirk.

A smirk that is wiped from my face as I hear his words, "Sebastian definitely shouldn't be with a woman like you. You're the kind who would get pregnant after one fuck, and he'd be yours forever."

Tears. Damn tears.

No.

If there is one thing I'm good at, it's *not* crying. Or caring. Or thinking about these foolish people. I don't need their approval. I'm happy with who I am. I don't want to be invited to their dumb parties. I don't want one of their elites to be my first, or my second, or third.

Kade did me a favor. I almost made a huge mistake giving Sebastian something so precious. He would have ruined me. And not in the 'now I have high expectations for sex' kind of way. He would have torn my heart to shreds when he made me realize he only fucked me because I looked hot for a moment in a dress, and I was his new infatuation. Or the more likely scenario, he was drunk and he'd already fucked all the women at his party.

I'll keep my virginity until I find a guy who thinks of me as somebody.

I storm down the stairs, and I feel everyone gawking.

Shit.

I'm only wearing a white T-shirt and my panties. I didn't think to pick up the shorts I dropped.

I hear the snickers. This should be the most embarrassing moment of the night. It's not. And I refuse to go back upstairs to put more clothes on. Not even to retrieve my dress and shoes I left upstairs. I refuse.

Instead, I keep walking through the crowd searching for Serena, but I can't find her anywhere. I didn't bring my phone. There was nowhere to hide it in my dress, and I didn't want to keep up with a purse. So I can't call her or an Uber to take me home. Not that I could afford an Uber even if I had my phone.

I should have waited for Kade to call me a car before I kneed him in the balls.

I grin again, thinking about how he's going to spend the rest of his night with an ice pack to his crotch.

Worth it.

I step out into the chilly night, my arms wrapping around myself and my legs sprouting goosebumps. My feet tingle from the cold concrete. *When did it get so cold out? It's almost May. It's supposed to be warm.*

I look down the long driveway that leads to a dark street. I live four miles from here. It's nothing, and if I jogged, I'd be home in twenty minutes.

But I don't have any shoes on.

It's cold.

It's dark.

And I'm pissed and frustrated, when I should be satisfied and blissfully ignorant. I should be asleep upstairs in Sebastian's bed.

Instead, I'm walking home in the dark. *Fuck my life.*

3

KADE

WHAT THE HELL is wrong with me?

My dick is hard, and for once in my life, I didn't take advantage of a woman I desperately wanted. Her eyes were a fierce shade of blue, the curl in her shoulder length blonde hair hung loose, and her body, *damn*. Her abs alone had me drooling and wanting to fuck her without thinking about the consequences. Her muscles rippled through her body. I've never seen a more toned body on a woman. And I can only imagine the positions I could put her in.

But she is too young and inexperienced for me. And I don't do Sebastian's sloppy seconds. I shouldn't be hard.

But I am. Painstakingly *hard*. I'm cursing for wearing such tight pants. I consider taking them off and jacking off, before heading back down, but I don't have time.

She kneed me in the balls, and yea, that hurt like hell, but it's nothing compared to how my dick aches at not fucking her. Her body was screaming for me to fuck her. I should receive a medal for chivalry after this is all over. Sebastian would have fucked her and hurt her, I would have fucker her and demolished her.

I jog out of the room to chase after her but stop after only making it to the door. I bend over trying to deal with the agony.

Twinging, throbbing pain that won't subside until I spend my night with an ice pack on my balls or by fucking a woman in my bed. I prefer the latter. At least if I'm fucking, my dick will stop suffering.

Stop being a wuss.

I force myself to start running again, and I jog down the stairs ignoring the torment, biting my lip, so I don't let out girlish screams bursting to be let out with every step I take. *Damn, Larkyn.*

The pounding in my head returns when I step foot back downstairs, the house full of beating music. *I'm too old for this shit*, I think. Most people are far too drunk at this point. Women are stripping, and I see more bras and exposed breasts than at a strip club. Men are taking advantage, pressing women up against walls, and trying to sneak them upstairs.

Ugh.

I like partying, but not like this. This is sloppy and gross. I much prefer to hang out in one of the bars I own. More control, and fewer teenagers.

I step over a mountain of broken glass. Sebastian should learn to serve these idiots with solo cups. Someone always cuts themselves on the broken glass inevitably covering the floor after a dozen people drop their glasses because they're too drunk to hold a fucking drink.

Sebastian thinks because he comes from money all his parties need to be fancy. Why can't he learn to have a college party without all the extravagance? It would suit these people better, no matter how they view themselves.

I search the main floor and peak out into the backyard, but I don't find Larkyn. She left. Had a friend take her home or called an Uber. Either way, she's no longer my problem. I need to forget about her.

I spot Sebastian out of the corner of my eye doing shots on Naomi's stomach.

I rub the back of my neck as I stare at him. He's never going to grow up. At least he is playing with a woman who understands what's at stake. She's on an even playing field with Sebastian. Unlike Larkyn, who was clueless about what she was getting herself into.

The TV is still hanging on the wall. Sebastian made it down in time to save his precious TV. And then, just as easily, forgot all about Larkyn. *Idiot.*

Smooth hands dance over my chest and wrap tightly around my neck as a boa constrictor wraps around its prey.

I pretend I can't breathe, motioning with my hands to my neck that Harlow's hands are too tight.

She laughs but doesn't loosen her grip on my neck.

"You can't resist me, so don't pretend. I like playing this game we have going on between us, but don't pretend we don't both know how this is going to end. I'm going to be naked in your bed by the end of the night," Harlow says.

I frown. No way in hell is that happening. I fucked her once, months ago. And I knew the second my dick touched her pussy it was a mistake. The sex was good, if not forgettable. Normally, it would have been fine. I wouldn't regret having sex with a woman as hot as Harlow, but fucking Harlow broke my one rule. I don't fuck women from Santa Barbara.

Women here aren't like women in LA. Women in LA know I'm only good for one fuck, and then they need to move on to the next millionaire or billionaire. Here though, they become attached. They want more. Women here are bred to search for a man with a name they can pass to their children and continue the legacy. And I happen to have a very powerful name in this town.

"Not going to fucking happen, Harlow. We had our one time, I don't go back for a second round," my voice sounds harsh, but I have to be cruel. She won't get the message if I'm not.

I untangle myself from her tentacles, as I try to disappear into the crowd. I should have stayed hidden in the shadows. I could watch the show without being noticed. But my brother had to go and be a dumbass and I have to save him, and the poor girl he almost ruined, like always.

Harlow yells after me, but I keep moving, only stopping to grab a beer from one of the waiters. I need it if I'm going to survive the rest of the night. I'd rather have another whiskey, but I need to stay sober to keep Sebastian out of trouble. I need some alcohol to keep myself from going off on Harlow, though.

Fuck this night.

I shouldn't have come back here, even if it was necessary.

I think I've finally evaded Harlow when a new warm body presses up against mine.

I don't recognize the woman, but she reeks of alcohol and vomit. Not an endearing combination.

I grab her shoulders to move her out of my way. She stumbles as I move her, and I hold her shoulder longer than I want.

"Kade King, I can't believe you're here. I've had such a big crush on you."

"You should drink some water," I say, flagging down a waiter and grabbing a glass of water to hand the woman.

She grins.

Shit, I know that grin. This is what I get for being nice and trying to help a woman.

"I want to have your babies Kade King!" she says, screaming.

My lips pull back tightly. I'm never coming to one of Sebastian's ridiculous parties again. In fact, this might be the last time I visit this town.

"Drink the water," I say, glancing around for her date or a friend to pass her off to. A man is standing behind her, eyeing her. I don't know if he's her date or not, but she's his problem now. I give him a, 'take care of her, don't fuck her,' glare and push her into his arms.

He looks happy, yet terrified. I roll my eyes and storm away. *Welcome to my world.*

Why do women think I want a baby? I already have one dealing with Sebastian.

I finish my loop around after thoroughly losing Harlow. I stand in the corner of the living room where Sebastian does another shot off Naomi, this time from between her boobs.

I nurse my beer, trying to blend into the corner as I keep an eye on my brother. He's done fucking everything up for me. This is the last major party of the year before graduation. He needs to make it through tonight without doing any damage.

"We need to talk," Harlow says, her body standing firmly in front of me, her hands crossed over her chest, and her face is fierce, in a don't mess with me sort of way.

I sigh as I glance at my brother grabbing Naomi's hand and leading her toward the garage.

Fuck.

He tries to drive drunk every fucking time.

Not going to happen tonight.

"We can talk later," I say, brushing past her rigid body.

"I'm pregnant," she says.

FUCK.

I stop dead in my tracks. I spin on my heels staring down at Harlow's belly. She's wearing her usual skin-tight dress that hugs her body like a second layer of skin. Her stomach is flat. Not even a hint of a bump.

I close my eyes trying to focus on when the last time I had sex with her was. I know it's been months, but when was it exactly... I rush through my flings over the last couple of months, and then I remember. It was the end of Sebastian's Christmas break. Early January. I came back after the previous party got out of hand and he was arrested for drunk driving. I was pissed and needed to let off some steam. Harlow was who I let off steam on.

It was definitely January. It's April now. If she is pregnant, there is no way it's mine.

I open my eyes calmly. My body has been calm this entire time in fact. Hearing a woman say she's pregnant would send most men's balls straight up inside their body. It would stop their hearts along with their breathing. It would shatter their world so they couldn't think straight or fuck another woman for months, even after the baby was confirmed not to be theirs.

Hearing a woman say she is pregnant doesn't have the same effect on me. Not because I want a baby. I sure as hell am not ready to be a father. But because I've heard the line used too many times. Women think they can trap a King if they say they are pregnant. I don't fuck without protection. I don't knock up women. And if she were pregnant, all my money and prestige would go to the baby, not her. I don't want a relationship. That's not who I am.

I turn away from her, not bothering to give her another second of my attention. I need to find Sebastian before he ruins the King name, again.

"Well? You're really going to walk out on the mother of your child?" she says, grabbing my arm.

I exhale to keep from pummeling her. I'm so tired of this shit.

I turn and look at her with a glare, my nostrils flare, and my frown burrows. She takes a step back, her hand falling from my arm.

"My lawyer will go with you to your next appointment to confirm you are pregnant."

She smiles brightly. She's pregnant, or she wouldn't be so smug about it.

"And to take a paternity test."

Her smile drops, and fear flickers in her eyes. The baby isn't mine. I don't know if she can take a paternity test at this point, or if we'd need to wait until the baby is born. But I don't have to wait. Her eyes confirmed what she wouldn't tell me.

In some weird way, I wish she was pregnant. Not because I want to deal with Harlow Hill for the rest of my life, but because if I had a child, an heir to my inheritance, maybe it would stop other women from trying so hard to make me theirs. If they realized Harlow was getting nothing, and I planned on turning my entire empire over to my first born, maybe the harassment would stop.

I could put out in every interview I don't want a sibling for my child. I don't want children fighting over running my company the way Sebastian and I fought over my father's. Maybe all this chaos would stop. *Maybe having a child wouldn't be the worst thing in the world?*

My eyes bulge thinking about it. I've gone mad. Having a child would destroy everything I've worked to build on my own.

I leave Harlow speechless, and I start jogging toward the garage, leaving my unfinished beer with a waiter on my way.

The Jaguar is gone. *Shit.*

Every. Fucking. Time.

I shake my head and run to my Aston Martin. My blood is boiling as I start the car up and zip out of the garage, dodging drunk college kids as I drive as fast as I can in the direction I know Sebastian drove.

He's predictable; I'll give him that. Why can't he be predictably responsible? The kind of kid who can throw a party without one issue. Where he fucks the women in his bedroom and passes out afterward. Like normal college students.

The lawyer I hired shouldn't have fought to scrub Sebastian's last DUI from his record. Sebastian should have lost his driver's license. Although, I doubt that would have stopped him. I should take his cars away, but he'd buy a new one.

I'm installing one of those breathalyzer tests on his cars so his cars won't start without him being sober. And since there are no sober people at his parties, he would never be able to leave.

My face burns red, and I grip the wheel tighter when I spot his red Jag on Highway 101, leading toward his favorite cliffside spot overlooking the beach. Naomi is in the passenger seat, and he has his arm draped around her back.

Why he thinks he needs to bring women here, I'll never understand. He's a King. Any woman at his party would fuck him. He doesn't need to be charming or sober. He can be sloppy drunk, barely able to get his dick up, and any woman at his party would praise him for how great the sex was.

I don't think he does this to impress the woman. He does this to piss me off. He hates me trying to control his life, and this is his fucked up way of trying to fight back. That, and he likes his fast cars almost as much as he likes his women.

I sigh.

I don't know how I'm going to let him take over any of my clubs. I want to give him one club. *One* single club. The one here in Santa

Barbara. So there is no reason for me ever to return to this fucking town. And he can prove he is capable of doing more than finding trouble.

Then, I might let him run a few more parts of the business. *Maybe.* Or he'll decide he hates running a business and will live off his trust fund and name our father left us.

I stick my hand out the window, the chilly air cooling my warm skin. I try to calm myself down so when I beat Sebastian's ass when he stops, I don't break his nose like last time. Though he deserves worse.

Squealing breaks bring me back to reality.

Sebastian swerves.

I slow and pass him, as his car tumbles into the ditch on the side of the road. Flipping once and landing upside down.

I scream, my voice high pitched as I witness the accident.

I pull my car off the road in front of his wrecked car slamming on the brakes, and jump out, preparing myself for the worst. I sprint to the upside down driver's door.

I grab the door handle to open the door, but it won't move. The window is open, but luckily it was too cold to put the top down, or this could be a lot worse.

I reach inside, undoing his seat belt.

"You okay, Sebastian?" I ask.

He coughs and smiles. "That was fucking insane!"

I exhale a breath I didn't realize I'd been holding. He's fine, just drunk. I pull him out of the car and inspect him for a second. He has a small cut above his eyebrow, but he seems fine. I'll call an ambulance after I check on Naomi so a doctor can check him out, and he's booked for drunk driving, again.

But he'll be fine, because as much as I want to kill him for being so stupid, he's still my brother. The only person who loves me. I won't let him rot in jail, or ruin his life for fucking up again. I will find a way to put an end to this. Even if it means taking away every one of his fucking cars.

When I ensure Sebastian is okay, I race over to the passenger side and pull the door open. Naomi has undone her seatbelt and falls into my arms smiling.

"That was wild!" she shouts, equally drunk and happy. I inspect her quickly, and she doesn't appear to have a scratch on her either. Which is good, because her family would definitely sue if she's injured. They will probably sue anyway, unless Sebastian agrees to marry her, or some shit like that.

I sigh, pulling my phone out to report the accident to the police, and call for an ambulance for the two crazy idiots that are now laughing, holding each other like they got out of the theater after watching a hilarious movie, instead of being lucky for surviving a car accident.

"911, what's your emergency?"

I exhale again, trying to remain calm. This isn't the time for lectures. That will come tomorrow, when Sebastian's no longer drunk.

"I need to report an accident on Highway 101, just past exit seventy-one."

"How many cars are involved?"

"One."

"Can you tell if anyone was injured?"

"Both of the passengers in the car appear fine, besides a few minor cuts."

"The police and ambulance are on their way and should be there in..."

A moan grabs my attention, and I turn back around, ignoring the woman on the phone. I stare at Sebastian and Naomi who are both still cracking each other up. They didn't make those groans.

"Sir. What is your name sir? Any other information you can give me?" The woman keeps asking me questions, but I ignore her, pulling the phone from my ear as I move to the front of the car.

Moaning. It sounds like a woman's moan, and it sounds terrible.

I don't see anything, initially. I look under the front of the car and see nothing.

The moan grows louder. It hits my soul and sends me into a panic. There is someone out here.

My eyes scan the darkness, searching. I finally spot the white T-shirt reflecting the light from the Jags' headlights.

I run faster than I thought possible to her, bending down to a woman lying in the dirt on the side of the road. She's wearing nothing but a white T-shirt and underwear. Her toned legs stretch for miles. I would know her body anywhere.

Larkyn.

I search around for her bike or the car she was thrown from, but I find neither. She walked home. This is my fault. I should have made sure she got into a car, not walk on the side of a highway in the dark.

I grab the phone and pull it back to my ear.

"There is a woman injured. I think she was hit by the car while walking on the side of the highway," my voice is shaky as I speak.

"Is she conscious?"

"Larkyn? Can you talk to me?" I ask, tapping her gently on the shoulder.

A soft moan escapes her lips.

"She's not speaking, just moaning."

"I don't want you to move her. The ambulance is caught up in a storm, a tree fell blocking their way, but they should be there in less than ten minutes. Without moving her, check to see if you notice any obvious injuries."

My eyes water as they search over her body. She's injured, every-where. Blood coats her skin, but I can't tell where it's coming from.

The operator said not to flip her over, but there is so much blood pouring around her body. I need to know. I flip her over, cradling her head as I do, to prevent any damage.

I see a massive piece of glass sticking into her stomach, along with smaller pieces of sticks and glass all over her body.

She moans again but doesn't open her eyes. Her breathing is frail and shallow. I check her pulse, and it's just as weak. I don't know what to do about the blood. If it's better to leave the glass in, or not.

"There is a large piece of glass sticking out of her stomach and a lot of blood. She's barely breathing, and her pulse is weak," I tell the operator.

"Okay, stay with her and make sure she continues breathing but don't touch the glass."

"How much fucking longer?" I ask, knowing she won't make it much longer without assistance.

"Nine minutes."

My eyes widen as she strangles her breath. Her breathing stops for a second.

"Breathe Larkyn!" I shout, not allowing her to die in my arms.

The phone falls from my hands, and I glance over at my car, then Sebastian and Naomi. Both thankfully stopped laughing, realizing the seriousness of their fuckup.

The wind picks up, and I know it's going to be longer than nine minutes. Storms in this town come from nowhere, and destroy everything in their path. This is one of those times.

The hospital is five minutes away; less, if I drive as fast as I want to. I'm not waiting.

I scoop Larkyn into my arms and race toward the car.

"Get in the fucking car," I shout to Sebastian and Naomi.

They do, Sebastian sits in the back, holding out his arms to hold Larkyn, as I lower her into the car.

Her eyes flicker open at me, and I swear she peers into my soul at that moment. Then, they close again as if I imagined it.

"Make sure she's still breathing. If she stops, tell me," I shout at Sebastian as I hop into the driver's seat, speeding as fast as I've ever driven to the hospital. I hope Sebastian is now sober enough to notice if she is breathing or not.

Sebastian fucked up.

I fucked up.

And now Larkyn is paying the price.

She moans again, letting me know she's still breathing.

Thank fuck. Keep breathing Larkyn. I can't live with myself if you die.

4

LARKYN

A MACHINE BEEPS RHYTHMICALLY NEXT to my head. The sound isn't supposed to be heard. It's supposed to become background noise. But my headache controls me. It's as if you found all of the jackhammers in the world and used them all to drill into my head at the same time.

I'd take the jackhammers over what is happening in my head right now. My head is worse. A simple beeping is enough to make me want to rip off my ears and throw them at the machine, in hopes it will stop.

I keep my eyes closed, though I'm awake. Even with my eyelids shut, the light is too bright for my sensitive eyes to handle. Now I want to carve out my eyes, too.

Great, at this rate I won't have any body parts left.

"Larkyn, are you awake?" the evil bastard asks.

I lie still, hoping Kade will go away if he thinks I'm asleep.

"I saw you ball your hands into fists, and you frowned when you heard me speak, so I know you are awake. You might as well talk to me," the son of a bitch says.

Kade's not going away. He feels guilty for what happened. That guilt won't go away if he leaves. Maybe if I talk to him, he'll leave.

"Turn off the lights," I say.

I swear I feel the bastard grin. "I'm that bad to look at, huh?" Kade asks.

My lips tighten, but I refuse to frown or show any emotion for Kade. He and Sebastian are cruel. They don't get to witness my suffering.

"No, I have a headache that hurts like a motherfucker, and the light is making it worse," I say, not adding I don't want him to see me in pain.

Kade turns off the lights without any more argument.

I slowly open my eyes. My eyes don't burn from the light, but I wouldn't call the room dark. The closed blinds let in far too much light to dampen how much agony I'm in.

Kade narrows his eyes at me and reaches out to touch my hand, as he sits on the edge of my bed. I pull my hand away and hide it under the covers so he can't attempt to touch me again.

"You're pissed, that's good," Kade says.

"How is being pissed a good thing?"

He smirks. "Because it means you remember what happened. The doctor was afraid you might not remember. The accident might have fucked with your head."

"Of course I remember your brother almost fucking killing me!"

He cocks his head. "And yet, you're looking at me like you want to kill me as well, even though I saved your life."

I huff and glare at him. I want both King brothers out of my life. I don't want to think about either of them again. I wouldn't be in the hospital for the dozenth time if it weren't for these assholes.

I glance at the door, afraid Sebastian is going to walk in and want to apologize. I'm not ready for that. I don't want to see him. Ever.

"Don't worry, Sebastian isn't here," Kade says.

I exhale, after realizing I had been holding my breath.

"But Serena may walk in at any moment. She hasn't left you, except to get coffee and occasionally food when I demand she leave," Kade says.

I smile. At least I have one friend. But that means... If Kade knows Serena hasn't left my side, then he hasn't left my side either.

He looks at me with his big smoldering eyes, and my anger falls away. Kade did save my life, and then he stayed with me. I can hate his brother all I want, but I can't hate him.

Nope, definitely can't hate him when he's looking at me with hungry eyes.

I force my eyes away, and the bastard chuckles like he knows the effect he has on me.

"How are you feeling?" he asks.

"Like I got hit by a car."

He winces. "I'm sorry."

I sigh. Kade's sorry seems sincere. When he speaks, his whole body matches his mood. His eyes grow heavy, his voice softens, and his body stills.

"It's not your fault, but I feel like shit. I want to rip my head off..." I move to sit up more. "Fuck, that hurts." I grab my side.

He frowns. "You had a sizable piece of glass stuck in your large intestine. They removed the glass along with part of your intestine. They removed your appendix too."

My eyes widen. "What else?"

He blinks, and I swear I saw a tear there. "You have been unconscious for forty-eight hours. You have a concussion, that's why your head hurts so much. Glass in your stomach. Small shreds of glass in your legs, stomach, and head. A couple of broken ribs. Lots of internal bleeding. A couple of broken bones in your left wrist."

I look down and see the small cast on my left arm for the first time. *How did I not notice that?* Oh yea, because my fucking head hurts so badly I can't think of anything else.

"And a couple of broken bones in your ankle. The doctors were amazed you didn't break more bones."

The last part hurts the worst. Broken bones in my ankle. That will take forever to heal. I won't be able to run for months.

Tears.

Dammit.

No.

Kade holds my gaze, reaches out, and touches my hand over the covers.

I let him.

I need the comfort.

"The doctor wants you to stay in the hospital for another day or two. And then, she'll set you up with a rehab program to help you gain your strength back. She gave you pain medicine a half hour ago, but I can call her back if you want more?"

"No, thanks."

He runs his hand through his hair, and I permit myself to look at him closer. He's still wearing the suit he wore two nights ago. The collar is open with multiple buttons undone, revealing a chest that looks hot, dark, and delicious. Then, I see the red blotches. Blood. *My* blood.

"Do you want me to call your family? Your emergency contact lists Serena, so they called her. But she said she didn't have any of your family members' numbers, and they never found your cell phone."

"I didn't bring my cell phone. And, no." I don't offer him any more explanations. I sure as hell don't need my father lecturing me for walking home in the dark on a busy highway. If he finds out, I'll deal with the lecture later.

"Okay," he says, rubbing his neck.

My throat locks up, and my hand trembles a little in anger thinking about Sebastian, but I need to know. "How are Sebastian and his date doing?"

Kade moistens his lips and smiles softly. "Sebastian is a jackass, but he and Naomi are both fine. Sebastian was lucky, only a cut on his forehead requiring stitches. And Naomi has a little back pain from the collision."

I nod. I hate them, but I'm glad they aren't injured.

"Sebastian would like to apologize when you're ready to hear it. I told him that would probably be months or years from now. He understands. He's offered to give up his driver's license, and do some community service. He will also pay all of your hospital bills, and pay you well for your emotional damages."

The words Kade is speaking make sense, but I don't want to hear them.

"No, thanks."

Kade grimaces. "You can sue him, but you'll lose. Sebastian has a highly paid lawyer who doesn't lose. If you fight this, you will be out lawyer's fees and get no reimbursement. Sebastian won't lose his driver's license or do community service, and he definitely won't spend a night in jail, if that's what you are after, as much as he deserves it."

My eyes flicker to Kade's. Though he is defending his brother, his eyes say Sebastian deserves worse than he is getting.

"I'm not going to sue him. I don't want his money or apology or any of it. I don't want to think about Sebastian again."

Kade's body stiffens, and his face grows red before he pulls his phone out. "Make sure Larkyn's hospital bills are taken care of." Then, he ends the call.

I frown.

"You can't do that."

"I just did."

I sigh. I should let Kade pay my hospital bills. I don't have enough to cover them, and I don't want to have to go to my father for this.

"Paying for your hospital bills isn't enough though. What else can we do for you? Sebastian will do anything to make this right."

I peek under the covers and see the brace on my foot. I wince at the black and blue covering my legs. This accident is going to ruin my running career.

"He can't make this right. I don't want to be near him. And I sure as hell don't want his money."

"Then, let *me* make this right," Kade says, his head dropping a little in embarrassment.

"You did when you saved me."

He shakes his head. "That's not enough. I shouldn't have let you walk home that night. You wouldn't have been out there in the dark if I hadn't made sure you had a ride home, instead of treating you like crap. I'm sorry. Let me make it up to you."

Damn Kade, and his sincere apologies. His puppy dog eyes and sad face, which somehow still shows his dimples, make me want to grab his face and kiss him. Then accept his apology immediately. I restrain myself, mainly because moving that much would hurt like a motherfucker.

"Kade, I don't—"

"Stop, I'm making this up to you. I understand you don't want to deal with my brother, and you're right. He doesn't deserve to be forgiven any time soon. But let me be nice so that I can have a shot at forgiveness sometime in my lifetime."

He grins.

And I grin.

His grin reaches his eyes when he knows he's winning.

"I'm stubborn. I won't take no for an answer. So you might as well start thinking of ways I can help you."

I bite my lip, trying to stifle my smile, but it's a useless endeavor.

"Okay."

He tightens his grip on my hand over the covers, and I regret hiding my hand away in the first place.

"So what will it be? Money? A new car? A broken faucet that needs fixing?"

I raise an eyebrow. "You know how to fix a broken faucet?"

He shrugs. "I know how to hire a plumber."

I shake my head. Of course, his ways of helping are to give me money. I don't want his money, though. If I won't take my father's, I sure as hell am not taking a King's money.

What do I want?

To be healed, but Kade can't help me with that. He already covered my hospital bills.

I need a place to stay after graduation, but I don't want to take his money.

My car could use a tune-up, but no, no money.

Graduation is coming up. I could use a new dress for the graduation party my father is throwing, so for once, I could meet his unbelievably high standards. But again, that would require Kade's money.

My face lights up when the perfect idea creeps in. I shyly peek over at Kade. *Do I have the balls to ask him this?*

He's looking at me eagerly, squeezing my hand twice, trying to coax words out of my mouth. I don't have a choice but to ask him or come up with another way for him to pay me back, fast.

"My father is throwing me a graduation party in two weeks."

"Isn't that a bit early for a graduation party?"

I smirk. "Yes, but my father wants to throw it early, so he doesn't have to cancel and be embarrassed in front of his friends on graduation day if I don't graduate."

"Is that a possibility? I mean...don't answer that," he says, his cheeks flushing. He draws his hand back and grabs his neck, like his collar is too tight, though his collar is barely brushing against his neck.

I'm not offended by his words, so I continue, forcing the words out. "Take me to my graduation party, and pretend I'm yours for the night."

He sinks back in the chair next to my bed, like I pushed this conversation too far. But of course, I did. I asked Kade King to pretend to be mine for a night. It would ruin his reputation in Santa Barbara. If any of the wealthy women that run this town saw Kade King with me, the drama it would cause would never end. He can't go on a date with me. Even if it might be the only thing to make the disappointment in my father's eyes disappear.

"You mean, be your date for the night?" he asks.

I bite my lip again, considering not saying the next words, but I'm committed now. "No, I mean, pretend I'm your girlfriend for the night. It has to be more than just a date."

Kade's eyes narrow as he searches mine for the truth. For why I need him to pretend I'm his girlfriend. But he isn't going to find the truth. If he pretends to be my boyfriend, he might get answers. It would take him five minutes in my father's presence to figure out why I need him. But if he says no, he'll never know the reason for my embarrassment.

The silence stretches, and I can't take it any longer. If he wants to say no, he needs to say it and stop toying with my emotions.

"I understand," I say, but I can't continue. He should go.

"I'll pretend you're mine for as long as you want," he says, with a wink.

I chuckle. "The one night will be enough." I peer at his cocky grin and blush. I hope one night is enough.

5

KADE

Larkyn thinks I'm an ass. She has no idea how amazing I can be as a boyfriend. I'm about to blow her mind.

I'm supposed to meet her at her parent's house for the graduation party they are throwing for her. *Not happening.* If I were her boyfriend, I wouldn't be meeting her anywhere. I would pick her up in one of my fancy cars, and drive her around proudly. So that's what I'm doing. If I'm going to pretend she's mine, I'm doing this right.

Shortly after noon, I park the car outside the apartment building she shares with Serena. Thank god I got Serena's number while waiting for Larkyn to wake up in the hospital. She told me where Larkyn lives, so I'm able to pull this off. I haven't talked to Larkyn in two weeks, since she woke up in the hospital. My throat feels dry just thinking about what condition she's going to be in. The last time I saw her, she was beaten up, broken. All I could focus on was her bruises and pain. I can't imagine that two weeks will have changed much. She may even need crutches or a wheelchair to get around.

I run up the stairs to their floor, holding the flowers in my hand with a smirk on my face. I thought Larkyn would want me to do

44

something horrible to pay her back. Like, perform at a gay strip club. Or dress in drag. Something *creative.* Instead, when she said she wanted me to claim her as mine, it was like she granted my wish. She gave me an excuse to put my hands on her. To kiss her. Worship her. And I plan on cashing in on that excuse all night long.

I knock on the door with my smug grin, knowing that this simple gesture is sure to earn me big points with Larkyn.

The door opens, and instead of the smile I'm expecting, she frowns.

"What are you doing here? I told you to meet me at my house."

I roll my eyes. One thing I'm learning about Larkyn is she likes things her way. If she's going to be mine for the night, she needs to learn to let go, because I like doing things my way. And that includes bringing her flowers and driving her to the party.

I hold out the flowers, and she reluctantly takes the roses, unable to hide her growing smile behind the dark red flowers.

"You're my girlfriend for the night. If anyone saw us show up separately, the ruse would be ruined before the night even started."

She sighs. "You're right."

I grin. I like her saying I'm right. I finally take in her appearance. Her flawless skin is wrapped in a deep blue sundress that flares out at her hips and gives her just enough cleavage. I might have over-dressed a little in my dark grey suit complete with a tie, but it doesn't matter. I'm sure she wants me as her date to make an ex-boyfriend jealous. Being more dressed up than everyone else will make my job easier.

My smile drops. Her skin is *flawless.* I don't see a bruise or a cut. Either she heals quickly, or she's wearing a ton of makeup. It was hard for me to look at her before when she was in the hospital. Not because the bruises and cuts made her appear ugly, but because they reminded me of my role in her suffering.

I glance down at her hands grasping the flowers, then dart down quickly to the heels on both of her feet. No cast or brace on either. No crutches. No wheelchair. I might believe the bruises healed enough to be covered in makeup in two weeks, but I know there is no way her wrist or ankle healed this quickly. The doctors said it would be weeks or months before the braces could come off, and even then it would be a long road of training and exercises before she was back to her old self.

She takes a step back, motioning me inside, and then curses as her ankle gives out in her heals. I grab her hips, keeping her upright.

"Are you supposed to be wearing heels right now? I thought your doctors said to wear your braces for a few more weeks?"

"She's supposed to be using her braces. But she's a stubborn ass that won't listen to anyone," Serena says, taking the roses from Larkyn's hands and storming into the kitchen to put them in a vase.

Larkyn half frowns, half grimaces from the pain. "I'm not going to my graduation party and letting everyone stare at me in the braces."

I narrow my eyes, not understanding why it would matter if she were wearing her braces or not. Surely, everyone would understand she is still healing from an accident that wasn't her fault.

"That's because they would ask questions since you haven't—" Serena stops when Larkyn shoots daggers her way with her eyes.

I look between the two women, even more confused at what's going on.

Larkyn continues inside, and I keep my hands on her waist, afraid she is going to hurt herself. It also gives me an excuse to be touching her.

"You should at least wear flats, those heels look dangerous," I say, staring at the high spikes on her feet.

Larkyn glares at me with a growl that tells me to shut the hell up.

I grin. I like that look.

"No, she should wear her braces," Serena says.

"Will you two stop? It's my choice. I feel fine. I'm not used to walking in heels, but after wearing them a few more minutes, I'll be used to them." She shakes my hands off her body as she storms over to the kitchen to pick up her purse and throw the strap over her head to cross her body. Her purse is a light tan color, not flashy, like Larkyn.

She stomps past me, without a word to Serena or me, merely an evil glare.

"Have fun!" Serena shouts from the kitchen. Then she looks at me. "Don't keep your hands off her. Larkyn's stubborn. She won't tell you she's in pain and she is in agony since she stopped taking her pain medications almost immediately after she got home. And she couldn't walk in heels before; she definitely can't now."

My eyes turn to the sassy woman strutting out of the apartment, her ass swaying making her flowy dress swoosh side to side as she walks. I much prefer the dress she was wearing the other night that hugged her body a little too snugly. This one makes her look as innocent as she is. This one will force me to behave like a gentleman, instead of the cocky bastard, I want to be.

"Don't worry, I won't be able to keep my hands off her," I say, winking at Serena who is smiling, amused.

Shit. I may have just given her the wrong impression about what my intentions are with Larkyn. I won't fuck her. I won't hurt her. I'm paying back my debt to her, that's it.

I need to talk to Serena on her own and explain things. And also receive some advice on how to convince Larkyn to take my money.

I chase after Larkyn as she reaches the stairs. Of course, she decided to skip taking the elevator. She's a wreck walking on a flat surface. I can't imagine how she is on the stairs.

I reach her as she is taking her first step down and hold out my elbow to her, like I'm escorting her down the stairs at some grand ball.

"What are you doing?" she asks, her body tense as if she might slug me.

"I'm being a good date. Now shut up and stop asking me that."

"You don't have to pretend until we arrive at the party. For now, can't we just be us? Friendly toward each other and nothing more?"

"No."

I grab her hand and place it on mine. I only get one day with her. I'm not wasting a second of it being *friendly* toward her.

She sighs but lets me help her down the stairs under the illusion

I'm doing this because I'm pretending she's my date, instead of it being necessary to ensure she doesn't hurt herself.

I lead her to my McLaren, and she smirks when it comes into view.

"You couldn't pick me up in something nicer than this piece of trash?" she asks teasingly.

I smile. "Sorry, next time I'll pick you up in my horse and carriage, princess."

That earns me a smile, and I never want her to stop smiling. The smile reaches her deep eyes and makes the blonde in her hair shine. Her cheeks blush enough to be noticeable, but not so much that she appears embarrassed. Just happy. I haven't seen this look on her. I like it.

I open the door and help her inside, hating that I have to drop her warm hand to run around to the driver's side. I hop in quickly and throw my arm around her shoulders as I start driving toward the address she texted me to meet her at.

Her body tenses when I throw my arm over her shoulders. But she doesn't say anything. Maybe she'll finally give up, and try to enjoy herself a little. She might like being mine if she let herself benefit from the perks.

Her fingers fidget with the hem of her dress as I turn on the highway. I swear I hear her heartbeat speed to hummingbird levels. Her breathing catches in her throat. And her face turns pale white.

"What's wro—shit," I curse when I realize what's wrong. This is the same highway where my idiot brother ran her over and almost killed her.

I turn off at the next exit, almost running over a minivan, as she squeezes her eyes shut and grabs for anything to brace herself with. She finds my hand. And she grips it, as if she were to let go, she'd float away and get sucked up by a black hole.

My hand hurts like a bitch, but there is no way I would ever let her stop holding it. *Never.* I want her tiny hand gripping mine. I would take this over any of my usual daily activities in a heartbeat.

I pull the car over to the side of the road as she takes several deep breaths and stares out the windshield. Her grip slowly loosens, but I tighten my hand around hers, letting her know I'm not going anywhere.

Seconds pass. Or minutes. I don't know.

But finally, she turns her attention from staring at the field in front of us to me. Her big eyes are swollen as if she might cry, but won't let herself.

"I didn't realize how much driving on that road would affect me."

"I'm sorry. I wasn't thinking. I should have driven a different route."

She shakes her head. "I would have said you were crazy for taking a longer route when this was the most direct way. I'm stubborn like that. You would have driven on the highway, and only then would I have realized my mistake. I'm glad I was with someone the first time, instead of driving myself when the panic attack hit."

I grin, and reach over to her body, pulling her into my arms so I can hug her. She lets me. Exhaling another breath, this one goes deeper than her previous breaths, now that I'm holding her.

She gently leans back in her seat, and I reluctantly lean back in mine. But I still hold her hand, dammit. I'm not letting go.

"I'm better now. We should go if we want to make it to the party on time," she says, her voice steady.

I nod and start driving. "You're going to have to give me directions. I don't know how to go anyway but the highway."

"Keep going straight. I'll tell you when to turn."

I do as she says, and the silence stretches out between us. It's not uncomfortable, but I don't want her thinking too much about what just happened.

"Tell me about yourself," I say.

She raises an eyebrow and makes a face like that's the worst thing I've ever suggested.

I laugh and bring her hand to my lips and kiss the top of it without thinking.

Her teeth rake over her bottom lip as she tries to pretend she didn't enjoy the simple kiss on her hand. But she did. She shivered when my lips touched her skin.

"I should know something about you if I'm going to pretend I'm your boyfriend for the day. What if someone asks me what your favorite food is or if you prefer red or white wine and I don't know the answer?"

She scrunches her face as she thinks a moment. "I rarely drink, but usually red wine, I guess, if I was going to choose. I don't have a favorite food either, and trust me, no one will ask. The basics are I go to UC Santa Barbara, and I'm graduating in two weeks with a business degree with a minor in finance. My best friend is Serena. I've lived with her all four years of college. We moved into the apartment last year. I love running. That's what I spend most of my time doing. And I teach yoga classes at the YMCA. And I don't bring guys home ever. So be ready for everyone to be shocked as hell at the sight of you."

She eyes me brightly with a goofy smile.

I blink rapidly, trying to take everything in. Except, all I can focus is on one thing. "How can you not have a favorite food? It's not possible. My favorite things are sex and pizza. Preferably together, but I'll take them separately."

She bursts into laughter. Most of the women I've dated, I've hated their laughs. Not Larkyn's, though. I love her laugh. It's not too high-pitched. It's not pretty either. She doesn't laugh while trying to bat her eyelashes at me or hide some of it to keep it feminine. Her laugh is deep and glorious.

"Sorry, I'm just imagining Harlow with cheese and marinara all over her body. And her annoyed face when some of the sauce reached into her hair. It made my day to think of her like that."

I narrow my eyes, amused at her. "How do you know Harlow?"

Her laughter stops, and her cheeks blush. "I may have looked you up. I thought the same thing; that I should know something about you if I was going to pretend you're my boyfriend. Harlow was in a lot of the pictures I found. Unfortunately, I didn't know much about you before that night, only Sebastian."

My heart hurts, and my throat growls.

Her eyes widen and stare at my neck.

I don't know why I growled, but I hate that she thought of my brother, and not me.

Her face changes. It lights up like the sun outside, whizzing by over the rolling hills. We haven't passed any houses or towns in a while. Hopefully, she's not taking me somewhere where she can push me off a cliff.

"Don't worry, I don't think you have to worry about me thinking about Sebastian like *that* ever again," she winks.

I sigh and try to forget about my brother. "So you think you know everything you need to know about me?"

She grins. "You graduated from Stanford four years ago. You own several businesses. Real estate, whiskey line, but your love is the bars you own. You've dated, but don't seem to have a steady girl-friend. You're one of LA's sexiest bachelors according to the article with an accompanying naked picture." She wiggles her eyebrows.

I chuckle. "They didn't ask my permission to use that photograph!"

She laughs. "Why did a photograph exist where you were completely naked on a bed except for the sheets draped over your crotch?"

"I guess you don't know everything about me then."

She blushes, and her eyes alight like it's a challenge to figure out why I have the picture. If she figures it out, she won't like the answer. A woman took it after I slept with her. She just happened to be a photographer and sold it to the magazine. I didn't bother fighting it since it gave me and the business good press.

"What else do you know?"

"I know that the town loves you. You're a King. Your father left you an empire, and your mother left you when you were a kid. I know you have at least six cars and three homes across California."

"What about the important stuff? Like favorite food, drink, and sex position?"

That last part earns me a scowl, and she's as beautiful scowling as she is smiling. "Pizza apparently, scotch or whiskey I'd guess, but you'll be served neither at the party. My father's too cheap to serve anything like that. And sex position is any, as long as the woman is covered in marinara sauce."

I smirk and bring her hand to my lips again to kiss her.

This time she doesn't hide her smile. She reaches with her other hand to turn on the radio, and it blares a country love song. She raises her eyebrows. "Really?"

I shrug. "I happen to like a good country ballad."

She turns the volume down. "Even this cheesy romantic crap about doing anything to win a girl back and driving down a country road in your truck?" She pauses. "You don't own a truck, do you?"

I chuckle. "I don't own a truck. And yes, I happen to like the cheesy shit."

I turn the volume back up and start belting along with Kenny Chesney.

She shakes her head like I'm crazy. I never ask her what music she likes, but I plan on finding out. Just like I plan on letting her know I like a lot more than cheesy love songs. I happen to like all things romantic. Romance is sweet; it's just not real.

———

I pull up in front of her house, and my mouth drops. No way do her parents live here. I should have recognized the address. Some of the wealthiest families in Santa Barbara live here. It's not the most expensive house in this area, but it costs enough for me to be sure her family hangs in some of the highest circles of society. I'm surprised I didn't realize her family before.

Larkyn dresses like she doesn't come from money. Yet, she was relieved when I said I would pay her hospital bills, though she would never tell me that. Something doesn't add up.

She glances over at me and slowly pulls her hand out of mine. I let her pull away in my disbelief. *Dammit.*

"My parents are rich," she says shrugging. She's out of the car before I realize it.

I race after her to put my hand around her waist again.

"Stop running off on me. I'm your date, remember? Start pretending as if you like me."

She sighs. "Sorry, just distracted." Her body stands straight ahead in front of the large brick house with an arch over the front door and gorgeous deep pink flowers lining either side.

We go to the front door, and she rings the doorbell.

I study her. I thought this was her parents' house. This party is for her. *Why doesn't she just walk in?*

The door opens, and a gentleman dressed in a tuxedo answers it.

I thought I was going to be overdressed, but I'm underdressed. And Larkyn is way underdressed in her sundress.

Shit. I should have offered to buy Larkyn a dress for tonight if she didn't own one.

"Welcome, Miss Veil," the doorman says, holding the door out for us. "You're twenty minutes late, I believe."

She glares at him. "I know. And it's Larkyn Day. Call me Larkyn or if you insist, Miss Day. I'm not a Veil."

So many questions whiz around in my head, but at least one is answered. The reason I didn't recognize Larkyn came from money is that her last name doesn't match her parents'. The Veils have as much money as my father did. I didn't realize they had two daughters. Just—

"Anastasia," Larkyn says to her sister, who looks nothing like Larkyn.

Anastasia is wearing a sparkly red dress showing off voluptuous curves I happen to know she bought. I know because I've slept with her. *Shit. Shit. Shit.*

I try to hide my face by turning away from Anastasia and hoping she doesn't notice or remember who I am. She was pretty drunk that night. That night is one of the reasons I instated my don't date anyone from this town rule.

"Hello, Larkyn. It's nice to see you *finally* made it to the party our father is throwing in your honor. You would think you would be one of the first to arrive," Anastasia says.

I hate her. We are twenty minutes past when the invitation said to arrive. Most people come after the invitation time to a party.

I grip Larkyn closer to my body, knowing she needs the support if she's going to survive her horrible sister.

Larkyn leans into me, and she takes a deep breath against my chest, ignoring her sister.

"Where is our father?" Larkyn asks.

"Smoking a cigar. He needed something to calm his nerves after thinking you might not show up." Anastasia steps toward her sister glaring at her, still ignoring me. "But don't worry, I will be announcing a surprise to liven this party up."

Larkyn scowls. "Good, then the party can be all about you instead of me."

Anastasia smirks and notices the arm wrapped around Larkyn's body. She looks up at me, and she laughs.

"You always did go after my sloppy seconds," Anastasia says before brushing past us, still laughing.

Silence.

"What did Anastasia mean about sloppy seconds?" Larkyn asks, her body rigid as she forces her lips upward as guests walk by.

I can't lie. There is no point anyway.

"I slept with Anastasia in college."

She nods like she knew the answer.

"Great. Just great."

She struts forward confidently, and I know there is no way she is going to fall in her heels, not now. My hand slips from her side momentarily, before I catch back up. She takes two glasses of white wine from the waiter because white wine and champagne are the only options waiters are serving at this party. Then she dashes off out back, with me at her heels.

Five minutes pass without her talking to me. She hides in the corner at the backyard, sipping her wine and sculling. Hating me. Loathing her sister. And hiding from the party.

"I'm sorry. If it makes you feel any better, Anastasia was horrible in bed. It only happened once because we were drunk. And if I had seen you first, she wouldn't have been an option."

That makes her smile though she tries to hide it. "You're lying, but knowing she's bad in bed does make me feel better."

"She was awful, one of my worst lays. All fake, and she thought all she had to do was lie there and let me do all the work. Not that I mind being on top, but give me something. Kiss me, touch me, moan, anything," I say, probably pushing this too far.

Larkyn bites her lip and is silent as she stares at me with her big eyes. "I don't think I need any more details. Picturing the two of you together isn't exactly making my day better."

She takes another sip of her wine, and her gaze catches the attention of a herd of chatty women in sparkly floor-length dresses. It's Larkyn's party, but they give her nasty glares as they judge her sundress, appropriate for most graduation parties in the world, except in the world of snobs in this town. To these people, a dress like the one Larkyn is wearing is meant to be worn at casual events, not for a special occasion.

Larkyn's eyes drop, and she winces then curses under her breath. I'm not sure if it is because she is pissed at the women, or if her leg is aching again. She lifts her injured leg up and rests it on top of her other foot. She finishes her wine, planning on getting drunk to deal with both her pain and the disgusting stares.

I have a better idea.

I finish my wine, though the stuff is disgustingly sweet.

"Come on. I may not be able to take away the torment you are dealing with in your leg unless you let me take you home and forget about the party."

She snaps her head to me. "Not going to happen."

I nod. "But at least let me help you with your other problem."

"I don't have any other problems," she lies.

I link my fingers in her hands again, and she shivers. I'd smile, but I'm too pissed off. Yet, I do love how much something so simple affects her. I bet I could ask her any question right now and she'd answer because she's too focused on my thumb lazily tracing the outside of her hand. I don't know how many boyfriends she's had in her life, but none of them have known what to do with her body, that much is clear.

I take my time as she hobbles in pain across the grass to where the women are watching us with narrowed eyes like they can't figure out who I am.

Every time she winces or curses, I press a little further to a pressure point in her hand. Her hand warms, and she stops groaning in pain every time I do. Every curse earns her a kiss on the hand. Both the touch and the kiss seem to help because by the time we approach the women, she's smiling and I know that at least part of the smile is genuine.

"Hello, ladies. How do you know the woman of the hour?" I ask, pulling Larkyn against my side as I wrap my arm around her waist. I want to do a lot more, but that won't win over these kinds of women. These women already look at her like she's trash. I won't add to the stereotype it's clear these women are giving her.

"Oh, we've been best friends with her mother and father since before she was born. You know how families like ours run together forever. How do you know Miss Veil?" one of the women asks for the group. But everyone peers over their drinks, none of them recognizing me. *But then, why would they?* I rarely ever come back to this town.

I'm not going to convince these women by playing their games. They are too good, and Larkyn hasn't been playing for years if she ever played at all.

"I'm Kade King."

Eyes widen, and whispers ring out.

I grin. I have their attention now.

"I'm so glad you are back in town Mr. King. I don't think you've met my daughter, Aubrey, yet. I'll fetch her," the woman says.

I smirk. I'm sure the woman would like to introduce me to her daughter. But it's not happening.

Larkyn is glaring at the women. Pissed. I think she's angrier at them than she was at Sebastian.

I tug on her hand, watching her stumble in front of me for a second, so I have an excuse to pull her tight against my body. Pressing her back to my front. My cock grows uncomfortably hard in this position. But I'll deal with the pain.

"Down girl," I whisper into Larkyn's ear, before kissing her tenderly on the neck.

A moan escapes, and my dick is never becoming soft again. It's going to be hard the rest of the fucking night.

"Larkyn is my girlfriend," I say, kissing her cheek.

She closes her eyes as I do, and when she opens them again, her eyes are fierce balls of furry, ready to fight anyone who argues we are anything other than boyfriend and girlfriend.

My statement earns us more whispering and stares. I'm not sure if it helped Larkyn or not, but damn does it feel great to say, even if it's not the truth.

"That's nice. But really, you should meet Aubrey. She's graduating from law school in a couple of weeks, and I think the two of you would hit it off," the woman says.

My mouth drops open. I grew up in this world, with women like her. It's one of the reasons I hate this town. I'm tired of daughters pushed on me.

"That's nice, Mrs. Jackson. And feel free to introduce Aubrey to Kade. Maybe she can date him when I'm finished with him. She'll be waiting a long time though. Because I don't plan on giving him up, ever," Larkyn says, storming away, her hand interlocking with my hand automatically as she pulls me away.

I chase after her willingly.

She stops just before we make it to the pool area, which is surrounded by a younger crowd.

"I'm so sorry. I don't know what I was thinking. I'm just so tired of never being enough for these people. Of course, we aren't going to keep this ruse up forever. After today, you are free to date Aubrey or anyone else you are interested in. I can't stand that they always get to win."

I tuck a strand of her curls behind her ear. She wore her hair down, unlike most of the women here. She doesn't understand she's the most beautiful woman at the party. She's not afraid to be herself, while everyone here is too worried about impressing others to think for themselves.

"Don't worry about it. If you hadn't said it, I was going to. I can't stand for them to win either. After today is over, we will find a way to make our breakup epic. We will find a guy for you to date who is way better than me," I say, not liking the words spilling from my mouth.

She smiles weakly. "Thank you."

I nod.

Gripping her hair a little firmer now, I watch as she closes her eyes and her face molds to my hand.

Her eyes flicker open a second later when I stop. Mortified.

"I'm sorry. Did I just moan? I don't know what's gotten into me," she says, with pink cheeks.

The same thing that seems to have stirred my dick up, and won't calm down. I'm surprised she hasn't noticed. If she has, she hasn't commented on it or stared.

I hear the laughter from the crowd behind us. We may not be able to win with the older group, but the younger ones will be easier to convince. And if she has an ex-boyfriend here, that's where he'll be.

"Let's have some fun," I say, with playfulness in my eyes and grin.

She cocks her head to the side as I pull her quickly toward the crowd. She tries to keep up, but she can't in her heels on the uneven grass. So I scoop her up, making sure her dress is still covering her ass as I run with her in my arms toward the crowd that is now silent.

They are all staring at us. Studying us, to determine what is going on. Now is the time to make the biggest show I can.

She's laughing, but it's not enough.

I grab her neck and pull her lips to mine. We kiss. I intended to keep it pure. Innocent. Our lips mashing together, but nothing else. That went away the second her moist lips touched mine.

Her lips part for me, and I can't not jump at the invitation. I slip my tongue into her mouth, not expecting her to be good at kissing. *But damn. She knows how to kiss.*

Her tongue dances with mine as she makes soft whimpers against my lips. Her hands tangle in my hair. And my cock presses harder into her body. There is no hiding how she makes me feel now.

Larkyn slowly ends the kiss, somehow having more restraint than I do. There is a twinkle in her eye when she cocks her head to the side laughing. She loved that damn kiss as much as I did.

She mouths thank you.

But I don't want her to thank me. I want her to want me. I want this to be real. I could use a hot fling with someone as innocent and pure as her instead of dealing with the experienced wenches that only want two things: to bear my children and steal my money.

I hear the hooping and hollering from the guys. I feel the shocked expression and whispers from the girls. They believe the act. My dick has decided our show is more than just pretend too.

I need a distraction if I don't want to walk around all night with a hard-on. And we need a grand finale to cement in their minds our relationship status.

I give her a warning with my eyes.

"No," she squeals.

And then I toss us into the pool.

When we come up for air, Larkyn is laughing, and I pull her to my body to kiss her again.

Her lips taste even better now that her body is soaking wet, and fully pressed against my body. Other people start jumping in now that we have. She smiles against my lips, knowing she is now a hit, at least with the younger crowd. They've all been secretly dying for a chance to dive into the pool all day.

"Larkyn," a stern voice says over us, and my body freezes. I think my balls climb up in my body a little at the sound.

Larkyn sighs, like she was waiting for this to happen, but she doesn't try to wiggle out of my arms.

"Hello, father," she says, staring up at a man.

I follow her gaze. I'm used to fathers glaring at me with unease and trepidation. I'm used to them eyeing me suspiciously, not sure if they like me with their daughters. But then when they realize who I am, they are doing everything they can to impress me.

But I'm not sure meeting her father while soaking wet was my best idea. I just needed a distraction from what she was wearing to keep everyone from thinking too hard about us. Now it seems stupid.

"Are you going to introduce your friend and spend some time with your family at your party? Or are you just going to play, instead of handling your responsibilities, as always?" her father says.

Larkyn takes my hand and leads me to the stairs of the pool, where she climbs out, kicking her heels off on the top step. I guess the heels don't matter now she's soaking wet. She doesn't seem pissed at me for putting her in this predicament though.

Her father starts walking into the house, and we follow. I snatch a towel off one of the chairs and wrap it around Larkyn, who gives me a curt smile and her own warning stare before we head into the house.

Her father is now standing next to, what I presume is, her mother. Both dressed to the nines, while we are dripping on their marble floors. *Shit. Stupid.*

I open my mouth to start charming her mother. I know I can at least handle that, but Larkyn squeezes my hand, and I stop. She wants to handle this. I'll let her, as long as she includes the part where I'm her boyfriend.

Her father eyes me again as he puts his hand around his wife, pulling her to him uncomfortably.

"Mom, dad, this is Kade King, my boyfriend," Larkyn says.

Her mother smiles and her dad stiffens. I wasn't brought here to make an ex-boyfriend jealous. I was brought here to stick it to her parents.

I grin widely as I pull Larkyn to me and kiss her on the cheek.

"You've raised a wonderful daughter, Mr. And Mrs. Veil. And you have a beautiful home."

"Thank you," Mrs. Veil says.

Larkyn's father ignores me though and stares at his daughter. He shakes his head disappointedly, which confuses me.

Anastasia decides to join in on the fun, with a man in tow who looks like a sad puppy following his master's orders. They stand silently by, watching the exchange.

Larkyn stares her father down, daring him to deny we are dating.

"It's nice to meet you Mr. King, but can I offer you a piece of advice?" he asks, but it isn't a question. And he doesn't look at me when he speaks. He looks at Larkyn.

"Find another girl to date. Larkyn is only dating you for your money. I won't give her any money unless she gets a grown-up job, which she can't get without a degree. She thinks she doesn't have to work. Work is beneath her. She's just a spoiled, rich girl who will take everything you have without giving anything in return. She'll live off your money until there is nothing left. Larkyn is like her mother in that way," he says.

I see red. I've never punched anyone before, but right now I want to. I've only known Larkyn for a short period, but I know that almost every word he spoke is untrue. She doesn't care about my money. She wouldn't even take it when she should have. I don't know how smart she is. I don't know if she will graduate or get a job after college, but I know she is fully capable of taking care of herself.

I open my mouth to yell at the man when I realize Larkyn is ready to defend herself.

Her mother, on the other hand, looks bored. Likes she's heard this conversation too many times to care anymore.

Anastasia is smiling smugly, behind her father.

"Excuse me, I need to talk to my father. Alone," Larkyn says, pulling out of my arms.

I grab her hand at the last second, jerking her to me so I can taste her lips one last time, and prove to her father I am her boyfriend. That I'm not letting her go easily.

She gets lost in our kiss, forgetting her family is here until her father clears his throat.

She lowers herself down, after having to stand on her tiptoes to kiss me. I think I could get used to our height difference. Her body is so tiny I could easily throw her around in bed.

She walks away confidently, without any sign of the trauma that occurred to her body.

I'm left standing with the rest of her family. Her mother turns away to the bar to grab another drink, leaving me alone with Anastasia and her date.

Nope, I'm not going to stay around and make conversation with this bitch.

I follow after Larkyn, so I can be near whenever she finishes talking to her father. She might need comforting after dealing with him. I thought my father was an asshole; this man is just as bad or worse.

They dart into what I assume is an office, and Larkyn gives me a thank you, but I got this smile and wink before closing the door behind her, leaving me alone in the hallway still dripping wet.

I really don't know what I was thinking.

I remove my jacket, now ruined, along with my tie, and start unbuttoning my shirt as I eavesdrop on the conversation behind the door.

I can't hear everything, but I do hear…

You're broke.

No job.

No degree.

No future.

Kade isn't going to save you. You're not worth the trouble.

All words spoken by her father. He's yelling. Her voice must be softer, calmer because I can't hear a word she is saying.

I sigh.

She needs me more than I thought. She needs me more than just for tonight.

I swallow hard, rubbing my neck, trying to figure out what to do next.

Anastasia walks over and places her hand on my bare chest. "Too bad we never got a second chance. We were good together."

I frown, grab her hand, and remove it from my chest before she touches the priceless piece of jewelry that always hangs from my neck.

"Any chance we could work out if we gave it another shot?" she asks, moving her hips side to side as she bats her eyelashes at me.

"I thought you were here with a date?" I ask.

"I am, and he's great. Tall, handsome, rich. Just not as rich as you." She says *you* with a raspiness to her voice meant to seduce me.

"No." I don't give her any of the other words I'm thinking. I'm sick of women acting like this around me because I'm wealthy. I need to find a solution to my problem.

She sighs. "Too bad. Oh well, make sure you and Larkyn get a good seat to my announcement."

"Announcement?" I ask although I remember her mentioning something about a surprise earlier.

She nods. "We have big news we're sharing in about fifteen minutes if father ever gets done lecturing Larkyn. I don't know why he wastes his time talking to her. She's never going to listen. She's a lost cause. I don't know why my family decided to adopt her in the first place.

"My mother thought I needed a sister, I guess, and she didn't want to fuck up her plastic surgery to have a second child of her own. So instead, she picked up some trash off the street and expected her to flourish in our world. Oh, well. She's not our problem anymore."

Anastasia rests her hand on my bare chest again, while I burn with rage.

"What the hell is wrong with you?" I spat out.

She grins. "Don't even try to defend her. I know the two of you aren't actually together. I saw her at Sebastian's party. I heard about the car accident. This is a pity date. Nothing more. Call me when you want a real woman," she winks before walking off, but not before I spot the flashy diamond on an important finger.

Shit.

Anastasia is going to announce she's engaged at Larkyn's graduation party.

Not fucking happening.

I stare at the door, trying to come up with a plan to ruin Anastasia's night and make Larkyn's.

I grasp for the ring hanging around my neck on a gold chain, as I always do when I need comfort.

And a solution forms. One I'm not sure if Larkyn will ever agree to. But it's the perfect plan. One that will solve both of our problems. Women will no longer hit on me. And Larkyn will be able to show up her family and get everything she's ever wanted. Money, security, and affection.

I need a few things. New clothes here, fast. And a diamond ring. Good thing I always carry a diamond ring with me.

6

LARKYN

"You can't live off your winnings as a runner! You'll never make enough money. And don't think I haven't noticed you're practically limping. Did you injure yourself again? How do you expect to be a good runner if you keep injuring yourself?" my father yells.

I pull the towel tighter around my body, trying to hold myself back from attacking as I want. My father doesn't know about the car accident. None of my family does. And I don't plan on telling any of them.

"I'll make enough. I'm still working as a yoga instructor. I'll be able to work more hours when classes are over next week. I'll survive."

He shakes his head, hanging it low like he can't even look at me. "You shouldn't just get by. You should find a real job. One in the business field, after you hopefully graduate."

"Stop. I'm graduating in two weeks. Just stop saying that."

"Fine. I'll accept you are graduating with a degree you will never use. What good is that? You have the skills, but won't use them? You'll be homeless or live off a man!"

I narrow my eyes. He has no idea what I want. He has no idea who I am or what my plans are.

65

"I won't be homeless or live off a man! I will make enough money to feed myself and put a roof over my head. That's all that matters. I don't care about money. I want to make a difference in people's lives." And I do, I just haven't figured out how I'm going to make a difference yet or what I want to do. All I know is I like running and helping other people stay fit. But I know it won't be sustainable to do forever.

"You can't make a difference without money. Charities, foundations run on money. So work hard at a big corporation, make your money, then start something like everyone else."

"No, I don't want to work at a big corporation."

Dad throws his hands up. We've had this same argument thousands of times before. I thought tonight with Kade on my arm he might stop. He might let me enjoy the night, but it made no difference.

He walks over to the bar and pours himself a drink as always. This is how he handles things. He drinks.

I won't stay another second and watch him drink his problems away. Drink *me* away.

I'm done.

I turn and storm out the door without a goodbye. The door swings open so hard it bounces back a little.

I expect Kade to be standing right outside the door waiting, but I don't see him. If he's with Anastasia, I'll chew him out too.

I turn down the hallway, and the AC hits my still soaking wet body. When I find him, I'll have him take me back to my apartment. I tried to make this day better, but it's impossible to do. If I don't find Kade soon, I'll call an Uber to take me home. I may not be able to afford it, but this is one of the few times I need to make an exception and figure it out because I can't stand being here for another minute. I have sixty-seconds to find Kade, and then I'm out of here.

I glance up and see Kade walking down the hallway toward me. He's not wet. He's changed clothes and is now wearing an even more dashing suit. This one is a dark blue and makes his grin shine. And he's holding something sparkly draped over his forearm.

I smile when I see him. Bringing him here may have been a horrible way for him to pay me back, but at least I got to spend some time with a great guy. I thought he was an asshole just like his brother, but he genuinely is a nice guy, even if he does date around too much. Maybe I've at least gained a friend out of all of this.

His arms wrap around my body when we meet, and his lips come down on mine. Passionately, not holding back, like I've been gone for days instead of minutes. His kiss is desperate for more, and as my lips part, I realize I never want him to stop kissing me. I didn't think it was possible for a man's kiss to ruin all other kisses for me. I've been kissed plenty of times, and they all had the same effect on me because they were pretty much all the same.

Kade's kisses, though, awaken parts of my body I didn't know existed. I feel *everything*. Excitement. Passion. Need. Ache. All of it. And I want what his kisses promise.

Then, I remember this is fake. He's kissing me because he's doing me a favor. Someone must be watching if he's kissing me.

He gently stops the kiss, his thumb tracing across my lips that are parted and useless after he devoured them.

"Your father was watching," he says, answering my unasked question.

I nod. I knew that's why Kade kissed me, but I just wish once he'd kiss me because he wants to. I don't need more than that, but I need to know on some level this was as real for him as it is beginning to be for me. I can't separate the pretend from how he makes my body feel. Which is very, very real.

He pushes the silky white fabric into my hands.

"What's this?" I ask.

He smirks, and puts his hands in his pockets, trying to act innocent. "Your new dress."

I stare at the beautiful white dress, decorated with gray lace and sparkles. I run the fabric through my hands, and it feels as good as it looks. It's meant to be worn, but I could just as easily use the heavenly fabric as a blanket in bed it's so soft.

"No, I just want to go home."

He narrows his eyes, determined as he grins at me. "I don't have time to argue with your stubbornness. I know today hasn't been perfect, but I have a plan to make it a whole heck of a lot better. We don't have a lot of time; I spilled wine on Anastasia's dress, but I know as soon as she's changed she will be ready to make whatever stupid announcement she's making. So hurry, and get changed."

I stare down at the gorgeous dress I would love to squeeze my body into. I know it would make me feel beautiful, and I need that right now.

"How did you get a dress so fast?"

He shrugs. "I have a friend in the fashion industry. He owes me plenty of favors, and was able to get a dress here quickly."

I try to think of the cons of changing into the dress. It means I'll have to stay, for at least a little while. I'll have to listen to Anastasia announce her engagement. I saw the ring. I know that's what she's planning. But if I have to listen to her steal the spotlight away from me, then I should at least do it feeling beautiful instead of like a wet mop.

"Fine. I'll change, and give you fifteen minutes to make this better. Then, we are leaving. Deal?"

He cocks his head to the side and smiles brightly. "Deal."

I rush into one of the spare bedrooms and change into the dress. It fits me better than any item of clothing I've ever worn. I don't know how Kade was able to get a dress here that is not only my size but tailored to my body.

I ring out my hair, letting my wet hair curl however it is going to curl. And I apply a little lipstick I find of my mother's in the adjoining bathroom.

I step back and stare at myself in the mirror. I look a little like a bride in the white dress. But I don't care. I love how I look. I look like a beautiful woman, instead of a girl playing dress up. I might even stay until the party ends to enjoy the dress longer.

I step back into the hallway where Kade is pacing back and forth. He freezes when he sees me, and his mouth drops open. And I swear

I see his cock harden in his pants. Maybe it's just my wild imagination, but I like to think I'm the one causing his package to grow.

"What do you think?" I ask, twirling around like a little girl.

His hands reach my waist as I spin, and he stops me. His eyes rake up and down my body.

"Beautiful."

I lick my lips wanting another kiss but knowing I'm not going to get one. I don't think I've ever heard a man call me beautiful before. And it feels damn good.

He tucks his hand gently around my neck and under my hair, staring intensely into my eyes before his lips press firmly against mine. I don't think about why he's kissing me. I don't search for anyone lurking in the hallway that might be the reason for the kiss. I just exist in a world where Kade King is kissing me because I don't want to ever live in any other world.

He stops, grinning against my lips. "That kiss was because I couldn't not kiss someone as beautiful as you."

My heart dances and my legs turn to mush as my body begins dropping to the floor. He holds me up like I'm a rag doll.

He grins wider, showing off his dimples beneath his five o'clock shadow that is beginning to form.

"I'd carry you, but then I'd take away from everyone getting to see how gorgeous you are in your dress."

I swallow and force my legs to work so I can stand. My legs are strong, muscular. Even if my ankle is in constant agony, my legs should be able to hold me up. I shouldn't need to rely on Kade to hold me up. But when I'm around him, my body forgets how to do anything other than kiss. I'm surprised I can still breathe without a constant reminder.

His hands slowly move down my side until he finds my hand and interlinks our hands.

"Come on, now for step two of my brilliant plan."

I laugh. "I'll be the judge of your plan after this is all over."

He shrugs. "How am I doing so far?"

We step outside to the patio near the gardens where everyone gathered. They stop talking and stare at us when we step out looking like a bride and groom on their wedding day. I know I won't ever look this good again, even on my wedding day, so I better enjoy this. There is no telling how much money this dress costs. Thousands of dollars at least.

"Pretty good," I say weakly, not sure how I feel about being the center of attention.

"My daughter and her date finally decided to join us," my father says, and everyone chuckles.

He raises his champagne glass as Kade and I am given our own champagne glasses by the waiter to match everyone else outside.

"I'd like to make a quick toast to my daughter Larkyn. To her new life after graduation. May she find her way, and not back under my roof."

The last part earns him chuckles, and everyone clinks their glasses as they drink to his toast. I've suddenly lost my ability to want to drink.

"To new beginnings. May you find a way to shove it to all these high-class idiots who don't know how amazing you are," Kade whispers in my ear, as he clinks his glass with mine.

I smile and drink my glass until it's empty. When I look up, I realize Kade has done the same. I don't know how many drinks he's had, but he better be able to drive me home later. I won't admit to him, but I enjoyed riding in his McLaren.

Anastasia grabs her fiancé's hand and starts to pull him forward as she glances at our father to let him know she's ready to make her announcement.

He smiles at her because of course, he's happy his princess has found love. But if I were announcing I was getting married, he'd think I was a gold digger who doesn't want to work.

"I think we should go. I changed my mind. I can't watch this, no matter how beautiful I feel," I whisper into Kade's ear, pulling his hand to lead him out of here quickly. I don't care if Anastasia knows why I'm leaving, I can't stay.

Kade kisses the top of my hand, and I'm thankful he's going to go without a fight.

A hand tugs me to the center of the crowd with Kade being the one forcing me in.

I glare at him, not liking whatever he's doing.

He flashes me his handsome grin and gives me a tiny wink.

I can't help but stop protesting when he looks at me like he is now.

"Thank you, Mr. Veil, for your toast, but I'd like to offer one of my own. My toast is to the most wonderful woman I've ever met. To a woman, I'm desperately in love with, and can't imagine living without."

I bite my lip to keep from grinning at his fake words. I don't care that they are fake. I love hearing them. I could live in this fantasy world forever. Even deal with my stupid family and their friends if it meant hearing him say such wonderful things about me.

"I love you so much, Larkyn. You're beautiful, smart, feisty, stubborn. And I couldn't have built a more perfect woman for myself if I tried. I've been searching for a woman like you for a long time. And I kick myself every day for not finding you sooner, especially when you were this close to me."

His words have a bit of truth to them, even though I know he means as friends. He's sad we weren't friends earlier. I am too, but I'm sure we will keep in touch after this day is over and make up for lost time.

Kade holds my hand tighter, as he bends down on one knee.

My eyes widen staring at him, and the crowd gasps all at once at the sight of him on one knee.

He pulls something out of his jacket pocket. But I can't focus on the object, all I can do is stare into his eyes and try to figure out what the hell is happening.

"Larkyn Day, I love you. Marry me?"

Yep, he's lost his damn mind.

He's smirking, and I know he thinks he's come up with the perfect plan to stop Anastasia. And he has. I just don't think he's thought this through. He's making my dreams come true today, only to crush me tomorrow. We aren't in love. We aren't getting married. This is all a ruse. And tomorrow it will all be over. We can keep pretending for a while, but we aren't getting married.

He winks at me though, and I can't help but go along with his ridiculous plan. Even if it's going to hurt me tomorrow, it will be worth it today.

"Yes," I say, barely getting the words out.

"She said yes!" he shouts so the crowd can hear my answer.

Cheering and applause break out, and Kade stands up and slips a ring onto my finger. *Where the hell did he get a ring?*

And then he kisses me. Hard. Long. A kiss that makes me forget this isn't real. That Kade King isn't mine. And I'm not his.

But today, I am.

When the kiss ends, people begin hurriedly approaching us, bombarding us with questions, and ogling the ring I haven't even had the chance to look at myself.

"Oh my god! Look at the size of the ring. Is it eight carats or ten?" the woman stares at Kade.

He smirks. "Ten."

My eyes come unglued as I stare at him. *How the hell does he have a ten carat engagement ring for a fake proposal?*

He shrugs at me knowing I have a lot of questions for him. I know he's rich and has a lot of friends. That's apparently how I'm wearing this expensive dress right now. But I don't care how many friends he has in the jewelry business. No one would lend him this expensive of a ring for one day, on this quick of a notice.

"Excuse me. I need to thank my fiancé. *Privately*," I say winking at them, knowing I just caused a new wave of gossip as they think I'm about to take Kade into one of the bedrooms to fuck him.

I grab Kade's hand, and I pull him into the house, but people continue to follow us in. As much as I like sticking it to my sister and family, I'm done with being the center of the attention and the reason for the gossip.

So I keep guiding Kade out the front of the house, and this time, he doesn't argue or pull me back to the crowd that has now gathered outside of the house.

"Thank you all for coming to celebrate our engagement and Larkyn's graduation. We would love some time to celebrate before we decide on a date. But it will be soon," Kade says, winking at the crowd that is asking us questions about when the wedding will be.

Kade opens the door to his car and helps me inside, before jumping in himself and speeding off.

I hit him playfully on the shoulder. "You're so bad. Why did you let them think there is going to be a wedding soon? And oh my god!" I grab the ring off my finger and thrust it into his hand.

"I can't be wearing a ring this expensive. If I lose it, I'll be paying you back my entire life. I'll have to sell my kidney to make a down payment on paying you back."

He smirks, pulls over abruptly, and shoves the ring back onto my finger.

"Did you hear me? I can't afford to pay you back if I lost this ring."

"I know. It's not on loan."

I narrow my eyes.

"How did you get the ring then? Please tell me you didn't steal it off of someone's finger when they weren't looking."

He laughs. "No, it belonged to my mother."

Shit.

"I can't wear it, it's irreplaceable," I say, trying to get the ring off, but it's now stuck on my swollen finger. *Great.*

I feel the panic rising in my chest.

"Stop," he says, holding onto my hand.

I freeze. If I don't move, there is no way I can lose the ring.

"I want you to wear the ring."

"Why?"

"Because I want to pretend marry you."

7

LARKYN

KADE'S LOST his damn mind.

Or he's drunker than I thought.

Or maybe he's high?

Except, he doesn't seem any of those things.

He's sitting in the driver's seat next to me, waiting for me to speak. But he's been waiting a long time; I've yet to find my voice or ability to move at all.

All I can do is stare down at the gorgeous ring that weighs heavy on my finger. Ten carats was what the woman said. That's *insane*. If I'm going to do this, I have to convince him at least to buy me a cheaper ring to wear, because I can't wear a ring this expensive or this sentimental to him.

What am I doing? I can't be seriously considering this. This is crazy! I don't even know why he would want to do this. He hardly knows me. He doesn't want to be fake married to me.

Kade grasps my hand again and pulls it to his luscious lips, planting a small kiss on the palm of my hand before interlinking our fingers together.

I close my eyes as the familiar tingling crawls up my arm and races through my body. It's such a sweet gesture. It's *his* gesture. It's

74

what he does when he wants to comfort me. If I was actually his, would he do more?

Would he be kissing me on the lips? Hugging me? Fucking me? Something else to make me forget about whatever I'm thinking?

If I said yes, I might find out.

No.

He said he wants to 'pretend marry' me. It wouldn't be any different than it was today. He would hold my hand and make polite conversations with people to make them think we are together. He would occasionally kiss my hand or kiss me on the lips. Nothing more.

But I would *get* to kiss him. And that alone would be worth the heartache of when this ended. Because this would end. Someone would find out. Or we wouldn't need each other any more.

Kade is a guy. He won't become emotionally attached, especially if there is no sex. He will use me to further his own goals, that's it.

But every brush of his lips against mine, every grin, every kind word, every touch of his hand will make me fall for him a little more until I'm completely in love with him. And then, I'll want this to be real.

Kade King is a gentleman. In fact, he's incredible. Other than the first night when he was trying to convince me to leave. That night, he was an ass. He wanted to fuck me, and we both knew it. And instead of admitting it, he treated me like dirt.

"You hungry?" Kade asks, as the car stops.

My eyes widen as I stare out the window. We're in the valet line of one of the most expensive steakhouses in town. I've never eaten here since it's not in my price range, but I'm drooling thinking about the food I've seen from Sebastian and his friends' Instagram posts of this place.

My stomach growls.

Kade laughs. "I'll take that as a yes."

I wince and nod.

He releases my hand, runs his hand through his hair, and jumps out to beat the valet to my door.

I stare at him wide-eyed, still not speaking, as he smirks. He picks my hand up off my lap, helping me stand. My ankle throbs as I stand, but I'm not going to let it ruin whatever is happening.

Kade is pretending to be my date and wants to fake marry me. That is all my brain can process at the moment.

I take a step, and my heel catches in the cobblestone.

Kade's prepared and tightens his grip on my arm.

"Sorry, I should have taken you home first so you could at least change shoes, but I couldn't resist bringing you here when you look this gorgeous in the dress."

I blush. He's making it harder for me to speak instead of easier.

We make it into the restaurant, only because Kade is holding me up.

"Mr. King!" the surprised hostess exclaims. "I'm so sorry if you made a reservation, it must have gotten lost. Give me one minute, and I'll make sure we have a table for you." She winks at Kade.

I grip his arm until I'm sure my nails are digging into his flesh and give her my best glare.

Kade chuckles and leans down to kiss me on the cheek.

"I think my arrangement is going to work out fantastically, but if you keep gripping my arm this hard, I won't be able to marry you because people will think you abuse me," he says.

I release my claws, but I still hold onto him, leaning harder into his chest. I can't believe this woman has the balls to flirt with Kade. She's the hostess. What happened to professionalism?

"We have a private table near the window overlooking the lake. I know it's not your usual table, but I think you will enjoy the new view," the hostess says.

I tense.

Kade nods and then leans into my ear again, causing shivers to roll through me. "Don't worry. I've never brought a date here."

I raise my eyebrow, not believing him as we follow the hostess.

"I haven't. I only bring business associates here. I can impress a date without bringing her here."

"Then, why am *I* here?"

He smiles. "I'm glad you haven't completely lost your voice. Because this is a mix of business and pleasure. And besides, you aren't like most woman. I need more than a fancy restaurant, fast car, and charm to convince you. You're too smart to fall for one of them alone. I need a mix of everything to win you over."

I blush again, liking his answer.

We keep walking, and every time we pass a table, the entire table stops their conversation to look up at us. For the first time in my life, I feel like I belong. These people don't know who I am, and they aren't judging me because Kade King is on my arm. My dress would win in any fight against any of the dresses in here on those who-wore-it-best shows. And I have a flashy ring, double the size of most in here, on my finger.

It feels strange, fitting into a crowd I've spent my whole life on the outskirts of. Not willingly trying to enter their world, but hating that I was never invited in.

Kade pulls out my chair, and I take a seat in the dark black chair, set in front of a white tablecloth with red flowers in the center. I turn my attention out the window, where strings of lights hang over the balcony, before the lake surrounded by flowers, fountains, and views. I didn't even know a lake existed back here, but it might be the most romantic spot in all of Santa Barbara.

Kade leans back in his chair, smirking like he thinks I'm going to be able to fix whatever problems he has.

I swallow. I can't even fix my problems. And I doubt fake marrying Kade will be the solution, however appealing it is.

A waiter appears and pours us both a glass of red wine. He also gives us a dish of bread with *butter*. I haven't had white bread with butter in ages. I only put healthy food into my body, but tonight, I'm eating anything placed in front of me.

"How did the waiter know we wanted red wine?" I ask.

Kade lifts the oversized wine glass out to me. I pick up my glass. It's so light. It must be real crystal.

"Because it's his job to know. I've come to this restaurant many times. He knows my preferences. And if either of us isn't happy with the wine, he will bring us a new glass of something else. He knows I prefer not to be disturbed or asked too many questions, so he won't, unless I let him know there is a problem."

"Oh."

"Now, to a night that will change both of our lives forever."

We clink our glasses together, and I taste the wine. It's good. I won't be asking to return my wine.

Kade watches me as I take another sip before I put the glass down. I need to drink slowly, I've already had more alcohol than I usually drink and I need a clear head if I'm going to make the correct decision.

I take a piece of bread and spread it with the butter before taking a bite.

I moan as the rich honey butter coats my tongue and slowly slips down my throat.

Kade cocks his head to the side.

"What?"

He shakes his head. "You're just sexy as hell when you do that."

I blush and put the piece of bread back on the plate.

"So tell me why you've decided we should get fake married. Because my theory is you're high or drunk."

He doesn't blink or react to my joke. He takes his piece of the bread and butters it before chomping down on it, making me wait. I hate waiting.

I raise an eyebrow.

Kade leans forward like he's about to tell me a secret.

"Because you need me."

I fold my arms and lean back with a sigh. "I don't need you or anyone else."

"Maybe. Or maybe you need *exactly* this."

I stop breathing, as I look into his dreamy eyes and cocky grin. He's going to win this. I need to make sure the terms are what I want. If not, I'm going to end up hurt.

"And why do I need this?" I ask, not looking at him, and instead, eating more of the crunchy bread that tastes like cake in my mouth.

"Because you need everything I'm offering. Money, a place to live, a job, and a way to prove that not only can you fit into the world your family lives in, but you can rule it. You can be the top of the top. You won't have to worry about your father, mother, sister, or anyone in this town, ever looking down on you again."

I bite my lip trying to think about his words before responding, but I have too much on my mind to be patient with words.

"I don't want—"

"I need your help too," he says, cutting me off.

I giggle. "How can I help you? You're a god in this town. I couldn't possibly help a man like you."

He leans back in his chair, as he waves over a female waiter.

"Hello, Mr. King. What can I do for you?" the woman says seductively while touching his forearm.

Kade doesn't smile back at her. He ignores her and instead narrows his eyes as he looks at me like he's undressing me.

I shift uncomfortably in my seat. I turn my attention away from Kade to the woman I hate. She doesn't get to touch him like that. I glare at her.

"This is Larkyn Day," Kade says, turning the waitress' attention toward me.

I snarl at her, and the woman hesitantly removes her hand from Kade's arm.

Better.

"She's going to be my wife. We got engaged this afternoon," Kade finishes.

"Congratulations," the woman says, taking a step away from Kade. "I'll make sure the manager knows, and he'll bring some complimentary champagne and dessert to help you celebrate."

"Thank you, Theresa," Kade says.

The woman practically runs off, like she can't get away from us fast enough.

"That is how you can help me."

I frown.

"I don't understand."

"Women hit on me constantly."

I snort. "And that's a problem?"

He growls in a throaty way. "Yes, it's a problem. I don't mind casual sex, but I'm not looking for a wife or heir. Every woman I date, especially the women in this town, are looking for a proposal the second I slip my dick inside them. They want my money and prestige that would come with getting my last name."

I blush when he says the word dick, which he positively notices because the edge of his lips curl up as he says the word.

"And I will help your problem how? You'll be fake married to me, the one thing you don't want."

"Exactly, I'll be married to you. A woman who can make women run away with just a look."

I huff. "That waiter did not run away because I looked at her."

He folds his arms across his chest and gives me an oh really look.

"She ran away because you said we were engaged," I say.

"Exactly, the combination of your scowl and the ring on your finger will keep the women away. I won't have to worry about fending off women because you'll do it for me."

"I think you're missing one essential part."

His eyes deepen. "And what's that?"

"That you won't be able to do the sleeping with any of these women part. I'll be fending off women, so I won't allow you to be married to me and fuck other women on the side. And if anyone in my family found out, it would defeat the purpose of me doing this."

He takes another bite of his bread, chewing, as a smirk forms. "Don't worry, I won't be fucking other women."

I swallow. I don't ask the follow up to my question, which is, does he plan on fucking me?

No. He can't be. He doesn't think of me in that way, and I'm far too inexperienced to be worth his time.

"So how would you see this working?" I ask.

"I'll have my lawyer write up all the details, so we don't have to worry about either of us getting hurt. But I'm thinking, stay married for one year. We would need to have a real wedding, and soon, for this to work. You could live with me. You can also work for my company if you want. And I'll pay you well for your time."

"Payment?" I ask, not sure why I didn't expect to get paid for this.

"Of course. If you were my real wife and we got divorced, you would earn half of my money. I think you deserve to be compensated well for helping me with my problem while I'm in town."

"And why do you need to be in town?" I ask.

His smile drops and I realize exactly why. Sebastian.

"Nevermind," I say.

"I'm thinking one million for one year of being married. If we decide to stay married longer than a year, we can renegotiate if our relationship still benefits us. We can..."

Kade continues rambling on and on, but I don't hear his words. All I hear is one million dollars. That would mean I could start any business I wanted. I would have earned the money.

No.

I couldn't use the money. At least, not for what I want.

I could get my family off my back.

I could have a place to live while I saved my own money to start my own business.

And I could spend it all while getting to kiss Kade anytime we were in public together.

It wouldn't be that bad.

I want to answer yes, but my heart still isn't sure I can survive this.

Especially when he grins like he knows everything I'm thinking. I need to find a way to make him grumpy, so my heart stops skipping every time he smiles.

"Do you have any terms you would like to add?" he asks.

"We would live mostly separate lives. No questions about where we come and go, or anything personal the other doesn't want to answer."

He nods.

"We only have to attend a maximum of two events for the other person a month, and it needs to be scheduled at least a week in advance."

He thinks for a minute. "Two should usually work, but exceptions may need to be made as long as it doesn't interfere with the other person's personal life."

"We don't sleep with anyone else or cheat on each other."

He smirks. "I thought I already made it clear that wouldn't be a problem."

I nod, trying to rack my brain for more.

Steaks are placed in front of us, and we both dig in, starving after not getting to eat much at my parents' party.

"I'll have my lawyer start writing everything we've discussed in a contract, but text or call me any time if you think of anything else that needs to be added. I'll also make sure my lawyer includes a way to amend the contract in a month, so if something we didn't anticipate having to deal with arises, we can add it to the contract."

I nod, unable to answer as I chew my last bite of food.

Kade reaches across the table and grabs my hand. "You don't need to decide now. We will both think about it, and I'll have a meeting scheduled for us with my lawyer at the end of the week. You can decide then. In the meantime, we can pretend to be engaged."

I smile, enjoying pretending to be engaged already.

"Now as my fiancée, would you like to stay and have champagne and dessert, or would you like to do something else, like a movie?"

My stomach is stuffed, and I'm tired of living in his world. I need something relaxed to make sure I can at least tolerate his choice in movies.

"Movie."

He grins. "Good choice."

He grabs my hand and helps me up from the table.

"Don't you have to pay first?" I ask.

He places his hand on my waist as he leads me out. "No, I have a tab."

We slip through the restaurant and into his car and drive to the movie theater in silence, as his hand squeezes mine gently.

"I know I said this at the restaurant already, but I'm sorry I didn't stop by your place first so you could at least put on flat shoes," he says, as we walk into the theater.

"No way. I've never worn a dress this fancy, and I don't care if we arc going to see a movie, I'm not changing out of it until tonight. I'm not a dress person usually, but then again, I've never worn a thousand dollar dress."

"Nine thousand, actually," he says, smirking.

I stare down at the white dress. I'm afraid I'm going to get butter on it when he orders popcorn.

We head into the dark theater to watch a romantic comedy, to my surprise. Kade is probably just trying to give me what he thinks I want, to convince me to fake marry him.

"Are you wanting to return the dress after this? Because I'm afraid I'm going to get butter all over it."

He eyes the dress and chuckles. "Even if I wanted to return it, I would have to pry it out of your hands, which would be impossible. But don't worry, you'll have plenty of more opportunities to wear more nice dresses."

I smile and pop a piece of popcorn into my mouth as he drapes his arm around the back of my shoulders. It feels incredibly normal. I lean back against his arm with ease.

I moan softly, as I pop a piece of popcorn into my mouth. It has been years since I've eaten popcorn. It's not on my healthy diet.

"Fuck it," I hear Kade say, just before his lips crash down on mine in a kiss.

I close my eyes, kissing him back as the bag of popcorn drops from my hands onto the floor. His tongue slips into my mouth, whisking me away to another world. When he pulls away, he's panting hard staring into my eyes.

"What was that for?" I ask, assuming someone is nearby he wants to make jealous. But it's so dark in here I doubt that.

He smirks. "Because I wanted to."

I bite my lip.

"How are you going to survive a year without sex?" I ask. He's a sexual man, used to getting sex regularly.

He tucks a strand of hair behind my ear as I freeze.

"You didn't listen to a word I said after I said one million, did you?"

"I caught some of it." I wince.

He shakes his head. "I'll make sure the lawyer sends the paperwork tomorrow, so you have plenty of time to read everything and decide."

I nod.

He smiles.

"But to answer your question." He leans down, so his lips brush against my ear. "I plan on fucking you any chance you'll give me."

I'm mush. My muscles don't work. My voice has closed up. I'm not even sure if my heart is beating in my chest. He just rocked my world with one sentence.

My eyes meet his, trying to understand him.

"I've wanted to fuck you since the moment I saw you in my brother's room. I just didn't think it was the best idea to fuck you that night. You were drunk, clearly inexperienced, and you were my brother's date."

I nod.

"I know you are inexperienced, and probably used to taking things slow. So that's what I plan on doing. Getting to know each other better. Go on dates. And when you're ready, I'll fuck you like you've never been fucked before."

I swallow. "I've never been fucked before."

His eyes deepen, along with his voice. "I know."

Cocky bastard.

"As I said, we can take as long as you want. Or no time at all, but I want you Larkyn. And I plan on getting what I want. So if you agree to fake marry me, know that I also plan on seducing you."

I lick my lip. *How could I be so lucky to get everything I've ever wanted?* I can lose my virginity to the sexiest man in town, who also happens to be the most caring man in town. I get one million dollars and the guarantee that Kade will fuck only me for a year. It's the kind of deal women dream about getting.

My eyes sparkle as I look at him.

"Sorry about the popcorn. I can get you another one," Kade says, still being the gentleman that he is. But I know he can be a bad boy when he wants to. And that's the version of him I want tonight.

"No, I don't want popcorn. I don't want to watch the movie either."

"No? What do you want then?"

"I want you to fuck me, and convince me to fake marry you, if for no other reason than I get your cock any night I want."

8

KADE

Larkyn wants me to fuck her.

I thought I would need to convince her over weeks or months. She's the type of woman that needs persuading. Not because she's a prude, but because she's been hurt before. I don't know Larkyn well, but I can feel the damage she carries around with her. She has an unhealthy relationship with her family. I'm guessing she has a reason not to trust men in her life.

But she's choosing me.

She wants me to be her first. A second ago, it was all I wanted. When I kissed her, it took everything in my body not to pull her into the closest bathroom, hike up her dress, and fuck her against a bathroom stall.

I've never wanted a woman so badly.

Larkyn's different. She doesn't want me for my money. She took the time to get to know something about me before wanting me to fuck her. She's not after my millions; I will have to practically force her to take the money that she would get if she married me.

But right now, I wish I'd just gotten a hotel near the movie theater. It would have been faster. Instead, I'm driving her the fifteen minutes to my house.

86

Stupid, stupid, stupid.

She giggles as I run another red light. "You'd think you were the one who hasn't had sex before."

I growl, which makes her smile fuller.

God, I love her smiling. She only seems to do it around me. When she was with her family, she did nothing but frown. She should say yes to pretend marry me, if for no other reason than she might smile more.

"How long has it been?" she asks, beaming at me, and I know she's teasing.

"Not as long as it's been for you."

She bites her lip and kicks off her heels, putting them up on the dashboard. Usually, that would drive me mad, to have her dirty feet on my pristine dash. But with Larkyn, I want her comfortable. I thought she might be a wreck about having sex with me. But she's at ease. The second her begging words left her mouth, the panic evaporated, and a calm overtook her.

I kiss her hand again, wishing I could be kissing her more. But I don't want to make her nervous of my driving. She's been through too much already.

"It's been three or four months," I finally answer her question. I usually would never tell a woman something so personal, but she deserves to know. She opened up to me about being a virgin, even though I had guessed as much.

Her jaw drops open, and her eyes light up. "No way! I call bullshit. The great Kade King has had sex in the last three months. I bet you've had sex this week."

I shake my head. "Nope, last time was when I was home over Christmas visiting my brother. I made a mistake with Harlow. I haven't wanted a woman since."

She puffs out her lips in a huff. Her eyes cut to me, as she folds her arms across her chest.

"I'm telling the truth," I say, taking my eyes off the road for a second to see her annoyed expression.

"I know. I just can't believe I have to take back everything bad I ever thought about you."

I laugh, grab her hand, and kiss it again. I've never kissed a woman's hand before, but I can't stop doing it with Larkyn since it is the only place I can touch her right now without risking crashing.

"Be honest; you didn't think that many bad things about me, did you?"

"No, but each time you shatter my preconceptions about you it makes it that much harder to…" she stops.

"Oh, hell no. You aren't getting off that easy. You finish that sentence."

"And, if I don't?"

"Then, no sex."

She chuckles, and her eyes deepen as she realizes I'm telling the truth.

"You're serious? You wouldn't have sex with me if I didn't finish that sentence?"

"Yep. I've been through plenty of droughts before. I can hold out until you tell me."

She stares at my dick, which is giving me away by pressing against the zipper of my pants.

"I doubt that," she chuckles. "But fine. I'll answer. I'm afraid I'm going to fall in love with you if we do this."

I frown, my head snapping to her. "If we have sex?"

"Not sex. If we pretend marry. Live together. Are friends. Continue to have sex. All of it. I'm afraid I'll fall in love with you, and you won't feel the same. I'll get hurt."

Fuck, that's a lot to take in.

Her eyes widen when I pull through the gate.

"This is your house?" she asks, her body leaning forward so she can get a better view out the window.

"Yes, I prefer condos. I have a condo in LA and New York, but I thought I should own at least one house. Makes me feel more like a grownup. Besides, there aren't any nice condos nearby."

As we pull up to the door, we both undo our seatbelts and stare up at my modern mansion. I thought if I designed it as modern as possible, it would feel more like a condo instead of a house. It would feel more like mine. Instead, all it feels is cold.

I open my door and go around to open hers, still thinking about what she said. I can understand why she might think that, but it's not something she should worry about. No one ever falls in love with me. Not after they get to know me. I'm putting on the charm now because I like her and want something from her. But as soon as that changes, I'll be an ass. She'll figure it out soon enough.

I help her out of the car onto her bare feet, her heels dangling in her hands. I pull her against my body roughly. Her breath catches, and her body stiffens against mine.

"I'll hurt you long before you fall in love with me. We'll fight, I'll sleep in a hotel for a night or two, and then we will go back to being friends. That is how our story ends. You don't have to worry about falling in love with me. You were right. I'm a cocky asshole."

She smiles, but her eyes don't believe me.

I sigh. She's about to find out how much of a bad boy I can be. I should back off. Let her think about this more. Find a way to protect her heart. But I'm not going to do that. Instead, I'm going to move faster.

I kiss her. Her head tilts to the side as her lips part wider, giving me more access to her tantalizing tongue. If she's half as good at sex as she is at kissing, I'm in trouble. My head is already spinning with thoughts of her. If fucking her is incredible, I won't be going to work for days.

Her tiny body is pressed against mine as I start walking her backward, toward the entrance to my house. She winces when she takes an awkward step back.

"See, I can't even remember that you have a hurt leg? How much of an ass does that make me?" I ask.

She grins against my lips, her eyes closed. "The biggest."

I scoop her up, but instead of holding her bridal style, I throw her over my shoulder and smack her ass, making sure she's at least a little-pissed off at me for manhandling her. It will make the sex better.

"Dammit, Kade!"

I laugh as I open the door.

"Oh sorry, I thought I should try to be a gentleman, and carry you with your hurt leg and all."

"No, you aren't. You're a jerk. You could carry me sweetly. Stop trying to be an ass and just be yourself."

"This is me, baby. Get used to it."

I storm through my house, upstairs to my bedroom, and toss her onto my bed. She falls in a huff. Her white, lace dress covers most of my dark blue comforter.

She looks like heaven, and she's about to find out how much of a devil I can be.

She's smiling behind her glare. She's pretending to be mad at me, just like I'm pretending to drive her crazy so she won't fall for me. Not that she would on the first night anyway.

Larkyn glances around, taking in the large room with floor to ceiling windows looking out to the woods behind my house.

"Why don't you have blinds?" she asks, trying to see if anyone can peer into my bedroom.

I take my time removing my jacket, tie, and shirt.

She finally looks my way, and her body blushes red at the sight of my bare chest. She bites her lip as she examines the tattoos on my chest. She rapidly blinks, like she can't believe what her eyes are seeing.

"Never seen a shirtless man before?" I tease.

She grabs the single throw pillow on my bed, and tosses it at me, but misses.

"Of course I have. The tattoos caught me off guard. Maybe you're the bad boy I originally thought you were."

I kick off my shoes and lower my pants and boxer briefs in one push.

"Maybe I am," I say, winking at her. Her eyes try desperately to stay on my chest instead of looking at my throbbing cock, which grows larger every second she stares at me with those big eyes of hers.

"It's okay, you can look," I say, walking toward her.

She swallows. "Um…"

Speechless, perfect. This is going to be fun, torturing her.

She finally takes a peek, and her hand covers her mouth to hold in her gasp. Her eyes are almost popping out of her head, and her cheeks are red.

I laugh. "First time seeing a cock?"

"No, just…um…yours is…um."

"You like it?"

"Yes," she breathes, finally gaining the confidence to look me in the eyes. And when she does, everything disappears. The embarrassment. The playfulness. The tinge of anger.

It's all replaced with lust.

She wants to fuck me. She's desperate for it. *Good.*

I pull open the drawer and find a condom, tossing it on the bed, so I don't have to find one later.

She bites her lip and runs her hands over my abs.

"I like these," she says.

I grin.

I flip her over and am rewarded with a whimper.

I unzip and pull off her dress sharply, before flipping her back over to get my own glimpse of her abs.

"I like these," I growl in return, before lowering my head to kiss her smooth stomach, rippling with muscles.

She grins and runs her hands through my hair, as I work my way up her body. Kissing over her white bra and cleavage, to her neck, and finally finding her mouth.

So many whimpers escape her lips, and this time her cheeks flush with need instead of embarrassment.

She arches her back as I kiss her, forcing my cock into her stomach. I swear I almost come like a fifteen-year-old boy from the touch of her body against mine.

What's wrong with me?

I need to slow this down if I want a chance at making her come on my cock and not embarrass myself. It's just because it's been so long without sex. That's all. It has nothing to do with the particular woman underneath me.

"How could a woman as beautiful and intelligent as you still be a virgin?" I ask, as I slow my kisses on her neck.

The question was meant to be rhetorical. It was meant to be a compliment, but from the way her body has stilled, I don't think she took it that way.

I stop, leaning off her body.

"I didn't mean anything by it. I just meant you are so incredible. I can't believe how lucky I am that I get to be with you first. I'm amazing in bed, so you're pretty lucky that you get to learn from the best," I say, with a wink.

She doesn't smile. She doesn't move.

"I should tell you before we do this," she says, sitting up, pushing my naked body back.

I narrow my eyes at her, not understanding her words.

"I don't want you to find out later, think I was hiding it, and it ruin our friendship," she says.

I tuck a strand of her hair behind her ear, but it does nothing to tame the wildness of her hair that already looks like I fucked her.

"There is nothing you could tell me that will make me stop wanting to fuck you right now."

She takes a deep breath before looking at me in the same way. And if she keeps staring at me like she is now, she won't have time to say anything.

"Then tell me. Because I can't wait any longer to fuck you."

She bites her lip, and this looks like it's going to be a long conversation.

"Actually, lay back," I say.

"Why?" She raises an eyebrow.

I sigh. "Will you just do what I say?"

"No."

I shake my head. "You trust me to be your first, but not to give you a simple command?"

She blushes.

I grab her legs, spreading them on either side of my body as I pull her roughly until she's lying on her back. Then, my face buries between her legs.

She gasps when I kiss over her panties to her most sensitive area.

"I can't talk if you keep doing that," she says, arching her back as I pull her panties down.

"What if I do this?"

I lick my tongue slowly over her slit, then up to her bud, swollen and ready for me.

She gasps again, gripping my bedspread.

"You need to stop."

I lick again, and her legs clasp against my head. There is no way I'm stopping.

"Has anyone licked you before, Larkyn?" I ask.

"No," she moans, as I continue.

"Good. Then, I get the pleasure of tasting you as you come on my face for the first time."

"Don't stop," she pants when I slow my tongue again.

I grin and speed up my pace. Not relenting or letting her get a second to think about whatever has her worried that I won't want to do this with her.

Her body tightens, her eyes roll back, and her hands grasp the comforter so forcefully, I think she might rip a hole in it.

"Come, Larkyn," I whisper against her pussy as I continue torturing her with my mouth.

Her legs lock my head in a headlock, she cries out, and her lips grip my tongue as her orgasm rips through her.

I lick every drop of cum off her body, letting her know how much I enjoyed that, and how much more I'm going to enjoy fucking her and making her come again with my cock.

I move up her body while she pants on the bed, exhausted and alive after the pleasure I brought her.

I smirk as I pop her bra open, and let my mouth come down on one of her sensitive nipples.

"Kade, I can't again—"

I silence her with a flick of my tongue on her nipple, and she's mine again.

She claws at my back as I continue my assault on her body, finding every sensitive area I can and exploiting it. Making it *mine*.

Her breasts, neck, and just above her hip are all sensitive areas I'll have to remember for the future.

"You still with me?" I ask, nerves slipping in as I reach for the condom.

She swallows hard, as her eyes lazily drop to my cock. I want her mouth on my dick, but that will have to wait until later. Right now, I need to make her feel even more incredible than she did with her last orgasm.

She nods, answering my question.

"Good, because I'm about to rock your world."

"That's cheesy," she says with a grin, as my lips come down and kiss her.

When I pull back, I tear the condom open with my teeth and sheath myself with it before resting between her legs.

Her breathing slows, and I feel the slickness escaping her, trying to welcome me in.

I need her permission. One more time first. And now I'm nervous. Why? Because I don't want to screw this up. Whatever this is between us, I like it. I like helping her, and I think she would like helping me.

Sex changes things. But it won't change us.

I don't ask her again with words. Instead, I press my cock at her entrance as I kiss her. Giving her a warning that if she doesn't stop me, she's mine. And I'm hers. I'll be her first.

"I'm not a virgin," she whispers.

I stop, but my dick doesn't soften. I don't give a fuck if she's a virgin or not.

"Doesn't matter."

"I was raped at nineteen, that's why I'm technically not," she says.

I suck in a breath, searching in her eyes for the pain. It's there, but tampered. She hasn't thought about that night for a long time.

"You're a virgin, then," I say, letting her know that whatever that asshole did to her doesn't mean he took her virginity.

I'm taking it.

She smiles. "I've waited a long time to find the perfect guy to be my first."

I smirk. "I'm pretty perfect, aren't I?"

She gives me a wicked stare. "Too perfect."

I kiss her lips. I'll stop and spend the rest of the night listening to her story.

"You can tell me every detail of how the guy raped you. I can be that guy for you. Or I can be the guy who fucks you and destroys his memory in your mind. Makes it all but disappear. No longer mattering. I know he's practically gone anyway because you aren't broken. You're strong. So which guy do you want me to be?" I know what guy I want to be, but she has to choose.

She looks away, and I'm afraid she's going to choose the talking route. After all of this, she's going to be the woman I thought she was all along. Cautious. Thinking with her brain, instead of her heart.

"Be the guy that fucks my brains out, and makes me an insatiable sex addict," she says, with a wicked glance.

"My pleasure." My cock slides into her with ease, her slick entrance coating me as I push inside.

My eyes stay on her, even as my lips kiss her, looking for any signs that this too much for her. That I'm bringing back nightmares or thoughts of him. I will be asking more questions later because I want to make sure the bastard is in prison. No one gets to hurt Larkyn Day ever again.

Her eyes stay open too.

"Incredible," she says, smiling.

I realize that I'm not moving. I'm frozen except for my lips kissing hers. I've been too afraid that I will physically or emotionally hurt her if I move.

"That's what I was thinking about you," I say, as I start to rock in out of her body. Treasuring every bit of her body as I do.

Her moans.

Her grin.

Her gaze.

Her body is holding onto me like she will never let me go.

I feel her building the faster I move, so I move faster and faster. I cradle her body tenderly in my arms while fucking her like no woman I have before.

I don't have to say a word. She doesn't either. We look at each other, and we come, together.

Both of our orgasms shoot through us like a fire that can't be contained.

I collapse next to her on the bed. I'm spent. I only fucked her once. Usually, I fuck a woman at least twice, but fucking Larkyn is like fucking a million women at once. Better actually, because Larkyn is the only woman I've fucked who is only interested in my dick and me. Nothing else. Not my money, my fancy cars, or my expensive condos. She doesn't want a baby to make me hers. She doesn't even want a real marriage. This isn't a trap. It's just her and me, fucking.

Larkyn begins to move off the bed, but I grab her hips and force her down, my body her trapping her.

"Where are you going?"

"Home, I didn't think you would enjoy having a woman sleep with you in your bed. Even one you might be fake marrying soon."

I frown. Usually, I would hate women that think they are going to sleep over after sex. But the fact that Larkyn didn't assume she was staying makes me like her even more.

"You're staying."

"What?" Her eyes blink rapidly.

"I want you here in my bed. If I fuck you, you're staying. You don't get to slink out in the night."

She narrows her eyes studying me.

"Even if I was living with you?"

"If I fuck you, you're mine for the night. You don't get to sleep alone." I want to add ever to the end of my sentence but don't. I want her in my bed for the entire year. So I can have my way with her whenever I want, but I think it might be too much to ask of her.

I roll off her and pull her to me as I pull the covers over our naked bodies. Her body fits snuggly in the crook of mine. Her head rests against my arm, and she's so small I doubt my arm will ever tire of having her lay on it all night.

"Yes," she says.

"What?" I ask, rolling her over to look at me.

"I'll fake marry you," she says grinning.

Yes, such a beautiful word.

"Good. Now get some sleep, so you have enough strength for me to fuck you in the morning."

She giggles as I wrap my arms around her again. "I have another condition though."

"Which is?"

"I want you to get me a smaller ring."

I laugh.

"Or a fake one to replace this one. I can't wear this expensive of a ring."

I kiss her on the lips. "No, you deserve the best."

The absolute best. She deserves everything. And I plan on giving her everything. I have to remember that it's okay to be an ass, too. Because there is no way, I'm letting her fall in love with me and ruin us. And I couldn't live with myself if I hurt her.

9

LARKYN

It's been a week since I slept with Kade.

It's what I wanted. A week apart after he rocked my world and made me realize what I've been missing all these years. I regret not having sex sooner if it is always that amazing. I'm afraid it might only be *that* incredible with Kade, and not any of other guys.

Kade has, mostly, respected my wishes to stay away. Only because I told him I needed to study for my final exams. I didn't need to study. I have straight A's and could have failed every one of my tests and still graduated. But Kade didn't know that. So he stayed away, except for a few naughty text messages telling me how much he missed my body.

I glance up at the stage where some rich man is speaking, trying to be inspirational. Saying things about how we are the future, and graduating from a prestigious school like this means we can do anything. It's the usual words. Nothing will make a difference in any of our lives. Thousands of students sit in chairs next to me, all waiting for him to finish talking so we can throw our graduation caps in the air and celebrate.

Only problem is, I don't have any family here to celebrate with. I texted my father on Thursday when it was official that I was graduating on Friday. He texted back that he had a meeting in Chicago and couldn't be here. My mother is too drunk to come. And Anastasia won't attend anything that isn't all about her, especially after I overshadowed her engagement with my own.

I stare down at my bare finger. I chose not to wear the ring today. Today is about me.

My family isn't here.

Kade isn't here.

Today, I'm on my own.

The man finally stops talking, and we throw our caps up in the air. We are graduates now. But I find myself wondering why I bothered attending the ceremony. I should have just stayed home to packed and had the school mail me my diploma. And I should have texted Kade to hang out instead. I need to text him so we can talk about the documents his lawyer sent over earlier this week.

I catch my cap as it falls. My immediate thought is to text Kade to see if he's busy tonight so we can talk, and do other things… I bite my lip as my mind is clouded with thoughts of having sex with Kade again.

But I know Serena is going to want me to hang out with her and her family to celebrate graduating. And then I should really start packing. We have to be out of our apartment in a week.

I start walking across the auditorium floor to the other side, where I know Serena was sitting, to meet her.

"Beautiful and intelligent, how lucky am I?" I hear Kade say from behind me.

I grin. I've never smiled so much in my life as I have the few days I've spent with Kade.

I turn around. "And why are you lucky?"

He holds out the most massive bouquet of flowers in the auditorium to me. I take it from him, barely able to wrap my hands around the stems.

"Because I get to spend the next year with you."

I try to hide my smile, but it's impossible. "And why do you think that? I haven't officially signed any papers yet."

"You already said yes. Twice," he winks as he says twice, and I know he's referring to me coming twice the last time we were together.

I reach into my oversized purse that is draped over my shoulder and hand him the papers I signed last night.

He grins like an idiot, as he takes the papers from me and flips to the last page with my signature. He takes a pen from his pocket and signs it as well.

"Now it's official. You're mine for the year."

My hands tremble a little at that thought. I want nothing more than to be his. I just need to remind my body that despite his words and actions, I'm not his.

He glances down at my hand. "Why aren't you wearing your ring?"

I sigh.

"Because I wanted one last day where I belonged to myself, and not to you."

He frowns and pulls the ring out of his pocket. He grabs my hand and places it into my hand.

"For when you're ready to be mine," he says.

I stare at the ring in the palm of my hand. Take a deep breath. And slip the heavy diamond onto my finger. I signed the papers. We are getting married next weekend. I might as well get used to wearing the enormous rock. I don't know how he has the ring. Did Serena let him in?

He smiles, and the smile is almost worth the cost of having to wear something so flashy.

"Where is your family? Are we headed to another graduation party?" he asks, as he drapes his arm over my shoulders and looks around to find my family.

"They aren't here."

He narrows his eyes, searching mine for answers.

"I'm sorry."

"It doesn't matter. My family doesn't matter. But I wouldn't expect them to attend the wedding either. They want nothing to do with me unless I do as I'm told."

He hugs me tight against his chest as the flowers rest by my side so my face can sink into his body. I take a deep breath and smell his deep cologne. It shouldn't comfort me, but it does.

"Oh my god! Are you two together?" Serena squeals, looking from Kade down to me.

I try to step out of his arms, but he holds me tight. He's always touching me or holding me. Something I'm afraid I'll get used to far too quickly.

I nod and blush.

"Getting married, actually," Kade says.

Serena's mouth drops, along with the diploma and graduation cap she was holding. She glances down and quickly picks it up again.

"You can't be serious? I didn't even know you were... I mean, when did this happen?" Serena asks, flustered and staring right at me. I know she's annoyed that I have been hiding Kade and I's relationship from her.

I wince. "It's a long story."

"A story you will be giving me every detail of later."

I nod.

"Good."

Serena looks behind her where her family is waiting for her.

"So I'm guessing you're a no then for celebrating with my family and me?" Serena asks with a smug expression on her face as she crosses her arms.

I nod, biting my lip.

She shakes her head and runs over to hug me. Kade drops his arm from my shoulders as she wraps her arms around me.

"I mean *every* detail later," Serena says, winking.

"Don't worry, I'll tell you everything. You're my maid of honor after all."

Her face lights up, and her grin reaches her eyes. "Damn right, I am," she says, as she struts away.

"We should celebrate. What is your favorite restaurant?" Kade asks.

"I don't eat out much. I don't have a favorite restaurant."

Kade sighs as he stands next to me, staring, as people continue walking by us. Every person that walks by stares at Kade and then to me with wide-eyes or a glare. They don't believe we belong together. And we don't.

"I have the perfect seafood restaurant to try. Do you like sushi?"

I stare down at the flowers and diploma I'm still holding. I'm supposed to go to a restaurant to celebrate with family and friends. Except my family is a no-show, and I just turned down my best friend. And I'm marrying a man that I've slept with once, and might as well be a complete stranger.

"I have a better idea," I reach up, grab his neck, and kiss him on the lips, slipping my tongue into his mouth. Our bodies collide, and I drop the flowers, along with my diploma to the ground.

He's not really mine. He's not really mine. He's not really mine.

But when he grabs my face and deepens the kiss, moaning into my mouth, I forget that he's not mine.

"I like your idea better; food can wait until after. Your place or mine?"

I grin.

"Mine's closer."

———

I open the door to my apartment with Kade's lips locked on mine when my leg hits a box that shouldn't be sitting in the entryway.

I pause the kiss and stare into my apartment. Boxes are everywhere. Boxes that weren't here when I left this morning.

"What?" I can't speak because I don't even know what questions to ask.

I turn to Kade who has a smirk on his face. "*You.* What did you do?"

"I hired movers to box everything up. Your lease ends in a few days, and I knew you'd say yes. So I went ahead and had them get started packing so you can move in with me ASAP."

I frown. "I'm not moving in with you until we are married."

He sighs. "I figured you'd say that. But your stuff is already packed. All of it. You can't exactly stay here."

I narrow my eyes and cross my arms. "I can and I will."

He shakes his head. "So stubborn."

I hold my ground. I may have signed the papers, but I'm not letting him think he can control me. He can't. Ever. And he certainly isn't going to start now.

"Fine. You can stay here until we get married next week."

I grin. "Thanks, but I don't need your permission."

I start walking toward the bedroom as Kade follows me. I stop abruptly and turn to Kade.

"Wait, how did you get into my apartment without me knowing? How did you get the ring back?" I ask holding up my hand.

He shrugs.

"Kade," I say sternly.

"I like you being all bossy. I got Serena's number at the hospital. It happened to come in handy."

"She knows?"

"Not all the details, like about how good I was in bed, but I'm sure you'll fill her in on that later. But yea, she knows."

Pink flushes my cheeks as I think back to Serena's reaction. "But she said..." I trail off.

Kade raises an eyebrow at me, smiling.

"Damn, she's a good actress," I mumble.

I open the door to my bedroom and gasp. My bed frame is in pieces, covered in bubble wrap, while my mattress is sandwiched between my wall and half a dozen boxes.

I pout. *Why can't I have this one thing? All I want is to have Kade fuck me in my bed to celebrate graduating from college. Why is it so hard for the universe to understand?*

I turn to Kade. "I guess we should have gone to your place."

He smirks, and his eyes darken as he walks toward me in his designer jeans and dark buttoned up shirt that reveals the hint of muscles lying beneath his shirt. I eye the growing hardness trapped in his jeans. He still wants me.

His thumb caresses my face as he kisses me again, harder than he should since we don't have a place to fuck unless we use Serena's bed. And I'm not going to deal with her wrath if she found out or came home early.

"Who says I need a bed to fuck you?"

I lick my lips, and my pussy aches as he speaks. I've had sex once. I'm not an idiot, but we don't have a bed. Or a couch. Or even a table to have sex on. I don't know what's left.

Kade grabs my hips, and we move backward until my back hits the wall behind me. He grins as his lips find mine again. Tasting and swirling around my tongue, making me lose my mind.

His hand slips under my dress, pushing it up, and finds my bare ass beneath the thong I'm wearing. His fingers hook the edge of my lace thong and pull them down until they fall to my feet. He watches them hit my ankles, and then I step out of them still wearing my heels.

"You found some prettier lingerie, huh?" he asks, as he kisses my neck.

"I didn't think you were too fond of my plain cotton panties."

He gives me a wicked grin. "They were starting to grow on me. And remind me to punish you later for wearing heels again and no brace."

His hand slips up my backside again before slapping me on the ass.

I let out a yelp.

"My doctor said I don't need to wear my braces any longer."

He eyes me suspiciously. "I doubt that."

"It's true." I kiss him on the lips and undo his pants to shut him up. I shove them down along with his boxer briefs, and immediately feel his erection in my stomach pressing hard, begging me to enter.

He spanks me again.

I gasp.

"You aren't going to be able to distract me with sex all the time you know." He steps back and pulls his shirt off until he's naked.

I bite my lip. I may not be able to, but I sure will try.

He picks up his pants and pulls out a condom. He sheaths himself with the latex before returning to kiss me hard against the wall. He shoves my dress up, grabs my ass, and I impale myself on his cock.

My hands grab onto his hair as he thrusts inside me, holding me up while fucking me against the wall. He rocks harder and harder inside me, knowing that he doesn't have to do much to make me come. My moaning gives me away; I'm very close to giving into the desires deep in my belly that are begging to explode out.

I try to speak. But everything that comes out of my mouth is a mix of a moan, groan, and holy hell pant.

His eyes sear into mine, as our tongues dance together. He knows what he's doing to me. But I seem to be doing the same to him.

He growls, and my body tightens around his cock, I can't hold on any longer. I come, and it's like a thousand fireworks go off in my body all at once. Last time, I came because his tongue was on my clit dancing. I came a second time that night, because of how much he stirred my body from the first orgasm.

But now, he made me come with just his cock, and I never want to come without his cock again.

He doesn't lower me immediately after we both come. Nor does he remove his cock. We stay locked, holding on to every last fleeting moment of pleasure. Because even though this is only the second time we've fucked, our time together is only for a year. And our agreement doesn't mean that we have to have sex for the entire year either. Although, I plan on taking advantage of every day of our year together.

He nibbles on my lip. "I'm hungry and need a shower. Let's order food, and then shower together while we wait for the food."

"Shower together?" I ask, stupidly.

He chuckles. "I forget how inexperienced you are when you fuck me like that. But yes, I plan on fucking you every way I can, in every place I can. Shower, kitchen, bedroom, living room, public places, everywhere."

He gently lowers me down to my feet. He winks and picks up his jeans to dig out his phone.

I lean against the wall, smiling like an idiot.

"Sushi, okay?" Kade asks.

"Yes," I say, taking a step forward. But my heels don't hold me, and I fall in a heap to the floor. My injured wrist catches myself on the floor, and the sharp pain immediately reminds me that although most of the bruises have healed enough to be covered with makeup, my wrist and leg have not.

Kade is kneeling in front of me in seconds. He gently holds out his hand to me, as I hold my injured wrist tenderly.

"Let me see," he says sternly.

I hold out my wrist that is red and inflamed. He takes it in his hand eyeing it carefully with concern on his face before he kisses it carefully.

"I'll go get some ice and see if I can find any painkillers," he says.

He leaves me sitting naked on the carpet of my bedroom as he heads to the kitchen.

"This changes nothing! We are still having shower sex!" I holler after him.

I hear him chuckle. "Only if you wear your brace," he hollers back as I listen to him open the freezer and scrape out some ice.

"Fine!" I shout back. My wrist hurts, and I'll do anything for another opportunity to have sex with Kade. We are going to need some boundaries if this is how I feel after only the second time fucking. Maybe the more we do it, the less effect it will have on me.

I try moving my wrist, but it burns to move it at all, so instead, I lie it carefully on my knee. I kick off my heels that I never plan on wearing again. They are the damn reason I keep falling. I wait patiently for Kade to return.

I don't know if it's the pain in my wrist, or if Kade is really slow at getting ice that makes the time move by so slowly.

"Kade, I only need a small bag of ice. Not an iceberg large enough to sink the Titanic," I shout.

Nothing.

I sigh. *Did he just leave?*

I use my good arm to push myself up into a standing position. Fuck, my ankle hurts too. I should put some ice on it as well. I grab Kade's shirt and slip it on, before walking to the kitchen where Kade is.

He doesn't look at me when I enter.

"What are you doing?" I ask. He's standing in my kitchen holding a bag of ice.

"I need to go," he says.

He walks to me and hands me the bag of ice. Then continues back to my bedroom. I take a deep breath, trying not to be upset. We aren't dating; of course, he can go and not tell me why. He doesn't need a reason. We are a fake relationship. This isn't real. We have sex and pretend we are together. That's all this is.

But the tears threatening my eyes say I want this to be more.

Dammit.

I can't be feeling this way already. I blink back the tears and put the ice on my wrist.

Kade reappears from my bedroom moments later in his jeans. He walks over to me, and I think he's going to give me an explanation or at least say he's sorry.

"I'm going to need my shirt," Kade says.

"Oh," is all that leaves my mouth. I quickly remove the shirt until I'm standing naked in front of him, and he's fully dressed.

And then, he walks out my front door without a goodbye, a kiss on the cheek, or any words at all.

I hate him.

Good.

That's what I wanted. To know that he can live up to his bad boy reputation and be just as bad to me as everyone else. It will stop me from feeling special. And will help me remember that after the year is up, I'll return to being nothing to him.

I head to the shower. I don't want to smell like him and be reminded of him all night. So I shower and put on a shirt and sweatpants that I find at the top of one of the boxes labeled clothing. I spend a few minutes digging my bathroom items out of boxes, and then I grab the ice I left in the freezer before my shower. I head to Serena's bed to ice my ankle and wrist. I guess I'm sleeping in her bed with her for the next few nights. Good thing she has a king-sized bed.

I'll spend the night icing my sore body and watching horror movies to distract myself from being pissed at Kade for walking out without an explanation.

A knock on the door stops me in my tracks. *Did Kade decide to come back?*

I walk to the door carefully, so I don't fall and injure myself again. I open the door.

"Delivery for a Miss Day," the man says, dressed in jeans and a dark shirt.

"I'm sorry, but I didn't order anything."

He holds out the bag to me. "It's already been paid for by a Mr. King who said to tell you he is incredibly sorry and to give you this note."

I take the note and the bag from him before going back inside. I place the bag on my kitchen counter and read the note.

Larkyn,

I'm sorry I left without a goodbye or explanation. I'm not used to being accountable to another person. A family emergency came up that I need to take care of. So sorry to cut our night short. I'll make up the shower sex to you soon. Promise. Stop being stubborn and ice your ankle and wrist. And wear your braces. I'll punish you if you don't.

—Kade

109

Dammit.

One note and a container of sushi and I like him again. I can't even go one night without hating him. My heart doesn't stand a chance at not falling in love during this next year.

10

KADE

I'm getting married to the perfect woman. Not because I love her or want a normal marriage with her, but because she is exactly what I need to make my problems go away. Women will stop hitting on me and trying to trap me by getting pregnant. And after we get divorced, women will realize that Larkyn got almost nothing in the divorce. One million is nothing to these women. They will realize I'm not worth the effort. It's a brilliant plan.

Now I have to stand at the end of the aisle with Axel, my best friend, and hope Larkyn actually walks down the aisle and marries me, instead of making me look like a fool by not showing up. She's signed the contract, and the money will be deposited in her account the second she says 'I do,' but it's still a lot to ask of her.

I've barely seen Larkyn this week. The handful of times I've seen her were when we were meeting to decide which cake or flowers we were going to use. Or when we met with the overly ambitious wedding planner, I hired to get the wedding planned in less than a week at the five-star hotel I'm currently standing in. I'll give it to our wedding planner and Serena; together they made a great team and somehow came in under the budget I gave them, while giving me everything I wanted.

Larkyn didn't have an opinion about any of the details. I was afraid I was even going to have to pick out her wedding dress for her. Luckily, I didn't, so I have no idea what she is going to look like walking toward me. For all I know, she will be in jeans and a tank top.

I haven't had time to fully explain to Larkyn since I walked out on her. She's still pissed; she has a right to be. But I'll spend this week making it up to her, because I don't plan on leaving her side after we say our vows.

If I play my cards right, I'll get her to work for me as my assistant so she can go with me everywhere. I grin, liking that idea too much. I would never get any work done with her so near, driving my cock mad, stopping to fuck her every time we were alone. But I won't be getting any work done without her.

Sebastian shifts in his seat in the front row, and my grin drops. He's under strict instructions to not fuck up today. I don't know whether to thank him for running over Larkyn or to kill him. He's the reason I'm getting married right now. But he's also the reason Larkyn's pissed at me and might back out. I had to fix another one of his fucking problems the night I walked out on her, just like I always do. He's got one year to get his shit together; after that, I'm done helping him.

The music changes, and I turn my attention down the long aisle lined with flowers. The doors open, and Serena starts walking in a lavender dress. It's a good sign seeing her smiling and winking at me. Her hair is swept to the side in defined dark curls.

When she gets to me, I ask, "Is Larkyn here? How is she?"

She smiles. "Look for yourself."

I swivel my head as the main doors close, then reopen with a new song. Larkyn is standing there, on the arm of her father.

I exhale for the first time in minutes. Her father came and is walking her down the aisle. He better have after the lecture I gave him. But I don't give a damn about him right now.

All I can focus on is the goddess floating toward me. Larkyn isn't wearing a giant expensive dress. It's a simple, understated dress.

Spaghetti straps hug her shoulders, lace covers the bodice, and chevron fabric hangs down from her chest. Compared to everything else in the room, she looks simple. There is no way she spent much money on the dress. But she looks even more stunning because she isn't over the top. She's just herself. Hair down and curled. No veil, only a few white flowers in her hair. And flat shoes.

I grin. At least she listened to one of my requests. I won't have to worry about her falling and injuring herself every second of the reception.

Larkyn and her father stop a foot from me. He gives me a stern look before holding out his daughter's hand to me. I take it, without giving a shit about the man who has treated his daughter like crap for the last twenty years.

"You look like an angel. So beautiful," I croak out, my voice breaking because it's so dry from gaping at her.

She blushes. "I used my own money to buy the dress. I wanted something that was mine to wear. I hope it's enough."

My eyes widen. "It's more than enough." I kiss her gently on the cheek.

"You still pissed at me?" I ask.

She licks her lips as her eyes tear through my tuxedo. "I can't stay mad at you, no matter how hard I try."

I smirk. "Good, because I really need the hot wedding sex tonight. This week has been torture for me."

She bites her lip. "Me too."

Damn, that's sexy.

"You ready?" I ask, eyeing the impatient minister out of the corner of my eye.

She smirks. "Yes."

We're married.

I'm not sure it has sunk in yet, but the ring on my finger tells me otherwise. And the look in my bride's eyes tells me it's true.

"You got me a simple ring," Larkyn says, holding up the plain gold band I bought her to serve as her wedding ring. "Does that mean I don't have to wear the enormous engagement ring all the time?"

My lips thin a little. The engagement ring has a lot of sentimental value to me. I'd love for her to wear it always, although I know it's not realistic for her to. It's too big and doesn't fit her style. I should tell her why the ring means so much to me, and why I want her to wear it, but I'm not ready to share my story, yet.

I kiss her hand where both rings rest as we sit in the backseat of a limo on the way to my house. I thought about getting a hotel room for the night, but I don't want her in a hotel room. I want her at my house where she belongs.

"You only have to wear it to parties or events you attend with me."

She relaxes her head on my shoulder. "We need to get a safe for it when I'm not wearing it, so I don't lose it."

I kiss the top of her head. My life is perfect. Everyone believed our wedding to be real. No woman hit on me at the reception. In fact, most of the single woman tried to give me a wide berth when walking near me. Larkyn's family seemed to believe what we have is real. Her father even appeared a bit proud when he looked at Larkyn, though he will never admit it to her.

"So are you whisking me to an exotic place for our honeymoon?" she asks, yawning.

I pull her closer into me, and she cuddles her head against my chest. We have at least a thirty-minute drive from here to my house.

"No, sorry," I say chuckling.

"That's okay. I was hoping we could stay at your place. I'm too exhausted to want to travel all over the world."

I stroke her hair, loving having her head against my chest. "We will go on a belated honeymoon in the fall or around the holidays if you want. Now isn't a good time with everything going on at work." *Or with Sebastian*, I think, but don't tell Larkyn. I need to keep my thoughts of my brother private from Larkyn.

"Stressed?" she asks.

"Not as much anymore, now that we are married," I say.

Her eyes flutter open, and I can see she has a dark thought.

"What?"

She licks her lips. "I can help you relieve some stress."

Yes. God, yes.

"I think I've flipped a switch in your head and changed you from innocent to sex goddess," I say, loving the look she's giving me.

I think she's going to straddle my lap so I can fuck her in the back of the limo, but she doesn't.

Instead, her hands go for the button and zipper on my pants. She undoes my pants and slowly pushes them down, along with my underwear until my cock springs free.

She eyes me as she licks her lips again. She hesitates for a second and grasps my cock firmly with her hand. Rubbing it up and down gently.

I gasp. She has never touched my cock with her hand. Either she wasn't brave enough, or I never gave her the chance.

She grins when she sees my reaction.

"You don't ever have to ask to touch me like this," I say between heated breaths.

She keeps her gorgeous, big eyes on me as she lowers her lips and sucks the head.

My eyes roll back in my head as a curse leaves my lips at how incredible the blissful touch of her lips on me feels.

I open my eyes to watch as her mouth takes most of me in, and then slowly rakes her teeth back up my cock.

Sexy as hell.

I grip her hair, doing everything I can to not force her head back down over my cock. I want her to be in control. And she wouldn't let me take it from her right now even if I wanted to.

Her lips curl up as she sees what she's doing to me. Her head comes all the way off my cock as a drop of pre-cum coats the top. Her tongue licks across the tip, grabbing the drop of liquid off before she swallows it down.

I ache. Everywhere. *What is she doing to me?*

She smirks as if to show she knows exactly what she's doing. Suddenly her mouth comes down on my cock, until she has every bit of me in her mouth.

"Fuck," I moan, not able to hold back.

I buck underneath her mouth. She meets my thrusts and begins moving her mouth up and down, stroking me at the same speed I'm moving.

I can't breathe. I can't speak. All I can do is feel every bit of her mouth, tongue, and throat moving over me like an expert that has done this exact thing thousands of times before. I don't have to tell her what I want. She knows. She moves faster, harder when I want her to. She scrapes the tiniest bit of her teeth against my head and then swirls her tongue over the top before sucking me in again.

I growl, looking her dead in the eye, telling her I'm about to come, so stop sucking me if she doesn't want to taste my cum. I can't speak, so it's the only way I can warn her.

She grins around my cock and takes me in further as I shoot my load down her throat. My cock pulses over and over in her mouth, until she's milked every last drop from me.

When I finish, she neatly tucks me back into my pants with the broadest smile possible on her face.

"You've done that before," I say, watching her smirk.

"No."

"Then, how?"

She blushes.

"How?" I ask again.

"I did a few internet searches…" She winces and blushes like it's a bad thing.

I chuckle. "You watched porn?"

She nods.

I laugh, a full belly laugh. I grab her steaming red cheeks and kiss her on the lips. "You're incredible. Don't ever be ashamed of watching porn. I kind of like it."

She leans back like she's exhausted.

"Oh, you don't get to be tired yet."

"Why not?"

The driver pulls up into my driveway.

"Because it's my turn to repay the favor."

I open my door and jump out before pulling her out into my arms so I can carry her into our house.

"You don't have to carry me. We aren't really married."

I scowl. "We are *really* married."

She rolls her eyes. "We aren't in love. We aren't planning on staying married. We signed a contract. We aren't *really* married."

"A prenup."

She sighs. "A contract I can already see I need to amend."

I frown, stopping before I carry her inside. "Why?"

"Because you have to stop being so nice to me all the time. I told you, I can't like you. Only the sex part. You need to be more of a jerk to me."

"I was. I walked out on you after we had sex without a word."

"And then you sent me sushi and a note, making it all better. You can't keep doing that. You need to treat me like any of the other women you fucked and didn't want a relationship with. The boundaries get too confusing otherwise. You can't do anything a boyfriend would do for me unless we are in public." Her eyes darken and her lips tense, and I know she's serious.

"No, I like treating you well."

"You need to stop. I can't handle it. That's why we keep going weeks without seeing each other. Now that we are fake married, we have to have boundaries. Mine is that we can have sex and we can do public appearances together as husband and wife. Otherwise, you treat me like a roommate that you can barely tolerate. No date nights. No sleeping in my bed. No snuggling. No watching chick flicks with me. Nothing."

I hate every single word leaving her mouth.

"And if I don't agree?"

"No more sex."

Damn, she's serious. And stubborn. I am too, but I'm not going to win this fight tonight.

"Fine."

She grins. "Now put me down. You aren't carrying me over the threshold like I'm your bride."

I grin, because she just gave me the out I was looking for. "No."

"You just agreed—"

"I agreed to treat you like a roommate and be an ass on occasion. Tonight, I'm going to be an ass. You don't want me to carry you over the threshold, but I do. Get pissed at me."

She does. The pout on her face is adorable, but it isn't gentle. She's pissed. And as much as I want to kiss her pout away, I won't. She wants me to be a jerk, which means not giving her everything she wants. She'll be begging me to be *nice* in a matter of days.

I carry her into my house. I don't bother to flip on the lights. I don't need them for what I'm about to do.

"Fine, you made your point. Now put me down."

I walk over to my sturdy dining room table with a view out into the forest.

"Fine."

I return her to her feet roughly, not waiting for her to gain her balance before I spin her around and shove her stomach onto the top of the table.

"What are you doing?" she asks.

"Fucking you."

She gasps.

I growl.

She's not going to win this war. She's not going to fall in love with me no matter what I do. I always fuck up relationships. She might as well get over this insistence that we can't be nice to each other and let me do what I want.

I undo my pants quickly, pushing them down as I hike up her dress. I've never fucked her from behind. She's never been fucked from behind. Each new thing I try with her is her first. I love being the first to teach her new things. I jerk her panties down, tearing them to rip them off her body.

She gasps again as my hand finds her pussy, flicking my thumb across her clit. She tries to move off the table, but my hand on her back keeps her down. I kick her legs apart as my cock pushes against her entrance.

"I'm going to fuck you without a condom unless you tell me to stop," I say.

She swallows at my words and takes a deep breath. "Fuck me."

I slide in, in one punishing thrust.

Larkyn cries out, grasping onto the side of the table as I slam into her.

I wait for a second, letting her get used to my cock inside her. From this angle, I can get so much deeper than before.

"This is how I fuck women who mean nothing to me," I whisper in her ear as I thrust in and out. Not touching her clit. Or building her in any way.

She bites her lip to keep from telling me to stop.

My hand reaches down between her legs and finds the bundle of nerves I know will set her off.

"This is how I fuck women I care about," I say, rubbing her clit and nibbling on her ear.

"You choose."

I stop suddenly.

She growls.

"Which will it be?"

"Make me come, you asshole."

I smile. I win this round.

I find the sweet spot again as I thrust hard until we both come.

I pull out and tuck myself back in. I just fucked a woman without a condom. A first for her and me. It felt fantastic.

She slowly climbs off the table and lowers her wedding dress to glower at me.

I cock my head to the side. "I'll show you to your bedroom. The movers finished moving you in while we were at our wedding."

I walk down the hallway to the door right next to mine. It isn't the second largest room in my house, but I wanted her close to me, even though I still plan on getting her in my bed as often as I can.

Her eyes widen when she sees the room, like I just showed her into a room fit for a queen. I guess I did compared to the place she used to occupy.

"You like it?" I ask.

She nods.

"Or you could always stay in my room tonight. I'd be happy to fuck again or snuggle if that's what you prefer."

She ignores me and runs her hands over the silk fabric of the white bedspread I bought for her. I let her keep her old bed because it is a decent bed, but the shaggy bedspread had to go.

"What happens tomorrow?" she asks.

I smile. "Tomorrow, I plan on staying home and fucking my wife as many times as she will let me."

Her eyes grow heavy with lust. She will let me fuck her plenty.

"And then, we can go shopping for a couple of dresses for events you'll be attending the rest of the month."

She frowns. "I don't need you to pay for nice dresses for me."

I sigh. Pick my battles and don't fight. "Fine. I don't have to be at work again until Tuesday. Have you found a job yet?"

She narrows her eyes. "I already have a job."

"At the yoga studio?"

She nods.

I frown. "Have you applied for any jobs, now that you graduated with a business degree? I have some openings at my company. You could come work for me. Just get me a resume, and let me know what area you are interested in working in."

"No, I have a job. I'm not going to work for you."

I study her. Something doesn't add up.

"One million dollars doesn't go as far as you think. Especially if you spend it all on dresses for events with me, instead of letting me pay for them."

She glares at me. "Don't worry; I make enough money."

"I just thought you would want to get a job in a big corporation now that you've graduated."

She falls back on her bed. "You sound like my father."

I wince. I pushed too far. "Sorry, I didn't mean to push. Just trying to understand so I know when I'll be seeing you."

She closes her eyes, and I know she'll be asleep in seconds.

I want to know what she's planning on doing with the money I gave her. Maybe then it will give me more insight into her.

"Other than sex, do you have any plans for tomorrow?"

"I'm going to run."

"But your ankle is still injured."

"I have a doctor's note saying it's safe for me to train again. I heal quickly." Her eyes and smile are bright again as she says it.

I smile and walk over to her. I pull her up so I can kiss her firmly. She melts in my arms, and I know I could convince her to sleep in my bed if I tried at all. But I'm going to respect her wishes and treat her like she's a roommate. It's the only way to convince her to sleep in my bed long-term.

I pull back, and she looks desperate for another kiss. Her body leans forward, and her eyes are still closed, waiting for another kiss that isn't coming.

"I'll see you tomorrow to train. I'll enjoy kicking your ass, roommate."

"I figured you'd be the type to get up at five am to workout," I say, stretching as Larkyn sits on one of my barstools with her elbows leaning on my granite counter, sipping a cup of coffee.

Larkyn narrows her eyes at me. "I am. I'm surprised you're up this early."

I grin and pour myself a cup of coffee from the pot she left on. "I also happen to be a morning person who prefers to workout in the early morning hours before most people are awake."

I lift my coffee cup to my lips. Larkyn doesn't smile at me. Her lips turn downward before she yawns.

"Tired?" I ask.

She nods.

I smile.

"Why does me being tired make you happy?"

I smirk at her deviously as I walk over to her, and lean down by her ear to whisper, even though nobody else is in the house to hear me. "Because it means I'm winning."

She scoffs and slams her coffee cup down harder than she intended to, and she winces. "Sorry. But you are not winning. I slept poorly on my first night in a new place. I always do."

"You would have slept just fine if you were in my bed."

She scowls and stands up pressing her tiny body against mine. "No, I wouldn't have, because we would have fucked all night long."

A slow smile curls up until it reaches my eyes. "You think I can last all night long?" I pause pretending to think. "You're right I can. You would have at least had a more enjoyable experience than tossing and turning all night, dreaming about me."

Finally, she takes a step back with a tiny smile of her own on her lips.

"What's that smile for?" I ask, taking another drink of my coffee while I check her body out in her running shorts and neon pink sports bra. Her abs flex with every movement of her body. Damn, I've only been awake for five minutes, and I already want to fuck her. I've never needed sex as much as when I'm around her. I pride myself on being in control of my body, and not needing sex unless I choose it.

"Nothing, just realized that I'm winning."

I frown. "It doesn't look like it from where I'm standing."

She holds her head high. "That's because you're too focused on trying to be as big of a jerk as possible until it pisses me off and I give in and want you to return to the charming man you were before. It's not going to work. I prefer a challenge. I prefer to take care of myself. I don't need you taking care of me or being nice to me. All I need is your cock at the end of the night."

I raise my eyebrows. "Only at the end of the night?"

"Yes," she breathes, but it's a lie. She wants me right now. Her breath sped up, her cheeks flushed, and her eyes glossed over with thoughts of me fucking her.

"So what does our workout consist of today? Some walking, light jogging, weight lifting, stretches, what?" I ask, trying to keep my eyes on her face instead of her abs and legs.

She smirks. "I was thinking an easy ten-mile run to warm up, and then some lifting. I saw the gym you have in the basement."

I cross my arms over my chest and glare at her. "Your doctor did not give you permission to run ten miles your first time out."

She mimics my move, crossing her arms over her chest. "She permitted me to return to my normal activities. These are my normal activities. I have a race coming up in less than a month, and I'd prefer not to get last place."

I narrow my eyes. "Fine. We will do things your way. But I'm coming with you so I can carry you home or call a cab when you're two miles in and you can't move any further. Deal?"

She rolls her eyes. "Back to worrying about me so quickly."

"I never said I wouldn't worry about you. Just that I'd be an ass rather than a gentleman. One wince from you, and I'll be carrying you over my shoulder caveman style."

She huffs. "Fine, let's go."

"You're wearing that?" I ask, when I don't see her reach for a tank top or T-shirt.

She cocks her head to the side, putting her hands on her hips and pushing her chest out. "You have a problem with what I'm wearing?"

I stare at her chest. I do. No one should see her body, but me. But now isn't the time to argue. I'll save it for when she's in pain and doesn't want me to call a car in about a mile. "Nope."

She heads out my front door, stretching her arms a little as she walks out into the dark sky. The sun has barely started to rise and provide enough light to know that it isn't the middle of the night. I predict we are back home before the sun entirely comes up. I should take her out to brunch or something. I lock the front door, turn around, and she's gone.

Dammit.

I sprint down my driveway, squinting as I look from left to right to see which direction she went. To the left is a flat stretch, to the right a giant hill. Of course, she chose the harder path. That seems to be her preferred method.

I run, chasing after her as she finishes climbing the hill. My lungs burn, and my legs ache when I finally catch her.

"What happened to warming up first?" I ask, as I inhale hard, trying to recover.

She smirks, keeping a perfect rhythm and form. She's barely out of breath despite tackling a huge hill and running expertly. She isn't jogging; she's fucking running.

"I already warmed up."

"Huh?" is all I can get out between aching pants.

"I didn't wake up at five, I woke up at four, stretched, and warmed up a little on your treadmill in the basement."

My eyes widen. "You've already been working out for an hour?"

She nods, although I don't see a drop of sweat.

"What race are you training for?" I finally ask, as she continues to sprint. I glance down at her taped ankle, but it doesn't seem to be giving her any trouble.

"The LA marathon."

I freeze, stopping for a moment to stumble and fall into my neighbor's grass.

"Come on you pansy! I don't have time to stop. I'm out of shape and need to get faster," Larkyn shouts. She doesn't hesitate for a second to stop and check on me. She just keeps running.

Shit.

I'm way out of my league. I workout. I run. I lift. I sprint. But I don't run marathons. I never have. No desire. It's too much work for not enough gain. I prefer crushing people when I take over their businesses.

I pull myself off the ground and chase after Larkyn. And I know that for the next ten miles, that is what I'm going to be doing.

Chasing her.

———

I collapse onto my sofa after the ten miles, which felt more like twenty, because Larkyn chose the hardest fucking route she could find. There were thirty-three hills on the route. Thirty-three! Insane. And she said that was her easy run day. I don't want to know what her hard day is.

I pant over and over, covered in sweat. I ditched my T-shirt somewhere around mile three. And there is no way I'm walking, or even getting in one of my cars, to go back and get it.

Larkyn walks by me, and into the kitchen. I hear her opening cabinets, and then I hear the ice as it clinks in a glass.

She walks back, and stands over me, smirking.

"I don't know how you are standing. Or moving at all," I pant.

She walks over to me and holds out a glass of water. I take it, chugging the entire glass in one gulp.

She takes a seat near my feet, and props her foot up on my ottoman before placing a bag of ice on her foot.

I raise an eyebrow. "Your ankle hurt?"

"No, but it will. I pushed it hard."

"Why?"

She stills and takes a sip of her water. I don't think she is going to answer me.

"Because I like competing against myself. I like being healthy. I like being this fit. And I like winning." She smirks at me when she says winning.

Dammit. She really does plan on winning our little battle with each other.

She smiles with her eyes as she gazes at me. "I'm surprised you were able to keep up."

I moan. "I'm not moving off this couch the rest of the week. You killed me."

"I didn't ask you to come with me. I usually prefer running on my own. No one to hold me back."

"Don't worry. I don't plan on running with you again."

She leans her head back with a massive grin on her face. She thinks she's won. One less thing for her to worry about.

"I plan on driving next to you in my car as I yell profanities at you."

Her head pops back up fast, looking at me with wide-eyes and thinned lips. She's terrified that I would really do that. And I think I just might.

Suddenly, my tastes for making her squirm change. I want to make her squirm, but for very different reasons. I'm tired of our game where I annoy the crap out of her, so she doesn't fall in love with me. I want to make her writhe under my grasp as I lick her most sensitive of parts, and taste how delicious her juices taste mixed with the sweet sweat misted over her body.

"No," she says, noticing my reaction before I say anything or move.

I laugh. "I want to taste you."

"No," she says again, her voice shaky. She wants me too, but is afraid. "I'm gross and I smell. At least let me shower first."

I smirk. "No, I want you as you are."

She takes off up the stairs. I jump off the couch, and chase after her.

She may be fast, but I'm stronger. She won't win this. I'll catch her. And when I do, I'll give her the best orgasm of her life.

Life is perfect with her. We've only been married one day, but this is precisely what I imagined. Fun. Flirting. And sex. Nothing serious.

My phone buzzes, and I glance at my Apple Watch to see the message. I freeze, not liking what it says. It's from my lawyer. All the money we deposited into her account is gone. All one million of it. I don't know what she did with the money, but I'm about to find out.

First, though, I'll fuck her. Then, I'll ask about the money, I think, as I grab the bathroom door. She thinks she can lock herself inside and shower before I can get to her.

"You might as well give up. You're not going to win."

"Never," she squeals as I grab her.

Never. Such a meaningless word. Similar to *forever.* Neither exists. I might want her forever. I might hate her never. But both are untrue. Because as much as I thought I knew who Larkyn Day is, I'm wrong. She tricked me into giving her money she desperately needed for something. And if I'm not careful, she's going to take more from me. More money, more of my time, more of my heart. Until there is nothing left, but an empty shell.

I thought I married her to keep women like her away, but what if she is the devil I've been trying to save myself from all along?

11

LARKYN

Not the war, but this fight.

He catches my arm, and I freeze. I don't want him to fuck me when I'm this gross. I don't want him to find me disgusting and think I usually smell like this. If he fucks me now, it will be a long time before he fucks me again.

I sweat a lot when I run. And that sweat smells like ass. As much as it would help me if he suddenly didn't want to have sex with me anymore, I don't think that I could survive a whole year in his house with him without sex.

My heart is conflicted though as he pulls me close. I want to fuck him, but I also don't know whether to knee him in the balls or thank him for running with me. I hate him acting like he can control me, which is what he was doing running with me. He thought he could persuade me to stop.

But I also want to thank him for giving me the motivation to keep running. That hurt like a motherfucker, but it was necessary if I'm going to get back into marathon shape.

"Tell me no," Kade says, as I'm pressed against his body, straddling the doorway between the bathroom and my bedroom.

"No."

He smirks, knowing that I would say no.

I take a breath, trying to calm my breathing so I can keep a clear head.

He takes a step back, not touching me, but still close enough I can smell the sweat dripping off his body. He grins to show me his damn dimples, and my legs go weak.

I grab the doorframe to stay upright, when I want to be holding onto him.

"Tell me to leave," he says.

"Lea—"

He grabs my shorts and shoves them down. Kneels before me and grabs my thighs while his mouth attacks my pussy.

Jesus.

He lifts me up as my legs go around his shoulders, and his tongue dances across my bud. I grab his head tightly to remind myself to hold on and not let my head fall backward like I want, as noises leave my mouth I didn't know existed.

He drops me on my bed and kneels at the edge as his head comes down on my pussy again. He nips at my clit.

I bite my lip to keep him from knowing how much I like what he's doing.

"Tell me to stop," he breathes against the lips between my legs.

"Don't you dare stop!" I arch my back until my body is pressed against his mouth again.

He smirks and attacks. His tongue moves faster, matching the pulse of my blood, which is all pooled between my legs instead of in my head.

I come, screaming Kade's damn name.

He wipes his mouth with the back of his hand as he climbs up my body.

"Don't you ever tell me, or any man, not to fuck you because you think you are gross. You are fucking amazing. Even more amazing after you just kicked my ass running ten miles. Don't you dare. Promise?" His lips twitch as he talks and the smile I'm so used to vanishes. He's serious, and I'm afraid he won't let me off the bed until I've taken his oath.

"I promise."

He stills, and when he finally believes my words, he leans back. He climbs back on my bed making himself comfortable, smiling with his arms behind his head, so that I can see every glorious inch of his toned body all the way to the v-shape that disappears beneath his shorts, hiding the one part of his body mine is still aching for.

"Good, now fuck me to prove you don't find me gross."

Damn, that slow smile is contagious.

I pull the bra off my body and attack. My legs part over his legs and I lower myself until I find the hardness push against my groin like I was expecting. Our lips lock, and I taste his sweat mixed with my cum.

It's the opposite of gross. It's what pleasure, pain, hard work, and desire taste like. How could that taste bad? More importantly, how could I have ever thought that he would find me gross? He can't resist me, just like I can't resist his glistening body.

I can't wait to have him in me. He knows I can't either.

His pants are down, and I feel his slick cock against my entrance.

He doesn't wait for me to permit him to fuck me without a condom this time. He just does. And I don't blame him. Fucking without a barrier is so much hotter than fucking with one.

I thrust on top of him. Loving being in control of everything. Speed. Depth. Angles. And controlling when Kade gets to come. Because I plan on torturing him a little, just like he has me.

I stop suddenly, pretending I need to catch my breath.

"Not happening, sweetie. You don't get to taunt me. You forget I'm more experienced at this than you." Kade starts thrusting.

I pout. I forgot that he can thrust from underneath me just as easily as he can on top.

He kisses me again, and the pout melts away.

He nibbles on my lips as he comes inside me, just as my body pulses my orgasm around him.

He collapses back, exhausted. But that just energized me more. *Who knew sex would turn me into a sex fiend?*

"We have to wait at least another twenty minutes before we do that again. You exhaust me, woman."

I smile.

"I need to go lift anyway." I consider staying and asking him about why we aren't using a condom. But it doesn't matter. I'm on birth control, and I'm clean. And as much as I don't want to admit it, I trust Kade. I trust him too much.

I start to climb off of him, but Kade grabs my hand stopping me.

"I have a question first."

I pause and sit back down on his cock that is just beginning to stir again. *Twenty minutes, my ass.*

"What did you do with the money?"

"How do you know?"

"I have my ways."

"You have lawyers and people that work at the bank you mean?"

He shrugs.

I frown. *Why is he asking me about the money? And why does he seem so pissed about it?* I open my mouth to tell him what I did with the money, but then I stop.

"It's none of your business what I did with the money." I climb off of him. He tries to keep me on him, but I jerk my arm free and stand next to my bed pissed. Butt naked, but pissed.

"Yes, it is my business. It's my money. You are my wife. I need to know if you did anything illegal or if you are going to need more. Because if you already spent everything, I don't know how you expect to buy things like dresses to the parties you are supposed to be attending with me."

I glare at him. I've never been so angry with him before. If he's doing this to keep up his end of the deal of being an ass, then he's doing a good job. Seconds ago, I could have loved him for making me feel wanted. Now there is nothing but hate.

"I didn't do anything illegal. And don't worry about the dresses.

I'll make sure I wear something worthy of being your wife, and you won't have to pay me another dime."

"Tell me what you did with the money."

"No. It's none of your business. Our contract never had any stipulations about me telling you what I did with the money or that I had to spend it a certain way." I grab a new pair of shorts and bra and put them on. "Now, I'm going to lift. Enjoy the rest of your day, you bastard."

———

"Damn, I need to spend more time in the gym. Or at least I need to watch my back, because I'm pretty sure my wife could beat me up," Kade says, standing in the doorway of the basement gym as I push the bar with way too much weight on it over my head.

I should have taken today easy. I haven't lifted in weeks, and my wrist is still fragile. But Kade pissed me off. So I taped up my wrist and went full out. I'll regret it later.

"What do you want?" I ask, racking the bar and sitting up to wipe the sweat from my forehead, not even bothering to look at Kade. I'm too tired to give him my full glare.

I hear him walk toward me, but I keep my eyes focused on the floor like the black spongy material that makes up the floor is interesting.

"You don't even have any music playing or the TV on," Kade says, stopping next to me.

I turn to him and snarl. "I couldn't figure out how to work your ridiculous sound system, and I don't watch much TV. I don't need entertainment to workout."

He grins, displaying his damn dimples. He's changed. He's wearing dark jeans and a black T-shirt that fits him too well. My insides curl, and my heart speeds up. *How the hell does he melt my anger for him with just a grin? I really am in trouble.*

I lower my eyebrows and frown. He doesn't get to know what he's doing to me.

I lean back down and lift the bar off the rack. I've already finished my reps, but I need a distraction from the sex god that is standing over me looking at me like he can control all my emotions.

My arms wobble a little as I lower the bar to my chest.

"I need your help," Kade says, putting his hands in his pocket.

My eyes cut to him as I push the bar up. He looks so sincere. Innocent, even. His eyes are big, and he bites his lip, like he can't believe he even admitted that to me.

I lower the bar again to my chest, and this time, I can barely push the bar up. Kade grabs it as my arms wobble, and he helps me rack the bar.

I pant heavily, but I'm not sure if it's because I'm tired or want Kade to climb on top of me and fuck me on this bench.

"I need you to bartend with me tonight at King's," Kade says.

I smirk. "No."

He sighs rubbing his neck. "I figured you would say that."

"Then you are learning. Why would I want to help you out?"

"Because you are my wife, and I'm paying you to help me."

I snarl. I hate Kade. I don't know how I go from liking to hating so quickly.

"Well, that has me convinced." I roll my eyes.

"Please?"

"No."

"Why not? What else are you going to do tonight?"

I get up and walk over to the large tank of water and fill a paper cup with water before washing it down. I feel his eyes on my ass, and when I turn around, they are on my flattened breasts, squashed beneath the sports bra I'm wearing.

I raise my eyebrows. "Really? You're checking me out while asking me for help? That's not going to work."

He cocks his head and smiles, as he purposefully stares harder at my breasts.

"Just honoring our contract and making sure you hate me. Is it working?"

I toss the empty cup into the trashcan. "Yes."

"Good, now go shower. You have ten minutes, and we need to leave."

"I'm not helping you."

"Yes, you are. I've been far too nice to you lately. I need the opportunity to make you mad at me." He wiggles his eyebrows.

I giggle. *Dammit, no.*

He chuckles. "See, you like me way too much right now. A night of me bossing you around ought to fix that."

I sigh. Kade's right. I need to be angry. And I don't exactly have anything to do tonight unless you count taking a long bath and icing my entire body all night to make the soreness go away.

"Fine."

His eyes twinkle at my surrender.

"Good, now shower and put on jeans and a black shirt. You have five minutes until we leave."

I frown. "I thought I had ten."

He shrugs. "Four now."

"I hate you," I say, racing past him to go shower.

"I know."

12

KADE

I'm going to kill him.

That's all I could think about when I got the phone call from Axel, my best friend, and manager of most of my bars, telling me Sebastian didn't show up tonight. Sebastian is supposed to be managing this bar. I'm giving him an opportunity to learn before he takes it over from Axel and me. But if he keeps being a no-show, he'll be lucky if I let him run a lemonade stand.

I throw my arm around Larkyn's shoulder as I lead her into one of my favorite places in the world. I stare at her face, as hard as it is for me to pull my eyes away from her ass in her skin tight jeans, or her breasts in her black T-shirt. Or the curl that has fallen out of her perfect bun.

Instead, I gaze at her gorgeous makeup-free face. She yelled at me and said she didn't even have time to put makeup on before I demanded that we leave. But she's the type of woman I doubt would wear makeup anyway. And I'm glad she's isn't wearing any. It shows off her freckles and sun-kissed cheeks.

"Welcome to King's," I say, opening the door for her. I try to keep

134

my voice level, so she doesn't realize the importance of the place, and I can get her honest reaction.

We stop just inside, and Larkyn soaks everything in. Her gaze floats around the bubbles of tables scattered throughout the room. The triple high ceiling that makes the bar look more significant than it is. And the booths that sit on the edge of the floors above, giving the perfect view of the dance floor below.

A slow smile spreads on her face, and a twinkle sparks in her eyes.

My heart beats again, seeing her expression. She likes the place.

She bites her lip as she finally tears her eyes away from the sparkle of the room to me. "This is your favorite place in the world, isn't it?"

I narrow my eyes. "No," I lie.

She smirks and stares back at the room that is alive with people, despite it only being seven in the evening. This place usually doesn't start getting crowded until nine.

"It's fantastic. I usually prefer to be alone, but this place makes me feel alive, more than I've felt in years."

I grin. "It's my second favorite place in the world."

She laughs. "I knew it. What's your first?"

I shake my head and place my hand on the small of her back. "I'd tell you, but it'd make you fall in love with me."

She licks her bottom lip slowly. "Oh, yea? I doubt that."

"Good of you to finally show up," Axel says, holding a tray of empty glasses.

I shrug. "I had to wait for Larkyn to shower. I figured we could use the extra help."

Axel rakes his eyes over Larkyn. I know he's doing it to piss me off, but I'll still kick his ass later. I hold Larkyn closer to me and look down at her finger to notice she's wearing her engagement ring with her wedding ring. Good, I need her to be mine tonight.

"Make sure you keep this one in line tonight. Kade hasn't bartended in ages." Axel winks at Larkyn.

Larkyn laughs. "I'll make sure Kade works his butt off."

"Good. Nice to see you again Larkyn." Axel leans over and kisses her on the cheek.

I glare at him like I'm about to punch him in the face. He smirks as he finishes the kiss.

"I've got to go. It seems one of the waitresses and both of our best bartenders called in sick all in the same night. We need you to cover the main bar," Axel says, before walking away.

Larkyn's eyes follow him, and she blushes a little. Axel's good looking. He's tall, with a beard and a man bun to go with his muscular physique. But she's mine, not his.

"Are you done ogling my best friend, wifey?"

She cocks her head to look at me. "Are you jealous?"

"No, just reminding you that you are *my wife*. So start acting like it."

She shakes her head. "You got this being a jerk thing down."

I sigh. "Come on, let's get you set up at the bar."

I show her the bar, where everything is, and how to work the cash register.

And then we both get swept away with a barrage of people.

"Larkyn, I need you to make two old fashioneds, a lemon drop, a manhattan, and two cosmos. That is if you know how to make all of those," I say.

She gives me her best 'I'm going to punch you later' stare while beginning to get the glasses out for the most complicated drinks anyone could order.

I'm busy pouring five beers for the men sitting at the bar.

"Seriously?" she asks, eyeing me as the sticky syrupy sugar from the lemon drop gets all over her hands.

I finish pouring the beers and hand them to the two guys.

"What?" I ask, faking innocent.

She slides the two old fashioneds to me and carries the lemon drop and manhattan to the other two men waiting.

She smiles at them a little too brightly, and when one of the men hands her his credit card, she lets her hand stroke his hand for just a second first.

I growl as I follow her to the cash register.

"Not cool," I growl in her ear. "You're mine. Remember?"

She bites her lip trying to hold back a grin. "Then start making some of the complicated drinks yourself. You can start by making two cosmos for those women standing over there. I need to wash my hands. I'm tired of getting sticky sugar all over my hands from all the sweet drinks these women keep ordering."

I press my lips against her ear. "I'll make the drinks if you stop flirting with the customers."

Her breath catches. "If I stop flirting, I don't make as many tips."

My tongue traces around the edge of her ear. "If you keep flirting, I'm going to throw you over my shoulder, carry you to the bathroom, and fuck you until you remember, you're *mine*."

Her teeth rake over her bottom lip. "Then, I'll definitely keep flirting."

I growl. I should have said something less sexy, although I'm desperate to fuck Larkyn in the bathroom. The first break we get, that's precisely what I'm doing. *Where is Axel when I need him?*

I release Larkyn as I head over to make the two cosmos. When I finish, I carry them down the bar to the two waiting women.

"Sorry for the wait," I say, sliding the drinks across the bar to the two blonde beauties.

"I'd wait forever to be served by you," one of the women says, as she strokes my forearm and bats her eyelashes at me.

"I'm Jane." She takes a sip of her drink. "This is delicious, how did you make it?" She leans forward, flashing me her cleavage.

I cock my head to the side with a smile, knowing that Larkyn is watching me. I'm about to piss her off.

"I'd love to show you exactly how I make it," I say, winking at her as I lean in.

I feel hands on my chest from behind me. I stare down at the ring that Larkyn has strategically placed firmly on my chest so there is no way Jane could miss it.

"Hello, hubby," Larkyn says, turning my face toward her before she kisses me on the lips, making sure she slides her tongue into my mouth.

She breaks away as she grins seductively at me, before turning her attention to the two women. "Can we get you two anything?" Larkyn asks, staring the women down.

"Nope," Jane says awkwardly, as she and her friend carry their drinks away.

Larkyn frowns at me.

"What? I make better tips if I flirt a little," I say, repeating her words.

"Fine, no more flirting from either of us."

I grab her at the waist as she tries to leave to take another man's order. I pull her to me and kiss her again. I can't get enough of her lips. Her sweet, perfume. Her moans. I can never get enough of her.

She pulls away with a dreamy look on her face. She can't get enough of me either.

I swat her ass as she walks away to make more drinks.

The night continues, and we both continue teasing each other. Bossing each other around while flirting and kissing any chance we get.

A crowd forms and I have to move fast to keep up. I haven't talked to Larkyn in half an hour. Nor flirted or kissed or even brushed against her. We've been too busy. Finally, I get a break when a group of guys orders shots of tequila. I glance across the bar to check on Larkyn.

Larkyn brings a man his whiskey with a scowl on her face.

I frown, but try to be patient. I know Larkyn can handle herself with touchy men. I've seen her do it all night. And as much as I want to jump in and defend her honor, I don't. I've pushed her far enough tonight, and I don't want to push too far and not get to fuck her tonight.

But then he grips her arm far too tightly and pulls her chest over the bar and kisses her.

Hell no.

I storm across the bar toward the man whose lips press against my wife's. She tries to push him away, but he digs his fingers deeper into her arm.

I push him away from her, and then before I can think, my fist makes contact with his face. Blood pours from his nose, but it's not enough. I punch him again.

The man laughs as he steps out of reach before I punch him again.

"I'm going to sue. I should get a pretty penny for getting punched by royalty like you."

"Get the fuck out!" I yell.

The man laughs. I look over at Axel who motions for our security team to grab him and take him out. Two of my security guys catch the man and start walking him out. The man grins as blood drips down his face and he flashes a look to Larkyn behind me.

Good thing I have a security team to handle creeps like this or I might have ended up in jail tonight after I killed him. I need to get a grip on myself if I would kill someone just for kissing Larkyn.

"Man, that guy was creepy," I say, joking as I turn to face Larkyn who I assume is going to give me a hard time for punching the guy instead of letting her handle him herself.

That's not what I see.

Larkyn's frozen. Her eyes are wide and unblinking. Her mouth tightens into a grimace. And her face is pale white.

"Larkyn, are you okay?" I ask, moving in front of her as I put my arms on her biceps. I try gently shaking like that would someone get rid of the shock she's in.

It doesn't work.

"Larkyn?" I ask, my voice catching in my throat.

Something is seriously wrong.

"Larkyn, talk to me. What's going on?"

Silence.

She does finally blink. Otherwise, she's still frozen. She's not going to talk to me here.

The bar has started to slow down, as it's well past midnight, but there are still plenty of people hanging around the bar looking for drinks.

I motion to Axel who delivers two drinks to one of his tables and then jogs over to us.

"Take over for us," I say.

Axel takes one look at Larkyn, and he does as I say, hopping into the bar.

I wrap my arms around Larkyn's shoulders and lead her to the manager's office in the back. I get her to sit on the couch, and then I close the door behind me, making sure to lock it before I take a seat next to her.

And then I wait. I stroke her hair and hold her hand and hope that whatever just happened back there didn't break her. Because I'm not ready to give her up yet. If she's broken, she won't want to stay mine.

"I hate him," are the words that finally leave her mouth.

I exhale and sink back into the couch, still searching her eyes for signs of life. Her cheeks have pinked, her lips are moist, and her breathing is steady.

"I hate him, too," I say, with a tiny smile.

"I shouldn't have let him get to me like that."

"No." I grab her face so that she can see how entirely wrong she is. This is not her fault. "Don't blame yourself for anything. He kissed you. He touched you. However you reacted, is perfectly acceptable. He was in the wrong, not you."

She nods, but her eyes say she doesn't agree with me.

I frown. I don't know how to get through to her. "You're plenty strong. You don't have to punch every guy that hurts you, though. That's why you have me."

A tear falls down her cheek. I rub it when it hits my thumb.

"Hey, it's okay. You're okay," I say, pulling her into my lap so that I can hold her as firmly as I want.

She starts bawling, and I don't understand. Larkyn is fierce, strong, invincible. She didn't cry when her father said she was worthless. She didn't cry when she was in agonizing pain in the hospital. She didn't cry when she injured her leg. But she's crying now. Full sobs. That man was way out of line, but it was just a kiss. I don't understand why she would be this upset.

And then it hits me. Larkyn was raped. Of course, a man touching her without her permission would upset her.

I hold her tighter, hating that I put her in this position, and didn't immediately try to protect her.

"His name is Nathan Watts."

I slowly ease back so that I can look at her as she speaks. "You know him?"

She nods and swallows like it's hard to get the next words out. "He was…he raped me."

My eyes widen, and my body chills as she speaks. I should talk. Say something. But now I've lost the ability to speak.

"We used to date. Freshman year. It was serious. I was madly in love with him."

Now my heart has stopped. Because it feels like someone has stabbed me when she mentions loving another guy, yet doesn't ever want to love me.

"But I was young. I wanted to take things slowly. Nathan was a senior. I was a freshman. I didn't want to jump into bed with him. We dated two months before I was ready."

I narrow my eyes, not understanding how it ended so badly if she was in love with this guy. How she was even still a virgin when I had her.

"Nathan was taking me to a party. I think it might have even been one of your parties. Anyway, I got all dressed up and decided that night was the night. We went to dinner, stopped by the party for about five minutes, and then he took me back to his apartment."

I nod, needing to hear the end of this story more than I need to breathe.

"And then, I changed my mind. It just didn't feel right. I wanted to wait a little longer. I said I'd had too much to drink, which was true, and I felt sick. I didn't want my first time to be when I was drunk.

"Nathan disagreed. He wouldn't stop. I fought for about five seconds before I grew still. I couldn't move. Or breathe. I didn't even tell him to stop."

She looks me in the eye. "Just like tonight."

"No." I stroke her again, feeling her wet, tear-stained cheeks. "You did not have to say no. He knew that you didn't want him to kiss you. Just like he knew you didn't want to have sex with him. This is not your fault."

She nods and smiles as a tear falls down her cheek again. And I can't help myself. She's so beautiful. She thinks she's weak right now, but I've never seen her stronger.

I lean down and kiss her tenderly on the lips, as the tears that have fallen over her cheeks cover her mouth. The tears continue, and I know I need to stop. This isn't what she needs right now. She needs comfort, not a man to grope her.

I pull back. "I'm sorry."

She sucks in a breath, and I think she's going to start bawling again, or yell at me for kissing her when she needed me to be her friend.

Her body tenses.

Fuck, I screwed up.

Her arms grab my cheeks, and her lips attack mine. Her tongue pushes into my mouth. Her body lands on mine.

"Don't ever tell me you are sorry for kissing me again. You are the only thing keeping me grounded. I don't usually like men that punch other men, but what you did for me...what you're doing for me now. I've never been more turned on in my life."

She bites her lip and then she grabs my shirt and lifts it off. I see the twinkle return to her eyes when she stares down at my chest. I did something right for once.

"I'm so glad you were my first," she says pulling her shirt off, revealing a far too sexy bra.

I growl. "I'm happy you're my first wife."

She laughs.

I smirk, as comfortable as it would be to fuck her on the couch, it just isn't enough.

"What?" she asks, smiling at my mischievous look.

"I'm going to fuck you on the desk."

She eyes the desk behind me covered in papers and electronics.

"No, we can't. We might break it or—"

I plant my lips on hers as I lift her up. Her legs wrap around my waist while I carry her over to the desk without protest.

And then, I sweep everything off into a mound on the floor.

"Oh my god!" Larkyn squeals.

I grin, loving the sound falling from her lips.

"You did not just do that," Larkyn says, laughing.

"I did. This is my bar. I can do what I want."

She stares down at the computer, which hardly has a scratch on it.

"What if we broke it?"

I kiss her again as I lower her to the desk. "Then, I'll buy a new one."

"Simple as that, huh? Just throw some money at it and problem fixed."

I look into her eyes, knowing that she thinks that's how I fix all of my problems including any I have with her.

"When the problem is simple, yes. Anything more complicated requires a kiss from you."

She hooks her legs around me and pulls my body to her as she kisses me. I'm usually not the kind of guy that cares much about the kiss, except that it leads to the much more enjoyable part. The sex part.

But when Larkyn kisses me, I lose my damn mind. I don't think about anything else. I feel the kiss everywhere in my body. And I moan like it's the only reaction my body can ever muster.

I grab her jeans and undo them expertly with one hand, while never having to glance down at what I'm doing and stop kissing Larkyn.

I kiss down her chest as my hand slips underneath the delicate thong she's wearing.

She is hot in anything, but seeing her in these lacey things makes her even hotter. Knowing that she is wearing them for me almost makes me come without fucking her.

When I kiss back up her body, she stops me just before I get to her lips by pressing her finger to my lips.

"How did I get so lucky to find someone like you?"

I shake my head and then nibble on her finger. "I'm the lucky one."

She moans, and I undo my pants releasing my cock before settling between her legs.

"Fuck me, Kade," she says, knowing tonight I need her explicit permission.

At her words, I slide inside, filling her as her moans fill the room.

I kiss her hard while I fuck her, taking with me all the pain and heartache she's feeling. I don't want her ever to feel that way again. I need to protect her. I won't let another man hurt her ever. Including me.

So as much as a new feeling is floating up through my body making me feel things toward Larkyn that I didn't think were possible, I push them back down. I will not feel anything more than I already do toward Larkyn. I can't.

"Come, beautiful. Let go of the pain."

She does, and it's the most exquisite sound that leaves her mouth. I genuinely think she let go in that moment. I come right after her, filling her with my cum.

When we finish, I carry her back to the couch and pick up her clothes, handing them to her. We both get dressed as I stare at her beautiful flushed body and the smile that hasn't left her lips since she came.

"How are you feeling?" I ask.

She bites her lip and yanks at my shirt, pulling me toward her. "Like you're the best husband ever."

I grin, but when I look into her eyes and see something more, I know I've fucked up. I quickly stand before her.

"I need to call my friends at the police department and see if I can get Nathan locked up, or at least a restraining order so that he can't come around you anymore."

She sighs. "Thank you. You can try. Nathan got out of prison a couple of weeks ago, so maybe that will help."

I kiss her, needing to take away the memory.

"He went to prison after he raped you?" I ask.

She shakes her head and stares at me with her big eyes as she curls up on the couch like she might fall asleep.

"No. I reported him, but they didn't have enough evidence to arrest him. Especially since we were dating. It was just his word against mine. But the police did a thorough investigation, and it turned out, he was selling pot and cocaine. He went to prison for possession."

I frown. I hate that she never got her justice. I know there isn't much I can do now, but I have enough connections to get a restraining order.

I pull out my phone. "I'm going to make a couple of calls and see what I can do to fix this. Then, I'll take you home."

I lean down and kiss her on the forehead.

She smiles up at me. "Thank you, hubby."

I swallow as she calls me hubby again. She likes calling me her husband or hubby. I love hearing it fall from her lips, but it's a problem. I promised I wouldn't hurt her. And right now the way we both feel, I'm going to hurt her.

I step outside the office to make the calls to protect her. Tonight, I can be her prince. But tomorrow, I need to bring back the ass she hates. After hearing her story tonight, it's more important than ever that I keep her from falling in love with me. She deserves better than a man who only cares about money, his work, and getting laid.

13

LARKYN

THE LAST FEW weeks have crept by. Kade has mostly left me alone. He's been busy working, while I've tried to teach as many yoga classes as possible to save as much money as I can. After teaching, I've spent most of my time training for the race today. Or hanging out with Serena. I need to stop meeting up with Serena though. All she wants to talk about is Kade.

Are we serious? Do I like him? Have I fallen in love?

It's exhausting. I can't handle talking to her anymore.

But I miss Kade. He's been traveling for work weekly. And even when is home, he's been working late. He's barely even made time to fuck me. I don't know how he has so much restraint. I've spent every night in this big empty house touching myself, making myself come. But it is nothing like when Kade fucks me.

And somehow, Nathan is back in prison. I don't know what he did, but Kade called me a couple of days after his release and said Nathan violated his parole and is back in prison.

I toss my running shoes into my bag and zip it shut. I swing the bag over my shoulder as I hear a knock on my bedroom door.

I grin. *Kade.*

"Come in."

Kade opens the door slowly and moves just inside my doorway. He's dressed in jeans and a buttoned-down shirt.

My smile drops from my face, and I almost drop the bag from my shoulder; the sight of his outfit knocks me so off balance. He's not coming to see me race.

"I wanted to pop in to wish you luck today. Sorry, I can't make it to your race today. Work calls."

I nod and give him a fake smile. But I can't say thank you. I don't open my mouth at all, because if I do, I know what's going to come out. True feelings that I don't want Kade to know about.

He hesitates in my doorway, before walking over to me, squeezing my body against his, and wrapping his arms around my back. My face buries in his chest. I smell the familiar musk of his aftershave. And I almost tell him to hell with the race and work. I need him to fuck me right now. Against the wall. In the bed. On the floor for all I care. I need his cock.

But he releases me before I have a chance to kiss him. If I had brushed my lips against his, everything would be different.

I didn't.

So now, Kade is walking away, out of my bedroom.

"Good luck, Larkyn. Text me how the race goes." And then he's out my bedroom door as he presses his phone to his ear to take a call. He doesn't even want me to call him afterward, just text. That's how much I mean to him.

I thought after Kade punched Nathan, I meant more to him than just a fake relationship where I help him fend off women. Apparently, not. I'm not even sure he thinks he needs me around to fend off women anymore, since we haven't been out in public in weeks.

I head to my old Toyota Corolla and drive off to the race. It's five in the morning. I didn't even ask Kade what he's doing up this early. But I guess running a billion dollar empire requires Kade to work all hours of the day and night.

———

As I'm running the race, all I can think about is Kade.

Kade, treating me like a queen.

Kade, being an ass.

Kade, in his sexy suits.

Kade, naked in my bed.

Kade, bossing me around.

Kade, comforting me when I cry.

He's a distraction. From everything. I should be focused on my pace, form, and where I'm planting my feet.

But I can't stop.

All I think about is Kade's grin.

His dimples.

His giant eyes, staring at me lovingly. Like I'm really his. But I'm not.

Shit…

My body crashes into the concrete, as my ankle twists beneath my body.

Fuck.

Runners jump around me, not bothering to stop and check on me. I don't blame them. They want to win. Get sponsors, same as me.

I glance down at my fitness watch, tracking my pace and mileage. Nine miles in a record pace. I could have won. Or at least finished in the top five.

Now, my dreams are gone.

I will never win a marathon. My body will heal eventually, but my heart isn't in it anymore. I like running. It used to be my whole life, but now all I can think about is Kade. I've turned into my mother. The one person I hate for not having her own life.

I need more.

But how can I, when my entire life revolves around Kade?

I don't know. But I need to get my shit together.

I force myself up into a standing position. Gravel and rocks fall from my body as I dust myself off. I hop on my good leg as a tear trickles down my cheek toward the nearest first aid station.

I'm not sad that my running career is over. Running made me feel alive, but it didn't serve the purpose of helping other people.

I'm sad that I don't know what comes next or how to go about achieving my purpose of helping other people. I love teaching yoga, but I hardly earn enough to feed myself. I don't need much money, but I need more than the thousand dollars I earn a month.

"Let me help you," a man in a red first aid shirt says, draping my arm over his shoulders.

"Thanks," I say, faking a smile at the good-looking man. Usually, I would be entranced with a man like him. Especially with my arm draped over his shoulders and our bodies so close together. Today, I feel nothing. I feel like a sex addict, but the only man that can quench my thirst is Kade.

"I'm Jeremy," the man says.

"Larkyn."

He smiles. "Sit here, Larkyn." He pulls up a folding chair behind me.

I ease myself down onto the chair as Jeremy lifts my leg up so he can inspect my ankle. He slowly removes my shoes, as my swollen ankle reddens.

"You need to have it looked at by a doctor."

I nod.

"Anyone I should call to help you get home?"

I shake my head. "Call me a cab. I'll pick up my car later."

Jeremy frowns, but pulls out his phone.

"I can take you home," Sebastian's voice rings out behind me.

Jeremy looks from Sebastian back to me. He raises an eyebrow, asking me without words if he should leave me alone with the man.

I smile at Jeremy, who walks over to a table a few feet away and starts organizing supplies.

"What are you doing here?" I ask, as Sebastian squats in front of me. He doesn't look good. His hair is disheveled, and he needs a haircut. His eyes are bloodshot. His clothes have dirt stains. And his breath reeks of alcohol.

"I came to apologize."

I exhale. I don't know why he doesn't make me anxious. Maybe because he's so good looking or that I almost slept with him. I don't know.

"That's nice of you Sebastian, but I'm not looking for an apology. I think you need to focus on getting the help you need and taking care of yourself."

"Please, Larkyn, I need to…" Sebastian stumbles over my leg as he stands up.

I wince as he hits my ankle and his hands flail, trying to grab onto my shoulders to keep his balance.

Before I realize what is happening, Sebastian is knocked on his ass, lying on the ground.

Blood spews from his lip, as a fist comes down on his face again. Sebastian holds his hands up to protect his face, but he doesn't fight back.

"Don't ever touch Larkyn again. You understand?" Kade says.

Kade.

My eyes widen as I grasp my injured ankle. I don't know whether I'm happy or afraid to see Kade here. I'm happy that's he's here. He lied to me and came to my race. But the way he's looking at his brother terrifies me.

Kade's eyes are dark, his face red, and fist balled, while his other hand tightens around Sebastian's throat.

"We are through Sebastian. You're on your own. I'm tired of fixing things for you. Don't call me asking for my help anymore. Don't ask me for money. Don't ask me to even be there for you as your brother. I'm done helping you," Kade says.

Kade huffs out a breath through his nose, and it might as well be fire. He finally turns toward me after taking more breaths to calm himself down. While Sebastian, is still in a heap on the ground. Several of the medics are staring at the scene, not sure if they should help Sebastian or stay out of it.

"You okay?" Kade asks me.

I nod.

"Sebastian didn't hurt me, and my ankle was already hurt."

"Your ankle, okay?"

"I twisted it. It will be fine. I just need to rest it."

Kade stares down at my ankle with the same intensity one might stare at a bomb waiting for it to go off.

"I'm fine," I say again.

Kade grimaces at me and then scoops me up in his arms.

I don't fight with him. Even if I could walk, I wouldn't argue with him. I like him carrying me. I like being in his arms again. Just being near him.

"You lied to me," I say.

He ignores me. "Where did you park?"

"The west parking lot."

He swallows, and I can hear him breathe, each breath strong and deep as we walk.

"Why did you come and not tell me?"

"Because I didn't want you to think I like you."

"You like me?" I ask with a smile.

"Of course, but that's all it is. *Like.*"

My eyes drop. I don't want him to see the pain in my eyes.

"You were too harsh on Sebastian. He didn't even touch me. You don't need to punch every guy that touches me."

He growls, and I know he disagrees.

Kade helps me into my car, and then he goes to the driver's seat.

"Home?" he asks.

"Drop me off at the yoga studio. I said I would help with any classes after I finished my race."

His eyes widen, and he rubs his head. But it looks more like he's doing something with his hands to keep from strangling me.

"No."

He doesn't say anything else. Just a no.

"No? You don't get to tell me what to do."

"When you are acting crazy and may have just had a concussion, then I do."

I frown, but don't argue. Honestly, I want to spend the rest of the day with Kade.

"You're lucky I'm not taking you straight to the doctor."

"It's just a sprain. I'm fine."

He rolls his eyes as more steam leaves his nostrils.

My car makes a weird noise as Kade speeds up, ending the silence that has spread between us.

"You need to buy a new car. This one is about to break down any minute."

I frown. "I happen to like my car."

"Buy a new one."

"No."

He sighs and rubs his neck again.

"Why did you punch Sebastian? I want the truth."

He keeps driving, ignoring me, and I give up pushing. It seems that we aren't on the same page anymore. We can't even carry on a simple conversation.

Kade pulls the car into the driveway of his house, and he shuts off the engine, but doesn't get out to help me. I sit too and wait. I could hop in the house on my good leg, but I don't want to. I want Kade's arms around me again.

"Our father died when I was fifteen. Sebastian was only twelve. Lung cancer."

I suck in a breath as Kade finally speaks.

"I'm so sorry," I say.

He stares into my eyes and touches my cheek like he needs my touch to be strong enough to continue speaking.

"Our father was abusive. He wasn't a nice man. Sebastian and I were happy to see him gone."

I place my hand on his, trying to bring him comfort.

"My mother though..." He takes a deep breath. "From what I remember about her, she was amazing. She divorced my father when I was six. She didn't have anything. No money. No job. No skills. But she loved Sebastian and I. Fought for custody of us. But she didn't have the means to fight our father's numerous lawyers."

I tighten my grip on his hand.

"She died of a broken heart."

A tear trickles down my cheek. He hurts. So much. And I can't do anything to make it better.

"Sebastian started acting out after our father died. He partied. Drank, smoked weed. All of it.

"I thought it was just a phase that would pass. But he's never been able to get over our parents' deaths or the emotional abuse he suffered from our father.

"I don't know how to help Sebastian. I don't think I can help him. I know I should give up on him, but I can't keep fighting for him when he keeps screwing up."

His voice trembles and breaks, as tears slip down his cheek.

I grab his head and cradle him against my chest, crying as well. I open my mouth numerous times, trying to find words to comfort him, but there are no words. Nothing I can say will make any of it better. I want to say Sebastian will get better. With help, he'll clean up his life. But I don't know that.

So instead, I get out of the car, walking tenderly on my injured foot to Kade's side, and I lead Kade out of my car and into the house. His eyes are sad, but he doesn't fight me. Tonight, it's my turn to take care of him.

I guide him slowly to his bedroom until he's sitting on the edge of the bed. Then, I remove his shoes. Followed by his jeans and shirt.

I remove my running shorts and bra, and pull on one of his T-shirts before climbing into the bed next to him and snuggling against his chest.

This is the first time I've slept in his bed, since the first time he fucked me. Tonight isn't about sex. Tonight is about comforting a man I'm falling for.

14

KADE

LARKYN IS an angel when she sleeps. Her head is curled up against my chest as her arm and leg are draped over my waist.

I've never slept with a woman in my bed before without having sex with her first. It was exactly what I needed. A night holding a woman I care about.

But it makes my feelings for her confused. *What am I supposed to do now?*

Tell her I'm falling in love with her, and I want to try a relationship for real? Or keep trying to push her away every time we do something that moves toward getting too close?

I run my hand through her sweaty hair. My lips curl up. She really does reek. She never showered after her race yesterday. She just curled up in my bed with me and made my pain go away.

If I were a better man, I'd spend the day telling her I love her and want her to be mine. I'm not a better man though. I barely even have enough emotions to care about my brother. I don't have enough to share with her too. I lose my temper often. I love my job too much to have time with anyone else. And my brother is a mess. I don't want to bring her into my troubles.

A loud snore escapes her.

I laugh. *So much for being an angel.*

And then the slow puddle of drool starts slipping from the corner of her mouth onto my chest. Usually, I would be disgusted. But there is nothing that Larkyn can do to make me turn up my nose at her.

I want to lie in bed with her all day, until I'm covered in drool and have heard every one of her cute adorable sounds she makes as she sleeps. But I need to deal with Sebastian. If Larkyn helped me realize anything, it's that I need to be tougher on Sebastian. And that ultimately, it's up to him, if he wants to change or not. As much as I threatened never to see him again yesterday, it's just not true.

Although, if he comes near Larkyn again or lays a hand on her, I'll punch him so hard he ends up in the hospital.

So with a heavy sigh, I carefully lift Larkyn's arms and legs off of me and slip out slowly, replacing my body with a pillow for her to wrap herself around. She smiles in her sleep, but otherwise doesn't stir.

It's early, but Larkyn usually gets up early, so I'm surprised she doesn't wake up. I grab my phone and type a quick message to her, so she knows I didn't abandon her. But then I hit delete.

If Larkyn wakes up without a message from me, that's a good thing. Last night, we shared too many emotions. Too many tears were shed together. Too much love was sparked between us. I have to keep my promise. That at the end of the year together, we will part as friends who spent a very enjoyable year together. Nothing more.

I slip out of the house without making a noise, jump into my McLaren, and take off toward Sebastian's apartment. I get to his door and pound on the door with my fist. He better fucking be here.

I don't hear anything at first, but my second round of pounding must have woken him up, because I hear loud stomps as he walks to the door. He opens it wearily, and I see the bruising that has formed around his eye. His eyes are still bloodshot from the alcohol. I take one whiff of his breath and know that he isn't hungover. He's drunk. At least he didn't drive anywhere. I took away all his cars and made sure to freeze his account for any payments larger than a thousand dollars, so he can't buy a new one.

I storm into his apartment and make myself comfortable on his couch. I need to calm the hell down if I'm going to survive this without killing him.

Sebastian takes his time walking over to a chair opposite me, stumbling into a seat before he picks up a beer and starts drinking from it.

I sigh. I see the pain in his eyes. Our father fucked him up. He emotionally and physically abused us both, then left us with no one to love. I was able to use that anger and funnel it into my businesses. But Sebastian, he's sensitive. He turned to drugs and alcohol, and now, there is nothing left of him.

"Let me help you," I say, keeping my voice calm.

Sebastian chuckles. "You can't help me. I ran a woman off the road. I almost killed her. And now the two of you are married or fucking or whatever the hell you are doing."

I take a deep breath, trying not to judge him. He's a good person. He just needs help. And I have no idea how to help him.

I rub the back of my head and look around his apartment, which is in desperate need of cleaning. Empty beer and whiskey bottles scatter the floor and tables. I can smell the rotting pizza in the kitchen from here. And I'm sure if I look closely, I'll notice ants, or possibly even mice, at home in his disaster of an apartment. Usually, I would call a cleaning service to help him. But I'm not going to this time. This time, he has to want to get better. I can't stay here and watch him slowly kill himself, but I can't keep fixing all of his problems, or he'll never get better.

"You need to go to rehab. Stop using alcohol and drugs as a way to crush your feelings; then you can figure out what you are doing."

He laughs. "Yea, because you are the model of healthy relationships."

I narrow my eyes, not understanding. "I have a great life. I work hard. I have great friends. I have an awesome brother when he's sober. I'm married to a beautiful woman. What more could I need?"

He shakes his head as he drinks the rest of the beer in the bottle that I want to rip from his hands.

"You are fake married. You may have friends, but you've never let a woman in. You won't because you're afraid if you really love someone, you might eventually turn into dad and treat her like crap. You're afraid you will drive away or hurt a woman, just like our father did to our mother.

"Just because you don't use drugs and alcohol doesn't mean that you are any better than me. You may seem to have your life together from the outside, but you still have no idea how to have a healthy relationship."

Every word he speaks is true. I don't know how to have a healthy relationship, especially with a woman. And I don't want one. I'm perfectly happy on my own.

I get up from the couch. I can't keep having this conversation with him.

"I want my business, Kade."

I glare at him. Hating that that's all I am to him.

"No."

He returns my glare as he stands up. Although, he's not that intimidating when he can barely stand upright.

"You don't have a choice. Father's will says that when I graduate from college, I am to be allowed to have one of the businesses."

My hands ball into fists next to my side, but I keep my composure and don't hit him again. If I do, I'm afraid it would do some serious damage. It might make me feel better, but it won't do anything to make Sebastian change his life.

"When you get sober, I'll give you one of the businesses."

I walk past him, ignoring him.

"That's not fair. Maybe having a responsibility, like having a company to run, would make me sober."

He looks at me, and my heart cools a little. He's just a lost boy that wants better, but isn't willing to do the work to help himself.

"You can't use a company as a reason to get sober. People rely on you to keep the company running. If you fuck it up, you'll be hurting other people. Whereas if you drink alone here, you'll just be hurting yourself."

"Why not? You do."

I stop in my tracks. Anger floods through my body until I'm trembling.

"I didn't come here to talk about me. I'm not the one with the problem. I came here to talk about you. Get your shit together."

A corner of his lip turns up.

"I'll have my lawyer talk to your lawyer about which company you will be passing onto me."

I grunt as I storm out of his apartment. He's not getting any of the businesses I've worked hard to grow until he proves to me that he takes his responsibilities seriously and is sober. I don't care if I have to spend all my time and energy fighting him in court, proving he isn't well enough to take over any of my businesses.

He's not tearing apart anything I've built. I came here wanting to get close to my brother again so that we could run the King empire together, but now I want nothing more than to go back LA and forget this town.

―――――

I open the door to my bedroom, but Larkyn isn't there. It's after eight in the morning. *What did I expect?*

I walk down to her bedroom and knock on her door, but hear nothing.

I sigh. I'm going to need a drink soon to get through the day. I should make a couple calls to my lawyer first and maybe go for a run or something to get rid of my frustration. I head to my office. I open the double doors and slam them shut behind me.

Larkyn jumps as she sits on the couch in the corner of my office.

I cock my head to the side, as I slip my hand into my pockets, looking at her.

Her big eyes look surprised to see me home.

"Sorry, I didn't mean to intrude. Your office has the best light in the morning."

I walk over and sit down on the edge of the couch while she stays curled up in the corner with a book in her lap.

"It's okay. I'm glad you're here."

She smiles at me with sadness in her eyes.

"You went to see Sebastian."

I nod.

"It didn't go well, did it?"

"No, it didn't. I don't know how to get him help. He won't listen to me about going to rehab, and now he's demanding he gets one of the businesses that are owed to him."

She bites her lip as she puts down her book and scoots closer to me in her short skirt and tank top. She almost never wears skirts, so I don't know why she's wearing one today, but all I want to do is lift the skirt up and fuck away my feelings.

She places her hand on top of my hand.

"You were planning on giving him part of the bar business?"

"Yes. It's my favorite business, and I thought he would enjoy running it with me. We could split the bars in half or run them jointly. Or I'd be willing to give up that part, if it made him happy."

"And now?"

"Now, I don't want to give him any part of any of the businesses until he shows me he's responsible enough to take them over."

She strokes my hand with her thumb. And I feel it all the way to my groin. *Damn, I want her.*

My phone buzzes in my pocket. I pull it out, glancing at the name across the screen.

"My lawyer. I need to take this," I say.

"I'll go," she says, reaching for her book.

"Stay, you being close may help me keep my temper."

She licks her lip, and I almost consider not answering and fucking her. But if my lawyer is calling this early, it means Sebastian already contacted his lawyer.

"Yes," I answer.

"Sebastian's lawyer called."

"I was expecting that."

"Good, then you know that you have to give him one of the businesses. You don't have a choice. It doesn't matter if he is sober or not. Especially since you helped bury his most recent transgressions. You have no proof that he is sober or not. And if you do have proof, he'll end up in jail."

I run my hands through my hair. "Then what do you suggest."

"Give him the bars. They are the riskiest and least lucrative part of the business. And he won't have to do much, the managers at each bar basically run it themselves."

"Fuck, I can't give him the bars." I just fucking can't. They are my heart and soul. I could give the bars to him if he were sober. If he took this seriously, but not in his current state. I can't watch him destroy something I love.

I glance over at Larkyn who gets off the couch and wraps her arms around me as I stand in front of my desk. I start thinking through the financials of the other businesses, trying to figure out one that would hurt the King empire less or that he could run without even showing up, but I can't come up with any solution. The bars are the best solution.

"Give him the bars," I say, begrudgingly. Feeling my heart shatter, as I force each word out.

"Wait," Larkyn says suddenly.

I frown.

"Tell him you'll call him back in five," Larkyn says, looking at me with a big smile.

"Let me think about it for a few minutes, and I'll call you back."

I hang up and look at Larkyn as I cock my head to the side. "What?"

She sits down at my desk, flipping through my papers, like she knows exactly what she's doing.

"How often do you come into my office?" I ask.

She blushes. "Most mornings when I'm not teaching a class."

"And how often do you snoop?" I ask, as I sit on the edge of the desk with my arms folded and a scowl on my face.

She winces. "Just a couple of times. I find your business models and financials interesting."

I raise an eyebrow. "No one, but my accountant, finds this kind of stuff interesting."

She shrugs and grins when she holds up the paper she was looking for. She starts skimming the paper with her eyes.

"Here," she holds the paper up to me, which I realize is my father's will.

"I've read my father's will before."

She nods. "Of course, but did you read the part about the business that is to be given to Sebastian when he graduates from college? You are required to give him a main part of the business or any part that Sebastian chooses."

"Uh-huh, got that part."

She shakes her head. "You need to find something that Sebastian loves. Buy the business no matter how small, and then give him that."

I smile weakly, if Sebastian wasn't so far gone, her plan might work. But I don't think Sebastian cares about anything other than where his next drink is coming from and hurting me.

"The whiskey line makes you a lot of money. Your hotel line makes you more. And your bars, although they don't make you a lot of money, you are in love with them. If you give him any one of the businesses, he'll be filing for bankruptcy in a year. But maybe, if you give him something he's passionate about, he'll be more serious about it. Or at least if he fails, it will be on his own and not destroy you or your father's legacy."

I lean down and kiss her on the lips. "Thank you."

She rakes her teeth over her bottom lip as she leans back in the chair. "I'm more than a pretty face, you know."

I nod. "You definitely are. So why don't you have a real job?"

She shakes her head, her smile immediately dropping off her face like it never existed at all. "I don't want to talk about it."

"You bad at interviews or something? Because I can tell you if you are, I'd hire you in a second. I have trouble getting my own people to read shit like this. And you did it for fun, and actually understood everything."

She rolls her eyes. "I don't want a job."

"Why not? You need a job to make money. Work for me."

She gets up, storming across the room to distance herself from me.

"I had plenty of job offers when I graduated. I had one offer from Apple to run an entire project that would've paid me six figures."

My eyes pop open.

"I turned them down."

"Why?"

She fidgets with the hem of her skirt, pulling it up too high on her thigh.

"Because I didn't want to work for a corporation."

I smirk. "Because you want to freeload off a man like me and live in a fantasy world where you can run and teach a few yoga classes and yet still live in a fancy house."

Her eyes bulge, her cheeks redden, and her lips tense along with her entire body. She looks like I just slapped her. I wouldn't be surprised if her face swells and forms a bruise even though I didn't physically touch her. She is beyond pissed. This is her kryptonite. She doesn't like it when I talk about needing a man to pay her bills.

"I can't believe I never saw how big of an ass you were before. I'm done running, at least in any professional sort of sense. And I teach yoga because I love it. And no, I don't plan on living off a man. Ever. I want more than just to teach yoga classes, but I want more than just sitting behind a desk making someone else's dream a reality."

I shake my head. "Yea, so that's why you agreed to our little arrangement. You get to live in the fancy house, while barely working. And you get a million dollars. What'd you do with the money, Larkyn?"

I pushed too far. I can see it in her eyes. Her ankle is still swollen, but she storms out so fast, you'd never know she was injured.

"I need you to go with me to a cocktail hour this weekend," I holler after her, hoping she will stop being pissed at me by this weekend.

"Go to hell!"

Yep, I pushed way too far this time. But it's for the best. Larkyn is better off without me.

15

LARKYN

K**ADE IS AN ASS.**

He's worse than an ass. He's a cocky, arrogant, son of a bitch. He has no right to tell me I'm just living off him, when the only reason he is as rich as he is, is because of his father. Kade may have taken the businesses to the next level, but he got a whole lot of a head start from his father.

Just because I don't want to follow the same path and take money from my own father, doesn't mean I'm a spoiled princess. I thought he knew that about me, but apparently not.

I slip the diamond bracelet onto my wrist. I should tell Kade what I did with the money. It was his money first. He should know how I spent it. But not tonight. Tonight, I'm going to be the perfect date and act as if he doesn't affect me. Tonight, I'm going to show him just how committed I am to pulling my weight in this deal. That I'm my own person, and my life doesn't fall to pieces when he yells at me.

I step out into the hallway on my much too high heels and storm down the five feet to his bedroom. I should consider moving my stuff to the bedroom on the other side of the house. It's much bigger than my current room and gets more morning sun, which I love. I know the only reason he put me in this room was so I could be feet away from him.

I knock loudly on his bedroom door and wait. I push my hip to the side, posing as best as I know how. I don't smile, I don't want to appear fake, but I do moisten my lips and give little pout.

The door creeps open slowly until I see Kade standing in the doorway, looking as gorgeous as I've ever seen him. Dark grey pants with a white buttoned shirt, open at the top, with a dark grey jacket over it. He's shaved, but left just the right amount of stubble on his cheeks. And he's grinning like he knows just how much effort it took me to be standing in his doorway right now.

"I thought you weren't coming," he says, rolling his eyes up and down my body.

I can't focus when his eyes do that. So I wait until he's thoroughly checked out the slip on my dress that skirts the line between being slutty and sexy. Until his eyes finish their trail up the pink and grey dress.

"Finished?" I ask, swaying my hip out even more.

"Never."

I sigh. "I never said I wasn't coming. Just that you were an ass."

"That implied you weren't coming."

I roll my eyes and can't help but let my eyes linger behind him to his unmade bed. His bed is a million times better than my bed, maybe because Kade is always in it. I can't help that no matter how angry I am with Kade, I still want to end up in his bed tonight. *How pathetic does that make me?*

"I'm here. Are we going to this thing or not?"

"Absolutely."

He holds out his hand to me, but I turn and storm down the stairs to wait in the garage. We hop into his McLaren and take off to his event. And some-fucking-how, my hand finds its way into his. Honestly, I'm fucking screwed, because even when I hate him, I want him.

———

"What is this event?" I ask, as we step into his bar. I never even asked where the event was, but I'm glad it's here. We both feel comfortable in his bar.

"Don't be mad."

I raise an eyebrow. "What the hell did you bring me to?"

He looks straight ahead, with a panicked look on his face. Our fingers are still interconnected, and I can feel a coldness shoot through his body.

I turn to see what he's looking at. Anastasia. Her fiancé. And my fucking family.

"Care to explain?"

He swallows and takes a deep breath, like that's going to save him.

"Anastasia booked her engagement party here."

"That doesn't mean that we have to be here!"

"She invited me as well. And unfortunately, I can't turn down an invitation to go to my wife's sister's engagement party. It wouldn't represent my kind-hearted appearance I've worked so hard to build."

"You mean your jerk, bastard, slutty reputation. The one that I married you to try to fix?"

He smirks. "Behave or don't. I don't care. I just got an excuse to have my wife get all dressed up and go to an event with me. No matter how boring."

"You so owe me for this."

He wiggles his eyebrows. "And how will I ever repay you?"

His hand slides down the back of my dress, stopping on my ass.

I blush. *Damn him.* He's going to get me naked in one of the bathroom stalls most likely. *Ugh, why did I have to fake marry such a good-looking man?*

He brings his hand back up to a more appropriate spot in the middle of my back and guides me forward.

"You came. I didn't think the Kings had time for our measly little family anymore," Anastasia says, wrapping her arms around her fiancé. He doesn't speak; he just stands stoically. He's more of an accessory for Anastasia than a person.

"Of course, I wouldn't miss my sister's engagement party."

Anastasia holds out her ring to me. "What do you think? Is it too big?"

I want to say yes. It's far too big. And the only reason she has an updated version, twice the size of mine, is to compete with me.

"It looks great."

I take Kade's hand and excuse us toward the bar.

"I need drinks. Lots and lots of drinks, if I'm going to survive the night," I say, as we stand at the bar waiting for Axel to serve us.

Kade grins and motions for Axel.

"What can I get you, boss?"

Kade frowns. "Don't call me boss."

"We want two shots of tequila, and then I want a whiskey."

Kade eyes me out of the corner of his eye. "The same," he says to Axel. "Whiskey? Really?" he asks me.

I nod. "I need something strong to get through tonight. I don't care what it tastes like."

Axel returns quickly with our drinks, even though there is a long line formed around the bar of people that were here first.

"Thanks." I grab the first shot and down it, then snatch the second out of Kade's hand and drink his too.

Kade chuckles. "You better not get too drunk tonight. I wouldn't want to take advantage of you tonight," he whispers into my ear.

"You are absolutely going to take advantage of me tonight. I need something positive in my life tonight."

He laughs again, and I fall in love. I swear. All it takes now is a laugh, a smile, a look from him, and it's as if I've developed amnesia. I can't remember the bad, only the good.

"So what's the plan for tonight?" I ask.

"You stay by my side all night," Kade says, nodding toward a group of women that are eyeing him as if they are going to eat him up.

I smile. "Of course."

"We will stay long enough for your family to realize we are still happily in love, and then I'm going to fuck you in the back of my car. And then again in the foyer of my house. Then my bedroom. And anywhere else I can think of."

I choke a little on my whiskey.

Kade grins as he slowly sips his own.

I don't care he dragged me to my evil sister's engagement party. He probably did it to piss me off, but it's not working. Something about his charming smile makes it hard to stay too mad at him.

His phone buzzes, and he pulls it out without checking the number first.

"Hello, Sebastian," he says, with a hint of distaste in his voice.

I bite my lip to keep from smiling, because I know exactly what this call is about.

I can hear part of Sebastian's conversation as I lean against Kade's chest. But Kade doesn't speak. I look up, and the shocked expression tells me he can't.

I laugh and take the phone from Kade. He lets go of it easily.

"Hey, Sebastian. Kade has gone into a little bit of shock. Don't worry, I'm here with him. But know he loves you and is very happy for you." I end the call.

Kade stills, even more, if it's possible.

"Kade?"

"Sebastian is going to rehab."

I nod.

"He said you called him yesterday."

I nod.

"He said you were the one that convinced him."

I nod.

"Um… How is that? I mean…How?"

I smile. "I think Sebastian just needed to hear that he was forgiven. That what happened wasn't his fault. And then when he is done with rehab, he can choose any path he wants."

"I…uh…thank you."

"You're welcome."

"You're incredible."

His lips touch mine, telling me just how incredible I am. His tongue sweeps into my mouth, and he might as well be sweeping me off my feet right now, that's how good the kiss is.

He tucks my hair behind my ear as he breaks the kiss. His lips tighten like he wants to say more but can't.

And I feel uneasy. I'm completely flushed, and I need a minute apart to cool down if I don't seriously want him to fuck me in the bathroom.

"Excuse me a moment. I need to use the ladies room."

I step out from his clutches and race to the bathroom. When I get there, I splash water on my face, not caring if it messes up my makeup. The water doesn't help, because I have butterflies dancing in my stomach all the way up to my chest.

I don't know what's real and what's pretend anymore. I don't know if that feeling deep in my gut is because I love him or hate him. I don't know if I wear the ring on my finger because I'm supposed to or if because I want this to be real.

I don't know anything anymore. All I know is that in a few minutes I have to step back out of this bathroom and pretend like nothing's changed. But I know deep in my heart, the second he thanked me for helping his brother made me want to spend the rest of my life loving him. Even if Kade doesn't always deserve it.

I dry off my hands, and then I walk back out to the party. Anastasia hasn't made any speeches, danced under a spotlight, or had all the attention on her in any way yet. So I expect when I walk back out that it will be about time for her to capture everyone's attention.

What I don't expect is for her lips to be pressed against my husband's.

I storm across the dance floor, not caring who I take out on my path. My heels clank against the floor so loudly I'm sure everyone can hear me. I glare at Anastasia even though I'm still twenty feet away. I've never hated her so much in my life. I don't know what she is thinking, kissing Kade. I know she is used to getting her way. But this is taking things too far. She can't just kiss Kade and expect he will fall madly in love with her, divorce me, and marry her. That's insane to think that. But I don't know any other reason she would have for kissing my husband than to torment me.

I get closer, and I start running. Planning on tearing the bitch from his lips and pulling her by the hair until I can throw her out with the trash.

Kade finally wiggles out of her grasp. And he looks pissed. Eyes dark, lips stern, and cheeks red.

"Get the fuck out of my bar!" Kade screams.

Anastasia folds her arms and raises an eyebrow. "Excuse me? I paid to be here. Not to mention, I'm your sister-in-law. You can't just kick my guests and me out."

Kade senses me and looks up. He struts over to me and holds me tight against his body.

"You are no sister-in-law. You aren't even a sister. You are a piece of trash that needs to leave now. Stop trying to manipulate your sister and me."

The entire crowd in the room has fallen silent. All eyes are on us. But I no longer care what any of them think. I'm just happy to have Kade hold me in his arms and defend me against my supposed family.

"You don't get to kiss me and get away with it. I want you out of my bar and out of our lives until you can apologize."

Anastasia's eyes panic when he mentions the kiss. And then she looks to me like I might save her.

"Out," I say, with the same fire in my voice as Kade.

Anastasia pouts before looking around the room at all the prying eyes. It only takes her a moment to decide it might be best if she walks away. Her fiancé comes out of the bathroom, and several people point outside, telling him to follow Anastasia out.

"This is unacceptable, Larkyn," my father says to me sternly.

"Get the fuck out, Father," I say. I've had enough. I'm tired of being mistreated by my family. I'm tired of them thinking they are better than me. I'm tired of being told I'm wasting my life. I no longer care about any of it.

"Out, everyone, now," Kade's voice booms.

Axel and the other employees get to work shoeing everyone out the door. While I stay tucked in Kade's arm.

"I'm sorry," we both say simultaneously to each other as the crowd starts to file out.

I smile.

"I shouldn't have even engaged with Anastasia. I knew she was trouble and only wanted me for one thing. I should have been prepared for her kiss."

I shake my head. "I shouldn't have ever left you alone. I knew better. And you did warn me not to leave you alone."

He kisses me gently on the lips. "Don't ever leave me again."

His words sound so sincere, but I know they aren't. Time is ticking away. Less than nine months remain until our time is up.

"You okay, Larkyn? I'll swear Anastasia was the one that instigated the kiss and Kade was just an honest bystander who broke the kiss the second he could," Axel says.

I bite my lip with a smile. "You don't have to worry about defending Kade's honor," I tease.

Axel smiles. "Good. Anything I can get you? Need a stiff drink after that?"

I look up at Kade with dreamy eyes. There is only one thing I want right now to make me feel better.

"No, um…we are good," I say, stumbling over my words.

Axel looks from me to Kade and takes a hint. "I'm sending the staff home. The party didn't last long, so there isn't much to clean up. I'll have tomorrow's shift clean everything up before we open."

I swallow, my mouth dry as I stare up at Kade. He's handsome, and loving, and kind, and everything I've ever wanted in a husband. And he's my husband. Too bad this isn't real.

Kade watches Axel walk out of the bar, out of the corner of his eye. And then he grabs my ass, pulling me flush against his body as his lips crash into mine. We aren't going to make it home. We aren't going to make it anywhere. We need each other far too much after the emotional chemistry we have felt all evening.

Between me saving Sebastian, and him protecting me, we both owe each other a lot.

And we are about to make good on paying each other back.

I jump up, and he catches me as my legs wrap around his body. Our lips stay locked together in a dance that moves faster and faster, showing our true desperation.

"I can't wait. I have to have you—"

His lips cut me off.

And he drops me into one of the couches sitting around a low table, near one of the bars, as his body crashes on top of mine.

I grab his pants fumbling with the button until I can finally jerk his pants down.

I don't wait for him to remove my underwear, I push them down myself as his hand slides up my ass.

"Someone's impatient."

I tug on his bottom lip with my mouth, punishing him for stopping to do something as silly as talking.

He grins against my lips. "I don't know how I ever survived without you."

"Shut up and fuck me."

That makes him chuckle.

He slides his hand between my legs, finding the sweet spot that only he knows where it is.

I moan as his fingers move over my body, igniting me and making me want him to be his forever.

Our eyes meet as his cock nestles in between my legs.

He opens his mouth, and I'm afraid of what he might say. We both feel vulnerable right now. We both just showed we care about each other more than we have ever let on. And that scares the crap out of me, because if he doesn't tell me he loves me, or at least what he is feeling is real, then I might explode in pain.

He hesitates, and it can't be good, so I kiss him, and it takes away whatever he was about to say away.

His cock pushes inside me, and I arch my back, begging his body to go deeper inside mine. Our eyes meet together, as bodies entwine. Our eyes stay open, together, as we both come.

We stay together a long time, neither of us speaking or moving. Kade finally pulls out of me, does his pants up, and then helps me up from the booth.

We both have so many things to say, but neither of us says them. Instead, we walk to Kade's car, and he drives us home with nothing but the radio to keep us company.

I try not to let my mind race, but it's difficult. All I can think about is how much I care about him. How much I want this to be real.

I rest my head against the window and close my eyes. If I sleep, maybe in the morning I'll have a different perspective on my life. Instead of the heartache, I feel at the thought of losing Kade.

The car eventually stops as I doze off to sleep. I feel myself being lifted into Kade's arms, but my eyes are far too heavy to open. My head flops against his chest, and my breathing is heavy as Kade carries me inside and into my bed. He doesn't bother undressing me; he pulls the covers over me as he sits on the edge of the bed.

I want him to climb in the bed next to me, but I know that would only make things worse. Our feelings are clouded enough.

Kade leans forward and kisses me softly on the lips. A perfect kiss to take with me as I fall asleep.

"I love you Larkyn," Kade whispers, thinking I'm asleep. But I hear his words, or I dream them.

"But you can never be mine."

16

KADE

HOW THE FUCK did I fall in love with Larkyn?

I have no idea, but it's a problem. I'm breaking the one promise she swore she needed above everything else. I fell in love, and now I'm going to hurt her. And I'm pretty sure she is in love with me, or at least has feelings toward me too.

I need to talk to Larkyn. We need a new plan if we are going to survive these next several months without hurting each other. I just have no idea what the plan is.

"I made dinner for you," Larkyn says, coming into my office and putting her arms around my chest like it's the most natural thing to do.

Dinner would be the perfect time to talk to her. Tell her we need more boundaries. That she needs to start treating me like an ass too, because I'm falling far too hard for her.

"Sounds great, what did you make?"

She grins far too wickedly. "Your favorite."

I raise an eyebrow as I follow Larkyn, who is basically dancing with giddy excitement, as she runs back to the kitchen.

I follow her at a slower pace, enjoying watching her show from behind.

174

And then I smell it. Garlic bread and marinara sauce.

I grin. "You remembered."

She laughs, as she stirs the big pot and begins scooping out food into a bowl.

I can't contain myself. I wrap my arms around her as I take a bite over her shoulder.

It tastes horrible.

I make a scrunched up face, unable to hide my disgust. Maybe this is just what we need. A playful, relaxed night where we have to order take out and realize we aren't perfect for each other.

She pouts.

"Your *first time* making spaghetti?" I ask.

She nods, biting her lip.

Her eyes turn to slits of lust. "But I have a way to make it taste better."

I raise an eyebrow. "By throwing it in the trash and starting over?"

She giggles. "No, you're lucky I like you or I might consider that too mean."

"It's not mean. It's the truth. That is the worst thing I've ever tasted. You somehow managed to burn it, and the seasoning is all off. Did you use cumin? You know that is usually used in Mexican dishes, not Italian?"

Larkyn turns, holding a spoonful of the sauce up to my lips. "Oh come on, it isn't that bad. Try it again."

I close my lips tightly. "Nope, I'm not eating another bite."

She cocks her head to the side as her hips pop out. She stands taller until her breasts are fully popping out of the low cut sundress she's wearing. She has a twinkle in her eye that I know means I should run. Far, far away, because whatever she is about to do is trouble.

Instead, I stand intrigued like the idiot I am.

She turns the spoon over, and red marinara sauce drips down onto her breasts.

"Oops," she says, smiling slyly.

Fuck.

My mouth falls open, and an instinct that is all man and testosterone takes over my brain. I forget about how bad the sauce is. I forget about talking to her. All I can think about is licking the marinara sauce off her tits.

I'm to her body in second. My tongue runs down her neck and over her breasts until I'm licking every drop of the sauce clean from her tits. More drips down between her breasts that I can't reach.

I rip the dress open, as she stumbles backward into the counter. She grabs another scoopful of sauce and rubs it over her chest and stomach.

It shouldn't turn me on, but it does. Anything she does turns me on. I remember back to the conversation when I told her I would love a woman to be covered in marinara sauce. It was a fantasy. One that I never thought to act upon. But seeing her covered in red sauce makes me do a weird cross between laughing and wanting.

She looks hot and ridiculous at the same time. And I've never wanted a woman more. Not because she looks sexy, but because she planned this. She made me spaghetti so that she could seduce me with a wild fantasy I once told her.

I set her up on the counter and spread her legs apart. Her hands run through my hair, rubbing red sauce all over my head until it's dripping down my face. I move to wipe it off with the back of my hand, but she leans down and slowly rubs her tongue up from my chin, over my lips, then nose.

I growl. "When did you become so sexy?"

She blushes. "I've always been sexy."

I rake my teeth over my bottom lip. She's right about that.

She grabs the hem of my shirt and lifts it off, making sure she covers my chest with the marinara. She reaches for my pants, but I really don't want sauce all over my cock. So I use my left hand, that is still relatively clean, to lower my pants and release my cock.

She reaches down to stroke me. It takes every drop of strength I have to push her hand away. I want her hand on me. Desperately. But I don't want to be covered in red, sticky sauce.

So instead, I push into her opening as I grab her ass and surrender my body to her. I've never felt this way before whenever I've had sex with a woman. I don't just want to bring her pleasure. I want to make her mine in every way possible. I want to rule her world and her mind. I want her to never think about anything other than me.

She smiles at me, then arches her back, and I lose her pretty eyes to the pleasure pulsing through her body.

"Look at me, beautiful."

She slowly tilts her head back to me and forces her eyes open.

"Gorgeous."

She blushes and stays with me as I feel us both building.

I try to tell her everything with my body. That I love her.

That I want more than a fake marriage.

But I'm terrified of hurting her.

I don't know how to protect her from the damage I'm capable of. Because for as much crap as I give Sebastian, I've been there. I've never abused alcohol and drugs, but I've buried myself in women or work. No matter what damage it caused other people.

I don't know how to treat Larkyn as a partner. I don't know how to truly let her into my life.

I come inside her as she screams her own orgasm. And as much as I desperately tried to tell her how I'm feeling, she doesn't have a clue at my inner turmoil.

Larkyn grins mischievously, as she fluffs my hair that is drenched in the disgusting sauce.

"I told you I could make it taste better," she says, with a wink.

I laugh and lift her off the counter. "Sorry, but it tasted disgusting the entire time. You have officially squashed any more dreams of getting to lick marinara sauce of your body."

She grabs a handful of the sauce from the pot next to me and flings it at me.

I duck, and the sauce scatters on the floor around me, but mostly misses me.

I grab her, lifting her up before she has a chance to attack me with the gross liquid again.

She squeals and flails in my arms as I carry her to the shower in her bedroom.

"Why aren't we showering in yours? Your shower is bigger."

I chuckle. I put her down on her feet in the shower. "Because I didn't want to drip gross marinara sauce in my bedroom or shower."

She scoops some off her chest and rubs it into my face while I grimace.

"Don't lie, you love it."

I turn the water on and watch her squeal as the cold water comes down on top of her. I love the sound. Just like I love everything about her.

I should break up with her. It would be the right thing to do. Release her from our contract. Set her up in a nice home and let her live her life in peace.

But my heart has fallen into the deepest part of love. I can't stop it. I can't control it. And I know that this is going to end horribly. Because I'm less than perfect. I'm a human with plenty of flaws. And one of those flaws is going to come crashing into our lives and screw us both, until I'm left with nothing, but heartache and pain.

I love her. But I'm not enough for her. She's going to realize it as soon as I fuck up. I've managed to hang on this long, maybe I can stop myself from fucking up for years, so that I can at least have some more time with her.

Or maybe, I should break up with her, and spare her the heartbreak before she falls in love with me.

1 7

LARKYN

"So what should we celebrate with? Wine? Champagne? Whiskey? Margaritas?" Serena asks, as I sit across from her at our favorite lunch spot.

"And what exactly are we celebrating?" I lean back in my chair. We are definitely celebrating something, Serena just doesn't know what it is yet.

"Spending time with each other, for one. It's been four months since you got married and we've barely hung out. So we are celebrating us getting back together again."

I laugh. "Fine, order whatever alcohol you want."

"Margs it is then."

I smile sweetly at her. "How are things going with work?"

"I'm doing amazing. I've already been promoted and got a huge raise. I've fixed their ridiculous filing system. My employers have realized they can't live without me."

I chuckle. "Sounds like you have thoroughly charmed them."

She nods. "Enough about my boring job though. How are Kade and you doing?"

I can't look her in the eye as I fidget with the napkin in my lap. "We are good."

She squints trying to look for something. "We're good. That's all I get? How's the sex?"

I laugh nervously. "Amazing. Not that I have a lot to compare to—"

Serena snickers.

"But I have no complaints in the sex department."

"So what's the problem?"

"I don't have a problem."

She stares at me, deadpanned. "You have a problem." She turns to the waiter. "Two margaritas please."

I sigh. "It isn't real."

Serena rolls her eyes. "I've seen the way that boy looks at you; it's real."

I tense. I know she's right. That we have feelings toward each other. But neither of us have acted on them in four months. It's been over a month since Kade said he loved me when he thought I was asleep. He's not mentioned anything like it since. Not one word. And my own heart has flipped back and forth so many times; I'm not sure what I feel anymore. One second I love him, the next I hate him.

"What about the job or life search as you call it? Have you figured out what you want to do with your life?"

I lick my lips, trying to find the words to tell her what I've been hiding for two weeks now. I need to tell someone, and she's that someone. But as soon as the words leave my mouth, I have to actually act on the words. I sure as hell don't have time to look for a meaningful job when I'm holding in a secret that will change my life forever.

"No, I haven't found anything."

Serena frowns. But the frown doesn't last as our server places two large margaritas in front of both of us. She lifts her glass up, and I do the same.

"To many more sleepless nights, as we both get to fuck two of the hottest and most endowed guys in town," Serena says.

I clink my glass with hers and then set mine down.

She studies me a moment. Looking me up and down. "Oh my god!" she squeals.

"Shh," I say, not wanting her to blurt out her next words too loudly.

"You're pregnant," she whisper-yells, as she leans across the table. At least she attempted to be quiet.

I nod.

"Does Kade know? Was it planned?"

I shake my head.

"Were you using protection?"

"The pill."

"When are you going to tell Kade?"

I shrug.

Serena laughs and gets up from the table and comes over to hug me. "At least I get to drink two margaritas for lunch."

I smile and lean into her chest. I don't know what I'm going to do. I'm pregnant. With Kade King's child. We are fake married. We aren't even in a real relationship. But we are having a baby. And I have no idea how Kade is going to react when I tell him.

———

I've been avoiding Kade all day.

I've gone to the grocery store multiple times to pick up things I forgot on previous trips.

I went to the post office to get stamps, not that I have anything to mail.

I filled my car up with gas and drove through two separate car washes.

I thought somehow doing those mindless tasks would bring me some clarity of mind and help me figure out how to tell my fake husband we are pregnant. *For real.*

How do I tell a man, who thought this was nothing more than a fake arrangement, that we are now bonded together for life, whether we want to be or not?

How do I even start that conversation?

I don't have the answers as I slowly walk into his house. I close the door carefully, hoping if he doesn't hear me enter, I can stall having the conversation for a little longer.

Stop being a chicken.

I clear my throat. "Kade?" I holler as I walk into the kitchen. It's around dinner time, but he's not in the kitchen. I hear voices down the hallway where his office is. Maybe he has a client back there, or Axel is over discussing things as they usually do?

I start walking down the hallway toward his office. I need to tell him I'm home and ask if we can chat later. Otherwise, I'll lose my nerve again and won't talk to him until tomorrow or the next day or the next.

My hand raises over his closed door to knock. He never closes the door, so it's strange it's closed now. My hand stops in midair.

"This is your child, Kade," a woman's voice says.

I still. *Did Kade knock up more women than just me?*

Kade laughs, like it's the funniest thing in the world. "The child isn't mine, Harlow. I can do the math. The last time we had sex was in January. This child is too young to be mine."

"I'm filing to sue you for child support. Or you can give me five million to make this all go away. It will be far less than what I get when I win my case."

"No. I want a paternity test, because there is no way that child is mine." A pause. And I feel tears threatening my eyes.

"And even if the child is mine. So what? I'll provide child support. I'll make sure the child has the money he's owed. But that's it. You aren't getting a penny of my money. I'll make sure every penny I give you goes to the child. And even then, your child won't inherit anything. You won't mean anything to me. I never wanted a child. Certainly not yours."

Tears pour out of my eyes like lava. They burn more and more, the heavier they flow out. I don't care if he knocked up Harlow. I don't care if he has a child other than the baby growing inside me. All I can focus on is five little words. *I never wanted a child.*

I force my legs to run away to my bedroom where I let all the tears fall. And in their place, the anger comes.

All the times that Kade has been a jerk to me flood my head. And most of all, the fact that even though he might feel love for me, he's never acted on those feelings. He doesn't want me.

He doesn't want our baby.

I won't listen to him cause me pain. But I can't stay here either. I want out.

I head to the bathroom, dry my eyes, and pinch my cheeks, trying to look like I haven't spent the last ten minutes crying, and then I storm toward the kitchen where I can hear Kade cooking.

"Hey, dinner will be ready in ten minutes," Kade says.

I can't wait ten minutes.

I pull the heavy ring off my finger and place it on the counter.

Kade raises an eyebrow. "Something wrong with the ring?"

"No, something is wrong with whatever this is that we are doing."

He stops stirring the delicious smelling Asian dish he is making and faces me.

"I'm sorry Larkyn, but I don't understand, and I've had a shitty day, so I'd love it if you could speak plain English and get whatever fight we are about to have over with."

"I'll make this easy for you then. I want out of our contract. I'm done being fake married to you."

He blinks rapidly, and then narrows his eyes at me, as he cockily crosses his arms. "You can't be serious."

"I am."

"Why?"

"Because I'm tired. This isn't what I thought it would be."

He cocks his head to one side. "And what did you think would happen?"

"I thought that you would buy me jewelry every other week, take me to fancy parties, and go on nice vacations with me. I thought I would get to enjoy more of the perks of being your wife," I say, lying through my teeth. I don't care about any of those things, but I know that money is sensitive with Kade. It's the main thing we've fought over. What I did with his money. And after Harlow tried to blackmail him for money, I have no doubt he is very sensitive about the subject now.

He narrows his eyes like he's looking through to my soul. "What would it take for you to stay?"

I wasn't expecting him to talk so calmly about this or to ask me that question, but I know my answer immediately.

"I want five million dollars," I say, lying. All I want is his heart. I want him to love his future child the way that I do. But that's asking too much.

He doesn't even flinch, and I think he might say fine. He'll do it. Maybe if he's willing to pay me five million dollars when he just denied it to Harlow, that means I'm special to him. Instead, he stands stoically looking at me while he reads me like an open book.

"What did you do with the money I gave you?"

I can feel my stomach clenching as he speaks. I'm about to be sick. I can't stay here much longer without upchucking. And yet I can't force myself to leave because I know these are our last moments together.

"I bought the most expensive house I could afford with it."

His eyes drop in disappointment. "Then, I'll have my lawyer draw up the terms to release you from my contract."

He walks toward me looking me dead in the eyes. I can't move. All I can do is smell his familiar smell of a deep cologne. I take in the last flicker of his dark eyes, and the curve of his lips as he frowns.

"You owe me nothing. And I owe you nothing. I'll put into the media that the divorce was amicable. And then we are done." When he says the word done, he turns and walks back to his pot, stirring it like we didn't just have the soul-crushing conversation we just had.

Contrastingly, it takes everything in my body to turn and walk to my bedroom before my stomach empties into the toilet. I don't know where I'm moving or what I'm doing with my life. I don't know if, in a few years, I'm going to regret ever agreeing to fake marry Kade or if I'm going to appreciate it because I love our child so much. I can't think beyond this moment. Because in this moment, I'm pregnant, and alone.

18

KADE

"WHAT ARE you still doing here? I can handle this, go home," Axel says next to me, as I clean the bar for the fifth time.

"I know you can handle it, but I want tonight to go perfectly," I say, ignoring him as I continue to clean. I don't add that it has been three months since I've seen Larkyn, and I'm losing my damn mind. I can't think, I can't sleep, the only time I can even pretend to function well is when I'm at work, and that's only because there is something for me to focus on to keep my mind off things.

"Go home. You hired me to be the manager. Now let me do my job and go home. I've dealt with plenty of corporate events before. I can handle making sure the bar is clean." Axel snatches the rag out of my hand.

I glare at him.

Axel looks back at me sadly, like I'm a stray puppy without a home or something.

"I'm fine. Don't look at me that way."

He shakes his head. "You are anything but fine."

"Yeah, you're an idiot," Sebastian says, taking a seat at the bar across from me.

186

"Should you be in the bar after just getting finished with your treatment program?" I ask.

"Bars aren't a trigger for me."

I frown. "What are your triggers then?"

"Anger, resentment, feeling betrayed, losing focus, and parties. No party, no need to drink."

"There is a party here tonight. You can't stay."

"I don't plan on staying."

I roll my eyes. "You just plan on calling me an idiot again and then leaving?'

He shrugs. "Something like that."

Ugh, I need a drink, but I'm not drinking in front of Sebastian. He's been sober for two months now. I won't be the reason he screws that up. Which is also why I'm not letting him hang out in the bar.

"Well, tell me how much of an idiot I am so that we can get on with our lives."

Sebastian gives a smug smile to Axel, who leans against the bar to join our conversation.

"You're an idiot because you broke up with Larkyn; filed for divorce even. You need to call her," Sebastian says.

"No, she made her decision. She doesn't want to be with me."

"Just call her," Sebastian says.

"No, that's enough. If you just came here to talk about Larkyn, I'm done," I say, giving Sebastian a warning glance. He may be my brother, and he may be getting his life together, but I've slugged him before, I'll do it again if he pisses me off.

Sebastian nods slowly, his head bobbing several times. "Fair enough. Then, I guess I don't have anything else to say." He turns toward Axel. "Can you get me a club soda?"

Axel tightens his lips and then makes a club soda for Sebastian and himself. He slides the drink to Sebastian.

"Have you heard from Larkyn lately? I know she used to love this bar," Sebastian says, staring at Axel.

"I know what you are doing, and it's not going to work," I say, annoyed.

"No, she hasn't come in lately. How has she been?" Axel asks, both men ignoring me completely.

"She's doing well. Really well, actually," Sebastian answers.

"That's awesome. Where has she been working? Is she still at the yoga studio?" Axel asks.

Sebastian grins. "No, actually, Larkyn and I started a business together. A non-profit. It's a healing center meant to help people that are struggling. It provides them a place to stay, people to talk to, and connects them with the treatment they may need. Larkyn's been running it with me. She occasionally helps teach a yoga or fitness class, but she mainly runs it as my business partner."

I listen to Sebastian. I can't help it. But then I already knew what she was doing because as much as I should leave her alone, I can't help but stalk her online.

"Is she seeing anyone?" Axel asks, his eyes cutting to me.

I growl.

Both men smirk. "Not that I'm aware of, but then again, we are only business partners. She doesn't tell me everything," Sebastian says.

"Okay, you've had your fun. Get out," I say, annoyed with both my best friend and brother.

Sebastian and Axel laugh. Sebastian stands. "Fine, fine. I'm going."

Sebastian's phone buzzes, and he pulls it out of his pocket. "Hey, Larkyn." He smirks at me as he answers the phone.

My blood is boiling, but I also really want to hear her voice on the other side of the phone, so much that I lean over the bar so that if an opportunity presents itself, I can snatch the phone out of Sebastion's hands.

"Wait Larkyn, slow down. What do you mean he's out?"

My heart stops. I don't know what's happening, but I hate the way Sebastian's voice just hiked up several octaves higher.

"No, don't leave your house. You have a security system, and he shouldn't be able to find where you live. I'll be there in five. Lock all the doors, and arm the security system until I get there. And try to relax. He's not going to come straight for you after getting out of prison. I'll call my lawyer on the way over and see what's happening with his case and if he'll end up back in prison soon," Sebastian says.

"Nathan got released on bail?" I ask, unable to contain my anger in my voice.

Sebastian nods.

"I have to go," I say, as I hop over the bar and start running toward my car. I hear Sebastian behind me, but don't wait for him.

I run and jump into my McLaren in one motion, enter the address I know she's lives at into my phone, and then take off as the directions appear on my phone. I've never driven by Larkyn's house, but I had my lawyer find her new address for emergencies like this or for when I couldn't stand to be apart from her for another second.

If Nathan so much as lays a hand on her, I'll kill him. Larkyn has been through enough. He doesn't get to touch her. Ever. She's mine.

He was supposed to stay locked up this time. I reported that he was dealing cocaine again, even though, I didn't have evidence. Just a hunch. My statement was enough for his parole officer to do a random search. Turns out he was dealing again. He was supposed to be locked up again for years.

It takes me five minutes to get to the address. I park my car, but don't even bother to turn off the ignition. I need to get to her. Last time Nathan was released, he went straight for her. I won't let him hurt her again.

I run up the driveway and take in the cute modest house in front of me. It definitely isn't a million dollar house, but I wasn't expecting it to be. It looks exactly like Larkyn. Independent, adorable, and perfect.

I knock on the door, pounding loudly with everything I have while I beg her to answer. She can hate me, but I need to see that she is alright.

The door creeps open the tiniest crack so that I can only see her head as she peers around the door.

"What are you doing here?" she asks.

"What are you doing answering the door when there is a known criminal on the loose?"

She frowns. "I saw you on my security camera Sebastian helped me install." She nods toward the corner of her porch. I see the tiny camera staring right at me.

"Let me in. I want to stay with you until Nathan goes back to prison."

She shakes her head. "I don't think that is a good idea. Sebastian will be here any minute to help. And I've already spoken with the police. There is nothing we can do until his next trial date later this month. He's out on bail."

"Please, let me stay. I won't be able to breathe if I don't know you are safe," I say, looking deep into her eyes and I can see her caving. She wants me here as much as I want to be here.

I put my hand on the door, gently pushing it open, hoping that once it's open, she will invite me in.

We both stop breathing as the door swings open, and I get a full view of her. She's beautiful, but there is something different about her I can't place. She's happier than she was with me, maybe that's it. I can't keep my eyes off her body. I scan her body up and down. Over her tight jeans and stomach that is protruding the tiniest bit over her jeans.

I narrow my eyes and look again. There's a bump. Not a huge bump, but definitely a bump. One that is very noticeable on her usually smooth, rock hard stomach.

My eyes meet Larkyn's, and her eyes glisten with moisture. She's about to cry.

"You're pregnant?" I ask.

She nods, swallowing hard.

"It's mine, isn't it?"

She nods.

"Larkyn, I'm so sorry, I was an ass." A smile creeps up on my face as I realize I'm going to be a dad, and the woman I love is going to be the mother. This is my chance to change things, to make things right.

"No," she says, as I move toward her.

I stop. "Please let me fix this. We are having a baby together. Let me fix things."

Her lip trembles, but she doesn't back down. "There is no together. No us. I'm having a baby, and you can be in this baby's life or not. I'm not looking for money, or child support, or inheritance. I would love for my child to have a father, so if you would like to be in my baby's life, then we can get our lawyers together to discuss a custody arrangement. Otherwise, I don't want to see you again."

"Larkyn, please let me explain—"

Her eyes aren't looking at me anymore; they are looking past me.

I glance behind me and see Sebastian standing on the foot of the porch.

"I can go if you two need more time to talk. I'll do whatever you want me to do, Larkyn," Sebastian says, ignoring me.

"Come in," she says, and Sebastian steps inside her home. A man she once hated for almost running her over; she now welcomes in so easily. But me, a man who loves her, she views as a betrayer. I still don't know what sparked her to fight with me the night she left, but it was clear she wanted out, that's why she said what she did.

"Please," I beg, as I bend down on one knee, like that will somehow convince her.

"I'm sorry," she says, closing the door.

And then I'm alone on her porch.

So instead, I say what I need to say to her, to her front door, and hope she's listening. "It was all fake. The reason we aren't together. The fighting. All fake. I love you, Larkyn. I was an ass because that's what you needed. I would do anything for you, and I thought I was doing the right thing by pushing us away from each other. But I was wrong. We belong together.

"I know you are upset about how I kept pressuring you about what you did with the money. But I've known all along what you did with the money. I've always known. You didn't use it to buy this house. And I love you more for it."

No answer. Not that I was expecting one. I let my hand rest

against the door for a second, needing to be as close to her as possible.

And then I walk over to the bench on her porch and sit down on it. I'm not moving from this spot until I see Larkyn again. She needs to know I'm here for her and our baby no matter what. And that starts with actions, then maybe she'll listen to my words.

19

LARKYN

"KADE IS SLEEPING on your front porch," Sebastian says, peering through my blinds.

"So?"

Sebastian drops the blind he had lifted up and walks over to the small white couch to sit next to me. I found this couch at a thrift store, and I love it.

"So, don't you think you should give him another chance?"

"No."

"You gave me another chance and look how that turned out," he says, wiggling his eyebrows to try to make me laugh. It's not going to work.

I sip my tea. "No."

Sebastian sighs. "You have to talk to him at some point. He is your baby's father."

"That's what I have lawyers for." I tuck my feet underneath me as I rest my teacup on my leg.

Sebastian reaches out and touches my leg lovingly. "I'm meeting with a few people this morning to work on the building construction. I can cancel if you want me to stay here."

"No, I'm fine. Besides, I have my trusty guard outside."

Sebastian gives me a weak smile. "You two had better have talked to each other and made up by the time I return."

"Don't count on it," I say, returning to my tea.

Sebastian gets up and walks out my front door. I peak around to see if Kade will try to sneak in before Sebastian has a chance to lock it, but I see no signs of Kade. *Maybe he went home?*

I finish my tea, and it's mid-morning, but I'm already exhausted. I don't have any meetings today, but I do have a lot of emails to go through. First, I need a nap; then I'll get to the emails.

I grab the grey throw draped over the back of the couch and pull it over me, curling up on the couch. I should be thinking about how I'm going to get the courage to talk to Kade, but all I can focus on right now is sleep.

———

I feel his hot breath on my neck.

I smile.

Kade.

I don't care that he snuck into my house. Or that he's breathing over me. Or that he woke me up from a much-needed nap. I'm just happy he's fighting to be in my life.

I open my eyes. And jump to my feet when I see the eyes staring back at me. They don't belong to Kade. These eyes are far too evil.

"Nathan," I say, stepping backward trying to reach for my phone on the coffee table behind me. But when I reach the coffee table, I feel nothing.

Nathan smirks. "Looking for this?" he asks, holding the phone up.

I take a deep breath and stare at the door behind me. Kade will hear. I need to talk loudly, and he'll call the police. But when I glance out the window and see it's dark outside, my confidence fades. *How did I sleep the entire day away? Where is Sebastian? And did Kade manage to sleep on my front porch for another night?*

"What do you want, Nathan?" I ask, trying to think of what to do next to keep Nathan occupied.

"I'm here for you, of course."

I nod. Trying to stay calm as I grasp my belly. *I won't let him hurt you*, I think.

"You don't want to do this, Nathan. You are free. You should go live your life."

He glares at me. "I'm out on bail. I'll be going back as soon as you testify against me. You're nothing but a fucking liar."

I swallow. "I won't testify to anything. I can't. What happened between us was a long time ago."

Nathan steps closer to me, and I freeze, just like before. I can't save myself. I'm not strong enough.

He reaches out to grab my arm, and finally, I snap awake.

"No," I cry loudly, not this time. I swat his hand away and run toward the front door.

I grab the doorknob and pull, but the door is locked with three different locks. *Why didn't I think about how to make a quick escape?*

I turn the first lock.

Then, the second.

I reach for the third, high up on the door, when Nathan's hands squeeze my neck.

I cry out as he pulls me away from the door.

"Help!" I scream, finally finding my voice. "Someone help me!"

Glass breaks in the window over the porch, and Kade's body comes barreling through. He doesn't stop until he reaches us, knocking us both to the ground as he goes after Nathan. I roll away from the two men as I watch Kade punch Nathan in the face over and over. Blood spews everywhere. And Kade easily wins the fight.

"Call 911," Kade says, pulling his phone from his pocket and holding down Nathan.

I call, and within minutes we hear the police sirens. Kade gets a few more punches in before the police arrive. They handcuff Nathan and take our statements. They all insist I go to the hospital, but I don't want to spend the day in the hospital, so instead, I have a medic check me out, and after promising to make a doctor appoint-ment for tomorrow, just in case, we are left alone.

"You're safe now," Kade says, stroking my face. "I guess I should go too." He glances toward my front door.

"No."

His face lights up, but the sternness of my face dissipates any happiness on his. This isn't going to be an easy conversation.

"I love you, Larkyn," Kade says.

I bite my lip. I've been waiting months to hear him say those words to me and mean them.

I nod, because I can't force my lips to say them back. Not until I hear more. Because if I admit I love him, and this doesn't work out between us, my heart will break worse than when Nathan attacked.

"I know you set up a foundation to help people. That's what the money went to. I know that money is now being used to start the non-profit with Sebastian to help people heal from whatever pain they are dealing with."

I nod. I'm sure Sebastian eventually told him the truth.

"What you don't know is I've always known. From the first day you set up an account to use the money for charity, I knew. My lawyer tracked the money and found out for me. You can talk to him if you want. He'd never lie for me. It's a problem really." He smiles and sticks his hands in his pockets as his adorable dimples form on his cheeks.

"If you knew, then why did you constantly ask me? Why did you make me feel like a gold-digger for taking the money?"

"Because you asked me to."

"Huh?"

"Because you asked me to be an ass so you wouldn't fall in love with me. So I was an ass. I knew that was a sensitive topic for both of us that I could easily play up and piss you off with. That's all it ever was."

I think back to all the times he screwed with me, and I know he's telling the truth. I asked him to make me hate him so that I wouldn't fall in love. And every time we got close to falling in love, he did something that made me mad.

"I'm not leaving you. Or our baby. Ever."

I shake my head. His words aren't enough. "I heard you with Harlow."

"I told her the truth. There is no way her baby is mine."

I nod. "I know. I heard you say you never want children. I don't want to trap you with a baby. This will never work."

Kade's eyes narrow, and he walks out of my living room. Then out the front door. While I stand frozen.

I don't know what he's doing or if he's coming back. And I hate that I don't know if he's coming back.

A few minutes later he returns with papers in his hand. He thrusts them into mine.

"Read this paragraph," Kade says, pointing to the third paragraph.

I start reading the page that I realize is the contract I signed a few months ago when we agreed to fake marry. But I don't believe what I'm reading.

"You added this page. This wasn't here on the contract I signed."

He frowns. "This paragraph was included the whole time. You just didn't read the contract very well."

I shake my head. "I read the contract front to back ten times before I signed it. I know better than to sign a contract like that without reading it first."

"Go get your copy of the contract."

I sigh. This is pointless, but I walk to my makeshift office in the corner of my dining room. I dig through the stack of papers until I find the contract, and then I bring it back and thrust it into Kade's hands. He flips through the pages, but can't find the one he's looking for.

He flips to the third page, studies the paper for a second and then begins pulling at the corner. Two pages are stuck together. And when he pulls them apart, and I see the paragraph. Tears fall from my face, most likely forming puddles on the floor near my feet.

"You wanted a baby this whole time. It's encouraged in the contract, but ultimately up to me if I want to pursue or not. You think I'm the perfect woman to have a baby with, and you want an heir because you are probably never going to get married for love. And you would love a child with a woman you care about, to love, to be your heir, and keep other women from trying to get knocked up so their child would become your heir," I say, paraphrasing all the important parts of the contract.

He nods.

"You want this baby?" I ask.

"As much as I want to spend the rest of my life loving you."

He wipes the tears from my eyes. "Will you have me? Let me try to make up for all the horrible things I've done to you. Love you and this baby and—"

I don't let him finish. My lips land on his in the most passionate kiss. "I've always been yours, from our first kiss, to the first time we had sex. Even when you pissed me off, it didn't make me love you less. It just made me mad."

"Then, you'll let me love you for real, forever?"

"You can love me for as long as you can stand me," I say, still sobbing as our bodies collide together.

He kisses me over and over.

"I'll never get enough of you, beautiful. I loved you even when you wouldn't let me. I just didn't know how to convince you to love me through your fear."

"Now you don't have to, because I'll never be afraid again as long as I have you."

"When do I get that five million bonus in the contract for having your baby?" I tease, not believing he thought I would ever be after his money.

He smirks. "I think I owe you half of my money, my businesses, and my heart. We may have been fake married in our hearts, but on paper, our marriage is very real."

I smile. "I like real."

EPILOGUE

KADE

"You are not proposing to me again," Larkyn says, brushing past me to rearrange the flowers at the entrance of the sanctuary that she and my brother created together. I'm a little jealous, actually, that he gets to work with her every day. They've created something incredible, and today is the grand opening.

I smirk. "How did you know I'm planning on proposing again?"

She flashes me a glare, but all I can do is laugh, because her heart isn't in it and it turns more into a half smile, half grimace.

"Because I know you. You won't leave my side, you bought me a new dress to wear today, and you bought enough flowers to fill my entire house."

"Our house," I say, referring to her home that we moved into together. I wasn't sure I would like the smaller, more modest home. But I love that there are fewer places for her to escape to and hide away from me. And I like that it gives us a fresh start.

"And can't I just do something nice for you?" I ask.

"No, you are up to something."

Larkyn grabs the vase of flowers and moves them from the right side of the front desk to the left side.

I wrap my arms around her stomach from behind and feel her

relax in my arms. I love that I simply have to touch her and she melts.

"Everything is going to be perfect. Now stop fussing, and kiss me," I say into her ear.

Her head leans into me as I speak in her ear. I turn her head toward me as I kiss her, not able to let go of her stomach, where our baby is due any day now. She turns her body toward me to deepen the kiss and her arms wrap around my waist. I grin against her lips when her hands grab my ass, then slide toward the front of my slacks shocking me. I might get to fuck her in her office.

"Ah, hah! What is this?" she asks, pulling a tiny box out of my pocket.

I shrug. "I don't remember putting that in there."

She glances down at my mother's ring that hasn't left her finger since the night we told each other we loved each other and wanted to make this real. I would never replace that ring with another.

"You didn't buy me another ring, did you?" she asks, exacerbated with the idea of me buying her more jewelry.

I grin. "Open it and find out."

She eyes me and the box carefully. And then opens it. She smiles and shakes her head, as she pulls the tiny handmade heart out with a note attached that says: *You're mine forever.*

She looks at me unsteadily as her eyes grow bigger, and I know, if I do this right, she'll cry, and I'll get to see her gorgeous tear-streamed face filled with love.

"I didn't want to propose. I know you don't want me to. And I don't either, but I wanted something special to cement our new relationship before this baby comes," I say, placing my hand on her stomach.

Her lip trembles.

"We don't need a redo. Everything I've ever felt for you was real. The pretending, the marriage, the love. All of it real. The only thing fake was when I treated you like crap."

"I don't want a redo either."

"We don't have to get married again, or go through a proposal or any of that. I just wanted you to know that I will spend the rest of my life finding ways to tell you and show you how much I love you, forever."

She kisses me, and I forget about my speech or what I was planning next. I know I need to wrap this up soon so we can officially open her business to the public. But I need a few more stolen moments with her. As soon as her business is open, and we have this baby, I know my stolen moments with her will be few.

"I'll be yours forever, as long as you promise never to be an ass again."

I smirk. I love calling herself mine. I love it when she calls me her husband or her baby daddy or any of the words she uses to describe me too. She loves me. And I love her. I was afraid, for far too long, of screwing up and becoming my father, but the only thing I needed all this time was the right woman, one that I didn't want to screw up with.

"Can I be an ass twice a year?"

She raises an eyebrow at me.

"Never being an ass is too hard," I say.

She laughs, and I can't believe I'm lucky enough to get to listen to her laugh for the rest of my life.

"Fine, but you'll be sleeping on the couch any time you are a jerk. And you have to do cute things like making me handmade hearts to win me back after you fuck up. But no more pretending to be a jerk because you enjoy watching me squirm."

I smile; I never want to be fake with her ever again. "Deal."

———

Thank you so much for reading! Sebastian has his own story to tell! Keep reading for Pretend We're Over!

PRETEND WE'RE OVER

BOOK 2

PROLOGUE

MILLIE

I OPEN MY EYES, and I'm staring at the hottest man I've ever seen in real life. And he's in my bed! Well, technically not *my* bed—we are in the honeymoon suite of the Paris Hotel. So not my bed, but it doesn't matter because he's naked and adorable, and any minute now I'm going to wake up and realize that this is all a dream.

I pinch myself.

But Sebastian King is still in my bed. I'm still staring at his muscled chest. A chest I could reach out and touch and—

A blaring alarm goes off, and I squeeze my eyes shut. I'm not ready for Sebastian to realize I'm awake yet. I need time to process —to put everything in order in my head.

Everything is fuzzy at best. I remember coming to this hotel room with Sebastian to wait for our friends—Oaklee and Boden. This is their room. *So how did we end up using it?*

I don't know.

But here we are. Two people, who are basically strangers, in bed together—strangers who turned quickly into enemies.

We don't belong in bed together. We don't belong together period. Yet, here we are.

I open my eyes, letting him know that I'm awake. And that's

when the accusations begin. I blame him, tell him it's all his fault, even though I know it's not.

I just wish I remembered what happened. *We couldn't have fucked each other?* I don't do one night stands. I don't do men in general. I've sworn them off for the time being.

And yet, all the evidence points to us fucking.

Us waking up in the same bed.

Him completely naked.

Me wearing his shirt and boxers.

The opened condom wrapper.

There is no denying that we fucked.

I grip the shirt I'm wearing tighter. Of course, the first man I've fucked in forever, I can't even remember.

I sigh—*this is just my life.*

I won't let it get me down, though. The fucking isn't the part I have a problem with.

"I think you should put some clothes on," I say.

"Why? Are you hoping for a round two? Because I don't—"

"No, that's not it."

"Then what? Does my naked body make you uncomfortable?"

He hasn't figured it out yet. There is one clue that he hasn't found yet.

I hold up my left hand, flashing the pretty rock that wasn't there yesterday.

He shakes his head, not understanding.

God, he's such an idiot.

I point to the ring, pointing out the obvious.

"Fuck, Millie, you're engaged?"

I roll my eyes. He thinks he fucked an engaged woman. I would never, ever cheat.

"No. At least, I don't think I'm just engaged." I think a lot more than just getting engaged happened last night.

"Is that Oaklee's ring? Are you safeguarding it?"

I shake my head. Oaklee's ring is pink; this one is gold.

"Okay...what am I missing?" he asks.

I nod my head in the direction of his left hand, unable to find the words.

His eyes follow my gaze.

"No way," he says, staring at the gold ring he's sporting on his left ring finger.

"No!" he says again.

I wince but force myself to say the words. "I think we got married last night."

1

SEBASTIAN

"I'm getting married tomorrow!" Boden yells through the heavy beat of the bass in the bar's too-loud sound system. He slams down his shot glass before throwing it back.

We all follow suit—all twenty of us. Ten males, ten females all gathered in one section of a strip club on the Las Vegas strip.

This would be most men's heaven. Half-naked women are dancing all around and over us. We have unlimited alcohol, and the only thing that will stop us is the night ending, which by the look of the happy couple, should have already ended. But it's just past eleven at night—the night is still young.

Boden, the groom, is getting handsier and handsier with the woman dancing all over him as he tucks dollar bills into her thong. While Oaklee, the bride, keeps getting more and more sloshed, pretending she's completely okay with what her soon to be husband is doing. She's not, but she won't start her marriage by nagging.

"Can I get you another drink?" A waiter wearing tight black shorts and a shirt that barely covers her double D boobs asks me. She picks up the shot glasses littering the table in front of me.

Before I can answer, I feel all surrounding eyes on me. My

209

brother, Kade, looks at me with suspicion. My sister-in-law, Larkyn, looks at me with pride in her eyes like she knows I'm going to say the right thing. My friend, Shepherd, looks at me nervously, like he's going to be the one to pick up the pieces if I fall off the wagon.

It's been over ten years—over a decade of sobriety. And still, everyone thinks that I'm one mistake from falling back into my old ways. I'm not a twenty-something alcoholic anymore. I'm not addicted to drugs. I'm sober. I'm clean.

I haven't put one toe out of step this entire time, but the way all of my friends and family are acting, it's clear they think I am one wrong choice away from turning into the old Sebastian—the fuck up. The boy who was hell-bent on destroying my own life by drinking away the pain.

They're right. That's the life of an addict. I'm always one wrong choice away from throwing away all the work I've done, but that's why I live the way I do. I don't put myself into these situations often. I don't go to bars, strip clubs, or anywhere with temptation.

The only reason I'm in the most tempting place of all is because my best friend is getting married—the last of my friend group to do so. I wouldn't miss it, even though he chose the worst place in the world for a recovering addict like me.

When Boden told me, he was the only one not concerned that I might slip into old habits. He doesn't understand that for an addict like me, I'm either drinking or recovering, there is no middle ground. It's something I've learned running a healing and recovery center with Larkyn—you are either doing the program, or you're an addict. Once you stop, it's all over.

"Just a club soda with lime, thanks," I say.

The waitress smiles at me before getting Shepherd's order.

"See, told you he wouldn't slip up," Larkyn says, giving me a wink as she snuggles into Kades's shoulder.

He looks at me with a tightness in his jaw and a squint to his eyes like he doesn't believe me. But then, he never does. He's my older brother, he's married, has three children, and an empire to run. He still looks at me as the screwup. I'm single and work for my sister-in-law, not exactly grown-up in his eyes. He thinks the only way I can be happy and show that I'm an adult is if I live my life like him—married with kids.

He doesn't realize that's exactly what would cause me to fall back into old habits.

The waitress returns with our drinks, and I take my drink that looks like a mixed vodka drink. I don't usually care to order drinks that make me feel like I'm drinking, but here in this club, I just want to fit in with as few questions as possible.

Oaklee stumbles over onto the couch I'm sitting on. We all turn our attention to her. She's wearing a white dress complete with a sash that reads 'bride' and a sparkly tiara. Her outfit is screaming for attention, but her eyes keep cutting over to Boden, whose buttoned-down shirt is now open as a woman dances over him with her tits in his face.

"So, are you ready to get married tomorrow?" Larkyn asks her.

"Of course, I've never been more excited," Oaklee answers, pretending to look at Larkyn, but still staring at her fiancé.

"What about you, Sebastian? When are you getting married?" Val, one of the bridesmaids, asks, as she sits on Shepherd's, her husband's, lap.

I frown at her but notice that her question has even gained the attention of Oaklee. So I guess it's worth it to make Oaklee feel better while, Boden, my best friend, makes an ass of himself. Oaklee seems cool, but she's not that cool. She may not bring this up for years to come, but someday, she will. When they are fighting about whose turn it is to cook dinner, or why he bought another bottle of fancy liquor when they can barely afford to pay for little Oaklee's dance classes, this will come back up. And on that day, Boden will wish he had listened to me when I told him having strippers at a joint bachelor and bachelorette party was a bad idea. There is one male stripper, but other than one obligatory striptease, Oaklee hasn't let him anywhere near her. While Boden has been attached to one stripper or another all night.

"Not anytime soon," I chuckle and give her a wicked grin making it seem like I like playing the field. Really, it's just self-preservation keeping me from getting married. Every person here is married, or is about to be married, except me. We are in our mid-thirties. That's what happens. I'm the only lone wolf left, and it's going to stay that way.

Val rolls her eyes at me as she strokes her husband's face. "You just don't realize what you're missing. Still such a boy."

I take a deep breath to stop from bulldozing over her and telling her that I'm not a boy. I'm all man. Choosing not to get married doesn't make me a boy. She thinks I spend my nights plowing into any girl I can get into my bed. Sure, I fuck often, but I treat every woman I'm with well. I'm not a playboy. I just don't want to get married.

"What about Simone? I thought you two were getting serious?" Oaklee asks, looking at me with big red-shot eyes, slurring her words. I stare at the drink in her hand. She's had more than enough to drink tonight, but she has no intention of stopping anytime soon. This is her last night of freedom. Her last night to party before marriage, and she's not going to let her soon to be husband outdo her, even though we all know he can drink her under the table.

"Nah, we weren't serious. We only dated two months," I answer.

"For you, that's a long time."

I stiffen. *Don't let her comment bother you. She doesn't mean anything by it.*

"I think Simone's already engaged to Reece," Larkyn says, trying to cover for me, but she's only going to make it worse.

Simone and I stopped 'dating' last month. The fact that she's already engaged makes me look worse, not better.

"When did you and Simone break up?" Oaklee asks.

I give Larkyn an annoyed glare before turning sweetly to Oaklee. "We were never really together."

She smirks. "So, you just fucked?"

"If that's what you want to call it, yes. We fucked. We weren't ever in an emotionally committed relationship. We were always free to see other people." In fact, we only fucked once. That's my rule. One night of fun and then move on. It just took me a while to get to the one night with Simone. She kept holding out hope that if we dated a while first, by the time we had our one night together, I would want more.

"You're such a slut, Sebastian. You're thirty now. When are you going to stop sleeping with other people's wives?"

My lips fall. "Simone wasn't married. She wasn't engaged. She—"

"She was clearly dating this man if she's already engaged while you two were fucking. You could have ruined something special. Maybe Simone thought she had a chance to change you, to get you to propose."

I run my hand through my hair and then sip on my bubbly water. For the first time all night, I wish it was spiked with something so I could deal with these women.

Simone knew what she was getting when it came to me—amazing sex. That's it. That's all I ever offered her.

"Actually, I think Simone rekindled an old relationship right after she and Sebastian stopped...well, whatever they were doing. They realized they weren't getting any younger, and wanted to get married right away," Larkyn says, once again trying to save me, and once again, putting her foot in her mouth.

"Exactly, at our age, you should want to get married and get settled down. That's the mature, proper thing to do," Oaklee says smugly before looking dreamily over at her almost-husband who had his hands down a lady's thong.

"Charming," I say under my breath.

"What did you say?" Oaklee asks, turning back to me.

"You heard me. Not everyone is cut out for marriage. I just happen to think that it's mature to realize you shouldn't get married before you pop the question."

Oaklee pouts, full lip out, and I swear there are tears behind her eyes.

Shit.

I was too harsh. I shouldn't have said that to a woman who is clearly having doubts about getting married tomorrow. I know my best friend. He's a good guy, just an idiot when it comes to reading other people.

I lean over and pull her into a hug before I whisper into her ear, "Boden's a good guy. You two are great together. You found one of the good ones; I'm just not like Boden. I'd make a terrible husband."

I hear her sniffle into my shoulder. *Fuck, is she really crying?*

I try to glance down without pulling her away and exposing her tears, but I can't. All I hear are her gentle sobs.

Larkyn and Kade stand up and walk over to us. "The sitter called. We have to go," Larkyn says.

"Oaklee, did you hear that?" I ask.

More soft sobbing.

"Um...okay. I'll get a ride back to the hotel soon. And um... Oaklee, we'll see you tomorrow," I say.

Kade just shakes his head at me, and I can read his silent words. *You're the asshole who made the bride cry the night before her wedding. You figure out how to get out of this mess.*

Larkyn squeezes my shoulder as if to say good luck. *Get her a drink,* Larkyn mouths at me.

I raise my eyebrows. *Really?* This woman doesn't need more alcohol. She needs a bed and to sleep it off.

Larkyn smiles sweetly. "Have a goodnight, Oaklee. I can't wait until tomorrow." She strokes Oaklee's hair and then is gone.

The rest of the bridal party gets back to doing shots, sloppy dancing, and lap dances. Leaving me alone with Oaklee, who I swear has turned from sobbing to snoring.

"Oaklee?" I ask, trying to unglue her from my shoulder.

"Hmm." She rocks back.

"What are you drinking? I should get you another drink. Why don't you go pull that fiancé of yours onto the dance floor?"

Her eyes light up. "I want another one of those fizzy drinks that light up."

I smile. "Can do."

Then I turn to her fiancé, who thankfully is done with the lap dances. "Dance with your fiancé!"

He grins, and I push Oaklee into his arms, while I carry my own drink toward the bar to go buy Oaklee another drink. Not that she needs it, but it gives me something to do until I can leave. I don't have the excuse of kids like Larkyn and Kade do. As everyone pointed out, I'm single. I'll be expected to close down the club with the rest of them.

I'm walking toward the bar when I'm ambushed from the side, a swish of hair, makeup, and freckled skin knocks into me, jarring my glass from my hand. Some of it splatters onto my dark jeans, but that's the thing about not drinking, it's just water.

I look up, expecting to see a drunk woman wearing nine-inch heels, a heavy cast of makeup, and a tight skirt. What I get is jeans, a black tee with the name of some band I've never heard of, and off-white sneakers. Her makeup is tame compared to all the other women here. The only thing I got right was her mane of strawberry blonde hair in thick waves around her face. Her hair isn't high-lighted or cut in professional layers; her hair is as wild as the twinkle in her green eyes. The only thing that tells me she's part of our party is the sash she's wearing across her body with the word 'bridesmaid' on it.

"Oh my god! I'm so sorry," the woman says. She starts trying to brush off the liquid on my pants with her hand, like that is somehow going to magically soak up the splotches of club soda on my pants.

"What are you doing?" I ask.

She blushes. It's an adorable shade of pink below her pale, freckled covered cheeks that make her look like she's about fifteen. But one glance below her adorable cheeks tells me she's all woman. Even though she's wearing an oversized T-shirt and jeans, it doesn't hide the swell of her breasts and the curve of her hips, leaving me watering. She may not be my normal type, but I can appreciate a beautiful woman's body when I see it.

"Sorry." She immediately stops trying to dry up the water on my pants and realizes her hand had slipped dangerously close to copping a feel.

Her gaze drops to the shattered glass on the floor. "I'm so sorry. Let me buy you a new drink to make it up to you. I'm not usually a stumbling drunk like this."

She's rambling. It's enchanting, but she's in the bridal party. Everyone is married in the bridal party, except me, and I don't flirt with other men's women.

"No," I say.

"No? Please, I insist...What's your name?"

"Sebastian. And you don't need to buy me a drink. All the drinks are free, courtesy of the bride and groom."

"Oh, I know, I just meant that I should at least order you another drink and get it for you so that you can keep enjoying whatever you were doing. Another lap dance or whatever or..." Her cheeks blush again as she blinks rapidly like she's batting her eyes, but I don't think she realizes she's doing it. "I'm Millie, by the way. Amelia, actually, but everyone calls me Millie. I'm getting you a drink. I—"

"Millie," I say, putting my hands on her shoulders, trying to get her to stop rambling. "You really don't need to get me a drink."

"No, but I insist. I don't want you to think of me as the drunk who spilled your drink all over you. What were you drinking?" She looks me up and down and then to the drink on the floor.

"Vodka?" she asks.

"No."

She scrunches her nose up as she tries again. "Gin?"

"No."

"What were you drinking then?"

I sigh. I don't like telling people that I'm not drinking. They never understand why, especially in a setting like this. It's not that I'm embarrassed to be a recovering alcoholic, but I don't usually broadcast it.

"Club soda with lime," I finally answer.

"Oh." Just one syllable, but I know more is about to spill out of her. "Well, I don't feel so bad now because club soda shouldn't stain."

She holds up her own drink. "I should switch to club soda; it's more fun than what I'm drinking."

I study her clear drink in her hand for the first time. "Which is?"

"Water." Her cheeks burn red again. "I'm on a diet. Alcohol is one of the biggest culprits of weight gain."

I blink rapidly, taking in her words. *Diet?* What beautiful woman like her needs to be on a diet? But I don't ask more. If it's just an excuse to not explain why she's not drinking, who am I to judge? She could be an addict like me, or pregnant and not ready to tell yet. There could be a million reasons why and none of them matter to me. After this weekend, I doubt I'll ever see Millie again. She must be one of Oaklee's friends. And as much as I like Boden, I don't plan on hanging out with his wife's friends after this weekend.

I realize that she's stopped talking and is staring at me, waiting for something, but I was more fascinated with the way her lips moved than what was coming out of them.

I'm an ass.

"I don't want a hangover tomorrow."

She nods. "I'll go get you that drink."

I shake my head as I put my hands in my pocket to keep from touching the curves in front of me hidden beneath layers of clothes. There is something about her that intrigues me. But whatever mystery she's hiding, it will stay hidden.

I didn't spot a ring on her finger, but if my pregnant theory is correct, her hands may be too swollen to wear her ring. I remember when it happened to Larkyn. I don't know which of the lucky bastards here gets to call her his wife, but he's definitely lucky. She seems more real than any of the other chicks here, even if she is a little strange.

She and I would never work, though. A woman like Millie is looking for forever. She expects a good man who flatters her and brings her romantic gifts—I'm not that man. I'm focused, disciplined. I work out two times a day, eat three perfect meals, meditate, journal, and crunch numbers to keep the business afloat. That's my day. I don't have room for a woman like Millie. A woman who is wild and untamed and seems to dance to her own drum. I have room for an occasional fuck, nothing more.

"Don't bother with the drink, I've had enough anyway." And with that, I start toward the group of guys chatting with Boden. I need to get away from her before I make a mistake. A man like me can't make a single mistake. For me, a single mistake leads to a lifetime of fuck ups, and I've worked too hard to mess it all up now.

2

MILLIE

I watch Sebastian walk away toward the groom. *God, his ass looks great in those jeans.* It's tight and firm, and damn do I want to run my tongue all over it…

"Earth to Millie," Oaklee says, snapping me out of my haze.

"What?" I say, taking a seat next to Oaklee and across from Cynthia.

"What are you staring at?" Oaklee asks, sitting up in her chair to get a better look.

"Nothing," I mumble into my water.

"That's not nothing. That's Sebastian King," Oaklee says, her voice rising higher as she speaks.

"Sebastian, who?" Of course, his last name has to be King—figures. He looks like royalty in his deep blue shirt, dark jeans, and muscles for days.

"Sebastian King," Oaklee says again before pulling the straw of her fruity drink into her mouth and staring at me with a knowing smile.

I lean back in my chair. "Am I supposed to know the name or something?"

"No, but you should definitely get to know the man. He's cute."

"So? There are a lot of cute men here."

"He's single. He's like the only man here who is our age and still single."

I huff. "So because he's the only single man here, that means I should go after him? Sorry, but I'll pass."

Oaklee and Cynthia trade glances. "No, you should go after him because he's hot."

I still, trying not to react because my friends mean well. Really, they do, but they don't understand my life. They don't understand that a man like Sebastian King would never go after a woman like me. Even if he did, I'm not interested. My life is too complicated to get involved with a guy right now.

"Please. There are plenty of hot, single men here."

"Where?" Oaklee asks, batting her eyelashes at me.

We scour the room, but every man my eyes turn to seems to be coupled off.

"What about him?" I point to a man in tight jeans, tattoos, and long hair. He's not really my type, he's kind of got a biker vibe going on, but I'm trying to prove a point, not actually date the guy.

"Gay," Cynthia answers.

"No, he's—" I start, but then a skinny man in leather walks over and kisses him firmly on the lips. "Fine, he's gay. That doesn't mean..."

"Honey, you're thirty-two and at the last of your single friends' weddings. I'm not saying there aren't single men out there. There are plenty, but not here. Even if there were plenty of single men in this bar, Sebastian King would still top them all. I mean, look at the guy," Cynthia says.

We all turn to Sebastian. He's talking with two of the grooms-men, who are both married. He really is the only single guy in this room. *How could that be?* We are only in our early thirties. Plenty of people don't get married until later in life. *How did I end up with friends who all took the plunge by thirty?*

Sebastian cocks his head toward us. He must have felt the three pairs of eyes staring, and at least one woman drooling in his direction. He frowns when he spots me staring and then quickly turns back to his conversation.

I exhale a breath. If he hadn't already made it clear he wasn't interested, that one look did it.

"He's so dreamy," Oaklee says.

"Down girl, you're getting married tomorrow, remember?"

"It doesn't mean that I can't look at attractive men. Sebastian has always been good looking, but in the last couple of years, he's somehow grown more muscle, more chiseled, more refined. And that dimple just above his jaw is swoon-worthy," Oaklee says.

I let my eyes drift. I haven't seen said dimple yet, because he has yet to smile in my direction. Shepherd makes him laugh and what do you know, he does have the sexiest dimple. I want to put my tongue in it and...

"What?" I ask when I notice Oaklee and Cynthia staring at me again.

"We all agree Sebastian is cute. You already bumped into him."

I moan. "Don't remind me. I literally bumped into him and made him spill his drink."

"So? That's a classic meet-cute moment—an adorable story to tell your kids someday."

"We won't be telling our kids anything because there won't be any kids. There won't be anything. Sebastian isn't interested."

"Are you kidding me? You're hot as hell, Millie. Why wouldn't he want to go out with you?" Oaklee asks.

I stare down at my clothes. I had every intention of wearing a dress and heels tonight like all the other girls here, but I don't usually wear dresses. So when I packed the single dress I own, I didn't think to try it on first. I didn't expect the zipper to snap when I put it on tonight, only moments before we were supposed to leave —the consequences of the ice cream and wine I've been consuming to drown out my feelings lately.

And it wasn't like I could borrow a dress from my abnormally skinny friends. They are a size zero, while I'm a twelve. The dress was a size ten. It was a struggle to fit my thick thighs and large breasts into the dress on a good day, let alone with the ten-pound weight gain I'm currently carrying around.

I look back up at Oaklee. I'm not going to spell out for her why a sculpted man like Sebastian wouldn't go for a soft curvy woman like me. Even in the best shape of my life, I never looked skinny or fit. I've always been curvy. I don't have a problem with that, but Sebastian King is too arrogant to be knocked off his high throne to consider dating a woman like me.

"Trust me, after basically plowing him over and spilling his drink all over him, he's not attracted to me."

Oaklee frowns. "I'm sure he's just wasted like all the other guys here. He didn't realize you were flirting with him."

"He wasn't drunk." *He didn't even have a single drink, just like me.*

"Well, he isn't dating anyone. He's a single guy. And it's not like he has a lot of choices here," Oaklee says absentmindedly. "Oh my god!" She looks at me. "I didn't mean...I'm sorry, Millie."

I down the rest of my water, but it does nothing for me. *Screw my diet. I need a drink.*

A waitress passes, and I jerk two shot glasses off her tray. She tries to stop me as the shots aren't for me, but I don't give a damn. I have some catching up to do. I throw both shots down, while Oaklee and Cynthia stare at me.

"Millie, I'm really sorry. I didn't mean to imply that you were Sebastian's only choice. You're hot as hell and the smartest, funniest chick here. You are..." Oaklee keeps talking, but I ignore her. She's a bitch, but we've been friends for years. It's not the first time she's said something like this to me. We are always honest with each other, and she means well.

"I just don't want you to be alone forever, Millie. It's time you get back out there," Oaklee says, squeezing my hand with pity in her eyes.

Dammit. I thought we had gotten past the pity.

"I'm fine, Oak."

"I know you are. I just worry about you, now that I'm getting married. You'll be alone, again."

I sigh. We've been through this before. Oaklee and I have technically been roommates for the last six months, not that she's spent much time at our place. She's been practically living with Boden the whole time.

"Go talk to Sebastian," she says.

"I will, but not so that I can date him. I don't think he's dating material."

"Then what?"

I wink at her, and she smiles. "As long as you get back out there. It's been too long. And for what it's worth, you and Sebastian would make a cute couple."

I roll my eyes. She thinks everyone would make a cute couple. She's in love and just wants that for everyone else.

I start to walk toward Sebastian.

"Wait!" Oaklee says.

I stop and turn toward her. She studies me a second, then runs her hand through my hair, giving me a deep side part, before she pulls out some red lipstick from her purse and applies it to my lips.

"You finished?" I ask. I'm used to Oaklee using me like a dress-up doll. This isn't the first time she's put makeup on me or fixed my hair.

"One more thing." She grabs the hem of my shirt and rips it.

"What are you doing?" I screech as she rips my favorite Lumineers T-shirt.

She looks down at my shirt that now ends just below my boobs. She knows that I'm not wearing a bra, I hate the things—so constricting.

"I can't go over to him like this. He's already seen me normal. This is…"

"Sexy?"

I look down as I cross my arms over my now bare stomach.

Oaklee quickly knocks my hands down and attempts to give me a confidence-inducing look.

I take a deep breath. I look sexy. I have curves—curves men find attractive, even if I'm not as thin as Oaklee and Cynthia.

"Perfect, go get him." She slaps my ass as I walk toward Sebastian. I'm not his usual type, but as I walk toward Sebastian, I feel men's eyes on me. Oaklee did good work. I stand taller, feeling sexy as I let my hips sway back and forth. My boobs are playing peek a boo with the bottom of my shirt, and my red lips and overdone hair scream fuck me. And that's exactly what I want—to fuck Sebastian. I'm not looking for a date. I'm definitely not looking for a husband —just one night of passion.

Sebastian doesn't notice me approach. That's okay. I like it better this way. It gives me a moment to study him and decide my opening line. I don't want to make a fool of myself again and do something stupid like spill his drink all over him again.

"I think she might be pregnant," Shepherd says.

"Who? You mean Millie?" Sebastian asks.

Just then, Shepherd notices me approaching the group. "Um…hi, Millie."

But it's not Shepherd I'm pissed at. I turn my anger at Sebastian, who is now eyeing me up and down, obviously noticing the changes Oaklee made. He doesn't drag his eyes up and down slowly like I had hoped. His eyes race like he's trying to find the next bumble I made—assuming I did something stupid or clumsy, not like this look is sexy and intentional.

"Millie, uh…" Sebastian grips his neck as he stares at me.

"Why do you think I'm pregnant?" I ask.

Sebastian doesn't hide his glance. He stares straight at my bare stomach. A stomach that protrudes just a little over my jeans, but apparently enough to make me look pregnant.

"You're unbelievable. You know what, I thought…never mind. You are a disgusting pig who only finds women who are model thin attractive. You wouldn't know what to do with a real woman like me anyway!"

He blinks at me rapidly, like he doesn't understand a word I'm saying, which is fine by me. I'm glad I found out what kind of ass Sebastian is before I slept with him. I've sworn off assholes, even hot assholes. I've been down that road before, and it almost killed me. I've done too much work on myself to let a jerk like him call me fat. I'm out of here.

3

SEBASTIAN

I FUCKED UP. I'm an asshole, but I'm not usually so cruel.

I adjust my tie as I stand uncomfortably in my suit, leaning against the door of the groom's room where we are getting ready in the small chapel, hoping that Millie walks by and I can talk to her before the wedding.

"Shut the door, Sebastian. Oaklee will kill me if I get a glance of her before the wedding," Boden says.

I sigh and wait one more second before closing the door and leaving any hopes of talking to Millie before the wedding. I should have tracked her down last night after she stormed off with tears in her eyes; tears I caused because I was stupid. I thought she was pregnant because she wasn't drinking, nothing else. I thought she was trying to hide her stomach beneath her baggy clothes. A statement she made abundantly false when she walked back over to me with her T-shirt ripped so high that I could see the undersides of her breasts.

I always thought women in tight dresses were sexy, but I'm beginning to think the cut off T-shirt look is hotter. It was clear that she wasn't pregnant, but by then, I'd already opened my big mouth and effectively called her fat.

"Shots!" Boden says, as Shepherd begins passing out shot glasses.

Ugh, really? I can't even avoid alcohol during the wedding.

I stand next to Kade, who reluctantly hands me a shot glass. A bottle of tequila is passed around, and everyone pours a shot into their glass, everyone but me.

"To Boden," Shepherd shouts.

We all clink our glasses, and then everyone but me drinks their shot.

I look at my best friend, who pours himself a second shot and takes it quickly. A man shouldn't need to do two shots before walking down the aisle. *But what would I know about it?* I'm the only man here not married or about to be.

Kade looks at me looking at Boden. He doesn't have to speak for me to know that he agrees with me, but there is no sense in jinxing their marriage right now. *Who am I to judge?* If they are happy, that's all that matters.

Brittany, the wedding coordinator, pokes her head in the door. "It's time! If I could have you all line up, we will get you walking down the aisle."

We line up in order. I'm the last, just before Boden, as I'm his best man.

"Who am I walking with?" I ask Boden. I flew in late last night and didn't make the rehearsal, so I never found out.

"Millie. She's Oaklee's maid of honor," Boden answers.

Fuck me. Now I really wish I had found her and talked to her before the wedding.

One by one, each of us are led out of the small room and into the hallway where we meet up with the bridesmaid we are to walk down the aisle. In everyone's case but me, their bridesmaid is also their significant other.

My heart thumps, trying to come up with a way to fix this. The church is small and quaint. It's pretty enough, but I don't know why we had to fly to Vegas when they were just going to get married in a church just like they could back in Santa Barbara.

The door opens again, and I walk out into the hallway where

Millie is already waiting at the double doors that lead into the chapel.

I hold out my arm, and she reluctantly puts her arm through.

"I'm sorry," I say, leaning over to Millie.

"Shh," Brittany gives me a look, and then the doors are opened. A crowd of a hundred and fifty stares at us.

I put on my best fake smile, and Millie does the same next to me. She's wearing the same lavender dress that all the other bridesmaids are wearing, except Millies has an extra sash that's darker to mark that she's the maid of honor. It matches my boutonniere.

We start walking forward, away from Brittany, who can no longer call us out for talking while we walk.

"I'm sorry," I try again.

"Now's not the time," Millie says through a clenched smile. I notice that her hand is barely touching my arm, trying to pretend I don't exist at all.

"Please, we need to talk. I'm so sorry."

"Little late for that."

"I'm sorry. Let me buy you a drink and apologize for real." We are close to the end of the short aisle. We are about to run out of time together, and I can't have her glaring at me the entire ceremony.

"I don't need a pity date right now."

"It's not a pity date. It's—"

And then it's too late. She's walking away from me toward her spot near the altar, and I'm left standing in front of my brother.

"Why is Millie glaring at you like that?" Kade asks.

I glance over, and I feel the full fury of her. Fortunately, it gives me an excuse to really take her in, instead of trying to come up with words to apologize. Her strawberry blonde hair is curled and pulled back on one side with a sparkly clip. Her face is painted, but it's tame compared to what it was last night with the red lipstick. The dress falls straight on the women behind her, but hers curves in at her waist before swelling out over her ass. *Did she walk in heels?* I glance down at her feet and smile. She's wearing white Adidas tennis shoes.

Millie notices that I'm smiling at her, which only deepens her glare. I fucked up, but making it up to her is going to be fun.

"No reason," I answer Kade, feeling happier than I have in a long time. I just found someone who is going to make this weekend bearable. Tomorrow I can go back to my normal life.

The music changes, and we all turn as Boden leads Oaklee down the aisle. Oaklee's parents died a few years ago. She doesn't have a brother, so Boden decided to walk her down the aisle himself. Just another thing that feels off about this wedding.

I turn my sights back on Millie when the happy couple reaches us. She's no longer looking at me. In fact, she seems to be trying to look anywhere but me.

I smile wider. *Why didn't I notice it before?* I know Millie and I had a rough start, and we don't belong together, but that won't stop us from enjoying tonight. I let my tongue run around my mouth like a warm-up for what I plan on doing to her body later.

"Do you take this man to be your husband?" The minster has been talking for a while, but I haven't been paying attention. I've been too busy undressing Millie in my head and imagining all the sounds she's going to make tonight when I get her back to my hotel room.

"Ah," Oaklee grabs her stomach.

That breaks me from my daydreams as I stare at her. I may not have been to rehearsal, but I know the appropriate response to that question is, 'I do.' And from what I can tell, Oaklee hasn't said the magic words yet.

The room is silent as everyone stares at Oaklee.

Boden's head tilts slightly, but otherwise, he doesn't move. He doesn't so much as mutter a single syllable to ask her what's wrong.

Oh god, oh god, oh god. This moment drags forever. I hate uncomfortable silence. I want to speak, do something to fix it. That's what I would do at work: jump in and save everyone. But I'm not at work.

This isn't my life. And I don't get involved in fixing relationships, just people.

My eyes flick from the back of Boden's head to Oaklee. She swallows hard, as she releases Boden's hands and grabs at her neck like she can't breathe. Her face turns green. She's about to be sick…

And then she runs. She takes off like a sprinter back down the aisle. Her dress is hiked up, and her heels are clanking loudly with each step against the hard floor.

"Fuck," Boden mutters under his breath, before running after her.

And then twenty groomsmen and bridesmaids are left standing in front of a congregation of almost two hundred without a clue what to do.

Millie steps forward. "The flu has been going around, and—"

In June? Not believable, Millie.

"And this morning, Oaklee woke up with a small fever."

I chuckle, *yea, she was hungover from last night.*

"But she was so excited to get married today, that she fought through it. It seems like the illness finally caught up with her."

The crowd stares at her bewildered, not having a clue what to say or do. It's not like they are used to witnessing a bride running out on her own wedding. We've all seen the *Runaway Bride* plenty of times, we all know our role is to sit back and laugh and be cynical while the groom chases after the bride to no avail.

"If you could just give us a moment, I'll go check on the bride, and then hopefully we can continue the festivities," Millie finishes, and then she is walking hurriedly out of the chapel. She's on a mission, but won't let anyone see her frazzled, adding to the chaos that is this wedding.

I doubt a single thing Millie said was true, but I do know that even if it is true, there is no way Oaklee will be stepping foot back in this chapel anytime soon. You don't come back from this level of embarrassment.

The minister looks at me, and I realize now that Millie is gone, I'm the one expected to hold everyone's attention.

I glance at the pianist. "Play until I get back."

She hurriedly returns to the piano and begins playing a soft song.

"Where are you going?" Kade hisses behind me, knowing he will be the next expected to entertain the crowd if I leave.

"Getting the groom back," I say. I start walking towards the exit and see my nieces and nephew sitting in the front row. I turn my head to Kade just as I leave and mouth, *Get Hazel to sing.* That adorable little girl could entertain a crowd for hours.

I get back to the small entryway that leads in two directions—to the bathrooms and to the two dressing rooms. I don't know which way everyone went. I listen carefully for voices coming from either direction. Instead, I hear the start of an engine from outside.

Fuck. Why did I agree to be Boden's best man? From now on, I'm not just swearing off getting married myself, but being in other people's weddings. It's too much responsibility for someone who doesn't believe in the constitution of marriage.

I push the doors open and go outside, hoping like hell the bride hasn't actually taken off, and that this is all a big misunderstanding.

4

MILLIE

I THOUGHT OAKLEE WAS SICK—I truly did. I saw the way her face turned green. I heard the heavy breathing and saw the glisten of sweat on her neck. All the signs pointed to her being sick.

So when I gave my little speech, I thought I was speaking the truth. *Well, okay, maybe I thought she was hungover, but that still classifies as sick.* I knew they should have had the bachelor and bachelorette parties earlier instead of the night before the wedding, but it wasn't up to me.

I thought Oaklee was sick, until I watched her run out the front door instead of turning toward the bathroom.

She turned to see who was chasing her, and I saw the fear in her eyes.

Oaklee isn't sick—she's running, I just don't know why.

I watch as Oaklee speaks to the limo driver before rounding the limo and heading to the backseat. Boden stands nearby, shouting at her for running out. She stops at the last second before climbing in and begins yelling back.

I stand back a second, but when I see the tears flowing down Oaklee's cheeks, and watch as Boden doesn't do a damn thing to stop it, I lose my cool and run up to Oaklee. I take her hand and squeeze hard, just letting her know I'm here but won't interfere unless she wants me to.

She squeezes back like she always does. Other than holding her hand, I don't have a clue what to do next.

The church door opens, and I'm afraid the entire congregation is going to run out and witness, well, whatever this is…

Instead, Sebastian King runs down the three steps and then over to us.

"What are you doing?" I snap at him while Oaklee and Boden continue to shout at each other. They don't even realize that Sebastian is here, or seem to care that I'm here, other than I'm holding onto Oaklee's hand for support.

"Same as you. I'm the best man. I'm trying to fix this mess." Sebastian looks at the arguing couple for the first time. "Not that I think this is fixable."

I frown and turn back to the couple, listening for the first time to the words they are saying.

"Oh, you're going to fix this, huh?" Oaklee turns her attention to Sebastian.

"I can't fix this, but I can help. Only you two can fix this," Sebastian answers. It's surprisingly mature and rational sounding coming from him.

"Where were *you* last night when Boden had his tongue down some slut's throat?" Oaklee releases my hand and storms toward Sebastian; her anger deflected off Boden for a moment. "Where were *you*?" She pushes a finger against Sebastian's hard chest. He doesn't move an inch; he doesn't seem bothered by the red hot female unleashing all her rage on him.

"I'm not your fiancé's keeper," Sebastian says.

She laughs. "Of course not. You're just his bad influence. Because, to answer my question, *you* were right next to him, sticking your tongue down another woman's throat instead of telling him to do the right thing. *You're* no better than *he* is."

My mouth falls open as I watch Oaklee storm towards the limo and climb in without looking back at the two idiots. *Well, one is an idiot, the other is a cheating asshole.*

I can't believe Boden cheated on Oaklee. She had to have gotten that part wrong. Or he had to have been manipulated in some way. Boden and Oaklee are perfect together—both so strong and fierce. He rocks the business world; she rules the courtroom. They have the perfect life. There is no way I'm watching it fall apart.

Both of the men are still staring at the door to the limo, like Oaklee might come back any second. Like this is all one big lie, and any second she's going to just walk back out, laugh this off, kiss Boden, and then they are going to go back into the church and get married.

But I know Oaklee—she's as stubborn as she is smart. And whatever Boden did, she won't forgive him easily. As much as she loves him, she won't marry him until she's forgiven him.

I climb into the back of the limo and find Oaklee has made her way to the midsection, where the bar is stocked with a chilled bottle of champagne and two flute glasses. She's working on getting the cork off, but each time she tries, she just ends up breaking off another piece of cork with the cheap knife she's using.

"Here, let me—"

She snarls at me, and I snap my mouth shut. *Okay then.*

I sit next to her while I wait to see if the guys are going to get their acts together and climb in before Oaklee orders the driver to leave.

"Get your ass in there," I hear Sebastian shout.

Interesting—I would have thought for sure he'd abandon his friend by now. Or at least told him to give up on fixing his marriage. He was there when Boden was sucking face with a woman who wasn't his fiancée. Sebastian was probably kissing a married woman —ruining two marriages in one night.

I feel my chest constrict as I imagine Sebastian kissing another woman after our fight. I spent my night tossing and turning, replaying our conversation over and over, while he was out kissing some floozy, not giving me a second thought.

"Get out!" Oaklee and I shout at the same time.

"No," Sebastian says, shoving Boden in the car. Boden just slumps in the back, staring out the window. Sebastian closes the door, and then I hear the driver start the limo.

"I'll just drive around the neighborhood until you give me more clear directions," the driver says before rolling the divider up.

We start moving, and all of us fall silent for a second, not sure what to do next.

Oaklee is still fussing with the champagne bottle, trying to get it open.

Boden is staring out the window, but I don't think any thoughts are playing in his head.

And Sebastian is staring at me with intense eyes.

Sebastian takes a deep breath before breaking his gaze from mine and looking back and forth between the unhappy couple. He breaks the silence first.

"Now, I've been to a lot of counseling sessions. Not a ton of marriage sessions, but enough to know that nothing will get better if you two don't talk to each other. No matter if you decide to get married today or not, you won't be able to move on with your lives until you talk to each other. So who wants to go first?"

He's been in a lot of counseling sessions? For what?

Sebastian looks between Oaklee and Boden, waiting for one of them to speak, but it's clear they don't want to talk.

"Oaklee, you seemed to have plenty to say before, would you like to start? Tell Boden why you are upset with him," Sebastian tries in a surprisingly calm voice. *Is he a therapist? No, there is no way. I've never seen a therapist in as good of shape as him, or one as cruel as him.*

Oaklee hisses at him.

"Okay, Boden, why don't you start? Tell Oaklee why you're upset? Or maybe apologize for what you did?" Sebastian tries again.

Nothing.

"Good job, Dr. King. It doesn't look like your little therapy session is going to work," I say.

Sebastian leans back, "Then, by all means, you give it a try if you think you know what's best."

Dammit. I didn't think before I gave my smart-aleck comment, which is why I don't usually say hurtful things. I don't like dealing with trouble.

"Oaklee, it sounds like you are upset that Boden kissed another woman. Is that true?"

She laughs deviously. "You think I'm upset about a little *kiss?* Are you serious? I'm not upset that the asshat kissed another woman. I'm upset he *fucked* her!"

My mouth drops. I thought it was an innocent kiss—a drunken mistake. But there is no way you can mistakingly slip your dick into a woman who isn't your fiancée. That's not a mistake, that's a choice.

I stare at Boden wide-eyed, and then I glance at Sebastian, who doesn't look at all surprised by what Oaklee is saying.

"You knew?" I ask, looking at Sebastian.

He doesn't answer me with his words, but I don't need his words. His silence proves his guilt. He helped break up a relationship, one destined for marriage, for forever.

Oaklee continues to fumble with the bottle. Boden stares out the window like he's in a daze, and Sebastian smirks like he's enjoying ruining other people's lives.

I'm the helpless optimist stuck in the middle of all these fucked up people. I grab the bottle and knife from Oaklee's hands and slice the cork off in one pop.

Champagne spills onto my lap, but I don't care. I just need the fucking champagne.

"Flutes," I say calmly to Oaklee, who grabs one and holds it out to me. I pour, expecting her to drink from one and I the other. Instead, when I fill both glasses, she crawls over to Boden and hands him one, sloshing some of the liquid onto his pants.

He takes it wordlessly. Then she hands the other to Sebastian, who stares at it like it's a foreign object to him.

Oaklee sits back next to me and rips the bottle from my hand before finding a wine glass. She pours champagne into the glass before handing it to me.

And then she holds the bottle out.

"To realizing what an ass Boden was before I married him," Oaklee says.

"To kicking said asshole to the curb," I say, holding my glass out.

Boden's eyes flicker to us, and then he gives Oaklee an angry smile. "To finding out how much of a prude you were before I gave you half of everything I own."

Boden looks to Sebastian, who is watching us all like we are crazy.

"Your turn, buddy," Boden says.

We are all holding our glasses out, or in Oaklee's case, the entire bottle. We are all waiting on Sebastian before taking a drink.

Sebastian sits up in his seat, reluctantly, and holds his champagne flute out gingerly, only in his fingertips. His eyes scan to the three of us. "To not losing myself while I save all of you."

I frown. Of course, his was selfish; he didn't even back his friend like I did for Oaklee. And as for saving us, Sebastian is as far from a knight in shining armor as you can get. He won't be saving anyone.

"Happy wedding day," Oaklee says, and then she lifts the bottle to her lips.

I do the same.

As does Boden.

Sebastian just stares at his glass like it's piss we are asking him to drink.

Boden and I finish our glasses in one chug. Oaklee stops halfway through drinking what's left in the bottle and stares at Sebastian. "Drink!"

He startles, coming out of his daze. He opens his mouth like he's going to say something but then thinks better of it.

Boden even opens his mouth and is about to snatch the drink from his friend when Sebastian tosses his champagne back in one gulp.

Oaklee smiles like she just got Sebastian to drink poison, before finishing her bottle.

I can't help but feel like I've been left out of something very important, as Oaklee lowers the partition and tells the driver to head to the hotel.

5

SEBASTIAN

I broke my sobriety.

I had a drink.

Champagne.

God, I can't believe that champagne is what I broke my sobriety with. That stuff was disgustingly sweet. I swipe my tongue around my mouth, trying to dispel the liquid there, but there is no use. I'm going to taste the disgusting sweetness judging me forever.

I should have said something, but I didn't feel like I had a choice. The way Oaklee was looking at me with a vengeance. She knows why I don't drink; I'm a recovering alcoholic. She knows I run a freaking recovery center for goodness sakes. But she blames me for Boden's actions.

Maybe she has a right to—I'm Boden's best friend after all. I should have said something. Put a stop to his idiocy, or told him to call off the wedding.

But I didn't.

Although, I didn't do what she's accusing me of either. Last night, I left shortly after Millie did—close to midnight. The party went on until three or four in the morning. I don't know what Boden did, but I wasn't there. I wasn't by his side, but I sure didn't have another woman's tongue down my mouth. The only tongue I want is currently sitting a few feet away from me, fuming.

Millie seems sweet and kind, but the glares she's shooting my direction tell me not to ignore what she would do for her friend. I'm the enemy, and she will toss a grenade my way if I'm not careful.

So I took my punishment. I drank the alcohol. I ended over a decade of perfect control. I've seen addicts fall off the wagon before—when the pain got to be too much, when the cravings became too strong, when the peer pressure got to them, and they thought one drink wouldn't cause them to backtrack. I've never seen any of them be able to take one drink and not go all in. That's why they call it an addiction. We can't stop after just one.

I'll have to deal with the consequences for myself later, whatever they are. However big the setback, this is just a setback. I won't let it become anything more.

Oaklee finishes her bottle, satisfied that I served my punishment. *Thank God there was only one bottle of champagne in the limo.* She'd have me chug a bottle to get back at me if she could. It's not a mystery why she's taking her anger out on me instead of Boden. She may hate what he did, but she still loves him. Being mad at me doesn't hurt her. Being mad at Boden changes her entire life. Once they talk, they will realize there is nothing to fix. Boden doesn't love her the way she deserves.

Fuck marriage.

Marriage is an antiquated institution in today's age. We don't need to be legally tied to another person to raise kids or show our love. Love rarely lasts a lifetime anyway.

Marriage is something we do to make ourselves feel better. To pretend that our significant other will never leave us, no matter how big of an ass we act like. They are trapped, stuck with us forever. It's all a lie. People have no problem getting divorced; the only hold up is the paperwork. But that isn't enough to keep people together.

Marriage doesn't work—Oaklee just figured that out before it was too late. No amount of pretty dresses, fancy gifts, or playing princess for a day was enough for her to go through with it in the end.

After some rude directions from Oaklee, the limo pulls up in front of the Paris hotel. I didn't know where the happy couple was staying tonight, but I guess it makes sense that the Paris hotel seemed like the most romantic choice to them.

I step out of the limo, and Boden follows me. He looks straight ahead as he walks inside and up to the front desk to check-in without a word.

Oaklee and Millie enter next. Oaklee rips her veil from her head as she enters the lobby and looks around at all the people staring at her. Even in Vegas, people still stare at a woman in a big fluffy white dress.

"I'm going to get a drink," Oaklee says, marching toward the bar.

Millie nods but doesn't follow her. Instead, she stomps over to me.

"This is all your fault," Mille says, pushing a finger into my chest. One little touch sends zings through my body, firing me up, making me want her more. She's so bossy and determined and…

"Did you just growl at me?" Millie folds her arms and takes a step back. I can see the heat in her eyes. I may not have noticed the sound I made involuntarily, but her body sure did. I let my eyes glide down her. Her nipples have pebbled, her eyes heated, and she's biting on her lip aggressively like she's angry at herself for finding me attractive.

I smile wide. "I most definitely did. Want to hear me do it again?" I make a bold move, swiping my hand through her hair and gripping her neck to pull her closer.

For a moment, her body takes control instead of her mind. She lets me hold her. Lets me pull her until our bodies are flush against each other.

We fit perfectly. Most women are too short, too skinny. But Millie's body curves into mine, filling every hard inch of me with her softness.

It's unnerving how well our bodies fit, when it's so clear that we don't belong together.

"No, focus." Millie swipes at my arm, forcing me to let go of my hold on her.

I put my hands in my pockets as I stare at Oaklee with a fruity drink sitting at the bar. She's mindlessly drinking through the straw as she stares off into space.

I glance behind me, where Boden is taking his damn time getting a room.

It's clear to me what needs to happen next, but I want to know what Millie thinks.

"Do you think they belong together?" I ask.

"Yes, of course."

God, she's a romantic.

I roll my eyes.

"Do you?" She pushes back.

"No. I thought this marriage was destined to fail after six months. I'm glad they figured it out before signing the damn papers."

Her head snaps back like I just crushed all her little romantic dreams. "But they've been together five years. They met in grad school and started dating their final year. They moved to Santa Barbra together. Traveled the world together. They belong together."

"Doesn't matter." I shake my head.

"So you don't believe in love?"

I sigh. Now she wants to get all philosophical on me. And the more I talk, the more I show how different we are, the more likely it is that we will be spending the night apart. I'll be with Boden trying to keep him from blowing all his money gambling or on strippers. She'll be holding Oaklee's hair back after she drinks too much and keeping her from drunk dialing all her exes.

Either way I slice it, tonight is not going to go well so I might as well tell Millie exactly what I think.

"I believe love between two adults doesn't last. Oaklee and

Boden were in love at one point. But people grow, they change, their annoying habits set in and they realize that whatever love they felt has a limit. Fairytale romance doesn't exist. The only love that is real and everlasting is between a parent and child."

Millie glares at me. "You're so cynical. Just because you haven't found love, doesn't mean it doesn't exist. What about your brother? Isn't he happily married?"

"Kade and Larkyn are the exception to the rule. And they only truly work because they have kids and work hard to make it work. They don't stay together because of how in love they are."

Millie raises an eyebrow. "Who is the woman, and what did she do to hurt you?"

I chuckle. "Why do you think I was hurt by a woman to feel this way?"

"Just a hunch."

"Well, you're wrong."

"So what do we do with Oaklee and Boden? Get Boden a stripper while I hope there is enough alcohol for Oaklee to drown out her pain?" Millie asks with plenty of snark.

"No, we lock them in their suite together and force them to hash things out."

Millie blinks rapidly at me.

"What?" I say.

"You just surprise me, that's all. I assumed you thought their relationship was a lost cause."

"Oh, I think it is. But I'm not the one who gets to decide. They have to decide if the relationship is over or not. They have to be the ones to decide if we call the limo and drive back to the wedding or if I call Kade and tell him to send everyone home."

"Are you a counselor or psychologist or something? Because I think you would make a terrible counselor if you don't believe in love or marriage."

"Good thing I'm not a counselor then." And with that, I turn and walk away before Millie starts digging any more into my past. She doesn't need to know my history in order to decide if she wants to sleep with me or not. That's the only decision she needs to make, because that is all I can ever offer her.

I snag the room keys from Boden and then whistle to Oaklee. "Let's go." To my surprise, all four of us end up in the same elevator together. I stare at the buttons as the lift starts ascending to the top floor.

Please, mother of god, don't let us get stuck on this elevator.

6

MILLIE

I WATCH the numbers rise higher and higher as we head to the top floor. Boden sprung for the Napoleon Suite at the Paris hotel, and Oaklee showed me the pictures. It's one of the most romantic rooms I've ever seen.

Sebastian can be heartless all he wants, but all we have to do is get them into that room, and they will fall in love all over again. With the pretty decor, the champagne, the chocolate-covered strawberries, and the heavenly looking bed—there is no way they don't fall head over heels in love again. They may not make it back to the chapel today, but they will salvage their relationship and get married in the courthouse or with one of those Elvis impersonators that are so famous around here.

Everyone saw Oaklee almost get sick. We will just tell them she got sick, and they had a quick wedding before heading out on their honeymoon after Oaklee felt better. Everyone will understand that. There will be nothing for Oaklee and Boden to be embarrassed about. This was just cold feet. Just a big misunderstanding when it came to Boden kissing another woman. He was just drunk and trying to sabotage his wedding because he was scared.

I smile to myself. This will all be fixed, just as soon as we get them to their honeymoon suite.

The elevator stops suddenly on the 17th floor instead of the top floor, but the doors don't open.

"What's happening?" Oaklee asks, her voice high-pitched and worried.

Boden stares at her like she's an alien.

Sebastian closes his eyes; this is his nightmare. He then steps to the panel and hits the call button.

"Hello?" a bright woman's voice says through the speaker.

"Hi, uh, we are in the elevator on the North side. And we are stuck," Sebastian says.

Oaklee sucks her pink liquid through the straw quickly now.

Boden cringes.

I stare wide-eyed. *Good job, universe. You couldn't just let us get to the room first before you started playing matchmaker.*

"I'll send for emergency services immediately. Everyone remain calm. This does happen from time to time, and almost always, the elevator starts moving again before the emergency response team arrives," the happy lady says like we aren't stuck in an elevator.

Sebastian releases the button and then turns, staring us all down individually like he's assessing each of our ability to get this elevator moving again ourselves.

"Don't look at me like that, this isn't my fault," I say, snarkily.

Sebastian ignores me and walks between Boden and Oaklee, who are standing about as far apart as humanly possible in the small space. I stand in the middle at the back, and Sebastian stands in the middle at the front, now facing all of us.

"Well, since we now have nothing but time on our hands, I think it's time you two talked to each other," Sebastian says.

My eyebrows shoot up. *He's going to get them to talk? Here? Really?* Wait until we get to the fancy, romantic room where they will have no hope but to fall in love again.

Apparently, Sebastian either can't read my frustration or disagrees with my strategy.

"I have nothing else to say," Oaklee says, slurping on her drink until the last of the pink liquid is gone from the cup.

Sebastian takes the cup from her hands.

"Hey!" she says.

"It's empty." Sebastian holds it up so she can see it's empty. She folds her arms, no longer having something to hold onto.

"Boden, I think you should start. Look at Oaklee and tell her how you feel."

Nothing.

Sebastian takes a deep breath, and if possible, his voice gets quieter, calmer. All the muscles in his body relax as he speaks. "Tell Oaklee how it hurt to have her walk out on your wedding day."

Boden glares at Sebastian. "It hurt like hell. I don't know what has gotten into her. She can't just walk out on me on my wedding day! I thought we were in this together, forever."

"And I thought we had agreed to be monogamous," Oaklee yells back.

They look at each other finally, and they're definitely about to kill each other.

Good job, idiot, I mouth to Sebastian.

He ignores me.

"Thank you for looking at each other. Conversation works better when you are watching and listening to the other person's feelings."

Both of them bare their teeth to each other like vampires about to suck all the blood out of the other. I don't think this is what Sebastian had in mind when he said that.

"Now, Oaklee, tell Boden how upset you were to hear that he kissed another woman last night."

"I didn't—" Boden starts but shuts up when Sebastian gives him a look.

"I felt like he's a lying cheating bastard! Like he never loved me at all," Oaklee's voice breaks as she says it.

I reach over and take her hand in mine and squeeze three times, our secret signal to tell each other we love each other and are here for each other. We got the idea from a Taylor Swift song and have been doing it ever since.

She squeezes back, sucking the sobs back down as she stands strong in front of Boden.

"You think I never loved you? Really, Oaklee? I loved you with all of my heart." Boden steps forward toward her.

What is happening?

"Loved?" Oaklee asks through a terrified hiccup.

"Love—I still love you, Oaklee. I will never stop loving you. I fucked up. I thought you cared more about our wedding than me. I was stupid, and I made a drunken mistake. It doesn't mean that I ever stopped loving you."

I blink as I look between the two of them.

And then, before I realize what is happening, Oaklee releases my hand, and she jumps on Boden. His hands grab her ass. Hers go around his neck. Their lips hungrily devour each other in between *I love you*'s and *I'm so sorry*'s.

And then past it all, I see Sebastian. He's leaning against the doors with a smug smile and cocked head as if to say, *I gave you what you wanted. I got them back together, now what are you going to do for me?*

I suck in a breath, but I can't tear my eyes from him. I'm hot and bothered. My panties are wet. My nipples hard. I want him.

No, it's just because I'm going through a dry spell. That's all. Sebastian King is hot, and he knows it. But I have to be attracted to the man underneath in order to sleep with a man, not just find him physically attractive. He's cynical and has a cruel streak, not the type of man I want in my bed even for one night. I bet he's a selfish lover, making it all about him, not even caring if his partner comes or not.

He strokes his stubbled chin with his hand. I know he shaved, but the stubble has started to grow back already. I can imagine it against my thigh, his tongue at my slit, his fingers in—

"Millie," Sebastian says, breaking my trance.

"Yes?"

"The doors are opened."

"Oh." I look behind him and see that the doors are, in fact, open. Oaklee and Boden are long gone.

I step off the elevator with Sebastian right behind me.

"Where did they go?" I ask.

"Not sure, we are only on the 17th floor, not their suite floor. They couldn't have gone far. Let's go to the room and hope that's where they're headed," Sebastian says.

"Just not on the elevator," we both say at the same time.

I smile and follow Sebastian to the stairs. We head up to the top floor and make our way to the corner suite. Sebastian puts the keycard in and waits for it to turn green before entering. I follow after him.

There is no Oaklee or Boden. For one, Sebastian has both keys. And they weren't waiting outside the door.

I pull my phone from my bra.

Sebastian stares at my chest.

"Really?" I say, and he smiles before turning his attention on the beautiful suite I haven't let myself enjoy yet. I've always wanted a fairy tale wedding. I've wanted a romantic honeymoon. *What girl doesn't?* But I know it's not in the cards for me.

Once Sebastian has adverted his eyes from my chest, I dial Oaklee's number. She doesn't answer. I leave her a voicemail telling her we are waiting in the suite, reminding her of the room number, and to meet us here when they are ready.

"No luck?" Sebastian asks.

"Nope."

I look past Sebastian into the room for the first time, but it's not just a room. It's a whole series of rooms.

I'm speechless. I know my mouth is hanging open, but I don't care.

Sebastian opens his mouth to say something, but I just hold a finger up, silencing him.

He's quiet while I take in the suite of rooms. Everything is decorated in red and gold accents, making me feel like I just stepped into a royal palace. Every room has its own chandelier perfectly designed to fit each of the three bedrooms. There is a baby grand piano, a wet bar, and a room that holds a jacuzzi tub as big as a kingsized bed.

But that isn't what takes my breath away. It's the roses scattered on the bed—the chocolates. The romantic note lying on the bed from Boden to Oaklee, that I promise to myself I won't read no matter how much I want my heart to swoon at his beautiful words.

And then I see the most romantic part of all—the Eiffel Tower view out the window.

"Wow," I say, taking in the beautiful view right out the bedroom window.

Sebastian, who has been following behind me wordlessly, finally speaks.

"You know it's fake, right? The real Eiffel Tower is in Paris. Does that squash your fairy tale?"

"Of course I know it's not the real Eiffel Tower. But it is a real structure, and it's still beautiful." I flip him off.

"Did sweet Millie just flip me off?"

"I did. And I'm not sweet."

Sebastian leans forward until his lips are right over my ear, and I can feel his hot breath on my sensitive flesh.

"How about I kiss you and find out just how sweet you are?"

If my mouth hadn't already fallen open, it did with his words. I clear my throat and step away before I do something dangerous to my health like fuck him in this bed—a bed that Oaklee and Boden are supposed to be fucking in.

"Maybe you should try calling Boden; see if he answers you."

Sebastian pulls out his phone and starts texting.

"I said call."

"I'm aware, Bossypants. But since the last time I called Boden was after his grandmother died, I think it's better that I text. He might respond to a text; he won't answer if I call."

I nod, he's got a point. I quickly pull out my phone and send Oaklee a text as I walk back to the living room, realizing that the bedroom is dangerous.

"So what should we do while we wait? Someone should call and let the minister know what's happening," I say.

"I already called Kade and told him to tell everyone that Oaklee is sick, so there won't be a wedding today. They should enjoy the food and drink if they want, though."

"Good, that's good. Even if they reconcile, they probably won't want to get married at the chapel still. We should look into places they can get married around here." I pull out my phone again.

"Or, we could use one of the dozen bedrooms in this place while we wait." Sebastian winks at me.

"First, there are only three bedrooms, not a dozen."

"You got me there."

"Second, unless you plan on napping in one of them until they get back, the bedrooms will not be getting used."

"Yes, Bossypants."

"Will you stop calling me that? I'm not bossy."

He chuckles. "Yes, you are. You are also adorable and beautiful and so damn sexy."

"Just stop. You've already apologized for calling me fat. No need to continue trying to flatter me."

"I never called you fat."

"No, you just assumed I was pregnant."

He frowns at his loss for words. *Hurry back, Oaklee. I can't stand to be here much longer.*

I spot the wet bar and walk over to it. I'm going to need a drink to get through this wait with Sebastian. And because I'm nice, I decide to make a drink for Sebastian too.

"What are you drinking while we wait?" I ask.

He looks at me with a stern expression I don't understand. My mouth goes dry. *How is serious Sebastian sexier than flirty Sebastian?*

I'm in trouble.

7

SEBASTIAN

AN ALARM BLARES in my ear. I don't remember setting an alarm, but I don't remember falling asleep either. I don't even remember what I'm supposed to be doing this morning.

I reach over to my nightstand to hit it off like I always do. But when I wack the alarm, it keeps blaring.

Dammit.

I force my eyes open, even though I don't want to wake up. My body is begging me to go back to sleep. When I open my eyes, I realize I'm not in my bedroom.

I'm somewhere far fancier.

I blink rapidly, assuming this is a dream. I would never stay in a hotel this foo-fooie, but every time I look around, red and gold accents are staring back at me.

I grab the still-blaring alarm and find the switch to turn the bastard off. Then I flop back and look up at a bright chandelier staring down at me.

Where the hell am I?

I glance down at myself—I'm naked, which is normal. I always sleep in the nude. When I shift in the bed, my back creaks. This

252

mattress is far too soft for me, and I know when I stand up, I'm going to have a massive crick in my neck and back.

But that won't be the only thing hurting. I turn my head just slightly, and the pounding headache I'm rewarded with terrifies me.

Not because of the pain. I can handle a little pain. But because what the clues all lead to—the headache, the tiredness, the loss of memory. They all point to one thing—I drank last night.

That's not who I am anymore. I thought I was past this part of my life.

I turn my head, and the culprit of my drinking snores next to me —Millie Raine.

I always knew a woman would be my downfall. I just didn't expect sweet Millie Raine to be the one to take me down. But apparently, she did.

I smile, looking at her drooling on her pillow as she sleeps soundly, most likely sleeping off her own hangover. For a moment, she looks peaceful and happy. And falling off the wagon almost seems worth it since I get to wake up next to her this morning.

I got Millie Raine in my bed. *What could be better?* The only problem is I don't remember what happened last night. I don't remember our first kiss. I don't remember how her body felt in my hands. I don't remember what thrusting inside of her felt like. I don't remember my one night with Millie. And as badly as I want it, there won't be a second night. That's my rule, and it's kept me safe thus far.

Millie is the reason I'm drunk; I remember her offering me a drink. I remember Oaklee pushing me to drink in the limo. Women are my downfall. And as much as I want Millie, I need to get as far away from here as possible. I can't have a second night where I get to remember. Hopefully, with time my memory of tonight will come back, and I can relive last night over and over. But for now, Millie is off-limits.

Suddenly, Millie's eyes fly open as if she knew I was staring at her.

She smiles at me at first, like she's happy that I'm here in bed with her, but it won't last. The rational side of her brain will return soon, and the happy memories will disappear.

Her smile drops suddenly, and she sits up quickly before realizing that might not be a good idea. She grips her pounding head.

I sit up slowly next to her.

"How are you feeling?" I ask.

"Like I got run over by an elephant. My head is pounding. My body aches everywhere. I'm afraid if I breathe too hard, whatever poison is in my stomach is going to explode everywhere."

I laugh. "Same."

Her eyes turn to me as she takes in my naked chest. Her eyes run over every ridge, every hard line, every muscle.

I hold my breath as she examines me, but I can feel the heat bouncing from her eyes. Her fingers are itching to touch me, and if I let myself breathe, I know I'm going to let her. That is the absolute last thing I should be doing.

Finally, her gaze meets my eyes, and she blushes.

"Sorry, I didn't mean to stare."

"Yes, you did."

She clears her throat, but it does nothing to reduce the blush to her face. "So, uh, what happened?"

"What happened?" I cock my head, making her spell it out.

"Did we...?"

"Did we, what?"

"Did we have sex?" She finally gets the words out.

I smirk. "I'm completely naked. And you are wearing my shirt and boxers."

She stares down at herself for the first time, taking in my clothes she's wearing.

"What do you think?" I ask smugly. I got Millie into my bed. *Except you can't remember fucking her, you asshole.*

Semantics.

"Oh god," she flies out of bed and then starts running her hands up and down her body and then grips her head. "Why can't I remember last night?"

"Because we got drunk."

She frowns. "I've never blacked out drunk before." She grips her body like she's trying to hug herself.

I understand the feeling. It doesn't feel good to not remember. Unfortunately, I've had too many of those days myself. It's a scary thought, not remembering moments of your own life.

"*You*—did you put something in my drink?" She accuses me with a glare.

"What? You really think I put something in your drink?"

"Yes. I've been drunk plenty of times before, and this has never happened to me. It has to be because of you."

I jump out of bed, ready to fight back.

Her eyes drop, and I remember I'm naked. *Well, I'm not going to back down now.*

"I didn't drug you!"

"Yes, you did. You drugged me and raped me!"

I chuckle. "Oh, sweetheart, I wouldn't need to drug you to have my way with you. From the way you are staring at my cock, it wouldn't take much to convince you to ride me."

This time her face turns bright red as she rages at me. "I would never fuck you!"

I shrug. "Too late to make that statement, sweetheart. Seems like you already did."

She huffs, flipping her hair off her face as she does. "I don't believe you. What happened last night?"

I sigh and cross my arms to mimic hers. "I don't remember either."

"What?"

"I. Don't. Remember."

She narrows her eyes.

"You don't remember what happened?" she persists.

"Nope, just like you don't."

She grips my shirt she's wearing tighter. "So we…?"

"Fucked? Most likely. Unless you usually allow men to sleep naked next to you who you haven't fucked?"

She shakes her head, her big green eyes staring at me all inno-cent-like. *Damn, I wish I remembered.* I have a feeling it was a night to remember.

"And I'm guessing you are sore. Most women are after I fuck them." I wink.

She rolls her eyes before she collects her thoughts.

"Did we use protection? Are you clean?"

"I'm clean." And I search the floor for evidence. Our clothes are scattered haphazardly around, and then I see the glint of foil that I'm looking for. I pick up the ripped square and hold it up to her.

She gasps like this is a mystery novel, and I just found the murder weapon.

"I'd say we fucked. Unless you can think of another use for a condom."

She looks away, like she's embarrassed.

"It wasn't…" Now I'm the one at a loss of words.

"It wasn't?" She smiles at me because she knows what I'm afraid to ask.

"It wasn't your first time, was it?" It's another one of my rules. I don't fuck women more than once, and I don't do virgins. Sure, it makes me sound like an asshole, but it's all about self-preservation.

She bats her eyelashes at me, eyelashes that still have a thin layer of smudged mascara on them from last night.

"No," she finally puts me out of my misery.

I let out a long breath. "Good. We can move on then. We had our one night together; now we can go back to Santa Barbara and continue on with our lives."

Millie stills as if my words hurt her.

Jesus, is she one of those women who will date a man no matter how clearly wrong he is for her just because she slept with him? Instead of admitting that sometimes she likes to fuck men just to fuck them?

I rub my neck, and her eyes fall to my dick again. "Can we just admit the sex was great, but that we don't belong together? That we shouldn't waste each other's time dating?"

"I think you should put clothes on."

"Why? Are you hoping for a round two? Because I don't—"

"No, that's not it."

"Then what? Does my naked body make you uncomfortable?"

She holds up her left hand like that's supposed to mean something to me.

I shake my head, not understanding.

She points to her ring finger, where a large diamond sits.

"Fuck, Millie. You're engaged?" I don't fuck engaged women. Or married women. That's where I draw my line. Except apparently, I do fuck taken women. I need to know who she's engaged to so I can apologize and let him punch me, which I clearly deserve for fucking his fiancée.

"No, at least, I don't think I'm *just* engaged."

She's talking gibberish. "Is that Oaklee's ring? Are you safeguarding it?"

She shakes her head; that isn't true either. Oaklee's ring is pink; this one is gold. I was with Boden when he picked it out.

"Okay…what am I missing?" I ask.

Her head nods in my direction. I follow her gaze to my left hand, where a gold band sits.

"No way," I say, staring at my ring that wasn't there last night. My gaze lifts to Millie's ring, that now that I think of it, also wasn't on her hand last time I checked.

"No!" I say again.

Millie winces but forces herself to say the words. "I think we got married last night."

8

MILLIE

"WHAT DO you mean we got married? Why would we do that?" Sebastian asks, finally picking up his suit pants and putting them on.

I'm happy not to have the distraction anymore, but Jesus, do I wish I could remember getting fucked by that cock. I've been soaking wet and ready the entire time he's been standing naked in front of me.

"I don't know. But we are both wearing rings that weren't there last night, so it's just a guess."

He frowns as he stares at his ring, trying to remember last night. I try to remember last night too, but it's all a fog. We must have really hit the alcohol to not remember anything after we stepped foot inside this suite.

We hear buzzing, and we both kneel down to search through our clothes for our phones. We both find ours at the same time, both ringing.

Oaklee.

Kade.

"Fuck, do you think they know?" I ask.

"No, we don't even know what happened. I'm sure they don't." Sebastian answers his phone.

So I hit accept and put my phone to my ear, not having a clue what I'm going to hear when I answer. "Hello?"

"Millie! Oh my god! How was the wedding night sex?" Oaklee shouts at me.

I gulp. *This doesn't sound good.* "Um…wedding sex?"

"Oh, don't even act like you two didn't do it."

"Umm…" *How do I respond to her? How do I make this go away?*

"Eek, I just can't believe it! I want to hear all the details when you come meet everyone for brunch! You are not missing brunch. I don't care how good the sex was last night, get your ass down here in the next twenty minutes before everyone arrives and quizzes me about why Boden and I didn't get married last night."

"But you're going to get married today, right?"

Now it's Oaklee who has gone silent.

What am I missing?

"Just get your cute butt down here. You saved my ass. You're all anyone can talk about."

Shit.

Oaklee ends the call before I can ask anything more. I stare at my phone a second in a gaze, and then I see Sebastian standing in the entry to the living room in the same way.

"So everyone thinks we're married," Sebastian says, looking from the phone to his ring.

"No, we can't be. There would be a marriage license. I'm sure these rings are fake, worthless. We must have gotten them in a vending machine or something."

Sebastian walks over to me and grabs my left hand with his calloused fingers. Fingers that have touched my body, but I can't remember what they felt like. If the electricity in my hand is any indication, the sex last night was like fire racing through my body.

"The rings don't look fake to me," Sebastian says, running his thumb over my diamond.

I pull my hand out of his grasp so I can think clearly. "Then we can get it annulled. It will be like it never happened."

He nods. "That's a good idea."

We are both silent as our minds go somewhere else.

"What about brunch?" Sebastian asks. "We could hide up here until our flight this afternoon."

As much as I want to, I won't do that to Oaklee. I don't know what's going on between her and Boden, but I need to see her. And our friends might have some insight into what happened last night. Surely, we didn't actually get married. It was probably some act to distract from the pain Oaklee is feeling if she isn't married.

"No, we have to go," I say.

"And say what? We don't know what happened last night."

Sebastian follows me back to the bedroom—the scene of the crime.

"What are you doing?" he asks, as I walk into the closet.

I pull out one of Oaklee's dresses and khakis and a button-down from Boden's suitcase—luggage they had brought up when the room was ready yesterday. "Here, put this on."

"I'm not wearing Boden's clothes."

"Well, there is no time to go back to your hotel room to get dressed. So yes, you are."

I hold up the dress that I know is going to show off my every curve. Sebastian stares at it, his eyes imagining it on my body.

"Fine, if you're going to wear that, I can manage wearing Boden's preppy clothes."

"Good." I walk into the bathroom and shut the door in Sebastian's face.

"If we are husband and wife, I should really get to see you undress!" he yells through the door.

"We aren't, so you don't get to look!" I shout back as I change out of Sebastian's clothes. Oaklee wants us downstairs in twenty minutes, so I don't have time to shower and get ready.

I stare at the shower. I should shower. I should remove all evidence of Sebastian from my body, get his scent off of me.

I take a deep breath, breathing in his shirt. It smells like pine and fresh grass and man. It smells like Sebastian. I fold the shirt up neatly along with his boxers and put them on the edge of the counter.

Then I flip the shower on and step under the cool spray. I can't get sentimental when it comes to Sebastian. He's not mine. It doesn't matter if we are technically married or not. It doesn't matter if we slept together or not. We aren't together.

I step out, quickly blow dry my hair, and slip into one of Oaklee's dresses. I don't have time for makeup. I don't have time to search through Oaklee's bag to find hers. So instead, I pinch my cheeks. I don't wear makeup that often anyway, I'm more a tomboy than a girlie girl.

I open the door and find Sebastian. He turns when I step out, staring at me with his intense smolder that would have me jumping back into bed with him.

"That won't work," I say.

"What won't?"

"That look you are giving me won't convince me to fuck you again."

He leans in close.

I hold my breath, so I can't breathe him in. I'm strong enough to fight his good looks, but there is something about his smell that makes me weak in the knees and ready to do something stupid for him.

"Good thing I wasn't asking then. Because I only fuck women once."

I roll my eyes and start walking toward the door. "Of course you do. You're one of those man-whores who thinks his dick is so special that it can only grace a woman's pussy once. When in reality, no woman would make the mistake of fucking your disgusting dick twice."

I reach the door and grab the handle, but Sebastian slams his hand on the door, preventing me from opening it.

"Oh, sweet Millie, by the time I'm done with you, you'll be begging to ride my cock again."

"No way in hell."

And then he runs the back of fingers softy down my cheek. I melt on the inside at how gentle and warm his touch is.

This is the man I want.

The kind of man who puts my needs above his own.

But this is just pretend for Sebastian. In reality, he's selfish. I don't even know if he made me come last night.

I grab his hand forcefully, letting him know I won't deal with his crap.

"Want to make a bet?" I ask.

He grins. "My sweet Millie, I never thought you'd gamble on something as dirty as this."

"We are in Vegas," I say.

"I bet that you will be begging to be back in my bed by the end of our time together."

"And when I resist?"

"I'll get down on my knees and worship your body at your feet. I'm a king; I never kneel." He winks at me.

We both exit the room and enter the elevator to take us to brunch. *Please, don't get stuck.*

I look at Sebastian watching the elevator with the same trepidation.

When the doors open on the bottom floor, we both let out a breath. But I'm not sure if I'm relieved or disappointed. Being stuck on the elevator sounds better than dealing with this brunch.

"I resist, you become my servant for one day, Mr. King."

"Deal," he says.

"What about you? What do you get if I give in and beg for you?"

He smirks as he steps between the open doors.

"You—I get you."

9

SEBASTIAN

"CONGRATULATIONS!" The room breaks out in one big cheer as Millie and I step into the room of the restaurant that has been reserved for us. It was supposed to be Oaklee and Boden's send-off brunch before their honeymoon with the wedding party and a few other special guests, but it appears the news has spread that Millie and I got married instead.

Millie freezes in shock as she stares at all our friends hooping and hollering for us.

I'm just as shocked as she is, even though we both should have known this is what was going to go down. There was no hope that news like this hadn't spread. For all we know, they were all at our wedding.

I go through the options in my head of surviving this.

One—say we were drunk and did it for fun to distract everyone and that we are getting it annulled immediately.

Two—deny, deny, deny. No one has proof that we are married. We don't have a marriage license. No one can prove shit.

Three—it was a one-night stand turned insta-love. We fell hard and instantly and just had to get married immediately.

263

I look at Millie, whose cheeks are redder than I've ever seen them as people start throwing questions our way.

Option one is the most honest, but also embarrassing and reckless.

Option two isn't feasible. Everyone already thinks we are married.

And option three isn't believable.

But there is another option…

I take Millie's hand in mine, marveling at how perfect her small hand fits my larger one.

"What are you doing?" Millie hisses through a fake smile.

"I'm getting us through this with the least bit of embarrassment possible."

"How?"

"Trust me."

She snickers. "I don't even know you."

"Well, then it wasn't very smart for you to marry me, was it?"

She frowns, but at least she doesn't look embarrassed anymore, which is an improvement.

"Thanks! I'm so lucky to have found the love of my life. Millie is the most incredible woman I've ever met. Only she could get me to settle down," I say, gripping Millie's hand as we walk into the banquet room covered in flowers. Everyone is either holding a mimosa or bloody mary.

There is a table at the far end that says bride and groom on each of the seats. I notice that Oaklee is sitting to the left of the table, which means we are expected to sit in the chairs.

"We can't sit there. That's for—" Millie starts.

"Oaklee isn't sitting in the chair, and I don't know where Boden is. Come on, just follow along, and we will get out of here unscathed."

Millie reluctantly follows me to the chairs labeled Bride and Groom and takes a seat next to me.

"How did you meet?" Val asks. "Tell us your love story!" She practically squeaks.

"Umm," Millie is expected to answer, but I take over.

"Millie got a job in my marketing department. We've been dating secretly for months. Millie didn't think it was appropriate to let it be known that she was dating her boss."

Everyone laughs. "No way, Millie is wild. She wouldn't care that she's dating the boss," Val teases.

Millie's eyes cut to mine, and I raise a brow. *Apparently, Millie is wilder than I thought.*

"Just how wild we talking?" I ask Millie at the same time Millie asks me, "You work at a marketing firm?"

"Not really," but I don't say more about my job.

"My wild ways are overblown."

I smile and throw an arm around the back of a chair as a waitress places two mimosas in front of us.

I look up and find Larkyn looking at me curiously. If my story checked out, there would be no way she wouldn't know that Millie and I were dating. She knows everything that happens in the center. And she's one of my best friends. I tell her everything. I'll tell her the truth later. Kade is looking at me with a surprising amount of pride on his face, not usual coming from my brother. So I'm going to enjoy this ride for as long as I can.

I reach forward, grabbing my glass before realizing I picked up the damn mimosa instead of the water glass. I set it down abruptly and pick up the water glass.

"You okay?" Millie asks, noticing my move.

"Yes, just still hungover and don't want to drink."

"I know what you mean. I'd be happy never drinking again."

I nod and stare at the mimosa. I'm surprised the cravings haven't kicked in. But so far, I don't crave alcohol any more than usual. It's going to be damn embarrassing when I go back to the center and have to start my sober countdown all over again.

"So it was an opposites attract situation?" Shepherd asks.

I frown. "What do you mean?"

"I just mean that Millie is fun, outgoing, adventurous, and kind. And you're serious, responsible, and well...a bit boring." Shepherd smiles when he calls me boring, knowing that I'm going to punch him for that later.

"I just mean your life is so routined, and hers isn't. How does that work?"

I realize that I know practically nothing about Millie's life. I don't know what she does for a living. I don't even know if she lives in Santa Barbara with me so that my meet-cute story could be true or not. And I sure didn't take Millie for adventurous and spontaneous. To me, she's just sweet, kind, adorably sexy, Millie.

"Ooh, show us the ring!" Oaklee squeals.

Millie holds out her hand, and all the bridesmaids swarm. Oohing and awing over the ring I must have bought her. I don't know how much it cost me, but it doesn't matter. I have more money than I know what to do with.

"When did you propose?" Oaklee asks.

"Weeks ago. We just didn't want to overshadow your big day."

"That's so romantic."

"Why'd you get married so fast?" Val asks.

"Well, we were in Vegas and thought, what the heck? All our friends were here to celebrate with. And we just knew now was the time. We didn't want to wait," I say.

One of the bridesmaids rubs her tummy as if to ask if Millie is pregnant.

I glare at her. "No, that's not what this is. We are in love. We didn't want to wait," I say to her sternly through a tightened jaw.

She drops it.

Just then, brunch arrives. Everyone turns their attention to the food, so the conversation turns away from us.

Oaklee takes this moment to move to our table, though, leaving us no room for alone time.

Just a little bit longer, I think. Once this meal is over, everyone will go their separate ways, leaving Millie and I time to get our marriage annulled quietly and spread rumors that we decided to be just friends. And more importantly, give me time to win our bet. I may not fuck women more than once, but with Millie, I'd like to make an exception since neither of us can remember our first time.

"Where's Boden?" Millie asks Oaklee.

I frown at Millie. It's not really the most important question to be asking Oaklee when we have her all alone to ourselves right now. The questions we should be asking are what happened last night and how in the world did we end up married.

Oaklee sighs. "He's gone."

"Gone? How could that be? Last we saw you two you were making out and—" Millie says.

"And then we had an epic fight and decided to break up for good." A tear escapes Oaklee's eyes, and Millie grabs her and pulls her into a tight hug.

"Oh, Oaklee, I'm so sorry. What do you need? What can I do to make this better for you? Do we need to go up to the room and order gallons of ice cream?"

"No, nothing like that. Just keep being the center of attention. No one asks about Boden when they are focused on the surprise wedding of the century."

"Oaklee, about that…"

"We will keep all the focus on us, don't worry," I wink at Oaklee, and she smiles back.

"I knew you two would make the perfect match for each other. I just didn't realize you were dating. You were so mean to each other," Oaklee says, giving Millie a sly smile.

Millie exchanges a glance with me. "Yea, well, we were trying to keep our relationship on the down-low."

"I'm glad you aren't doing that anymore. I told everyone Boden is in our room sick with the same bug that I had and that we will reschedule or have a smaller wedding later. But it isn't true. He's probably at a strip club and already found another woman he's fucking by now."

Millie takes Oaklee's hand and squeezes three times. She squeezes three times back.

"I know," Oaklee says. And for a moment, she and Millie share a secret conversation without me.

I know Oaklee will be one of the few people who eventually learns the truth about Millie and I's relationship, but for some reason, the thought of the two of us being together makes her happy, so I guess we will pretend around everyone, at least for today. Tomorrow we return to our own lives.

"Ooh!" Oaklee starts jumping up and down excitedly.

Millie grins, seeing her friend so happy, but I know better. I cock my head suspiciously in her direction as I cut my eyes around the room. Thankfully, no one is paying us much attention.

"You have to stop jumping up and down so you can tell us what you're thinking," Millie laughs at her obnoxious friend.

Oaklee stops jumping and grabs both of our hands. "You should go on our honeymoon."

"Oh no, we couldn't do that," I say, terrified. I have a life to get back to. And if I know Boden's dumb ass, their honeymoon was probably planned for Florida. *No, thank you.*

Millie shakes her head. "I think you should go, Oaklee. Maybe take a close friend to go with you. It could be healing."

Oaklee shakes her head. "Nope, I don't want to go and sulk. I want someone who is actually going to enjoy it to use it. It will be my thank you for taking the attention off of me."

"Oaklee, I really don't think—" Millie starts.

"I'm not taking no for an answer. You are going. You deserve a honeymoon after that crappy Elvis impersonator wedding you had and getting married in lavender instead of white. I'm going to do this for you. I just need to get the names changed on the flight and reservations."

Oaklee pulls out her phone and starts making calls.

"Shit, well, how are we going to get out of this?"

Millie bites her lip. "I think we should go."

"What? We can't go. I have a life to get back to!"

Millie takes my hand and strokes the back of it. I instantly feel calm. *How did she do that?*

I stare at her holding my hand so casually, like we've been doing it for months.

"I know, I have a life to get back to as well. But surely since you're the boss, you can take a week off from work. I can get time off. And it will give us time away from everyone to figure out what to do about our situation."

"I'm not spending a week in some crappy motel in Florida. If we are going on a 'honeymoon,' we are going somewhere nice at least."

Millie laughs. "They weren't going to Florida for their honeymoon. Oaklee booked the most expensive hotel in Maui."

"Hawaii?"

She nods.

I frown. "I guess I could spend a week in Hawaii."

She laughs harder. "So accommodating of you to spend a free week in Hawaii. It's very noble of you, King."

Apparently, that's my new nickname. I've been called that plenty of times before, but somehow, hearing it fall from Millie's lips gets my heart beating a little faster in my chest.

Clinking of silverware against glass gets our attention.

"What are they doing?" I ask as everyone taps their forks, spoons, and knives against their champagne flutes.

Millie sighs. "They want us to kiss."

The corner of my lip curls up. "Oh, do they? *They* aren't the only ones."

"I'm not kissing you. I'd lose the bet."

"No, the bet was that you'd be begging me to fuck you by the end of our time together. Which apparently, just extended to a week in romantic Hawaii. A show kiss isn't you begging."

"Fine." She plasters a fake smile and is about to lean over to give me a chicken peck on the lips. That's not going to fly—with me or them.

So instead, I grab her hips and jerk her up. The room erupts in hoops and hollers and yelling for us to kiss.

Her eyes light with fire as if to say, *you wouldn't dare.*

Oh, honey, you have no idea how far I would dare.

I dip her back away from the room. And then I lower my head over hers. My hand is running up the side of her smooth black dress that clings to her full hips and breasts. She should be wearing white, not black, but no one argues when it's Millie we are talking about. She's my sweet, bossypants.

She licks her lips, waiting for the kiss, but she doesn't close her eyes, which excites me even more. She doesn't play by the rules. She likes to watch.

"Are you going to kiss me or not?" she dares me.

I lower my lips, and she parts hers, preparing for more than a chicken peck.

I stop just short. Our lips are so close that if I'm not careful, they'll collide. But I'm very careful. I don't want the first kiss I remember with this woman to be in front of a crowd. I want our first kiss to be because she's begging for it.

Instead of kissing her, I breathe my hot breath into her mouth.

"I won't kiss you, sweetheart, until you beg me to. Which based on how fast you're breathing and how hard your heart is thumping, is going to be very soon. And once I kiss you, you'll be begging for more."

I run my hand through her hair, messing up her hair just enough for everyone to believe that we've kissed, and then I pull her up.

Millie bites on her bottom lip and blushes as the crowd cheers. *Oh, my dear sweet Millie, I'm going to enjoy getting you back into my bed.*

10

MILLIE

THE BRUNCH WAS HELL. Going on a honeymoon is going to be like burning in an inferno. Resisting Sebastian to win a bet and keep my pride is going to be unbearable.

The hotel had our bags brought to this room, so Sebastian and I have been spending the last hour getting ready before our flight and avoiding each other. Well, I've been avoiding him. He's been as obnoxious as possible, trying to get me to fuck him in this bed before we leave.

Not going to happen.

And as beautiful as this hotel is, if I was going to use my one night in the sack with Sebastian, I wouldn't use it now, I'd wait until I get to Hawaii.

Nope—get those thoughts right out of my head. Sebastian and I are not happening. I'm not fucking him again. The first time was a mistake. If I fucked him again, it would mean I'm a screwup. And I finally have my life together. I'm not going to let a man take me down a dark path again.

I pull the zipper on my backpack after changing into my own clothes of shorts and a tank top.

My phone buzzes in my pocket. I pull it out, expecting Oaklee to

271

be calling with more details about my honeymoon. She's my closest friend. She lived with me. I don't know how she thinks Sebastian and I have been having a secret relationship for months now. She's delusional if she thinks Sebastian and I belong in the same room, let alone married to each other.

I freeze when I see the text isn't from Oaklee.

An unknown number flashes on the screen.

No.

No.

NO.

This can't be happening. I was free. I was…

I click on the text message and open it, even though I know better. I should just delete it.

Unknown number: Where R U?

My body reacts immediately to the threat. It may not seem like a threatening text message, but I know better.

Chills worse than I would feel in an old mansion filled with ghosts dance down my spine.

My ribs constrict around my lungs, rocking them with fear.

Sweat drips down my neck as anxiety spreads.

Not again.

I swipe the message, deleting it before I toss the phone on the bed. If I stop touching it, it can no longer have an effect on me.

I close my eyes and take several deep breaths as I wash the images out of my head, scrubbing my brain clean like I'm Cloroxing a bathroom, that's how hard I force the dangerous thoughts out of my head.

Sebastian opens the door from the bathroom as he sings a Justin Bieber song about how yummy I am and then switches to how his only intentions are to get me into his bed.

"You know you are combining his songs, right? And when Bieber sings those lyrics, he's being sweet, not an asshole," I ask, keeping my eyes closed.

"I'm just improving his lyrics."

I open my eyes and see his crooked grin as he dries his wet hair. And then I make the mistake of glancing down and see that once again, Sebastian is completely naked.

"Goddammit, what is it with you and not wearing clothes?" I cover my eyes with my hands.

He chuckles. "Don't pretend that you don't like what you see. And we are married after all. If I can't prance around naked, what benefit is there to being married?"

"Can't you wait to dance around naked with your next wife?"

"This will be my only marriage, so I have to take full advantage."

I lower my hands to look at him. He can't be serious. Yet, the playful gleam in his eyes is gone. I may not know Sebastian King very well, but I doubt his statement was anything but honest.

"Just get dressed and packed. The car will be here in ten minutes to take us to the airport."

His lazy eyes run down my body until they land on the bottom of my short shorts that barely cover my ass. Shorts that I think are a little too short, but Oaklee says I look smoking in. I just wear them because they are comfortable, but now that Sebastian sees me in them, I regret packing them. I can't read him. I don't know if he finds my ass attractive or if he thinks it's too large.

His pregnant comment still stings. Even though he defended me in the room during brunch. He thought I was pregnant. He basically called me fat. And now he's staring at my ass in the same way.

He tilts his head. "What are you thinking?"

"That you now have eight minutes to get dressed and packed before the car arrives for us."

He shakes his head slowly as he walks to me. "Liar. What are you thinking?" His voice is soft and dreamy, like melted chocolate. He's trying to caress me with his words to pull the truth from me.

And why not tell him? We are going to be stuck together for the next week.

"I'm thinking that you think my ass is too big."

His brow furrows, his jaw tenses, and his eyes darken. "Look at me, Millie."

I do.

"No." He cups my chin, dragging my eyes down his naked body to his rock hard cock.

I bite my lip to keep from saying something stupid.

"I'm hard because of you. I'm extremely attracted to you, Millie. All of you. Your natural beauty. Your freckles. Your sparkling green eyes. Your full breasts. Your curvy hips. And your ass—god, your ass might be my favorite part of you. I wish I could remember how it felt in my hands."

My mouth falls open.

And he takes a step back, his hand falling away from my chin. I don't know if he's stepping back because he wants me to get a better look at his body or because he needs to put distance between us, so he doesn't jump me.

Silently, he turns and gets dressed. I do my best not to stare. Not to crave him. Not to want him.

"Moron," I whisper under my breath.

"What was that?"

"I said, moron."

He buttons his jeans. "You called me a moron, why?"

"Just ensuring that I win our little bet."

He laughs hard. The muscles in his belly contract, drawing my attention to them, until I see his smile that reaches up to his crystal blue eyes.

He takes my breath away; that's how good looking he is.

"Jerk," I say.

And it makes him laugh again.

"You are something else, Millie Raine."

I blush but don't respond.

He grabs a T-shirt and finally puts it on. Then he finishes his look with a worn-out baseball cap. He zips up his bag and then turns to me.

"Where is your bag?"

I pick up my backpack. "Right here." I sling it over my shoulder.

He frowns. "That's your suitcase? How are you going to survive a week in Hawaii?"

"I only packed enough for two overnights, so I didn't need much."

He holds up his rolling suitcase on wheels. "This is a normal size suitcase for a weekend trip."

I shrug. "I travel light. And all I need when we get to Hawaii is a swimsuit anyway."

"Hopefully one of those red thong bikinis that cover practically nothing?"

I laugh. "Nope, a full wetsuit that covers every bit of me."

His smile drops before he recovers. "That's okay, I like the catsuit look as well."

He rolls his suitcase out while I carry my backpack. We take the elevator down, both of us staring intently at the numbers as we descend. The doors finally open on the bottom floor, and we both exhale a deep breath at the same time and then laugh at how ridiculous we are being. We were trapped in an elevator for all of two minutes. It wasn't a big deal.

As we walk to the lobby, cheering starts in along with bubbles floating all around us. Apparently, the wedding party has decided to wish us well on our way.

Before I realize what's happening, Sebastian takes my hand in his. Just like the last time he touched my hand, there's a spark followed by a warmth spreading through my body.

It's just because our hands fit together so well, that's all. There is nothing else to read into.

Sebastian leads me through the weave of people as we make our way through the lobby. We get outside to the waiting car that says 'Just married' on the back.

Just married.

I still can't believe those words.

"Kiss, kiss, kiss," the crowd starts chanting again.

Sebastian hands our bags to the driver, and then he flashes his signature grin showing off his white teeth. This smile is fake, unlike the other ones I've seen from him. He's putting on a show for the crowd, and I prepare myself for an untimely kiss.

But maybe if he finally kisses me, I'll get over him. I'll realize he's just a man, and I'm just horny. It's nothing some quality time with my vibrator can't fix.

He flicks his baseball cap off and then leans in. I part my lips waiting for his kiss. At the last second, he puts the cap over our faces, hiding them from the world as he leans in as close as he can get without kissing me.

"Are you begging yet?"

"Are you done being a prick yet?"

He smirks. "Keep calling me names, Millie. It only means I'm getting under your skin and getting closer to winning."

I exhale my breath—a mistake because it means I have to inhale, and all I breathe in is him.

The hollers grow louder, and eventually, Sebastian lets go of me. He opens the door to the car, and I slide in. He follows after, and then we are driving toward the airport.

There will be no more people to put on a show for. We are all alone. We don't have to pretend anymore. We could even change our flights and head home early, and no one could stop us.

We are silent as we both get lost in our phones. Until the texts start in again…

Where r u?

Call me.

I need you.

· · ·

You can't hide from me.

I'll find you.

Delete all.

"Shoot," I breathe.

Sebastian looks at me. "We don't have to go to Hawaii, you know. No one would know."

I nod. "I know."

"But maybe we should. We could both use a break."

"And the trip is already paid for, nonrefundable. It seems silly not to go."

"So, we're going."

"We're going."

"I, uh, talked to my lawyer," he says while I fidget with my phone, thinking about the deleted messages.

"He said that he could get our marriage annulled before we get back. I'll cover the costs of the legal fees."

My mind is racing with so many thoughts. *Could being married to Sebastian save me from my past?*

I glance up at Sebastian, who is oblivious to the thoughts in my head. I have to tread carefully, to get him to agree to my plan.

"About that…"

11

SEBASTIAN

"What do you mean you don't want me to use my lawyer?" I ask as we stand in line to board our plane.

She runs her hand through her hair, making it look even more wild and untamed. If I didn't know better, I'd think she had a quick fuck in the bathroom before boarding. But the look is just Millie—a little wild, a little messy, and probably an animal in the bedroom. *Too bad I can't remember.*

We are headed to Hawaii for an all-paid, week-long vacation. I'm going to win our little bet. I'll get my one night yet. One that this time, I'll make sure I don't forget.

Millie mumbles something under her breath that I don't catch.

"What was that?" I ask.

"Sir, your ticket," the flight person says. I hold out my phone, and she scans it, then scans Millie's.

"Have a nice flight," she says.

We walk down the ramp. Me pulling my carry on, Millie still sporting her backpack that somehow fits a weekend's worth of clothes. I'm okay with her not having many clothes. It means she can spend more time naked around me.

"Window or aisle?" Millie asks when we get to our seats in first class. Boden really went all out for this honeymoon. I texted him in the limo, but he never responded to me. I don't know where he is. I just hope he's taking the breakup as well as Oaklee is.

"Aisle," I say.

Millie smiles. "Good, I prefer the window."

We both take our seats after I put my bag in the overhead compartment, and Millie squeezes her bag under the seat in front of us. We look like a happily married couple, which is why you should never believe appearances. They can be faked.

"Welcome, Mr. and Mrs. King. Can I get you some champagne before we take off?" our flight attendant asks.

"No!" Millie and I both answer at the same time, equally emphatically that we don't want any champagne.

"Hungover?" he asks us.

We both nod.

He chuckles. "How about some coffee then?"

"Yes, please," I answer.

Millie nods as well.

"I'll be right back with your drinks, Mr. and Mrs. King." And then he leaves us.

"Do you know that you do this blinking and wincing thing every time someone calls us Mr. and Mrs. King?" Millie asks.

I turn my head toward her. "I don't think I do."

"You do."

"Is that a problem? We aren't really married."

"Actually, we are."

I roll my eyes. "Fine, we're married, but not by choice. And we won't be for much longer. As I said, I spoke with my lawyer—"

"Why do you have a lawyer? I don't have a lawyer who I can call when I get into trouble. Why do you?"

I sigh and look down the aisle to where our flight attendant is preparing our coffee. *Hurry up, man, I'm going to need it to survive this flight.*

My legs start bouncing up and down, and my heart races—all the familiar signs of a craving starting. Now, I really want that coffee.

"Here you go, Mr. and Mrs. King." We are both handed our coffees, and I grip mine like it's the only thing keeping me from raiding the liquor cabinet for bourbon, my liquor of choice.

"Thank you," Millie says brightly when I don't say anything. Our flight attendant returns my smile and leaves us.

"Are you rude to everyone like that?" she asks.

"I wasn't rude." I grip my cup tighter.

"Yes, you were. And now the vein in your forehead is popping out. The one that pops out when you're mad."

I shake my head. "Can you stop overanalyzing me so we can talk about our situation, and then I can put my headphones on and spend the rest of my flight watching the latest Fast and Furious movie?"

She makes a disgusted face.

"Really? You don't like Fast and Furious? It's like we weren't meant to spend the rest of our lives together."

She chews on her bottom lip.

"What? Spit it out."

"Um…I just don't want to get lawyers involved."

I sip on my coffee again.

Millie puts her hand on my forearm like she's trying to calm me, which only makes my breath fly. I glance at the couple sitting next to us, sipping mimosas and enjoying life. And suddenly, I want a mimosa.

No, it's just the addiction talking. I don't want a damn mimosa.

I turn back to Millie.

"You can't be serious?"

Millie looks at me nervously—she's serious.

"I told you I'd pay for legal fees. That includes *your* legal fees." There is no way I can get this annulled or even divorced without a lawyer. Kade would kill me. I don't know if I should trust Millie or not yet, but if she finds out how big my bank account is before the annulment or divorce goes through, I'm going to be out a lot of money. Not that I care, but I'm not going to let a complete stranger take half my money.

"It's not that..." Millie looks out the window like she's lost in thought as she once again mumbles under her breath, talking to herself. If I didn't work with mentally ill people all day, if I wasn't mentally unstable myself, I might think Millie is losing it.

I let her be for a moment, even though I want to quiz her about what's going on in her head. The flight attendant collects our mugs, and then we are asked to turn off our cell phones before takeoff.

Millie turns hers off like she can't turn it off fast enough and then practically throws it into her backpack. I assume that Oaklee or our friends have been texting her with a million questions about our relationship the same way my friends have been.

Then we are taking off, my fingers now dancing on the armrest.

Millie stares at them. And I think she's going to ask another question about why I'm behaving this way. I'm sure she'll find out I'm a recovering alcoholic at some point, but I'm not in the mood to share my life story right now.

Instead of asking a question, though, Millie simply takes my hand and holds it. I stare at our interlocked fingers that just fit together, and I feel calmer and electric at the same time. Like I've just been plugged into an outlet, and I'm charged, ready to fire but also grounded at the same time.

The plane begins to take off, and Millie squeezes my hand three times like she did with Oaklee. I realize that she must assume I'm a nervous flyer.

"What does that mean when you squeeze my hand three times? I saw you do it with Oaklee."

She smiles at me softly but doesn't answer. Which is okay because I don't want to talk too much either. She would just force me to talk too.

"I think we should stay married," Millie hits me with words I never expected to hear. From her. From anyone.

I blink over and over, making sure this isn't a dream. And then I remove my hand from her grasp because maybe she thinks there is something between us that isn't there.

She glances down at our now separated hands.

"Millie, I like you, but I don't want to be married to you. I'm sorry if you think there is something going on between us but—"

"No, I don't think there is anything between us. I think you are an arrogant jerk. Trust me, I don't think we fit well together."

I narrow my eyes. "Okay, then I don't follow your logic. If you are afraid of what everyone is going to say when we go home, I think we can just play it low for a few months and then announce that we quietly separated. Our only shared friends are Oaklee and Boden, who we can tell the truth to if you want. And then we can just bury ourselves in our work and tell Oaklee in a few months to say we rushed into marriage too fast and just decided to remain friends. It can't be more embarrassing than Oaklee running out at her own wedding."

"I'm not worried about being embarrassed. Trust me, having people find out the truth is one of the least embarrassing moments of my life."

"Okay…" I rub the back of my head, not understanding.

Her eyes go to my shirt that has risen up, and her eyes sink into my abs, getting lost in my body for a moment. I welcome her heated stare, except I'm worried that my body is why she wants to stay married.

"Do you think staying married is the only way I'll bend my rule and fuck you again, because I already told you, I'd gladly wave my rule and fuck you again. I think we both deserve a do-over," I ask after I put my arms down.

She shakes her head. "You're so full of yourself. I'm not fucking you again."

"Are you trying to get me to fall in love with you?" trying to figure out her reason.

"No."

"Only believe in sex after marriage?"

"No."

"Need to be married to get a promotion?"

"No."

"Need to be married to inherit?"

She sighs. "This isn't about money."

Good, because baby, you aren't getting any of mine.

I pull out a piece of gum and start smacking it, knowing it will help my antsy body.

I rub my chin, trying to figure her out. Millie Raine isn't like any woman I've ever met, though, so I don't know how to figure her out.

"Why?"

She looks out the window again, all joking gone. There's a reason. She just doesn't want to tell me.

Well, too bad, if she wants me to stay married to her, she better damn well tell me why.

"Don't you want your first marriage to be with someone you love?" I ask.

She snaps her head with a soft chuckle, but it's hiding pain. Her green eyes dilate; her eyelashes blink faster, trying to keep the pain inside.

"Don't you?" She throws my question back at me.

"Since this will be the only time I'm married, that's not an option for me."

"A good looking guy like you only thinks he's going to be fake married to me for however long I convince you to stay married to me, and doesn't expect to be taken by some Miss America, living in the dream house with the two-point-five kids and golden retriever? I'd bet that you'll be married to the woman of your dreams in the next two years."

"I'd say I'm way more likely to win my bet than you are yours." I lean closer to her and watch her squirm away in her seat, knowing that if I so much as breathe on her, she's going to be begging me to help her join the mile high club.

I nod at her with heated eyes. "My point taken. Now, you didn't answer my question, you deflected. Don't you want your first marriage to be with someone you love?"

She looks down at her nails. I notice they have little flecks of black nail polish still on them that she's obviously picked off instead of removing with nail polish remover.

Finally, she looks back up at me with determination in her eyes, like how she answers this one question is going to persuade me to stay married to her.

"I won't marry again after this, either."

I freeze. No way is this woman planning on not getting married. She's not conventional. I expect her to tell me that she's a musician or a travel blogger instead of a school teacher or medical professional or lawyer like most of the women I know. But every woman I know wants to get married. Hell, every man I know does too. Except, maybe Boden.

"What do you mean?"

Her chest rises as she takes a deep breath and looks me dead in the eye, like she's trying to talk to my soul.

"I mean—I'm just like you. I don't want to get married. This, whatever this is, will be my last marriage. I'm not a romantic. I don't believe in happily ever after. I believe marriage only works between two people who want it to work, usually because of their children. I don't want a house. I don't want children. I've gotten by pretty well on my own. I'm happy. I don't want to get married. You and I may differ on a lot of things, but we don't differ on this."

"Then why did you think Oaklee and Boden should get married? You wanted them to get back together."

"Because despite what I believe, I thought that's what they wanted. I thought they might be the exception to my rule that everlasting love doesn't exist. I was wrong about their marriage, but not about this. Love isn't real. Love is just lust well hidden."

Her words hit me like a bullet. I've said those exact words to Larkyn before when she asked why I didn't want to get married. Larkyn and Kade are my exception just like Oaklee and Boden were hers.

"So why do you want to stay married to me if you don't believe in marriage?" I ask, sitting on the edge of my seat, entranced that no matter how different we are, I may have just found the one woman on the planet who feels the same way as me.

"Maybe I just want to pretend that love exists for a little while longer before I return to being cynical." Her words are a lie. I know it, she knows I know it. But her words strike me. Like a blow from a sword, they weaken me. They may not be true for her, but they are true for me. For once, it would be nice to not live in my perfect bubble with my perfect routine and life all planned out. It would be nice to pretend that I could be like everyone else. That I could believe in love even if that love isn't real.

I stare at Millie. She stares back and lets me see a flicker of her pain behind her green eyes.

The reason Millie wants to stay married to me is serious. It's hiding her pain. I want to know why. And someday, I'll know why, but not today.

Today, I just have to decide if I'll go along with her plan even though all I'll get out of it is spending more time with her in hopes of winning my bet and getting to fuck her again. I get to get everyone off my back about getting married. When this is all over, I can say if a marriage couldn't work between me and Millie, a woman who is lovable in every way, then how could a marriage between me and anyone work?

I don't know all the details. I don't know what is expected of me.

All I know is that with a single look, my entire world just changed. I will do whatever this woman wants, something I thought was only reserved for Larkyn and Kade and their kids. But for some unexplainable reason, I want to help Millie.

"I know it's a lot to ask. I think we should stay married—" Millie starts rambling, but I've already made my decision. I don't need any more persuading.

I lean over and press Millie's lips together to get her to stop talking. And then I give her my answer, letting her know that I'm all in.

"How long?"

12

MILLIE

"I'm not considering; I'm doing this."

I lean in close, too shocked to remember that it's a mistake getting near this man. His scent is like honey to a bee, except he's the honey and the bee. If I fall for him, I'm going to get stung.

"You are?"

He chuckles. "I want details, Millie. Not more questions. How long?"

He's agreed. I don't know why. *What does he get out of this?* Not much. At least, not much that he's making clear. Maybe he thinks I'm going to fuck him every night that we're married. I'm going to have to put that in the rules—no fucking. That's the only way our 'marriage' is going to survive.

"One year?" I ask.

He cocks his head with a sly look. He can sense my fear. I know he's dying to know the truth, why I want to stay married to him, but I'm not revealing anything.

"Six months," he counters.

"Deal." I'll take him for as long as I can get. Six months gives me plenty of time to figure out a solution.

"Where do you live?" he asks.

"I share an apartment with Oaklee."

"Then I guess you are moving in with me. There is no way in hell I'm living with Oaklee. She's a diva."

I laugh, thinking about all the makeup and hair products everywhere in our apartment. Her needing her sparkling water and special protein shakes every morning. And how she complains about me being messy.

"She's definitely a diva. Where do you live?"

"I have my own apartment downtown. On 9th street. Does that work for you?"

"Shouldn't be a problem."

"Good, I have plenty of furniture. So you can either keep your stuff at Oaklee's or put it in storage. I'll make sure there is closet space for you."

"How generous of you."

"Own any pets?"

"No, you?"

"Nope. I don't have a spare parking space."

"I don't have a car, so I won't be needing one."

"Night owl or early riser?"

"Night owl."

He frowns.

"Let me guess; you're an early riser?"

He nods.

"What is your rent?" I ask.

"You don't need to worry about paying rent."

"I want to. Oaklee can easily cover the rent on the old place. And after our marriage is dissolved, I won't be moving back anyway. So I can cover my fair share. It's the least I can do since you are agreeing to this."

"Really, it's not a problem," he tries to assure me.

"Will you just tell me what your rent is?"

"Two thousand."

"See, that wasn't so hard. I can easily cover that." The old rent was fifteen hundred between Oaklee & I, so it won't be much of an increase.

Sebastian grips the armrests, his jaw set tightly, and his eyes flicking to the flight attendant who is now going through the first-class cabin pouring wine. He must really be a nervous flyer by the way he keeps tensing and glaring at the flight attendant. I know he has a monster of a hangover like me.

"You know I've heard that sometimes if you drink a little in the morning, it can cure a hangover," I say.

"I'm good," he practically growls at me.

Okay—I won't make the mistake of trying to be nice again.

He runs his hand through his unruly hair and then looks at me as he lets out a sigh. "I'm sorry. I'm just…"

"A nervous flyer? A crabby hungover monster? Or just naturally a jerk?"

He smiles. "Hungover. Do you want some wine?"

I shake my head.

"More coffee?"

I nod.

We wait until we get more coffee in our systems before we finish our conversation.

"So we agreed to six months and that we will live at my place, what else do we need to discuss?" he asks after he drinks half of his new cup of coffee.

"Sex," I blurt out without thinking. The older woman sitting next to us gives me a scowl around her husband, who is smiling at me.

Sebastian grins. "My favorite conversation."

I roll my eyes. "I just meant that you need to know I won't be fucking you just because we are staying married. Nothing has changed."

"I think *everything's* changed. But I will definitely fuck you again before our time is over. Not because we are married but because I have every intention of winning our little wager." He leans in again, in what is quickly becoming his signature move. He likes watching me squirm. He knows how badly my body craves his. If I let my guard down for a single second, I'll be fucking him, which is a horrible idea.

Why is it a bad idea again?

It just is, I tell my inner conscious. *It just is, for so many reasons.*

"I'll fuck you, because you want me to. You can fight it. Actually, I prefer it that way. I always enjoy a good chase. But no matter how much you tell yourself that we shouldn't, in the end, it will happen because it's the best damn idea either of us have ever had."

My entire body flushes, not just my cheeks. My nipples pebble. My panties flood. My breath catches. My heart races.

Damn him. He knows exactly how to push my buttons. He thinks he's going to win, and maybe he's right. But if he wants a chase, a chase he'll get. He'll be begging for me long before I'm begging for him.

I purse my lips and let out a long slow breath to try and calm my raging hormones. And then I throw it back at him.

I lean over in his seat, pushing him back with the air between us. Neither of us touches each other, but it doesn't matter. We know the game we're playing. The first to beg, the first to touch, loses.

I run my tongue over my bottom lip and watch his eyes watch my lips. I let my thumb pull down on my bottom lip and then let it fall down my body, my neck, stopping just above the curve of my breasts.

He's practically panting as he watches me.

"Game on, Mr. King."

When I say his name, I know I just won this battle. The large bulge in his pants confirms it.

I laugh and fall back into my seat.

"I'm going to enjoy being married to you, Mrs. King," he finally says, when he's caught his breath again.

"You are going to have the worse case of blue balls ever."

"Oh, I doubt that."

Which makes me frown. "Um...that leads me to my next term."

His eyebrows shoot up. "Which is?"

"We can't fuck other people while we are married. I know we

won't be fucking each other. I have no right to ask, but I just…" I can't handle being married to a cheater. I can't handle anyone finding out that Sebastian fucked other women while being married to me, even if our marriage isn't real.

"I don't want to fuck anyone else. Just you. If I have to be celibate for six months in order to get you once, it will be worth it, sweetheart."

I swoon at his words. *How is a guy like him not taken?* I know he's cocky, and he sometimes says the wrong thing, but when he says the right thing—oh my god, he's the perfect man.

"How does this end?" I ask, knowing this is the last major point we need to figure out.

"How do you want it to end?"

"I want it to be believable, but I don't want either of us to be at fault."

He nods. "Well, everyone seemed to believe that we were together easily enough. It should be easy enough to convince everyone that it just didn't work out, that we decided we are better off just friends. That I wasn't suitable for marriage."

We both aren't suitable for marriage, but I don't tell him that.

"We need an event. Something where we can stage a fight or show off how well we don't work together," I say.

"Larkyn's birthday is just shy of six months away. We can stage a fight. We can pretend we're over, that we didn't work. Then when we announce we're getting divorced a few weeks later, it won't come as a shock."

I nod. *Six months*—I have six months of protection. Six months to pretend that my life isn't what it really is. Six months to escape my own reality.

I glance over at the sexy god sitting next to me. Maybe I should enjoy my time with him, enjoy the escape. If I'm smart, I'll start pretending it's over now, before my heart does something stupid, like fall for him. A charming man like Sebastian King is easy to fall for—that's the real reason I can't have sex with him. If I fuck him, I'll want to keep him forever, and he's not mine to keep.

13

SEBASTIAN

"Here is your suite, Mr. and Mrs. King," the manager says as he holds the door open to us.

"Holy shit," Millie and I both say at the same time when we enter top floor suite that Boden and Oaklee reserved. Boden has money like me; I'm just surprised he sprung for this nice of a suite and didn't cancel, or at least try to get his money back. If I was a better man, I'd offer to pay him back, but I'm not going to.

"Your luggage is already in the closet. There are champagne and chocolates for you by the minibar. Do you need anything else, Mr. and Mrs. King?"

"No, thank you." I tip him as he leaves, and then we are alone in a beautiful suite with an incredible view.

"Can you believe this? Have you ever stayed anywhere so nice before?" Millie runs out onto our private balcony, complete with a jacuzzi tub.

I'm silent. I don't want to ruin the moment.

But Millie's big eyes don't miss a beat. "Oh my god. You have, haven't you?"

I nod but don't elaborate.

291

"Well, don't ruin this for me. I may never stay anywhere this nice again."

I walk over and lean against the railing next to her. "I won't ruin anything. And even though I've stayed in hotels this nice before, I've never been to Hawaii."

"You're going to love it! It's one of my favorite places I've ever been to."

"You travel a lot?"

She nods but doesn't elaborate either.

We both stand next to each other in silence, enjoying the ocean breeze and sun on our faces. I may not have realized it before we came, but this is exactly what I need. It's been a long time since I've gone on a vacation or been out of my normal routine. One week here with Millie might finally prove to myself that my life is perfect and that I can handle a week vacation a year.

"We should go snorkeling! And hiking to the volcano. Oh, and surfing! You know how to surf, right? If not, I can teach you. And dancing! I love dancing."

I chuckle, a grin slipping back onto my face as I listen to all the things Millie is excited to do. I haven't smiled this much in years, but find myself grinning all the time when I'm around Millie.

"You're laughing at me. You think this is all a bad idea. Well, what do you want to do, Mr. Boring?"

I laugh again. "Actually, it all sounds great, Millie. I'm up for whatever you want to do this week."

Her eyes narrow as she tries to figure out if I'm lying or telling the truth. "You sure Mr. Stick-Up-His-Ass is up for an adventure?"

"I am. I'll say yes to anything this week."

"Anything?" Her eyes light up.

"Anything." My eyes sear with all the dirty thoughts I'm thinking.

She notices, and her eyes turn fiery.

She grabs my hand and pulls me back inside. I'm hoping her first choice of activity will involve us both getting naked and using the ginormous bed or jacuzzi, but when she drops my hand and picks up a brochure, I know that's not where her head is.

Too bad. My cock twitches in my pants. I've never been this hard without a release. Six months and only one night of sex with this woman is going to be a nightmare.

Something catches Millie's attention, and I follow her gaze to the bottle of champagne chilling.

Do I tell her that I won't be drinking? Do I tell her why? It will be such a buzz kill. I've been sober for ten years.

No, I've been sober one day. I don't care if it was just one night. It was a slip-up. A major slip up that led me to getting fucking married. Although, I might take the fresh start with my sobriety if it means I get to spend a week in this hotel with Millie.

"I don't think we should drink this trip," Millie says, which sounds like music to my ears.

"Oh? Why do you say that?" I ask as casually as I can.

"Last time we got drunk, we ended up married to complete strangers. Who knows what we would do if we did it again."

I nod, agreeing.

"And besides, I'm on a diet. This should be a healthy vacation. We'll spend our time doing fun, adventurous things instead of gorging on gluttonous food and alcohol that is only going to mean I leave fifteen pounds heavier."

I frown. I don't know why Millie insists she needs to lose weight. She looks fucking incredible—perfect curves in all the right places.

It's because you basically called her fat, you jackass.

I sigh. I need to fix this.

"I agree that this should be a healthy vacation. One where we do things that are good for us instead of indulging in drinking, but not because we might gain fifteen pounds. Even if you gained fifteen pounds, you'd still look smoking hot."

"But you—"

"I know what I said. I was an idiot. I should have never assumed you were pregnant just because you were the only one not drinking that night. I'm sorry. I thought everyone in the bridal party was married except me. I knew you weren't drinking and just jumped to conclusions. I don't think you are fat; far from it. You're beautiful."

Millie gives me a relaxed smile, one where she keeps her lips pressed together instead of letting her smile reach her eyes. She doesn't fully believe me, which means I'm going to have to prove it to her.

"Can we start over? We didn't get off on the best of foot, but I really think we could have fun together this week."

Millie nods. "Yes, let's start over." She grabs two champagne flutes. *Dammit, I thought we were past the drinking thing.* She digs through the mini-fridge and pulls out some sparkling water and fills our glasses.

"To starting over," she says, as she hands me a glass.

"To being Mr. and Mrs. King."

She smiles bigger now. "I'm still not fucking you, Mr. King."

"Oh, we will see about that. There is only one bed, after all, I don't think you'll be able to resist having me sleep next to you every night and not fuck me."

"This suite is huge. I'm sure you can sleep on the couch, or the hotel can bring up a cot for you to sleep on."

I step closer to her, into her space. She doesn't step back. She's too determined to not let me affect her.

"I don't think the hotel would know what to do if the couple in the honeymoon suite asked for a cot."

"You're full of shit, Mr. King. You don't give a fuck what the hotel staff thinks of us."

"But *you* do."

She cocks her head and folds her arms. "Actually, I don't. But the bed is huge. I think we can manage to sleep next to each other like adults and not fuck like bunnies. Unlike you, I don't have sex with someone just because they share a bed with me."

"I don't either, Mrs. King. But I'm very much going to enjoy fucking *my wife*."

Her breath catches. I got the reaction I wanted. Now it's time for the real fun.

14

MILLIE

THE ENTIRE DAY has been one activity after the other. We've been going non-stop since we left the room early in the afternoon.

We've explored the city, went zip-lining, and then finished the day off with a jet ski tour. We haven't had time to stop, even to enjoy a romantic meal together all day, which was intentional.

I don't want to give Sebastian any opportunity to say sweet things that makes my heart go pitter-patter. Staying in a honeymoon suite in Hawaii with a hot man like Sebastian is just asking for trouble, so I need to keep us out of that hotel room as much as possible. We will only return when we are both seconds away from crashing.

Sebastian, to his credit, has been a good sport. He hasn't complained once about the crazy schedule I've made us keep. His only attempt at romance was when we were renting jet skis, suggesting that we share one. I quickly said I wanted my own, and he didn't protest too hard. And when I looked back at him, he seemed to be having a good time driving his own jet ski.

But now it's getting dark. The day is ending, and I'm running out of excuses for us not to go back to our hotel room.

"Let's go for a walk on the beach," I say.

"Lead the way," Sebastian says, just like he has all day. He's gone along with every activity. I wonder if he will truly let me decide every activity of this vacation. So far, he has.

I kick off my flip flops. Sebastian does the same as we walk along the hotel's beach in the moonlight. We pass a few couples holding hands. If we were really here on our honeymoon, we would be doing the same. Although, if we were really here on our honeymoon, I doubt I would be making an excuse to not go back to our hotel room right now. In fact, we'd probably spend our entire time in the hotel room.

"So we haven't had time to talk much. What do you do for a living?" I ask.

"Nope, we aren't going to go there."

I frown. "How are we going to pretend to be married to each other if we don't know anything about each other when we return?"

"First of all, we will know all the important things, like you hate pineapple, and I hate sushi."

"Which is absolutely ridiculous, by the way. Who hates sushi?"

He ignores me. "I'll know that you snore and how long it takes you to do your makeup."

"I don't snore and five minutes."

He chuckles. "I guess we'll find out tonight."

"But what about our jobs, our mothers' names, where we grew up? We should know the answers to those questions."

He nods. "We will. We can talk about all of that on the flight home. But I don't want this to feel like a first date. First dates suck. I want this to be fun, an adventure. We can learn the important things about each other after we leave. Agreed?"

"You know for a man who claims he isn't adventurous; you sure got this adventure thing down pretty fast," I say.

"I'm adventurous when I want to be."

"Good, because I've decided our next activity."

He looks around in the dark. Only the moonlight and the lights from the hotel in the distance pierce the darkness.

"I assume you mean go back to the hotel to sit in the jacuzzi? I don't think there is anything else to do at midnight."

"You are such an old man." I grab the hem of my tank top and pull it over my head.

He blinks his surprise as I stand in my sports bra. I should have had us wear our swimsuits under our clothes, but I only brought one, and it's not the most comfortable thing to wear all day.

"What are you doing?" he asks.

"What are *we* doing, you mean." I shimmy out of my jean shorts until I'm standing in front of him in just my sports bra and thong. Even in the darkness, I can see his eyes heat at the sight of my body. He wasn't lying when he said he found me attractive.

"Strip," I say.

I don't have to tell him twice. He removes his shirt and khaki shorts in record time, not even asking why we are stripping in the middle of a public beach. The darkness makes it hard to see every groove of muscle on his body, but I don't have to take in every wave of his muscles to know how ripped he is. I already have the memory of his shirtless body to fill in any gaps.

I turn around before I lose my nerve, and then I pull my sports bra off.

"Millie, what are you doing?"

I slip my panties down, and then I'm running into the waves. "Skinny dipping!"

I don't wait for Sebastian. If I do, I'm going to catch sight of his naked body again. I'm going to see what lies beneath the bulge in his boxers, and this isn't about that. It's about doing something crazy and adventurous.

Sebastian seems plenty adventurous to me. We're married for goodness sakes; if that isn't fearless, I don't know what is. But I get the feeling that other than his hookups, he usually isn't too adventurous. He must have a boring desk job or something.

I hear Sebastian splashing in the waves behind me, and I dive under. Chills immediately set in as soon as my head dunks under the water. It's springtime in Hawaii at night. There is a reason no one else is in the water—it's fricking cold.

My head rises out of the water and comes face to face with a soaking and very naked Sebastian.

"You're crazy! This water is so cold," he says.

"You said you were up for anything. I wanted to see how far I could push you. Ever skinny-dipped before?"

He shakes his head. His eyes go to my bare shoulders and chest that bob up and down with the waves, threatening to reveal more of my body to him.

I shiver. We need to head back before we freeze to death and ruin our vacation on the first day.

"Come here," he says. His voice is calm and trusting. He holds out his arms and waits.

I move closer, suspecting it's a trap. When his arms go around me, I realize he's just being a gentleman. He's warming my body against his—it's sweet.

"We should head back before my cock falls off from hypothermia."

I laugh, and we start swimming back. We get close to where the water will no longer hide my nakedness from him.

"Go on, I'll turn around until you're dressed."

"Nope, we go together. It's too cold to wait in the water." I grab his hand and pull him toward our clothes. Neither of us looks below the other's eyes, no matter how badly we both want to, as we slip our clothes back onto our soaking bodies.

"You're shivering," Sebastian says.

I look up at him. He's put his shorts back on but not his shirt. Water drips down his chest in beads, bouncing over his rock hard muscles.

When my gaze meets his, there is a familiar grin. "Put your arms up."

I frown, not understanding, but I do what he says. He slips his T-shirt down over my body.

"Better?" he asks.

I tremble again, but I'm not sure if it's from being cold or his touch.

He frowns. "Let's get you inside and warmed up." He takes my hand, our fingers melding together like all the other couples on the beach. But they don't stay together for long and then Sebastian has me pulled against his side. His arm is draped over my shoulders, and his hand runs up and down my bicep, trying to keep me warm as we race back to the hotel.

All I can focus on is his touch against my skin. His arm over my shoulders. His smell is filling my nostrils.

"Still cold?" Sebastian asks as we enter the lobby.

"Nope." In fact, I'm burning hot from his touch. An unfamiliar ache grows in my belly—want, desire, lust. Things I haven't felt in such a long time.

We enter the elevator—our nemesis. Sebastian hits the button for the top floor and then holds me tighter to his side.

"You don't have to keep doing that. I'm warm."

"I know." His answer is confusing; I have no idea what that means.

I stare ahead as the numbers climb, his arm feeling surprisingly perfect around me, even if he's turning my hormones upside down with need. The numbers jump from ten to the eleventh floor, and I panic. I don't want to be stuck in an elevator alone with Sebastian. Not when we are soaked. Not when both of our minds are on the reckless thing we just did. Reckless because we were naked, and it spurred our desire, not because I was afraid we'd get caught.

"I think for once I'm hoping it will get stuck," Sebastian whispers in my ear, his voice somehow dropping an octave.

"Oh yea, why's that?" My voice grows raspy as I speak.

"I'm pretty sure I'll win our bet if we get stuck."

Just then, the doors open on the top floor. "Maybe you'll have better luck next time."

We step out. Sebastian's arm is no longer around me as I strut to the door and pull the room key out of my pocket. It flashes green, and then I step inside, feeling burning hot even though I'm dripping wet.

"What are we doing now?" Sebastian asks, making me jump.

I turn around to face him. "What do you mean?"

"You're in charge of all our activities. What are we doing now?"

I'm staring at his chest again. Damn, he has a nice chest. *Why does he have to have such a nice chest?*

"Millie, does the next activity involve us ogling each other? If so, you need to remove a layer of clothing to make it fair." He winks at me.

I breathe again. The shiver returns.

"I think I should be the one to decide the evening's activities, or at least tonight's activity," Sebastian says.

And just like that, my breath is gone again. I nod.

He laughs.

"Let's warm-up in the jacuzzi. Your nipples are rock hard; you must be freezing."

I look down and, for the first time, I realize that you can see straight through the two layers of shirts I'm wearing. I should be embarrassed, but Sebastian's heated gaze keeps me from feeling anything but want.

I want him.

You shouldn't.

Maybe I should?

Just get a redo on the one time. Something to remember this time.

No, Millie.

Sebastian's eyes flicker back and forth over my forehead like he can read my mind.

"Where's your suit? I can get it for you," Sebastian says.

He's just as affected as I am. If we are going to fuck, it's going to be because he begged for it, not because I did. I don't usually strut around naked; it's not my style. But I want to with Sebastian.

He thinks I'm wild, and I am, but not in this way.

I grab the bottom of both of the shirts I'm wearing and lift them over my head, still facing Sebastian. He's frozen as he stares at me, not hiding where his gaze is this time—on my breasts.

I let him take in my body. I let the memory burn into his brain. My next move is even bolder—I undo the button on my jean shorts and slide them down my body until I'm naked in front of him.

His hand balls into a fist, and he bites his knuckles to keep from begging for me. I can see how close he is to breaking.

Give in, Sebastian. I want you, too.

But he doesn't.

Soon, one of us is going to break. It's only a matter of time.

"My first wife is hot."

I blush.

He steps closer and drops his shorts.

Fuck me.

He's gorgeous.

His cock is hard, just like every other part of him.

"So is my husband."

"You ready to put our last activity on the table?"

"Are you?" My eyes cut down to his cock, which is very ready.

"Just say the word, Mrs. King."

"Not until you beg, Mr. King."

And then I turn and strut toward the jacuzzi on our private balcony.

"Fuck, you're good, Millie," I hear Sebastian curse under his breath.

I know. And if I'm lucky, I'll get to fuck him and win the bet at the same time. I'll get the fantasy husband for one day. I just have to remember it's a fantasy. In real life, I'll never get the perfect husband.

15

SEBASTIAN

WATCHING Millie's naked body walk away from me and not at least trying to get her into bed was one of the hardest things I've ever done. It takes all of my restraint to not beg her, to not literally get down on my knees to let me fuck her.

Millie Raine is the hottest woman I've ever seen. She's got more confidence than Taylor Swift does when she struts around on stage. Her body is fit and curvy, and I want to grab onto every one of those curves.

Why the hell did I make a bet saying that she would be begging me? I'll be the one begging. She's a predator. When she removed her clothes, she knew exactly what she was doing—winning.

I don't care that she's winning. I want her to win. I just hope she decides to collect on her prize. I hope she lets me worship her body, taste between her legs. I want it all, and if she won't let my cock enter her body, I at least want to touch and taste every part she'll let me.

"You coming?" she yells as she hits the buttons on the jacuzzi, turning it on and leaning over the tub in plain view.

My mouth is dry. I'm at a loss for words. So I don't answer with my words, I just head out onto the balcony.

She climbs the two stairs leading up to the hot tub.

"Here, let me," I say, holding my hand out like a gentleman. I've been acting nice all day, even though my thoughts have been anything but gentlemanly. They have been dirty, debasing, and needy.

She takes my hand, her eyes practically glowing with victory as she sinks beneath the bubbles. I follow after her. She scoots over; I assume to give me room to sit by her, but I sit opposite her in the tub.

We've both teased each other enough. We're both single. Technically we're married. We should fuck. There is no reason not to.

"You win," I say, hoping if I let her win that we can both stop this charade pretending we don't want to fuck each other and just do it already.

She laughs. "I win, huh? I thought I was going to be begging you for sex?"

"Your body is, your mouth just hasn't gotten there yet, and I'm an impatient man."

"If you want to fuck me, why are you sitting way over there?"

"I'm not going to touch you until you tell me to. I'm not asking you to beg. I'm just asking you to tell me it's what you want."

She shakes her head. "Nope. Not going to do that. Just because you are ready to beg me for sex doesn't mean I'm going to fuck you."

"You can't deny that you want me. I can see your desire in your eyes."

She bats her eyelashes but doesn't deny it. She doesn't confirm she wants me either. The nibble of her teeth on her bottom lip lets me know how twisted up inside she is.

"It doesn't matter what I want. It matters what's good for me. And fucking you isn't good for me."

"It will be very good for you."

"We're friends. We are going to be living together for months. I don't want sex to get in the way."

"Sex doesn't have to get in the way."

"It will, though. It always does." She looks off in the distance, and

I realize she says that because sex has gotten in the way for her in the past. That's why she's so hesitant to fuck me now.

"If we don't fuck, we are always going to wonder. We've fucked before, but neither of us remember. We need to fuck so we can remember. So we don't always wonder what happened between us, we'll know."

"We could remember still."

"Do you remember?"

"No."

"I don't think the memory is coming back, unless we fuck."

She chuckles. "Is sex your answer for everything?"

"Yes." I wiggle my ears, and my dimple drives into my cheek. She laughs at both.

"I had a good day with you, Sebastian."

I sigh. It seems she's done talking about sex.

"You don't fight fair," I say, looking down at her naked body covered in bubbles.

"Neither do you."

I sink lower into the bubbles, up to my chin. "I had a good day too, Millie." *A really good day.* I can't recall a day where I laughed more than I did today with Millie. No matter what happens between us, I shouldn't ruin it. Millie would make a great friend.

She would also make someone a good wife someday. That's a topic I need to dig deeper on. A woman like Millie should definitely get married, not because she needs a guy, but because she's so fucking incredible.

"What crazy things do you have planned for us tomorrow?"

"Who says I have a plan? I didn't today."

I smile at that, before yawning.

"It's past someone's bedtime," she laughs, as I yawn two more times.

"I told you, I'm an early bird, not a night owl."

She yawns too. "I think it's time for bed."

I climb out of the tub, feeling her gaze on me as I dry off and then wrap the towel around my waist before waiting to see what she's going to do. *Is she going to be as brave leaving the tub as she was going in?* All she has to do to get me to leave is say the words.

But when she stands, water dripping down her naked body, it's too much for me. I grab one of the towels and hold it up, blocking my view of her body.

She smirks and then wraps the towel around her.

I turn and walk inside. "You can have the bathroom first."

"Thanks."

She grabs her clothes; I assume to go to the bathroom to change. Instead, she drops her towel and then pulls an oversized T-shirt over her body.

"You're sleeping like that?" I gape.

"Do you have a problem with that?"

I moan. My cock is throbbing. My body is aching for her. She's not even wearing any underwear.

"Nope. I uh…" I run my hand through my wet hair. "I think I'll sleep on the couch after all."

"The bed is plenty big enough."

"Um…fuck."

She laughs at my words. "I'll put on panties if it will help."

I don't think it will help. I don't think anything will help.

There is a buzzing coming from her bag that draws her attention —giving me time to compose myself. She may not need to go to the bathroom, but I need to go jack off if I'm going to have any hope of falling asleep.

I grab my toiletry bag and head toward the bathroom. Once I'm done in the bathroom, I exit and glance over at Millie sitting on the bed. The phone is pressed to her ear, she must be listening to a voicemail, but her face is as white as a ghost.

"Everything okay, Millie?" I ask.

She stops breathing, her body growing paler.

Fuck. Whatever is in that voicemail isn't good. *Did something happen to Oaklee? To some of her other friends? Is it her parents? A sibling? Is someone in the hospital? Did someone die?*

A million scenarios go through my head. I'm actually really good in a crisis. I know all the steps you should take. I know how to stop someone from having a panic attack. I know the stages of grief. I know how to help her get through a five-hour flight back home while dealing with the news that someone died, if that's what I have to do.

I just don't want to. I don't want our time here to end. It barely got started. Once we return home, our lives will change. The flirting will end. The possibilities will close. We will go through the motions of pretending for a few months, and then this will end, it will all be over. I'm not ready to go back to my old life.

I kneel down in front of her, putting my counselor hat on, hoping that in a few minutes, I can take it back off again and go back to being the asshole who's trying to get in her pants. I'm still just wearing a towel around my waist. Kneeling practically naked in front of her should draw a smart comment from her.

Instead, she acts like I'm not here.

She's in shock. I've seen it before.

Slowly, I reach up and place my hand around the phone pressed to her ear. She doesn't flinch. She still doesn't acknowledge I'm here.

Carefully, I take the phone from her hand. When I do, her gaze finally meets mine.

"It's okay. Whatever happened, it will be okay. I just need you to focus on your breathing. In and out…"

Her breathing is shallow. She's not focused on her breathing. Her head is still wherever the phone call took her.

I stare at the phone a second. It's unlocked. I could listen to the voicemail myself and understand what I'm dealing with, but even though technically I'm her husband, I won't breach her confidentiality like that.

"Millie, breathe with me." I take her hand and press it to my bare chest.

I stifle down my own moan at the touch of her hand on my skin. My cock is throbbing beneath my towel as I kneel between her spread, bare legs.

"In," I take a deep breath, and Millie does the same.

"Out." She exhales with me.

"Good, one more time." We breathe together in and out in long, slow breaths. Our eyes lock, and slowly, I see the light return to her eyes. She's coming back to me. When she realizes that she's touching me and I'm between her naked legs, she jumps back.

"It's okay, nothing is going to happen."

She nods.

"Do you want to tell me what happened?" I don't know if I want to know, or I want to pretend that everything is okay more. I just want more time without the baggage that is our lives. I want more pretend, even if I'm curious about her life.

She shakes her head.

I nod.

"You don't have to tell me anything, but do we need to head back home early?"

She shakes her head, emphatically. "No, I don't want to go anywhere."

Her words are music to me. Her voice is soft and sweet, and it's practically begging me to be the one to lose—the one to beg for more, for sex, for her.

God, do I want to. I want her more than I've ever wanted anything.

But I won't have her when she's so vulnerable. When we fuck again, it will be because we both want it, not because she's scared and wants to use me to forget whatever was on the other end of that voicemail.

"We should try to sleep. We have a big day ahead of us tomorrow."

She smiles at that.

I stand up to give her space, but she grabs my hand, seeming to know that if I leave, I'll come to my senses and sleep on the couch.

"Stay," she says.

Fuck, I curse under my breath.

Stay.

I can't deny her what she wants, not when she's this emotional. *But Jesus, this is going to test me.*

I nod.

Then I watch as she scoots up in the bed and starts pulling the covers back. I'm still just wearing a towel; I should at least find my boxers to put on, but then she's patting the spot in the bed next to her.

Fuck it.

We are both adults. It doesn't matter what we are wearing. We are just going to sleep.

I remove my towel, climb into the bed, and pull the covers up over us, doing my best to tuck her in. She seems unsettled next to me. I turn off the lamp, and then we are lying in darkness.

She sits up suddenly. "Can I?"

I know what's she asking even though she doesn't say the word. I can feel her fear. And right now, I'm the only person in her world who can take away the fear.

No matter what happens tonight—*I will not fuck her tonight. I will not fuck Millie.* I repeat my mantra over and over in my head.

Then I pull her to my chest. Her head rests perfectly on my shoulder, her body fitting like a glove to mine. She takes a deep breath, relaxing into me. Minutes later, she's snoring.

I smile. I knew she was a snorer. I won't be able to sleep. I've slept for years alone in my bed, but I could listen to the soft sounds she makes all night. It will be worth the lack of sleep.

I kiss her forehead, breathing in the salty ocean water and sand still stuck to her hair. Something stirs deep inside me, a feeling I've never felt before. A feeling I didn't know I could feel.

Want.

I want her. Not just to fuck her. I want more with her. I want to feel everything with her, even if our time together is limited. I want to protect her.

What are you doing to me, Millie?

And then I close my eyes, and the strangest thing happens. I fall into a deep, content sleep.

16

MILLIE

I'm warm, too warm, but also so damn comfortable that I don't want to move. Maybe if I just kick the covers off, I can sleep some more without being so hot.

I kick, knocking the comforter and sheet to the floor. Not what I intended, but I feel so much better. The sun is warming my skin through the large window. Quickly, I realize that the main source of heat isn't the sun or the covers, it's the very hot, naked man that I'm practically groping.

"Oh my god!" I squeal when I realize he's naked—completely naked. My thigh is draped over his waist, and his cock is straining against my leg. My hand is gripping his pec, and his hand is gripping my ass.

Sebastian stirs awake from my outburst. I might have been a little too dramatic.

"You're naked," I exclaim in horror. Right now, my memory of last night is a little foggy. In fact, I don't think I've ever slept harder or better, except maybe the night that got us in this mess in the first place.

He chuckles. "You're observant."

I pull my body back, ripping myself from him even though what

I really want to do is snuggle deeper into his shoulder, grip his cock, and then climb on top of him and fuck him awake.

Instead, I do the right thing, which is to act like he's a hot stovetop I can't touch.

"Did we? We didn't fuck again, did we?" I ask in horror. If I fucked this man again, and have no memory of it, I'm going to kill my brain for having such shitty memory. It's not fair that my body gets to experience such pleasure, and I can't relive the moments over and over again. I remember every embarrassing comment I've made, but I don't remember Sebastian King fucking me.

He stretches his arms over his head, and his cock rests back against his hard stomach. "No, we didn't have sex."

I let out a long breath.

"But we can change that." He winks at me.

The memories start coming back. The voicemail that ruined our perfect day. Sebastian being kind and holding me while I fell asleep. He kept my demons away last night. He was so sweet. He was the kind of guy women could fall for.

Thank god he's back to his playful, joking, sex-focused self this morning.

"Are you ready to beg?"

"Are you?"

I smile. We don't have to talk about what happened last night. I just need a few more days without thinking about the voicemail—about him. I need this. I need to be carefree and fun Millie again. I haven't been her in years. Sebastian lets me be her. He wants me to be her.

I pull on the hem of my shirt. Last night it seemed like a good idea to sleep in just this T-shirt. Now, in the bright daylight, I feel vulnerable. I feel naked, even though Sebastian is the one who is naked. I'm covered, but all my old insecurities come flying back.

"Don't," he says.

I narrow my eyes as I bring my knees up to my chest.

"Don't think you're less than. I don't know who made you feel that way but don't let them win. You are incredible, Millie. My cock thinks so, and so do I."

I stare down at his dick—hard, long, and thick.

"It's just because it's morning. That happens to all guys in the morning."

"No, it's because it's you."

He rolls over and grabs my hands pulling them away from my legs so he can look at me. "I'm not the man who can give you the happily ever after that you deserve, but I am the man who can remind you of how beautiful and incredible you are. If I could choose any other woman to be fake married to, I wouldn't. You're the only person I would want to be fake married to."

I shake my head.

"And before you go thinking that was just a line I tell women to get into my bed, know that you're truly the only woman I've ever been fake married to."

I laugh. "I'm still not fucking you."

"I didn't say that so that you would fuck me. I said it because it's true. I've never met a woman like you, Millie. Don't let anyone stifle you."

My stomach growls. "I think it's time for breakfast."

"More like lunch."

"What?" I frown, looking over at the clock on the nightstand. "Oh my god! It's twelve-thirty. I haven't slept in this long since college."

I look at Sebastian. "Me neither."

We stare at each other. Both of us know that we should leave this bed before we do something stupid. *Although, maybe it isn't stupid?* We have chemistry. We're adults. In six months, we are going to be nothing but a bad memory. Maybe we should fuck and get each other out of our systems.

"Can I plan today?" Sebastian says suddenly.

"I thought I got to decide all our activities this week?"

"Please?"

"What do you have in mind?"

He shakes his head. "Nope, if I'm in charge, it's a surprise, just like when you choose the activities."

I sigh. "Fine, but whatever activities you have planned, we have to keep our clothes on."

"That wasn't the deal when *you* did it."

I fold my arms over my chest. "That's my condition. Take it or leave it." I know it's hypocritical. I had us skinny dip yesterday. But that was before we spent all night snuggling naked in each other's arms. If we fuck, I want to make sure I have a clear head. I need to make a pros and cons list. I need to talk to Oaklee. *But how do I ask Oaklee if I should fuck Sebastian without explaining everything else?* Of course, she'll say I should fuck my husband.

"Fine, I don't need you naked to have my way with you." He winks and then stretches and gets out of the bed. Then I'm staring at his naked ass, hard and muscly, until he covers it with the towel that I remember he came to bed with.

Dammit, why did I insist on wearing clothes today?

"Are you trying to outdo me on being more adventurous?" I ask, panting behind Sebastian.

He laughs. "When you chose the activities, we zip-lined, jet skied, and skinny-dipped all in one day. All we're doing today is going for a hike."

"Yea, a hike across the entire island." I lift my arms over my head, trying to catch my breath. I'm wearing jean shorts and a tank top. I have a Hawaii ball cap and cheap sunglasses from the hotel gift shop, but none of it is doing much to block out the heat. Even though it's only spring, it's hot in this jungle. Sweat trickles down the back of my neck.

"We've only been hiking an hour. We have two hours left to reach the waterfall."

"Two hours! Are you serious?"

I sit down on a rock, not believing that Mr. Not Adventurous really planned this long of a hike.

He hands me a bottle of water. I take it and start chugging.

"The worst is over. It's mostly flat from here on out."

"It's not the incline that's getting to me; it's the heat. And the fact that I hardly ever work out."

Sebastian stretches his arms over his head until the T-shirt he's wearing rides up. He's not sweating at all, and I haven't heard him breathe hard once. This is a leisurely stroll for him.

"Why not?"

I shrug. "I'm not a gym rat. And I don't usually have time to explore the outdoors like this and get exercise that way."

"You should really try working out—"

I put my hand up. "I'm going to stop you right there. I agree. I don't need a lecture from a guy who has the body of Greek god."

"Actually, I prefer a Roman god; they were more ripped."

I roll my eyes.

Why can't I remember that one night? Maybe if I had the memory, I wouldn't want him so badly. Maybe he's terrible in bed. Who am I kidding? He's probably incredible in bed. If I remembered, I'd only want a repeat, which apparently the Roman god won't do.

"I thought you preferred to be called King."

"Only when I'm making you come."

I sigh. "We really shouldn't."

"Why not? It would be fun."

My heart thumps in my chest, but not because I'm out of breath from the hike. "How much fun it would or wouldn't be isn't the problem."

"Then tell me what you're worried about, and I can fix it for you."

"Just like that?"

"Just like that." His eyes twinkle with his promise. He truly thinks he can solve any of my reservations around us having sex.

"If we fuck, are you going to fall in love with me?" he asks.

"No." I'm not capable of loving anyone.

"Are you going to get emotionally attached?"

I shrug. "I don't think so."

He scrunches his mouth until it's pursed together as he thinks. "You won't."

"How do you know?"

"I'm an ass, you've said so yourself. And once we fuck, I'll pick up my asshole game so you can't possibly grow attached. Problem solved."

"I'd prefer nice, sexless Sebastian to asshole Sebastian who I get to fuck all the time."

He shakes his head. "That's the wrong choice. Being with asshole Sebastian is totally worth the mind-blowing orgasms I could give you."

I laugh. "I can give myself mind-blowing orgasms, thank you very much. I just need a friend."

His eyebrows raise. "A friend who is fake married to you to protect you from something that you won't tell me about?"

I nod. "Exactly."

"You should be glad I like you, Mills. I wouldn't be fake married with no benefits to just anyone."

"Mills? You're giving me a nickname now?"

"I could go back to calling you Mrs. King."

"Nope, I like Mills."

He holds out his hand to help me up. Reluctantly, I take it.

He pulls me up, and our bodies near.

"How about we make a deal?" he asks, his breath hot against my neck. I like this kind of hotness.

"I thought we already had a deal and a bet?"

His eyes darken. "We don't have an arrangement."

I laugh.

"You finish this hike with me, and I'll give you a kiss when we reach the top."

"I don't get anything out of that deal."

He grabs my hips and jerks me tight to him until our lips are hovering just over each other's. I stare into his deep eyes, and I've never wanted to kiss him more.

"Are you sure about that? I think you get a romantic kiss over-looking a waterfall in Hawaii on the only honeymoon you may ever take. You get to remember how it feels to be kissed by a man who truly wants you. You get to know how it feels to be desired desper-ately. And you'll be reminded that you are a sexual creature who deserves to have the best sex of her life. Then you'll realize that you do want to be married after all, not because you need a man, but because you deserve to be fucked like a queen every damn day. That's what you'll get."

I can't breathe. I can't respond.

Sebastian's eyes flicker over mine, and then he steps back and holds out his hand. I take it gladly. I've never wanted a kiss more than I do now. This hike just got a lot longer. Unbearably long.

"Maybe I can get that kiss now," I say.

He turns to me with serious eyes. "No. I'll kiss you when we make it to the waterfall. A woman like you deserves the best first kiss."

"But this won't be our first kiss."

He frowns. "Yes, it will. It's the only first kiss that matters."

17

SEBASTIAN

I SHOULD'VE KISSED HER. **Right then and there.**

We've been hiking for almost two hours since the moment she told me to kiss her, and I refused until we made it to the waterfall.

Big mistake.

I've been hiking with a hard-on the entire time, not the most comfortable thing in the world.

But I'm determined to give her the best kiss I can. I want it to be romantic and perfect and magical. I want it to make her believe in love again. Not that she should fall in love with me, but that love and magic can exist. I don't want her to turn cynical like me.

Our kiss isn't going to be magical, that is if we even make it to the waterfall. We were supposed to arrive at the waterfall twenty minutes ago. I'm pretty sure we're lost, but I won't tell Millie that.

When, or if, we ever make it, the kiss is going to be far from perfect. We are both covered in sweat from the incredible heat. Millie has about a dozen mosquito bites because I forgot to pack repellent, and I have a sunburn on my forehead because I didn't wear a hat.

Our muscles ache, and even though I still have two bottles of water and a granola bar in my backpack, we are dehydrated and

316

hungry. I didn't plan this well. I was just focused on getting us to the waterfall, on giving Millie a magical moment.

Millie deserves it. She deserves the perfect kiss. And dammit, we didn't come all this way to not let it happen.

All hope is lost.

Suddenly, Millie starts singing 'Heart Attack' by Demi Lovato. She's completely out of breath. Her hands rest on her hips as she tries to suck in more oxygen with each step, but it doesn't stop her from trying to belt out lyrics about not falling in love.

"For real, I think I'm going to have a heart attack." Millie folds her arms over her head, her chest rising and falling, panting. Her cheeks are red, her face is dripping sweat, and her hair is a mess, tied back behind her ball cap. There are sweat stains all over her shirt, and her freckled legs have red swollen spots from mosquitos and where she's gotten too much sun.

"Maybe you should stop singing then. You sound like a dying horse."

"I. Do. Not." She pants between each word.

"You. Do. Too." I pant just like her to prove her point.

"I think you're trying to kill me. But I hate to tell you, if you kill me I don't have any money for you to collect and I don't have a life insurance policy. So there is nothing to gain by killing me," Millie teases me.

I laugh, knowing that Millie is just kidding, but it is a thought that has crossed my mind. A strategy that she might be trying to do to me—marrying me to take half of my money. "I'm not trying to kill you, but you are trying to kill me with that voice of yours."

"Well then, you sing. I didn't bring my phone, and I need music to keep me entertained."

"I thought the very thought of kissing me was enough to keep you occupied." It sure is enough to keep my thoughts off how bad of a plan this was. All I want to do is kiss her. One kiss and I know I can convince her to repeat our one forgotten night.

"Sing, pretty boy."

"I'll sing, you drink." I toss her a water bottle. She catches it and starts drinking.

I wrack my brain, trying to think of a song. What comes out is 'Mercy' by Shawn Mendes. I sing a few bars before I hear Millie chuckling behind me.

"It wasn't as bad as your singing," I say.

She laughs. "That's not why I'm laughing."

"Why are you laughing?"

"Because the only songs you know are boy bands."

I stop, and Millie slams into my back.

"Shawn Mendes isn't a boy band. Neither is Justin Bieber," I say, remembering the earlier song I sang to her.

She laughs harder. "Stop, you're making it harder to breathe."

So then I start singing Maroon 5's 'Harder to Breathe.'

"That's a real boy band," I say.

"Oh my god, seriously stop. I can't—"

I turn, and she runs smack dab into me, chest to chest. Face to face. I'm standing downhill from her, so we are actually at eye level with each other. We breathe into each other. Our mouths are hovering over each other but not crossing the line.

Millie leans forward, her pink lips so close to mine. I want them. It doesn't matter that we haven't found the waterfall yet. It doesn't matter that I'm not in control. What matters is that we want to kiss.

"Kiss me," she whispers.

"Are you begging, Mills?"

Her lips part, and her tongue slides through, licking her bottom lip, making it perfectly clear what she'd like me to do.

I swallow hard. This is what I wanted. I wanted her to initiate. I wanted her to beg. I wanted her to want me. To want to be kissed. To want to be fucked.

"Yes, just like your body is. Your lips have parted. Your breath has caught. You've leaned closer. Caught us both entirely out of breath so that we can't think and stop this. We are both begging—now kiss me," she says.

Suddenly, I spot the waterfall trickling behind her through the trees. I grab her hand and yank her in that direction.

"What are you doing?" she squeals. "Sebastian, I'm tired. I don't care about the damn perfect waterfall, just—"

She gasps when she sees the sight. It's the most beautiful, magical vision. I never knew things like this existed in real life. It looks completely untouched by mankind even though a trail leads right to it. Not very many people have ventured four hours through the steamy jungle to see the simple flow of water over a cliff into a small pool of water surrounded by flowers and greenery that seem to only exist in Hawaii. I've never seen anything like it.

"It's—," Millie breathes in, trying to find the right words to describe how incredible it is, but I don't give her time to think. I want to give her the perfect kiss. Partially because I want to spark her to search for her own happily ever after again, but also because I want to be her best first kiss. I want her to compare all men to me. I want to be impossible to top, so that when a man finally tops it, she can know he is the real deal.

A kiss by a man who truly loves her doesn't need to be done near a waterfall in Hawaii, the best kiss of her life just needs to be given by a man who loves her. He can kiss her by a dumpster filled with rotting fish and sewage, and it will still be the best damn kiss of her life.

I grab her neck, my thumbs caressing her jawline, and before she catches her breath, I close the gap, and our mouths meet for the first time that either of us remembers.

I forget about where we are. I forget about the waterfall. The sweet scent of the flowers. The beautiful roar of the water.

The seconds our lips touch, I'm consumed by her—her smell, her taste, her touch. It overpowers everything else. All I can feel is her.

She smells like juniper breeze. She tastes like strawberry jam. She feels like heaven in my arms.

This was supposed to be the best damn kiss of her life, but it's quickly becoming mine. I've never had a kiss like this—one that literally took my breath away, along with all of my thoughts and senses.

I don't know what is going on in Millie's head, but I hear the moans she's making, her hands digging into my chest, pulling me tighter against her, our hips slamming together. Her tongue begs for more in my mouth, and I give it to her. Our tongues glide over each other's in a teasing dance.

This kiss has to end before I yank all her clothes off and fuck her in the middle of the rain forest. That might sound romantic as hell, but I doubt when we have splinters and poison ivy and ticks, it will still feel that romantic. I want Millie in a proper bed—my bed. I want her in that heavenly bed back at our hotel.

I pull away before she realizes the kiss is over, and I watch for a split second where her lips kiss the air between us wanting more.

Her eyes flutter open, slowly coming back to reality.

I'm still stuck in the fantasy. *What the hell was that?* There is no way that was normal. A kiss like that is a once in a lifetime kiss.

"Was that…?" I ask, even though I have no idea what I'm asking.

"Hmm," she says back, oblivious that my question made no sense.

We both take deep breaths, still pressed against each other everywhere but our lips. I'm not big on kissing. It's just a prelude to the fucking, but Jesus effing Christ—I think I've been wrong all my life. That kiss flipped my heart upside down. It wrecked my soul. It made me harder than I've ever been. It was more than just a tease—it was the whole show.

Yes, I still want to fuck her, but I'm more than satisfied just kissing her.

Millie is the first to actually articulate her thoughts into words. "If you kissed me like that back in Vegas, then it's no wonder that we ended up married. How could I let someone who kisses me like that go?"

She's so bold with her words, so Millie. I'm thankful, because it reminds me that I can't let her fall for me. I have to be a little cruel. I have to be a bit of the asshole I'm supposed to be. I have to keep her feelings out of this. Just remind her that perfect kisses exist. That love can exist if both people believe in it. I just don't.

I snicker. "Don't go getting soft on me, Mills. I made you climb a mountain to earn that kiss. I didn't kiss you until you begged."

She steps back, and I step forward. I grab her hips, pulling her tightly against my steel cock. "And I won't fuck you until you open your pretty little mouth to me, get down on your knees to worship my cock, and plead with me to enter you."

"Asshole," she curses when I release her.

"Tease," I curse back. But Millie is anything but a tease. She's the whole package. And I think for a moment that I'm wrong in trying to push her into dating again, finding a man again. No man could be worthy of her.

She glares at me, but there is a softness to her eyes when she looks at me. She knows I'm acting mean to keep her safe, to keep her from falling for me. I look away, needing a moment to think about my next move...

"Son of a bitch," I yell as something stings my neck.

"Don't move," Millie says so calmly and sure.

I freeze. Well, everything but my heart freezes. My heart pounds a million miles a minute in my chest, still dreaming about that damn kiss. I know I'm in danger. This special moment is over, but all I can think is, *why did I stop kissing her?*

1 8

MILLIE

MY HEART TEETERS on the edge of so many feelings. The hurt I felt after he acted like a grade-A asshole. The fear I feel at watching what he just stumbled into. And yet the strongest emotion is still tied to that kiss.

I've been kissed before, but not like that.

That kiss was jaw-dropping, inside turning, a let's ride off into the sunset on our white horse kind of a kiss. I can't even figure out why the kiss was so incredible. He had great technique, sure. The spot he chose to kiss me was magical, the most beautiful natural place I've ever seen, and I've traveled the world. But we were also exhausted, sweaty, and sunburnt. We don't like each other, we hardly know each other, and yet...

I want a repeat. I want him to kiss me again and again.

He's kissed me before, but somehow I forgot. I don't know how that's possible when I know that I'll be thinking of this long after Sebastian and I get divorced and go our separate ways. That kiss renewed my hope in humanity, in love.

It shouldn't. Sebastian King doesn't do love. Neither do I. Yet it felt like the universe was trying to tell us something with that kiss.

I'm horny as hell and haven't gotten laid in forever. That's it. We

322

just need to fuck, and then we will be out of each other's systems. But no more kissing; kissing is dangerous. Kissing caused my heart to flutter—a heart I thought I'd locked away and protected with castle walls, a draw bridge, and a moat. I didn't think anyone, especially Sebastian King, had a shot at getting through, and yet, my heart did strange things during that kiss.

Focus.

"Son of a bitch, that hurt," Sebastian says, slapping his neck again.

"Don't move."

"Millie, what's going on?"

Sebastian huffed off because he was a jerk after our kiss. A kiss that affected him just like it did me. A kiss that caused him to lash out to avoid either of us getting feelings. A reaction that caused him to not realize that his foot is stuck in a fallen beehive. The bees he has thoroughly pissed off will come at him hard as soon as he removes his foot.

I have to remain calm though, I don't want him to panic and take a misstep and fall over the cliff a few feet behind him.

"Sebastian, are you allergic to bees?" I ask.

"No, I don't think so."

I nod. "Good. You're standing on a beehive, and when you lift your foot, they're all going to come after us. I'm going to count to three, and then we're going to run as fast as we can. Understand?"

His eyes are big as he nods.

I swallow down my fear. Bees are harmless; they don't usually attack unless threatened, but we just threatened a whole bunch of them.

"One…two…three!"

We immediately sprint as fast as we can while a swarm of angry bees lurches out of the hive. We run through trees and jump over bushes to get away as fast as possible.

I know we have to get to the water. That's our best chance of avoiding more stings, but we are at the top of the waterfall. We have to climb down. We have to—

"Jump!" I shout at him.

"Are you crazy?"

"We have to."

"We could break our necks! Why are we jumping?" He slaps his legs as more bees sting him.

He's right. I shouldn't risk his life to save mine. *Think!*

The bees are getting closer. Stay calm; they won't hurt you if you stay calm.

Sebastian looks at me closer. "Millie, are you allergic?"

I don't answer. We are miles away from civilization. It doesn't matter if I'm allergic or not. What matters is that I make sure Sebastian is okay. He may not be allergic, but the number of stings he's getting can't be good for anyone.

"Millie?" he asks again.

"Let's climb down around the side and get you into the water where the bees can't get to you."

"Jesus." His eyes peer over the edge, and then before either of us can think about what he's doing, he's grabbed me by the hand, and we are both jumping over the waterfall and into the pool of water below.

I scream as our bodies fall, having no idea how deep the water is. It's thrilling and dangerous, and exactly who Sebastian thinks I am.

We hit the water, our hands coming apart on contact. My legs hit the floor too fast, but not enough to break them or seriously hurt me. Sebastian is taller and heavier, so he hit the bottom before I did.

We both break the surface, breathing fast.

"There is never a dull moment with you, is there, Millie?"

I laugh nervously. "Nope, my life is just one crazy adventure after the next."

He laughs with me, finding my hand in the water and pulling me to him.

"Are you okay? Your foot—"

"Is fine," he finishes, taking my face in his hands as we continue to pant. Apparently, neither of us are ever able to catch our breaths around each other.

"Why did you stay when a single sting from one of those bees could have killed you?"

"You were in danger. I couldn't leave you."

"You should have run."

"You shouldn't have jumped."

I let my hands roam his face and neck where I see a few red bumps, but the bees seem to have vanished like I thought they would when we jumped into the water.

Sebastian thinks I'm wild—I am, but not in love. In love, I don't take risks, not anymore. I don't risk anything with a man. But for a second, I risk it all.

I grab Sebastian's neck and pull us together as our mouths connect. Open, raw, rough—we devour each other. Our first kiss was perfect, sweet, magical. This kiss is hungry, carnal, and intimate.

The water pushes us closer together, smashing us together until I can feel all of him. Everywhere I touch is hard—his chest, his arms, his cock. All of him is muscle and man. All of him begs me to touch him.

I forget about the consequences. I just want him. This is pretend; this isn't real. But for a moment we had a very real moment. We risked our health for the other, and that brought us closer together. It turned the tables and made me want him.

I shouldn't. This is when I should demand he be a jerk. When I should turn wild and crazy. This is when we should ensure that we are our worst because we are vulnerable. Our hearts are open after the beautiful moment we just had. And hearts are designed to fall in love and then break.

I vowed I wouldn't let that happen again.

And yet, here I am kissing Sebastian like he's my real husband. My body is sliding up and down his, humping him in the water, begging him to remove our clothes and take me right here, right now.

"Sebastian," I breathe through the sloppy kiss, one that fires through my body and practically makes me come. *Jesus, it's been too long. That's all this is. Too long since I've been fucked. I don't feel anything else.*

"Mmm," he moans back, unable to detangle his mouth from mine. His hands slide up my body under my shirt, moving so close to my breasts.

Yes.

Yes!

Just a little closer...

When suddenly, he's gone. He's no longer kissing me. He's no longer feeling me. No longer seconds away from taking me in this pool of water.

I open my eyes.

"Why did you stop?" I ask, afraid he's come to his senses and no longer finds me attractive.

"I'm not going to fuck you for the first time either of us remembers in this freezing pool, with me covered in bee stings, and you risking your life being out here where you could get stung."

I shiver, realizing how cool the water is for the first time. He's right. We shouldn't fuck here. But hiking back four hours to get back will seem like an eternity.

I pout.

He chuckles. "We don't have to hike the four hours back. There is a thirty-minute hike to where we can have a car pick us up."

"Thank God!"

He laughs harder. He holds out his hand, and I take it as he helps me out of the pool.

He hisses when he steps out. For the first time, I see the damage of jumping into the water caused him. His ankle is swollen and bruised.

"Sebastian, your ankle, I'm so sorry. I shouldn't have made you jump."

He turns and shakes his head. "And I shouldn't have put you at risk in the first place." He tucks a strand of hair behind my ear.

"Let me help you create a makeshift brace or something to make it easier to walk."

Sebastian brushes me off. "I'm fine."

Just like that, he's back to being cold with me except when we are being intimate.

"Ouch," I wack my neck after something sharp hits me.

I don't think twice about it. I'm too busy thinking about Sebastian and how to get him to stop being so hot and cold. I know I wanted him to be a jerk to me to protect my heart, but…

"Millie." Sebastian's voice drops, and the twinkle in his eyes is now replaced with absolute fear.

I don't know what he's so afraid of.

Then the burning on my neck hits me. Already, I can feel my tongue swelling, my throat closing. I know better than to travel without my epi-pen. But when I'm around Sebastian, I forget everything but him.

"Fuck," I say, knowing that might be the last word I ever say. We are thirty minutes from a road. Thirty minutes from cell phone service. I'm about to swell up bigger than Sebastian's ankle.

I take a shaky breath. At least I'll die having had the perfect first kiss, and the dirtiest second kiss. I'll die without having my heart broken again.

19

SEBASTIAN

MY NIGHTMARE HAPPENED. The thing we were trying to prevent—
Millie got stung.

I realized it before she did. I tried not to react, hoping that if I
kept her calm, then she wouldn't actually feel sick. But I'm not a
good enough actor to hide my fear.

Now Millie is standing in front of me, gripping her neck. I know
how bad her neck stings. I have small bites all over my body that all
burn. But unlike her, my entire body isn't swelling up.

"What do I do?" I ask, knowing that time isn't our friend. I have
to get her help.

"Get us somewhere where we can call 911," Millie says so calmly
like she's just telling me directions to drive to her favorite diner—
not giving me instructions that can save her life.

I nod. "The road is close from this direction." I pull out my cell. I
don't have any service, but I should once we get a bit closer to the
road.

Millie takes a breath, and it's already garbled. I can hear the
wheezing, the struggle to breathe.

"What else?"

She shakes her head gently, giving me a fake smile that's meant to reassure me. but I see right through it. "We take our time walking toward the road together. There is nothing else we can do."

"How long do we have?"

"We'll make it," she gives me a wink.

"Yea, we will." I grab her hand and drape it over my back. "Climb on."

"Sebastian, your ankle. You can't carry me."

"Millie, climb on my back right the hell now."

She does. She may be wild, but my voice can tame her. *Good to know.*

And then I start running.

"Sebastian, slow—" Her voice catches, and she struggles to get any more words out.

"Do not tell me to slow down because I won't."

She doesn't ask me again. I run down the mountain through the trees and branches that have fallen on the path. I don't feel my ankle as I run. All I focus on is Millie, listening to her breath and hoping that I can run fast enough to save her.

I've saved people before, but never have I felt such urgency, such responsibility and need to save someone. If I fail, not only will the world lose an incredible woman, but I will never be the same. Losing Millie would be like losing a piece of me.

"You shouldn't have—" Millie takes a deep breath while I hang onto her every word.

"…stopped kissing me."

I laugh. "Are you trying to make a joke?"

She nods against my neck.

"Well, it's a horrible one."

"You," she takes a broken inhale. "Then," she exhales painfully.

"If you didn't want to fuck me, you should have just told me no. You didn't have to fake almost dying." My joke sucks worse than hers, but I hear the faintest chuckle behind me. It made her smile.

I need to keep talking. I need to distract her from whatever pain she's feeling.

"I'm going to try and guess why you wanted to stay fake married to me since you won't tell me and there is no way those Kylie Jenner sized lips are going to tell me now."

More chuckles, but these ones are softer.

Keep breathing, baby. Don't die on me.

I keep running as I think of the most ridiculous reasons I can think of.

"You have to be married to inherit an English estate."

Laugh.

"You are a princess in line to the Monaco throne and are trying to live a normal married life before being forced to marry a prince."

Laugh.

"You're secretly in love with me and think you're going to make me fall head over heels before our six months together is up."

She laughs, but it's barely audible. It deflates me. I have no jokes left in me.

You're running from something and need me to protect you.

The guess has floated through my head before, and right now, it seems like the most plausible.

Millie makes a sound, but it doesn't sound like anything I've ever heard before, and I've heard countless people on the edge of death before. Most of those people wanted to die, but the sound Millie makes is a cry to live. If she had use of her voice, it would be a warrior cry instead of the soft moan of a woman whose body is swollen and making it impossible to breathe.

The sound tells me time is up. I have to get her to a hospital as quickly as possible.

I pull out my phone—one bar.

I dial 911 and then hold it to my ear.

"What's your emergency?" I hear on the other line.

"My fr—wife was stung by a bee, and she's having an allergic reaction. We are hiking near Waimoku Falls and are headed to the road. We are less than five minutes away and need an ambulance."

"Okay, sir. I have an ambulance on its way. Is she walking on her own?"

"No, I'm carrying her."

"Is she breathing?"

I feel the heat of her breath against my neck.

"Barely."

"Okay. Keep monitoring her breathing. If she stops breathing at any point, I need you to communicate to me what is happening, and I can walk you through steps to clear her airway and give her CPR until the ambulance arrives."

"Okay," I breathe back, hating how easy it is for me to breathe and how hard it is for her to breathe. If I could give her all my breaths right now, I would.

But all I can do is keep running forward and hope I make it there in time. *So close.*

I run faster.

Then I see the road. I hear sirens in the distance.

"We made it, Millie. We made it," I say out of breath from running.

The ambulance roars to a stop in front of us, and the paramedics jump out, racing to take Millie from me and put her on a stretcher. One of them stops in front of me.

"You riding with us?"

"Yes, I'm her husband."

He nods, and I follow him into the back where they've already loaded Millie into the ambulance and begun working on her. She has an oxygen mask on and an IV in her arm.

The second the door shuts, the ambulance starts flying.

"Is she...?" I ask one of the paramedics who is administering medicine through her IV.

"My job is to get her to the hospital alive, and I will. You'll have to talk to a doctor about her long term prognosis."

I nod and don't ask any more questions as we drive. Millie's hand is within reach, so I take it and hold onto her, giving her all of my comfort and hope.

"You got this, Millie," I whisper.

We arrive at the hospital, and the doors fly open. I hop out and curse when my foot hits the pavement, but I don't give a damn about my foot. All I care about is Millie.

The paramedics pull Millie out on a gurney and then pass her off to a team at the hospital. I try to follow through the doors when a nurse stops me.

"You'll have to wait here," she says.

"But I'm her husband." I hold up my hand with my ring like I need to prove that I'm her husband or something.

She nods. "Come with me."

I follow her, and then suddenly she stops outside a door. "Sit on the exam table, and I'll have someone examine your foot."

"My foot is fine; my wife isn't. I won't leave her."

"Get your ass on the table so I can set your foot quickly while the ER docs look over your wife. They won't let you in the room anyway, and you won't be any good to her with a broken ankle."

"My ankle isn't broken."

She raises her eyebrows. "I'm fifty-three years old. I've been doing this a long time. I know a broken ankle when I see one. I know you want to be with your wife, so give me twenty minutes to set it and put it in a cast to heal it until you have an orthopedic doc take a look. Or you can be stubborn, in which case I'll make you wait for a doc to look at it, which could take hours before you see your wife. Now, which will it be?"

I frown, ready to argue.

"Twenty minutes. I promise I'll get you to your wife as soon as they will let you see her."

"Fine." I step inside the room, trying to prove to her that my ankle isn't broken, but there is no hiding it.

I sit on the table and let her quickly put my foot in a cast.

"Do you want pain meds?" she asks.

"I'm an alcoholic and drug addict. No, I don't want drugs."

She nods. "Wheelchair?"

I hop down, giving her my answer.

She smiles at me. "I'll have some crutches brought to her room. Follow me, and I'll take you to your wife."

Luckily, Millie is just in the room over. I can't breathe though when I see her hooked up to so many tubes and IVs. She even has one shoved down her throat.

My nurse takes the chart and looks it over quickly as the other nurses and docs are still working on Millie. She looks from the chart to the machine with her vitals and then squeezes my hand. "Your wife is going to be okay, thanks to you. Now, go hold her hand until we get her moved up to another room."

I nod, choking back tears and words, and then I go to Millie. When I squeeze her hand three times, I swear I feel her squeeze back three times. That's all I need to know that everything is going to be okay. We are going to make it.

I look down at her hand. I have no idea how I'm going to let go of her hand in six months.

20

MILLIE

SEBASTIAN SQUEEZES my hand three times. He doesn't know the meaning; at least, I don't think he does. But he saw Oaklee and me do it. He's letting me know he's here for me. He's letting me know that he cares more than any words he could ever say.

I smile inside even though I can't show him what it means to me that he's here, that he saved me. Not only that, but once he saved me, he stayed. He didn't leave. He stayed.

I try to squeeze his hand back, but I feel so weak that I barely moved my fingers at all.

"I'm here; it's going to be okay. I'm here."

Those words stayed with me while I dreamed. I wish I dreamed of my future. Instead, I dreamed of my past. Even dreaming about a future without Sebastian would have been better than reliving everything.

My dreams didn't take a different form. I didn't dream of a bright light or falling or clowns or whatever it is that people dream about that is a metaphor for their real fear. No, for every second that I was unconscious, I relived every heartbreak, every mistake, every drop of pain my life has contained.

It gives me motivation to open my eyes even faster, to get away

334

from my past and live my present, even if my future is back to reliving my pain.

I open my eyes, afraid that Sebastian is gone. That I dreamed Sebastian King up. Or that once I open them, I'll remember he's nothing more than an egocentric ass, who is only in this relationship to get laid.

I open my eyes, and I see him. He's sitting in a chair next to my bed, slumped over face first on the edge, drooling onto my pillow, making the softest most adorable snores. He looks exhausted, even though he's sleeping. I can tell by the ways his eyes are twitching, his mouth is moving, and the adorable yet painful soft snores he exhales. What catches my breath, though, isn't the broken man, it's that he's still holding my hand.

"He hasn't let go," a woman says.

I glance away from Sebastian to the other side of my hospital room, where a nurse is pressing on the monitor next to my bed.

I'm surprised these are the first words she says after I woke up. She didn't ask me how I'm feeling or tell me a doctor will be in to check on me soon. *No—she needed to tell me about Sebastian.*

"I'm Rebecca, one of your nurses."

I smile weakly.

"You have a good hubby there. He hasn't left your side. Hasn't let go of your hand. I had to force him to get a quick cast put on his ankle. And the only reason I've been able to get food or coffee in him is if he can eat it one-handed."

I look away from her and back at Sebastian. He's too good. He shouldn't have stayed, at least, not like that. He should have gone back to the hotel to sleep and checked in on me during normal visitation hours.

I study him closer, looking at the bee stings that speckle his arms, neck, and cheeks. They're now covered in a lotion to reduce swelling and itching. I try to glance over the bed to see his ankle, but I can't with the way the bed is situated.

"I'm sorry your honeymoon was ruined, but if I can give you a piece of advice, don't let this ruin your relationship. He's a keeper."

She winks at me and then leaves without checking on any of my vitals or asking me any questions. *Does that make her a terrible nurse or just skilled at sensing what people need?* Because right now, I just want a moment alone with Sebastian.

I run my hand through his fluffy hair that still is coated with saltwater and sand from our dip in the pool.

"This didn't ruin anything. If anything, it stopped me from doing something stupid that I'll end up regretting." A kiss is intense enough. If I let this go any further, there is no way I'd survive it; no way I wouldn't fall for him. And me falling for handsome men like Sebastian King would ruin me.

Sebastian's eyes open. I don't know if he heard my confession or not, but when he looks at me, really looks at me, with all the emotion in the world, my confession doesn't matter.

I want to jump his bones.

"Mills, you're awake."

I nod, realizing that I still haven't spoken out loud to him.

"Thank God." If my heart wasn't a crumbled mess before, it is now. He climbs up into the bed next to me, cradling me against his chest as we both exhale a deep breath. For a split second, this feels real. Like it would have really mattered if I had died, and wouldn't just be an inconvenience he had to deal with.

The way he presses my head against his heart, I know that he'd mourn me far longer than any other acquaintance.

What does that mean? Does he have feelings?

He can't. He's already said he doesn't feel things like that. And we haven't known each other long enough to catch feelings. Being in a hospital like this just does something to people. No matter what, it would have been traumatic watching me swell up like a balloon, about to die at any second.

But the reality hits me, and I feel tears in my eyes. Our life may only stay connected for six months, but I will forever owe my life to him. He saved me. He ran on an injured ankle to save me.

"My superman," I whisper, blinking back my tears.

He pulls away; his expression falls into one of twisted agony.

"I'm not your superman. I'm the arrogant playboy who just wants to get into your pants. Just ask the nurse, I hit on her earlier."

I take a deep breath. "Jerk." Even though he's the farthest thing from it.

"That's me, sweetheart." His knuckles brush over my cheek. "I can't wait to get you back to the hotel to play doctor and nurse." The twinkle returns to his eyes.

This is who he thinks he is. Or maybe this is what he thinks I need per our arrangement.

But something changed here in Hawaii. I saw a portal to a different side of him. I saw the man willing to go through hell to save me. No man has ever done that for me before.

Sebastian tries to pull away, to climb off the bed. I know once he does, that he'll go back to pretending. That's all we do with each other—pretend. I just don't know when we are pretending and when we are being real.

He doesn't fight me as I pull him back. He doesn't touch me either, though. I don't need him to touch me. I need to look at him. I need to thank him.

I try to stare into his eyes when I say the words, but my eyes fall to his lips, the part of him I need connected to me.

"Thank you." I don't say what for. I don't think he would accept me getting mushy on him right now. We are both in too vulnerable a state to go expressing anything genuine right now.

I think he's going to pull away again. I think the moment is over.

Then he gives me another shock. He fills the gap between us, his lips carefully sweeping against mine. I could almost not even classify it as a kiss, that's how gentle he's being.

For a second, our lips are just brushing as we both breathe in each other's souls. Somehow this is more intimate than either of our previous kisses. We aren't touching anywhere except our lips.

And then like lightning, we both strike at the same time. We each deepen the kiss, turning it into more than just a thank you, more than just a sweet moment of understanding that we can brush off.

This kiss hints at feelings that both of us promised we would never have. It breaks all the rules we set. This kiss isn't about remembering what lead us to be married. It isn't a gut reaction after a near-death experience.

This kiss is the realest thing in our fake marriage.

We separate, at least our lips do. But I stole a part of him with that kiss, and he stole a part of me. Which part, I'm not sure, but I'll never be fully alone again.

"Don't scare me like that again," he whispers so softly before kissing my forehead, a kiss that transfers even more of himself to me.

Then he turns and walks out the door for the first time since I arrived. The moment was too much for either of us to handle. I'm not sure what it means, but I know that whatever that was, it wasn't pretend.

And that scares the hell out me.

2 1

SEBASTIAN

I SPIN my wedding ring around on my finger. It's a type of ring I never thought I'd be wearing, and don't even remember purchasing.

It's still strange being married. And yet each time I've spoken to someone else—the nurse at the hospital, the waiter at dinner, the butler at the hotel—calling Millie my wife falls off my tongue easier and easier.

She isn't my wife, in any sense of the word. We haven't fucked. We've barely kissed. We know nothing about each other's history. And for the past week, we've hardly talked to each other except when necessary. We know a line was crossed that day.

Our first kiss toed the line.

Our second pushed us over.

Our third sent us tumbling over a cliff.

Not to mention our experiences rescuing each other from death. There is no going back. No pretending that I can just be her asshole and her my wild plaything.

Something was stirred in both of us that day, some emotion that neither of us thought we could feel. And yet, we did.

But over the last few days, we've squashed any feelings we've had. The day Millie was released from the hospital, we went to different sides of the hotel suite and stayed there. I didn't take care of her, and she didn't pamper me. It was an unspoken agreement. We didn't share a bed. We rarely ate dinner together. We both spent our days watching TV alone.

And it worked.

Now we can be in the same room and there are no longer any feelings, just sexual tension, exactly what I wanted.

"It's still raining. Doesn't look like we will get to enjoy the beach or go on any other adventures before we have to leave tomorrow," Millie says.

I stand from the couch on my good leg and hobble over without the help of my crutches. After Millie woke up, I eventually got my ankle x-rayed. As the nurse told me, it was broken. Several weeks in the cast and then physical therapy after is my future.

I stare, getting lost in the beautiful woman with the strawberry streaks in her hair, the freckles, and a single bee sting on her neck. I'd break my ankle all over again if it meant saving her. I'd break every bone in my body for her.

That doesn't mean I have feelings for her. It just means I don't want to see a woman like her get hurt when I can do something to fix it.

"I don't think we should go on any more adventures. The last one about killed us both," I joke.

She laughs. Apparently, no joke is too soon with her, which makes her even more intriguing to me.

"Probably not. I think Mother Nature is trying to tell us we shouldn't be together."

"Nah, it's just probably monsoon season or something."

She shakes her head slowly. "That's in the fall. It's spring. I talked with the concierge, and he said that before we came, they hadn't gotten more than a sprinkle in over a month. I think we are bad luck or something."

I take a deep breath, and all I get is Millie. I haven't been this close to her in days. I haven't gotten the honor of smelling her. Her scent is always a little different each day. Some days she smells like lavender, other days peppermint, sometimes like the ocean, and then sometimes it's sugar and spice. Today, she smells like fire, like spice, like want.

Millie is wearing jean shorts and a T-shirt, and I bet if I slipped a finger in her panties, she'd be wet. Maybe not because of me, but because sex is already on her brain.

"Actually, I think we should have one last adventure," I say.

She folds her arms in front of her chest and looks at me. "You can't be serious. It's raining. Your cast can't get wet. And I'm not taking any more chances that one of us gets hurt."

"We won't go outside. In fact, we won't leave this hotel. How much trouble can we get into if we don't even go outside?"

She raises her eyebrows as a glint of a smirk touches her lips. "This is us we are talking about. Somehow we ended up married, broke your ankle, and almost killed me. Anything is possible."

"True, but this will be worth it. We have one last night before we get back to reality. One night before we learn the truth about each other. Before we leave paradise. Before we start pretending that we're already over so people aren't shocked when we finally are. The small risk is worth one last awesome night." My chest tightens when I talk about us one day being over. We were never something to begin with, I remind myself.

"What do you have in mind?"

"We get dressed up in our finest clothes. Have a romantic dinner. See where things take us. Pretend for one day that we are a real married couple; that we are really on our honeymoon."

She opens her mouth to talk, but I press further.

"Pretend I'm not in this cast and that you didn't almost die. Pretend that we love each other because we both know love isn't actually in the cards for us. We are in the most beautiful place in the world, in one of the most expensive hotel rooms, and we are two of the hottest people in the world."

She blushes at that. "One night?" Her eyes light up, telling me she knows exactly what this means. We are using our one night, our one redo—tonight. This is it, there won't be a repeat. If we are going to live together, we need to get this out of our systems. Tonight should be the night. We won't get a better setting.

"One night," I answer her.

Her eyes rake up and down my body in heated waves, even though I'm only wearing boxers and a ratty T-shirt. Even though I smell and haven't showered in two days, I can tell she'd let me fuck her right here right now if I just said the word.

But I want tonight to be perfect. If we only get one night together, I want it to be the best fucking night. A night that we will never forget, unlike last time. And if we are really lucky, it will trigger the memories of that night too.

I flick a piece of her hair back off her shoulder, the only touch I allow myself for now. "Go shower, do your hair and makeup, wear your nicest dress and your sexiest lingerie." I wink at her when she's about to protest the lingerie part.

"Go," I push her in the direction of the shower. Luckily, there are two bathrooms, so we can both get ready at the same time. I hope she gets dressed slowly because I have an unforgettable night planned.

22

MILLIE

MY HAND SHAKES as I try to run my eyeliner over my upper lid, resulting in a wavy line.

Fuck.

I put the eyeliner tube down and pick up some Kleenex to wipe it off, but all I do is smear the black liner everywhere. I toss the Kleenex in the sink. I'm going to have to use remover to get it off.

Instead, I grip the sink, knowing the problem isn't with my makeup, it's with me. I'm so nervous.

My hair is curled, and I'm wearing a simple black dress that dips down, showing off plenty of cleavage, while also hugging the curves of my stomach, waist, and hips. I feel sexy as hell in this dress, but only a man who likes plenty of curves will find me attractive. I'm not a stick-thin model. I have breasts, a waist, an ass.

Some men think that's what they want until they see me naked, and then they change their minds. Or they talk to me after about losing some weight, going on a diet, exercising more.

Sebastian has already seen me naked, though, and his eyes told me he had no complaints. It only strengthened his resolve to fuck me more.

He did mention me exercising more, but it had nothing to do with my weight, rather my stamina—that I can get behind.

I take a deep breath. This is about one night. He's not going to want to fuck me again after tonight. Those are his rules. He isn't trying to date me; he isn't trying to trap me permanently. It's just about one night of sex. One night where we are anything but ourselves.

One night to remember forever.

I stare at myself in the mirror. I'm a wild child. I don't do makeup or dresses. I don't usually curl my hair or wear heels. In fact, I had to call down to the gift shop to see if they had any. Luckily for me, they had one nice pair of black strappy heels.

This isn't me, I say to myself as I look at half of the makeup and curls in my hair.

Tonight it is. It only makes me want to dress up and wear more makeup. I want to impress Sebastian. I want his jaw to drop, his eyes to bulge, his heart to race frantically when he sees me. I want him to not be able to keep his hands off me. I want him to fuck me against the door because he can't wait until after dinner.

I take the makeup remover wipes and clean my face from the black smudges. Then I start again with a renewed sense of purpose. My hands don't shake this time. I'm in control. I'm going to look like a freaking goddess that he can't resist.

There is a gentle knock at the bathroom door twenty minutes later.

"There's no rush, just want to make sure you're okay," Sebastian says through the door.

I smile. It's been two hours since we decided on this plan. I've never spent this long getting ready before. I've also never looked hotter. Every inch of me has been shaved or waxed. My hair has never been this curled. My makeup is flawless. The dress is one of Oaklee's she slipped into my suitcase somehow. It fits too tightly, but that only makes it more perfect. I stand in the heels full of confidence. Tonight I won't stumble, I won't fall, I won't make a fool of myself. Tonight is going to be perfect.

I take my time walking to the door, for one to ensure that I don't stumble, and two because Sebastian's voice sounded just a little nervous, a little needy, and a little greedy. I like Sebastian King a little off-kilter.

I open the bathroom door. Sebastian is standing in the opening with a bouquet of exotic flowers in his hands. I don't notice his reaction right away because I'm too busy drooling at how well he wears a suit. I remember back to the wedding, how well his tux fit him then.

But this is one of his own suits, and it looks like it's been glued to his biceps, his stomach, his thick thighs. His hair is styled but not overly so. His beard has been shaved into perfect stubble. The only part of him that isn't completely perfect is the cast around his ankle and the crutches leaning against the wall behind him.

Finally, I notice his reaction, and it's nothing like I expected. I can't read him. It's like he's gone into shock or something. His expression is blank. His eyes are blank. His mouth doesn't drop open like I expected. He doesn't even move to hand me the flowers.

"Sebastian? Are you okay?" I try to hide my worry, but I can't. Not after everything we've gone through together. He could be having a heart attack or something for all I know.

He exhales and comes to life in a split second. "No, I'm not okay, but it has nothing to do with a stroke or whatever you must be thinking. It has to do with how incredibly beautiful you are, Mrs. King. How hard it's going to be to sit through an entire meal with you and not be able to touch you like I want."

I grin, pulling my bottom lip into my mouth. I don't think he could have said more perfect words to me.

"We don't have to go to dinner," I say.

He steps forward, not at all hobbling on his ankle that must throb every time he puts any weight on it. But the way his eyes shine as he watches me tells me he doesn't feel any pain. The only pain he feels is in having to wait to have me.

He holds out the flowers to me, and I take them, inhaling a deep floral breath.

"Yes, we do have to go to dinner." He reaches out and strokes the side of my face with his knuckles. "You're going to need your strength for what I have planned for you."

My eyes darken, and I have an insatiable ache between my legs. "I thought you only fucked women once?"

He shakes his head. "I said one night, not one fuck."

I suck in a shaky breath. *No, I will not let him affect me. I will not let him make me nervous.*

"Are you ready, Mrs. King?"

I nod. "Yes, Mr. King. The sooner we go to dinner, the sooner we can come back..." I let my hand trail down my chest, and he watches.

"Jesus, you're mean," he growls into my ear.

"You're the one who insists on dinner."

He clears his throat and then holds out his arm like a gentleman. I hook my arm through his, thankful to have his arm keeping me on my feet as I walk in heels for the first time in years. Sebastian is steady on his feet even though one is in a cast.

"You sure you don't need your crutches?"

"I'm sure."

Sebastian deposits the flowers in a vase he's already prepared, and then we are walking out of the room toward dinner. The anticipation is killing me; I can't wait until we walk back into the room after dinner.

It's only for one night. I have to remember that, because if I don't, I'm going to let Sebastian ruin me. I'm going to let him take my heart, and that can't happen.

Maybe it will help me remember what happened that night. Sebastian seems to think us getting married was my idea, but if he knew my past at all, he'd know that is the last thing I would ever suggest to anyone.

We head into the empty elevator, and Sebastian hits the button for one floor up where the restaurant sits.

Nervous tension fills the small space as the doors close. Every nerve in my body is shooting off, begging to be touched, begging to go back to the hotel room and fuck. Dinner is going to be a struggle unless I get a little taste first.

"Kiss me," I say.

He looks at me but doesn't move.

"Please, kiss me," I beg, my voice heady and needy.

I grab his neck, not giving him a choice, but his lips were already halfway to crashing down on mine. He tastes fresh, minty, and hot. My tongue licks over his, pulling the kiss deeper. My lust demands that he doesn't stop with just this kiss, tempting him until he can't resist me.

The elevator creeps up. *Please, get stuck. Please.* I don't need a bed. I'm just as happy getting fucked against the wall of this elevator.

But the doors do open on the top floor. Sebastian grabs both of my cheeks, pulling my face away to end the heated kiss. I breathe hard and fast, while he seems barely phased.

"Not fair," I whisper.

He chuckles quietly. His eyes glance down between us, and I follow his gaze until I see his hardness straining against his zipper. "Oh, Mills, I'm definitely affected. But I still want to have dinner with you first."

I shake my head. "You're supposed to be an asshole. I might just want to keep you as my husband, otherwise."

"Trust me, Mills. When I'm through with you, you won't want to keep me. But you might want more than one night with me," he breathes on my neck before taking my arm in his and leading me off the elevator like nothing just happened.

We walk side by side to the hostess stand.

"Mr. and Mrs. King," the hostess says without asking for our names. "I have the private room all ready for you. If you will just follow me."

My eyebrows shoot up. "Private room?"

Sebastian kisses the back of my hand. "Only the best for my wife."

We follow the hostess to an outdoor patio. Turns out the private room is an outdoor terrace with a small intimate table for two overlooking the ocean, romantic lights hanging overhead, and roses everywhere.

I blink back tears. "You did all of this for me?"

"I arranged it. I didn't actually decorate the space myself. Don't give me too much credit."

Sebastian pulls out my chair for me and then sits across from me. I try to catch my breath. No man has ever done anything remotely this romantic for me.

"Stop," Sebastian says with a grin. "This is all pretend, remember? Tonight we aren't ourselves. We are pretending to be married, so go all in."

"So you won't be yourself later? You'll be pretending to be good at sex, because if last time was any indication, it was very forgettable."

He chuckles in his deep and sexy way. The way that makes my stomach do somersaults.

I look around but don't find any menu. Our glasses are already filled with champagne.

"We're breaking our healthy vacation rule?"

"We're breaking all the rules tonight."

I blush. "And what are we eating?"

"Does it matter?" His gaze is heated and electric.

Nope, it doesn't matter at all.

My question is answered, though, as our waiter brings over some heavenly smelling bread. I don't do carbs very often, but I'm eating everything in front of me tonight.

"Welcome, Mr. and Mrs. King. Tonight, we are doing a tasting of the chef's menu created especially for you. Do you have any allergies or preferences I should be aware of?"

I shake my head, as does Sebastian.

"Excellent. Enjoy the bread and champagne. I'll have another course for you soon."

I hold up my champagne glass, and Sebastian mirrors me. "To breaking all the rules."

The corner of his mouth lifts in approval. And then we clink our glasses together before taking a sip, not breaking eye contact.

"So what are we going to talk about on this extravagant date that just prolongs what we both want?"

Sebastian's eyes light up. "We talk about who we wish we were."

"What if I'm perfectly happy with who I really am?"

"You're not. But even if you are completely content, there must be some part of you that you wish you could change. Something you've always wanted to try or do."

"Astronaut," I say immediately.

"That's hot. I'm married to a smart astronaut." He scrapes his teeth over his bottom lip and practically purrs at me.

"Yes, you are, and I'm about to leave on a mission soon, so we better make tonight a night to remember."

He laughs at my role-playing. I don't know why I said astronaut. It just sounded fun and as far away from my actual life as possible. "What about you, hubs? What's your story?"

His jaw twitches, and then he says, "Bartender."

I raise my brows up, and my grin stretches across my face. "Really? I chose something original, and you chose bartender?"

He shrugs and then sips his champagne. "Maybe I'm looking for something more ordinary. Or maybe I think bartenders are sexy, and you'll find me sexy if I'm a bartender."

"Well, you're in luck, I do find bartenders sexy."

Course after course comes out after that. I continue to pretend to be the nerdy astronaut, while he pretends to be the sexy bartender. Neither of us mention our real life. We keep that separate. He's right, it's fun to be someone else for a night under the stars with the ocean waves crashing in the distance.

But even with all the pretend, neither of us can stop thinking about what is going to happen after dessert is over. So much so, I'm starting to get second thoughts. Not about the sex, but about protecting my heart.

"I'm going to the restroom a minute," I say after I finish my dessert. Not because I have to go, but because I need some space to think.

Sebastian nods.

While I'm standing to go into the restroom, all the lights in the hotel go out. Suddenly, I'm standing in the darkness with only the moonlight lighting the small patio.

"Sebastian?" I ask. I can no longer see him, but I feel him move close.

"Don't think, just be."

Then his lips find mine in the darkness, and I forget about my doubts. I forget that I shouldn't be falling for him, and I just fall.

"Fuck me, Mr. King."

"Oh, I plan on it, Mrs. King."

The lights flicker back on at our declaration. Then we race to get back to our hotel room. As much as I'm okay with fucking him on the balcony or in the elevator, we both still prefer the bedroom.

23

SEBASTIAN

I SHOULD HAVE HAD us eat dinner in our hotel room. There is no way we will make it the one floor down before I devour her. Her taste is so addicting, more addicting than any drug I've ever taken.

I know I have to be careful with her, but I crave sex, I demand all of her.

I saw the doubt in her eyes before she got up from the table, thank goodness for the darkness to give me a chance to change her mind. If she turned me down tonight, I'd go insane. I need her more than I need oxygen. She's my sole focus.

Millie slams against me while the elevator doors close. My ankle throbs as I'm putting too much weight on it, but I don't care. I'd cut off my leg if it meant fucking her.

The doors open, and we keep our mouths locked, stumbling hard into the hallway wall opposite the elevator.

"Ow," Millie groans.

I bite her bottom lip, giving her an entirely different kind of pain to complain about. I'm rewarded with the most delicious moan that runs from her lips and hits me straight in the cock. These last few days together have been torture not getting to fuck her, but now, it's finally happening.

Millie pushes me away and then jumps into my arms, wrapping her legs around me. I grab her ass in my hands, thankful to have her in my arms. This will be so much easier to get her back to the bedroom as fast as possible so that I can have my way with her.

My ankle can barely hold my own weight, though, and her's sets me off balance entirely. I slam her back into the wall, trying to keep us upright.

She pants against my lips. "I need you, now."

Her words are enough to get me to fly. I don't know if I literally fly, levitate, or teleport us to the hotel room, but somehow we make it there in record time. I rest her back against the bedroom wall, not wanting to let go of her.

"God, you are the sexiest minx I've ever seen," I kiss down her face, over every ounce of caked-on makeup, as my hand rides up her thigh to grip her ass.

Our kisses are hungry and unstoppable. I kiss down her throat, begging it to make more intoxicating dirty sounds, but somehow, that gives her a second to think—a second to realize what we are doing.

"I—I can't," she says suddenly.

I stop kissing her neck but don't remove my hand from her ass.

I stare at her in the eyes. I'll honor her wish, if this is what she really wants, but I can see it's not because she doesn't want me. She's terrified.

The entire time I've known Millie, she's been the most confident person I know. But right now, she looks timid—like she wants to crawl into a closet and lock herself away from the world.

I think I know why, and it kills me. If she ever tells me the truth, I'm going to kill the bastard who made her feel this way.

But I'm not going to let the monster take away a moment meant to be pure ecstasy.

"Talk to me, Mills."

She bites my lip, and I know I'm not getting another word out of her.

"Do you want to fuck me?"

"Yes," she whispers.

"What's stopping you?"

Again there is a flash of doubt behind her eyes. "I won't hurt you," I whisper.

"I know, that's not it…"

She hugs her middle. She doesn't think she's enough.

Jesus, this woman is more than enough. She's more magnificent than any woman I've ever seen. She risked her life to help me. She took me on the craziest adventures. She got me to marry her somehow that night. I have no doubt that it was her that caused us to be husband and wife. At first, I wanted to yell at her for it. But now, I'm beyond thankful to her.

If she doesn't want to fuck me, then fine. But I refuse to let her think less of herself. I refuse to let whatever haunting words another man has said to her play in her head while I do nothing. If I do anything, I'm going to ensure that my words replace his.

Thunder rolls overhead, and I hear the pitter-patter of the rain pick up again. It had stopped momentarily during our dinner but must have started again. This time I don't curse the rain. I welcome it.

I tighten my grip on her ass. "Hold on."

I walk determinedly outside with her still in my arms.

"Sebastian! What are you doing?" she squeals as I throw the door to our balcony open, the rain immediately pelting us with its heavy drops. It won't take long until we are soaked—*perfect.*

"Sebastian!" She pounds her fists against my chest, trying to get me to let her go so she can escape the drumming rain.

I'm determined, though. Nothing is going to make me let her go, not until she understands something. I'm more determined to make her see the truth than I am to fuck her, which is the absolute oppo-site of how I should feel. I shouldn't be emotional about my fake wife.

Another crack of thunder sparks overhead, and I push those thoughts out and focus on my goal.

"Will you stop squirming?" I say.

"Will you get us back inside before we add getting hypothermia or struck by lightning to the list of things that have gone wrong on this trip?"

I smirk. "The odds of us getting struck by lightning are like a million to one."

She shakes her head, trying harder to get out of my arms. "No, not if you are outside on a high balcony during a thunderstorm. The odds are like one in ten."

I laugh. "Stop fighting me, and I'll tell you why we are out here. Only then will I let us go back inside."

She stops squirming and hitting me. I walk us over to one of the lounge chairs. I sit down with her straddling my lap, and then I take the sleeve of my shirt and wipe over her eyes.

"Stop! You're going to get my makeup all over you."

My eyes slice through the rain to her, telling her to stop fighting me.

She does.

I keep wiping until all the makeup is gone from her face. "You don't need this. You're the most gorgeous woman without it. You don't need to hide behind it."

I grab her ankles and remove each of her heels. "Just like you don't need these."

She sucks in a breath as I grab the back of her dress. "And you don't need this dress." I rip it open at the back but don't remove it. My point is made.

"Do you feel my cock?" I ask, knowing that she can feel how hard I am for her as she straddles my lap.

She nods her head slowly, heat flowing through her body, making her cheeks flush. I'm sure her panties are soaked, and not from the rain. But I won't push us any further than this unless she wants to, even if she gives me the biggest case of blue balls that have ever been recorded.

Her hands curl around the back of my neck, stroking my hair between her fingertips.

"You're smart and sexy and adventurous," I say.

She breathes in all of my words, considering them.

"Let go of all the words that hurt you. Let go of the past and just be present with me now."

She exhales sharply.

"You are the most confident person I've ever met. Don't let go of that version of you. That part of you isn't pretend, no matter how much you think it is. I've seen the confident, brave woman. The woman who risked getting stung by a deadly bee to help me. That woman isn't afraid of anything."

She bites her lip, and I think I've gotten through to her, even though I suspect I've ruined the mood. Fucking in the rain isn't nearly as sexy as it is in the movies. In real life, it's wet and cold and uncomfortable.

Her hands leave my body, and then she grabs the straps of her dress and slides them off her shoulders. Then her hands push the rest of the fabric down until it's bunched at her waist.

I can't breathe. My mouth falls open, and rain drips down my face blurring my view of her fucking incredible body.

"Fuck me, Sebastian."

24

MILLIE

SEBASTIAN KING IS A PLAYER. I know that. I know that he knows how to feed me lines to get me into bed.

But when he spoke, it didn't feel like a line. It felt like the truth. Maybe I'm naive, but I want to fuck him. I want this. I want to feel like his queen, if only for one night. So I push all my doubts and insecurities out of my head, and I let the confident, smart-aleck Millie take over.

"Fuck me, Sebastian. And this time, make sure I remember." I nip at his earlobe as I elicit a deep throaty growl in response to my demand.

I expect that he's going to take me here in the rain. I shiver, though.

"Oh, I will. But first, I need to warm you up."

He scoops me back in his arms, somehow not missing a step even though he's walking on a cast. A cast he wasn't supposed to get wet—*oops*.

He devours my mouth again as he carries me back inside. I've never felt this beautiful, this wanted. I don't know how Sebastian was able to read between the lines. *How was he able to figure out that*

I'm not this confident woman when it comes to men? Somehow, he did exactly what I needed.

He tosses me down on the bed and then walks calmly into the bathroom. I stare at his soaked ass and shirt clinging to his back as he walks. When he returns, his shirt is off. Water droplets cling to his sharp chest, and he has two towels draped over his shoulder.

I reach out to take one from him, but he shakes his head. I lay back in anticipation as he uses one of the towels to wipe the water from my face, then down my neck. I suck in a breath when he rubs the towel over my bra, my nipples hardening, wishing there was less fabric between us. I never realized that a man taking care of me like this is the sexiest thing a man has ever done for me.

I'm in heaven as he continues down my body, over my underwear, and then down my legs. My mouth runs dry as he finishes, then steps back and dries off his chest while never breaking eye contact.

I'm practically naked in front of him, in my bra and panties with my dress around my waist. I've flaunted my naked body in front of him before, but I've never felt this exposed. He sees beyond my flesh. He knows my fears and anxieties without me speaking them. I don't know how but him trying to take care of me makes this experience all the more incredible.

"Don't worry, Millie. When I fuck you, there won't be anything gentlemanly about it." He grins, and if my panties weren't already soaked, they are now.

And then he's undoing his pants and pulling them down until he's naked and glistening from the rain still against his skin. I try to keep my eyes from descending down his body, but I can't help it. And when I see his cock, I panic.

He's impressive. He's a sex god. He's charming, and I'm—

Sebastian leans down and kisses me, stopping me from finishing my thoughts. His tongue sweeps into my mouth, claiming me as his, causing my tongue to swell and my lips to tingle from his touch.

"Don't think about anything except that kiss."

My brain floods with images of that kiss. I burn the image, the taste, the touch, the feeling into my head. There is no way I'll forget this night.

I regret drinking those glasses of champagne during dinner. I don't want anything to impede my ability to remember.

"Strip," Sebastian says as he sits on the edge of the bed.

I sit up as his appreciative eyes travel down my body. I unhook my bra, immediately, letting the wet material fall to the floor. I know my boobs look good, but the rest of me has more curves than most men accept as beautiful. I let my dress and panties fall next, and then I hear Sebastian gasp.

"Come here." Sebastian hooks his finger at me as he lays back. I walk over to him, he grabs my hips, and then I'm straddling his face.

"I've wanted to eat you out since you strutted around naked after leaving the hot tub. I've been dying to know what you taste like."

I've never had a man eat me out before. I've never had a man go down on me. I've never had a man make me come from his tongue.

I should tell him. I tense. My thighs straighten, keeping his tongue from diving into my body.

His eyes flicker to mine—*he realizes the truth*.

"Tell me," he commands.

"What?"

"Tell me. Once you do, you'll be free of it. It will be just words. I'm about to devour you, and I sure as hell won't stop until you come. I don't care about the failure of men before me. I don't care if they were too dumb to taste you here. Too inexperienced to make you come. Say it so that you can be free."

"I've never had a man go down on me before."

"Good girl."

And then his tongue sweeps over my clit. It's like a shot of lightning through my entire body. I jolt at the explosive touch.

Sebastian grabs my thighs, keeping my body against his mouth as he hums lightly, adding vibration as he licks me.

I grab his hair, holding on as the pleasure intensifies. I never realized that having a man lick me like this could be so good. I lose my mind as he continues torturing me with his tongue.

My body tightens more and more with each lick, until my thighs are clenched around his head. I'm not sure he can breathe with me over him like this, but he doesn't seem to care. And I—I can barely think.

Please, remember this.

He changes everything when he pushes two fingers into my slit. I gasp as he fills me with his fingers. His tongue dances over my clit as he moans over it like it's the most delicious thing he's ever tasted.

"Sebastian," I whisper, suddenly going quiet. Everything stills for a moment, even the rain and thunder stops cracking.

I swear I can hear my own heartbeat. I can feel the blood flowing between my legs in gentle pulses. It's the quiet before the storm.

And then, the storm lets loose.

I arch my back, and my body convulses, rattling as an orgasm rolls through me like thunder. I yell out Sebastian's name as my body shudders.

"I've never felt…" I pant.

Sebastian smirks beneath me. "There is a reason they call me the king."

I laugh and blush before rolling off him. But he grabs my hip, stopping me from rolling all the way away from him.

"I'm not done with you yet, wifey."

My heart races when he calls me wifey, but I quickly shut it down. *This is just about sex, remember heart? Just sex. No feelings. Feelings lead us to get hurt.*

He rolls me onto my back as he grabs a condom and sheaths himself before settling between my legs.

"No man has ever made me come before—thank you." I like sex. I like it because it makes me feel powerful. It makes men weak. It makes men want me. But that's the only reason, not because it's ever felt this good for me.

He smiles at me with his crooked grin that makes him look like a boy instead of a man. "You're about to come twice in one night."

"Sebastian, I can't."

He growls at me. "You can—trust me."

I nod. I do trust him, and that's beginning to become a problem.

His thumb presses over my sensitive clit. There is no way I'm ready to come again. But Jesus, my body responds to that one touch. And then he's pushing inside of me.

"Holy fucking Sebastian," I say as he fills me to the brim.

He chuckles—it's deep and masculine and relaxes me. He pushes further in, stuffing me completely, and that's when I realize he's not all the way inside me.

"Kiss me," he moans as he lowers himself over me.

I kiss him. I focus on the kiss, letting it consume me. That is until he thrusts, and my body soars.

"You're mine, Mrs. King," he growls against my ear.

I've never liked being claimed. I'm an independent, modern woman. But when he goes all caveman like this, I want him to do it again.

"Say it."

"I'm yours, Mr. King."

"And?"

"You're mine." *At least for tonight.*

And then everything changes. He's no longer the gentleman; he's the king. He pounds into me like he owns my body. His thumb plays my clit like it belongs to him. His tongue dips into my mouth like it's our millionth kiss instead of our tenth.

Our bodies are like magnets, pushing and pulling together as Sebastian thrusts harder and faster. He demands everything from my body, not letting this be anything but incredible. My body is going to remember every thrust, every look, every moan. I'll remember it all because he burned it into my memory.

My body is sizzling with need, but I'm still greedy for more. I grab his ass, sinking him deeper inside me. He responds by pushing my legs back until there is no way he can thrust any deeper, until we feel completely connected to each other.

I feel the undeniable need to speak—to explain to him what he's doing to my body. To tell him how appreciative I am. But I can't form words. All I can give him is breathy cries and moans of pleasure.

"I know," he whispers over my lips before pulling them roughly into his mouth.

And then it happens. Sebastian's body goes rigid, my body explodes, gripping him harder than a vice grip, my orgasm pulses around his cock. It's an experience I've never had before. Sebastian gave me two unforgettable experiences in one night. *How will my heart survive letting him go?*

Sebastian resumes his rocking into my body. His growl is penetrating my broken heart and fills a spot in my soul as he releases his own orgasm.

I'm used to men who pull out immediately feeding me some garbage about how good it was and then falling asleep snoring moments later. Those men meant something to me. I expect even less from Sebastian, my fake husband.

What I don't expect is for him to stay inside me far longer than necessary, like he can't bear to pull out and end the intimate side of our relationship.

"Do you remember?" he asks, referring to the first time we must have done this.

I shake my head with heavy breaths.

"Me neither," he says, stroking my face. "Which is a damn shame, if it was anything like this."

I feel the same way. I'm sure our first round of sex was good, but I didn't realize until now exactly what I was missing out by not remembering. Now I do, and it feels like an enormous loss.

Sebastian pulls out, and as he does, a loud, ominous crack of thunder booms through us like Mother Nature isn't happy with our separation either.

Join the club, I think to myself.

Sebastian gets up and goes to use the bathroom, and I wait for my turn in it. There are two bathrooms in the suite, but all my stuff is in this one. I don't want to have to walk down the hall to the other one.

Sebastian stands over me just as I'm about to roll off the bed for my turn in the bathroom.

"Where are you going?" he asks.

"Bathroom."

He shakes his head. "You're not escaping that easily."

He grabs me by the midriff and pulls me back into bed with him. He has a washcloth, and he takes his time cleaning between my legs. Then he pulls my back to his front before draping us with the covers.

He's spooning me. This was the last thing I expected him to do.

My heart hammers as he holds me—somehow, this feels more intimate than the actual sex.

"Tell me about your darkness," he says into my hair.

And for the first time in forever, I want to.

SEBASTIAN

I FEEL Millie's heart racing against my chest as I hold her. Her breathing hasn't slowed, and she's still hot. It does nothing to help me regain my composure. Even after going to the bathroom and coming back, I still haven't returned to my normal in control state.

I've never felt anything like I did when I entered Millie. It was like I was coming home, becoming grounded in a way I didn't know was possible to feel with another person. She filled some part of me that I didn't know was empty.

And now I'm spooning and snuggling with her in bed—something I never do. I'm not doing it out of obligation. I want to hold her—all night or maybe even longer than that…

I want her to talk to me. I want to know what she's thinking. What she's feeling. What she desires. What she needs.

However, I know the most important place to start is her darkest secret, the man or men who hurt her. We are in our thirties. She should have had dozens of orgasms by dozens of men by now. She should have experienced a whole world of men. Instead, she found the assholes. No wonder she calls me that—it's her defense mechanism.

"Tell me about your darkness." I choose my words carefully. She can tell me anything. My words make no assumptions that her darkness is another man, but if I had to guess, it is.

A man she dated treated her wrong.

Her father abused her.

An uncle touched her.

Something happened that caused her to not be able to experience an orgasm with a man—until now.

I feel a strange, wicked pride knowing I was the man to end her dry spell, to conquer the darkness that she has yet to share with me. But I don't focus on that. I want to hear her. I want the truth.

This is completely out of character for me. Usually, I just bang women and send them on the way, usually the same night, definitely before breakfast.

But I crave every word Millie is going to say. I want her to want me, to need me, to let me help her. I shouldn't want to. It feels too much like therapy, like work. I'm not a therapist, but I might as well be because the work I do is therapy. But I never bring my work home. Until now.

I'm not sure I've earned her words yet, so it doesn't surprise me that she doesn't immediately spill all of the dark things that have happened to her. A real husband would already know, but I'm just the fake stand-in helping her escape her past.

I hold her in my arms, hoping it brings her enough comfort to talk. I've heard enough people spill their guts to know that the most important part is just being patient, just being there for her to open up when she's ready.

My fingers wander to her spine, and I trace down it, watching as chills roll through her body with a shudder, bringing life back into her.

"I'm here. I'll wait all night. And if that isn't long enough, I'll wait as long as it takes. Even if we aren't together anymore."

She sucks in a breath, like she's sucking in all my words and using them for strength.

I suck in a breath too because if she's about to tell me what happened, then I need to be prepared for the monster she is about to call out. And I'm going to want to kill that monster.

Millie is the most confident person I've ever met. At least, that's what she exudes. She's confident and adventurous and fun, but it's all an act. It may be who she wants to be, but it's hiding the truth. It's hiding the lack of confidence, the pain that someone caused her.

Maybe she's able to play so confidently because her darkness isn't that vast. Or maybe she's an actress in real life. Tomorrow when we head home, I'll learn who she really is—her job title, where she lives, what she does in the real world. But I don't care about any of that, because what we experienced here was the real us. The parts of us that matter, that we hide from the world. Hopefully, we can take more of these parts back to the real world instead of just having to pretend.

"I don't know if I could pin it on one moment or a series of moments," she starts.

And suddenly, I can't breathe. My mind goes to all of the darkest of places—she was raped, abused, tortured. I'm not going to survive her words.

"I've never had a particularly bad experience with men. Never had a man take things too far. Never been hurt by a man. Never been abused—nothing like that."

I exhale a breath and grip her tighter, like that will somehow protect her from ever being hurt.

I want to talk, to tell her to continue, but the silence is easier for her to fill if I don't. So I wait for her to continue. I'm patient, and eventually, she does.

"But I've never found a relationship that was particularly amazing either. Never found that once in a lifetime kind of love that people talk about."

I hang onto her every word, wanting to know more. I'm an excellent listener. I have all the patience in the world, but I've never struggled so hard to keep my mouth shut as I am right now.

"I thought I had found it. Numerous times, with numerous men. But each time, I was wrong."

I kiss her shoulder, rewarding her for talking, but she still hasn't told me anything specific. *I need details, Mills! I need to know whose ass to kick.*

"Every time I thought I'd found my happily ever after, something happened—a car accident killed the first man I thought I loved."

My heart breaks for her.

"I guess I became broken, numb to the world after that. With each man I was with after, I tried so hard to be perfect. I tried to have the perfect relationship, afraid that if I wasn't enough, it would be taken from me."

She cries, I feel her warm tears falling onto my arm wrapped around her front. Still, I don't let myself comfort her beyond holding her.

"I thought I was enough to keep them. I tried to be the perfect partner. I lost weight or gained weight to be beautiful in their eyes. I learned to cook fabulous meals and would be exactly what they wanted in bed. Sometimes I was wild; other times, I was innocent, adventurous, whatever it was they craved. But it was never enough to keep them. Eventually, they all left."

She sucks back a sob. I squeeze her as tight as I can.

Just get it all out, baby. Get it all out.

"I know I'm not good enough to be in a relationship. To get married. I would never make a good wife. And I can't handle any more heartbreak. But thank you for giving me a night where, for once, I felt worthy."

I can't take it anymore. She may not feel she was abused. But whatever these men did to her, it was borderline abuse. They wrecked her confidence. Destroyed her hope for a real relationship. And I won't have it.

I turn her toward me until we are lying on the pillow eye to eye. What I have to say is important, and I need her to start believing my words. It's the first step toward healing. I take her hands in mine.

"Millie, you weren't the one who failed in your relationships—they were. Those guys weren't worthy of you. Even the guy who died, he never even gave you an orgasm. That's not love. That's not romance. That's a man who doesn't realize your worth. Millie, you are incredible, and you would make an incredible wife someday if that's what you want. Don't let any man or any past relationship tell you differently."

My heart throbs as I speak. I could be that man. I could be the man who shows her her worth. Who values her above everything else. Who loves her.

Now that's just crazy, my mind reminds me. *You're a bachelor for life. Millie might make a great wife, but you would make a terrible real husband.*

"Do you hear me?"

She nods.

"Do you believe me?"

"Yes."

I kiss her sweetly on the forehead, but it's as much for me as it is to comfort her.

"Now, tell me about the man who keeps texting and calling you, the man you are afraid of. What of him?"

Her eyes flick to the phone on the nightstand like she just now thought of him, and I curse myself for bringing him up and ruining this moment, but I need to know. I need to know who she's running from.

"He's an ex."

"Did he hurt you?"

She shakes her head. "Trust me, it was me—not him that broke us up."

I frown. I know deep into my heart that it wasn't Millie who messed up the relationship. She's not capable of doing anything wrong, anything to make a man leave. But I know now isn't the time to argue.

"It's him you're running from, right? He's the reason we are going to be fake married for six months? So you can show him that you've moved on, and he'll leave you alone?"

"Yes," she breathes. "Will you help me?"

I pull her to my chest. "I'll do anything for you. If it means staying married for longer than six months, I'll do that too."

She shakes her head, but this time, I don't let her speak. I might just need this relationship to last longer than six months myself. Already, I can't imagine the pain at her leaving.

2 6

MILLIE

I can't describe how I felt. I can't describe how I feel now. I just can't...

It was beyond incredible. No man has ever fucked me like that—in a way that was both about fucking and, dare I say it, lovemaking.

Sebastian King fucked me hard and fast, but he also made love to my body, caressing and stroking it until I bent to his will. Until I wasn't in my head anymore. Until all I could feel were the thousands of tiny explosions dancing all over my body as I came.

I came—during sex with a man.

I thought I was incapable. I thought I just couldn't. I thought... well, I thought I wasn't worthy of an orgasm. That Mother Nature decided that because of all the fucked up things I've done that I would never orgasm with a man. It was the world's way of keeping me away from men because I wasn't good for them, and they weren't good for me.

But what if I was wrong?

What if I just hadn't found the right man?

There is a loud knock at our door. I squint my eyes open. I'm exhausted after our round of fucking last night.

369

The pounding doesn't stop. Sebastian must be a heavy sleeper because his naked ass doesn't stir at all.

I sigh and then grab one of the hotel's white robes before slugging to the door and opening it.

"Mrs. King, I'm here to take your bags down. The car is here to take you to the airport."

"Shit!"

"Mrs. King?" the young bellhop says.

"Um…give us five minutes."

"But the car—"

"Tell the car to wait."

I close the door gently in his face and then run back to the bedroom. I stop abruptly when I see Sebastian sleeping so peacefully stretched out on his stomach, completely naked in all his glory.

I bite my nails as I smile at him, remembering everything. I may not ever remember our real first time together, but there is no way I'll ever forget last night. I'll file it away to relive over and over and over and over again.

And hopefully, Sebastian is up for breaking his little rule—it's the least I can do to thank him for staying married to me a little longer.

But that's for later, right now we have to get to the car and to the airport.

"Sebastian," I grab his ankle and shake it, but it does nothing. He doesn't move.

"Sebastian!" I holler louder as I round the bed.

"Sebastian!" I yell even louder as I shake his back.

He turns and smacks me right in the nose.

"Jesus," I curse as my eyes water, and I see stars.

"Oh my god, Millie. I'm so sorry!" Sebastian jumps out of bed, and tries to access my nose, but I don't lower my arms.

"I'm fine. We have to go, though." My words are muffled as my hands cover my mouth and nose.

"Let me see," Sebastian says, gently touching my wrists.

Slowly, I lower my hands, and the look of concern on Sebastian's face intensifies. His eyes darken, his jaw twitches, his forehead wrinkles as his thumb traces the bridge of my nose.

"The good news is it doesn't look broken. The bad news is it's bleeding and most likely going to bruise."

"We have to pack. Our car to the airport is here," I say, sounding nasally, the taste of iron spilling onto my lip.

"First, you need to put some ice on your nose and eye." Sebastian heads to the kitchenette, hobbling on his cast, and I follow after, tilting my head back to keep the blood from dripping everywhere.

"Sit," he says.

I do, and then he hands me a bag of ice to hold against my face. I move to get up. "Stay," he says, blocking me from getting up.

"But we have to go."

"I'll take care of the packing. You take care of that nose."

I nod as a sneaking smile spreads. I don't know how Sebastian thinks he won't make a good husband someday. He's such a sweetheart.

After that moment, though, the rest of the day goes to hell. Our car leaves, assuming that we changed our flight, so we have to take a crowded bus that only had two seats left on opposite ends of the bus. We were late for our flight and had to change to a flight that flew through Seattle and then on to Los Angeles, which meant we didn't have first-class seats together anymore. Instead, we both sat in two middle economy seats on opposite sides of the plane.

By the time we landed, we had barely spoken to each other all day. We were crabby. And we hadn't talked about the future at all.

We had an agreement that we'd learn all there was to learn about each other as we flew back home. We'd tell each other the truth about ourselves.

Instead, we weren't even close enough to talk. And as we ride back in the back of a cab to Sebastian's house with his crutches between us, I feel like the high we were on before we left is gone.

The world is back to being against us.

The truths we are supposed to share, stay hidden.

I think back to the other part of the night—the part that was equally as special and memorable as the sex part. The part that was tender and kind and intimate. Sebastian looked into my soul and found the darkness.

He thinks the guys I've been with are the problems.

My phone buzzes, and I stare down at the text message from my ex.

Sebastian thinks the stalker is my problem.

"We're here," Sebastian says.

He climbs out and wheels his suitcase up to the elevator. I follow with my backpack. Once inside the elevator, there is no spark. Nothing moves us from the misery we feel. When the doors open onto the top floor and Sebastian leads me to a door, I hope everything will change once we get inside.

And it does, but not because Sebastian suddenly starts talking to me, but because I learn one truth about Sebastian. He's fucking rich. Like billionaire, I own half the town, rich. My mouth gapes as I follow him inside his apartment.

Now we are going to talk. Now is the time to discuss if we are going to have a conversation about who we are, if we are going to fuck again.

Which better be yes, because there is no way I'm going to survive living under the same roof as him if we don't.

"I'm beat, and I have a meeting at six in the morning I have to get to. There are two spare bedrooms, choose either, and if there is any food in the fridge, you're welcome to it. I'll give you the grand tour tomorrow after I get off work."

My mouth falls wider. *Is he serious? Are we seriously not going to talk? About anything?*

"Um…sure, I get it. I have to be up early, too," I lie. In fact, other than packing up a few items to bring over from my old apartment, I have nothing to do tomorrow.

"Goodnight, Millie," Sebastian says, not even looking back at me.

He's back to being the asshole that I thought was all a lie. In reality, this is who he is. The man who doesn't care once he's fucked a woman. The man who is now done with me.

I stomp down the hall to one of the spare bedrooms and collapse on the bed. My face is swollen, along with my feet from being in an airplane all day. My stomach rumbles, and my face is oily. I should shower, and eat, but the only strength I have now is barely enough to lift the comforter up and crawl under.

Sebastian's right to stay away from me, though. He thinks the men in my life were the problem in my relationships. He doesn't realize the truth—I'm the problem.

27

SEBASTIAN

MY ALARM WAKES me up at five-thirty. Like a robot, I go through my normal routine.

I put on my workout clothes and guzzle a glass of water. I meditate for fifteen minutes on my balcony before heading to my workout room. I spend ten minutes stretching, before forty-five minutes on the bike instead of the treadmill, the only change to my routine due to my fucked up ankle, and thirty minutes lifting weights.

I grab a second glass of water.

I shower.

I get dressed.

I make a cup of coffee and a protein smoothie.

Then I head out the door, using one crutch as I hobble along.

When I park at my office, I take a deep breath. My routine is so ingrained into my life that I didn't even stop to think about Millie.

Millie—my heart lurches in my chest, begging me to turn the car around and go after her. To find out how she slept last night. To feed her breakfast. To find out everything about her.

To fuck my routine.

Blow off work and just spend every waking second with her.

I want to learn what she does for a living. I want to tell her what I do. I want to ask all the questions I've been avoiding.

For a moment, I let the desire grow. I let myself think about that night. *Was that really only two nights ago that I was fucking her in a resort suite in Hawaii?*

Why didn't I fuck her every night? Now reality is going to get in the way.

Who am I kidding? Reality already got in the way the second we left for the airport yesterday. Everything that could go wrong, did. Maybe that was for the best, because if I'd sat with her in first-class and talked all the way home, I would have fallen for her. Just a little. Just enough that I wouldn't be able to push her out my head. Just enough that I would actually turn the car around and head back to her.

Instead, I've become an asshole again. I ignored her all night and didn't even wake her before I left. She's going to hate me, but it's for the best.

Just like it's for the best that I get back into my routine and go inside my office like nothing's changed. I'm the same man. I'll go to work and continue on with my normal life. I'm just helping a friend away from her ex—that's all.

I climb out of my car and grab my crutch—cursing it to hell as I use it to walk inside. I can mostly walk without the need of the crutch the way the cast was done, but the doctor told me to keep off my foot as much as possible would help it heal, so I'm trying to behave.

I hobble on my crutch inside the healing and rehab center where my office is.

"Oh my god, Sebastian, what happened?" Shelly, the receptionist, asks as I walk inside.

"Just a small accident while I was in Hawaii. I should be able to get the cast off in a few weeks."

"That must have ruined your honeymoon."

I pause. It should have completely ruined it, but after that night, everything changed.

"How is Mrs. King doing? Are you going to have a reception or a big wedding to celebrate?"

Jesus, what's with all the questions? I run my hand through my hair, the back of my neck perspiring a little as I think about how to answer her question.

"No, we liked the spontaneousness of the wedding. I don't think we will have a big reception or anything."

Shelly pouts. "You should. I'm sure your wife would love to have a big wedding to celebrate. And I want a chance to hook up with a sexy groomsman." She bats her eyes seductively at me. I know she doesn't mean anything by it; Shelly is like another sister to me.

"We'll think about it," I say to get away.

I frown as I hobble along to my office. The rest of my day will go better. Shelly is nosy, that's all.

However, news of my wedding and ankle spreads around the office until even patients are coming up to me congratulating me and wanting to hear the story of how I broke my ankle rescuing my wife.

Eventually, Shelly got me to spill, and then she blabbed to everyone until I eventually had to lock myself in my office to get any work done. My day is usually about answering emails, taking meetings, ensuring the staff has everything they need and are up to date about the latest techniques to help our patients.

I also handle the financials. We're a non-profit that helps people. My salary barely covers my car payment, not that I need it. My family owns a restaurant chain, several bars, and a few hotels. Money isn't an issue. And money wouldn't get me out of bed every morning anyway.

But by lunch, I've had enough. When another loud knock raps my door, I decide it's time to work from home the rest of the day. I can't handle any more questions about Millie. *How did we meet? How did I propose? How did I break my ankle? What does she do for a living?*

The questions are endless.

I hop on my one good foot to the door to turn away whoever is at the door. When I throw it open, I realize that I shouldn't have opened it.

Kade and Larkyn are smiling at me with knowing expressions on their faces.

"What are you two doing here?" I ask my brother and sister-in-law. Kade works in an office building uptown, taking care of the part of the business that makes money. And although Larkyn runs the non-profit with me, she doesn't usually come into the office but a couple of times a week, usually preferring to work from home where she can be near her kids.

"Taking you out to lunch."

"I was going to skip lunch and head home."

"To Millie?" Larkyn's eyes light up.

"No, my ankle is just killing me," I lie.

Larkyn frowns. "You should invite Millie to meet us for lunch. Where does she work? We can pick a spot where she can meet us."

"No," Kade says suddenly.

Both Larkyn and I snap our heads to him.

"We need to talk with just Sebastian," Kade says.

My brother and I exchange icy glances. Of all the people that I have to convince that my marriage is real, Kade is the toughest. He knows me better than anyone. He knows that all I've talked about for years is never wanting to get married.

And then all of a sudden, bam, I'm married. I know it's going to lead to some suspicions, and I'd rather be anywhere but at lunch with them.

———

"When did you and Millie start dating?" Kade asks me.

"Six months ago," I answer, lying through my teeth.

"Oh, it's so romantic. Why didn't you tell us you were dating and getting serious?" Larkyn asks.

"Because I knew you'd do this." I stare at my brother as I pop a bite of my salad into my mouth, challenging him to be different. To not criticize me, or say that my marriage is going to fail. That I'm not cut out for marriage. I already know all of this. I don't need my brother telling me.

Larkyn looks from me to Kade, completely oblivious to our battle of wills.

"We just want to know because we love you. Now, tell us about the honeymoon and the romantic way you saved her and ended up breaking your ankle," Larkyn asks.

I sigh and then go into the story of us hiking and how I ended up hurting my ankle before carrying her to safety.

Larkyn swoons, but Kade looks at me like he isn't buying it. He's not buying that I'm spontaneous, or adventurous, or married for that matter.

"Excuse me, I need to go the bathroom before we leave," Larkyn says, getting up from her wicker seat where we are sitting on the terrace of an upscale restaurant. She squeezes my shoulder. "You have no idea how happy I am that you found someone. I was worried about you, but you look so happy now. We need to plan a get together soon so we can get to know her better."

I nod.

"I'll meet you in the lobby in a second," Kade says to Larkyn before she leaves. And then he turns to me, and I know he's about to give me a big brother speech.

"Alright, let's hear it. I'm not cut out for marriage. I'm making a big mistake. I jumped into marriage too early."

Kade just stares at me.

"Out with it."

He reaches into the pocket of his suit and pulls out a stack of papers. His life could have been my life. If I was normal. If I wasn't addicted to drugs and alcohol. I could have worked in a big office in a suit and gone to client meetings where I drank fine whiskey and made deals like him.

Instead, I wear jeans and a company T-shirt every day. My office is surrounded by patients who are detoxing and cursing and vomiting. Trust me, detoxing isn't a pretty sight. There is nothing fancy about my life. The only part of my life that is anything like I expected as a kid is the high-rise apartment. And that is just because of my inheritance.

I may not be trusted or want to work in the family business, but that doesn't mean that I haven't earned every drop of money that I inherited. I just earn mine by staying sober and keeping out of the newspapers, while Kade earns it by working hard in a fancy office.

If Kade only knew the truth, that technically I'm not sober anymore. I broke my ten-year sobriety, and that's what led to me making a stupid decision and getting married to Millie in the first place.

Kade tosses the papers on the table without a word. I glance down.

"What's this?"

"Your prenup."

I frown as I pick up the papers that he had drawn up for me. I don't read them over, but I see mine and Millie's full name on them. Rose—her middle name is Rose. Beautiful.

"Hey," Kade snaps his fingers in front of my eyes. I dazed off thinking of Millie.

"We don't have much time to talk before Larkyn comes looking for us."

"Why are you handing me a prenup? We're already married. And what are you doing getting involved in my business anyway?"

"The prenup is to protect you. It doesn't matter that you are married, you can still sign a prenup after, especially since you got married so fast. That, or you can get it annulled now before things get messy." He tosses a second set of papers in front of me—annulment papers.

That pisses me off. "That's all Millie and I are to you, a big joke? One you can just toss some papers at and make go away?"

"No, actually. I don't think you are a big joke. That's why I want to protect you. Because when this fails, and it will because you haven't known her long enough, you will be protected."

"I don't need a prenup!" I stand up.

Kade does, too, in his incredibly calm way. "If she truly loves you, she'll sign the prenup. It's incredibly generous and just protects the family assets you wouldn't want to give up anyway."

"You mean *you* wouldn't want to give up. You're the only one who cares about the business."

"Read it. It protects the healing and recovery center too. She could get half otherwise."

I hadn't thought of that. My life's work—Millie could take part of it. She could demand it since we are legally married, even if everything else is fake.

Kade holds the paper against my chest, begging me to take it.

"And if she signs it, you'll leave us alone. You will accept our marriage. You won't secretly be betting on when it will fail. You won't tell me I told you so if it does."

Kade nods.

I snatch the papers and head home, intent on getting Millie to sign them, but end up mindlessly driving around for a while to blow off steam.

Millie will sign them because she doesn't give a fuck about my money. And this is all fake, I try to calm myself as I drive.

But Kade is right. Eventually, this marriage will end, in less than six months in fact, and whether he says it or not, he'll be thinking it.

When I get to my apartment several hours later, I have every intent on having Millie sign it. On finding a way we can stay friends and put the physical part of our relationship aside.

And then I see her, standing in my kitchen in nothing but a towel, her hair wet from a shower.

I forget about the prenup.

I forget about how weak my heart is right now.

All I want to do is fuck her.

2 8

MILLIE

I SHOULD HAVE EXPECTED Sebastian to walk in. It's six in the evening. That's when most people get off work.

But for some reason, it didn't register with me. I wasn't planning on letting Sebastian see me standing in his kitchen in nothing but a towel, and yet, that's exactly what happened.

"What are you doing?" are the first words out of Sebastian's mouth.

My heart flutters because even though his words are an accusation that I shouldn't be standing here, tempting him, his eyes are filled with desire. The tightness in his body tells me he's holding back, standing in the doorway because if he comes any closer, he's going to do something he regrets.

"Am I not allowed to shower?" I ask as I feel my pulse beating in my throat.

"You're allowed to shower. Did you come home from work early?"

"No."

He blinks, not expecting that.

"Did you just finish working out?"

"No."

381

His eyes slide down my body, taking in the swell of my breasts over the towel, the curve around my hips, and then down my bare thighs. I relish in the feel of his heated gaze over my body, how he appreciates every bit of my body, and I remember exactly what he did to it.

Only one night.

That's all we get. Those were his words. I try to remind my body of that, but he's turned on a desire that I don't know how to turn off.

"Why are you only now showering then?" His voice is low and deep, but I think it's more out of lust than anger. He's trying to make sense of me, trying to understand why I'm standing here in a towel tempting him.

"Because night time is when my day usually starts."

His forehead wrinkles. "What do you mean your day usually starts now?"

I shrug. "I'm a night owl. I work at night, not during the day. Hawaii was the opposite of my normal life." Everything about Hawaii was out of character for me.

He nods like he understands, and I suspect everything about Hawaii for him was also out of the norm.

"We should talk," I say.

He nods again but doesn't speak. His eyes stay locked on my body. He doesn't look like he wants to talk. He looks like he wants to devour me.

Finally, he speaks. "Go get dressed. Then we can have dinner together."

I nod and hurry to my room to get dressed. Mostly so I don't do something stupid like jump into his arms and kiss him against his will. It's clear that he still finds me attractive, but is just as much of an ass as I thought.

I gathered the rest of my things from the apartment that I shared with Oaklee, which wasn't much. I left my bed at Oaklee's, so it was mainly just a bit more clothes and toiletries. I select a pair of jeans and stretchy top and put them on before combing my wet hair, but I don't bother blow-drying it. Then I head back out to the kitchen.

I assume Sebastian will order takeout for us, or he has a chef who cooks for him, so I'm surprised to find him standing in his expansive kitchen behind his large stainless stovetop cooking.

"You cook?" I ask.

"Yes," he says, offering nothing more than a one-word answer.

"I thought we were going to talk. That means you have to say more than one-word answers."

"We will."

Great, now we are onto two-word sentences. We are never going to get through this night.

Sebastian continues to face the stovetop as he cooks. We are going to need some alcohol to get through this night. I'm going to need it to tell him about my past and keep my desire for him at bay. And he's going to need it to loosen him up and stop making him such a giant prick.

I glance around the room but don't spot a bar or place where he keeps his alcohol. I head to the fridge, hoping he has some white wine or champagne chilled as both are my favorite.

His fridge is perfectly organized. It looks like a celeb's fridge who his giving a house tour for Architecture Digest. Like it's been organized and cleaned for a special occasion. But there is no way it is; he didn't know that he'd be bringing back a wife when he went to his friend's wedding.

I easily scan the fridge filled with lean meats, vegetables, fruit, and water. There is nothing unhealthy in his fridge. But then I spot what I'm looking for. There is a single bottle of white wine chilling in the fridge. I remove it and then go in search of wine glasses. I open almost every cabinet before finding two wine glasses pushed far into the back of a cabinet.

Seems strange for a bachelor. Most men I know who live alone have their alcohol on display or in the easiest cabinet. He must just not be a wine drinker.

I pour us both a glass, and I take a sip as I watch him work at the stove in his jeans and T-shirt that says something about healing on the front. It's not what I expected. I expected him to be wearing a suit when he returned to work. Instead, he's wearing casual clothes. Not that I'm complaining, his ass looks great in his dark jeans, but it just goes to show how much we need to have a conversation. I have no idea how he made the millions he obviously has to own an apartment like this.

Sebastian plates the food he's been hard at work at and then finally turns to see what I've been doing. He frowns when he sees the wine glasses I'm holding.

"I'm sorry if you were saving this bottle for something, I'll buy you a new one," I say as a vein pops out on his forehead.

"It's fine, I just don't usually drink wine on a Monday."

"Oh, I just thought the alcohol was needed for us to get through this conversation."

I follow Sebastian to the small two-seater dining table that I doubt he ever eats at. That is until he pulls his chair back, and I see the scuff marks on the floor where he's obviously pulled out his chair on a regular basis. When I pull my chair out, I see no such marks.

"Do you usually have dinner at this table by yourself?"

"Yes."

Back to one-word answers.

I sigh, deciding we both need some food in our systems and definitely lots of wine. The food Sebastian cooked is delicious and simple—grilled chicken, asparagus, and a green salad.

"You're a good cook."

"Thank you." And then he looks up as if he knew what he was going to see when he did. "Look." He nods in the direction of the skyline behind him.

I turn, and my breath is taken away by the view of the sun setting behind the skyline.

"Wow."

"This is why I sit here to eat my dinner every night. It's peaceful and reminds me that life is precious and beautiful. That I deserve to live a life that is full of wondrous things. And I should protect my body so I'm able to enjoy such wonders."

I turn back, realizing what Sebastian just did was more incredible than the view. He let me into a part of his soul. And he did it without a drop of alcohol needed. He was brave.

Maybe this conversation will be easier than I think.

"What do you do for work?" Sebastian asks. It should be an easy question for me to answer after he bared his soul to me. And yet, it's one of the hardest. It's embarrassing for me to say.

But I need to tell him. I lift my wine glass, needing liquid courage to be brave like he was. I open my mouth to speak, when there is a knock at the door.

My eyes shift from Sebastian to the door.

"Are you expecting someone?" I ask.

He sighs and gets up, making it clear he knows who it is. I stay in my seat as he goes to open the door. It doesn't shock me when a skinny blonde looking model waltzes into the room. It doesn't take a detective to figure out who this woman is—someone who has shared a bed with Sebastian. Someone who might have shared multiple romps in his bed with him.

The woman stops dead in her high-heeled shoes and skin-tight white dress when she sees me. "Oh, did I interrupt something? I was just coming over to drink my wine and enjoy the sunset with you. I didn't mean to intrude."

Sure, you didn't.

I fidget in my seat as Sebastian wordlessly enters the room. We agreed that we wouldn't cheat while we were married to each other, but that was before we had our one night together. Before we returned to reality. Before hot neighbors showed back up in our lives.

I don't know how to introduce myself to this woman. If she is someone who Sebastian might want to see again after we get divorced, then I don't want to insert myself as his wife. So I wait for Sebastian to decide how to handle her.

"Chloe, this is Millie King," Sebastian says, stepping around the woman and helping me out of my chair.

He used his last name as mine, Chloe and I realize at the same time.

After a long pause, he puts the final nail in the coffin. "My wife."

Chloe gasps as shock rolls over her red lips, blue eyes, and curled blonde hair. She shifts her weight nervously. "I didn't realize when we were together that you were seeing someone else."

Her voice sounds hurt. She must be a recent conquest, and my heart breaks for her a little.

"I didn't cheat. Millie and I's relationship started recently, and we fell hard. I just knew I wanted to be with her forever." His fingers tangle with mine, and I feel like we are one. It's the first time I've ever had that feeling when a man holds my hand.

"I didn't realize you were looking for a wife. If I'd known, I would have wanted more than one night," Chloe says.

Sebastian shakes his head. "I wasn't looking for a wife." He turns to look at me before he says his next words that capture my heart. "I was looking for Millie."

Yep, my heart is his.

It's all an act. He's just saying this to make our marriage look more believable and get this woman to leave.

I look over at Chloe, and I see tears in her eyes. It's clear that Chloe had feelings for him, whether or not there was ever a hope of Sebastian returning her feelings.

"I'll, uh, just go then. It was nice meeting you, Millie."

"I'll walk you to the door," Sebastian says, putting his hand on the small of her back as he leads her out.

My jealously grows, watching the small gesture. He just told her I'm his wife, that he wanted me and no one else, and yet him touching her is what is pushing me to the edge. I grab the bottle of wine and pour myself more. I look at Sebastian's still full glass.

He returns as I hold the glass to my lips.

"I met her in the elevator."

I smile. "Is that how you pick up all your women?"

He ignores me, and I swear he can see down to my anxieties about that woman. "I brought her back here and fucked her."

I wince.

"I had my one night with her, and then I was done with her."

"It didn't look like you were done with her."

"She lives on my floor and works similar hours to me. She comes over twice a week, and we share a meal together, nothing more. She's just a woman I can talk to, but I only fucked her the one night. I didn't change my rules for her."

He sets my wine glass down on the table and takes my wrists in his hands.

"I wasn't finished with that," I say breathlessly.

"I'm not finished with you."

29

SEBASTIAN

I GRIP Millie's wrists in my hands. I can feel her pulse racing. But I don't need to feel her pulse, watch her breathing, or see the way her pupils dilate to know what she's thinking—the same thing I am.

Millie wants me. Just like I want her.

But we both feel an air of apprehension. Me, because I know what having her again will do to me. And her because she sees Chloe as a threat.

I can't do anything about my own apprehension, but I can do something to fix Millie's.

"She means nothing. She was nothing but a good fuck. She meant so little to me that I didn't even remember that Monday nights are the night she usually comes over because all I was thinking about is you."

She swallows so hard that I can see her throat bob. "You're allowed to have feelings for her. This is all pretend."

Her words are a knife to the gut, but I know they aren't true. She feels something when I hold her like this, when I kissed her, fucked her. If not, she wouldn't be jealous of a woman who means nothing to me.

"I know I am, but I don't. The only woman in the world I could possibly have feelings for is you, Millie."

She sucks in the tiniest of breaths. She doesn't want me to notice her reaction, but it's there. I notice everything about her. There is no way I'd miss her reaction to me telling her that I feel more for her. What, I've yet to figure out, but definitely more.

"Me too," she says, telling me she has feelings but no way to put them into words.

I nod solemnly. This wasn't supposed to happen. We weren't supposed to feel anything. But no matter what feelings we have, it won't change the result. We will eventually get divorced. It's what's for the best, for both of us.

"Where do you work?" Millie asks as we stand inches apart, our heated breath warming each other, her wrists still in my grasp.

"I'm half owner of a non-profit that focuses on the healing and recovery of addicts."

She smiles softly. "Such a sweetheart. You really aren't an asshole at all."

I smirk and pull her tight to me. My lips hover over hers, but not giving her the kiss that she's begging for. "I can still be an asshole when I want."

Her eyes gleam.

"What do you do?"

She takes a deep, steadying breath. "A little of everything."

"What does that mean?"

"It means I'm a wanderer who hasn't found her calling yet."

I frown at her non-answer. "What was your last job?"

"Security guard."

"Security guard? And the job before that?"

"I've also been a bartender, a photographer, a driver, and an event planner."

She really is a wanderer. Full of life and adventure. She's free. I can't handle that kind of disorganization in my life. I need order.

"My last real relationship was in college. Other than that, I just fuck women once and then move on to the next," I open myself to her.

"In the past, I've only done real relationships, no one night stands, until you. But I think you've changed me on that. I want more one nights and fewer relationships. All of my relationships have ended in heartbreak." I can feel her wounds as she speaks. I may not get all the details, but I can still feel the pain.

"I'm a control freak. I need order and the same routine every day."

"I'm messy. I like the freedom of not being tied down to any one person or job."

"I can't fuck you."

Her hands drop out of mine, and she backs away. I don't know if I let go, or she pulled them out at my admission. She grabs for her wine glass, like that might dull the sting of my words.

"Ask me," I say, stepping back into her space even though she shifts, begging for me to release her from this conversation. "Ask me why."

She clears her throat, but it comes out raspy anyway. "Why can't you fuck me?"

"I'm an addict."

Her eyes widen with surprise but no judgment.

"It used to be drugs and alcohol." I step closer again, and this time she doesn't retreat.

"I've been sober for over ten years. But I'm worried I might fall back into addiction again."

She opens her mouth to speak.

"I think I'm addicted to you." With my words, I pull her into a kiss—a desperate, heart wrenching, addicting kiss. One that I know there is no stopping. One where I will kiss and kiss and kiss until I've taken everything I need from Millie, but I won't stop until I've taken more than she's willing to give. That's the life of an addict.

I used to think it was alcohol's fault. In reality, I'm just addicted to pleasure, to joy, to life. That's why my life is regimented. But once Millie entered my life, I realized all the things I was missing.

Right now, I can't think about my addiction. All I can think about is feeding it.

Millie gasps when I let her breathe again. She's the only one with the power to stop me.

"I should stop you then," she pants heavily.

I nod. She should. I will only destroy her.

She thinks for a second then grabs onto my neck with one arm as she kisses me so hard our teeth clash and our tongues battle.

She moves to set the wine glass down on the table, but that's not where I want the wine glass. It's where I want her.

I sweep our dishes onto the floor. The clatter barely registers in my brain. I'm no longer in control; that's what happens when I become addicted. And I'm about to surrender all of my control to Millie.

I grab her hips and lift her up onto the table as I spread her legs and step between them. She finally sets the glass down behind her, less destructive and more in control than I am, and then she grabs my shirt, lifting it over my head. I work the buttons on her jeans and begin to pull them off.

"You know dresses give me better access," I say.

"I hate dresses, but if you promise me more orgasms if I wear them, then maybe I'll start."

I grin and then yank her pants and panties off before kneeling between her legs. Her eyes grow big as they watch me study her so intimately and closely.

I love every inch of her body. Every curve. Every freckle. Every imperfection. She doesn't try to hide who she is; she just is.

I grab her thighs, and then I plunge my tongue between her folds. She tastes so sweet, already drenched for me. But I want to give her as many orgasms as I can tonight. I remember how she screamed my name last time, and that sound is an addicting melody to me.

I try to slow my pace as I lick between her folds and find her clit. But I can't. Every pant she makes, every moan, every cry that brings her closer to orgasm is feeding my own addiction.

And then she's gripping my hair, screaming my name, as she comes around my tongue.

One orgasm isn't enough; I want more. So immediately I start licking again.

"Sebastian, I want your cock. Please."

I grin. She's right. I need to give her more than just my tongue.

I stand and shove her shirt up, needing to taste her breasts as her fingers fumble against my zipper.

Her nipples are hard and pointed. She's not wearing a bra beneath her shirt. I'm not even sure if the woman owns a bra, which makes me happy.

"Please," Millie says again, her voice full of need as she grabs at my hips.

I lean in close to her mouth as my tongue traces her full lips. "Be careful what you ask for, Millie. Once I start again, I won't stop."

Her cheeks blush. "Good, I don't want you to stop."

I pull a condom out of my back pocket before I push my jeans down. I sheath myself and barely push at her entrance, waiting.

"Fuck me, Sebastian. Show me how good it feels to be fucked by a King. Remind me what it's like to be claimed by a man who's addicted to me."

I give her a devilish grin. "You think you know what it felt like to be fucked by me before, but you have no idea. I was holding back. This time I'll give you everything."

I slam into her body with my last word so hard that the table she's lying on shakes roughly, her arms raise over her head, pushing back against the floor to ceiling window behind her to keep from slamming her head into the glass. I might have gone too far already.

But when the seductive gleam returns to her eyes, I know that she likes this new roughness. This animalistic desire to fuck her no matter the consequences. The uncontrollable nature of not even being able to make it to the bed down the hallway before I have her.

I thrust into her again, this thrust just as punishing as the first.

"More!" Millie screams.

Again I thrust, somehow sinking deeper into her, before pulling all the way out and doing it again and again. The wine glass shakes roughly next to her on the table.

Alcohol used to be my addiction, but I beat it. I got clean and healthy. Millie is my new one, but I'm not sure I'll ever want to beat this new addiction.

I grab the glass and lift it to my lips.

"What are you doing?" she asks, her voice more panicked now that I hold the glass in my hand than when I started fucking her.

"I'm not going to drink."

She exhales.

"Technically, I already broke my sobriety the night we got married. And then again when Oaklee forced me to drink, but I haven't since. I have no desire to drink."

I bring the glass to her lips and pour the wine over them, letting a little spill out. I trace the cool liquid down her breasts over her nipples that somehow harden even more at my touch.

Then I lean down and kiss her. "You're my new addiction."

One final thrust sends us both over the edge into our orgasms. Millie screams my name as pleasure overcomes her senses. I roar my own ecstasy. I slow my thrusts, but at the last thrust, the table creaks.

Millie grabs my arms, and I catch her hips, but it's too late, and we tumble to the floor in a pile of broken wood.

"Oh my god," we both laugh. This destruction feels as much an end as a new beginning. A table that I've sat at thousands of times is now gone. My routine and control—gone.

We keep laughing, my head resting against her chest as we lie naked in the rubble. But it won't stop me from wanting her again and again and again.

"You said you were a night owl?"

She nods.

"Do you have anywhere to be?"

"No."

"Good, because tonight I'm going to feed my addiction until you tell me to stop."

"What if I never tell you to stop?"

I shudder, because the answer scares me.

"Then, I'll never stop."

3 0

MILLIE

I PANT HARD, still not having caught my breath as I lie naked on top of the covers in Sebastian's penthouse bedroom. The sun has started peeking up over the buildings. We haven't slept one second. All we've done is fuck.

On the dining room table we broke.

The couch.

Against the wall.

In his bed.

We've fucked everywhere.

I didn't believe Sebastian at first when he said he'd get addicted, when he said that's why he only fucks women one time. He's afraid of what will happen if he has too much of a good thing.

I understand now. But there is no way I want this to stop. It's too good. I don't want to let him go.

I glance over at him. His hard chest rises and falls as he tries to catch his own breath. I let my eyes wander down his ribbed abs, down to his glorious cock. I've never been with a man who reads my body so well, who can anticipate my desires before I even realize them myself.

Sebastian starts to roll over toward me. He cups my head in his hands and presses a kiss against my lips.

I moan into the kiss. *We have to stop.*

"Sebastian, we should talk," I say. There is no way we can fuck again. It's not physically possible to go again. And yet, I feel him growing hard against my stomach, and my own wetness spills between my legs as he continues to kiss me.

He laughs when I push against his chest.

"I know, let's talk. But you're going to have to do it while we shower, I have to get to work."

I blink at him rapidly. "You're still going to work? You didn't sleep at all."

He pulls me out of bed as we walk naked toward his large shower, complete with a rain shower head and a dozen other nozzles that all point in different directions. He turns one of the knobs, and the rain shower head comes on before he turns back to me.

"If I don't go to work, I'm going to want to stay and keep fucking you. And as incredible as that sounds, I know that I've already made you sore enough. Our bodies need a break."

He steps into the shower, pulling me with him. When I step in and feel the warm water, I feel the familiar ache, and know that he's right. We need to stop, and if him going to work is the only way, then fine.

"So, I'm guessing our one night only deal went out the window?" I tease as he grabs the shampoo bottle. He squeezes some in his hand and then massages it into my scalp.

"I want to fuck you every day until we decide that our marriage is over," Sebastian says.

I exhale. Fucking Sebastian every day for the next five in a half months seems like heaven. Until he decides the pretending is over, then it will be hell.

"And when our marriage is over, how are you going to handle your uh...addiction problem? I don't want to be responsible for you becoming an alcoholic or something again." *Maybe we can keep fucking even after we are no longer married.*

He shakes his head. "I won't go back to drinking. I'll go through my usual process when it's time to break up. I'll do the therapy and detoxing."

"You'll detox yourself of me? How will that even work?" I ask as he tilts my head back to wash the shampoo from my hair. *How does this feel more intimate than anything else we've done all night?*

"I'll get rid of everything that reminds me of you. I'll give myself some time away from any of our mutual friends. I won't look you up on social media. I'll need a full break when this is over. It should be easy for our friends to understand since they think we will be going through a real divorce."

I nod. A complete break, cold turkey. That's what he's asking for. It's probably for the best.

"Okay. I can do that," I say.

And then he's running a bar of soap over my body, and I can barely think. My body tingles everywhere he touches.

"What about you?" he asks.

But I have no idea what he's talking about as his hand runs over my breast and down the front of my stomach. I'm seeing stars, and thinking of all the times he touched me last night.

"Millie?" He chuckles at my reaction.

"Hmm?"

He laughs and removes his hands and starts washing himself, which is just as distracting as having his hands on me.

"What about you? What do you need from me to make this work?" he asks again.

I pause. I need this to end right now before I fall head over heels in love with him.

"Just keep being an asshole when you can outside of the bedroom, so I remember that we aren't right for each other. Point out all our differences. This is just good sex, that's it."

He nods slowly. "Just good sex. Trust me, I'd make a terrible boyfriend. And an even more terrible husband. I work all day, have a rigid routine, and then would fuck you all night. You wouldn't get any sleep. It would be a horrible life."

"Horrible," I repeat his words under my breath. But it doesn't sound horrible. It sounds amazing. I've already experienced one night of his rigid routine, and it involved him cooking for me. And the lack of sleep doesn't bother me if it means I get all the orgasms. *What could be bad about this life?*

Sebastian steps under the water, washes the soap off his body, and then steps out to wrap himself in a towel while I gape.

"So what are you going to do today while I'm at work? Are you working tonight? I never got a clear answer on what job it is you are currently doing."

It's because I was fired from my last job, and I'm currently unemployed, but that's too embarrassing to talk about.

"I'm going over to Oaklee's to chat a bit. I'll convince her we're in love but are nervous we jumped in too fast, so when we get a divorce, she'll accept it. And I'll see if she'll spill any more details about how we decided to get married in the first place."

"Good idea. You can also arrange to have your stuff moved in," Sebastian says with the towel wrapped low around his hips as he walks to the closet to get dressed.

Yea, except I already moved all my stuff in, he just doesn't realize it yet. He's truly a king, and I'm a pauper. There is no way this could ever be real. I have nothing to offer him but sex. I have no career. No money. No furniture. All I come with is a lot of baggage.

I turn off the shower and am wrapping a towel around my body when Sebastian comes back into the bathroom with a scowl on his face. He thrusts my phone at me.

"We need to talk about your stalking ex."

I look down at the phone and see the text threats from an unknown number. I take the phone and hit delete, blocking yet another new number from my ex.

Sebastian tucks a strand of wet hair behind my ear. "Don't worry, we will find a way to handle him. We should go hang out with our friends tonight publicly, make a big splash so that news spreads to him, and he realizes he doesn't have a chance with you."

I nod.

"He's not dangerous, is he?"

"No, he would never hurt me. He just wants me back."

"Well, that's not going to happen. You're mine."

———

"What can I get you two to drink?" the waitress asks.

"Two white wines," I say, looking to Oaklee for clarification. We have shared many meals at this restaurant before, and we almost always enjoy our salads while sharing a bottle of white wine.

"Actually, uh, just water for me," Oaklee says.

I stare at her like she's just grown horns. I don't ever recall Oaklee turning down wine, which only signals I'm going to need alcohol to get through this conversation.

"Just the one glass then," I say, and the waitress leaves. I lean in across the booth. "Spill."

"What? You know I'm pregnant, I want to hear about how your honeymoon went. And how you're living with a gazillionaire in his incredible penthouse."

I did not know she was pregnant. She must have told me the night of our wedding. I attempt to wipe the shock off my face and distract her with an innocuous question.

"How do you know Sebastian is a gazillionaire?

Oaklee rolls her eyes. "Everyone knows."

I sigh. "Stop trying to distract me. You already know how the honeymoon went and living together is great, but we are so different, and everything moved so fast. I'm not sure it's going to work out. Just look at you and Boden. You've been together forever, and it didn't work out."

Oaklee turns somber.

"Are you two back together?"

"No."

"The baby is his, right?"

"Yes."

I nod, assuming already that it was. There is no way she could have fucked another man and found out she was pregnant by him after the wedding. And she's not a cheater.

"I know it would be better if we had gotten married, but I just couldn't…" She stares down at the glass of water in front of her, and I notice the tears watering her eyes.

"Oh, Oaklee." I run around to her side and hold her again, holding her head against my chest. "It's going to be alright. It's going to be better than alright. You are going to have a baby. You've always wanted a baby, and you're going to make a great mom."

I stroke her back as she sobs a little. "It wasn't supposed to be this way. He wasn't supposed to cheat. He wasn't supposed to hurt me. After I saw them together, I just couldn't go through with the wedding. I can't be married to a cheater."

I nod. "Of course, you can't."

Oaklee sits up slowly, and I wipe the tears from her eyes.

"Don't," she says.

I frown and pull my hands into my lap. "Why not?"

"Because I have more to say." She doesn't have to finish her sentence for me to know the rest of her sentence is going to hurt me. She has the same expression she did when she told me in the fifth grade that she accidentally killed my fish she was watching for me while I was on vacation.

"Sebastian was the one who set Boden up. He got him drunk. He found the women. He bought the hotel rooms. He's the reason Boden cheated."

I suck in a breath—*asshole*. But then, I already knew that. I know that Sebastian helped his friend cheat. And yet, it seems so out of character for Sebastian. It seems strange he would throw away ten years of sobriety on one night that led to his friend cheating.

I wish more than anything I could remember that night. I wish I could remember the events that led to Sebastian and I getting drunk, getting married, fucking in our hotel room. I wish I could remember it all because I know that there has to be an explanation for it all.

As much as I want to pretend that Sebastian is a pretentious jerk, deep down I don't think that's who he really is. *But maybe I'm wrong? Maybe he can hide his true self when his cock is deep inside me, and his thumb is playing with my clit?*

"I just think you should be careful where Sebastian is concerned."

"I get it. I'll be careful." I look away from Oaklee as I try to remember what happened. I try to reconcile the man who saved me and shares a bed with me with the man who would get drunk and help his friend cheat.

"Wait…" I say, as I realize something. "How long have you known you were pregnant?"

"Since two weeks before the wedding."

"So, at the bachelorette party and after the wedding, you weren't drinking?"

She shakes her head. "No, I replaced a lot of the wine and champagne with sparkling apple juice."

"So, the alcohol you made us drink in the limo wasn't really alcohol?"

"Correct."

"How drunk were Sebastian and I the night we got married?" I ask, hopeful that maybe Sebastian didn't actually drink. Maybe it was all a false assumption, and there is another reason we don't remember.

Oaklee shrugs. "You seemed pretty drunk."

I sigh. Nothing about that night makes sense to me. I stare down at my wedding ring. But it led me to an incredible guy. One I would have never spent time with if it wasn't for our mistakes that night. So I don't regret it, even if I have to give him up eventually.

Still, I should tell Sebastian what I know about that night, about not drinking in the limo. At least that will make him feel better and might trigger something about that night for him.

Right now, though, I have to be a friend. Sebastian may not be in my life for much longer, but Oaklee will be in my life forever.

I hug her again. "Come out with us tonight."

She smiles. "I'd love to. I want to see and hear all the stories about how you and Mr. Filthy Rich ended up together."

I lean my head against hers. *You and I both.*

My phone buzzes, and I don't have to look at it to know who it is.

"Is Trevor still trying to find you?" Oaklee says, her voice shaking a little.

"Yes."

Oaklee hugs me tighter.

"Don't worry, Sebastian will protect you. He has more than enough money and resources to protect you. Tell him to hire a bodyguard, though. You know Trevor, and he won't stop."

I nod, agreeing. But I'm afraid as soon as Trevor is no longer a threat, that will be the end of Sebastian and me. There will be no reason to stay together. So getting Trevor out of my life as quickly as possible no longer seems like the best idea.

31

SEBASTIAN

I HAVE EVERYTHING ARRANGED. I was supposed to pick Millie up at the condo at seven, and then we were going to meet everyone at the club for dancing and drinking. Well, everyone but me will drink. I'll focus on my new obsession—Millie.

I pick up my phone to text Millie. I smile when I see her programmed into my phone as 'Wifey.'

Me: Hey, wifey. I had a problem come up at work. I'll be twenty or thirty minutes late to pick you up. Looking forward to tonight.

Wifey: Hey, Hubby. I'm actually on my way back from Oaklee's. I'll just Uber to you, and then we can drive together. That way we aren't late.

Me: Perfect. See you soon.

. . .

And yet, I feel a tightening in my chest at the thought of Millie coming here. This is my baby. This is the best of me. I don't want her to see the best of me. I promised her she'd see me as nothing but a jerk outside of the bedroom. Tonight was supposed to be the start of showing our friends how incompatible we are.

"Sebastian, you're needed in room eleven," Shelly pokes her head in.

"Can't Jade handle it?"

"She went home for the day."

I sigh. So much for wrapping up my day before Millie gets here.

———

"It's okay, get out the anger if you need. Destroy the furniture. Rip apart your pillow. Do what you need to do, but don't give up. Your life depends on it. Don't you dare give up," I say to Zach, one of our newest patients.

He's nineteen—an adult by most people's standards. But I was younger than him when I started drinking, when I got addicted. And I can tell you, there is nothing about being a nineteen-year-old addict that makes you an adult. He needs help, and that's why we are here—to get him help. Without us, he'll be thrown in jail or end up dead if he keeps using like he is.

He grabs his chair and throws it against his bedroom window. It doesn't break, though. He isn't the first who has tried to break a window while staying at the rehab center.

"You're angry. I can understand that. Get your anger out; you'll feel better."

He glares at me, and I know he's about to turn his anger on me. He doesn't want to be here. He doesn't realize he has a problem, and we can't hold him here. I just hope he'll realize that he needs to be here.

He starts toward me, ready to bulldoze me over to escape. I stand firm, balancing on my good foot, and when he gets close, I wrap my arms around him and hold on for dear life.

At first, he fights, hitting me hard in the mouth, and I know he's knocked a tooth hard enough that it's bleeding.

"Shhh, it will be okay. It sucks, but it gets better. I just want to hug you, not restrain you." I soften my hold, showing that he can go if he wants, I won't physically stop him.

He hesitates. And then he collapses into my arms, a ball of emotions and tears and apologies and curses.

Zach grew up in a group home. He's been on his own since he aged out last year and most likely hasn't been hugged much in his life. That's all he's looking for—human connection.

We stand like that for a while. And after a bit longer, I get him to agree to go to a therapy session and to take our boxing class to get his anger out. Only when he's finally settled down, do I leave him with one of our therapists.

I have no idea how long I was in that room, but I suspect that Millie has been waiting for me for a while.

I sigh, hobbling out of the room, knowing I look like a mess. I see her standing in the hallway staring at me with big eyes.

"I'm sorry I'm so late," I say.

Her eyes seem watery, and she bites her bottom lip as she comes up to me.

"Hey, are you okay?" I ask, lifting her chin to meet my gaze as she walks up to me.

"Mmmhmmm," she says, dabbing at my bloodied lip with a Kleenex.

I search her eyes and see the want as she stares at me.

"You heard?" my shoulders drop.

She nods. "I didn't mean to. Shelly sent me down the hallway to your office. I heard your voice. I didn't realize it was a therapy session. I shouldn't have overheard."

"No, you shouldn't have." It goes against patient confidentiality. And also because of the way she's looking at me now, like I'm a good person. She's seen behind the mask that I put up to keep people out. Now there is no way to put the mask back on.

"This doesn't change anything. You're still an asshole to me," Millie smiles as she speaks.

"Good," I say, even though I know she doesn't mean it. She saw the best of me, the kindness and tenderness I have when I'm working with patients.

"Does that happen a lot?"

"Yes. We have therapists and doctors who are better at helping people. But sometimes my job is convincing people they should be here in the first place. And to deal with them when they get physical. I don't want my staff to be in danger, and I don't like drugging patients to calm them down. I must look like a mess, and I'm really sorry we are going to be late."

"You look like my Sebastian. And I think everyone will understand why we are late."

"Nope, they won't understand because everyone outside these walls only sees the asshole, the playboy, the jerk. They don't get to see this side of me."

Millie links her fingers through mine, startling me, but damn does it feel good to be connected like this. "Got it. Back to being your usual controlling mean self once we leave."

I nod as we walk outside, taking in her appearance for the first time. She's wearing jeans, a black V-neck shirt, and flats. She's not extremely girly, and she's not wearing a dress, but it doesn't stop me from wanting to jump her in the back of my Porsche before we go.

No, control yourself. We are already late.

We pull up in front of the club where we are meeting our friends, and we're over an hour late. Millie leans over to me. "Just so you know, I like you when you're caring and also when you are a prick. It makes no difference to me." And then she kisses my cheek.

I grab her wrist and pull her back to me. "Oh, yea?" I kiss her hard, yanking her bottom lip into my mouth as I nip until her lip is swollen. I drive my hand into my hair, fussing it up so everyone assumes why we were late. "I think you like it when I'm an asshole more than when I'm being sweet."

"Maybe I do." And then we both step out of the car and enter the club hand in hand. I use Millie as a crutch instead of using my actual crutches I hate.

Our friends holler at us from a circle of couches in the corner of the room as we arrive. It's mostly everyone who was at Oaklee's wedding with a few more of my co-workers I usually hang out with.

"You finally made it! Now, you can cover our drinks, you asshole," Boden shouts at me as he raises a glass from his seat.

I feel Millie glare at me. "You invited Boden?"

"Yes? He's my friend, and I thought we were trying to get Oaklee and him back together."

She shakes her head. "You're an idiot." She pulls away and goes to talk with Oaklee.

I run my hand through my hair, messing it up even more. My shirt is wrinkled and stained with a drop of my blood, and I haven't slept in twenty-four hours. I look like hell. I guess we are going to show our friends how incompatible Millie and I are tonight.

Millie and Oaklee head out onto the dance floor, while I walk over to Boden and take a seat.

"Be nice to Oaklee and Millie tonight," I say as I sit.

Boden rolls his eyes. "When am I anything but nice? And Oaklee's my ex. I'll be nice but not friendly. We're over. There is nothing that will cause us to get back together."

"Why? What happened?" I don't understand how you go from wanting to marry someone to not wanting to be in the same room with them.

Boden takes a swig of his beer. "Really? The king of one night stands is asking me why I don't want to give my ex a second chance."

"I'm not that guy anymore. I'm married now, remember?"

Boden laughs. "Okay, right."

"What is that supposed to mean?"

"It means marriage doesn't change anything. One woman, especially a woman like Millie, won't keep you satisfied for long. You'll be looking for something new and exciting in a matter of weeks if you haven't already."

I stand up and knock his beer from his hands.

"Hey, what was that?" Boden asks, bewildered.

"That was me holding back from kicking your ass. Don't you dare talk like that about my wife ever again. I'm not going to punch you because you're my friend, and it would ruin everyone's night, but keep your mouth shut if you don't want a black eye and a fat lip. Also, I won't be paying for your drinks tonight, so don't you dare start a tab under my name. And if you knew what was good for you, you'd leave now and apologize tomorrow if you want to remain friends."

I storm off. My rage is flowing through me. And for the first time in years, I want to drink. I want to pick a fight. I want—

My eyes catch Millie out of the corner of my eye, dancing, swaying her hips to the music. And then she sees me. And her body changes. Her eyes tell me to come to her. She'll fix it.

I want her. More than alcohol or fighting or fucking one night stands. I want her. This doesn't feel like any other addiction I've had. This doesn't feel shaky or reckless or controlling. This feels warm and welcoming and calming.

I head to where she's dancing with Oaklee. Millie whispers something in Oaklee's ear, and Oaklee walks away so it's just Millie and me.

We don't speak. Millie just leans into my chest, resting her head there as her arms go around my neck, and we slow dance together even though this song is fast. For a moment, the world stops, and it's just her and me.

Our hearts beat together, our hips sway in unison, our bodies become one. Too many feelings flood through me, feelings that I can't name. Feelings I shouldn't feel for a woman who I was only supposed to stay married to for six months. We are still at the beginning of our time together, but when you have such a short amount of time with someone, every moment feels too short.

I know that time is going to move too quickly, so I try to soak up every second I can with Millie. I try to remember it all. No matter how my heart is shifting, I know I'm not husband material. I'm too broken. One slip would destroy us.

"I'm scared," Millie whispers into my chest.

Her words hit me like a punch to the gut. She can't say what she's feeling either, but her words tell me she's scared of what we are feeling—scared of the pain that we could inflict upon each other.

"Me too." I kiss her hair, wishing I had the words to comfort her. I do work healing people, helping them recover from their addictions, but I don't have any words that can comfort her.

"Sorry to interrupt, but I need Millie a second," Oaklee says, tapping me on the shoulder.

Every muscle in my body is screaming to hold onto Millie and never let her go, but reluctantly, I run my hands down her arms until only our fingertips are touching, and then I let her go.

I watch as Millie and Oaklee head toward the bathroom until they are out of sight. Then I head back to where our group is, but Kade corners me before I make it back.

"Did she sign the prenup yet?" Kade asks.

"I don't give a damn about the prenup. I don't need her to sign it. We aren't getting divorced, so it doesn't matter anyway." My words aren't true, but what I mean is that Millie won't take half my money. She doesn't care about my money.

"Sebastian, I'm just trying to protect you. She needs to sign the prenup. I saw your little spat earlier. You may not plan on getting divorced, but it could still happen. Even the best of marriages, couples who are deeply in love still end up divorced. Love isn't always enough."

I push past him, the anxious desire to quell my anger returning. I head toward the bar as old habits take over and sit down at the bar. I won't actually order any alcohol, but I think this was a mistake—all of it.

I can't pretend we're together.

I can't pretend we're fighting.

I can't pretend anything with Millie.

But what can I offer her?

"What can I get you?" the man behind the bar asks me.

"Club soda."

He nods and then returns a moment later with my drink. When I grab the glass, I realize how much I feel like smashing the glass. I have pent up anger about Boden. About Kade. And even Millie. I don't know how I'm going to survive five more months. Five more months when I know this is all going to end.

I glance over my shoulder, hoping that Oaklee is no longer in need of Millie so we can get out of here. But I spot Oaklee talking with Larkyn.

I stand from the bar, leaving my drink on the counter, and head toward Oaklee.

"Where's Millie?" I ask her.

She frowns. "She said she was coming to find you."

"We'll help you find her," Larkyn says, being able to read the tinge of electric fear zipping through me. I can't explain the feeling, just that something doesn't seem right.

I nod and start walking through the crowded night club. Every woman with blonde colored hair I think is her, but each face I search ends up not being her.

Did she leave without telling me?

I pull my phone out of my pocket and dial her number. It rings and rings, but no answer.

I text her, but I don't get a response. No little dots form, letting me know she's texting me back.

And then, I panic. After the connection Millie and I shared, there is no way she'd just leave. She's not with any of our friends.

Something's wrong. She wanted to stay fake married to me because she was running from her ex. All the little hairs on my body stand up, and I know she's in danger. I had one job—to protect her. And I failed.

MILLIE

I SHOULD HAVE NEVER LEFT Sebastian.

That's the thought that keeps playing in my head as I follow Trevor into a corner of the club so we can talk.

I was safe in Sebastian's arms. And then I followed Oaklee to the bathroom so she could vent about Boden and ask for advice on how to tell him she's pregnant.

When I came out to find Sebastian, Trevor met me instead.

"What do you want, Trevor?"

"You're a hard woman to get ahold of."

I cross my arms and puff my chest, trying to act like I'm not intimidated by him. I won't let him bully me. I won't let him have any control over me. Even though we are in a dark corner of the club, we are still in public. Surely he's not going to do anything to harm me here.

"We're over, Trevor. I don't think there is any reason for us to talk or be in each other's lives. I've changed my number for a reason."

Trevor puts his forearm over my head and leans in until I'm trapped between him and the wall. Sweat forms on the back of my neck, my pulse jumps, and my breath hitches. My muscles stiffen, and my eyes dilate. My entire body goes into fight or flight mode.

I want to fly, but there is nowhere to run. All I have left to do is fight.

"We have a lot to talk about, actually," Trevor breathes over me.

"No, we have nothing to talk about. We are over." I try to push past him, ducking under his arm, but he lowers his arm at the last second, and my neck collides with his thick muscle.

Trevor grabs my left hand and jerks it up so he can inspect my ring. "This is some ring."

Chills run down my spine. I've never truly been afraid of Trevor until this moment.

"Let me go," I say calmly, hoping that if I stay calm, he'll release me.

"Not until we talk."

"You're done talking," Sebastian says, standing over Trevor. He doesn't move in. He doesn't charge. Three little words hang in the air, exuding control and power. Sebastian may not be in a suit. He may not rule a courtroom or boardroom, but he demands to be listened to when he speaks.

Trevor, though, isn't phased. He continues to grip my hand, holding my fingers so tightly that I can feel the blood struggling to get through my veins to the tips of my fingers.

"Let her go, now." Sebastian's voice is deeper, gruffer, and full of threats without using violent words.

"You must be her new husband. I'll let her go. I don't want anything to do with the whore. You'll soon learn that she makes a terrible wife. I just want—"

He doesn't get the rest of his words out. Instead, Sebastian's fist hits Trevor square in the jaw.

I stand frozen as I watch my fake husband pummel my ex's face —a man I once loved.

"Don't ever talk about my wife that way again. You're going to stop texting her. Stop calling her. Stop stalking her. First thing in the morning, we will be filing a restraining order against you. Trust me, we will get it. If you so much as come into the same room as us again, you'll be arrested," Sebastian says, before taking my hand and pulling me away from Trevor.

"You're shaking," Sebastian says as he pulls me tight against his body.

I look down at my hands and realize that I am.

"Come on, we're going," Sebastian continues to drape his arm around my body, holding me tightly to him as we make our way through the bar. I can't think. I can't focus on anything.

When we get to his car, Sebastian doesn't separate from me until he has me tucked into the passenger seat. Once in the driver's seat, he takes my hand again, holding it tightly as we drive back to his condo.

"Are you really going to file a restraining order?" I ask, surprising myself when those are the first words I speak.

Sebastian parks the car in his private spot below his penthouse and then looks at me, really looks at me, like he can understand everything I'm thinking from my eyes.

I wish he could. It would be easier than having to tell him everything. I have so much to say. About the events that led to us getting married. About Oaklee. About my past.

And yet, I have no idea where to start.

Sebastian unbuckles both of our seatbelts, still not speaking. "You're incredibly brave, you know that?"

"What?" I ask, breathlessly.

"You. Are. Brave."

He kisses the back of my hand.

"You. Are. Strong."

He lifts my chin and kisses one cheek.

"You. Are. Fierce."

He kisses my other cheek.

"You. Are. An. Incredible. Wife."

He kisses me on the lips like this is the last kiss he'll ever get. It's full of desperation. Or desire. Or longing for something he knows won't last.

"Yes, I'm going to file a restraining order. I'm going to make it clear to the fucking world that you are mine. And I'll make sure that you never have to be afraid of Trevor again."

He doesn't give me a chance to respond. Trevor left me speechless by getting physical. Sebastian is leaving me speechless because I didn't realize a man could be so kind, so loving.

He grabs ahold of my hand as he pulls me into the elevator. When the doors close, I wait for him to kiss me. For his hands to roam over my body. For him to show me exactly what he has planned once we reach his condo.

"Don't look so disappointed," he says.

I look up at him.

"I'm planning on fucking you, dirty girl. But both of us are already on edge. I don't want to spark any more anxiety or fear. I want to fuck you long and slow. I want to cherish you. Take my time with you. Remind you of how incredible I think you are."

Make love to you, my mind fills in what he's not saying.

And God, do I want that. We've fucked a lot in our time together, but he's never been gentle and sweet when he's inside me. I get the sense he wants to slow time down. He wants to worship my body. And I can't think of a better way to spend the evening.

When the elevator opens, he lifts me up, cradling me in his arms as he kisses me so gently that if my eyes weren't open, I wouldn't be sure he actually kissed me. Once inside, he kicks off his shoe before carrying me straight to his bedroom, hobbling on his cast.

He lays me down on the bed. His body hovers over mine.

"You okay?" he asks, his eyes burning into my body, looking for any clue of pain that Trevor might have caused.

"He didn't hurt me."

Sebastian shakes his head. "The fact that you don't realize he did hurt you means he hurt you."

I frown but don't have time to think before he's kissing me. His tongue is darting into my mouth, possessing me, and controlling me.

I grab onto the neck of his shirt, holding him close to me, gripping it so tightly, afraid that he's going to pull away. If he stops kissing me, I might speak. I might tell him about my past, about everything. And if I speak, he won't want to keep kissing me. He'll think the worst of me.

Sebastian lifts his head from my lips.

"Don't stop," I beg.

His smile shines down on me, warming me and helping me to forget the pain. He lifts his shirt off over his head, and I no longer have anything to hold onto to keep him close except his skin. So my fingers claw at his chest, begging him to keep kissing me.

He starts his kisses again, but he doesn't kiss my lips. He kisses everywhere else, worshipping my body as he works his way down my body. He pushes my shirt up so he can access my skin.

"How did I get so lucky to have a woman like you even for a short while?" His tongue licks over the bottom of my breast and up to my nipple.

I moan in delight as he licks over my pointed tip.

"I'm not as nice and perfect as you think I am."

"No, you're messy as fuck," he grins with my nipple in his mouth before biting down. "My bathroom looks like makeup and hair products have exploded everywhere."

I open my mouth to protest and say that's not what I meant about not being nice or perfect, but Sebastian shoves his fingers in my mouth, silencing me as his tongue lingers then traces down my stomach to just over where my jeans rest.

"Suck," Sebastian demands.

I suck his fingers.

"You're also a blanket hog. I never wake up with any blankets anymore. You have all of them, hiding your naked body from me."

He removes his fingers from my mouth, and I open to tell him to give me a real critique when his fingers slip under my jeans and find my clit. His fingers swirl around, and I know I won't be able to talk except in moans and groans until he stops.

His eyes light up; his smirk grows as he watches me be teased by his fingers.

"You're also spontaneous to a fault—too trusting, stubborn, secretive, bold, merciless, forgiving." He stops teasing me and grips my jeans, yanking them down before he delivers his final blow. "And none of that makes you anything but the perfect wife."

Our eyes hold each other as I search for any part of him that doesn't believe his statement. He believes I'm the perfect wife. *Maybe because I've been so different than I was in other relationships? Maybe he hasn't dealt with me long enough to realize that my spontaneous, fun, flirtatious manner can cause problems? Or maybe he truly believes it?*

I look down and realize he's naked as he settles between us. "You're perfect, Millie. Believe that, no matter what I or any other man says."

His words hammer through me, making me chill.

He reaches back to grab a condom, but I stop him with my hand. I'm on birth control. I don't say it with my words, but he knows. There is a trust between us. I guess that's what happens when you save each other's lives. When you care about each other more than anything else.

He spreads my legs and enters slowly, like he needs to move slowly so he can remember every inch as he slides inside me. When he's filled me, he grabs my hips and holds me close before his lips land on mine again, kissing me tenderly as he rocks into me.

Every thrust, kiss, touch is all saying the same thing. The one thing we are both too scared to say—I love you.

Those are words we will never say. Because if we do, we'd have to stop pretending. Those words would make this real. And despite the feeling being true, love isn't enough. It's not enough for him to no longer be an addict, or to become spontaneous enough for a life with me.

And I'm too out of control, too purposeless, too me to ever be with him for real. Not to mention my past or how we came together.

So I cherish every moment as he thrusts in and out, knowing it might be the only time I'm ever truly loved like this.

Our orgasms come too fast. We explode, our love dancing around the room, but still never spoken.

Sebastian pulls out and then wraps his arms and legs around me, holding me tight against his chest, not even giving me a moment to clean myself off.

"I'm not good for you, Millie. You deserve better," Sebastian whispers, telling me why he can't be with me.

"I'm no good for you either," I whisper back.

33

SEBASTIAN

I no longer struggle to remember to call Millie my wife. I think about her constantly—at work, at home, in the shower —everywhere.

And my most important task has been protecting her.

I got the restraining order against her ex filed the next day. Because of who I know and how much money I have, that was easy.

I hired a private investigator to keep an eye on him and make sure he wouldn't be coming for Millie.

And I hired a security guard to protect her whenever she leaves the condo. Not that she's super happy with that or finds it necessary, but my private investigator found a prior domestic abuse call on Trevor's record. A fact that I'll keep to myself. I don't want to worry her more than necessary. She said he never hurt her, but that doesn't mean he won't to get her back.

I lean down and kiss Millie on the cheek. She rolls over and groans. "I should get up."

I laugh. "It's seven in the morning. You went to sleep like two hours ago. You should sleep, I'll see you when I get off work."

She grabs my shirt and pulls me back to her. "Or you could stay."

She kisses me with everything she has, which is surprisingly a lot for being completely asleep.

I laugh and pull myself away from her. "I have to go to work. And you need your sleep so I can enjoy you when I get back."

"You can enjoy me now."

So tempting.

"I can't. I have to go to work. Are you working tonight?" I ask. Millie got a job at an emergency response call center this week, which has severely reduced our time together. It only makes every moment that much more fleeting. And her security guard that much more important.

She sighs. "Yes."

"See you for dinner before you go?"

"Am I dinner?" She bats her eyelashes at me.

"Definitely." I pull her bottom lip into my mouth and kiss her harder than I intended to. Now she's starting to wake up fully.

"Go back to sleep, my beautiful wife."

She smiles with her eyes closed, pulling her sheets up higher around her neck. It takes everything I have to walk away from her and go to work—*five more months*. I have five more months to enjoy every second with her.

I need to find a way to convince her to quit her job, and I need to cut back at work so we can spend all of that time together. Because I don't have the strength to keep walking away from her like this.

34

MILLIE

"Sᴇʙᴀsᴛɪᴀɴ?" I ask as I creek the door open to his condo.

No answer.

I exhale a breath as I push the door all the way open. We have three months left until we decided to stop pretending we are married and file for divorce. But if Sebastian sees what I'm carrying in this box, he might decide to call it quits early.

A small whimper comes from the box as I flip the lid up. A ball of brown fluff jumps up and licks me in the face.

"You're lucky Sebastian isn't here, or we might already be kicked to the curb." I bob the first of the five puppies on the nose as I carry them into the kitchen.

"Where should I put the dog supplies?" Andrew, my security guard asks.

"In the kitchen. Thanks, Andrew."

He puts the bag of supplies on the counter. "Are you all set for the rest of the day?"

"Yep."

"See you tomorrow, then."

I nod with a small sigh. Trevor hasn't bothered, texted, or called in two months. I don't know why I still need a security guard to follow me around everywhere.

I set the box of puppies down the floor, and they all start crying, trying to get out of the box. I tilt it and let them out and do my best to corral them in the tiled kitchen by moving some dining chairs and the trash can.

"Stay in the kitchen, guys. I know you're hungry. I'll feed you." I start digging through the bag of dog food and bowls I got from the shelter. I mix the food with some supplemental formula the volunteers gave me. They said the puppies could eat solid food now, but that it might help to give them some formula since they don't know their exact age or how long they've gone without their mother's milk.

"Alright, everyone, dinner's ready." I set the bowl down and wait...

One, two, three...I'm missing two.

"Looking for this?" Sebastian asks, holding up one of the puppies with a stern look on his face.

I wince and try my best cute guilty face as I reach out for the puppy in his arms.

"I didn't realize you were home," I say as the puppy nibbles on my chin.

He looks to the furball in my arms. "Obviously."

"So, you aren't a fan of dogs?"

"It's not that I don't like dogs. I have enough people to take care of in my life; I don't need more to take care of. And I particularly don't care for untrained little beasts that will pee on everything and destroy my furniture."

I hold up the puppy. "This little guy won't destroy your furniture, will you?" He licks my nose, and I smile before turning to Sebastian. "See? He agrees."

Sebastian shakes his head. "Where did you get the puppies?"

"A volunteer at the shelter called me."

"And why would a volunteer from a shelter call you?"

"Because I've fostered stray dogs and cats before, so when they can't find a home for them, they call me. The puppies will get adopted easily, but they need a little special care until they fatten up a little. They are malnourished after being away from their mother and need to be eating solid food before they can be adopted."

"How long?" His voice is stern, but he's not that pissed at me. He's just trying to hold onto his control. This isn't the first time in the last three months that I've pushed him out of his comfort zone.

"Two weeks."

He sighs. "Just keep them in the kitchen, that way we can minimize the damage."

"Um...about that..." I spot the last missing puppy peeing on the rug behind him in the living room.

Sebastian follows my gaze to catch the puppy in the act. He goes to pick up the runt. I expect Sebastian to scold him, but instead, he lets the pup lick his face before lowering him over the temporary barrier I set up to keep them in the kitchen. Then Sebastian digs into my bag of supplies, which mostly just consists of dog food, formula, and bowls.

"There's a pet store two blocks from here. I'll walk there and see if they have some puppy gates and pee pads."

"You're the best, hubby." I smile brightly, hoping it will earn me a smile before he leaves. Instead, I get a grumpy grimace.

"You're lucky I like you, wifey."

I smile at his comment before going back to taking care of the puppies. "You guys better behave, so he doesn't try to kick you out."

When Sebastian returns thirty minutes later with not only a gate and pee pads but dog toys and adorable little collars, he obviously isn't upset they are here. He looks at them the same way he looks at me—with adoration and love. *Maybe my spontaneousness is rubbing off on him after all?*

That is until the next morning when we wake up to five very naughty puppies. But even then, he helped clean up the mess and snuggled with me and one of the pups on the couch afterward. And as I lie resting my head on his chest, I have to remember—this isn't real, and I only have three more months left.

3 5

SEBASTIAN

"It must feel good to have the cast off. I know you weren't expecting to have it on this long, but I'm glad we waited the extra time to ensure it healed properly," the doctor says as he removes my cast.

"Uh, yea, feels great," I say because that's what I'm supposed to say. But in fact, it feels horrible. Of course, I want the cast off, but it means I only have weeks left until the six-month time limit is up. Until we are to stage a fight. Until we are supposed to file for divorce.

Trevor hasn't been bothering Millie. In fact, he seems to have moved on and is dating another woman in his office. Millie is safe.

We've been married long enough that it won't be embarrassing when we break it off, but not too long that our friends won't encourage us to fight to stay together.

Oaklee probably already knows the truth about our relationship.

Larkyn suspects.

Kade thinks I should have already divorced her.

Boden is an idiot who I haven't spoken to in months.

There is no reason we need to keep the act up. No outside reason to stay together.

Except, my own heart. My own addiction to her.

I thought these six-months would move slowly. I thought her spontaneous and adventurous spirit would drive me mad with the need to control everything. Instead, it's brought me new life and focus on only controlling the important things in my life that keep me from turning back to drugs or alcohol.

"So you're a newlywed. That's exciting. How is married life?"

I should say it's horrible. She's controlling or she's messy or we bicker a lot, something to start the process of acting like there is trouble in our marriage. The last few weeks I've been trying to drop hints at work. Trying to say little things that bug me to Larkyn.

But every time I start to complain, somehow it comes out as a compliment. Somehow it makes it seem like we are more in love than ever. Every time I try to say how awful it is, it backfires. In the five months we've been together, we haven't had one real fight.

So instead of pretending our marriage is horrible, I just say, "It's great."

"Good, you're all set," the doctor says.

I hop off the table and put weight on my ankle for the first time now free of a cast. I'm thankful to have complete freedom during my last few weeks left with Millie.

When I get back to my penthouse, I don't expect Millie to be here. She's been working a lot in the evenings, and my appointment wasn't until after I got off work.

Shadow, the puppy that Millie ended up keeping, comes bouncing down the hallway to me when I enter. He's peed almost everywhere, ripped up carpet, chewed the legs off of two chairs, and destroyed all of my shoes, but he still makes me smile every time I see him. Another thing I'm going to miss when we get divorced and Millie takes him with her.

"Come on, buddy. Let's go get you fed."

I carry him to the kitchen when all of a sudden, Millie pops the cork on a bottle and yells, "Congrats!"

I startle, and Shadow barks happily at her as champagne spills everywhere.

"I thought you had to work?" I say with a large grin as I grab her and pull me to her as Shadow wiggles between us.

"I changed my days. I couldn't miss celebrating that you got your cast off."

"With champagne?" I raise an eyebrow.

"Non-alcoholic champagne."

"What's the point then?"

"It's fun to drink out of the flutes, that's the point. I also ordered in dinner since you know I can't cook and macaroons, your favorite, for dessert."

"How do you know my favorite dessert?"

"I asked Larkyn."

"You've been hanging out with Larkyn?"

She kisses me, playfully. "Yea, I can see why you two are such good friends. And I get the best dirt on you."

"I don't like you hanging out with her," I say, pulling her lip into my mouth.

"Too bad. I learned your guilty pleasure is watching Keeping Up with the Kardashians."

"Stop," I say, kissing her again. And then I spot the food behind her. "Sushi? Really? You know I hate sushi."

She bites her lip to try to hold back her huge smile, but she can't. In fact, her entire body screams light, bright, and happy. She's wearing a bright blue sundress making her eyes sparkle. Her hair is loose in messy waves, and she's painted her nails a bright pink color.

"I want you to give sushi a second chance. And if you hate it, that's what the macaroons and fake champagne are for." She's so excited to have me try the new sushi that there is no way I can turn her down.

I put Shadow down, and he goes to work chewing on my shoelaces.

"I'll try, but only because I plan on eating you for dessert."

She blushes with a twinkle in her eye as she looks at my healed ankle. "I can't wait to see what you can do now that you're completely healed."

I laugh and dip her before kissing her again. "Oh, my dirty girl. I think we should skip dinner."

She pushes me back. "Nope, you just don't want to try any of the sushi I got. There is no getting out of this. Put your charming grin and lustful words away. We are eating and celebrating first."

"But my way is celebrating."

Her cheeks puff out from grinning so much as she shakes her head.

"Sit." She points to the new table we bought together after we broke the last one.

I sit, and she carries over a large assortment of sushi before sitting down across from me. I focus on looking at how beautiful and incredible she is instead of on the gross raw fish in front of me.

She pours the bubbly sugar water into two glasses and hands one to me. "To finally getting your cast off."

I clink my glass with hers.

"Now, what is it that you don't like about sushi?"

"It's undercooked and cold, and the texture and smell is..." I shiver at the thought.

She laughs. "Try this one." She picks up a piece with her chopsticks and holds it up to my mouth. She waits patiently for me to open. I would do anything she asked. All I want to do is make her happy. Maybe it's my addiction to her talking. Or maybe...

I open my mouth, and she puts the sushi into my mouth before I can finish my thought. I start chewing, surprised that it's warm, has a tough texture instead of the chewiness I'm used to, and doesn't have a strong fish smell or taste.

I swallow.

Millie claps excitedly like I just won a race or something.

"What do you think?"

"Not bad."

"Yes!" She makes a pumping gesture with her hands. "I knew I'd get you to like it."

I stare at the plate of 'sushi,' but most of it is cooked, not raw, so no wonder I like it.

"I'm not sure you can call this sushi."

"We have to start with baby steps. I'll get you to be more adventurous eventually."

I scourer over the sushi pieces. "Where are the raw ones?"

She points to the corner closest to her. I pick up my chopsticks and get one of the pieces.

"You're going to try one?"

I nod.

"Close your eyes when you do."

I scrunch my nose in confusion but do as she says, not sure how this will help. I pop the bite into my mouth, feeling the cool, salty, fishiness of the bite. At the same time, I feel her lips come down on my throat as I swallow.

I moan as the bite goes down.

I open my eyes and find Millie straddling my lap.

"What are you doing?"

"Making sure you have a good experience with sushi. Did you like it?"

"I'll eat sushi all day if it means you'll kiss my throat like that."

Her eyes darken. "I changed my mind."

"About what?"

"I can't wait until after dinner." She grabs my neck as her lips land on my mouth harshly, like there is no possible way she can get enough of my lips and tongue.

I grab onto her hips, yanking her body tight against mine as I kiss her back. I love that she's always pushing me to try new things, but right now, all I want is her—just her.

I wish I could say the words, but for now, my kisses will have to do. Kisses that I'm addicted to. These kisses are the only thing keeping me sane right now.

Her hips start moving, grinding over my lap as her body craves more.

I lift my hips, pushing my erection into her, wanting her to feel as good as she possibly can. The moment is full of frenzy and lust. This moment very much feels like before, when we broke the table.

"Don't break the table," Millie says with heavy breaths as she keeps kissing me as I lift her up.

"We won't." But I also know there is no way I'll make it to the bedroom either. I need inside her.

Thank God she's wearing a dress. And when I slide my hand up her inner thigh, I realize she has no panties either. I spread her wetness around as I lift her up, trying to find a place to fuck her without having to wait.

Her fingers are already fumbling at my zipper, trying to get my pants down. And then she's reaching into my pants and grabs my cock.

I growl as she takes hold of me. There is no way we are making it to the bedroom.

I press her back against the wall as I push my pants down with a gleam in my eye. "Good thing my ankle is all better, so I can do this."

My cock pushes at her entrance as she holds on tightly to my body. She arches her back and moans as I push deeper.

Then our mouths are locked together again. Her hands fist my hair, and I pound into her, pushing her closer and closer to her orgasm while chasing my own. I can't get enough of this woman.

I've fucked dozens of women over the years to the point that my friends and family have thought of me as a manwhore. But none of the women I've been with come close to making me feel the way I do when I'm with Millie.

I thrust harder into her, until I'm sure we are making a dent in the wall. Her moans only grow louder, more desperate. I know her body well. I know what to do to prolong her orgasm and what to do to make her come immediately. I know how to tease her and how to please her. I know how to make her screaming angry and how to worship her. And there hasn't been one moment where I haven't loved everything about her.

I love her.

I've never said those words to a woman before. Never even thought them. But I think them now. And for the first time, I want to say them. I want to shout them from the rooftops.

I don't think while I'm thrusting inside her is the best time to say those words for the first time. So I stay silent, vowing to find the perfect way to say the words.

But I have to say something.

I wait until we've both come. Until we are both floating high and then I mutter the closest thing I've ever said to 'I love you.'

"I don't want to pretend anymore."

3 6

MILLIE

I DON'T WANT to pretend anymore.

Those words. He's said them before.

He's said them before…

Suddenly, it all comes flooding back.

How we ended up together.

Why we ended up together.

What the plan was.

I go white. My heart jumps to my throat. My hand trembles, still grasping onto Sebastian's neck.

"Baby, are you okay?" Sebastian asks still inside me, able to sense everything about me without saying a word.

I kiss him softly, not able to speak. Sebastian just told me that he wants more than just pretend. He just fucked me like he didn't want this to end. And I can't even speak because my thoughts are racing a million miles a minute trying to process how I remember, how I forgot.

I was drunk, so drunk. That's how I forgot.

And now I remember everything.

"Shower with me?" Sebastian asks, as he sets me on my feet.

I nod, still speechless.

430

He doesn't speak either as we walk toward his bathroom—both of us shedding the rest of our clothes as we walk. Sebastian turns the water on, and I get us fresh towels, needing a moment alone to compose myself.

Oaklee led me to believe that what Sebastian did that night was the problem. And at the time, I thought he was the problem. But I ruin everything. I ruin every relationship I've ever been in. Turns out, I ruined any chance Sebastian or I ever had before our relationship even started.

I hang the towels next to the shower and then step under the water, where Sebastian is already waiting for me. He wordlessly starts washing me, but I know he's studying me. I'm not usually this quiet. He knows something is wrong.

I should say something—anything. But I can't. Because I can't believe what I've done.

And I don't know how to fix it. Or if it can be fixed. I don't know...

No, I can fix it. It will be a process, but I can fix it.

But Sebastian will never forgive me. It's too much to forgive. There is no chance at more. In less than two weeks, this ends as planned. The most I can hope for is that he never finds out the truth and that he can think back to our time together with some small joy. Despite how we got together, he has become more than that. He has become my everything.

"I'm sorry—I shouldn't have said that," Sebastian finally says, and he pulls me into his bare chest.

"No, you shouldn't have."

"I'm sorry."

"Me too. If I were looking for a husband, I would choose you. I'm just not looking. That's not what I want."

"I understand." His voice is firm and strong, but there is an undertone of confusion beneath his strength. Inside, he wants more. So much more.

After we speak, everything shifts once again. Gone is the lust and charge between us. Now we are just two empty vessels headed toward the end. And our end was never supposed to end in happily ever after. Our end is just that—an end.

I can't think about what that will mean, though. Hopefully, tomorrow we can go back to some level of normalcy so that we can enjoy our final two weeks. But if not, then I'll remember tonight forever.

We both get dressed and climb into the bed.

"I don't want this to change, yet," I say.

"It won't." Sebastian pulls me onto his chest as he snuggles with me.

He says things won't change, but it has. Usually, he would have fucked me again, feeding his addiction of me, but it seems he's trying to wean off me already.

It's for the best.

Twenty minutes later, Sebastian is snoring, and I'm still wide awake, thinking about all the things I have to do. All the things I have to fix before our time is up so Sebastian doesn't get hurt.

But all I can think about is how badly my heart is breaking. *Is his breaking too?*

I know my eyes aren't going to close. I want to remember every moment of our time together. I'll sleep when he's at work tomorrow.

I run my hand through his gorgeous thick hair. "I'm so sorry, Sebastian. So sorry...I ruined everything."

A tear spills from my eye and lands on his cheek.

"I love you. And in a different world, I would stay married to you, and it would be more real than any other love in the world. But I fucked up, and now I'm just going to have to love you from afar."

37

SEBASTIAN

I HOLD Millie's wedding ring as I sit on the couch. She's currently in the shower getting ready to go over to Kade and Larkyn's tonight. It's Larkyn's birthday, and Kade is throwing her a big party.

It's supposed to be the night where we fake a fight and tell everyone how miserable we are together. Then Millie will ask Oaklee if she can stay with her tonight. They will have a pity party and talk about how horrible their men are, and then eventually, one of us will file for divorce, and that will be that.

That's how everything is supposed to go. That's been the plan all this time—for six months now.

And yet, these last two weeks have been the hardest of my life. Every moment has been moving toward today. And as much as I applied the breaks, swerved, done everything I could to stop us, to slow down time, nothing has worked.

To make matters worse, Millie won't talk to me at all about us except to plan today.

She's afraid—and I can understand why. Her ex is a piece of work. The more my private investigator looked into him, the more criminal charges he dug up. I can understand why she's afraid to enter a real relationship again.

But that's what we've been doing for months now. I can't remember the last time I did pretend with her. I can't remember ever pretending. Every moment with Millie has felt real.

I twist Millie's ring around on my pinky finger, examining it. I wish it would jog my memory. I wish I would remember where I got the ring. I wish I could remember our wedding night. Maybe it's for the best, though. Because if I remembered that night, things might not have led me here.

I'm supposed to pretend we are bickering and fighting. But I can't, no matter how hard I try. Millie doesn't want to talk to me. She doesn't trust me. She doesn't trust that I love her. She doesn't trust that this is real. So I'll just have to show her how real we really are.

"Sebastian?" Millie says as she pads down the hallway. I tuck her ring into my pocket. "Have you seen my wedding ring?"

I shake my head. "Nope, I haven't seen it."

"Huh. I took it off to shower and put it on the bathroom counter, but it's not there anymore."

"I can help you look for it. But if we are supposed to be fighting, maybe it's best that you're not wearing it."

She rubs her bare finger. It doesn't look right without her wedding ring on her finger. And the way her face falls, I know she'd rather be wearing it. But I have something special planned for tonight that involves it.

"Yea, I guess you're right."

"You look beautiful, by the way." I stand and take her hands in mine, trying to get her to stop thinking about her missing ring. I kiss her cheek, careful not to mess up her hair or makeup.

"Thanks, I feel weird wearing a dress. It's not usually my style, but I know how much you like me in a dress."

"I like you in anything. Dresses are my favorite because I can do this." I lift her dress and find her cunt bare. Once again, she's not wearing panties or a bra.

She gasps as I touch her. "Sebastian, don't. I can't—"

But then she's coming. It's not a full explosion, but enough to take the edge off and give her a beautiful glow.

She blushes when I remove my hand. "You ready to go?"

She nods, her pink lips gaping, still in shock of what I just did to her. I take her hand in mine, and then we head to the suburbs where Kade and Larkyn live.

I park on the street outside the house. Millie and I haven't spoken much on the drive over. We just held hands in comforting silence. These could be our last moments together as a couple. Tonight, Millie could end up sleeping at Oaklee's, or I could end up sleeping here at Kade's.

I can't let that happen. I'll do everything I can to change her mind. It might not be fair to do this publicly, but I think it's the only way she'll listen to me—the only way we have a shot at a future. And right now, I'm not ready to give up.

"You ready?" she asks. It's a loaded question. She doesn't know the thoughts racing through my head. She doesn't know how far I'll fight to keep her, but she's about to.

I grip her hand tighter. "Yes."

Her eyes shake back and forth like she's reading my thoughts running across my forehead, but of course, she can't.

"We'll stay friends after this? Maybe meet up on some island somewhere for a weekend or something every couple of years and just hang out? No matter what happens after tonight," she says suddenly.

I do my best to hold back my grin, but I feel it all the way in my toes. She still wants more. Whether she says it or not, she wants more. That is all I need—hope.

"Yes, no matter what, we will still be in each other's lives."

Her lips pull back into a thin smile, and then she bites her bottom lip like she isn't sure that's enough.

It's nowhere near enough, baby. Soon you'll realize you can have everything you never knew you wanted.

Once out of the car, though, I try to take Millie's hand back in mine, but she pulls away. *And so it begins.*

Larkyn and Kade's house is a nice suburban home with a large garage, plenty of space, four bedrooms, three baths. It's beautiful and homey, but not too big. It doesn't show off the true wealth that Kade has. Larkyn didn't want her kids growing up in something too grand.

There was a time when I thought a house like this would be the last thing I want. But when the kids come running at me, and I scoop each of them up, my heart all of a sudden feels empty. I've never wanted kids, never thought I'd be a good father, but I want to learn to be one. Millie would help me become a good father. And she'd make a great mother. I want everything with her.

"Millie, Sebastian, I'm so glad you could make it," Larkyn walks over and gives each of us a hug.

I watch Millie closely. I don't touch her. I don't put my hands on her. But I also won't be the one to start a fight.

"Happy birthday, sis," I say.

"Thank you!"

"Is my big brother treating you well?"

"Of course, he went all out for the party. He's out back arranging a band for dancing later."

I smile. I love that my brother takes such good care of Larkyn.

"He's spoiling me," she says.

"No, he's loving you. And you deserve every bit of it."

She lights up. "Enough about me, I want to hear about how you two are doing! It's been weeks since I've seen you together."

I keep my mouth shut, waiting for Millie to speak first. If she wants to fake a fight, here is her chance. An awkward silence spreads between us.

"Picture! I take picture," Iris says.

"Oh goodness, yes, you should get a pic of us," Larkyn says to her child.

Larkyn stands next to me, leaving Millie no choice but to stand closer to me. I put my arms around her as the squirt takes our picture.

But as soon as she's finished, Millie runs off, with some mumbled excuse about finding Oaklee.

"What's going on?" Larkyn asks, as soon as Millie is out of earshot.

I flash her a wicked grin. "I'm proposing to Millie tonight."

"I'm confused since I thought you already did that."

"If I did, I don't remember."

Larkyn's eyes widen. "I knew it! I knew you weren't together the night you got married. We weren't there, but I knew you couldn't have been hiding a woman like Millie from us. So why did you get married? Why pretend?"

I shake my head. "It's a long story, but I want to make it real."

She claps her hands together, excitedly. "Oh my god. You fell in love. I never thought I'd see the day."

"You thought I had married Millie but didn't love her?"

"Well, I thought there was some reason you weren't telling me at first. But lately, every time I've seen you two together, you are all over each other. So if you are going to propose tonight, why does Millie look like she's about to explode into a million tears?"

"Because tonight was the night we were supposed to end it."

"Oh."

"Yea, oh. Instead…" I pull out the ring. "I'm going to propose."

She looks at it closer with recognition in her gaze.

"You know where the ring came from," I say.

She frowns. "Maybe."

"Where?"

Her eyes flicker up at me. "You don't remember that night?"

"No."

She smiles. "Let's just say it's the perfect ring for you two."

"Tell me."

"Nope. Now, go win your girl. But be careful with big gestures, and don't take her first reaction as her truthful reaction. Give her time to realize that you love her for real. That will take time."

"I will."

I turn and start to head off to look for Millie and avoid Kade. I don't want to hear him yell at me for not getting her to sign the damn prenup again.

I bump into a caterer. I get tackled by Henry, one of Larkyn and Kade's kids. But I don't find Millie.

I head out back to where the band is setting up, and then I see her in a heated discussion with the guitarist.

I run over, afraid that the man will hurt her when I hear him speak. "You took half my fucking money! That makes you a gold digger!"

I step between the man and Millie. "Sir, step back."

He growls, looking from Millie to me. "You, her new husband?"

"Yes, and if you speak to my wife again, I'm going to punch you."

He laughs. "I'm done with her. Tell the Kings I'm sorry, but I can't play tonight, not with her here."

"And you are?"

"Her ex-husband, Noah. And a piece of advice from one ex-husband to you, her next victim—make sure you get a good lawyer when she files for divorce. Which will be about six months after the wedding. That's when she knows she's been married long enough to ask for half of everything. She has an excellent lawyer."

He stomps off, and I can't process what he said.

"Let me explain, please," Millie says quietly from behind me.

I turn slowly. I notice others in the backyard, watching us closely, but I no longer care what anyone thinks. I just want the truth. I want to know my future with her isn't at risk.

"Is what he said true? Were you married before?"

She sucks in a breath and then nods. "Yes."

"And the rest?"

"True," she says without hesitation.

I look at her through a new light. *Do I even know her at all?*

Millie has her arms wrapped around her chest, and she looks like she's about to be sick.

"What else? What else haven't you told me?" My voice is angry. I can't hide it, and I can't keep everyone in the yard from noticing our fight either.

"I've been married three times," she says softly.

Three.

Fucking.

Times.

Holy shit. She's thirty. How does someone get married three times? Unless the bastard was telling the truth. Unless she really is a gold digger. Spots rich men to marry and then fucks them over with a divorce settlement. That's why she never works a real job. It all makes sense.

I take a step back when she reaches her hand out to touch me. I can't handle her touch right now. I need to get out of here. I need…

"That's what you get, you asshole," Oaklee says, coming up to support her friend. Her pregnant belly is round beneath her black maxi dress.

"That's what I get?"

"You hurt us, so we found your weakness. We got you drunk and then tricked you into marrying her so she could take half your money and pay you back for what you did. You'll lose half of everything," Oaklee continues.

I look at Millie dead in the eyes, and I know without her reacting that it's all true.

"How long have you remembered? This entire time?"

Millie swallows hard, and I realize I don't want to hear the answer.

I hold up my hand, stopping her from speaking as I feel all eyes on me. I feel the ring in my pocket—a ring of unknown origin. But one I plan on throwing into the ocean as soon as possible.

My heart has never beat faster, never been more panicked, more pained, more broken. I look at the only woman I ever imagined as my wife. A wife that will be able to take half of everything I own. She said it was pretend, but it wasn't, it was real. The marriage certificate was real. Legally, we existed. And emotionally, I fell for her. This is as real as it gets.

I thought I'd make it real tonight. I thought I'd cement us together forever.

It became real, but we won't be locked together forever.

And then I say the words that I thought I'd only say under false pretenses, but they have never been truer.

"We're over."

3 8

MILLIE

I thought I was prepared to hear him say those words. But hearing them with all of the pain in his voice rips through me like an ax.

Our fight was supposed to be pretend, but there was nothing fake about our fight. It was completely real.

The crowd is quiet as we stand. They part when Sebastian heads back into the house.

I close my eyes, needing some strength before I chase after him.

"It's for the best," Oaklee says next to me.

I open my eyes, sending her a glare. "You have no idea what you've done."

"That was the plan all along, though."

"I didn't remember the plan until the other night. And he didn't deserve that."

"But—"

"We were wrong. It was a mistake. Boden did what he did on his own."

"Are you sure?"

I nod.

"Shit."

I don't have time to explain everything to Oaklee. I start running, even though I'm wearing uncomfortable wedge heels that I struggle to run in, I run.

I was prepared to say goodbye tonight, but only on good terms. Only if we parted as friends. I can't part Sebastian like this.

I see Larkyn in the house, who gives me a puzzled look then points to the front door. I'll have to thank her later. I run out the front door and see Sebastian about ten feet from his car.

I open my mouth, but if he hears me coming, he might get in the car and take off before I get to him. So I run, flying as fast as I can and I fling myself in front of him just as he reaches his car.

"Listen. Please."

"I don't need to hear any more. Not from a liar like you."

"Sebastian, just listen. It's not what you think."

"There isn't any possible explanation you could give me for not telling me you were married three times, stole money from unsuspecting men like a leech, and then are trying to pull the same thing on me. You're a con-woman."

I wince at his harsh words. I deserve that, but it doesn't help the situation. He doesn't understand why.

"And you were an asshole when I first met you!"

"I called you fat. I didn't try to steal half your wealth."

"I thought you had been helping Boden cheat on Oaklee. I thought you were a monster."

"And I thought I loved you. I guess we were both wrong."

There is a crack of lighting when he says his final sentence, followed by the rain pouring down in sheets.

Just like that, the world declares us over. *We're over.*

It's for the best.

"I'll see you in court," Sebastian says, pulling his door open to escape the rain.

"I don't want your money."

"And I don't want you."

His door slams shut, and then he's driving off.

Leaving me breathless as I stand in the rain.

I don't know how long I stand there in the pouring rain. Eventually, Larkyn finds me and brings me inside, wrapping me in a blanket.

"I'm sorry, I'll call an Uber and get out of your way."

"No, you're staying here tonight. I know Sebastian needs his space. And Oaklee doesn't seem like the best friend of yours to be around."

"But you're Sebastian's family. I shouldn't be here. Not when I hurt him."

She smiles as she hugs me. "That's exactly why you should be here. Now tell me everything."

So I do.

39

SEBASTIAN

I DROVE until I could find the shittiest, ugliest bar in town. The kind with cockroaches and everything is sticky where you walk. The kind that only serves one brand of beer and two brands of whiskey.

That's where I'm sitting, holding a whiskey glass in my hand filled with some cheap shot.

I haven't taken a sip, and yet, I still feel drunk.

The bartender walks back to me. There are only three other people in the bar. It's a slow night.

"Want to try the other whiskey? Or I can mix some fruity shit in it if that's what you need to get it down."

I glare up at the rude man. "I'm good."

He chuckles and then walks away.

I go back to staring at my glass, feeling the effects without drinking. I'm drunk not on the liquor, but on Millie. I'm drunk on the pain, the misery.

I realize there is no going back to my life before. Not after I've realized what I'm missing. Even if Millie faked everything, for me, it was real. And I want it. I just can't have it with Millie.

She's a liar.

A fraud.

A mistake.

A mistake that's going to take half my money. Not that I give a damn really. I don't need my wealth. I don't need any of it.

Millie was married three times.

She's a gold digger.

She remembered that night.

I wish I could remember. I wish I could understand what really happened. If I could rewind and remember, maybe I wouldn't be sitting here like a chump who just got his heart ripped out.

I can't shoot the whiskey. I can't drink. I won't do drugs. But I can find a woman to drown my misery in, not that I'll find one in this bar. It's probably why I chose it, so I wouldn't be tempted to do something that stupid.

"King?" A man says from behind me.

I turn, not in the mood to talk to anyone tonight. And when I see him, I'm really not in the mood.

"I wouldn't come any closer, not unless you want to get your ass beat again."

Trevor doesn't hesitate. He takes a seat at the bar next to me.

"I don't want to cause a fight. I'm here to apologize. I shouldn't have laid a finger on Millie."

"No, you shouldn't have." I grip the drink tighter, wishing I could drink it and not lose myself. "What do you want?"

He studies me a moment. "I'm here to talk about Millie."

"You want her, you can have her. We're through."

There's a pause and then a soft chuckle. "So she told you."

"Yea, she told me she's a fucking gold digger who has been married three times before me."

"Wait…you think Millie is a gold digger?"

"Yes. I met Noah. She took half his money. And that's the only reason she's married to me."

Trevor hangs his head low, and he shakes it. "Oh man, I'm going to regret this. I'm really enjoying watching you hang out your misery, but you don't have a damn clue what you're talking about."

"What?"

"You heard me. You don't have a clue. Millie is a lot of things. She's all over the place, wild, carefree, but she is not a gold digger. The one thing in the world Millie could care less about is money. Trust me, I was married to her for two years."

He might as well have punched me. The bastard was married to her longer than I will be.

"And why should I listen to a criminal like you?"

He laughs hard at that. "I'm not a criminal; I'm a lawyer. Your investigator must have spelled my name wrong, too. Trevor with an 'o' is me, a lawyer, but Trever with an 'e' has a nasty rap sheet. We share the same last name. I found out about it when I got mistaken for him during my bar exam, so don't kick yourself for screwing it up.

"In regards to Millie, I never hurt her physically. I would never lay a hand on a woman. We just didn't belong together, and I'm afraid I hurt her in more ways than I realized at the time. I know that, now that I'm in a good relationship, which is why I'm here."

"I'm confused. If you are in a good relationship, why did you stalk Millie?"

"Because I needed to give her this." He lays a stack of papers in front of me. "Make sure she gets them. And if I were you, I would listen to her before you throw away what you have. Millie and I didn't work out, but that doesn't mean I don't know what a catch she is. I saw the two of you together. You fit. We didn't. She was looking for a man who could tame her. But she doesn't need to be tamed, you know that."

I narrow my eyes and watch as he leaves. "And don't worry, she can't get half your money. But if you aren't careful, she'll get away with half of your heart."

MILLIE

I NEED to get up off the couch I've been sleeping on all night in Larkyn and Kade's home. I need to pick myself up. I need to start over. And I need to explain and apologize to Sebastian.

Not because I deserve forgiveness, but because he deserves to hear the truth. He deserves to know what happened. He deserves to understand the pain that led to me hurting him.

I can't sit here on this couch, and yet, I'm putting off seing Sebastian because the next time I see him could be the last time. Having Sebastian in my life, even when he's upset with me, seems better than not having him in my life at all.

And then I feel him. Without looking up, I know he's here. Apparently, today is going to be the last day I see him.

"Can we talk?" I ask as I look up at him. I should be the one to speak.

"No."

His word cuts through me. But he continues toward me even though he said no. *Does he want me to leave?* I can understand since this is his brother and sister in law's house.

He sits down on the couch next to me silently before finally saying, "We can't talk. You should talk, and I can listen."

He leans back, not giving me a clue to how he's feeling. To what he's thinking. But it's clear he won't be talking. This is my chance to come clean about everything. To tell him everything.

"His name was Gavin. We grew up together. Had that epic kind of love that you just know is going to last forever. Except it didn't." I swallow, it's been a long time since I talked about Gavin. But it's where my story starts—the first man who ever destroyed me.

"We were twenty when he proposed. We were poor. Neither of us went to college. We both worked three jobs a piece just to survive, but we were happy. We were going to have forever." My voice cracks, reliving the pain.

"I said yes immediately. We got married in the courthouse that weekend. It wasn't much, but it was enough for us. But then things changed.

"Small things at first. He wanted more. More money, more stability. He tried to tame me. To convince me that we shouldn't live so spontaneously. I needed to focus on one career instead of twenty. I needed to lose weight so I was more appealing. I needed to...the needs just kept continuing, and I tried so hard to be what he wanted. I loved him, of course. I wanted to make him happy."

I stare at my hands as I talk. I'm not telling Sebastian this so he'll give me sympathy. I'm telling him so he can understand. No, I'm telling him so I can let the past go. So I can realize that although I loved him, he wasn't right for me. No man has been, except maybe Sebastian.

"Our relationship was chaos, a complete storm. I didn't realize the signs, I didn't realize I was drowning. We never got the chance to fix it, before he suddenly died. A fluke seizure while he was driving, and then he was just gone."

I close my eyes feeling the pain of the hole he left in my heart. "I struggled with him gone. I thought I needed a man to make me whole. I didn't realize that what Gavin had done to me did lasting damage. I didn't realize that what he did was abuse. I just thought I needed a man because that had been my entire life, and it was gone. Something was missing, so I tried to fill it."

I take a deep breath. "So I married Noah. But he was worse. I barely got out with the money I brought in. And I vowed after him to stay away from men. But then Trevor entered. He was actually a good man. He was smart and intelligent and settled. He worked as a lawyer and helped me focus my passions into one. He got me to work as a photographer. And as much as I loved the work, it wasn't who I was. I like to bounce around. I don't need money or status to make me happy."

I look at Sebastian for the first time. "That wasn't what this was about. I never wanted your money; I still don't."

Sebastian sits still as a statue, unmoving. He doesn't say anything. He's just listening.

So I continue.

"At first, I couldn't remember that night. I couldn't remember what happened or why, same as you. That wasn't a lie. I never meant to lie to you; I just didn't think my past mattered. I didn't want you to try to convince me that I was abused in any way. I'm not a victim. I don't need help.

"That's what I thought. I didn't realize that my first love really messed me up, that the abuse wasn't physical, it wasn't in my face every day, but it was there. It's going to take a lot more healing, but I realize that now. When we got together, we were never supposed to last, and I didn't want to heal."

I look at Sebastian again. "You were the one who helped me heal. You helped me realize that I was hurt. That my past relationships weren't healthy. And I've been getting help. That's why I've been talking with Larkyn. She's been getting me counseling."

I exhale another breath. "Here is what I remember of that night."

———

I order a drink at the hotel bar next to Sebastian while we wait, hoping that soon we will hear from Oaklee or Boden to let us know they want to head to chapel to get married still. Or at least to tell us something.

Just as I get my drink, though, I see Oaklee in her wedding dress with mascara stained tears running down her eyes.

I exchange a glance with Sebastian.

"Go, I'll pay for your drink and then find Boden. Here's my number." He takes my phone and programs his number into it. "Text me and keep me in the loop, and I'll do the same."

I nod and then run to her, pulling her back into my arms. I had hoped they would work it out. They needed to work it out. They love each other. They seemed to be working it out in the elevator.

"Talk to me, Oaklee. Tell me what happened."

"I can't. I just can't."

"Shh, it's okay. What can I do to help? Do you want me to get you a different room? Do you want to change out of your dress? Get a drink?"

"I don't know," she sobs.

I take a deep breath and walk us over the hotel desk clerk. "Can you get us a room with a double bed and have her bags brought from the honeymoon suite?"

An hour later, Oaklee and I have both changed clothes and are settled into a new hotel room. But she still hasn't talked to me.

"Where is Boden?" she asks.

"Let me find out."

I pull up my phone to text Sebastian. He types back the name of a club.

I show Oaklee against my better judgment.

"Let's go," she says.

"Why are we going to the club? Oaklee, you need to tell me what happened. Why didn't you get married? Why did you break up?"

"I'm pregnant. I told him, and he ran. He said he didn't believe it was his, and that he never wanted kids."

"Oh, sweetie." I hold her as we both cry and cry and cry.

Finally, she pulls away. "Let's go."

"I don't think that's a good idea."

She flashes me a look that says she's going, whether I'm coming or not. Boden is about to get his balls chopped off by one angry woman. I can't stop her, but I can join her. That's what best friends do.

"Let's go." I grab my purse, and then we head to the club to go chew Boden out.

The club isn't just any club. It's a strip club, which I guess shouldn't surprise me. What does surprise me is what we see. Boden and Sebastian with two women dancing over them. Both seem to be making out with the women, and Sebastian seems to be encouraging Boden to go further.

The scene stops me in my tracks, but it doesn't stop Oaklee. She marches over to Boden and slaps him square in the face and yells something at him before I can stop her.

Sebastian realizes what's happening and stands before she slaps him too.

I walk over to her and give them both a stern look. "Come on, Oaklee, they aren't worth it."

I lead her to the bar and order us both two drinks before I realize what I'm doing.

Sebastian comes up and sits next to us. "Boden's gone. You don't have to worry about him anymore." There's a pause. "I'm sorry."

Oaklee and I ignore him as I drink down my drink. Oaklee eventually pushes her drink in front of Sebastian.

"Drink this. You're a fucking asshole, and I'm not going to let you go enjoy yourself. Tonight, you are going to drink because I'm pregnant and can't drink. So you're going to. Both of you. We are going to drown in my sorrows and come up with a plan that doesn't leave me completely embarrassed to face all of my friends and family tomorrow."

"You could tell them that Boden is a cheating bastard who is skirting his responsibility to his kid?" I say. "There is no shame in that."

"I can't," Oaklee breaks. "We need something else to focus on."

Sebastian starts to open his mouth, but I give him a threatening look. *If you do anything, and I mean anything, that will hurt my friend, I will castrate you right now.*

He gives me a nod. "Boden is an asshole. I'll do whatever I can to help you, Oaklee. Just tell me how to fix this."

She glares at him. "For now, drink."

I down mine and order another. I assume Sebastian does as well because when Oaklee waves the bartender down, he brings us two more shots. That's how we continue—drinking shot after shot while we listen to Oaklee's pain.

"We need a diversion—something to draw attention away from what happened. We will say I was sick, and there will be redo at some point. But we need a different focus, something big," Oaklee says.

"Like what?" I ask.

She glances between the two of us. "Like you two eloping."

I gasp.

"Um, what now? How is that going to help anything? Or be remotely believable?"

"You two are the most unlikely people to get married. Everyone knows that. But if you got married, no one would care that I didn't."

I'm too stunned to process her words. She has to be kidding.

Oaklee ignores my response and gives Sebastian a smug expression. "You said you would do anything to help me. This is what I want."

"Okay," Sebastian says.

"Okay? What are you crazy?"

Oaklee grabs my arm. "Excuse us for just a moment." She pulls me into the bathroom, and I shake her off.

"Have you gone insane? Why do you want us to get married? How will that solve anything? I don't want to marry the guy who helped your almost-husband cheat."

She smiles. "Marry him. Save me from complete embarrassment. And then take half his money."

"What? I don't want his money."

"Okay, fine, just make him think you are going to. Get him to sign a prenup to give you half by sneaking it in the marriage license. The man is filthy rich and a jerk. You don't have to actually take half but just put that fear into him. Show him that no man messes with us."

"Shouldn't we be hurting Boden right now, not Sebastian?"

"Are you my best friend or not?"

"I am."

"Then help me mess with him. We will find a way to make Boden pay too."

"Fine. If Sebastian agrees to it, then okay."

"Eek! This is just what I need tonight, a distraction!" She pulls out her phone to arrange a marriage license and prenup on short notice. Then she starts calling chapels and then her friend, Val, who will make sure everyone else shows up.

Meanwhile, I panic. Full-blown panic. "He's never going to fall for this. He will never sign the prenup. He will never get married. He'll get it annulled tomorrow."

"Then, we will mess with him until tomorrow."

I sigh and leave Oaklee alone in the bathroom and am immediately met with Sebastian.

"She's lost it. We aren't getting married."

He frowns. "Why not?"

"Because it's crazy! It won't fix anything."

"Maybe, maybe not. I never thought I'd get married."

"Well, I've been married three times. I think that's enough. I don't want to get married again."

He chuckles. "Perfect. Neither of us believes in the institution of marriage. So it will mean nothing, and we can just help out our friend. I fucked up, and I feel bad. And you want to help her. She's a mess. She needs this. We can get it annulled or get a divorce in a few months. But tonight, I think it would help."

"You're mad."

"I know." He leans in close. "Plus, I think it will be really fun to be married to you."

His lips brush my skin and tease me with want and desire. "I'm not fucking you just because we're married."

"Oh, but I think you will. It will be fun to play our own little game between just us."

His eyes are playful and light. He has no idea I plan to destroy him—that that's what Oaklee really wants.

I fold my arms over my chest. "You haven't proposed, and I don't see a ring, so until that happens, I won't give you my answer."

He smirks as he kneels down before me and produces a ring.

I'm stunned. *How did he come up with a ring so suddenly?*

"Millie Raine, will you marry me?"

"Yes." *Wait, yes? Did I just say yes?*

He grins and puts the ring on my finger.

"I'm going to need another shot," I say.

———

I look up at Sebastian again. "We got married in front of everyone. And then you signed the prenup papers giving me half. You were too drunk to notice them in with the marriage license."

His jaw twitches, but he still doesn't say anything.

"After that, we passed out drunk in the honeymoon suite, and you know the rest. The only other part you don't know is why I kept it from you when I remembered. That was selfish. I knew I'd never be with you for real, what I had done was too terrible.

"But I was hoping to still have a tiny piece of you in my life. So I tried to change the prenup so you wouldn't have to give me anything. I tried to keep what happened hidden, hoping we could part friends. I know it was wrong, but I just couldn't bear to live a life without you in it. I'm sorry."

A long silence stretches. I said what I needed to say. There is nothing left for me to say, and when it's clear that Sebastian isn't going to speak, I say, "I should go."

"No."

I fall back into my seat like the full weight of the world just crashed down on me.

"It's my turn to talk and your turn to listen."

I bite my trembling lip and fist my hands, trying to keep my anxiety in.

"You should have told me that you'd been married before."

I wince.

"But I understand why you didn't."

He takes a deep breath. "I was wrong to not have stopped Boden. I didn't even realize what was happening, and then the next thing I knew half-naked women were dancing on us. He was kissing them and telling me about how he had cheated over the course of months. When you came to the club, I was chewing him out, not encouraging him.

"But I'm not upset with you for thinking I was. I should have never been friends with someone like Boden. And I understand why you did what you thought you did."

I feel tears wallowing in my eyes. This is the part where he says we're over again—that we can't even be friends.

"But I wasn't drunk that night."

I tilt my head, unsure of what he said.

"I knew that Oaklee and you were trying to get me to drink, so I pretended too. I was completely sober walking down the aisle, and you know why? Because when you followed Oaklee into that bathroom, a woman came up to me. She had overheard our conversation and said she had just lost her husband of over forty years. She saw the way I looked at you and said it was the same way her husband looked at her. And then she handed me her and her husband's wedding rings. Told me to marry you, that it would change my life. That it would be the best decision I ever made, and it was."

Tears are flowing now because I don't understand, and all I feel is a million emotions.

"Her words hit me like I was wasting my life. I didn't know if we would work out or stay married, but I planned to try. I vowed to live a real life, one where I might get hurt instead of playing it safe so that I wouldn't. I wanted real, not pretend. And that's what I vowed to do."

He scoots closer to me but doesn't touch me yet.

"When I signed that prenup, I knew what I was signing, and I didn't care. If you wanted my money, then you could've taken it. But I didn't think that was who you were. I saw you as someone who deeply cared about her friend, that's it."

I nod. "I'm sorry."

He lifts my chin. "I'm not. Because I fell in love with the most beautiful woman with a huge heart. A woman who pushes me out of my comfort zone. A woman who fights for justice for her friend. A woman who loves me so much that she spent all the money she had on lawyers trying to get the prenup we signed changed."

"How do you know about that?"

"I have friends who would do anything for me too."

"You mean Larkyn?"

He nods.

"So you've known this whole time? How could you forget if you weren't drunk?"

"After you passed out in our suite, Boden came back to get his things. We got into a fight. He knocked me out when he pushed me into the bedpost. My huge headache when I woke up was from our fight."

The pieces all start making sense. "And the condom?"

"Boden fucked a random woman in there while we were getting married."

"What a giant fucking cunt."

"He's no longer my friend. And if I meet him again, I'll kick his ass."

"I couldn't get the prenup changed. I'm sorry. I don't want your money, though. I'll sign the divorce papers, and I don't want your money." *I just want you.*

"About that." Sebastian pulls a small stack of papers out and lays them in front of me.

"My divorce papers with Trevor? Why do you have them?" I flip through them, not understanding, and then I get to the final page.

"Oh my god. I didn't sign the last page. What does this mean?" I'm so confused.

"It means, technically, you are still married to him. And both he and I would really like you to sign them. He would like to get married soon, and so would I."

I frown. Sebastian wants to get married. *So quickly?*

I swallow down my pain. "Do you have a pen?"

He holds one out, and I sign quickly. "I'll make sure he gets these, and we file again as soon as possible."

"Good."

"I'll have my things moved out of your condo today. But this means that our marriage was never real? The prenup never real?"

His face falls apart. "Legally, no. But us being together was the most real thing I've ever experienced. I love you, Millie. I. Love. You. I don't care how we started. I don't care about the lies or manipulation. And I don't want a fresh start. I just want us together, for real."

"I love you too, Sebastian King. I've loved you since you saved me in Hawaii. And it's been real for me this whole time too. I have some more healing to do personally, and I know we have wounds we've caused each other that need time to mend, but I want to be with you. However you'll have me."

He leans down and kisses me. It's full of everything—hope, love, a future. I could get lost in it forever.

"Well, Millie Raine, I want you as my wife. I've never known you as anything except my wife, and I'm not about to change that now." He holds out the ring that the old woman from the bar gave to him. "Millie, will you spend the rest of your life with me and one day marry me for real?"

"This is already real, but yes, I'll marry you." And then he slips the ring on my finger. A ring I never plan on taking off.

I never thought I'd get my happily ever after. I know I'm strong enough to live a happy life without it, but I'm glad that Sebastian King gets to be part of my happily ever after.

EPILOGUE

SEBASTIAN

I COMB my hair one more time in the hotel suite mirror before I prepare to walk out onto the beautiful beach in Santa Barbara to get married. We considered getting married in Las Vegas, where this all started, but we chose the beach. We wanted to keep it simple, and this made the most sense.

The wedding will be small. Only Larkyn, Kade, and their kids on my side. Oaklee and her newborn baby on Millie's.

After I proposed, we agreed to live together a year. Millie didn't want to get married again until she had finished her therapy and was sure this marriage would last. I agreed that I would wait.

We waited three months. That's all the waiting either of us could stand. Millie's past no longer haunts her. And I couldn't wait to be tied to her forever.

There is a knock on the door. I look over at Kade, who is getting ready in the suite with me. The women and kids are getting ready in Millie's suite.

I glance at the clock; I have twenty minutes until the wedding still, so I don't know who would be knocking.

Kade opens the door, and Oaklee is standing in the hallway. "Can I talk to Sebastian alone for a moment?"

Kade looks to me, waiting for my response. For a while, Kade was the only one not sure about Millie and I's relationship. He wanted us to slow down. He still wanted a prenup to protect us both, but he's come around. He hasn't pushed the prenup topic in the last month.

Oaklee and I's relationship still needs more work. I was in the waiting room while Millie was in the delivery room when Eddie was born. Oaklee hasn't forgiven me for my part with Boden, and I haven't forgiven her for her plan to ruin me.

I nod at Kade, though. I know Oaklee won't ruin my wedding day.

Kade brushes past Oaklee, giving her a warning glance before leaving. Then Oaklee steps inside.

"Is something wrong with Millie?" I ask, suddenly worried that's why Oaklee is here. Did Millie get cold feet? Is she sick?

Oaklee smiles at my worried expression. "Millie is head over heels in love with you. She can't wait to marry you. She's been ready for over an hour and has almost stormed over and demanded the wedding get moved up an hour so she can see you again. There is nothing wrong with Millie."

I exhale a deep breath, relief flooding me. "Then, why are you here?"

"To apologize." Oaklee sits down on the couch in the small living area.

I sit down on the loveseat opposite her.

"There is no need to apologize. We both did what we did."

She shakes her head. "I'm going to be standing beside your wife when you get married. I need to apologize. I need you to know I have no ill will toward you. That I'm sorry for blaming you for Boden's actions. I don't want you to worry that I'm secretly trying to sabotage you."

"Thank you for apologizing. It really wasn't necessary. I know why you did what you did. And I'm sorry I couldn't stop Boden from cheating and hurting you."

She looks off in the distance, like I brought up painful memories for her.

"I'm sorry. But for what it's worth, you are a great mother and don't need that jerk in your life."

She smiles. "Thank you. And I know. So we're good?"

"We're good."

She exhales an anxious breath and then bites her lip as she stands. "I do have one surprise though planned for the wedding."

"Which is?"

"You'll see."

"Oaklee, I don't like surprises."

She opens the door of the suite to the hallway. "I know, but Millie loves surprises. Now, let's get you two married for real."

I follow Oaklee into the hallway, where Kade, Larkyn, and their kids are waiting.

"Ready?" Kade asks.

I nod.

Together we walk out of the hotel and down to the beach where a small arch sits near the ocean. That's when I realize my surprise.

The woman from the club in Las Vegas is standing under the arch. The woman who gave me the wedding rings and told me to be brave. The woman who told me to get married. The woman who changed my life.

My mouth falls open as I walk to her. "What are you doing here?"

She smiles at my shock. "Your friend Oaklee got my number at the club. She thought I might want the rings back when the marriage failed, but I knew it wouldn't. When she called to ask if I wanted to marry you, I couldn't pass up the opportunity. I'm Grace, by the way."

I pull the woman into a hug. "Thank you, Grace. You have no idea how thankful I am."

"I'm thankful the rings now belong to two people who will also be married until their dying breath."

A roll of thunder jolts us apart. I look up at the storm clouds brewing in the distance. "Not today, clouds."

But I don't have time to focus on the weather because Kade and

Larkyn's kids start walking down the beach, dropping rose petals as they walk. Larkyn walks down after in a pale pink dress and bouquet of exotic-looking flowers.

She winks at me before gathering the kids to stand next to Kade.

Next come Oaklee and baby Eddie with a large flower tied around his head. She reaches me and then says, "If you hurt her, we will hurt you."

I smile. "I'm glad Millie has a friend like you."

Then I turn back toward the hotel stairs that lead down to the beach, and I get my first glimpse of Millie in her white dress, holding a bouquet of exotic flowers that matches Larkyn's.

Kade, Larkyn, and Oaklee all offered to walk her down the aisle, but Millie wouldn't have it. She said she wanted to walk herself down the aisle.

Tears water in my eyes as she walks toward me. I'm impatient, though, and meet her halfway down the beach and walk her the rest of the way.

"You look beautiful."

"So do you."

Those are the only words we can get out through the tears threatening both of our eyes as Grace starts the ceremony. She keeps it short and sweet, knowing the weather could ruin it any minute. When it starts sprinkling, she says, "Rain is good luck on your wedding day. Not that you two need it. You're going to love each other forever."

"Yes, we are," I say, looking into Millie's eyes.

"And with that, I pronounce you husband and wife."

I grip Millie, vowing to never let her go as I kiss her deeply and passionately. As soon as we kiss, the rain stops, the clouds part, and the sun finally comes out.

"Seems like the weather is happy you two finally said 'I do,'" Grace says.

Millie and I exchange loving glances. I grab Millie's hand, and we lead the charge, jumping into the ocean to celebrate getting married with everyone following us.

"So are you going to tell me where we are going on our honeymoon, yet? I've been thinking we should go back to Hawaii," Millie says.

"Nope, not telling you. I thought you were Mrs. Adventurous. You don't need to know until we get there." Although, she's already guessed the plan. We are going back to Hawaii and then New Zealand and then Australia. We are taking two weeks off, so we have time for a repeat in Hawaii and a little new adventure.

"No, now I'm Mrs. King. I can't believe how lucky I am to have fallen in love with a King."

"Not as lucky as I am that I'm married to you." I kiss her hard in the ocean, our hands find each other and intertwine, and I feel for her ring on her left finger. A ring that gave me the final push to start living my life instead of hiding in fear.

I'm about to start the adventure of a lifetime being married to Millie—an adventure that I know will never end.

———

Thank you so much for reading Pretend We're Over! Oaklee has her own story to tell! Keep reading for Pretend You're Her!

PRETEND YOU'RE HER

BOOK 3

1

OAKLEE

I wouldn't consider this my best moment. It's not my worst moment. I've done far worse when I thought I was being betrayed, but this is definitely not my finest moment.

I'm not usually a stalker. Honestly, I'm not, but I'm desperate. I don't have much of a choice, so I guess I'm a stalker now.

I look down at the bundle beneath my coat, snuggled up against my chest, not phased in the least by what I'm doing or the snowflakes that now cover my coat. He's still fast asleep as I make my way inside the hotel. I hope he stays that way a little while longer so he doesn't completely ruin my plan.

Who am I kidding? I don't have a plan.

"Are you here for the Spade and Brooks wedding?" the receptionist asks as I make my way to the front desk.

"I am." *Just please don't ask for my name or invite because I wasn't invited.*

That's right—not only am I stalking, but I'm also crashing a wedding.

The woman with warm hazel eyes and bright red lips smiles at me. "The wedding will start in about twenty minutes on the back terrace overlooking the mountains. Would you like to check-in before the ceremony or wait until after?"

"After," I say with a nervous smile. This hotel is beautiful and extravagant, the kind the wealthy book to get away from real life. They ski the slopes in the morning, shop in the expensive stores in the afternoon, and eat at their fancy restaurants in the evening. I will not be doing any of those things while I'm here in Aspen, Colorado. And I won't be staying in this hotel, unless I convince the man I'm stalking to take pity on me and give me his room.

I walk briskly past the receptionist in search of said terrace. I can't believe the wedding is outside as a foot of snow blankets the ground, but as I walk toward the back of the hotel to see guests gathering just inside the terrace, I realize why.

The view takes my breath away. It's a winter wonderland outside. The terrace juts out over the cliffside with a picturesque view of snow-covered trees and mountains behind it. There are about fifty chairs facing the mountains and a few decorative heaters throughout. Most of the snow has been cleared, so only a light dusting covers the ground. I couldn't imagine getting married inside the hotel when that is the other option, no matter how cold it is outside.

I turn my attention from the view and look at the crowd before me. Busy in conversation, no one notices me as I approach, which will make my stalking and crashing easier. I'm here for a good reason, and it has nothing to do with the incredible view, expensive champagne, or the charcuterie tray you know the happy couple will be serving after the wedding.

I'm here to find a man—one man in specific.

The crowd is smushed together in the hall. It's not a large crowd, which will make finding my target easier, but it also means it will be harder for me to blend in and pretend I belong.

I don't even know the names of the bride and groom. *What did the receptionist say again? Brooks and...?*

My eyes scan quickly behind my dark sunglasses and under the brim of my hat that I wore so that he won't recognize me until it's too late, knowing I have less than twenty minutes before the ceremony starts. I'm not sure if it's best to approach him before or after, but I just need to see him. Once I do, then I can make a plan.

I spy his dark locks easily enough, but it's his laugh booming through the room that tells me I've found him. It's a laugh full of confidence and a life of ease—one with no responsibilities. I used to like his laugh, but now I find it infuriating.

I suck in a breath. I was so sure I'd know exactly what to do, exactly what to say when I found him. I told myself I wouldn't care if I made a scene or ruined someone's wedding—talking to Boden Vaughn is too important.

Now that I'm here and I've found him, I'm frozen. I don't have a clue what to do.

It turns out Eddie, my son, doesn't have a problem screaming his frustration at his father. Eddie's sudden shrieking cry is like nothing I've heard since the ear infection he had when he was three months old.

Unzipping my coat, I look down to see what's making my son scream bloody murder in the carrier against my chest.

"Shh, it's okay, mommy's got you," I whisper, bouncing as I look him over but finding no sign of injury.

My son slowly stops screaming, but it doesn't stop the room from silencing and everyone's eyes from peering at me. Many of the older women are smiling and cooing at Eddie, while several of the younger men are ghost-faced at the sight of a small child. I don't care about any of the stares, except one—Boden's.

Connecting with my own are Boden's deep brown eyes, the same eyes he gave to Eddie. And my disguise does little to hide myself from him. He knows exactly who I am the second he gazes at me.

"Can we talk?" I ask.

He doesn't blink. He's probably in shock. Boden has never laid eyes on Eddie, even though he knows of his existence, and Eddie is almost six months old. This probably wasn't the best way to introduce him to his son, but I didn't have much of an option.

Boden has been MIA since I told him I was pregnant. I hired a private detective to find him, only to discover he had moved across the country from me. I didn't want to fly with a six-month-old all the way across the country, but then I found out Boden would be in Aspen—a much shorter flight for me. This is as good as any other place to talk.

Boden turns and starts slowly walking out of the hall.

I follow, assuming he wants to talk, just not here in front of everyone. But the second he turns down the hallway, he bolts.

"Really, Boden?!" I holler after him as I start running, too. I won't be able to catch him between my heeled boots and the sixteen pounds of baby strapped to my chest, but I need to try.

"Don't be such a fucking coward! We need to talk!" I shout. I'm usually more responsible with my language around Eddie, but I'm too infuriated with my ex to care at the moment.

Boden makes a sharp left turn, and I do the same, only to come to an abrupt halt when I almost run into the chest of a man who is definitely not my ex.

My eyes skim up his body, slowly—too slowly to be doing anything but checking him out. But I can't help myself. His tux fits him too perfectly, molding to every one of his thick thighs, the jacket rolling over his muscular biceps. I get up to his face and almost swoon at his chiseled jaw with just the lightest dusting of facial hair, piercing green eyes, and textured dark brown hair trimmed high on the sides.

Jesus, this man is sexy.

"Madison?" the man asks me, startled as he blinks rapidly like he can't believe what he's seeing.

I don't know who Madison is, but I'm not her. Before I can open my mouth to respond, he shakes it off like he just realized that, of course, I'm not Madison. I'd guess that he's had too much to drink if he's mistaking me for another woman.

I'm inches away from his body. I suck in a low breath, and a deep earthy, musky scent fills my nostrils. No whiff of alcohol under his breath.

"You smell good," I say.

"I do?"

"Like expensive cologne and…"

"And?" I can almost hear the amusement in his voice.

I chew my bottom lip. "And burnt coffee and sweat."

I look up at the man, not the least bit embarrassed by my statement. It's the truth, and I don't get embarrassed for telling the truth.

I expect him to laugh or shake his head, but instead, he's scowling. I'm about to be told off. He knows I haven't been invited to his wedding, and I've just insulted him by calling him sweaty and smelling of burnt coffee. *You'd think his rich ass could at least afford quality coffee.*

"I said you smelled good first—" I start, but he interrupts me.

"Are you okay?" he asks me, his eyes narrowing in concern.

Oh, he's concerned about me? He's not annoyed that I crashed his wedding, just gave his guests something to talk about, and insulted him.

"Yes, I'm sorry," I say, looking past him to see that Boden already has a beer in his hand and is talking loudly with the other groomsmen. It appears I won't be having that conversation with him right now.

The handsome man looks from me to Boden, trying to piece together what just happened.

Eddie takes that moment to cry again. At least this time his moans are at a much more normal tone.

"You sure you're okay?" he asks me as I bounce Eddie, trying to soothe him.

"I am. I just got lost. Can you point me in the direction of the ceremony?"

The man frowns, obviously not believing me. I'm guessing now is the moment he'll call for security and kick me out.

"It's down that hallway and to your left. Your son is welcome at the ceremony, but we hired a woman from a local daycare if you'd prefer. She comes with the highest recommendations. You're also welcome to hang out in the babysitting room if you need some privacy to breastfeed or change a diaper. It's just past the main hall, the first door on the right," he gently explains.

I smile at him. "Thank you."

He doesn't smile back. He's a strange man. He spoke in kind phrases to me, but he didn't smile. He must be one of those tough, corporate men who make like a million dollars an hour and never smiles—that must be it.

I turn and walk back down the hallway with thoughts of the stranger overflowing my rage at Boden. I bounce Eddie as I walk, and thankfully, he falls back asleep as I approach the hall.

I prepare myself for the onslaught of questioning looks again, but apparently, it's getting close to the wedding time. All of the guests have moved outside and have started taking their seats.

An usher walks over to me, holding his arm out. "Bride or groom?"

I don't know how to answer that until I replay the conversation with the stranger in my head. 'We hired a woman,' he said. He must be the groom. No wonder he smells like burnt coffee, sweat, and nerves—he's about to get married.

"Groom," I say, deciding I should sit on his side since he's the only one of the pair I've actually had a conversation with or even ever laid eyes on.

The usher nods, and I take his arm as he leads me outside. I brace myself for cold and for Eddie to wake up again, but it almost feels warmer outside than inside.

I glance around the terrace and spot more heaters than I first saw. They blend into the scenery, so this place still looks magical but also comfy and warm.

"The ceremony should start soon," the usher says with a smile as he drops me off in the last row.

I nod and take a seat, wrapping my jacket tighter around Eddie. While it's warm, I don't want the falling snowflakes to wake him.

My mind drifts to Boden as I wait for the ceremony to start. We were supposed to get married. We made it all the way to the eve of our wedding before I realized who Boden is—a lying, backstabbing cheater. He cheated on me the night of his bachelor party. Luckily, I had the sense to run back down the aisle the next day before I was tied to him for the rest of my life.

I laugh to myself at that thought—thinking I'd saved myself from ever having to think about Boden again.

I stare down at Eddie. I don't regret fucking Boden. If I hadn't, I wouldn't have Eddie. And Eddie is the greatest thing in my life. I just regret that having him tied me to his father for the rest of my life.

Not that Boden wants to be tied to me. If it were up to him, he'd never see me or his son ever again. Hence, the stalking and wedding crashing.

I wouldn't be here if I didn't need Boden's help. Well, actually not just his help—I need him to fix the things he screwed up in my life. If I'm lucky, he'll own up to the fact that he should be a father to Eddie, even if he isn't who I'd choose for him. Having a father in your life is better than not—even a cheating scumbag who runs from his responsibilities but not before riddling us with his debts.

Eddie stirs, which means I'll have no way to quiet him without feeding him. I pull my phone out and check the time. The ceremony is about to start any minute.

I sigh. As much as I'd love to watch the romantic fairytale wedding, my son comes first. Maybe I'll find a quiet spot inside to feed him that still has a view. I can still corner Boden at the reception to talk. It seems he's in the wedding after all, so it's not like he can run.

I get up and make my way inside, thankful the wedding seems to be running a few minutes behind.

I spot a small sitting area looking out the giant windows and decide that's the best place for me. The groom mentioned having a room I could go to, but I don't want to invite any unwanted questions. Plus, the view here is great.

Eddie starts to fuss.

"You hungry, buddy?" I ask, even though I know he is. I begin to adjust him in the carrier so I can breastfeed him.

He coos in response, making me instantly smile and relax as I push the sleeve of my black dress to the side, along with my bra. I don't have a fancy nursing bra or nursing dress, so more of my boob ends up visible than ideal, but I don't care as I latch Eddie. I don't need any of the fancy things to take care of my son. He just needs love.

I frown. As much as I wish that were true, kids need a lot more than just love to survive. If Boden won't give Eddie the love, at least he can pay child support and make sure Eddie's basic needs are met.

I relax into my chair, trying not to think about Boden as I feed Eddie in the most beautiful place I've ever fed him. But as I switch boobs and the ceremony still hasn't started yet, I realize something must be wrong.

I look behind me just in time to see the groom walking with a determined expression toward the doors that lead out to the terrace.

I don't spot any of his groomsmen behind him—something is wrong. I don't know if the wedding is being called off or something less dramatic, but at this moment, I feel for the man. I know what a failed wedding feels like.

He pauses at the terrace door, his hand on the door. His head turns, and he spots me.

I freeze, trying to sink into the couch. He doesn't appear to be in a good mood, and I'm sure he isn't happy to see an uninvited woman casually breastfeeding her child with her boobs on full display just outside the entrance to his wedding ceremony.

He doesn't move for a second, just staring at me and my son. I can't read his expression. I have no idea what thoughts are going through his head, but if he is going to come over here to yell at me, he has another thing coming. I will defend my right to breastfeed anywhere, anytime.

He releases his grip on the door and starts to walk toward us.

Fuck.

I've told many a stranger to fuck off dozens of times, but the intensity of his stare has me tongue-tied.

He stops a foot in front of us and rubs the back of his neck nervously. More sweat beads on his forehead, but somehow it makes him look even sexier. He's a real man, with real problems. He's not a model from a catalog.

"I need your help," he says.

I cock my head and look behind me, although I don't find anyone else he would be talking to. "Me? You don't even know me."

He nods. "Exactly. Other than Boden, no one else knows you either."

"Okay? I'm not following."

He clenches his jaw, and then a bashful smile takes over his face. "Will you pretend to be my bride?"

2

OAKLEE

"Umm....what?" I must have misheard him. I must be hallucinating. I really should eat something. I don't think I've eaten anything since I got on the plane, and that was almost eight hours ago.

The man chuckles, putting his hands in his pockets. "You heard me."

"Umm…I'm really going to need you to repeat yourself because what I heard was crazy."

"Not crazy, exactly…"

"Yes, crazy is exactly what it is when a complete stranger asks you to marry them," I half-whisper, half-yell.

"I'm not asking you to marry me, just stand in and pretend to marry me."

I shake my head. "I don't understand. Where is your bride?"

He sighs, massaging the back of his head as he slumps onto the couch next to me. Eddie looks up from where he's still feeding on my breast, reaching his arm out toward the stranger in greeting. I quickly bat his hand down to keep from bothering the man.

"Madison missed her flight. She won't get in for hours, if at all tonight. There's a massive snow storm rolling in."

Madison is his wife-to-be. Strange that he mistook me for her.

"Okay…so just wait until she gets in and do the wedding right."

"She won't make it tonight," he says.

"Okay, well, do it tomorrow or the next day or fly everyone back out here next weekend and have a redo. If you have an open bar, your guests won't mind showing back up a second time. I'm sure you have the money to afford it."

He raises an eyebrow. "You think I'm made of money, don't you?"

I raise my own incredulous eyebrow. "You're getting married in Aspen, in a beautiful hotel, in the most picturesque place you could possibly get married. Yes, I think you have plenty of money."

"You're right; I do. But that doesn't mean I want to disappoint everyone by not getting married today."

I narrow my eyes at him. "Why is it so important that you get married today?" There has to be a reason he's not telling me for him to be propositioning me like this.

"It doesn't matter." He stares out the large window, and his eyes glaze over. There's a reason, and it's playing in his head.

"Your reason kind of does matter if you expect me to help you out," I snap.

He turns his attention back to me, and I see a heaviness in his eyes. "I don't expect you to help me out for free. I know you're here to see Boden. I can you help ensure that you two talk."

"I can do that myself."

He nods his head. "Yea, you seemed to be doing an excellent job of that by chasing him down the hallway and crashing my wedding."

I frown. "I don't feel guilty for crashing your wedding. If you think you're going to blackmail me or make me feel guilty enough to go along with your scheme, you need to think again."

"I'll pay you," he offers.

That catches my attention. "How much?"

"Fifty thousand for the day."

My mouth falls open. I should counter, ask for more money. But *fifty thousand* is enough to ensure Eddie and I don't get kicked out of our apartment for several months. Unfortunately, it's not enough money to pay off Boden's debts that somehow ended up in my name, but it's a good start.

My hand wraps around Eddie's cheek as I squeeze him to me. I can't believe I'm going to do this.

"But, how would this even work? Surely your family and friends would know I'm not Madison?"

He shakes his head. "None of my family or friends has ever met Madison."

I scrunch my nose. "Um, not to be rude, but are you sure you didn't imagine Madison? Like is she even real or just your imaginary friend?"

He laughs, his head falling back against the couch.

It makes me smile to see I've made him laugh, even if it is for ridiculous reasons.

He pulls out his phone and pulls up a picture before handing the phone to me. I stare down at it. It's a picture of him and a beautiful blonde woman. They're both smiling, and his arm is draped around her shoulders.

"Wow, she looks—"

"Exactly like you. So much like you that for a second I thought you were her," he says.

"Well, I wouldn't say exactly. We couldn't pull off being twins, but we could be sisters if I didn't know I'm an only child."

"Exactly. You'll be wearing a dress, a veil, and heavy makeup. Everyone will drink a lot, and by tomorrow no one will be any the wiser."

"But everyone saw me carrying Eddie in. Won't they think it's weird that I have a child one minute and the next I'm pretending to be childless and marrying you?" I just assume that they are childless. Based on how this guy looks, he doesn't seem like a man who has a child. There are no signs of sleep deprivation or spit. Or if they have a child—that child is not Eddie.

He raises an eyebrow as he motions toward my sunglasses and hat, and I get the message. No one got a good look at me. And if I change clothes and makeup, then no one will be any the wiser.

I stare down at the floor, contemplating, even though I already know what my answer will be. I don't have a choice. I'll do anything for my son. Even if I do succeed in getting Boden to pay child support and pay off his debts, my future is bleak at the moment.

"What exactly are you thinking?" he asks.

"I'm thinking you say exactly a lot."

He chuckles. "I guess I do."

"I'm also thinking I don't even know your name, and you don't know mine."

"Dax Spade," the man says, holding out his hand.

I tentatively put my clammy hand in his and find it rough and calloused. It surprises me and makes me wonder what he does for a living to make all his money. I assumed he's a trust fund baby, or he got handed his great grandfather's company and tonight is the deadline for getting married to get the money. At least that's how it usually goes in the romance novels I read.

But then why would his hands be so calloused?

"And you are?"

"Madison Brooks," I answer, giving him the name of his bride I'm supposed to play.

He grins, knowing he has me.

"Are you ready to get fake married, Ms. Brooks?"

I suck in a breath. "Let's do this."

———

Dax stands and holds out his hand to me just as Eddie finishes feeding, meaning my breast is now completely out and exposed to him. If Dax notices, he doesn't let on that my tit is on full display. His eyes never leave mine, even though I have yet to remove my sunglasses.

At least I know I'm not marrying a sleazeball. For some reason, the simple gesture makes me trust him more than I should for someone I just met and is paying me far too much money to pretend I'm his bride for a day.

I cover myself up and readjust Eddie in the carrier before taking Dax's hand again. My hand is tiny in his, but it also strangely feels right as he lifts me off the couch. Our eyes continue to peer into each other, and we both break into a smile. I was wrong about him —he smiles a lot, actually.

He leads me away from the hall and terrace as a young woman runs up to us.

"Mr. Spade, the wedding was supposed to start ten minutes ago!" the woman, who I assume is his wedding planner, says to him.

He nods. "Well, now it's going to start thirty, maybe even forty minutes, late."

"Mr. Spade!" she shrieks.

"Ms. Thompson, it's my wedding, and Ms. Brooks needs a little time to get ready as her flight was late. I'm sure you can find a way to entertain my guests so she can have a few extra minutes to get dressed."

Ms. Thompson looks to me. "Of course." And then she runs past us and out to the terrace to make our excuses.

"I take it Ms. Thompson has never seen the real Ms. Brooks either?" I ask skeptically.

"That would be correct."

Dax tries to take a step, our hands still interlocked, but I don't move. "Dax, why hasn't your soon-to-be wife ever met the wedding planner? That seems odd to me."

"You have a lot of questions, you know that?"

I shrug.

"Not that it's any of your business, but Madison travels a lot and trusted me enough to make all the wedding plans and to surprise her with a weekend to remember. We're a modern couple, not impeded by gender stereotypes. You know I even cook and clean sometimes, and Madison knows how to change the oil in her car."

"Sorry, I shouldn't have pried," I apologize.

"Now, we only have twenty minutes before Ms. Thompson will be banging on our door and dragging us out whether you are dressed are not. We better spend all of that time getting you dressed and prepared."

I nod, but then I stop after taking one step forward. "What about Eddie?"

Dax stops and looks down at Eddie like he's just seeing him for the first time. "Are you okay with dropping him with the daycare attendant I hired for the evening? I promise she comes with the best recommendations, and she only has two other children she's watching."

I nod, for some reason trusting this man to have chosen a competent woman.

Dax leads me to a room off the main hallway. He knocks first and then pushes the door open. "Mrs. Whitlock, I'd like you to meet Eddie."

He holds the door open for me as I tentatively walk through the door with Eddie still strapped to my chest.

A woman in her late forties looks at me with a bright smile and warm eyes. I instantly calm at handing over my child to this complete stranger.

She turns to Eddie. "It's nice to meet you, Eddie."

Eddie turns his little head and gives her a gummy smile back. It melts my heart and gets rid of any lingering doubt about this absurd plan.

"I've been a child educator for twenty years, I'm CPR certified, and I'll take great care of Eddie," she offers.

I nod, pulling Eddie out of the carrier on my chest and holding him out to her. He happily goes into her arms, instantly forgetting about me.

I sigh, but it's a happy sigh—just another sign of how much Eddie is growing up. This is one night in the grand scheme of things. One night I'm doing for Eddie. One night to make our lives slightly easier.

I turn to go when I realize I haven't given Mrs. Whitlock any supplies. No diapers. No bottles. No toys. No change of clothes.

"I have everything I need, and if I don't, I'll call you. Just write your name and number down the sheet at the front before you go," she says.

"Oh, okay. He's mostly breastfed, but he'll take any bottle and formula too. I just fed him, so he should be good for a while, and he just started solids." I continue to ramble everything this woman could possibly want to know about Eddie when I glance up and see Dax out of the corner of my eye.

He's watching me closely but not saying anything. He's not pressuring me to hurry up, even though he said we only have twenty minutes, and I'm going to need a lot of makeup and wardrobe changes for anyone to believe I remotely look like Madison.

But he's not pushing me at all. Not tapping his fingers or toes impatiently. Not constantly checking his watch or phone for the time. Not trying to hurry me along. He's just watching me.

I swallow hard, and my pulse speeds as I watch him watch me. Madison is one lucky woman. I don't know much about Dax, but I do know he's caring and sweet, and I could bask in his heady gaze forever and never get tired of him staring at me.

He cocks his head to the side as he stares at me, noticing my change in thoughts.

Jesus, he's observant. I'll have to remember that.

No, it doesn't matter. It's just for tonight. After tonight, I'll never see this man again.

"Let's do this," I say.

3

DAX

WHAT THE HELL am I doing?

The thought keeps flittering through my head as I lead the fake Madison down the hallway to the real bride's dressing room. Blasting through my head like a tornado warning is more like it.

This will never work. I don't even know why I suggested it, but I just saw her sitting there on the sofa, feeding her baby, and the words just came out. Words I never meant to speak. Thoughts I should never have had in the first place.

It's a crazy idea—one I never thought in a million years she'd agree to. Even after she agreed and I led her to the nursery to drop off Eddie, I thought she would back down, say this is insane, and then leave.

But she's desperate, really desperate. I could see it in her eyes when she was handing her child over to a complete stranger to watch so she can go through with my ridiculous, half-baked plan. She needs the money—most likely for something noble like helping her son. She'll do anything for him—even pretend to be someone she's not, marrying a complete stranger.

She's not the only one who's desperate.

I stop in front of the bridal suite and turn to face fake Madison.

"There's a dress hanging in the closet and any makeup and hair supplies you could need on the vanity."

She nods at me with a twinkle in her eye. "You're worried?" It's a question, but she said it more like a statement.

I put my hands in the pockets of my tux pants. "I am. It's not every day you get fake married to a complete stranger."

She puts her hand against my chest, and I can feel her warmth all the way through my clothes to my chest. "There's no need to worry, Dax. I'm a great actress, and I'm pretty good at hair and makeup. Just keep any of Madison's closest friends and family away from me all night, and I might be able to pull this off."

I nod solemnly and watch as she enters the room, closing the door behind her.

I run my hand through my hair and take a deep breath, but I can't get enough oxygen.

I'm going to hell for this.

No, no one will ever find out that she's not Madison. She'll get paid and be able to help her son. And I—I'll be in my own version of hell for the rest of my life, but I quickly push that vision out of my mind. I have things to do if this wedding is going to happen.

I run down the hallway to the groom's room and push it open. My dozen groomsmen all raise their drinks to me as I enter.

I grit my teeth and plaster on a fake smile. These men are supposed to be my friends. They are supposed to be here to support me. Instead, they've been getting drunk and haven't even noticed the wedding hasn't started on time.

"Good news. Madison just arrived, so the wedding should start soon. Finish your drinks and get your jackets on," I say.

The room toasts me again, but I ignore them. Instead, I look around at all the faces of the men who could realize that Madison is not actually Madison.

Madison works in a male-dominated field, and most of her friends are male. So when we decided who would be in our wedding party, only men's names came up. She doesn't have any bridesmaids, only groomsmen. Many men might not be comfortable with their wife having mostly male friends, but it doesn't bother me. She chose me, and I'm her best friend. I'm not threatened by any of them.

Three men, in particular, have me most worried about unveiling the scam we are about to attempt—Henry, Kenneth, and Boden. Thankfully, Henry is almost blackout drunk already. If Kenneth found out the truth, he'd just think it's funny and go along with the ruse. But Boden…I'm not sure what to think about him.

And I know fake Madison wants to talk to him—that's why she's here. But I don't think tonight is going to be the best night for them to talk.

"Boden," I call his name.

He walks over from the group of guys he's been talking to. I look him in the eyes and smell his breath. Thank god he doesn't seem to have been drinking too much yet.

"I need a favor," I say when I have his attention.

"Anything."

"I need you to drive Madison's parents to the airport as soon as the wedding ceremony is over."

Boden frowns. "I thought you hired a driver?"

I did, one I'm about to cancel as soon as this conversation is over. "They double booked and had to cancel on me. You're the only one with a car who's also sober enough to drive, and—"

"Absolutely, I'll do it. You can count on me." He pats me on the shoulder. "Told you, you should have made me your best man."

I return his shoulders pat with my own. "I can always count on you."

I stare into his eyes, the same eyes Eddie now shares, and I'm reminded of why he's so willing to help me out. He doesn't want to confront fake Madison and his son—a son he hasn't once spoken about to me. It's one of the many reasons why he isn't my best man.

I exhale a deep breath as I leave the groomsmen to go check on fake Madison. I've taken care of the most likely threats to our plan. Madison's parents were planning on leaving just after the ceremony anyway. Work has always come before their daughter. And with

Boden taking them soon after, fake Madison won't have to put on a very long act.

I make it back to the bridal suite and lift my fingers to knock on the door, but I stop myself.

Even with Madison's parents and Boden leaving shortly after the ceremony, there is no way we are going to pull this off. And even if we somehow do go unnoticed, there is no way I'm going to get out of this without consequences.

I stare at the door. I should stop this—tell everyone Madison got food poisoning or something. I'll pay fake Madison, though, for the trouble. I'll be left to deal with the aftermath on my own, but at least I'll have a clear conscious.

I knock on the door, ready to tell the kind stranger this was all a mistake.

The door cracks open. "Come in," her voice barely over a whisper.

I frown, not sure why she's suddenly shy. I don't know much about fake Madison, but our limited interaction was anything but timid. She's a firecracker ready to be unleashed upon the world. The only reason she'd probably ever hold her tongue is if it helped her son.

I step inside the room and close the door.

My eyes slowly rake up her body.

"Holy shit," I say.

She's fucking incredible.

I never saw the dress Madison chose, and it was a long shot to fit fake Madison, but it fits her like it was made for her, not Madison.

The dress has a boho feel—lots of see-through lace hinting at her underwear and bra underneath but doesn't actually reveal anything. There's a high slit on one thigh and a deep V-neck in the front. Her arms are covered in lace, making it feel like a winter dress. Although, the lace is doing nothing to keep her warm.

She's let her hair down in long curly blonde waves and applied thicker makeup to shape her features similar to the real Madison's.

She grins at me and then licks her lips. "Do you approve?"

I blink several times, not trusting my own voice. I'm going to say or do something stupid if I speak, so I decide it's better if I don't.

She laughs at my reaction as she walks over to the closet and pulls out the hanging veil. "Hopefully, this will cover me enough that no one will notice I'm not the real Madison."

She holds the veil out to me, and I take it from her, my gaze locking with hers. Suddenly she's not so talkative. Our eyes lock, and I think she's figured me out. I think she can read through all my bullshit and knows exactly who I am and what my motivations are.

But then she clears her throat. "Luckily, Madison is a traditionalist with how much this veil covers my face."

She turns around, and I gently place the comb of the veil into her hair. When she turns back around, she lifts the veil over her face.

"Ready to go get fake married? Although I guess technically, you're getting married for real. I'm like those stand-in representatives that kings and queens used for marriages back in the day," she says playfully.

I lift her veil so I can look her in the eyes without the thin netting separating us. There's nothing playful in my gaze as I stare at her. I want to tell her so many things, but I can't. I say it all with my eyes and hope it's enough that she'll forgive me later. Or at least she'll realize why I'm doing this.

"I'm ready to get married if you are," I say.

4

OAKLEE

"Ready?" Dax asks, holding his arm out to me.

I blink rapidly, trying to shake myself from the spell of his stare. For a moment, I think he's attracted to me. But then, when he speaks, I realize he's not looking at me with lust but rather with a sweet, appreciative gaze. His gaze tells me I look enough like Madison to pull this off, and he's thankful for what I'm doing.

He doesn't find me hot. He's about to get married. I'm just the stand-in.

"Ready," I say, hooking my arm through his without a second thought.

The moment my fingers brush his arm, a warmth spreads through me. The warmth says I'm safe with him. It's a feeling I've been seeking forever but have never actually found.

Dax looks down at me with a frown I don't understand, but he doesn't say anything.

He leads me out to the foyer, where I notice the groomsmen have started to gather. I quickly flip the veil back over my face, like that is somehow going to make it impossible for them to see me. Then I stop dead in my tracks, already recognizing the first way we're going to be found out.

"How am I supposed to convince Madison's father that I'm Madison when he walks me down the aisle?" Unless he has Alzheimer's or some other mental impairment, there is no way he's not going to notice I'm not his daughter.

"He isn't walking you down the aisle. I am," Dax says in a deep voice, stirring something in my core.

"Why?"

Dax keeps his eyes on the groomsmen just ahead, holding us back so they don't spot us.

"Madison isn't close to her parents. They're leaving as soon as the ceremony is over—something about needing to get back for a business meeting."

I frown. "It's Saturday. They aren't even staying for their daughter's reception?"

Dax just shrugs. I'm starting to realize why he wanted to have this wedding so quickly and didn't want to reschedule. Madison's parents are dicks.

The wedding planner spots us and gives Dax a thumbs up and a raised eyebrow. When Dax nods back, the volume of relief on her face is comical.

She opens the doors to the terrace, and the groomsmen start filing out.

"Are there any bridesmaids I need to be worried about?" I ask, my palms sweating. There are so many ways this could fail horribly. I can't imagine no one here knows who Madison is. It shouldn't really matter to me; I'm just doing this for the money. But I'd also rather not completely embarrass myself in front of a room full of strangers. And strangely, I don't want to embarrass Dax either.

"There aren't any bridesmaids, and I've already made sure the groomsmen won't be a problem."

I look up at him, studying his face. He does seem incredibly calm. For some reason, I believe no one is going to find out.

"You got them drunk, didn't you?" I tease.

He finally looks at me. "They did that all by themselves. But yes, that's one of the main reasons. The other is only a very select few people here have actually met Madison. Her only family is her parents, and they barely see her once a year. Everyone else here is either a friend or a guest her parents invited, but they don't really know her.

"We can do this. Just follow my lead and be Madison for the day. No matter what happens, I'm going to pay you, so you have nothing to worry about."

I frown. "I know, but I don't want to embarrass you. I want this to work."

He pats his hand on mine. "It will."

The last of the groomsmen starts his way down the aisle, but not before turning and looking directly at us.

My heart stops.

I can't breathe.

Boden stares right at me, and I think he's going to realize who I am. We aren't even going to make it down the aisle before we're called out.

Instead, he smiles at me and then looks to Dax. He mouths, 'Good luck' before turning away and walking down the aisle.

I exhale a deep breath.

"I told you. People see what they want to see. Boden would much rather see you as Madison than actually realize who you are," Dax says.

"That may be true, but it's different seeing me across the room compared to talking to him face to face at the reception."

"He won't be at the reception. He's taking Madison's parents to the airport."

"Oh."

Dax smiles down at me. "Now, stop worrying and let's go get married."

I laugh, shaking my head. "That doesn't ease my anxiety."

He laughs. "Well, you only have to be married to me for a day."

My heart does a little flip thinking about being married to Dax longer than just one day. Honestly, I don't think it would be a hardship.

"Good thing," I say.

The wedding planner starts waving us on frantically—show time.

This time Dax doesn't ask me if I'm ready. He doesn't ask me if I'm sure. Together, we both just start walking.

My nerves build with each step toward the terrace. *Should I be doing this? Is the money worth it?* I think of Eddie and know that it is.

We reach the closed doors leading to the waiting ceremony outside.

The doors are swung open, and cool air hits our faces.

I hear Dax take a deep breath in at the same time I do. As if we planned an in-sync entrance, we take a step outside at the same time.

Magic hits me. I felt it when I sat among the guests earlier. This place is magical, and that's all I feel as we walk down the aisle.

I don't have to force a smile onto my face; it's just there. I don't make eye contact with anyone, but I couldn't even if I wanted to. All I see is the panoramic view of mountains at the end of the aisle. I'm floating on a cloud as we walk together.

Abruptly, we're at the end of the aisle, and an officiant is talking as Dax and I turn to face each other. I don't know what I expected to see on his face, but I find Dax's smile to be just as bright as mine when he looks at me.

I know there are groomsmen on either side of us. I know Madison's family is sitting in the front row. I'm sure Dax's family is sitting across the aisle from them. But I don't care about any of the guests. I don't care about being found out as a fraud trying to trick all these people.

Right now, I can't help but enjoy this moment.

I don't know if I'll ever get married. The way my life is headed, I doubt I ever will. I don't trust men, not after my experience with Boden. So I'm not going to feel guilty about enjoying this fake wedding.

Dax takes my hands in his, and that tingly feeling returns, but it's probably just sweat mixed with cold air causing some sort of electric shock between us.

There are butterflies flutter in my stomach, but not in an anxious, nervous kind of way. It feels like my entire life is about to change, but I don't know how. It feels like I'm taking a leap of faith and starting something new, even though I know I'm not. After today, Dax and I will go back to being strangers.

"Repeat after me. I, Madison Brooks…"

Holy shit. We're already to the vows.

The second the officiant says 'Madison Brooks,' I come back down to earth. I'm not getting married for real. This isn't real.

"I Oa…Madison Brooks, take Dax Spade to be my husband." The words I'm saying are fake. But when I look at Dax, it doesn't matter what I'm saying—this feels real. He's looking at me with such love and sincerity.

He's just a good actor. If I were the real Madison, this is how he'd be looking at her. This is how the guests expect him to look at her. He's just imagining I'm her.

I still have the veil on, along with pounds of makeup. It must be easy for him to get lost in this moment. After all, he won't get a redo either. I'm sure he and the real Madison will say some fake vows or do some sort of private ceremony later when she finally arrives. But this is the only chance he'll make his vows in front of his family and friends.

My eyes start watering at the thought. Something so special was stolen from them.

I don't know why the wedding has to happen today. I don't know why Madison isn't here. But I do know Dax loves her desperately to be willing to make this happen for her.

Tears stream down my face, and I hope Madison is the kind of woman who would get emotional at her own wedding. At least I hope the veil is still hiding enough of my face that no one notices.

Dax notices, though.

He squeezes my hands and smiles like he's in love with me. It makes my heart tighten, and the tears fall faster.

This isn't real.

I'll never have this.

This isn't right.

No matter the reason, Dax should have waited to marry Madison for real, even if she doesn't get in until two in the morning. His love is too real, too big for her to miss out on.

But she's not here—I am. And it's too late to back out now.

"I, Dax Spade, take you to be my wife…" his throat cracks, and he has to clear it before he can continue. "I never thought we'd get to this point. I never thought this day would come. But I'm lucky to say I'm marrying the most beautiful, kind, generous woman I've ever met. I can't believe you entrusted me to be your husband, but I'm going to do my best every day to be the husband you deserve. I love you, and I'm so excited to spend the rest of my life with you."

If I wasn't already crying, I would be after that speech. I swear I see a tear fall from Dax's face before he quickly wipes it away.

The officiant speaks again, but all I can do is stare at Dax and imagine what it would be like if this were real. Maybe he proves that men like him exist in real life, and I should give men another chance.

But then I spot Boden behind him, and I know I'll never trust a man again.

"You may now kiss the bride," the officiant says.

Wait…how could I have forgotten about the kiss part?

Dax seems unfazed. He doesn't hesitate to start lifting the veil off my face—the only thing keeping me somewhat hidden and out of view of the guests.

I want to run away. The guests are going to realize I'm not Madison if my voice didn't already give it away. More importantly, I can't be Dax's first kiss as a married man!

It was one thing to pretend to be Madison while I said some meaningless words; it's another thing to kiss her man.

But as his head tilts and his lips lower over mine, I don't stop him.

I'm frozen.

He's just going to give me a quick peck. Or he'll tilt me back and just hover close, so the guests think we kissed. He's not going to actually kiss me.

But his lips inch closer, and my pulse beats faster. The butterflies in my stomach intensify.

He's going to kiss me.

And then he is.

The spark of electricity hits first—it's just static electricity caused by our bodies rubbing together, nothing more, I remind myself. The kiss is such a shock. I doubt I'll recover quickly enough to even feel the rest of the kiss. But then the warmth of his lips pushes through the shock. My lips part in a gasp at how incredible he feels.

I hear the crowd cheering us, but I'm lost in a dream. I don't hear them. I'm not sure I can trust my memory of this kiss. I'm pretty sure his tongue just slipped between my lips, but I can't be sure.

That can't be his tongue. He's in love with Madison. It was just my vivid imagination.

At least, I hope it was my imagination. If not, then maybe Mr. Magnificent is just an ass like Boden and every other guy I've ever met.

I'm not in a relationship, though. There's no reason for me not to enjoy this kiss, so I do. I would have pretended to be Madison for just this kiss, forget the money. I'm not going to turn down Mr. Magnificent's money, but damn, that kiss was something else.

"Peaches," Dax says as he pulls away.

"What?" I exhale.

"You taste like peaches." He gives me a crooked grin, and my face lights up in the bask of his glow. I can't process anything; my head is still spinning. I barely notice the officiant turning us to the crowd.

"I would like to introduce to you Mr. Spade and Mrs. Brooks—husband and wife."

Before I realize what's happening, Dax has lifted me in his arms, and he's racing down the aisle.

I'm married.

No, I'm fake married.

This fairytale ends after one night, but it's a dream I'm going to replay over and over again.

5

DAX

It hit me like a bomb, exploding through my body, penetrating every muscle and fiber of my being. It felt—oh god, I can't even think about how it felt.

Real.

It felt real, that kiss.

But it wasn't real. I mean, sure, it was a real kiss, but only in the sense that our lips were pressed together. There wasn't any feeling or emotion behind the kiss. No history or connection, but there was something...a spark. There was a physical connection I wasn't expecting.

I could have avoided the kiss. I could have tilted her back away from our guests and kissed her cheek or something.

But I didn't. I went for it.

I didn't think it would matter. I thought I'd kiss her and it would be like kissing any random stranger—sweet, awkward, and meaningless.

That's not at all what happened. It was sweet, but only because of how she tasted.

It was only awkward because I knew it shouldn't have felt that good.

And as far as meaningless goes—it felt like a shift in my life. Like that kiss is the start of something, but I haven't figured out what yet.

It was wrong for so many reasons, but not the obvious one. I know she felt something too. I can only imagine what is going through her head. As much as I doubt we have a future together, even as friends, I can't have her hating me. I can't have her thinking I'm a scumbag. I have enough of that in my life.

I carry her fast through the lobby and back into the bridal suite. I should ask her if she wants to check on her son, but I'm selfish and need to speak to her first. I don't put her down until I've kicked the door shut behind me.

I take a step back, giving her air and us space, so I don't do something stupid.

"What are you thinking?" I ask Peaches as I lean back against the door. That's what I've started calling her in my head since I kissed her and don't know her real name.

She chews on her bottom lip before it flickers into a smile. "I think that was the most insane thing I've ever done, and I can't believe we pulled it off."

Her smile is infectious, so I smile back at her despite my own nerves. "We still have the rest of the night. We could be found out."

She shrugs. "Everyone will be drunk, and I'll touch up my makeup before we head back out. No one will be able to tell."

I examine her face already covered in caked-on makeup, making it hard to distinguish her features. I'm not even sure I would be able to tell the difference between Madison and her if they were both wearing the same dress and makeup. Most people here haven't seen Madison in years; they won't notice either.

Her face drops. "I am sorry, though. I'm sorry Madison didn't get to experience her dream wedding and I did. I'm sorry I kissed you."

I shake my head. "Don't be sorry. Of all the things you might feel, sorry shouldn't be one of them."

"But I am sorry," she says barely over a whisper.

I study her carefully, suspecting the real reason she's sorry is because she enjoyed the kiss. But I need to know for sure.

"What are you really sorry for?" I ask, gently coaxing her.

She wordlessly shakes her head.

"I'm not sorry. And you shouldn't feel guilty about anything," I say.

"I kissed a married man. Or an almost married man. Or whatever you are. You're taken. You're not mine. I kissed you, and I enjoyed it!"

There—she finally said it.

"Madison won't care that we kissed. In fact, she'll find this whole thing hilarious." I put my hands in my pockets, studying her.

"What woman is okay with someone else kissing her man?"

"The secure in her relationship type. The trusting type. The very thankful for your help type," I reply.

Her face widens in disbelief as if she can't imagine, and maybe she can't. I don't know the full story of her relationship with Boden, but I'm guessing he fucked up her trust in men, in relationships.

"I don't believe you," she finally says.

"Why? What have I done to lose your trust so quickly?"

"You're friends with Boden. I'm suspicious of anyone who thinks he's a good person."

I sigh. She's probably right, but we don't have time to get into that now. Neither of us knows each other's pasts as far as Boden is concerned. And now isn't the time to have that conversation.

"Just trust me. We'll call Madison later and you'll see, but for now, please just trust me. We aren't going to hide anything from her. There's a photographer and videographer. She'll obviously be able to watch everything. I wouldn't be able to hide anything from her even if I wanted to. I'm not a cheater, and I promise I won't kiss you again unless it's absolutely necessary to keep the ruse up."

She folds her arms across her chest and simply stares at me, clearly in need of more reassurance.

"Let's try to have a good evening. Eat yummy food, drink extravagant champagne, and dance. Just focus on having a fun night you're getting paid to enjoy."

She sighs. "Okay."

There's a knock on the door. "Mr. Spade and Mrs. Brooks, are you ready to be introduced at the reception?" The wedding planner's voice sounds worried and anxious from the hallway. I need to remember to tip her well for putting up with the stress I've put her through.

I look to Peaches for an answer. I don't even know her real name. I know nothing about her, but I wish I did. We may not be destined for a romantic relationship, but we could be great friends. And I take care of my friends.

She walks over to the makeup stand to apply a new layer of lipstick and something else to her eyes before strutting over to me.

I hold out my hand, and she doesn't hesitate to put her hand in mine.

"Ready," she replies to the wedding planner.

I hold the door open for her, our fingers still linked as we walk out of the bridal suite.

We don't make it far before our wedding planner says, "Oh, Madison, your parents are leaving soon and wanted to say goodbye. I'll go flag them down for you before we announce you at the reception."

Peaches stops dead in her tracks, frantically whispering to me. "What do we do?"

I look behind her and see Ms. Thompson ushering Madison's parents toward us. I'm not panicked. Madison's parents are self-centered and usually only see Madison about once a year. They won't even look at her closely enough to see it's not their daughter.

But Peaches is about to have a panic attack, and I can't have that.

"Just follow my lead and don't speak unless you have to."

She nods.

I place my hand on her hip and gently guide Peaches back against a wall. Her breathing deepens, her lips part, and her eyes widen.

"Trust me," I whisper against her ear, causing her to shiver. I put one arm above her head, blocking anyone's view of her.

Keeping my lips close to her neck and ear, I pretend to kiss her. I'm not trying to get a reaction out of Peaches. In fact, I'm trying to calm her nerves, but as I breathe against her neck, I realize I'm eliciting the opposite reaction.

Goosebumps rise on her neck, and every few seconds shivers overtake her body. She wets her lips and closes her eyes.

"I'm not going to kiss you. Relax, Peaches."

"Peaches?" she breathes.

"That's what I'm calling you until you tell me your real name."

"What if I never tell you my real name?" She bites her lip to keep quiet, but the softest moan escapes her lips.

Jesus Christ, this woman makes it hard to keep control of myself. I harden at her sound, but I keep my body from pressing against her. I haven't even touched her, and she's moaning. I can't imagine the sounds she'd make if I actually did caress her.

"Madison, we're sorry we can't stay for the reception, but we have to leave if we are going to catch our flight. We have that important meeting tomorrow, and you know we aren't drinkers or partiers anyway," Madison's father starts speaking.

Peaches' eyes widen in panic, unsure of what to say or do. She just reacts. Next thing I know, her arms are around my neck, and her lips are pressed against mine.

I don't know how to react either, so I just go with it. And I like kissing her, even though it might complicate things. I grab the back of her head and press into her, blocking Madison's parent's view of her almost entirely.

Peaches grabs the back of my neck and tilts my head as her tongue presses at the seam of my lips.

My brain is no longer working. I part my lips for her, and her tongue instantly sweeps inside my mouth. The overwhelming taste of sweet peaches fills my mouth. It's a taste I want over and over again.

She doesn't stop at just kissing me—she devours me. Her lips press hard against mine, her tongue pushes deeper into me, and her grip on my neck tightens, petrified of what's going to happen when she lets go.

Oh, Peaches, don't you know I won't let anyone hurt you? I can't be your boyfriend or husband, but I can be your friend. I don't let anyone hurt my friends.

I tighten my grip on her waist and push against her, trying to tell her with my body what I can't with my words—she's safe.

Her kisses turn into moans, groans, and whimpers. I can't even remember why we are kissing, just that we are.

Is this right or wrong? Should we be doing this or not? I'm consumed by this kiss taking over my brain, my body, and my existence.

All I know is that I keep my hands firmly in place. I don't explore her body like my instincts scream for me to do. I don't grind against her like I want to. I just follow her lead and kiss her.

It's enough. *It's not enough.*

It's confusing as hell.

I shouldn't have any feelings as far as this woman is concerned. Not because Madison would care, but because I don't know this woman. I don't know anything about her other than she needs money and is willing to help me out. And she's a damn good kisser.

Slowly, reality sinks back in, and blood returns to my brain enough to remember why we were kissing in the first place. I listen carefully but don't hear anyone behind us. I look out of the corner of my eye, relieved to find we're alone.

I break the kiss.

"Peaches."

"Huh?" Her lips are swollen, and her eyes are barely open as she comes back from our haze.

Our lips hover over each other, and our breath is heavy as we pant against each other.

"Madison's parents are gone. We don't have to keep kissing," I say.

"Oh my god, I'm sorry! I shouldn't have kissed you again. Madison is going to kill me. I'm such a bad person; I just panicked."

"Peaches," I say calmly, grabbing her hands. "Madison is not going to care. You did nothing wrong. Let me worry about what she would be okay with or not. Let's just enjoy our night. Can you promise me you'll stop worrying and just have fun?"

She takes a deep breath. "Yes, but I'm going to rat you out to your wife."

"Rat me out?"

"I can feel your erection pressed against my stomach."

I laugh. "I think you and Madison will become great friends."

"You're still pressed against me," she persists.

"Sorry, but you were the one kissing me all hot and heavy. I can't help that my body reacted."

"Were you thinking of Madison while you kissed me?"

That's a dangerous question to answer. "Come on, wifey. We need to get to the reception."

She gives me a knowing smile and takes my hand as I lead her into the reception hall.

She thinks she's a bad person when really she's the sweetest angel I've met in a long time. I'm the only bad person around here. She'll figure that out soon enough.

6

OAKLEE

"I CAN CARRY HIM," I tell Dax as we ride up in the elevator.

"He's asleep against my shoulder. Do you really want to move him?"

"No, but if anyone sees you with a child, they won't know what to think."

He chuckles. "Most of our guests are drunk or already asleep. We have the entire top floor to ourselves. No one will see us."

I nod, realizing he's right.

"Besides, it won't be any better if they see you carrying him."

I look at Eddie asleep on Dax's shoulder, and I can't help but smile. This night has been the opposite of what I expected. I was expecting to have a fight with Boden, sleep in a cheap hotel, and introduce Boden to his son. If I was lucky, I'd have gotten Boden to realize he needed to be a part of Eddie's life.

Instead, I've lived a romantic fairytale all night. It's been difficult to remind myself it's completely fake because Dax is way too charming. And yet, somehow, he hasn't crossed a line. His kisses have been reserved after I kissed him to avoid talking to Madison's parents. His touch has been intimate and yet always appropriate. When he placed his hand on my back, it never lowered below my waist. When

501

we danced, he held me close, but he never pushed himself against me.

I had the time of my life. I ate delicious food, drank expensive champagne, danced, barely had to make small talk with anyone, and enjoyed an adult night in a winter wonderland with free babysitting.

But I've read enough books to know every fairytale night eventually ends. Cinderella turns back into just a girl after the ball, and that time is now for me. The biggest difference between me and Cinderella is that the prince eventually comes for her. I glance at Dax, who is gently rubbing Eddie's back and is completely content with him in his arms. He would make the perfect prince; he's just not my prince.

"You okay?" Dax asks me, noticing my sour mood.

I force a smile on my face, reminding myself I'll fly home tomorrow, and then I can let myself fall apart again.

"Mmmhmm," I nod.

He narrows his eyes. He doesn't know me well, but he's intuitive and seems to be able to read through me.

Luckily, the elevator doors open, and I don't have to continue this conversation with him.

Dax carries Eddie to the door of the penthouse suite, and I follow behind. I've been nervous about spending the night in the honeymoon suite all evening, but the second Dax opens the doors I relax. We have almost the entire floor to ourselves. There will be plenty of bedrooms and space, so we won't be sharing a room.

"I had the staff bring up a pack-n-play for Eddie to sleep in. I'll go see if I can find it," Dax says.

"Thank you," I say, my ovaries melting around this man. *Why couldn't I have gotten drunk and fucked a man like Dax? He'd never abandon his child.*

Dax turns a corner and searches down a hallway, while I stand frozen in the entryway. I'm not sure what to do. I'm not sure where to go. I'm not sure what comes next in my life.

My thumb instinctually rubs over the band on my finger. I should give it back to Dax; it isn't mine. Dax isn't mine. He belongs to another woman, and every time I think about it, my heart sinks.

What have I done?

Did I just ruin a marriage or help one?

I think about the woman Boden cheated on me with. *Am I that person now?*

"Stop," Dax says, appearing in the archway of the hallway. He no longer has Eddie in his arms. "Stop overthinking this. It's done and trust me when I say we did the right thing."

I nod, but I'm still not sure. "I'm going to go kiss Eddie goodnight."

"Second door on the left."

I scurry past him and down the hallway to eventually find Eddie asleep in a pack-n-play. I walk over to the side, lean down, and kiss Eddie.

"Goodnight, my sweet boy. I don't know what mess I just got us into, but at least we'll have some money to get us through these next couple of months until I can talk to your father."

I take a couple of minutes to just watch my son sleep, avoiding having to go talk to Dax. I could lie down on the bed, fake sleep, and avoid him entirely, but I need to talk to Dax. I have a flight to catch tomorrow, I still need to find a way to talk to Boden, and I need to make sure Dax pays me for tonight.

So I walk back toward the suite entrance still in the white wedding dress I've been wearing all night. I have a bag of things in the rental car I should go get so I can have something to sleep in besides this dress.

I find Dax in the bar area. "Do you want more champagne or something stronger?"

I probably shouldn't drink more at all, but I could use another drink.

"Champagne is fine," I reply.

Dax pours us both a glass of champagne and then grabs a tray of chocolate-covered strawberries. We move to the living room, sitting on either end of a couch with the tray between us.

"Your bag is in the room next to Eddie's."

My eyes widen. "My bag?"

"I probably should have asked first, but I knew you would need your stuff tonight. I didn't want you to worry about it or question if anyone would find out who you are that way. I found your keys in your coat pocket and asked the bellhop to bring up your luggage."

I'm speechless, but somehow I squeak out a 'thank you' before taking another sip of champagne. That was very thoughtful of him. *Does this man have any flaws?*

"Have a strawberry," Dax says.

I shake my head. "It's one thing to pretend to be Madison in public, but I'd feel horrible eating her romantic food you're supposed to share together when she gets here. Have you heard from her? Do you know when she'll arrive?" *Is she arriving before I leave and going to scream at me for fake marrying her husband?*

"She won't be getting in until tomorrow, just before we were supposed to leave for our honeymoon. I'll meet her at the airport."

"Where are you taking her on your honeymoon?"

"Fiji."

"Of course, nothing but the best," I say.

"She deserves it."

"I still think she's going to kick your ass once she finds out what you did."

He laughs. "She won't."

"You're that confident you know her that well? How long have you two been together?"

Dax is silent a moment as he studies me.

"Can't remember how long, can you? That's not a sign of a lasting relationship."

"No, I was just considering how to answer. I've known Madison since high school—we were best friends back then but never thought of dating. We actually managed to attend the same college together without dating."

"What changed?" I ask.

His eyes twinkle with dangerous thoughts, and I blush. "She's gorgeous. She's my best friend. I finally woke from my spell and realized what was right in front of my eyes."

"You got drunk and fucked her?"

He laughs again and shrugs. "Something like that."

I grin from behind my champagne glass. "I should go to bed. Eddie is going to be up by six, and then we need to get to the airport, but I wanted to talk about Boden and…"

"And how I'm going to pay you," he finishes my sentence.

I nod. I'm not usually a bashful person, but I am when it comes to asking for the amount of money we agreed on for this night.

"I'll make sure Boden talks to you soon."

"Thank you."

Then he gets up and heads down the hallway before returning with a checkbook in hand. He writes the check for fifty grand like he's writing a check to pay a grocery bill. He hands it to me with the recipient line blank.

He's still not going to ask me my name, although he could easily get it from Boden. I'm not sure why he doesn't want to know. *Easier to forget what we did if he doesn't know my name?*

"You'll always be 'Peaches' to me. And I don't want you to worry about me showing up in your life again. I won't," he says earnestly.

I nod and hold up the check. "Thank you."

"I'm the one who should be thanking you."

I shake my head, knowing we won't agree on this, but it won't stop me from cashing the check. He's rich, we agreed on a service and price, and I need this money. I move to get up, but Dax stops me.

"One more thing," he says.

I tilt my head and yawn. "What?"

"You don't believe that you did the right thing, but I want you to hear from the only person who will make you believe you did —Madison."

I blink rapidly, pretty sure I just hallucinated. He can't be asking me to talk to Madison. I thought I'd just slip out tomorrow, check in hand, and pretend this entire thing was a dream.

"I'm not sure if that's a good idea."

But Dax already has his phone out and has dialed her number.

"Hey, baby," he says with the phone facing him. It's then I realize that not only is he calling her, but it's a video call.

I look down at myself. I'm wearing her wedding dress. *Could this get any worse? This woman is going to want to murder me.*

"Hey, handsome," Madison says back.

What the hell do I do?

I should run. It would be a really good time for Eddie to wake up and start crying. But of course, his room is silent.

My pulse is going a million beats a minute. I've never wanted to run more. Okay, well, that isn't true…I wanted to run more after I found out Boden cheated on me the night before we were supposed to get married.

"Is she there?" Madison asks Dax.

Dax, to his credit, doesn't react. He doesn't immediately say I'm here. He waits for me. He's letting me choose, even though it's clear what he wants me to do.

Suck it up and talk to her, that's what the voice in my head says. *Suck. It. Up.*

I'm a strong, independent woman raising her son by herself. I've been through so much. I agreed to this arrangement. This woman deserves to talk to me after what I did. But I'm not strong enough to speak just yet, so I just nod at Dax.

The second I do, he answers Madison.

"She's here."

Slowly, he moves the tray of strawberries off the couch and slides down toward me. Every inch he gets closer to where I'm sitting makes me want to jump off the couch, run down the hallway, and lock myself in Eddie's bedroom until I can leave in the morning.

But then I feel Dax's hand grip mine. One quick squeeze and my pulse calms. I take a deep breath, and then Dax faces the phone toward me.

"Madison, meet the woman you should be forever grateful to," Dax says.

I stare at the phone—at the beautiful blonde woman who looks eerily similar to me. She has a wide smile, bright eyes, and perfect makeup despite the late hour.

"Thank you. Thank you so much! You have no idea how much this means to me," Madison says.

My eyes widen, and I'm sure I'm hallucinating. I never stay up past midnight, with Eddie constantly waking me up throughout the night and before five every morning.

"I'm not sure why you're thanking me. I'm not sure I understand any of this to be honest," I say.

Just then, I hear Eddie crying.

"I'll go check on him. You two talk," Dax says.

I frown, but now that I've started I need to continue this conversation. I deserve answers as much as she does. *Why couldn't Eddie have cried five minutes earlier?*

"It's complicated. I know I'm not the most traditional of brides. I never cared about the wedding. All I cared about was being married to Dax and having fun on the honeymoon. My parents, as you may have seen, are a pain in the ass. It took us two years to agree on a wedding date they could attend. And as it was I'm sure they left as soon as the ceremony was over."

I nod. "They did."

"Well, I'm beyond thankful to you. I know Dax and I could have just eloped, but I would have never heard the end of it from my parents. And as much as they drive me nuts, I want to make them happy. So truly, thank you. I'm sure Dax and I will have our only fun ceremony in Fiji."

"You don't need to thank me. Dax paid me well. I just feel bad you didn't get to experience the ceremony. It was so beautiful and wonderful. And this dress…" I gush.

Madison laughs. "I hate dresses, but the dress looks great on you. The pictures are going to look incredible. And I hate the cold, so thank you for preventing me from having to deal with it."

"You hate the cold? Then why have your wedding in the Colorado mountains in winter?"

"This was the only date for the next six months that worked for my parents. We figured if we were going to have to get married in the winter we might as well lean into it. Plus, Dax loves the cold weather, and it wouldn't matter to me where we got married. He got to decide where we had the ceremony, and I got to decide where we go on our honeymoon. He chose cold; I chose warm. Marriage is all about compromise, so I hear."

I smile. "Well, it seems like you two have got that part figured out well."

Just then, I hear a speaker voice in the background, and the phone shifts. I realize she's at an airport.

She sighs. "Well, that was the official cancelation of my flight. I need to go get some sleep so I make my flight tomorrow. This is why I hate the cold. It snowed a foot in Minneapolis, which is why I couldn't make it to my own wedding."

"I'm sorry." And I truly am.

"Don't be. Like I said, you did me a favor. I get the benefit of being married without having to deal with my annoying family or obnoxious friends," she says.

I nod, even though I still feel like I might be missing something. I do genuinely feel like she's happy that I stood in for her.

She's about to go when I remember the thing I'm most guilty about. The thing she might not be okay with.

"I kissed Dax," I spit out just as she starts saying her goodbyes to me.

She stops and then laughs. "Was it good?"

Oh, fuck. How do I answer that?

My cheeks burn bright red, and I suddenly feel like I'm sitting in a sauna. Sweat pours down the back of my neck.

She smiles brightly. "It was! I can tell!"

I give the slightest of nods. "I'm *so* sorry! I only kissed him when it was absolutely necessary to keep up the ruse. And I know it didn't mean anything to him."

Madison chuckles. "It's fine."

"I kissed your husband. It can't be fine."

"But it is. I'm not the jealous type. I know why you kissed. And I can't blame you, or even him, for enjoying the kiss."

"It won't happen again," I say.

Madison looks at something behind me with a knowing grin. "I need to go, but enjoy your night. Thank you again. And make sure Dax pays you well for what you did. You deserve it for putting up with my parents."

"Safe travels tomorrow, and thank you. I needed a night like tonight probably as much as you needed me to stand in front of your parents."

We end the call, and I take a deep calming breath, already knowing what's waiting for me behind me.

Dax.

I don't know how much of that conversation he heard. I don't know if he heard the part about me enjoying our kisses, but just like I had to face Madison, I need to face him.

When I turn, he doesn't give anything away. "Eddie went right back to sleep. I wasn't sure if he needed to be fed or not, but he's asleep again."

"Thank you."

He nods.

I stand up. "I'm going to bed."

"Thank you, Peaches. Thank you for everything."

"Thank you for the check," I say.

He gives the slightest shake of his head as his eyes penetrate through me. He wants to say more. I want to say more. But neither of us do. This is goodbye.

Tomorrow morning we will both figure out ways not to see each other. And that's for the best. This is the end of my fairytale life. Tomorrow, I'll go back to raising Eddie on my own and struggling to pay the bills. This time it will be a little easier, though. I have enough cash to survive for a while and a promise that I'll get to speak to Boden.

I wasn't sure what I was going to get when I crashed the wedding this weekend, but I ended up getting more than I could have ever imagined—I got hope. Hope that I can find love if I open my heart.

It's clear how much Dax and Madison love each other. They showed me love is real. My love story may not end up quite as fairy-tale-esque as theirs, but I can still find someone to spend my life with that makes me happy. It was worth the trip just to be reminded of that.

7

OAKLEE

My new perspective on life was short-lived. Less than a week later, reality hit like a battering ram through my heart, shattering any dreams of finding my own man who would love me like Dax loves Madison. Men like that are rare. I've only ever met two men like that—Dax and Sebastian. Both men are married. I doubt there are any good single men left in the world. And if there are, with my luck, I'll never find them.

I roll my shoulders back and hold my head high as I march into the bar. I wore my most modest dress with a jacket over it. My hair is half-up and half-down. I spent about five minutes on my makeup. My entire look says put together without trying too hard. I'm here for a meeting, not to be hit on.

The bar is busy, which I'm not surprised given it's a Friday night. It's been a long time since I stepped foot in a bar. I used to spend every weekend in one, but now, I feel out of place. I feel like everyone in here is ten years younger than me, when in truth, I've just lived a very different life these last few months.

There aren't a ton of open tables, but I find a two-seater near the back of the room. I can watch the door while also having some privacy when he arrives.

511

If he arrives.

"Can I get you something to drink?" a bartender asks shortly after I sit down.

"Yes, a glass of white wine."

He nods and smiles at me before returning to behind the bar to make my drink.

I fidget with the paper coaster on the table while I stare intently at the door. I'm fifteen minutes early.

He won't be early.

He'll be late.

I need at least one glass of wine in me before I have this conversation anyway.

The bartender returns with my wine, but he doesn't leave immediately. "Don't fret; no man in their right mind would stand you up."

I keep my eyes on the door as my hand finds the stem of the wineglass. "Even my lying, cheating ex who has completely balked his responsibility to his child and in no way provided for him?"

The bartender's mouth drops open as he struggles to find words.

"That's what I thought," I say before taking a sip of the wine.

The bartender leaves me alone while I drink my wine and try not to think about everything wrong with my life and how badly tonight could go. But of course, that's all I think about.

I think about how I lost my job at the art gallery. Finding a new job as a curator is going to take months. I'll have to start applying to other jobs just to pay the bills in the meantime.

I think about how my best friends Millie and Sebastian are leaving on a once in a lifetime trip around the world next week. I won't be able to rely on them to help watch Eddie.

I think about the fact that Dax hasn't texted, called, or made contact with me in any way after the wedding. Although, I didn't expect him to. He's probably currently sitting on a beach in Fiji with Madison enjoying married life. I knew once I left that hotel I'd never see him again. That night still feels like a dream. The only thing reminding me that it did, in fact, happen is the check burning a hole in my purse.

I should cash it. I need the money, and I earned it, but I decided to wait until after this meeting. There's a small chance Boden will do the right thing, step up and help take care of his son and his debts. It's a very small chance, but it's still a chance. Then I wouldn't need Dax's money. Then I could just keep the happy memory of that night without tarnishing it by taking Dax's money.

If Boden does show up tonight, I know I owe it all to Dax. I got a text message from Boden the night after I arrived home asking to meet him—alone. He said we had a lot to discuss, and he wanted to talk before he met Eddie.

I agreed.

So here I am—waiting.

I pull my phone out of my purse, set it on the table in front of me, and check the time.

Seven o'clock.

Let's see if Boden shows up.

Thirty minutes later, I've finished my glass of wine, and Boden has yet to show or text.

I text him asking if he's still planning on coming, but there's still no response ten minutes later.

I sigh.

Why didn't I get Dax's number? He might be my only shot of getting ahold of Boden.

The bartender returns. "Another drink?"

I shake my head. If Boden shows up, I want to have a clear head. If he doesn't, I'll need to be sober to get home. And besides, I can barely afford the one glass of wine, I can't afford another.

The bartender shrinks away without another word. It's clear he has no idea how to handle me.

I don't know how to handle me.

It almost makes me feel better about not being able to tip him well and taking up a valuable table on a Friday night. But then I see him intercept a group of guys headed my way, most likely to hit on me, and the guilt returns.

"Here, I thought you could use this," the bartender says thirty minutes later, setting another glass of wine on the table.

"If it's from a man, I don't accept, and I can't pa—"

"It's on the house."

I frown. "I can't accep—"

"You can. The bottle of wine is already opened. It's just going to get poured out tonight if you don't drink it, and I can't look at a sad girl like you all night and not do something about it. Drink it. Then go home and find a way to move on without him. He's no good for you. Trust me, it's better for your child to grow up with no father than a deadbeat one."

I accept the glass of wine. "What if I don't have a choice? What if I need the father's help?"

His eyes roll up and down my body. He's a good-looking man, and if I still believed in the possibility of love I might ask him out, but I don't. "You always have a choice. And I have a feeling that a strong, fierce woman like you doesn't need help from a shit-hole like him."

I smile. "How do you know I'm strong and fierce?"

"The way you walked in here tonight. Everyone's eyes fell on you —you demanded it. And yet you gave off the vibe that if anyone came near you without your permission, you'd murder them. You're a spitfire."

I shrug. "I used to be. I'm not sure what I am anymore."

"Drink your wine. Think about who you are, about who you want to be. And then walk out of this bar as that person."

"Thank you for the wine and advice. You're good at your job..." I wait for him to say his name, but he doesn't.

He shakes his head. "You don't care about my name. I'm not important."

"How do you know? Maybe this is the start of an epic love story between us?"

"It's not."

"How do you know?" I ask.

"I've already had my love story, and you're hung up on another guy."

I frown. He said 'had,' which means his life is tragic too. "I'm not hung up on my ex."

"I didn't say you were hung up on your ex. I just said you're hung up on someone."

My scowl deepens. That's worse. That means I'm hung up on a married man.

The bartender recognizes he struck a nerve. "Do you have a way to get back tonight?"

I nod and dig through my purse, looking for my wallet.

"Nope, both drinks are on the house."

"But—"

He leaves before I can force him to take my credit card.

I sigh, looking through my purse to find I'm out of cash. If he doesn't take my card there is no way to pay for my drink.

It's then that I spot the check from Dax.

I didn't want to cash it. I wanted Dax to realize I helped him because I think of him as a friend and look fondly on that night. But I don't have a choice. I'm going to cash it tomorrow, and then I'm going to find a job—any job that will pay the bills.

I down the rest of my wine in one gulp. I still don't know who I am. I haven't reflected on my life like the nice bartender said, but I do know one thing. I can't count on Boden for anything. And I know how to spend some of Dax's money—on a good lawyer.

The bartender is wrong if he thinks I can get out of this mess by myself. Sure, I can find a job and raise my son, but my life isn't that easy thanks to Boden. But it's not anyone's problem except my own. Not having to pay for a couple of glasses of wine aren't going to solve my problem, but it definitely doesn't hurt.

I get up from the table and head outside to my car.

I'm not going to give up talking to Boden. I'm going to make him take responsibility—if not for his son, then for all the unsettled accounts he saddled us with. I won't let him hurt his son like this.

How?

I have no fucking idea. Maybe I'll start with tracking down Dax or…

A large hand covers my mouth as another grips my waist, and suddenly I'm pushed against the side of my car.

I suck in a deep breath through my nose and try to remain calm. I was so caught up in my own thoughts that I didn't take the most basic precautions to ensure no one was following me.

I feel tears welling in my eyes and a panic attack rising in my throat.

No, I'm stronger than this. I won't let these men break me. I have to stay focused if I'm going to find a way out of this.

"You thought you could just ignore us and not pay up, Mrs. Vaughn, but we aren't patient men," the man's growly voice heats my ear.

Vaughn?

"I never married Boden. I'm not Mrs. Vaughn," I try to say, but the hand is still covering my mouth.

"We don't want to hurt you, but we will if we don't get what we are owed."

I suck in another breath through my nostrils and exhale angrily as the man holding me against the car gropes me, trying to prove his point. They have no problem hurting me if I don't give them what Boden owes them.

I don't know why they aren't going after Boden directly. Probably because he's a bloody coward who never shows his face. It wouldn't surprise me if Boden was planning on coming tonight and then got wind of these men being here and left me to fend for myself.

"Check her purse," one of the men says.

I try to use the car window's reflection to see how many men are behind me, but the street light's glare blinds me.

The man behind me yanks my purse off my arm and tosses it behind him. I can hear another man rummaging through my purse.

I know exactly what he'll find.

The blank check is held up against my cheek.

"We'll take this, but it is nowhere near what your husband owes us."

I'm finally able to get my elbow free enough to jab it into the chest of the man behind me.

He groans and releases his grip on me enough to speak.

"If it's my husband's debt, then why come after me? I'm not the one that owes you thousands of dollars."

I get a good look at the man holding the check. He's scrawny, and his menacing smile is missing some teeth.

"Millions—your husband owes us millions."

My mouth drops open.

Holy fuck.

Millions.

I don't know what to think about that.

"And a wife is always a husband's greatest weakness."

"My husband doesn't care about me. And I don't have that kind of money! If Boden owes you that amount, you're going to have to take it up with him."

The toothless man shakes his head and looks to the man behind me, who grips me roughly once again.

"It doesn't matter if Boden cares about you or not. You want to live?"

He waits for me to nod my head.

The man looks into my car and spots the car seat in the back.

"You want your child to live?"

My eyes pop out of my head, and my arms scratch at the man holding me like a feral cat until I draw blood, and he releases me.

"Don't you dare touch my son!"

The man tucks the check into his coat pocket. "We won't. You're going to get us the money."

I shake my head. "How? I don't have that kind of money. I just lost my job. I—"

"I don't care how you do it. You're a smart woman; you can figure it out." He looks me up and down. "And if not, I'm sure you can find someone willing to pay to use that pretty body of yours. You'll have the three million dollars paid off in no time."

I grind my teeth together. I want to kill him for threatening my son. I want to kill Boden for getting me into this mess. But I need to think sensibly. I can't kill anyone right now. They outnumber me. And the best way to protect my son is to agree to their terms.

"How do I contact you? And how long do I have?" I ask calmly, too calmly.

"You have a year to pay in full, but we expect monthly installments of at least fifty grand."

"How do I contact you?"

The man smirks. "We'll contact you. Don't you worry, Mrs. Vaughn."

And then both men disappear into the dark, while I'm left frozen.

I should call the police.

But I don't.

I should call Boden.

But I don't.

I should tell someone—ask for help.

But I don't.

Instead, I think about Eddie, whom my best friends are currently babysitting. I have to find a way to protect him.

I lost my job.

I've already drained my savings.

I don't have money for next month's rent.

I barely have enough money for food.

Boden opened a string of credit cards in my name. I now owe thousands of dollars in unpaid interest.

He also didn't pay his tax bill, which he somehow filed jointly with me, of course.

And now, I owe millions to some bookies thanks to Boden.

My blood is boiling as I hit the car door over and over again, my frustration finally exploding through me.

The tears come next, along with an overwhelming feeling of defeat.

My landlord is after me.

Creditors are after me.

The IRS is after me.

And now bookies are after me.

None of it is my fault.

All of it is Boden's.

I would regret ever meeting him if it wasn't for Eddie. Somehow, my son makes everything worth it.

I wipe my tears off and get into the car. I won't let Boden defeat me. I won't let any of his bills defeat me. And I won't let any of this mess near my son.

8

OAKLEE

"How was your date?" Millie asks as soon as she opens the door with a conspiring look on her face.

I may have lied to her just a little when I told her I was going on a date. I didn't want her to worry about me or ask any questions about Boden.

Right now, I'm thankful I lied to her.

I make a disgusted face.

She sighs. "That bad?"

I nod, not wanting to talk about it more. I hate lying to my best friend, but I don't even know where to start in confiding in her.

"Is Eddie asleep?" I ask.

"Yep, he went down about an hour ago. Let's get you a drink."

I shake my head. "I shouldn't drink. I've already had two, and I won't be able to drive back if I have more."

"You need a drink, Oaklee. And you're not driving anywhere tonight. We have plenty of spare rooms. Stay tonight and wash away the bad vibes of your date."

I exhale. I know she's right. I don't want to go back to my apartment alone tonight, not after what happened.

520

I follow her into the kitchen, where she immediately pulls out a bottle of my favorite white wine and starts pouring us both glasses.

I can hear her husband, Sebastian, approaching behind us. He doesn't speak at first, but I see Millie look up at him, and the two of them exchange a silent conversation.

"I'm going to bed. Wake me if you need anything. It's good to see you, Oaklee," Sebastian says.

I just nod at him as I sip my wine. I know he's only making himself scarce so Millie and I can talk. He's a good man, which is rare. He's the type of man I've resolved to never find.

"Let's go to the living room," Millie says.

I follow her, and we both take a seat on the couch, facing each other. The fireplace is turned on, and the lights are dimmed. I'm sure I just interrupted a romantic evening between her and Sebastian.

"So tell me honestly, how bad was the date?" Millie asks.

I decide to tell the truth to the best of my ability. "So bad he never showed up."

"Oh, Oaklee, I'm sorry. Men are assholes."

I raise my eyebrows. "All men?"

She shrugs. "Sebastian can be an asshole, too."

"He's not an asshole. Trust me, I've met my fair share of assholes —Sebastian isn't one." Even if I might have thought so at one point, I know differently now. Sebastian is one of the good ones.

Millie smiles dreamily. "He is a good guy, isn't he?"

I pretend to gag, and she laughs.

As she takes a sip of her wine, her expression changes. "Close your eyes."

"What? Why?"

"Can you just humor me?"

Sighing, I set my glass down on the end table next to me and close my eyes.

"Now, imagine your perfect man."

"Really, Millie? This isn't going to work."

"Well, nothing else has worked. I'm not saying you need a man to be happy, but I know you want one. Take fate into your own hands."

I roll my eyes in my head at the ridiculousness of this, but she's not going to let this go, so I'll play along.

I take a deep breath and let an image of a perfect man start to form in my head.

"What does he look like?" Millie whispers.

"He's tall, with dark wavy hair, piercing eyes, and a smile you have to earn from him."

"Good. What about his personality? His career? His aspirations?"

"He's kind. He's good with Eddie. He's honest, charming, confident, and thoughtful. He sees me for me and not just a piece of ass. He does the little things like hold my hand, compliment me, have a special nickname for me..." I trail off as I realize what I'm doing. The man my mind has manifested as the perfect man is the absolute wrong man for me. He's a married man, a man who called me Peaches.

Dammit. Why did I have to fall for a married man?

It's because I spent so little time with him. He's not perfect. When I first met Boden, I thought he was perfect too. When I first met Sebastian, I thought he was evil. I'm clearly not a good judge of character at first.

I open my eyes, and Millie's face is bright and excited, like the man I just described is about to materialize in front of us.

"You're going to find him. I know it. This year."

I shake my head and pick up my wine again. Millie has lost it.

"You have to believe it too! Otherwise, the manifestation won't happen. Manifest him. Manifest the life you want. Tell the universe exactly what you want to happen this year and it will."

I want Boden to take responsibility for all his debts, so I don't have them hanging over my head and bookies literally threatening me and my son to pay them back. I need that way more than I need a man.

I need a million dollars—at least that to pay off all the debts that Boden has somehow made me responsible for.

I hate asking for help, but I know when I'm in over my head. It was one thing when it was some credit cards and taxes that needed to be paid. I could fight with the companies to get my name removed from those bills, but it's an entirely different thing to owe bookies money. They don't care I'm not responsible for the gambling in the first place—they'll make me pay all the same.

I open my mouth to tell Millie everything when she speaks.

"So we have some news." She chews on her bottom lip but can't keep the glimmer out of her eyes.

"You're pregnant!" I say.

"Oh, no, not pregnant, but we've made some plans for the future."

"What?"

"We're selling the house and going to travel the world together."

My heart simultaneously sinks and grows. I'm excited for them. They want to travel, and they deserve to take this chance, but that means time without my best friend. It means I can't tell them what's been going on with me. It means I can't ask for their help. If I do, they won't go. And they deserve to go. They deserve to be happy.

"That's awesome! I'm so excited for you guys." I reach across the couch and hug my best friend.

"I'll miss you and Eddie. We will have to fly you both out to meet us along the way."

"We'd love that." I keep the forced smile on my lips as I sit back down.

They've earned this. They are some of the best people, the best friends I have ever known. Without them, I'd be lost.

I just don't know what I did to deserve the heartbreak and responsibility I now carry. I must have done something horrible in my previous life to deserve all this. All the manifesting in the world isn't going to save me.

9

DAX

"WE CAN'T MAKE IT," I say into my phone as I walk from my car toward the bank.

"Nope, not that either," I say, my blood pressure rising the longer this conversation goes on. My lawyer rattles on about events we are supposed to attend. Madison and I can't make it, and that's that.

I'm getting tired of getting pulled in a dozen different ways. If it's not my lawyer claiming we're legally required to attend an event, it's Madison's parents, Madison herself, or my friends. I just want to be left alone to live my life. *Why is that so hard?*

"I've got to go; I'll call you back." I end the call as I enter the bank, but not before I hear him sigh on the other end of the line. He knows I won't call him back.

I walk toward the back of the line when my heart stops.

Long blonde waves are my first clue, followed by a woman bouncing and hushing a small child in a carrier attached to her front.

I walk closer, unsure if I'm dreaming or if it's really her. I take a step behind her and am met by her familiar scent—citrus, lavender, and spit-up.

I smile, and Eddie spots me, giving me a huge smile.

524

She notices her child's reaction and turns. Her mouth falls open.

"What are you doing here?" she asks.

"Opening a new bank account and cashing a check. You know, the typical things you do at a bank."

She shakes her head. "I don't mean at the bank; I mean here, in this city."

"I live here."

She blinks as if she's hallucinating me.

"Well, I live here for the next six months. Then I'll be moving to New York City," I clarify.

She nods slowly, still attempting to comprehend my presence. I give her a moment and talk to her son instead. "Hey, Eddie. How are you doing? It seems like you've grown in the few weeks since I've last seen you."

He babbles his agreement which makes me smile brighter.

I look up, and she's staring at me like I've grown horns.

"Did Boden reach out to you?"

She huffs. "No. He never met up with me."

I frown. "He told me—"

"He texted me, set up a time and place for us to meet, and then bailed. I don't know what you see in him as a friend, but he's not a good man. He's a bad friend and an even shittier father. And you still need to uphold your end of the deal to convince him to talk to me." She points her finger at my chest like her problems are all my fault. Some of it definitely is, but I didn't realize he didn't talk to her. He told me he had.

I study her closer and realize a lot has changed in the three weeks since I last saw her. Deep lines have formed around her swollen, bloodshot eyes. Her skin is paler. Her hair has barely been brushed. There's dried spit up on her shirt she hasn't bothered to clean off.

I don't know a lot about her, but I do know that she cares about her appearance. She's usually bubbly and fierce and witty. But right now, she looks like life has dragged her through the wringer. I don't know what life has thrown her way, but it isn't good.

Other than ensuring that Boden speaks to her, I owe this woman nothing. In fact, I should run as far away from her as possible because nothing good can come to me talking to her. But I can't ignore what I see with my own eyes. And I can't let her suffer without offering to help.

"Let me buy you a coffee, and we can figure out how to get Boden to talk to you."

"Next," the bank teller says.

She looks from me to the bank employee, trying to decide who she's going to talk to. Go about her day and continue with the reason she's here or divert her plans, trust me again, and come talk to me?

"Sorry," she says to the attendant and then faces me. "I'm getting the most expensive drink and food item on the menu."

I chuckle. "Good. My wallet was feeling a little heavy today. I'd love some help lightening the load."

She gives me a dirty look, and I follow her outside.

Luckily, there's a coffee shop right next door to the bank, so we don't even bother moving our cars.

I hold the door open for her and wait behind her while she orders a drink.

"I'll have a shakerato, a french mousse cake, and a cappuccino."

I raise an eyebrow but don't say anything as I order a coffee and pay for everything.

Peaches is already settled in the corner with Eddie while I wait for the drinks and food. A moment later, I collect our order and sit down across from them.

"Did Eddie start drinking coffee since the last time I saw him?" I ask when I set down her fancy drink along with her cappuccino.

She picks up the cappuccino. "No, I prefer cappuccinos, but I wanted to make you pay for the most expensive drink on the menu. I told you I was going to make you pay for it and I don't back out when I make a promise."

I laugh. "You're something else, Peaches."

She shrugs.

"Tell me what happened with Boden."

"I already did. He texted to meet me and then didn't show up. He didn't respond to any of my text messages afterward and didn't answer any phone calls. He's a douchebag."

"I mean, what happened before? Why hasn't he met Eddie? Why aren't you on speaking terms?"

"Long story short, Boden cheated on me the night before our wedding. There was one moment of weakness on my part after that night, which resulted in Eddie. I have no regrets because Eddie is my world, but after that night we went our separate ways. I never intended to talk to him again, but a month later, I realized I was pregnant." She pauses and takes a sip of her coffee, looking off into the distance.

"At first, I didn't want anything to do with Boden. But eventually, I realized no matter how much of an ass I thought he was, he deserved to know he was going to have a child. So I called him, but he never answered. I texted, but he didn't answer. I decided it didn't matter. I had the means to support myself and great friends to be there for us."

I nod along, listening to her story, but she doesn't continue.

"What changed?" I prod her to continue.

She bites her bottom lip, contemplating if she should tell me more. Eddie cries, and she rocks him gently, trying to quiet him.

"I'm sorry. Of course you want Eddie's father in his life. Being a single mom can't be easy, and Boden should help out financially and otherwise."

Her eyes flutter up to meet mine, and she sees the sincerity in my words. She sees something else because she doesn't hesitate after that moment.

"I lost my job. I'm riddled with debt. My best friends are about to leave on a trip around the world and won't be nearby to help. I'm alone. I don't have enough money to pay rent next month. I've drained all my savings. I have no family that can help."

She takes a deep breath. "I would prefer to raise Eddie alone. I'm a strong, independent woman. I've survived my entire life by myself.

I've never relied on anyone, but..." she looks down at her son. "It's not about just me anymore. If it was, I'd starve rather than ask that man for money. But I won't let Boden hurt Eddie. Boden's the reason we're in trouble. The reason I don't have enough money to pay rent. I need his help. And I need your help to get Boden to help us."

I nod. "Of course, I'll do everything I can to help."

I'm still missing a lot of the story. She opened up to me more than I'm guessing she's opened up to most. I'm not even sure if she's opened up to her friends because if they are as great as she says, I doubt they would abandon her in her time of need. I gave her a check for fifty-grand I know she deposited. I don't know what she did with the money—*pay some bills, maybe?* Apparently, it wasn't enough for her to no longer feel desperate. But she needs help, so I'll help.

She just nods. She doesn't thank me. I'm not even sure she believes that I'll help since my help wasn't enough last time. But just like her, when I give my word, I keep it. And I made her a deal that if she helped me out, she'd get paid and I'd help her talk to Boden. I paid her for standing in for Madison, but I failed to get Boden to talk to her.

"Why are you friends with Boden? You seem like the complete opposite of him. You're so nice, and he's..." she sighs as she looks down at Eddie. I guess she's at her limit of badmouthing his father in front of him, even if he's too young to understand.

"I've known Boden my entire life," I say.

"So that's your excuse?"

I run my hand through my hair. "My relationship with Boden is complicated." *And if you think he's an ass, wait until you find out who I am. I'm a much bigger asshole than him.*

"How's married life?" she asks, diverting the conversation.

"It's good."

"It's good? That's all I get? I played your stand-in wife and all I get is, 'it's good?'"

I laugh. "Sorry, um...the honeymoon was great."

"I bet," she says with a knowing look.

I just shake my head with a grin. "Fiji was amazing. The weather was warm and relaxing. It was just what we needed."

"Sounds amazing."

"It was. But then we got back and life went back to our normal craziness."

"Which is?"

My phone buzzes, and I pull it out only to hit cancel.

"Sorry about that," I say.

But then it buzzes again and again and again. No matter how many times I hit cancel, it keeps buzzing. I finally just turn the phone off.

"Chaos—our lives are chaos."

She smiles and looks down at Eddie. "I can't believe your lives are any more chaotic than mine."

"You're probably right, but care to find out?"

"Huh?" she blinks at me, confused.

An idea forms as quickly as the first time I came up with an insane idea that involved Peaches.

She narrows her eyes at me. "You have that look again."

"What look?"

"You've just come up with a crazy idea."

I grin, liking that she knows me so well.

"Want to pretend to be Madison a little longer?" I ask with a smirk.

10

OAKLEE

"You can't be serious," I say, staring at him like he's lost his mind. It was one thing to play Madison for one day when everyone around us was mostly drunk, and I could hide beneath a layer of thick makeup, but pretending to be her anymore seems insane.

"I'm serious," he says, his face unbending.

"Did you fuck up? Does Madison already want a divorce, and you're trying to save face?" He must have cheated on her and doesn't want to tell his friends.

I stand to leave—this is a complete waste of my time. He's not going to help me with Boden—he's just as bad as him. He fooled me and kind of helped me. Now we should part ways before I end up getting in more trouble or end up hurting Madison.

He chuckles at my frustration, and it stops me in my tracks. It's the same chuckle I've only ever heard him use in response to me. I haven't spent much time with him, but I've barely seen him smile at anyone other than me.

"I'll have to tell Madison you said that. She'll get a kick out of it," he says.

I frown and glare at this man. *Is he my friend or enemy?*

Eddie wakes up fully now, and I know I need to change his

530

diaper. I'd rather do that in the bathroom than in my car, so maybe I shouldn't leave so quickly.

"I'll get you another coffee while you go change his diaper. Then we'll discuss terms," Dax says, somehow reading my mind. He quickly gets up and heads to the counter to order, not really giving me a chance to argue.

I sigh and go change Eddie's diaper. When I've returned, a new coffee is sitting in front of my seat. I'm tempted to grab it and run out the door, but it could be a long time before I can afford a simple cup of good coffee. I sigh and sit back down.

Dax smiles at Eddie as my son finally notices our guest. He struggles to get out of my arms and get a better look at the stranger. Except Eddie smiles at Dax and doesn't seem to think he's a stranger.

Dax holds out his arms and Eddie immediately does the same.

I groan but let Dax take Eddie in his arms. I'm really hoping Eddie spits up on Dax or something. But of course, my child takes to Dax immediately, playing with his watch while Dax turns his attention back to me.

"Madison is a pilot," he says suddenly.

"What?"

"She's a pilot. Her parents hate that she's a pilot. They'd rather her just attend social events and charity auctions, but Madison loves what she does. Her job takes her all over the world. I travel with her when I can, but I'm working on a contract that will keep me here for a few months. And Madison just got an awesome stint in Europe she couldn't turn down."

It sounds legit, but I've learned that I'm gullible and will fall for any story.

"There are some events that I should attend with Madison, but the real Madison can't make it. You would really be doing me a favor if you came with me."

"Even if I wanted to go along with your plan, someone would realize I'm not the real Madison."

He shakes his head. "They wouldn't, trust me. And if they do, who cares? You'll still get paid either way. It's a win-win for you."

"How exactly? Last time you made promises, and I did all the work but didn't get anything out of it."

His brow furrows. "I paid you fifty grand. And I'm still going to keep my promise to get you and Boden together; it will just take me longer than I realized."

I don't respond to his fifty grand comment. Sure, I got paid, but it didn't really help me beyond ensuring those guys didn't bash my head in or rape me the other night.

"Fine. You want to do this, then these are my terms—you provide us a place to live for the duration of our deal, you pay me twenty-grand an event, and you guarantee Boden and I talk. You'll do everything you can to convince him to do the right thing."

He pauses for a second and looks down at Eddie, who is now chewing on Dax's sleeve. His buttoned-down shirt probably cost more than my rent. Normally, I would try to stop the behavior, but I have a weird urge to make this man pay. I can't quite understand it because I also want to jump his bones. Going anywhere with him is a terrible idea.

"You'll live with me for the next six months, and then I'll help you move to a new place when I leave. I'll pay you thirty-grand an event, and I'll personally set up a meeting with Boden, you, and me within the month."

I narrow my eyes. "You don't want to live with a six-month-old."

Dax looks down at Eddie as he drools all over his shirt. "I do, actually. I've always wanted kids, but Madison isn't ready. It will help me get my fix without actually having to have a child. What other arguments against this do you have?"

I cross my arms and frown at him. "Why are you giving me more money than I asked for? It's very suspicious. You know paying me more won't make it any better if you fuck this up?"

He gives me a devious grin. "I am probably going to fuck this up. We barely know each other, but you need help; you're desperate.

And I could use some help too. So I know you'll say yes—you don't have a choice."

"I always have a choice," I spit back defiantly. But his offer is the only good option I have.

"So what do you say, Peaches?"

My shoulders slump, and I relax. "I say yes if you stop calling me Peaches."

His eyes light up, and Eddie smiles at him. "Not a chance."

11

OAKLEE

I KNEW HE WAS RICH; I just didn't realize he was mansion-level rich.

Holy fuck! I keep repeating in my head as I pull up to the gate at the entrance of his driveway.

Holy fuck, holy fuck, holy fuck!

I should have asked for a lot more money. *What would I have to do for him to pay me a million dollars?*

Ugh, don't go there. He's married, and as much as I want to think he's a bad man, he isn't. I only keep trying to make him out to be evil in my head.

I roll down my window and press the intercom button.

"Pull up to the garage door," Dax's deep voice says through the speaker as the iron gate opens.

I take a deep breath and roll up my window. "Eddie, I don't know what I've just gotten us into, but I hope I'm doing the right thing."

I pull up next to what looks like a five-car garage just as one of the garage doors opens, and Dax steps out with a frown on his face.

"Where's your stuff?" he asks when I get out of my Audi. Luckily I haven't gotten desperate enough to sell it or trade it in for something cheaper yet.

"In my trunk."

"You have a six-month-old, and you've been living in an apartment where I assume you had some furniture. I sent a truck to pick it up for you. Did the company not show?"

I pull Eddie out of his car seat and place him on my hip. "You said you had a bed I could use, and I have a pack-n-play for Eddie. We have two bags of our stuff."

"Where's your furniture and the rest of your stuff, Peaches?"

I glare at him. "Stop. Calling. Me. Peaches. My name is—"

"I know what your name is, but you'll be Peaches whenever you aren't playing Madison."

I sigh.

He stares me down, clearly unwilling to let me into his house until I tell him the truth.

"I sold it, okay? I sold everything I could."

He frowns. "I don't understand why you need so much money. You're living with me. I'll pay for your expenses while you're here."

"Well, since we aren't actually married and I won't be living here more than six months, I need to save as much as I can."

"I'll make sure Boden pays his fair share of child support."

I nod solemnly, but paying his fair share of child support is the least that Boden can do with his debts hanging over me. I don't tell Dax that, though. I'm too embarrassed I let Boden take advantage of me in the first place.

I shouldn't have let Boden access all of my credit cards. I shouldn't have given him everything he needed to put his bills in my name. I shouldn't have ever dated him. I shouldn't have said yes to marrying him. And I shouldn't have fucked him without protection even if it brought me Eddie.

I'm too proud to tell Dax any of that, though. I just need to talk with Boden; then I can figure out what to do.

"Let me show you around, and I'll unpack your car," Dax says, still frowning. It seems he's going to let this go for now, but I doubt he'll drop it forever. If we're living together for the next six months, I'm not sure I'm going to be able to hide all my secrets.

Dax leads me through the garage. "I'll get you a garage door opener and a code to the security gate and system."

"Are all of these cars yours?" I say wide-eyed as I look at the five fancy vehicles parked in the garage.

"Technically, four of them are Madison's. I just have the Porsche." He smirks at me.

"The motorcycle is Madison's?"

He nods.

I run my hand over the bike's handlebars. "I think I'm going to have to become more of a badass if I'm going to keep impersonating her."

"You're plenty badass, trust me."

I roll my eyes.

"You are." That's all he says, but something in his look forces me to believe him. The way his eyes lock onto mine and don't let go until I give him my faith—I've never had a man look at me that way.

I nod and look away before a tear slips out. He's a good man as much as I want him to be horrible. It would be easier to just do this job, take his money, and never think about him again, but his kindness makes it difficult. I can already tell that when we go our separate ways in six months it's going to hurt. Call it a premonition—this man is a heartbreaker, and he's about to break my heart.

He opens the door to the house and holds it ajar for me while I step inside.

I gasp. Despite how big the house looks outside, I can't believe how incredible the inside is. It's like I stepped into a different time, a different world, a different place.

The house was clearly built fifty years ago, but everything inside has been updated to the latest state-of-the-art design. Sharp edges, clean lines, quartz, stainless steel—I could go on and on admiring everything.

Dax doesn't give me a tour so much as he just lets me wander and follows behind with his hands in the pockets of his suit jacket. He watches me and answers my questions but leaves me to check everything out in my own time.

I stop suddenly in the formal dining room when I see a painting on the wall. My heart flutters at the sight, almost like it would if I saw a hot man for the first time and it was love at first sight. It's a similar feeling to how I felt when I first saw Dax.

"Is…oh my god…it can't be? Is it? Is it a Monet?"

"It is."

"It's real? Not a copy?" My brain can barely comprehend what I'm seeing.

"It is."

My heart stops as I stare at the beautiful piece of art. Now I'm curious what other art I'm going to find in this house.

Eddie doesn't appreciate art like I do, though, so the piece does nothing to stop his sudden crying.

It takes me a moment to tear my eyes away from the artwork to give my attention fully to Eddie.

"Is he hungry?" Dax asks.

"I don't think so; I just fed him before I came."

"Let me show you to your room if you want to help him relax. Then I'll carry your stuff in."

I nod and bounce a still-crying Eddie as I follow Dax upstairs.

Dax shows me a room bigger than my entire apartment, even without its adjoining nursery for Eddie. There's a bathroom suite connected as well. I could practically hide up here and never leave.

Dax runs downstairs to grab my stuff while I try everything I can to calm Eddie. After Dax brings his diaper bag up, I change Eddie's diaper even though it doesn't really need changing. I offer to feed Eddie, but he just turns his head away. I give him a pacifier even though he never really liked them in the first place. I sing to him. I bounce him. I try everything I can think of, but Eddie still doesn't quiet.

Dax stands in the doorway after bringing up the rest of my things.

"Are you sure you still want us living with you?" I ask sheepishly.

He shrugs. "My room is on the other side of the house. I doubt I'll even hear you."

"Of course, it is."

"Here, let me try," Dax says.

I raise an eyebrow. "You know you're doing enough. You don't have to add childcare to your list."

"I know, but I want to," he replies as he takes Eddie from my arms.

"You actually want to hold my son?"

He nods. "I want kids soon." He almost says more but stops himself.

"But Madison doesn't?"

He purses his lips and looks into Eddie's eyes before he smiles. He doesn't answer me, but that must be it. I guess it makes sense. She travels a lot, and she's a badass who likes her freedom. I'm shocked she even agreed to get married.

A realization breaks through my thoughts about Dax, and I shake my head in disbelief. "Eddie stopped crying. Maybe you should have kids soon; you have the magic touch. Just let Madison know you'll handle it every time your kid cries. I'll send her a pic of you holding him, and her ovaries will melt at the sight. Trust me, she'll be dying to have your babies," I tease.

"I'll just have to enjoy using my fathering skills on Eddie while you're here. I'm not sure if I'll ever be a father. I won't pressure Madison and..." he trails off painfully.

I made a mistake joking about it. Clearly, it's a sensitive subject for him and Madison. Some people don't want kids, and there's nothing wrong with that. I shouldn't pressure anyone. Hell, I wasn't even sure I wanted kids until I found out I was pregnant myself.

"Let's go downstairs, and I can see what we have for dinner," he says after a few minutes of relaxed silence from Eddie.

I nod and silently vow to keep my mouth shut about things I don't know. As Dax continues to hold Eddie, I follow them downstairs to the gourmet kitchen, fit for any chef.

I skip past Dax. "I'll cook dinner since you've got Eddie."

"Do you know how to cook?"

"Yes, thank you." I roll my eyes and open up his massive fridge.

Poking my head in the fridge and freezer, I'm relieved to spot a frozen pizza.

"How about pizza?" I hold up the box.

Dax chuckles, and I'm happy to see him laugh again after I put a downer on the evening by pushing the children subject. "Pizza would be perfect," he replies with a grin.

I walk over to the oven, while Dax walks to the bar. "Want any wine or a cocktail?"

"I'll take wine."

"White, right?"

"How do you know what wine I like?" I fiddle with the oven nobs, trying to figure out how to turn it on.

"You only drank champagne and white wine the night of the wedding, so I just assumed that's your preference."

"It is." I keep tweaking and pressing the oven knobs, but I refuse to ask for help. I'm going to figure this out.

I take until Dax finishes pouring our wine glasses to figure out the oven. I triumphantly stick the pizza in the oven.

Dax hands me a wine glass while he carries his own glass and Eddie to the living room. My son's head is now resting against Dax's shoulder, and he's drooling on his suit jacket.

I wince. "Eddie is drooling on your jacket. I'd offer to pay for dry cleaning, but..."

Dax laughs. "I think I'll survive."

I sit down on the couch, and Dax does the same. "So, if I can ask, what do you do for a living to be able to afford this mansion of a house?"

"Guess." Dax's smirk on his face is irresistible.

"Hmmm," I study him closely and try to think back to the night of the wedding. Did anyone give away any clues? I don't recall anyone mentioning his job. I've only ever seen him wear suits. He has some sort of contract to keep him in town, but he'll take another contract overseas when he's finished here. I can't really make sense of him, but I have to guess. "Lawyer?"

Dax chuckles. "Nope."

I frown and take a drink, narrowing my eyes. "Your turn."

"To guess what you do?"

I nod my head.

His cocky grin says he'll guess what I do on his first try. He won't, though; no one does. I run my tongue across my bottom lip, enjoying our game while we wait for food. It will be good to know each other a little better. It won't feel so strange sharing the same house if I know more about him.

"What's your guess?" I ask with a sly smile. Everyone thinks I work in the beauty industry, or I'm a hairstylist, or I work in PR, or I'm an interior designer. Jobs that are stereotypically girly or that people think don't require much intelligence.

No one ever sees me as a woman with a mind. They just see me as the girl who wears pretty dresses and makeup. The girl who got knocked up and ruined her life because she couldn't possibly take care of a child on her own.

They're all wrong. I could—I can. But first, I have to get rid of the yoke of debt and complications Boden brought into my life.

My jaw tenses as I wait, and I realize how much I care what Dax's answer is going to be. It started out as a fun game, but I care about what he thinks of me. I care about how he sees me. I've let him into my life more than most people. He knows more of my secrets than most. He might be the only person who has seen the new me—the real me. The me that I've become—a mother without my history of party girl mucking up his view of me.

I take a drink of my wine, hoping Dax doesn't realize how nervous I am for his answer. I look at Eddie still asleep in Dax's arms. My son obviously trusts him, so maybe I can too.

"Well, there are only two choices."

My eyebrows raise. "Only two? You only think I'm capable of doing two things?" my voice is a little snappier than it probably should be.

He shakes his head and pats Eddie's back to keep him asleep. "No, I meant after getting to know you a little better, I think there are only two things you would be satisfied doing. And you aren't the kind of woman who would settle, so I know you're doing one of two jobs."

I lift my glass to my lips again but then freeze. My heart does little flutters in my chest at his words.

Does he really know me that well?

"You're either an artist…"

My heart rate speeds up until my chest is beating unbelievably fast.

"But based on your lack of paint stains or sketch pads, I'm guessing you're an art curator or art historian."

I'm pretty sure my heart just flatlined. My eyes are locked on him, and I don't know what to say.

His dimples flash as he smiles widely. "I'm right, aren't I?"

I blink at him, still speechless.

He laughs, his head falling back on the couch, while he holds Eddie close to keep him from waking.

"How?" I breathe.

He frowns. "No one has ever recognized a single painting in my house. Every painting or statue in the wedding hotel you would take an extra second to look at as if you were trying to take it all in."

"I can't believe you noticed," I whisper.

"It's hard not to notice everything about you, Peaches."

Suddenly, I don't care that he calls me that ridiculous nickname. He sees me—he really sees me.

"Your turn again. What do you think I do?"

I take a long sip of my wine, swallowing hard as my face reddens. I don't know what to say. I wish I knew him as well as he apparently knows me. I feel like a terrible person for not paying attention to him.

I try to think about his personality combined with him always wearing a suit, but nothing obvious pops into my head. He seems like the responsible type. The type who went to a four-year college, maybe even got a master's degree or doctorate.

"Doctor?" I ask, suddenly self-conscious. He takes such good care of Eddie. I suddenly realize he must be a… "Pediatrician!"

Dax laughs. "Really? I've never held a child in my life besides Eddie, and I wouldn't last that long in school."

I frown. "You seem plenty smart and caring enough to be a doctor."

"Maybe, but I hated school."

"So you didn't go to college?"

He shakes his head.

I chew on my bottom lip, considering my choices. A job that requires a suit but no college degree.

"Stockbroker?" *That doesn't require a degree, right?*

He shakes his head.

"Flight attendant?" Maybe that's how he and Madison met.

He shakes his head.

"Software engineer?"

He shakes his head.

"Sports agent?"

He shakes his head no again.

Each time he shakes his head he gives nothing away. He doesn't offer any clues or seem offended that he guessed correctly on the first try, while I feel like I've guessed every job in the universe and still haven't figured it out.

But then suddenly, I have it. It's obvious. There are only two ways to make this kind of money that can afford a house like this and be able to pay me the kind of money he's paying me.

He either inherited it, worked for it, or Madison is somehow loaded. But considering the family and friends on his side I saw seemed like ordinary people at the wedding, I'm going with option two. He earned it.

"You're a business owner. You started your own business and made it big," I state it confidently, not like a question, just like he did when he guessed.

He doesn't move—*I've finally guessed correctly!* He's going to make me guess what business he actually started, but I honestly have no clue. It has to be a big business, but I can't figure it or him out.

But then I watch as Dax slowly shakes his head. He seems ashamed to be putting me through this torture.

"What? I didn't guess correctly? Really?"

"Sorry, but as much as you're an open book—I'm not."

I run my hand through my hair. "So, what do you do?"

He winces, hesitant to tell me.

"Oh, come on, it can't be that bad. You're not like a hitman or something, are you?" My voice doesn't sound as convinced as my head that he's not a murderer.

"You think I kill people for a living, and you're fine living in my house and letting me hold your son?"

"Fine, I don't think you're a murderer. But what do you do?"

"Head down that hallway, third door on the left," he says with a tilt of his head.

I narrow my eyes at him. "Why can't you just tell me?"

"I'd rather you see for yourself."

"You're a creepy dude; you know that? I didn't realize it at first, but you're creepy."

He chuckles. "I prefer the term mysterious."

I shake my head with a teasing smile. "Nope, creepy."

I'm too curious to find out the answer, so I quickly get up and walk down the hallway while Dax stays on the couch. I reach for the handle of the third door on the left with a clammy hand, turn the knob, open the door, and...

"It's a bathroom. You're a plumber?" I yell behind me.

Laughter rings through the house. "Sorry, I meant fourth door."

I sigh, my heart still racing as I make my way to the fourth door.

What the hell could he be? What could be hiding behind the door? And why does it send a tiny thrill through me to think it could be something sexual? Like he's Christian Grey or something? Maybe he's a high-end escort, so Madison is used to sharing him, and that's why me kissing him wasn't a big deal?

I let out a deep breath to let go of my anxiety, along with any hope of this being a sexual playroom or him being an escort. He's neither of those things. And I shouldn't be thinking like that. I'll never kiss Dax again, and he doesn't think of me that way.

Before I lose my nerve, I quickly turn the knob and push the door open. The room is dark and doesn't give away any of its secrets until I flip the lights on.

I purse my lips and tilt my head, trying to piece together what I'm supposed to decipher about his job from what I'm seeing. There's a large black desk with three huge monitors sitting on it, an expansive keyboard, an ergonomic mouse, big over-the-ear head-phones with a mouthpiece, and the most comfortable-looking chair I've ever seen.

I look around the room for more clues, but all I see are dark, almost black painted walls and blackout curtains covering the windows. It's like a dungeon in here. Unfortunately, not a sex dungeon. And I still don't have a clue what he does for a living.

"You're a vampire that barricades himself in this room while doing a boring office job?" I cock an eyebrow up, looking over my shoulder. I feel Dax's hot breath behind me, and it intensifies when he chuckles at my guess.

I don't allow myself to completely turn and look at him. One more flash of his pearly white teeth and adorable dimple, and I'm not sure I'll be able to control myself.

He's a married man, I keep trying to remind myself.

He hands me a baby monitor showing Eddie in his pack-n-play and brushes past me into his office. That little zip of electricity hits me deep in my core again as our fingertips brush against each other. If he feels the electricity, he doesn't acknowledge it as he sits behind the desk.

His scent overwhelms my senses, and my throat runs dry as I watch him roll his sleeves up, revealing thick veins that wrap around his forearms. Wondering if another particular part of him is veiny, my eyes drop down, but I catch myself.

"You don't happen to have a brother, do you?" I ask, my voice too breathy.

Dax stares at me for a second as if he doesn't know how to answer.

I blush, realizing I may have revealed too much about how I feel about him with that question.

"Sorry, forget I asked. I know you don't have a brother. I would have met him at the wedding. What is it that you do?"

Dax turns his eyes back to the screen as he places his headset on top of his head.

I walk behind the desk as he furiously types and moves the mouse on the screen.

My eyes widen as I see his screen. A sci-fi yet urban-looking world is filled with characters jumping all over the place. Each of the characters is dressed up differently and holding some kind of weapon. One character at the bottom of the screen seems to be running away from the screen and possibly controlled by Dax's mouse.

"You design video games?" I ask, wildly impressed.

Dax's face turns a crimson red as he stops what he's doing and removes the headset to face me. He runs his hand through his hair, tousling it. Between it and the bashful smile on his face, he turns ten years younger, with a sweet boyish charm to his grin.

"No, I'm a gamer. I play video games for a living."

I stare at him, then at the screen, and then back to him. "So you're a trust fund baby?"

He laughs as he stands up from his overly padded office chair. "No, my parents are teachers. They didn't leave me any money; they barely had enough money to live on themselves."

I frown. "I'm confused."

"I enter tournaments online and in-person, and I film myself playing and put it on YouTube."

"And you make money doing that?"

"Only if I win." His eyes light up.

"And do you win?"

His boyish grin widens, and I can't help but smile along with him, until he takes a step toward me into my personal space. I don't think he realizes he's doing it or that I'm quickly falling for him. If he was single and I didn't think the male species was a bunch of lying, cheating scumbags, I'd be jumping his bones right now.

Who am I kidding? I'd be all over him even if I didn't want to look at another man again after what Boden did to me.

I hold my breath, so his musk doesn't enter my nose again. I try to stare at the walls behind him, so I don't get lost in his warm eyes. But I can't escape his aura. I can't escape the longing I feel—the wish I had met him first. This kind man belongs with me, not Madison.

"Usually." His eyes drop to mine, and I finally look at him. He looks as lost as I am. "But there is this one game I've been playing that I keep getting burned in."

I don't ask what game it is. I don't ask if there's a hidden meaning behind his words. I don't ask if he's actually looking at me with longing in his eyes or if it's my imagination because neither answer is a good one.

I want him to want me, but that would make him a cheater, and I refuse to date a cheater. And if he doesn't want me, that makes me pathetic.

"I should go to bed," I say.

He nods, and I run out of his office to my bedroom. I throw the door shut, breathing too hard.

What is wrong with me?

Dax is just a kind man, offering me and Eddie a place to stay. He's basically my employer. I work for him, helping him out, and he pays me. That's all this is—a business arrangement.

My flashes of lust are just because I haven't been laid in a long time, that's all. I better get my feelings under control soon before I ruin everything.

12

DAX

"WHAT TIME IS IT THERE?" I ask as I smear toothpaste on my toothbrush and shove it into my mouth.

"Too early," Madison says into the phone and yawns as if to prove I'm interrupting her sleep by calling her. But I need to talk to her. I have a huge problem—and she's the only person in the world I can talk to about it.

"Are you sure you can't come to the charity fundraiser this week-end?" I ask as my toothbrush dangles from the corner of my mouth.

She laughs into the phone. "Is that really why you called me? You know my answer to that question."

The answer is the same as it always is—no. No, I can't attend an event. No, I can't actually stay in the country so we can live like a normal married couple. No, I don't want kids. No, no, no.

I sigh and spit the toothpaste out before rinsing my brush.

"I don't think we've thought this through, Madison. It was one thing for Oaklee to pretend to be you at the wedding ceremony, but how is she supposed to keep pretending to be you for the next six months? Someone is going to figure it out."

"No one will figure it out. It's been years since I've been seen at a public function. The girl looks exactly like me. She'll do a fine job, and in six months, we can all go our separate ways, and no one will be any the wiser."

"Oaklee. The girl's name saving your ass is Oaklee," I say through gritted teeth.

"What has you so on edge, Dax? It's not the charity event."

I yank off my shirt and toss it on the floor, not bothering to carry it to the hamper in the closet. I'm in a foul mood, and the only chance I have of getting out of it is to get a good night's sleep. But not before I have it out with Madison first.

"Your parents are going to be there. We fooled them once, but that was pure luck. How are we going to pull that off?"

"My parents and I haven't had a real conversation since I left their house when I was eighteen. They don't know anything about me—all they care about is that I show my face at these events and make them think I'll take over the family business and give them grandchildren they can turn into polite little socialites they can give their wealth to. They won't notice the woman on your arm isn't actually me."

I don't respond because it's true. And she knows it's not the real reason why I called.

"What's going on with you, Dax? What has you so wound up?"

I close my eyes, regretting calling Madison. She's been my best friend for years. She knows me better than anyone, and I know her better than anyone. I used to be able to talk to her about anything, but I'm not sure how I talk to her about this.

My mind has no issue playing out my problems like a sad romantic tragedy. It takes me back to earlier in the night when I showed Oaklee my gaming room. I let her into a tiny bit of my soul —of who I am.

The way she looked at me with such awe melted me. Her eyes practically glowed as she watched me do something I love. There was no judgment in her eyes like I see with a lot of women when I tell them what I do for a living. There was no calling me a boy that never grew up.

There was more to her gaze than just awe and appreciation.

There was something I dare not name, definitely not out loud and not even in my head. I can't say it. I can't think it. It's not fair.

Oaklee ran out of the room, confirming my suspicions even more about her feelings, and it kills me.

After she ran out, I went to her room to try and talk to her. I reached her door before realizing I had no idea what to say to her to make it better. Short of telling her the entire truth, there is nothing I could say to make it better.

Before I could walk away, though, I saw her holding Eddie, spinning around and singing to him. I've never seen anything more beautiful. She was in pajama pants with a hole in the knee. Her hair was up in a messy bun and strands were falling out around the base of her neck. She wasn't wearing a lick of makeup, but none of that mattered. All I saw when I looked at her was beauty. I saw a mom loving her child with everything in her.

My chest tightens as I think about what a woman like that deserves in a man. She is entitled to so much more than Boden. She definitely deserves more than a man like me. She thinks I'm a kind, generous man, but she doesn't know how much of a liar I truly am.

"You want her," Madison says suddenly.

"No," I snap back like it's absurd.

She chuckles. "You so want her—Oaklee. You want to date her. No, you've already fallen in love with her, haven't you?"

I don't answer her. Madison is too perceptive. I never should have called her.

"Oh, my dear, Dax. You can't beat yourself up. This is a good thing, not a problem. Enjoy your time with her. Maybe the two of you will hit it off and—"

"And what? We'll get married and live happily ever after? Everyone thinks she's you. She can't pretend to be you for the rest of her life. And besides, once she finds out the truth, she'll want nothing to do with me."

Madison sighs. "You're too harsh on yourself. Oaklee will fall for you the same way all women fall in love with you—you are incredible. The lies, the half-truths, the rest of it won't matter. If she falls for you and you for her, you'll figure everything else out."

"How?"

She's silent for a long time. She doesn't know how to solve anything because there isn't a way.

"I'll tell the truth when the moment is right. If you two fall in love with each other, I'll fix everything when the six months are up. You have nothing to worry about. Love is all that matters. Go for it. You deserve to be happy, Dax."

I end the call because I can't listen to Madison any longer. She's wrong. I don't deserve to be happy. Love is not the only thing that matters. There is no happily ever after for me. The only way this ends is in disaster and me breaking Oaklee's heart.

13

OAKLEE

I SMEAR a final touch of my lipstick on my lips before leaning back to take in the full picture. I clean up good—I know how to rock a skin-tight dress, sweep my hair to one side in long curls, give the perfect smoky eye and red lip, and walk in six-inch heels.

This used to be my world. I used to attend galas and charity events almost every weekend, until I lost my job and future husband. And until I got stacked with so much of his debt that I didn't have a choice but to sell all of my fancy dresses.

Luckily, Madison had plenty to spare, and we share a nearly identical size. I can tell she's slightly bustier than I am, and my hips stretch the dress a little bit more than hers would, but the average person won't be able to tell the difference.

Eddie is already down for the night, and I hired a high school girl off the internet to watch him for the night. I'm not worried about Eddie; I'm worried that this house will be too hard to resist throwing a big party at while we're away. Dax assured me that even if she did, he wouldn't care.

Still, I made sure to show her the security system so she'd know we can watch everything she does anyway. I'm hoping that will deter her from destroying Dax's house.

I peak into the theater room where the babysitter is already watching a movie with the baby monitor next to her.

"Do you need anything before I go?" I ask her.

Her eyes don't leave the TV. "Nope, I'm good."

I sigh at her lackluster response, but she's really only here in case of an emergency. Eddie sleeps through the night, so unless something happens, her job is to just watch movies all night until we return.

I close the door and start walking down the stairs as I hear Dax call up. "You ready?"

I stop, knowing Dax is at the bottom of the stairs looking all handsome in his tux. This is the cinderella moment. The moment where I descend the stairs, his eyes go to me, and because he's polite he'll tell me how beautiful I am, and I'll blush and let his words go to my heart more than I want to admit. And then I'll fall even more in love with a married man. I can't let that happen.

"Oaklee? Are you okay?" I can hear Dax's footsteps as he starts up the stairs.

"Wait!"

The footsteps stop.

"I'm coming down, but I need you to promise me something first."

"O-kay," Dax says cautiously.

"I need you to promise me that you won't say I'm beautiful. Don't say anything polite about my appearance. We are just two friends attending an event together. This night is all pretend. And when it's just the two of us, we won't pretend. We will just authentically be ourselves. So you don't get to call me beautiful."

"But I would tell my friend she was beautiful if she got all dressed up to attend a charity event with me just as my friend."

I wrinkle my nose, knowing he's right. "Just don't, okay? I get all embarrassed with compliments, and I can't handle them, so just don't," I lie. The real reason is my heart can't take hearing he thinks I'm beautiful while he's in love with another woman.

"Okay, I promise, no compliments. And I'll treat you as I would any other friend unless it's absolutely necessary tonight to help the lie. Satisfied?"

"Yes. I'm coming down."

And with that, I descend the stairs. I don't hesitate. I don't take my time ensuring I don't fall down the stairs. I practically run down the stairs, keeping my eyes down, and only find his until the very last second. I almost trip over him from coming down the stairs so fast.

He puts his hands on my shoulders to steady me, while his eyes rake over my face. His breath is hot on my lips, and his eyes dilate as he stares at me.

I should say something—a snarky comment to break the mood—but I can't come up with anything. My heart is pitter-pattering in my chest, yearning for him to say the words I just begged him not to say.

"Ugly," he says.

"What?" I crane my neck to look up at him.

He grins wickedly at me. "I've never seen anything so ugly in my life. Your dress is too tight, your hair too curled, and your makeup makes your eyes look too big. Horrible, all of it."

I bite my lip to hide my smile.

"Don't you dare smile. If you smile, it might make this hideous dress look good, and then I'll have to give you a compliment."

I roll my eyes, but my smile grows larger.

"You look pretty terrible yourself. Can your tux cling to your biceps anymore than it already does? Nobody likes a showoff, Dax," I tease.

He chuckles as I jokingly give a bicep a squeeze. My stomach does a little flip before I remove my hand.

I've got to stop touching him.

"The limo is out front," he says.

I nod and start walking in that direction, but his fingers brush mine before gripping them, stopping me.

I turn and look at him with big eyes.

"Seriously, Oaklee, you look amazing. You always do. I'm sorry you're not good at taking compliments and that it's probably because you've been treated poorly by men like Boden your whole life. But you should know you're beautiful, and intelligent, and funny, and the best fucking mom I've ever seen. And I'm honored to be your friend tonight."

I scowl at him. "You promised."

"Sorry. I'm not very good at keeping promises that are no good for either of us." He grins, expecting to be forgiven.

I sigh. *If he only knew how bad giving me compliments really was, he wouldn't give me any.*

I follow Dax to the limo, trying to stay grounded in why I'm doing this—to help Eddie. And Dax is doing this to help Madison. Neither of us is doing this for ourselves. I just hope we don't have to deal with the consequences if we're found out.

Dax holds the limo's back door open and holds out his hand to help me in, but I ignore him, hike up my dress, and climb in myself. Maybe if I'm cold to him, he'll stop being nice to me, making my heart skip a beat and making me believe in good men again.

Dax slides in next to me, and then a moment later, the driver heads toward the charity event.

I have a million questions I should be asking. *What is the event for? Who will we be talking to? How should I act? What should I know about Madison to pull this off?* So many questions, but instead, I stare with an unyielding gaze out the window, counting the trees as we drive by, trying to keep my focus on anything other than him. His cologne, the energy is buzzing off him, and his warm smile— blocking it out to stop the swarming butterflies in my stomach.

I'm so lost in counting the trees and keeping my mind occupied that I don't brace myself for the sudden stop.

The limo slams to a halt and doesn't keep me from stopping along with it. I fly forward, falling face-first toward the floor between the seats, only to land on a hard body instead.

I squeeze my eyes shut and try to hold my breath, not believing what just happened. My reaction doesn't stop Dax from being the perfect gentleman he is.

"Are you hurt?" His finger brushes my cheek, and I shudder.

I nod but don't open my eyes. I'm still holding my breath, trying to block out his scent.

"Oaklee? You aren't breathing. Where are you hurt?" Somehow he's scooped me up in his arms and climbed back onto the seat just as the driver continues on, unaware that he almost caused both of us to end up bruised and beaten.

Dax's hands race over my body, looking for signs of blood or an injury, which is the exact opposite of what I want him to be doing.

I grab his hands.

"Stop," I breathe, my eyes peeking open a crack. But it's enough to see the world of worry in his eyes.

He opens his mouth, I'm sure to ask what's wrong, but I put my finger up to his lips, shushing him. A zap of energy zips down from his lips to my core, igniting my desire for this man even more.

I really need to consider ending this arrangement sooner rather than later. I'm on track to become the thing I hate most in this world—a cheater.

Thankfully, the limo stops outside of the event room, and I scramble off his lap and out of the door before he can stop me. I know I have a part to play, but I'm going to need a lot of alcohol if I'm going to be able to pull this off. Hopefully, being intoxicated will help dull my senses when it comes to Dax.

1 4

DAX

I STARE at Oaklee racing up the stairs of the public library decorated for the event. I have no idea what just happened, but I'm going to find out.

I climb out of the limo myself, but the driver never gets out. It's a good thing, too, or I'd chew him out for his reckless driving. We'll find another way home.

I take the stairs two at a time until I make it to the top where a doorman is checking invitations at the door. I don't know how Oaklee got in without showing hers, but I guess he didn't question her. He was probably too stunned by her gorgeous looks to stop her.

I pull my invitation out and flash it to him before brushing past to find Oaklee. I scan the crowd quickly, already seeing several people noticing me and walking toward me to chat about my wedding, where Madison is, and hoping to gossip. It's why I'm here —to put my life on display, so Madison's family is happy. This is only a few months of living in their world for a lifetime of freedom.

But right now, none of that is my concern. I need to find Oaklee.

My guesses are she's hiding in the bathroom or at the bar. Many women might try to hide in the bathroom, but hiding isn't exactly Oaklee's style, or at least, I hope it isn't. I don't want to go into the

556

women's bathroom to drag her out. In this crowd, it would cause a scandal, and I don't want to make this any harder on Oaklee than it has to be.

I head toward the bar and find her, white wine in hand.

I inch next to her and motion to the bartender for a drink. "I'll take a white wine as well."

She raises her eyebrows at my choice but doesn't say anything.

"I expected you to order something harder too," I say to her.

"White wine is what the occasion calls for. It wouldn't be polite for a woman to be drinking anything else in a social situation like this. Besides, if I switch to whiskey, I'm afraid of what I might do. Wine is enough to take the edge off, but not too strong that I lose my wits."

I frown. "You're probably right about the other women gossiping if they see you drinking something stronger than champagne or fruity cocktail. But what are you really worried about? I know it's not the rumormongers."

Oaklee stares at her wine intensely, expecting it to somehow save her. But I'm a patient man, and I can wait until she tells me what's going on in her head. The only problem is the wealthy women here don't have any patience.

After just a few minutes, we're swarmed, and it's time to play the part.

"Madison? Is that really you? It's been ages since we've seen you at one of these events," Natalie, an old classmate, says. She's wearing a black dress two sizes too small, stiletto heels, and long blonde hair that is clearly mostly extensions.

Oaklee doesn't miss a beat, turning toward Natalie and hooking her arm into the crook of mine.

"I've been too busy planning my wedding and enjoying our honeymoon, but I know how important this charity is. I just had to see that Dax and I made the effort to leave the house in order to be here." Oaklee bats her eyelashes at me, and it's clear what she's implying—we spend all of our time in the bedroom having hot sex. "No matter how hard it was."

"I'm sure it's hard for a man like you, Dax, to come to such a sophisticated event like this. I know it's not really your crowd. I'm surprised you even own a tuxedo," Natalie squeaks.

There is it—the first insult of the night. But it won't be the last. I don't belong in this world. I have money, but not old money. I'm wealthy but not wealthy enough. And my 'job' is seen more as a hobby than a real profession. Everyone here will make sure I know that I'm only welcome because of who I'm married to.

I'm about to brush Natalie's comment off since I'm used to the vial words of the elite, but Oaklee is not okay with it.

"It's only hard for Dax to be here because of women like you. Dax is a perfect gentleman..." she starts.

A small crowd has gathered now, backing Natalie. She grins slyly, but her face barely moves. She's overdone it on the botox. But she's already ready with her comeback.

"Dax is anything but a gentleman. We went to school together, remember? You can't fool us, Madison. He was a loser, a loner, a druggie. He was barely smart enough to graduate. He didn't get into college. He's nothing more than trailer park trash. He's only here because of your money. You may have dressed him up in a fancy tux, but that doesn't mean he's changed who he is—he's still a drugged-up criminal who deserves to be in jail," Natalie spats.

Oaklee loses it. I'm used to her standing her ground and using her words to attack others, but Natalie pushed her too far. She launches herself at Natalie.

But if Oaklee touches a hair on Natalie's head, the cops will be called, and Oaklee will spend the night in jail. So as much as I'd love to see Oaklee beat the crap out of Natalie and know that she'd deserve it, I won't let Oaklee go to jail trying to protect me.

I step between them at the last second, grabbing onto Oaklee's arms and dragging her away before she breaks free of my hold or says something she'll regret.

I find a janitor's closet and shove her inside to calm her down. I keep my hold on her arms. I keep the lights off. And I take deep, calming breaths, hoping it will be enough to calm her down as well.

We don't speak, but I can feel her warm breath against my neck. I close my eyes, thankful it's too dark for her to see my reaction and how inappropriate it is.

"What a bitch," she says, and we both break out into laughter.

"Is everyone here that horrible?" she asks.

"No, just the people I went to school with who think I'm still the trailer park trash I was as a kid."

"I'm sorry. You shouldn't have to deal with that."

"And you don't need to defend me."

"What would Madison have done? Would she have just stood by and let those people attack you for your past? A past that isn't even your fault? It's not your fault you grew up poor."

I sigh. It's true; Madison would have done the same thing Oaklee did or worse.

"That's what I thought," Oaklee says, taking my silence as confirmation to her question.

Finally, I release Oaklee from my grip. "Well, it doesn't mean you can just attack anyone who insults me. If you do, it's going to be a long night."

"We should just leave then because it's going to be impossible for me not to attack anyone who insults you," she says.

"We can't just leave."

"Why not? It's clear we aren't wanted here."

"We just can't…"

"You don't have to pay me. But I don't think we should stay."

"Of course, I'll pay you," I say, my voice sharp and annoyed.

"Well, I don't accept, and I really don't think we should stay."

I'm not sure if I can endure an entire night of insult and attacks either, but leaving isn't an option either.

"Then let's compromise. We'll go talk to Madison's parents, you'll fake an illness, and then we can go home and split a bottle of wine while watching an action movie."

I can't make out Oaklee's face, but I can sense her frown nonetheless. "You don't accept my terms?"

"No," she says stubbornly.

"No? Don't you want to get out of here?"

"I do, but we aren't going home and just watching a movie."

"Then what are we doing?"

Despite the darkness of the closet, I can feel her smile, and it makes me smile. "Something fun."

"Like what?" I ask.

"Trust me." Her fingers find mine, and that familiar tingling shoots from her to me. I've never had such a strong reaction to the simple touch of a woman before. I wish I could explore the feeling more.

I grab the door behind me and push it open. "Let's get this over with."

15

OAKLEE

WE END up staying longer than I would like, but we only have to deal with one more person making a snide remark. It was some old bitch who I flipped off as we were walking away.

We only had to talk to Madison's parents for a brief moment, and Dax was right—they don't know their daughter at all. They didn't even bat an eye when they saw me, didn't remotely consider I'm not actually their daughter.

I want to ask Dax more about Madison's relationship with her family and friends and why none of them recognize her, but I don't. The second we walk out the doors, I want to forget all about this terrible night.

"Now what? You sure you don't want to go home and watch movies the rest of the night? I'll let you pick the movie, and we can relieve that babysitter. I'm not sure she's the most competent babysitter in the world anyway," he says.

He's trying to rouse me so we can go home, but not a chance. Tonight we need some fun.

"Call for the limo. I know just what we need tonight," I say.

Dax frowns. "We aren't getting back in that death trap. The driver clearly isn't capable of driving us safely."

"Uber then?" I ask, surprised he'll take a chance on an unknown driver.

The lines around his eyes deepen, but I can see the wheels turning behind his eyes. He pulls out his phone and calls for the limo after all. When the driver pulls around, Dax walks over to him and has a curt conversation beyond my earshot.

The driver stomps off, and I furrow my brow in confusion. Dax holds the passenger door open for me.

"You're driving?" I question.

He nods solemnly.

I grin in delight. This is going to be a night to remember.

I climb in, and Dax gets behind the wheel. I don't want to know what he said to the driver to get him to give us the limo for tonight.

"You know how to drive this thing?" I ask.

Dax shoots me a cocky look. "I play video games for a living. I can handle driving a limo."

"I'm not sure playing video games is at all the same as driving a limo."

"Trust me, I'm good," he says.

And I do trust him, despite the rumors I heard swirling all night about him. Despite the criminal comments, the druggie comments, the lowlife comments, I trust Dax. It's a feeling as much as how he's treated me.

"Where to?" Dax asks.

I bite my lip, trying to decide if I want to tell him or make it a mystery until we arrive.

"Turn left at the next light."

He nods and does as I say, unquestioningly.

We don't talk about anything else as Dax drives, and I tell him directions. But then suddenly, Dax makes a turn without me telling him to.

"Hey, I didn't tell you to turn there," I press.

"We're going to the art museum, right?"

I nod, surprised he can read me so well and that he even knows where the art museum is.

"This way is faster," he says, not looking at my reaction.

I'm speechless as he parks in front of the museum a few minutes later.

"You do know the museum is closed," he says.

"Yep." I open my door and climb out.

I hear his door slam and his footsteps behind me. He easily catches up to me as I walk toward the side door.

"Are we going to break into the museum?" There's a drop of sweat on his forehead. "I really don't want to go to jail tonight."

I look into his eyes and see at least some of the rumors are true. He's spent time in jail. The fear in his eyes is only possible for a man who knows what it's really like to spend a night in jail—possibly more than just a night.

I want to know what happened to him. I want to know how he became the person he is today. But that's not what tonight is about, so I don't ask. I'm not sure I'll ever ask.

I pull out a key from my purse.

"It's not breaking and entering if I have a key and security codes," I reassure him.

His eyes widen, but I can still see uneasiness in his eyes.

"I was laid off because the museum is struggling, not because I did something wrong. The owner let me keep my key. He knows how much this place means to me. It was the biggest perk of the job —getting to visit when there are no guests."

I'm not sure I've convinced him this is legal, but he nods, and I use my key to open the door.

He follows behind me after I enter the security code, and then I take his hand.

I shouldn't touch him; I know I shouldn't, but I want to calm him. And after the rough night we had, I can reward myself with a few seconds of his touch.

I lead him through the museum to a room at the back of the first floor. It's my favorite room. The art in here is of the stars, the universe. It speaks to me.

I force myself to let go of his hand as soon as I lead him into the room, and we both take in the art. I take a deep breath, finally being able to breathe again in my favorite place. I don't let myself look at Dax at first. I just look at the paintings on the walls, but after a while, my curiosity gets the better of me. I want to know if he's having as much of a visceral reaction to the art as I do every time I'm here.

But he isn't looking at the art—he's looking at me.

"This is your favorite place in the whole world, isn't it?" he asks.

I nod.

"I can see why. The art is incredible."

I smile, letting go of the breath I didn't realize I had been holding as I waited for his reaction. I wanted him to love this place as much as I do, and it appears he does.

He turns and faces a painting. "Are you going to ask me what I did?"

I walk over and stand next to him, looking at the painting of Saturn.

"What you did?" I ask.

"How I ended up in jail."

There's a heartbeat between us before I answer. "No."

"Aren't you curious?"

"A little, but your past doesn't matter to me."

"It should. I'm a criminal, a monster. You shouldn't be associated with me."

I shake my head. "I don't believe you. Whatever you did, there was a reason. You're not a criminal. You're not a monster."

"How do you know?"

"You would have come with me even if it risked going to jail, wouldn't you?"

He doesn't answer at first, but then he gives just the slightest nod of his head.

"I can't judge if you were a monster to other people, whether you hurt someone else or not. All I can judge you on is who you are to me. To me, you've been the man I needed at just the right moment. A friend who helped me..."

"Financially," he grumbles.

"And otherwise. If it wasn't for you, I'd be drowning myself in alcohol every night. You've given me hope that there are good men in the world."

"I shouldn't. Like I said, I'm a monster."

"You're not—"

"But what if I am?" he says firmly, turning to me. I face him head-on at his reaction.

I take a deep breath, unsure how to answer. His expression says he believes himself to be a monster. I barely know Dax; all I know is how he's treated me. Although, I'm not the best judge of character. I used to think Boden was amazing, and look how that turned out.

"Then you'll have to atone for your sins. But I've known plenty of bad men in my life, and none of them would have ever admitted their faults. None would have admitted they were bad people. That makes you better than them, at least. And until you prove me otherwise, you're not a monster to me. You're just a friend."

A friend I want so much more from.

16

OAKLEE

It's been a week since the charity event.

A week since Dax called me beautiful.

A week since his body pressed against mine accidentally in the limo.

A week since he bared a little of his soul to me.

A week since I fell a little harder for him.

A week of wishing I could change my feelings so I wouldn't want a married man.

A week since I decided I can't keep this charade up much longer. After today, I have to tell Dax this has to stop. I'm moving out, and I can't keep pretending to be Madison.

I'll have to find another way to make money, find a real job. But hopefully, after I meet with Boden today, I'll only need enough money to take care of Eddie and me instead of the mountains needed to pay off Boden's bookies.

"You sure you want to go in alone?" Dax asks from the driver's seat as he parks the car. The coffee shop parking lot is mostly empty, but Boden agreed to meet me here.

Wordlessly I store at the shop's glass door with a coffee cup etched on it and overhead bells that jingle anytime anyone enters or exits. It's a small local shop with only a handful of tables. Dax arranged the meeting, and I left Eddie with a babysitter.

I'm not sure if I want to go in alone. In fact, it's the last thing I want to do, but Dax shouldn't be mixed up in this any more than he already is. I need to confront Boden on my own.

And no matter what Dax says, he and Boden are friends. I can't trust that Dax would really be on my side. He would just be in the middle, trying to compromise. But when it comes to my son, there is no compromise.

I need Boden to take responsibility for credit card charges, the crooks that attacked me, all of it. I need him to start paying child support. I need him to be a father.

I tear my eyes from the door and look directly at Dax. His hands on the steering wheel tap nervously. His eyes are full of emotion and a little swollen, like he didn't sleep well last night.

He cares.

He might even be on my side.

But I can't rely on him.

I can't get used to relying on anyone. Everyone who has ever cared about me has turned out to fail me when I really needed them. The only person I can rely on is myself. I have a responsibility as a mother to take protect my child, so this meeting needs to go perfectly.

"I'm sure," I finally answer. Then before I lose my nerve and ask for his help, I get out of the car.

I walk straight into the coffee shop and up to the small counter, where I quickly order a black coffee. I look around the tables for Boden and keep my eye on the entrances for any sign of Boden.

He's not here—not surprising.

After what happened last time, I don't expect him to show up. The only reason I have any hope is that Dax assured me he would be here.

I wait at the small counter, collect my coffee, and then sit at the table right next to the entrance. It would be impossible for me to miss Boden coming in. At least, that's why I tell myself I chose this seat. It's not because I also have a view of where Dax's car is parked in the parking lot.

As I sit and wait, I don't let my eyes go to Dax, only the door.

A moment later, the door bells chime, and Boden walks in. He's wearing a suit like he's entering a business meeting instead of having a coffee to discuss his son and how he's going to provide for him.

Boden spots me but doesn't acknowledge me as he goes to the counter and orders a drink. As he waits for the drink to be made, he still refuses to look at me. Instead, he pulls out his phone and scrolls through it like I'm not twenty feet away from him like he hasn't been dodging me for months.

My blood boils as I wait, but I know it's a tactic. The more riled up I am, the less level-headed I'll be, and he'll win. I have to keep my cool, be the mature one, and do what's right by Eddie.

I may hate Boden for everything he's done, but Eddie deserves to have a father in his life—even a cheating, lying, manipulative one who pushed his overdue bills on me and almost got me killed.

Finally, Boden walks over to my table. He doesn't speak or greet me. He just takes a seat across from me.

I grip my coffee cup, staring at the black sludge and taking several deep breaths until I'm sure I won't kill Boden when I look at him. When I do look up, I'm surprised to see it's not just Boden sitting across from me but another man in a suit already pulling out some paperwork on the table.

I eye them both suspiciously, not knowing what to make of this unexpected guest. The man is obviously a lawyer—I know that without asking him who he is. *Is he here to negotiate child support and pay off the loans? Maybe I should have had Dax come in with me just to review the paperwork? Or I should have had Dax help me obtain my own lawyer?*

Don't sign anything today, I remind myself. No matter how good it seems, I need to have my own lawyer look at it to ensure Eddie is getting the best out of any agreement.

"We will be filing this today, ma'am," the lawyer says, sliding the papers across to me without introducing himself. The man looks to be in his early forties, well dressed, and all business.

I take the papers into my hands and start reading. It takes me a minute to realize what the papers are until I read the words 'sole custody.'

But it's not talking about giving me sole custody. Boden is filing for sole custody.

I don't look at the lawyer when I speak; I look directly at Boden. "What the hell is this?"

"I've decided to file for sole custody of Eddie. I want what is best for him, and I've come to realize that while you have tried your best to provide a safe and loving home for Eddie, you just aren't up for the job, Oaklee. It's best for everyone if Eddie resides with me. I'll be sure to give you supervised visitation once a month, and we can discuss increased visitation once you're back on your feet."

"Bullshit. You don't want sole custody. You haven't even met Eddie. You've taken no interest in your son since the moment I told you I was pregnant."

"I allowed him to live with you because I thought that was what was best. But I've since realized my mistake, and I'm fixing it," he replies.

I throw the papers back at both of them. "Fine, file, you aren't going to win. You haven't been in his life at all! You haven't paid a dime of child support. You haven't been there for any doctor's appointments, for any milestones, for anything. You're a gambler and a cheater and an addict. You won't win. All you'll do is waste everyone's time, and you'll still end up having to pay child support in the end and repay me for all the money you've gambled away."

Boden smiles slyly but doesn't say anything.

"I'm sorry to hear you feel that way ma'am, but my client has a very good case. You are no longer employed, you're homeless, and the amount of loans you've taken out is insurmountable. You owe millions of dollars. And it's come to our attention that you're abusing narcotics."

"What?" I gasp.

I look from the lawyer to Boden, only finding a gleam in his eyes. Somehow this jackass has fabricated evidence of me abusing drugs. Everything else he said is accurate, even if the reason I owe millions is the smug asshole sitting right in front of me. If they file this and win, I'll lose Eddie.

"What do you want?" I ask quietly.

My heart is beating a million miles a minute, waiting for their answer. I'll do whatever they want in order to ensure that Eddie is safe.

Boden looks to his lawyer, who quickly stands, gathers the papers, and walks out the door. The chimes of the bells ring in my ears like a wailing siren.

"Don't mess with me, Oaklee. You're not going to win. You want to keep Eddie? Then leave me the hell alone. You don't ask for child support. You don't ask for help paying off the loans. You stay the fuck out of my life. You don't send my friends after me. You don't talk to anyone about me ever again." Boden picks up his to-go cup of coffee and looks me dead in the eyes. "If I hear from you again, I'll file the paperwork. I'll take Eddie from you, and you'll never see your son again."

Tears well in my eyes as I realize I've lost. There is no way to keep Eddie safe. If I force the issue, Boden will most likely win physical custody in court. But if I remain silent, the mafia or whoever Boden owes money to will most likely kill me.

No, I won't let him win. I'll find a way to protect my son. I wasn't prepared for this meeting, but I'll find a way—I have to.

I grit my teeth, and even though the tears fall, I refuse to fall apart. I refuse to be weak.

"You haven't won. You just think you have. I'll find a way to protect my son. I always have, and I always will."

"You mean *our* son," Boden muses.

"No, I mean *my* son. You were just the sperm donor. He's mine. Mine to love. Mine to protect. And I will protect him."

Boden stands. "Then protect him; just keep me out of it."

"Pay off the loan sharks, and I will."

"Those are your loans, Oaklee, not mine." He sips his coffee nonchalantly as if talking about what he's having for dinner, not about decisions impacting the life or death of his child and ex-fiancée.

"You know that's not true," I seethe at him.

"I know they're after you, not me."

"Do you even care about your son? About his safety? About his future? About what would happen to him if I'm murdered because you didn't pay off your bills?"

Boden doesn't even hesitate. "I'm not even sure he's my son. You were sleeping around with other tons of guys when we were together."

"No, that was just you who was cheating."

Boden doesn't respond; he just turns toward the door. I don't know what to do. I feel like I've failed, but I have to try one more time.

"You really don't care if I'm murdered because of your gambling problem?" my voice carries throughout the coffee shop, but I don't care who hears me. I'm desperate.

Boden stops at the door and looks back at me shaking his head. "Stopping being so dramatic, Oaklee. No one is going to kill you. You owe some money. Pay them back, and they'll go away."

"I don't have that kind of money," I cry out, tears falling freely now as anguish overtakes my body.

"I'm sure your rich boyfriend will be able to pay off your loans." He smiles smugly and cocks his head. "What was that about not being a cheater? You do know he has a wife, right?"

My blood boils as my face heats bright red. I've never wanted to hit someone so badly in my life. I usually have a comeback for everything, but I can't think—all I see is red.

I wipe the tears from my eyes and run after Boden out of the coffee shop. He heads toward the same parking lot Dax is parked in. I spot his stupid Mercedes nearby, a car he could sell and pay for a big chunk of his loan immediately.

I don't know what I'm going to do when I catch him.

Hit him.

Take out my anger on him.

Yell at him some more.

Nothing will fix my problem, though.

The sound of a door slamming gets my attention, and I see Dax climbing out of his car and heading in our direction.

Another door slams to my right, and I see the lawyer getting out of his car.

I can't hit Boden. If I do, the lawyer will just use it as more evidence for Boden to get full custody. Or he'll blackmail me into leaving Boden alone.

I stop in my tracks, keeping my distance.

"What's wrong?" Dax asks as he approaches me. He lowers his head and gets a good look at my swollen eyes and the snot running down my face from crying so hard.

He looks at me a second longer, waiting for me to answer. When I don't answer, he says, "Stay here."

And then Dax marches toward Boden.

I wait, watching him until I see his fist balled at his side.

"Wait! Dax, don't—his lawyer is right there!" I scream.

But my words don't stop Dax. He doesn't know what Boden did to make me cry—all he knows is that he made me cry, and to him, that's unacceptable.

"You fucking bastard," Dax says as he grabs the back of Boden's shirt and punches him in the face.

I gasp as Dax pulls his fist back, and blood drips down Boden's face.

"Whatever you did, you're going to go home. You're going to clean yourself up. And then you're going to figure out how to apologize and make things right with Oaklee. Do you understand, Boden?" Dax says.

"Or what? You'll beat me up?" Boden snickers.

"You don't want to know what I'll do to you." Dax's face is furious, and his hands are still balled into fists at his sides, ready to punch him again.

Boden just shakes his head and laughs. "Dax, I'd like to introduce you to Michael Stewart. He's my lawyer and caught everything you just did on camera. So I won't be doing anything, but you'll be hearing from us after I press charges."

Dax glares at Boden. "Take me to court. You'll lose."

"Will I? I'm not the one who has a criminal record, am I? That would be you." Boden opens the door to his car and climbs in, while his lawyer walks back to his own car.

I can tell Dax wants to chase after him, but he doesn't. He turns away, and the second he looks at me, the rage is gone. He softens completely; his steps are tentative as he holds out his arms. He wants to wrap his arms around me and hold me in a hug, but he's waiting for permission.

I nod the slightest, and his arms envelop me, my head resting against his beating heart. I've never been more enraged, more scared, or more protected than I am right now.

And it's that last emotion of safety that scares me the most. I can't rely on Dax to protect me, and I sure as hell can't give in to what I'm feeling for him at this moment.

17

DAX

SOMEHOW I GET us back to my house without driving after Boden, without asking her any questions, and without driving someone off the road because of my rage.

Oaklee is deep in thought the entire drive. She doesn't look at me, but she doesn't stare out the window either. She's just lost in her own mind.

I held her hand the entire time, worried she was about to have a nervous breakdown, and I wasn't going to be able to do anything to stop it.

But now we're back, and I still don't know how to help her. I actually don't even really know what happened other than Boden is a fucking bastard who thinks he can hurt the mother of his child.

The babysitter approaches as I lead Oaklee inside.

"Do you mind staying for another hour or two? I'll pay you double."

The teenager's eyes light up. "Sure! I just put Eddie down for his nap."

I nod. "Just keep an eye on him for us."

"Will do. I'll be in the theater room watching a movie." She scurries off while I lead Oaklee in the direction of my bedroom. Why I lead her that way, I'm not entirely sure. I tell myself it's in the opposite direction of where the teenager just headed and will give us the most privacy.

Once inside my bedroom, I help her onto the bed and then climb up next to her, pulling her into my chest so I can hold her tight.

"Can you tell me what happened?" I ask in the gentlest voice I can muster while my hand strokes up and down her bicep.

I'm not sure I'm going to get any answers out of her, but I need to fix this. The only way I can do that is if she tells me what happened.

"He wants sole custody," she whispers.

It takes me a minute to register. "What? Boden wants full custody of Eddie? That can't be true. There is no way he wants the responsibility of being a parent."

"He doesn't—not really. He just wants to threaten me with it because he knows he'll get whatever he wants."

"And what does he want? What power does he have over you?"

She shakes her head. "It doesn't matter. He has me cornered. I can't win. Either way I choose will hurt Eddie."

I want to comfort her, tell her it will be alright. But I can't promise her that. I don't know what the future holds.

"I'm glad I punched him. I should have done worse. I'm sorry the meeting went so horribly. I feel responsible."

"Don't be. It's not your fault. And I'll try to talk to him so he won't file charges against you."

"He won't. Don't worry about that."

"Boden is vindictive. He won't let the fact that you punched him go unpunished."

"I don't want you worrying about me or a place to stay or money. I know we said six months, but Madison and I can help you for as long as you need. Madison will like having a baby in the house."

Oaklee leans forward, off my arm, breaking our physical contact. I feel the empty coldness immediately.

"I can't stay here, and I can't keep working for you."

"What? Why not?"

She pulls her knees toward her chest, resting her head on top of them.

"You know why." It comes out like an easy breath, but her words are anything but easy. Every word was hard, but a tiny bit of anxiety leaves her body as her words do. These aren't words she chose rashly. These are words she's been thinking about for a while.

"I think I do, but I want to hear you tell me why."

She stares straight ahead at the black TV on my wall. I shouldn't be persuading her to spill her feelings when she's already so vulnerable, and I've yet to share mine. But I need to know. I need to know if she feels the same way about me that I feel about her.

Time comes to a stop, or maybe it flies by. I don't know. It just feels like we are in a different dimension, a different world, just the two of us.

My hands are sweating, I'm grinding my teeth, and my heart is begging for an answer.

She takes her time turning to look at me, but I know she'll answer. She's brave like that. She wears her heart out in the open. Boden was a fool for letting her go.

"Do you ever wonder if you chose the wrong person to spend your life with? I thought Boden was the right person for me. My forever. I was wrong to think that. If he was my soulmate, then that's it. I'll never find someone else because my soulmate didn't love me back. Maybe you get more than one soulmate, or maybe I just chose wrong." Her gaze bores into me, searching for answers. "Is Madison your soulmate?"

"No," I say instantly, not trying to hide the truth any longer. Although the truth is going to hurt her.

"How do you know?"

"Because you are."

And then our lips collide. My brain yells at me to explain first, to tell her this isn't cheating. That we aren't hurting Madison, but the second our lips touch I'm lost to her. My brain no longer works. I can't think. I can't breathe. I'm just hers, damn the consequences.

I wish I was the only one who would suffer the consequences. I would pay anything and suffer everything if I could prevent her from feeling any pain I cause her. But I can't.

18

OAKLEE

I FORGOT how good his kisses are—out of this world. I'm pretty sure my soul just left my body, and I'm floating in space now. His tongue sweeps through me, hitting every nerve in my mouth and cascading tingles through my body.

He grabs my waist and pulls me on top of him. I wrap my arms around his neck as I straddle him and deepen the kiss. My heart beats furiously over his, wondering what's going to happen next.

What is going to happen next?

Shit.

I push against his chest, breaking the kiss.

"Fuck." I wipe my mouth on the sleeve of my shirt. Maybe if I wipe his saliva off, I'll wipe away what happened. I just became the one thing I hate most—a cheater.

"Fuck. What did we just do? What did you do! I can't believe you're a cheater, just like Boden."

I jump up, needing out of the house. I can't stay here for even one more night.

I can't breathe—there's not enough oxygen here. I can't believe what I just did. I didn't think things could get any worse, but they did. I've become the worst version of myself, the thing I despise more than anything else on this earth, and my heart broke in the process.

I fell for a married man. I thought he was kind and honorable, but he's a liar. He seduced me; maybe that was his goal from the start. It's probably why he chose me, why he hired me, why he invited me into his house. He didn't want a fake Madison; he wanted a whore to fuck.

I run down the hallway, trying to figure out what to do next. My brain can't process the simple things like packing my bags, getting Eddie, and loading us all in the car. *So then what? Where would we go?*

I'll figure that out later; I just—

"Oaklee!" Dax's voice is full of emotion, and my heart seizes. I need to close it off to him to prevent any more of his painful manipulations.

I try to force my legs to move quicker, to get away from here faster, but instead, they stop. I don't care what Dax has to say, but my body just reacts to him.

I stop and turn.

Dax is standing in front of me, closely but not touching me.

Dammit, does my body want him to touch me again. This is the last time I'll see him. If he could only touch me again, maybe I'll hate it. Maybe I'll realize I never wanted him. After learning he's willing to cheat on his wife, I'll hate him.

Touch me, my body screams at me. *Kiss me again. This time I'll hate it, I promise.*

He doesn't budge, but he runs his tongue over his bottom lip. He wants to kiss me again, but this time he keeps his lips to himself.

Our chests rise and fall heavily as desire swirls between us.

"I'm not a cheater," Dax says slowly, ensuring I hear every word he speaks. "And neither are you."

I shake my head, breaking eye contact with him. "We're both cheaters, Dax. I know we've kissed before, but each time it was under the pretense of me pretending to be Madison to help you both with her knowledge. This time was different. This time we weren't pretending—it was real."

"We're not cheaters," Dax repeats again.

"You can say that all you want, but it doesn't change anything. We're both cheaters. We didn't fuck each other, thank god, but we kissed, and we wanted more. If my brain didn't start working again, we would have taken things further. I don't know much about your relationship with Madison. I don't know if she's a forgiving woman or not, but with some therapy, you can still salvage your marriage, and I can move on with my life feeling minimal guilt for my actions. But I can't stay here. I have to leave before we let things go any further."

"You're not listening to me. We're. Not. Cheaters," he repeats.

I roll my eyes. It's just like guys to only think it's cheating if his dick enters my vagina. Everything else is acceptable.

"It is. You're married, last I checked."

"Legally, sure. Although, technically, you were the woman I said my vows to, not Madison."

"We aren't married, Dax. You made a vow to Madison, not me. You love her, not me. You just miss your wife, and I'm an easy stand-in for her, but no more. Nothing between us is real."

He sighs. "Madison and I aren't real."

My heart stammers to a stop.

"We've never dated, never so much as kissed."

My eyes open wide, and I can't blink, too afraid I'll miss anything of what he's trying to tell me. I need to study his every movement to tell if he's telling the truth or lying.

"Madison likes women. We've been best friends for years. Her parents didn't accept that she wouldn't someday marry a man, have children, and live the life they wanted her to."

I can't breathe as I process his words, and it doesn't make what he's saying any easier. Even if we didn't hurt Madison, what we did was still wrong, still unacceptable.

"Why marry her then? So her parents would leave her alone?"

"No, it was so she could inherit their fortune and finally be free of her family. Their will says she needed to be married by her thirtieth birthday and stay married for at least six months."

"Let me guess—her thirtieth birthday was the day after our fake wedding."

Dax nods, his shoulders relaxing as if he's relieved that I'm finally understanding. But I couldn't be further from understanding. Nothing can change between us; nothing should have happened.

He pulls out his phone and shows me a picture of Madison and what I can only assume is her girlfriend kissing on the beach looking so happy. So fucking happy—I want to be that happy.

Dax's body is feet away from mine. He's kept his distance, trying to give me space to decide what happens next. It seems his main goal is to ensure I don't feel guilty for the kiss.

I don't feel guilt anymore; he's proven his point. He's gotten under my skin, and my body is begging me to go for it. To taste him again. To free my desire and take what I want from him.

I want to be reckless with him. My brain can barely process right from wrong. I shouldn't do this, but I can't remember why. His marriage is fake, a scam. We wouldn't be hurting anyone else by doing this—except my own heart.

There are a million reasons why I shouldn't do this. I'll just end up hurt again. But for once, it seems like the temporary joy could be worth the impending heartbreak.

Dax stares at me as if reading my mind. He sees me process everything, raking his teeth over his bottom lip, but he doesn't say anything. He doesn't make a move toward me. This is entirely my decision, but it's clear how much he wants me.

I start toward him, outstretching my arm to touch him, but then I hesitate. This is going to hurt so badly. I already like him. If I fuck him, there's no telling how hard I'll fall for him. And the reasons why we can't be together are piling up, reasons I'm only just discovering.

"I tried not to fall for you. I tried not to want you. I failed. I'm sorry," he says.

"Same," I reply.

It didn't matter what we tried; we couldn't help it. It doesn't matter if I fuck him or not; my heart has already fallen.

Even if he's a liar, he's also the sweetest man I've ever met.

And I want him.

I fling myself at him, no longer thinking about how bad of an idea this is. If he's thinking about how wrong this is, he doesn't show it. His arms wrap around me tightly, and his lips press against mine like I've always belonged to him.

He pushes me against a wall, pressing my arms above my head and kissing down my jawline. Then he moves his lips to the spot behind my ear that sends tingles through my body.

He thinks he's got me. With other men, I've let them take control, but I've always wanted it for myself. Dax might be the first man I can be my full self with.

I shove him back with fire in my eyes.

He grins, and it's the sexiest thing I've ever seen.

My eyes glance down the hallway, knowing we're too close to Eddie's bedroom.

I grab Dax's hand and pull him down the hallway back toward his bedroom, not that he needs much persuading. As soon as we're back in his bedroom, he kicks his door shut, and I attack him at full force.

I grab the hem of his shirt and yank it over his head, kissing every inch of hard flesh I can find. I rake my nails down his rippled abs until I reach the top of his pants.

I undo them quickly and yank them down his body until I get the first hint of how hard he is for me beneath his boxers. Now it's my turn to chew on my bottom lip with a knowing grin.

"I want you so badly. I've wanted you since the second I ran into you at your wedding."

I wrap my arms around his neck and press my lips against his punishingly. This can't last forever, but I'm furious at him for not letting us do this sooner. We could have been fucking all this time if I'd known the truth. This will end. Once our agreement is over, I'll never see him again, but that didn't need to stop us from having some fun in the meantime.

"I've wanted you since I breathed in your scent, Peaches."

"I'm going to make you pay for calling me that," I say with a mischievous twinkle in my eyes.

He chuckles. "I expect nothing less from you."

And then I rip his boxers off his body and gasp at the sight of his body. He may be a nerd who plays video games for a living, but damn he's hot. I don't know when he has time to work out. I haven't seen a gym, but there must be one in this mansion to get a body like his.

"Are you drooling?" he asks, cocking his head and standing still, not the least bit embarrassed to be naked while I'm fully clothed.

"Just a little." I shove him onto the bed, forcing him to lie on his back. "But I'm about to drool all over you."

His eyes darken with need.

I climb on top of the bed, up his body, and eventually straddle his muscular thighs. Then I shed my shirt over my head, tossing it to the floor. I unhook my bra with my eyes on him, watching his reaction.

His gaze meanders down my body. He's enjoying taking me all in like he has a lifetime to spend with me instead of a few hours at best.

He takes my hand in his and kisses the back of it.

"Incredible," he says.

He flips my hand over and kisses my palm.

I gasp in response.

"Strong," he continues.

He takes one of my fingers in his mouth and sucks gently. I roll my hips over him as the sensation hits me like a wave.

"Feisty," he whispers.

I undo my pants and slide his hand into my pants. I raise an eyebrow at him, encouraging him to make a move. He does eagerly, moving his finger over my slit, spreading my wetness around.

"Determined."

I arch my back and reach behind me to grab his hard length. When I do, he lets out a feral growl.

"Mind-blowing."

He pulls me forward and rips down my jeans and thong off my

legs before setting me back on top of him. His words still ring in my ear as my bare skin connects with his.

God, I want mind-blowing sex.

I lean forward and kiss him. When my lips touch his and the intensity sparks through my body, I know I'm going to get it. His tongue glides through my mouth, pulling moans and cries out of me I didn't know I could make while I let my hands explore his body.

I should be patient. I should drag this out and remember every moment. But it has been too long, and every moment I wait is a moment my brain will start functioning again, and I'll put a stop to this.

"I want you," I hiss against his lips.

"Then have me."

With that, I guide his cock to my soaking entrance and sink onto his hard length. I feel tight as I take him inside me, but the promise of delicious euphoria keeps me pushing past the slight burn.

"Jesus, Dax," I moan as he thrusts inside me, not letting go of the intensity of the moment.

"Ride me, Oaklee. Ride me hard and fast or soft and slow. Use me until you feel good and you forget everything else."

I do. I rock my hips as he pounds into me. I grab onto his hair to get more traction. I take over the thrusting and slide up and down his cock while he kisses me.

His kisses are perfect. I left myself get lost in them because he knows just how I like to be kissed—the right amount of pressure, the right amount of tongue. It's like he's studied me, or we've done this millions of times, and he's learned a little tidbit about me each time.

I don't know how he knows my body so well, but I'm so thankful. I don't have to direct his every move like I did with Boden to feel good.

His hands slide up until he's caressing my breasts, massaging my pebbled nipples as I rock harder against him. I love the feel of his hands on my breasts, but when one moves down my body to find my clit I love that more.

I throw my head back as my first orgasm hits me hard like a freight train. It takes over my entire body.

When the second one hits, I lose all control of my mind and body as I shatter around him.

It's not enough, not enough of a release. I need more. I'm frantic as I chase that high again and again. I ride him harder, faster—a punishing speed.

I'm using him.

It takes me a second to realize he doesn't deserve it. He deserves more. I want him to feel as good as I do.

I focus my mind on what makes him feel good. I kiss him hard. I deepen the thrusts until he comes, screaming my name like it isn't the first time it's left his lips.

I collapse on top of him in pure bliss. He wraps his arms around me, holding me close as we both breathe hard.

"I wish we didn't have to pretend," I say.

"We don't," he breathes into my hair.

I start to drift to sleep, not taking his words too seriously. I need to rest before I comprehend all the mistakes I just made.

I lift my head off his bare chest, and I steal one last kiss from him. Later the weight of reality will hit me, and my brain will scream at me for fucking up so badly, but I need to enjoy it now.

19

DAX

I THOUGHT I would feel guilty. I thought I didn't deserve this—happiness. But damn does it feel good to be happy. I want to always feel this elated.

I hold Oaklee tight to my chest, knowing the second I loosen my grip, this bubble of bliss will burst. Her mind is clearly whirling with all the reasons we shouldn't have done that and won't do it again, but I've never been so sure of something in my life.

I want her.

I need her.

I can't live without her.

I know that after one taste. I've never felt this way about another person before. I've never wanted someone as much as I wanted to breathe. I'll do whatever it takes to become the man she wants back.

"Wait," I say into her tangled hair sprawled over my face.

She just hesitates for a second. One more heartbeat, that's all I get of her in my arms before she's pushing herself off of my chest and rolling over to the other side of the bed.

I groan, missing her in my arms already. Those brief moments weren't enough, not nearly enough.

"Shit, we fucked up," she says, her eyes wide.

586

I take a deep breath, knowing I need to remain calm. If she's going to be willing to give this a try, I have a lot of explaining to do.

"We didn't fuck up," I say evenly.

"We did! How can you say we didn't? We should have never done that! You're married or sort of married or whatever." She throws her arms in the air as she talks, which makes me grin.

"You lied to me. We barely even know each other. I have a son. I have my Boden problem. And—" She frowns. "Why are you smiling like that? Aren't you more upset?"

"You're the most adorable woman I've ever met, and I love how strong-willed you are. I can't help but grin. I like you a lot."

She pouts. "I don't want to be adorable. I want to be sexy."

I take her hand and kiss her palm again, watching as her eyes roll back in her head. Then I rake my eyes down her still naked body. "You're very sexy. But when you try to fight this thing between us, you're adorable."

My words seem to tame her a bit, although not enough to be out of the woods.

Her eyes grow wide, and she jumps out of the bed. "Oh my god! We need to get to the store right now!"

I narrow my eyes, trying to figure out what I'm missing. "I'm sorry, I'm not following. Why?"

"You fucking came in me, and I'm not on birth control, and as much as I love Eddie, I am not ready to have another child right now, especially by a man I'm pretending to be married to," she rambles.

I smirk at her.

"This is not funny. I'm not getting pregnant again unless I absolutely want another child. Get your ass up, and let's go get some emergency contraceptive."

"I can and I will, but you should know I didn't come in you."

She rolls her eyes. "Yes, you did. I heard the moaning, don't try to make me think you didn't."

I sigh and point to a wet spot on the sheets and a sticky spot on the inside of my thigh. "I didn't. I pulled out first. I know the pull-out method isn't the most reliable, and I'll happily go get you the morning after pill if you want.

"But first, can we finish our conversation? Then when I do go, I won't be afraid that you and Eddie are going to leave while I'm out?"

She shoots me an evil look, angered I must have guessed her plan.

I stand up and go to my dresser. After putting on some clean boxers, I toss Oaklee a T-shirt of mine.

"What's this?" she asks.

"Put it on so I can focus."

Now she smirks at me as she pulls the T-shirt over her head. I'm taller than her, but not by much. Although the shirt covers the important parts of her, I'm still very much distracted by what's still visible.

I sit on the edge of the bed and wait for her to do the same. When she doesn't, I start the conversation, hoping I can ease her mind enough eventually.

"Tell me what's going through your mind."

"I'm thinking I made a huge mistake. That was so reckless—I didn't even think of using condoms first. This can only happen the one time. There is no way this should happen again."

She starts to pace around my bedroom as she continues to stress.

"You're a liar, and I shouldn't trust you. I hope you were at least telling the truth when regarding Madison. Otherwise, I am a cheater. And you better not have gotten me pregnant."

"Is that all?" I ask calmly.

"Yep, that pretty much covers it." She stops in front of me and crosses her arms. It's a challenge, one I'll gladly accept.

"Want to know what I'm thinking?"

She cocks her head. "Maybe."

I grin—she's dying to know what I'm thinking. "I'm thinking I just had the best sex of my life. I've been fighting my feelings for you for too long because I didn't think I deserved you, not because I didn't think this could work. And I'm thinking I need to do everything in my power to convince you we should do that again and again and again…"

Her mouth gapes open a little, and then she snaps it shut. "We can't do that again."

"Why not?"

She looks flustered grasping for reasons. "Because it's messy…"

"Yes, sex is messy. But that's what laundry and showers are for," I grin at her.

She rolls her eyes. "You're so not funny. I mean, we could have sex until our business arrangement ends and then go our separate ways."

"We could, but that wouldn't be nearly enough time. We only have to stay fake married for six months. After six months, Madison and I are going to get divorced. She'll continue working as a pilot, and I intend to move to New York City. I will have helped her out, and we won't care what others say because neither of us will stay here. We will never see these people again.

"Her parents will shun her, but as they can't tell the difference between you and her, it will be a small loss in her life. She's barely spoken to them since she moved out when she was eighteen. And—"

"And what? Then you and I would be free to date? After I've been pretending to be her for months? I don't think so," she huffs.

"Why couldn't we? Once I divorce Madison, no one will care what I do. No one will even know. If we wanted to date, we could. But I understand if you wouldn't want to. I've lied to you, and that's not acceptable. I'm sorry."

"What did you get out of marrying Madison?" she asks.

"I got money to pay you for your time."

"And how much are you making out of this deal?" She raises her eyebrows as if assuming I'm getting paid a large sum. She doesn't understand I do this as part of my restitution to those I've wronged in my past, to pay for my sins.

"Nothing, I'm making nothing. All I want to do is help my friends—Madison, you, Eddie…" I open my mouth to say more but stop myself.

Tears well in her eyes. "I've been burned by a man before. A man I thought was good and loyal and kind. You lied to me. You kept the truth from me. And I still don't know what's truth or fiction, but I do know I'm not willing to risk getting hurt again."

"I understand. I don't want to hurt you. It's why I didn't tell you the truth. I just want to help you. I'll do whatever you want."

She chokes back tears. "Then help me move out."

My heart squeezes in my chest. *God, how did I fuck this up so badly? What could I have done differently for this to have ended better?*

"If that's what you really want, then, of course, I'll help you move out."

She nods, unable to say anything else.

"Mr. Spade," the babysitter's voice carries into the room from down the hallway. "I have to leave soon."

I stand and put a calming hand on Oaklee's shoulder. "I'll go relieve the babysitter. You take your time getting dressed, and then we can make a plan, okay?"

She nods again.

I pull on my jeans and a blue T-shirt before heading out into the hallway. I hand over a wad of cash, way more than what I agreed to pay her, thank her for staying extra, and then I pad down the hallway to find Eddie.

When I get to his room, he's wide awake in his crib, sucking on his thumb and looking around. He's most likely waiting for his mom to come in and hold him, but it's me instead.

"Did you have a good nap, buddy?" I ask as I walk over and pick him up. I haven't been around kids much, so I don't really know what I'm supposed to do next. Oaklee won't take long to get dressed, so I just hold him and talk to him, which he seems content with.

"I'm sorry I haven't got to spend more time getting to know you, buddy. I wish we had more time. I think you and I would have become best friends," I say.

He coos at that and smiles his gummy smile. I smile back at him, turning serious after a moment.

"I'm not sure what's going to happen next. I don't know how

things are going to work out between your mom and me. I'm not sure if your father is going to step up and be back in your life or not. I'm not sure of any of it, but what I do know is that if you need me—a month from now or years from now, I'll be here for you. And I hope your mom lets me stay in your life because I'd really like that."

I sway as I hold him. "You have the best mom in the whole world. She loves you more than life itself and would do anything for you. If you have any advice for me, let me know. Your mom doesn't want to have anything to do with me, and for good reason. But I promise if you help me get an in with her, I'll love her and spend the rest of my life making it up to her."

Eddie laughs at me and squeals like he agrees with me. Even though my heart is breaking at the thought of never getting to see him again, at never getting a chance with his mom, I can't help but laugh along with him.

"Dammit," I hear Oaklee say over my shoulder. I turn to find her leaning against a doorframe with tears welling in her eyes.

"What's wrong?" I ask. Jesus, what more could happen to this woman in the last five minutes since I've seen her? She has the worst luck.

She sighs in defeat, looking from me to Eddie, who giggles his approval of whatever she's about to say.

"Don't break my heart, Dax. And if you break his, you're a dead man," she threatens.

My eyebrows shoot up, and my heart stammers to a stop. I can't be hearing what I think I'm hearing.

"Really? You want to give us a try? For real?"

She can't contain her own smile.

I race to her, terrified she's going to change her mind again in the three steps it takes me to get to her. I hold her close, sandwiching Eddie between us and leaning in close, wanting to taste her lips again.

Eddie stills, looking up at us with his big eyes as if trying to decipher how his life is about to change. *I don't know either, man.*

I wait, needing Oaklee to definitively decide before I kiss her again. I vow now to do everything I can to not hurt her. I don't know how because I always end up hurting people I love, but I'll figure something out. I won't break their hearts.

Her eyes flitter back and forth, searching mine. I don't know if she sees what I'm thinking. I don't know if I helped her change her mind or if her mind was already made up. But everything goes silent before she speaks.

"No more pretend."

"No more pretend," I agree. Closing the distance, I kiss the woman I love.

20

OAKLEE

STEPPING out onto the busy downtown street, I know I didn't get the job before I'm even out the office building door. It was an HR position that only required having a college degree and would have paid well enough for me to survive. It wouldn't have been my dream job or anything, but it would have been a job. Even though the interview went well, I could feel the disappointment in the room. I'm sure I won't be getting that job.

Just like I didn't get the half a dozen other jobs I applied for today. I'm pretty sure the only places that will hire me are fast food restaurants, and I don't blame them. My heart isn't really into it. I want my old job back. I want to do something with art that doesn't involve teaching—I'd be a terrible teacher.

As I drive home, I realize exactly what's holding me back from getting a job—Dax.

I don't know what to do about him.

I don't know what I want when it comes to him.

And I sure as hell don't know what the future holds. I still can't see how a future with him is even possible after he lied to me.

But I do know that in a few months he's moving. *And if I get a job*

593

here, then what? We do long distance? As if our lives aren't complicated enough.

I need money, though. I need a lot of money.

I sigh and drive back to Dax's place.

When I step inside through the garage, I can already sense babysitting didn't go well. One whiff of the air tells me that it went very, very wrong.

"Dax?" I ask cautiously, not sure how his mood is going to be when I reach him. I don't have to go far into the house, and I can't hold back my smile as I see them.

Dax is lying on the floor with Eddie on his stomach, and they are looking at each other, Eddie with his gummy grin and Dax with a smile. But Dax's body shows exhaustion, not to mention the spit-up and avocado all over his shirt.

The kitchen reeks of burnt food, but there isn't smoke or an active fire, so that's good. I scan the room and find random toys, diapers, and clothes everywhere.

I bite my bottom lip with a grin. "So… how did it go?"

Dax turns his head to me and pops up on his feet with Eddie in his arms. He tries to brush the avocado remnants off his shirt, but it's now smooshed into his clothes.

"Great. Not a problem at all," Dax says cheerily.

I raise an eyebrow.

"Okay, so it was a bit harder than I thought it would be. But we both survived, although my living room did not. We got lots of bonding time, though."

Eddie yawns in Dax's arms.

"Did he nap?" I ask.

"Um…" Dax rubs the back of his head and avoids making eye contact with me.

I laugh, knowing how hard Eddie can be to get down for a nap. Eddie seems fine, just tired. Dax honestly looks like he needs a nap more.

"Give him to me."

Dax passes Eddie over.

"I'll put him down for a nap. You clean yourself up."

When I take Eddie from Dax, I laugh harder.

"What's so funny?" Dax asks.

"Um…your shirt. It isn't just covered in spit-up and avocado. Eddie had a blowout."

"A blow-what?" And then Dax looks down at his poop-covered shirt and chuckles. "I don't know how you do it."

I shrug. "You figure it out."

Our eyes meet, and I'm afraid of what he's going to say. Eddie is a lot of work, but Eddie and I are a package deal. If Dax isn't ready to have Eddie in his life, then he isn't ready to have me in his life either.

Dax reaches out and touches my cheek. "I want to figure it out." And then he kisses Eddie on top of the head.

I nod with a soft smile before taking Eddie upstairs for a nap.

Eddie falls asleep quickly, and then I return downstairs to search for Dax. My eyes widen in shock the second I step into the living room. It's like a cleaning crew came through in the five minutes I've been gone. I walk to the kitchen to find Dax scrubbing dishes —shirtless.

My heart melts a little watching him. Damn heart, falling for a man it shouldn't. At least he's a good man, a kind man, a caring man. He's not a cheater. He won't hurt me—I won't let him. Maybe he's worth taking a chance on because he could make me very, very happy.

I walk over to him, trying not to drool as I do. But I'm afraid the look in my eyes will give away exactly what I want.

He stops doing the dishes and watches me with hungry eyes. But then he takes in my appearance and remembers his manners. "How did your interviews go?"

"Fine, but I don't think I'll get any of the jobs."

He nods. "Is it bad that I'm not really sorry to hear that?"

I frown. "Yes, I need a job."

"I know, but I want you to find the right job, not just any job. I want you to find something that makes you happy. And in the meantime, I want you around me as much as possible."

"Do you?"

He nods.

I rake my teeth over my bottom lip and hold out my hand to him. He takes it gleefully.

A giggle escapes my throat as I lead him to his bedroom and then through the door to the bathroom.

He frowns when I turn on the shower instead of leading him to the bed, assuming I'm only interested in cleaning him off. If he thinks that, he doesn't know me well at all. But I'll change that.

The second the four shower heads are blasting hot water, I shove him into the oversized glass shower. Sex is what this shower was made for, but it makes me happy that it appears I'm his first.

He stumbles in, laughing and clinging to me. I'm pressed against his bare chest as the water rains down on us. My black dress becomes glued to my skin, and his jeans tighten onto his legs as they soak.

He tilts my head up and kisses me tenderly. I can barely see him with the water running over my eyelashes, but I don't need to see him to know how he feels.

"I want you so badly," he says.

"Then have me," I say, repeating his words from the other night.

He kisses me again with a different type of urgency. He's been wanting to do this all day and couldn't wait until I got home. I could get used to this kind of kiss.

Reaching down to find the top of his jeans, I need him naked— now. I need to feel him in my hand. I want to hear his growling moans of desire.

I peel his wet jeans down his thick legs until he can step out of them. He kicks them through the open part of the glass shower doorway.

"Why do I always end up naked first, while you remain dressed?" he growls into my ear.

"Because I want you more than you want me," I tease.

He spins me around in the shower and shoves his hardness against my ass. One of his arms presses underneath my breasts, holding me to him, while the other arm slinks up my bare leg, hiking my dress slowly higher and higher.

"Not possible. I need you. I've never been so hard in my life. Never slept so poorly because all I think about is you. Never wanted to turn my life upside down for someone," he whispers into my ear.

I shudder as he nips at my earlobe.

His hand pulls my dress up above my breasts, but he doesn't remove it. Instead, his hand slides around my thigh and comes to rest between my hips.

I hold my breath, waiting in delicious anticipation as he takes his sweet ass time moving his fingers to my clit. The second his fingers reach my bud, I gasp for air at the intensity of his touch.

I try to reach around to touch him, but his other hand twists and lifts my arms up to grip his neck as he pleasures me. My nails dig into his muscles as he kisses my throat. His fingers rub in slow circles over my most sensitive point. While continuing to build me higher and higher, he slips a finger inside, feeling how soaked I am.

I try to hold back my orgasm, letting it linger as long as possible, enjoying every moment, but it's impossible. His kisses, the heat of the shower, and his touch—his touch is everything.

I buckle as I come completely undone, only staying on my feet by gripping his neck and his arms keeping me standing. As soon as I'm composed, I turn, wanting to pleasure him but needing him inside me more. Maybe it's selfish to not make him come first before he fucks me, but his brain seems to be on the same wavelength.

I yank my wet dress over my head and throw it outside the shower. "Fuck me."

"With pleasure."

He scoops me into his arms, and I frown.

He chuckles. "I'm not going to fuck you without a condom again. I don't want you worrying about anything while you're coming on my cock."

I reach up and touch his gruff chin. "So considerate."

He shakes his head. "I'm not going to be considerate when I fuck you. I'm going to be rough and hard and punishing."

"Good, just how I like it." As he tosses me onto his bed, I allow my mind to escape my worries and focus only on him, before he walks over to his nightstand and starts rummaging through it.

"Hurry," I let out a wispy breath, desperate for him. He's barely touched me, and I already feel like I'm about to burst. It's been a long time since I've had frequent sex, and my body is insatiable. At least, that's what I keep telling myself. It couldn't be because the man I'm having sex with is incredible.

I don't know if Dax is taking his time digging through his drawer or if he really is unorganized, but it feels like a century passes before he returns to me. He tosses the retrieved condom on the bed next to me as he spreads my legs wide.

"What are you doing?" I pant, needing him to fuck me now. I've waited long enough, and he knows that—my voice is desperate.

He smirks. "Tasting you."

And then his mouth is between my legs, his tongue moving between my folds until he finds the bundle of sensitive nerves that shoot bliss straight through me. At first I want to yell at him to stop —it isn't necessary for me to come. I came yesterday just fine from sex, and none of the previous men I've been with were any good with the whole oral sex thing, so it's not something I'm used to.

I'm not sure what to do. I'm not normally this vulnerable and exposed. I'm not used to getting pleasure like this.

"Relax, baby. Close your eyes and block everything else out."

His tongue moves again, and the world falls away around me. My eyes roll back in my head as ecstasy washes through my body. I forget about the mess I'm in. I forget about Madison and Boden and everything else in my life, and I just feel him.

His tongue rolls over my clit again and again, sending shock-waves through me as I sink further into the bed, enveloped in his touch. The feeling of his warm breath against me is heaven.

And then an explosion of emotion comes, sweeping through my body with hurricane force. After the waves subside, I open my eyes to find Dax hovering over me with a goofy grin.

"You're a fucking wizard with your tongue." I could die at any moment and feel like I lived long enough because that orgasm was that good.

"I need to be inside you," he says.

I pull his neck toward me, his lips lowering down on mine. The rest of him slams into me as well. It's a jolt to my system, rough exactly like he promised, and it brings me to life in a new way. From a soft and gentle orgasm then to rough, erotic sex now—I want it all with him and everything in between.

I swallow a lump of doubt in my throat, unsure if I'll ever get a forever with him. The lump that says there are too many obstacles for this to ever actually work.

I rake my nails down his sculpted back.

"You're hot for a video game nerd, you know that?" I say between kisses.

He kisses me in a hard, appreciative way. "And you're hot for a nerdy art curator."

I gasp as he suddenly thrusts deep inside me, hitting a depth I didn't realize was possible. He palms one of my breasts, flicking his thumb across my nipple before pinching it hard, making me cry out. His eyes heat as he fucks me, knowing I need it rough to stay out of my head right now. He knows me better than I know myself.

How?

How does he know me so well?

It's like magic. If it wasn't impossible, I'd think he could read my mind.

Thrust after relentless thrust brings us both up and over the edge together. Our bodies needed each other to come.

He rolls us over, draping my body over his as we both catch our breath. But before I come close to catching mine or coming back to reality, he says, "Move to New York with me. Don't get a job here.

Once we get settled, find a job in New York. Move in with me—you and Eddie."

I blink, thinking I just imagined his words. But the way he's staring at me says he meant every word he said. I want to scream yes, but it's more complicated than I want to admit.

"Dax, I—"

He shakes his head. "I know there's a lot to work out, but don't think about all the logistics. Just answer with your heart. Do you want to move in with me? Do you want to move to New York City with me?"

Yes.

But that's not what I say. "I don't know. I can't just answer with my heart when I have Eddie to worry about."

"There is nothing to worry about logistically. I'll be officially divorced from Madison. You don't have to worry about money or—"

I put my fingers to his lips. "I'm not taking any more of your money, not now that we're together. I'll finish pretending to help you out, and as payment for letting us live with you, but I'm not taking your money. I need a job and…" I trail off.

And Boden riddled me with so many loans and now has mobsters after me to collect that I can't possibly move with you because it's my burden to bear, and you shouldn't be tied to someone who owes millions.

But I don't say any of that. If I did, he'd pay off the sharks without even asking me. And as much as I want to protect Eddie, I can't be in a relationship with a man who I owe that much to—not again. I need to figure out a way out myself, and I will. It's the only way I can stay in a relationship with Dax.

Dax frowns, disappointment clear on his face. He grips me tight, like he can already feel me slipping away.

I don't have a good answer for him. I don't know how any of this is going to work. All I know is that I want to try to figure it out.

"When the six months is up, when you're divorced, then I'll give you my answer." That's the best I can do.

I have less than six months to figure out how to either pay off the loans or convince Boden to. Less than six months to find a job in New York. Less than six months to keep pretending I'm someone else in public. Less than six months to decide if Dax is worth moving across the country for. It feels like an eternity and like not enough time at all.

21

DAX

A WEEK HAS GONE by since I asked Oaklee to move in with me, and we haven't talked about it since. But every day I feel the heaviness of that request, and I'm terrified of her deciding that I'm not worth it.

I love her. I haven't told her yet. My feelings have grown fast, but it's how I feel. I've never felt this way about anyone. I want her and Eddie in my life always, not just for the next few months. I'm already tired of her having to pretend. She, on the other hand, has been having a blast pretending to be Madison.

This last weekend we had to attend a runway event showing off the clothing company Madison's grandfather started and is now run by her parents. Oaklee had no problem playing dress-up. But instead of awkward hand-holding and chicken pecks, Oaklee put on a show. She practically groped me, much to the dismay of her parents, but the paparazzi loved it.

When the real Madison saw the pictures in the tabloids the next day, she squealed with delight. She was thrilled someone was able to stand up to her parents by just living their life.

Madison has been calling me every other day, asking when I'm going to propose to Oaklee. Each time I remind her that we're still married legally.

Thank god no one cares about video gamers the same way they care about heiresses to a fashion label. Once Madison and I are divorced, I can go back to living my life without the cameras in my face.

Today though, there is no pretending. Today is a simple Sunday afternoon at home with just the three of us.

"So, what do you want to do?" Oaklee asks, bouncing Eddie on her knee.

"Want to play a video game?" I ask.

Oaklee cringes. "You're going to crush me."

"I'll pick a game I'm no good at and hold Eddie while we play, so I'll have a disadvantage."

She purses her lips, considering my question. I know her, though —she's going to say yes, and she's going to do her damndest to beat me, not that I'm going to let her win.

"Fine, what are the stakes?"

"Stakes?"

"Yep. What do I get if I win?"

I shrug, confident that's not going to happen. "Whatever you want."

Her eyes cut to me, bright with desire. Apparently, if she wins, it will be something sexual. It's almost enough to let her win just to find out what's going on in that dirty mind of hers.

"And what do I get if I win?" I ask.

She shrugs in the same nonchalant way I just did. "Whatever you want," she teases.

I instantly harden thinking about what I want.

"Game on," I say.

I turn on the TV and grab our controllers, passing one to her. Grabbing Eddie from her lap and placing him in mine, I get settled in to kick her ass.

"You gonna help me win, Eddie?"

He coos in response.

"Good. Because your mom needs me to win, she just doesn't know it yet," I whisper so only he can hear me.

"What are you whispering about over there?" Oaklee asks.

"Nothing." I start the game and whistle, making Eddie laugh.

———

"Are you going to pout the entire time?" I ask, intertwining our fingers as we walk down to the beach.

"Yes, it's not fair. I demand a rematch," she whines.

"I'll play again anytime you want. You just won't win. You need to try a different game if you want to beat me. Chess, cards, basketball—I'm a terrible basketball player."

She glares at me. "I'm going to beat you at that video game."

"Maybe, someday. But you're going to have to play me millions of times for a chance at beating me."

"Then I'll play you millions of times."

My heart races at that thought—she plans on staying with me for years. I can't get my hopes up, though. There's still too much that could go wrong, too much that I could fuck up. Tonight is about getting one small part right.

"So what are we doing here? I thought for sure your victory prize would be some sexual fantasy of yours. You're just taking me to the beach. This is a silly way to celebrate your victory."

"Is it?" I raise my eyebrows.

"It is. You could have had me literally anything in your bedroom."

"I'll remember that for next time."

"So what are we doing, really?"

"We're having dinner on the beach."

She shakes her head at me and laughs. "I would have done that whether you won or not."

"I know." My eyes cut to her, but I don't give anything away. "It's killing you not knowing why I brought you here, isn't it?"

"No," she lies, followed by a heavy sigh a moment later. "Fine, yes, it's killing me! Just tell me what we're doing."

"Nope."

Her shoulders slump, and she pulls her hand free from mine. I laugh inside, knowing that's exactly how she would react. But this is exactly what she needs.

Something is preoccupying her mind, something to do with Boden, and I need to figure out what it is. I want her to open up to me about it so I can help her.

The best way to do that is to prove she can trust me. Even if she doesn't open up to me today, she'll have this relaxing evening with me. My victory reward is just spending an evening with me, not thinking about the past. I want a night to get to know each other a little better.

I drop the backpack I'm carrying and take a seat on the sand.

"What? No blanket?" Oaklee teases.

"Nope. Sit in the sand." I pat the spot next to me.

She folds her arms across her chest. "Is this it? You're going to make me sit next to you in the sand?"

"No, you're welcome to do whatever you like."

I start pulling out a bottle of white wine and pasta I packed for us, ignoring her.

She huffs adorably and then sits down next to me, taking the glass of wine from my outstretched hand.

I wait patiently for her to relax. I don't know her as well as I'd like, but sitting here on this little private stretch of beach will help her relax, even if only for a little while.

She takes a sip of her wine, and I watch as her tense shoulders slump, her breathing slows, and her fisted hand loosens.

"This is my favorite spot in the whole world," I say.

This catches her attention, and gone is the spunkiness from before. She takes in the spot more closely, trying to figure out why it's my favorite.

"I almost ruined my life once." I sip a drop of the wine. "No, I did ruin my life once. I got arrested multiple times. I did drugs. I stole. I hurt people I cared about."

She takes my hand back in hers as I speak.

"I love this spot because it's the exact spot where I hit rock bottom. I came here after I destroyed everything good in my life. I woke up drunk, high, and beaten up. I was in pain. I was suffering. I had no one. Everyone had abandoned me after my last stint in jail, and with good reason."

I don't give her details, and she doesn't ask for them. Sharing the worst parts of yourself with someone you love takes time and a lot of trust. I have to trust she won't hate me for my past, trust that she can understand and love me through the darkest parts. And if she can't, then we don't belong together.

"This is the spot I woke up. The sun rose, and I decided my life would change."

"Thank you for bringing me here and for telling me that. I know you have more to share, and I'll be here when you're ready to share it," she says.

I nod. "I do have one more thing to share."

"What's that?"

"I love you."

My words hit her slowly, needing a few seconds to process. Then the biggest smile I've ever seen spreads across her face. "Do you know you're the first man who has ever said those words to me first? I'm usually the one that says them first in a relationship."

"Is that a good thing or a bad thing?" I ask.

"A good thing. It means, for once, I think I found someone who loves me as much as I love him and isn't just saying it because I did. You're a good man, Dax."

I toss my wine glass, lean over, and roll her onto her back until I'm hovering over her. "Right now, I want to be a very bad man," I whisper into her ear.

She licks her lips in anticipation. "And I want to be a very dirty girl."

"Thank god for that." I didn't bring her here to fuck her, but as the sun sets, that's all I can think about.

The spot is private enough, but we could still be spotted at any moment. We'll have to be discreet.

"And thank god you're wearing a dress. Take off your underwear," I demand.

Her cheeks pink, and her eyes darken with thoughts of what we are about to do as she slips her thong down her body. I take them, tucking them into the pocket of my shorts.

"So bossy. Now what?" she wiggles beneath me, itching to be in control, but happy to let me take the lead.

"Now I'm going to fuck you, and you're not going to make a sound."

"Yes," she moans as I run my hand up her leg.

I smack the back of her thigh and bite down on her earlobe. "Not. A. Sound."

Her eyes darken, and she nods.

I want to fuck her, and I know she wants to fuck me, but I won't risk her getting caught. I won't risk her going to jail. I'll keep her body covered and any sign of what we are doing hidden.

I kiss her neck and then across her jawline as my hand inches up her thigh. I wish I could undress her, but that would be too risky. Instead, I listen carefully for any sign of others. As much as this will help her relax and feel good, she's also putting her trust in me. I won't let her down.

My hand slips between her legs and is immediately met with her wetness.

I groan.

"Not. A. Sound," she mocks me.

I growl low against her lips and spread her wetness from her slit to her clit. She wants to moan, but she manages to keep it in. I tease her as I kiss her, moving my hand slowly, then quickly driving her close to a release before suddenly stopping.

Her eyes scream that she can't take it anymore. She reaches for my shorts, trying to pull me to her in sheer desperation.

I grin against her lips. I know what she wants, and I'll give it to her.

I pull myself out of my shorts, slip a condom on quickly, and then push myself between her legs, hiking her dress up.

She grabs at me, not letting me slow down as I push inside her.

We both groan, unable to keep the sounds down as we form

together. And then there are no more sounds as we rock together in the sand.

Fucking in the sand isn't as romantic as it sounds. It's messy. The sand is coarse. The fear of being caught is always there.

None of that matters, though. I would fuck her on a bed of hot coals—that's how much I need her and her me. I can feel it in the way she responds to me. Every thrust brings me deeper inside her, until...

"I love you," she says, unable to keep the words in a second longer.

"I love you, too," I say back.

Those are the only words we speak, but they're everything. Our words break down another barrier as we release into each other.

"So this was your fantasy?" She smirks at me.

"My fantasy was hearing you say you love me." I wanted to learn more about her, and I did. I wanted her to trust me, and she did. And I trust her more than ever.

I didn't learn her secret, and she didn't learn mine, but I have faith that whatever hers is, I'll learn it soon enough. We'll have a lifetime together to learn everything there is to know about each other.

After all, there is something sexy about keeping the mystery between us alive as long as possible. There's just the tiniest fear left that that mystery could destroy us, but it's a risk we are both willing to take.

2 2

OAKLEE

I'VE BEEN PRETENDING to be Madison for five months.

Five months of going to charity events.

Five months of attending parties with her family, who doesn't so much as think twice about me not being their daughter.

Five months of attending fashion shows.

Five months of going to gaming events.

The five months should have been hell, pretending to be someone else. But they were the best five months of my life.

And it was mainly because of Dax. I'm head over heels for him. But I'm still nervous about how this is going to work after we stop pretending.

I wish I had met him in any other way.

Eddie crawls toward me while I apply the last of my makeup. I'm meeting Madison in person for the first time and if my shaky hand repeatedly stabbing me in the eye with the mascara is any indication, I'm nervous.

I've been pretending to be her all this time. I'm confident that what Dax told me about her is true, *but what if it's not?*

There's the tiniest bit of doubt that I shouldn't have trusted him.

609

I shouldn't have trusted any of them, and this was all a mistake. *Maybe Dax is no better than Boden?*

At least Boden has stopped sending his goons after me. I don't know why or what happened, but I haven't heard from the mobsters since that initial shake-down by my car. Maybe they did decide to go after him after all instead of me. That just leaves the credit card charges, which I've been able to make a dent in.

I hear the doorbell ring, and I quickly scoop Eddie up, my arms still shaking a little. Eddie grabs onto my hair, getting my attention.

"What is it?" I ask him.

He smiles at me and starts babbling.

I tighten my grip on him as my nerves decrease. As long as I have Eddie, everything will be okay. I'll learn more of the truth from Madison, and if it turns out Dax is just as terrible as Boden, then so be it. I got a temporary job here working at a library. It's enough to pay my own bills if I need to move out.

I walk into the living room and find a beautiful woman that looks like a twin sister of mine hugging Dax. She squeals when she sees me, letting go of him and racing over to me.

"Oh my god! I'm so excited to finally meet you. And this must be Eddie. He's incredible," Madison says.

"Thank you," I say, my lungs struggling to breathe as I sweat profusely, still nervous.

"You must have a million questions for me," Madison says.

I nod. "And I'm sure you have a million questions for me."

Madison looks from me to Dax. "Not really, but I'd love to chat. I'm only here a few hours, so we best make the most of things. Dax, honey, can you watch Eddie so Oaklee and I can have some girl time?"

Dax looks to me for permission, knowing that it's up to me if I want him to watch Eddie, not Madison. It's something I'm grateful for, even if Madison doesn't realize it herself.

I give the slightest nod, not entirely sure I want to be left alone with this woman. I'm still greatly confused by her, but I hand Eddie off to Dax all the same.

"I'll make margaritas," Madison says, taking my hand like we're besties and dragging me into the kitchen. Dax tries to give me a reassuring smile before taking Eddie to the theater room that we've turned into his playroom.

Madison knows her way around this kitchen as well as I do, even though she hasn't been here in at least five months. I know her and Dax used to live together, although according to Dax, Madison was always flying and rarely home.

"So start asking, ask me anything. I'm not shy, and I know you want to get your questions answered before the six months are up." She starts pouring tequila into a pitcher.

"Um…okay…yea, I have a lot of questions." My main one being about Dax—*is he as genuine as I think he is, or should I be worried?* But I don't want to start there.

She keeps mixing things into the pitcher like we're girlfriends who do this every week.

"Tell me about your childhood and parents. I'm still in shock every time I see them, and they don't realize I'm not you."

She pours the liquid into two glasses. "That's because you've probably spent more time with them than I have my entire life."

"That can't be true."

She hands me one of the glasses, and I sip it slowly.

"They hired a surrogate to carry me. Then, I had a nanny until I was old enough to be shipped off to a private boarding school. Then I went to college the second I turned eighteen, and after that, I went to flight school. I wanted to be a pilot, so I could get as far away from them as possible. They only had me to have someone to take over the family business."

I nod. "I'm sorry. That must be rough."

She shrugs. "It's my life. I've never known my parents to really care about me."

"Then, why try to please them? Why pretend to be dating Dax? Why pretend to marry him? Why pay me to pretend to marry him? Are you trying to get back at them at the end of the six-month term, or are you trying to please them? Do you need the inheritance money?"

"It's not about the money, or pleasing them, or retaliation. I hope they never realize the truth of how I tricked them; I just hope they find someone better to run the company and let me live my life. I like to travel. I like to date women, not be tied down in an old-school fashion business where I'm expected to marry a man and have a child I can pass it on to."

I don't know what to say. I'm sorry doesn't seem right, but what else is there to say?

"I'm doing it because of the relationship I had with my grand-mother," she says.

I look up, unsure what she means.

"My grandmother was the only person in my family who spent any time with me. The only person who really knew and under-stood me. She was the only person that knew I was gay. The only person who knew I wanted to travel the world, not run a clothing company. That's why I'm doing this."

She pauses and takes a sip of her margarita. "I want my grand-mother's things. My grandmother died suddenly, without a will, so all of her things passed to my grandfather. When he died, he included a stipulation that I would only inherit those things, the money, and eventually the company after I was married for six months. He thought marriage would tame me."

She smiles. "My grandmother knew it wouldn't. She knew I couldn't be tamed. I was born to be wild and free. I want her things —her ring, her wedding dress, her coin collection. I want the things that mattered to her so I can remember her always. I don't care about the money or anything else."

I touch her hand. "Thank you for sharing that with me. It helps me to understand and makes me feel good for helping you."

"You have no idea how grateful I am to you. There is no way I would have survived doing what you're doing—going to the stupid runway shows and events. I don't know how you do it."

I blush, and she laughs. "Well, sleeping with Dax helps, I'm sure."

"God, am I stupid for falling for him?" I bury my face in my hands, not able to hold back anymore. "I feel so stupid. Logistically, I have no idea how this will work. And then…"

Madison is quiet, studying me for a moment, and then she says, "You love him?"

"Yes."

"Does he love you?"

"Yes."

"Then, you'll figure everything else out. It's not my place to share his story, but you should know that Dax and I have been best friends for a long time. We've been through a lot together. He's a good man —not a perfect man, but a good one. You have to decide if that's enough for you."

I nod, sipping my drink. Dax is a good man. I've known that from the start. *But is he enough for Eddie and me?* I'm not sure, not until I know the whole truth. And not until we are done pretending.

23

DAX

OAKLEE IS in the shower while I'm laying in our bed with Eddie on my lap, jabbering at me.

I love mornings like these. It's a slow morning where we bring Eddie to our bedroom while we all eat breakfast in bed and then take turns showering and getting ready for the day. I don't know how many days like this we have left.

The six months is up in a week. Madison and I have already made plans to file for divorce the second the six months are up. I have movers scheduled for the week after that. I've already found a place that would be perfect for us in New York. And when I showed Oaklee, she obviously thought it's perfect too, but something is still holding her back from agreeing to move with me.

She hasn't said no either, though, so I'm still hopeful. She said she'd give me her answer when the six months are up, which means I only have a week to wait. That doesn't prevent my mind from agonizing over the possibilities while playing patty cake with Eddie.

If she says no, I have no idea how I'm going to be able to let go of her and Eddie. I won't be able to survive without them.

I've considered all options—buying an engagement ring, buying her a separate house in New York, helping her find a job there. But none of those things seem to address her issue, whatever it is.

The Boden problem seems to have resolved itself. He hasn't reached out, filed for custody, or even pressed charges against me for hitting him. So it can't be that.

We love each other, so that's not the problem.

I've told her more and more about my past, and she's told me more about hers. I don't think she's afraid of anything else I've done in my past.

The only thing I can think of is that she's terrified of how this whole fake relationship situation will end. Maybe she thinks people are going to find out that she pretended to be Madison this entire time.

What she doesn't realize is that it's not our problem; it's Madison's. I did everything I could to help Madison, and she knew the risks. It was never our intention to stay married forever. Madison knew I'd live my life after the six months, and she fully supports Oaklee and I being together. If that is Oaklee's problem, I don't know how else to convince her it's all okay.

"Dada," Eddie says, and my world stops.

My jaw falls open, and my eyes bulge as I look at him. A boy I've known for half his life. A boy I've fallen in love with as much as I have his mother. A boy I very much consider a son.

Tears well in my eyes at the words. I doubt he knows what they mean, but I hope he considers me his father. When he smiles at me, it's clear he considers me an important person in his life, but I want to be more. I want to be his Dada.

"Everything okay in here?" Oaklee says, poking her head through the bathroom doorway.

I quickly wipe my tears to hide them. "Yep, of course. We're just playing."

She smiles at us and then closes the door to finish getting ready.

I can't tell her about what just happened; I don't want it to influence her decision. And I don't want her to feel bad for missing a milestone. It was Eddie's first word, and Oaklee has been relentlessly trying to get him to say 'mama.'

I pull Eddie into a hug. Whether they move with me or not, at least I have this moment with him to remember.

24

OAKLEE

I'M RUNNING on fumes as I step into the coffee shop to grab a much-needed caffeine boost. I've been running errands all day and making calls to get everything set up for us to move to New York with Dax. He still doesn't know my answer yet, and I can't wait to tell him tonight.

I bought a bottle of our favorite wine, cake, and a shirt for Eddie that says 'I heart NY.' I even got a job at an art museum there. I talked to Millie and Sebastian about moving, I talked to Madison about it, and luckily Boden hasn't talked to me in months. There is nothing holding me here anymore. I want a fresh start with Dax in a new city.

I quickly order my drink and start scrolling through the messages on my phone, when I bump into someone.

"I'm sorry, excuse me," I say, not looking up from my phone.

A hand grabs my forearm, stopping me from moving. A sinking feeling hits me hard in the gut, and I can't breathe.

I stare up at the man before me—Boden.

What are the chances we run into each other at a random coffee shop? This isn't just a chance meeting. He followed me here.

"We need to talk," he says, tugging me toward a seat.

"

I rip my arm free. "We really don't."

He holds out some papers, and it doesn't make more than a quick scan to see they're custody papers for Eddie. That's all it takes, and he knows I'll do whatever he wants.

I nod solemnly.

I wait at the bar for my coffee and then make my way over to where he's seated, glaring at me.

I take a seat. "What do you want, Boden? I have a lot to do today, and I don't have time for your games."

"You haven't made payments."

"I've been making payments on the credit card loans, not that I should. You're the one who racked up the debt."

"That's not what I'm talking about, and you know it. The credit card debt is nothing compared to the loan sharks you're indebted to."

I shrug. "They left me alone. It seems they realized you're the one who should be paying, not me. Why should I pay it? Why should I pay any of it?"

"Because I racked up those credit card charges paying for your shit."

"I never asked you to do that. I was fully capable of taking care of myself."

"Yea, but I had to wine and dine you. You wanted flowers and jewelry and shit, stuff that costs money."

I roll my eyes. "All I wanted was a man who loved me and didn't cheat on me."

He scoffs. "Yea, that's why you're with Mr. Moneybags. Because he loves you, right? You aren't after his money at all."

"I'm not!"

Now it's his turn to roll his eyes. "Pay off the mobsters before you get hurt."

"Again, why should I? It's your problem, not mine. They left me alone."

"It's your problem because you are the reason I gambled money, to take care of you. You made me neurotic—your need for me to be fucking perfect all the time! I couldn't live up to it. No one can. I've paid off half; you should have to pay off the other half."

I shake my head. "I don't have that kind of money."

"Dax does."

"Actually, he doesn't." The mansion we currently live in is half Madison's—her money is the only reason we can afford it. Once we move to New York, we'll downsize a little. Dax has plenty of money, but not if he forfeits millions to Boden's goons.

Boden laughs like it's the most hilarious thing I've ever said. "He does. You're just too stupid to realize how much money he actually has. Here I thought you were his mistress for the cash. You're even stupider than I thought."

"I'm not stupid."

"You are—Dax is filthy rich. He could write a check to pay everything off and not even make a dent in what he has."

"You're wrong."

"I'm not."

"And how do you know how much money Dax has? Madison and him might be married, but they have a prenup; Dax doesn't get her money."

He shakes his head like I've lost my mind. "I know because I know every dark secret there is to know about Dax."

"That's right, your friendship. Well, I think when Dax punched you, that friendship ended."

"We were never friends."

"Then why were you a groomsman at his wedding."

"Because we're brothers."

An invisible slap leaves my entire face stung. "What?"

"Brothers. Dax and I are brothers."

"You never told me you had a brother."

"I was ashamed of him. The bastard ruined my life. I almost died because of him, and my family disowned him after that. He's been trying to make amends, which is why I was at his wedding."

"I don't understand..."

"Remember how I told you I was in a car accident when I was fifteen?"

I nod.

"Well, there's a lot more to that accident that I didn't tell you. Dax was eighteen, and he was taking us both home from a party. He was driving—drunk and high—and he slammed us into a tree. I broke my leg, several ribs, and had a horrible concussion. I almost bled out at the scene."

"And Dax?"

"He walked away with barely a scratch on him."

"I'm sorry that happened, but you were kids. Kids sometimes make stupid mistakes."

"I was in a lot of pain after that. My leg and back were always hurting. So Dax decided to get me some narcotics."

I cringe, not liking where this is going.

"I got addicted. He showed me how to gamble to make enough money to pay for them."

"You were kids," I whisper.

"Dax was eighteen; that's hardly a kid. He made me everything that I am—everything that you supposedly hate about me? It's because of him. He gave me my first beer, the drugs, the gambling— all him. He taught me how to lie, how to cheat, how to never get close to people. It's all fucking him."

"I'm sorry, Boden. I'm sorry about what you went through. I'm sorry that he hurt you. I'm sorry that your life has been hard. But it doesn't change anything."

"Doesn't it?"

I hesitate for just a second. "No."

He smirks, thinking he's got me. "How much is Dax making from pretending to be married to Madison?"

I gasp, not sure how he knows that exactly. "Nothing—he's just helping out a friend."

"You're always so gullible, Oaklee. Dax is making half. He gets fucking half. Do you know how much money that is? Hundreds of millions."

I frown. "He's not making anything."

"Ask him then if you're so sure. Ask him how much he's making. It's more than he can spend in a lifetime. And then tell me if he doesn't deserve to pay my gambling debt. Tell me if the man who has lied to you, a man who almost killed me, a man who destroyed our relationship doesn't deserve to pay for it?"

I blink, staring at him, unsure of what's true and what isn't.

"He's using you, Oaklee, to get the money from Madison. He's using you, all while playing house and pretending to be a good uncle, when the second the money has been transferred, he'll toss you to the side, just like he did me. He used to promise he'd help me get better, help me stop the addiction he started. He hasn't. Whatever promises he's made you, it will be the same."

Boden doesn't wait for my reply. He silently gets up, knowing he's destroyed my trust in Dax.

I don't know what's true anymore. I don't know Dax's side of the story. I'm not even sure I blame him for what happened between him and Boden. That's not what I'm upset about.

I'm upset that Dax lied—again. He told me he wouldn't. He hid the truth of who Boden is from me, and he lied when he said he wasn't getting any money from Madison. He lied—and I'm tired of being with liars.

2 5

DAX

I KNOCK on Eddie's bedroom door, gently cracking it open. It's not usually Eddie's nap time, but every once in a while, he throws us for a loop, so I'm quiet just in case.

My eyes widen, and my heart leaps when I step inside. There are suitcases and boxes everywhere. *Does this mean what I hope it means? She's finally going to give me an answer and move with me to New York! There's nothing else this could be.*

"Oaklee?" I call into the adjoining closet, where I can hear her packing up her things. "Can I come in?"

She doesn't answer, but I hear her sniffling.

"Oaklee? Please, can I come in?"

I stand outside, pressing my ear to the door, trying to figure out what's going on. I want to say its allergies or she caught a cold, but something isn't right.

"Did Boden do something?" It's the only person I can think of that would have her crying like that.

The door abruptly opens, and Oaklee is standing there with a glare on her face. I don't see Eddie, which has me even more worried.

622

"Boden didn't get custody, did he?" my voice is shaking at that thought.

"No, Eddie is with Millie, one of my friends. They're back in town for the week."

I nod slowly. "Okay? So what happened?"

Her eyes are puffy, and her cheeks bright pink. She's been crying for a while.

"What happened?" I reach out to hold her hand, hoping it will bring her some comfort, but she pulls away. "Are you upset with me?"

"No, you're just a liar—I've always known that. I'm not upset. I enjoyed the sex. I enjoyed the pretend. I enjoyed the payments. Now, it's time to go our separate ways." Her eyes don't meet mine as she talks. She's upset and trying to keep it together.

"Talk to me, Peaches. What happened?" Even if she decided she didn't want to go to New York with me, this isn't how she would tell me. Something happened.

"You tell me." Her eyes glare at me with a rage I've never seen before.

"I'm sorry? I don't know what I'm supposed to say."

"How about everything between us has been a lie!"

I flinch at her words but don't say anything. I need to know what happened.

"How about you and Boden are brothers! How about you're getting paid hundreds of millions of dollars by marrying Madison. No, by pretending to be married to Madison through me, while you give me pennies! How about you almost killed your brother in a car accident, got him hooked on drugs, and taught him how to gamble to make money! How about I'm a fucking fool for believing any of your bullshit!" Her voice cracks, and she pushes past me.

I should say something to stop her, something to defend myself, but I have nothing.

I hurt her—I don't deserve her. I always knew that. I always knew she should leave me. I knew I'd hurt her.

She swings back around the door, though, apparently not done with me. Tears are streaming down her face; mascara is running down her cheeks.

"Is that why you fucked me? Why you pretended to want more with me? Why you said you loved me?"

My eyes move over hers, not understanding, but I don't dare open my mouth. It's her turn to talk, not mine.

"You feel guilty about your past? It's the same reason you tried to befriend Boden, to help him? You agreed to help Madison, so you must have hurt her. You hurt people, and then you feel guilty and try to fix things? Is that what this was?" She waves between us. "Is that what it always was—guilt?"

It's the reason I do most things. I fuck up, and then I try to fix them. But it was never like that with her. With her, I just wanted her. I fell for her when I knew I shouldn't. I knew it would be messy. I knew it would hurt her to learn I'm related to Boden.

To make it worse, I hid the truth. I've been in and out of jail for half of my adult life. I hurt my brother. My parents don't even talk to me. I used to steal money from Madison. The only reason we're friends is because she's the most forgiving person in the world, and she's made mistakes too.

I can't ask Oaklee to forgive me—I can't expect her to. She's the most incredible woman, and I'm a fucking mess. She's already dated an asshole—my brother. She doesn't deserve to date another one.

I should have never let it go this far, but I thought I was changing. I thought I was becoming less of an asshole, but I was wrong.

This has to be the last time I fuck up. One more fuck up, which will also be the last lie I ever tell her.

"Yes, I felt guilty for not telling you the truth and for not knowing I had a nephew. I felt guilty for making you pretend to be Madison after I found out who you were. I asked you to move with me so I could take care of you when Boden couldn't."

I don't tell her the words I'm aching to say—I love you. The only reason I'm with you is because I love you. I'm a better person when I'm with you. I don't care about Boden. I don't care that Eddie is related to me. I don't care that we've been pretending to help someone else. I just love you, and I want a future with you despite everything.

I don't say any of that.

I don't fight for her to stay.

My words push her away, and she runs.

I watch her leave.

I doubt I'll ever see her or Eddie again, but maybe that's for the best. I'm a liar, a criminal, a former druggie, and all I do is fuck up people's lives.

26

OAKLEE

I'm NUMB, going through life like a zombie. I don't have emotions, not anymore.

I don't think about a future with Dax or any man.

I don't imagine I'll ever get life back in me after I've been so torn down. All I can do now is figure out how to put enough of the pieces of my life back together to be a good mom to Eddie.

Right now, I'm not a good mom. I'm not present. I go through the motions, but I'm not emotionally connected to him.

I take care of Eddie.

I go to work.

And then I come home to the two-bedroom apartment Millie and Sebastian are renting for me. All my cash is going to pay for the best lawyer in the city. I've had everything taken from me, but I won't let anyone take Eddie. I won't let them take his future.

I'm not paying off any more loans.

I'm not going to let Boden threaten me to get custody of him.

I'm not going to let some goons push me around.

And I'm not going to let Dax lie to me.

I'm done being hurt.

My sole focus is Eddie, and I know I'm a damn good mom. That's enough.

But the night haunts me—I can't get my brain to stop dreaming about him. Over and over, I wonder what happened and whether or not I got everything wrong listening to Boden.

What if I made a mistake? I know Dax lies; I've seen it firsthand. But what if the thing he's lying about is what he said when I left? What if Boden was the liar? What if...?

That's how I spend my nights—trapped in a realm of past possibilities.

I know I have to stop, but what if I'm wrong about Dax?

2 7

DAX

"God, Dax, you really need to take a shower. You smell and probably haven't shaven in weeks," Madison says as she hugs me the second she enters the door.

"It's only been a week."

She holds my shoulders and looks me up and down. "God, men are gross."

I roll my eyes at her and walk into the kitchen, pouring us both a cup of coffee.

"I'm sorry. You're not gross; you're just stupid."

"Really? I lost the woman I love and her son, who I think of as my own, and you're going to call me gross and stupid?"

She shrugs. "Well, you are."

"Some friend you are," I gruff.

She just smiles. "You're in love—I can't believe it."

"Well, believe it. But it doesn't matter because there's no way I'm getting Oaklee back. I hurt her. I don't deserve her."

"Jesus, will you stop? You've been this self-destroying fool for years, and it's got to stop."

I glare at her but don't say anything as I drink my coffee.

She sets her mug down and walks over to me, pulling me into a

628

gentle and sweet hug. It's the kind of hug meant to make me feel better. I wish it would, but it doesn't. It just hurts; I always hurt.

"You're too hard on yourself," she says.

"I'm not."

She shakes her head. "You are. You're the best guy I know. You're kind and caring and self-sacrificing."

"No, I lie and hurt people that get close to me. I always have."

"You really don't know yourself very well, do you?"

"Well, isn't what I said accurate? I've hurt you countless times."

"Yes, in your youth and when you were desperate. You never did it out of spite. You stole some shitty jewelry I didn't care about and cash out of my wallet so you could pay for food when your parents wouldn't feed you."

"For drugs and alcohol, you mean. I was an addict and a criminal, always in and out of jail."

"You were doing what it took to survive. You forget how abusive and neglectful your parents were. You forget I know the real story. I've seen your criminal record, and every time you went to jail, you were usually stealing something for your younger brother, not yourself."

She looks at me with such soft, caring eyes as she shakes my shoulder to compel me to listen.

"You're the reason he's even alive. You made sure he had food and clothes. You made sure he went to school. You took the rap so he could go to college. You. Saved. Him."

I shake my head. "I got him addicted to drugs. I taught him how to gamble. I made him a spoiled brat who didn't know how to take care of himself."

Madison runs her hand through my hair, clearly frustrated with me.

"You were a kid, and you did everything you could to help him. You weren't expected to be a parent, but you took on that role. You went to jail for him. And you've been beating yourself up about it every day since. When I asked for your help, you did it without a second thought, even though you knew you wouldn't get anything in return. You helped Oaklee and hid the truth from her because you thought she's better off without you."

Her eyes widen. "You're wrong, Dax. You are the best guy. But no one will ever be able to see it if you keep hiding the best parts of yourself from them. The only thing you are is a martyr. Stop lying to everyone and pretending you're a monster—you're not. Tell the truth and then see what happens."

28

OAKLEE

"Your loan has been paid off in full, ma'am," the teller says.

I frown, not understanding. I came here to collect all the debt paperwork for my lawyer. We were going to see if we could fight it in court, but instead, I'm being told the massive loan was paid off.

"Can you tell me who paid it?"

The woman smiles. "You?"

I shake my head. Even if I wanted to, I don't have that kind of money. Selling everything I own and draining my accounts wouldn't make a dent.

"Thanks," I say. Walking out of the bank, I'm more confused than ever.

A strange feeling of being watched comes over me, but I brush it off. As I reach my car, I recognize the feeling—Dax.

I turn to find him walking to me from his car.

"I can't deal with you today, Dax," I say, surprised to see him. I really thought I'd never see him again after I left, and he barely spoke. I thought that would be easiest—a clean break.

Instead, it's been torture wondering about him for the past two weeks. *Did he move? Does he still think about me? Did I get the whole truth?*

But now that he's here, I'm terrified.

"I know I shouldn't just show up, but I don't know how else to reach you. I need to talk to you. If it doesn't change anything, then so be it, but I need to tell you some things. You deserve the whole truth from me."

"I gave you a chance to talk to me when I left. You barely got out a couple of words and then clammed up."

"I was in shock and scared. I thought it was best for you to leave. I thought if you hated me, you wouldn't come back, and I couldn't hurt you again."

I hold in my breath. I want to talk to him. I want it all to be one big mistake, but I'm scared to hope. If I open my heart again and he shatters it, I'm not sure I'll survive.

I bite my lip, contemplating what I want to do, when I hear the footsteps behind me. I see a look of terror on Dax's face, and I know who's behind me.

"We meet again, Oaklee," the man says.

The same deep voice who threatened me at my car all those months ago is back. I turn slowly and come face to face with the business end of a gun.

"You're a confusing woman. Are you Oaklee or Madison?"

I fold my arms across my chest. "Depends who's asking."

He smirks. "I don't really care who you are, as long as I get my money."

"I'm not the one who owes you money; that would be my ex. Talk to him," I say, firmly and no longer afraid. He's not going to shoot me.

Clearly nervous for my safety, I watch Dax inch closer to me out of the corner of my eye. This man may need me alive, but I doubt he'd have any problem shooting Dax. I try to send a worried and cautious look to Dax, but he doesn't get the hint.

"I would take it up with your ex, except he doesn't have any money. I've already tried kidnapping and beating the money out of Boden—his face will never look the same again. He's not a very tough guy. If he had the money, he would have offered it up in exchange for his freedom." He looks to Dax. "You found yourself a sugar daddy, though. So you'll be the one paying."

Dax steps in front of me in one smooth motion. "I'll pay. Whatever she owes you, I'll pay it."

"Three million dollars."

Dax's eyes widen.

"I don't care who pays it, as long as it gets paid."

"Fine, I'll pay it. I just need to make a couple of calls, and I can get you the money, okay? But you're going to let her go."

The guy keeps his gun pointed at us.

"No, she's my leverage."

Dax shakes his head. "You still have Boden?"

The man nods. "In the trunk of my car. I have a guy watching him."

"Then, you have all the motivation you need to ensure I'll pay you," Dax says.

The guy frowns. "You care about her ex? I don't think so."

"No, I care about my brother," Dax says.

He chuckles in disbelief. "You know you guys are fucked up, right? Who dates their brother's girl?"

"I'm not Boden's girl. And I can make my own decisions about who I date," I snap.

"Well, not Boden's girl; you're coming with me until Mr. Moneybags here pays."

"No, take me. Oaklee will get you the money," Dax pleads.

I raise my eyebrows and whisper to Dax. "I can't do that. I don't have that kind of money or access to your accounts."

"Madison will help you."

I look at Dax. "Don't," I beg.

"I love you, and I'm sorry," he whispers back so quietly I'm not sure I heard him. And then, before I can protest again, he walks over to the shark's SUV and gets in the back, leaving me broken again.

———

"Madison!" I say out of breath into the phone. I'm franticly driving with one hand, trying to keep up with the SUV. Dax would yell at me to not risk my life for his, but I need to. I need to make sure he's okay, and I need the truth.

"Oaklee? What's wrong?" Madison replies.

"They have Dax."

"Who has Dax?"

I realize I don't have time to fill her in on all the crazy details.

"It doesn't matter. I need access to Dax's bank accounts."

"Okay—I can try to help with that. How much does he need?"

"Millions," I say as I take a sharp right behind the SUV. I don't know where the goons are going, but I keep following.

"Um…I can give you access to his accounts, but he doesn't have that kind of money."

"What do you mean? He got half of your inheritance!"

There's a pause. "He didn't. I would have given him half, but he didn't take anything. He did it as a favor to me."

"What? Seriously?"

"Yes."

"God, he's such a liar! And a fucking martyr."

"That's Dax. But he loves you. He just thinks he hurts people, so he pushes them away."

"Well, right now, I need a couple of million dollars to pay off some mobsters, so they don't kill him. Then I can kill him myself."

"When you're finished with him, I want a piece too. I'll send you the money."

"Thank you," I sigh, hanging up the phone. The SUV stops in front of a warehouse, and I swerve into a street parking spot. *What are they going to do to Dax?*

———

I sit in my car for an hour, waiting for Madison to send me the cash. I hate that I asked her for the money, but she has plenty. She can part with a couple million to save Dax and Boden.

The entire time I contemplate what I'm going to do. *What do I want to say to Dax? What comes next? What are they doing in that warehouse?*

Madison calls Dax to arrange the details of the transfer, while I sit and wait, feeling completely helpless. All I can do is sit here and hope they come out alive.

And then I see them—walking out of the warehouse toward my car. Boden is leaning on Dax for support, his face and clothes bloodied. Dax, thankfully, seems unharmed.

I jump out of my car and open the back door as they approach. To my surprise, I realize I'm just as worried about Boden as I am Dax.

"Do we need to get him to a hospital?" I ask Dax as he helps Boden into the backseat.

"It's up to him. I'm pretty sure his nose is broken, but everything else just seems bruised," Dax answers.

We both stare at Boden. "I'm fine."

He leans back against the headrest as Dax and I get into the front of my car. I start driving back to Dax's place. I'm not happy with either of them, but I'm glad they're both alive. I just don't know who I want to yell at first.

We're silent as I drive. No one talks about what just happened until I pull into Dax's driveway.

"I'm sorry, Oaklee. I know an apology isn't enough. I'm grateful to you—forever grateful," Boden says as he sits up.

I nod, not ready to accept his apology but not ready to yell at him yet, either.

"I'll sign full custody over to you. I'm not ready to be a father. I wish I could help more, but I just can't. I'm sorry," Boden says.

"I think that's for the best," I answer.

Boden nods, staring at me for a long while. Then he gets out of the car, leaving me alone with Dax.

"I'm sor—"

"No," I cut him off.

Dax just stares at me, looking lost and broken.

"Are you okay?" I ask.

"Yes, they didn't hurt me."

"Good." I pause. "I want the truth. No more lies. No more martyring yourself. Just tell me the truth."

"What do you want to know?" he asks hesitantly.

There are so many lies he told me, but I know where it starts—where all his trauma starts.

"Tell me about the night of the car accident with Boden."

He sucks in a breath like it hurts to talk about it. I'm sure it does, but I need the truth.

"I was driving Boden home from a party. He was drunk, completely wasted. He started throwing up in the car on the way back, and I drove faster." He pauses. "A car came out of nowhere and sideswiped us. I swerved, trying not to hit it, but I lost control. We spun until we hit a tree."

His eyes glaze over as he's back in that moment. "Boden was thrown from the car. I don't think he was wearing his seatbelt, and the airbags didn't go off. Meanwhile, I was trapped. I couldn't get my seatbelt off, and I couldn't find my phone to call for help."

Tears drip as he turns and looks at me, reliving the worst moment of his life.

"He was my brother, and he almost died because of me."

I can see the guilt that has eaten at him all his life. His entire life has been driven by it, but it wasn't his fault. It was an accident.

"Were you drinking?" I ask.

"No."

"Were you in your lane?"

"Yes."

"Were you speeding?"

"Barely."

"It was an accident. It wasn't your fault."

"But it felt like it was. And Boden's life spiraled after that. He hurt you, and—"

"And it wasn't your fault. His actions weren't your fault. His pain —not your fault. None of it is your fault. You have to stop feeling guilty for an accident and everything else that went wrong in your life. People make mistakes; you don't have to keep paying for them forever."

He closes his eyes and sucks in a breath as if no one has ever said those words to him. "I need a lot of help. Probably should start seeing a therapist."

I nod. "Probably."

"I promise you—no more lies, no more martyring myself, and no more hurting you." He looks deep into my eyes.

I want it to be enough, god, do I want to just take him back. But I'm just as scared as him. I have my son to think about. And our relationship, if you can call it that, has been riddled with lies and pretend and fear.

I hold out my hand to him, and Dax looks at it suspiciously.

"Will you just shake my hand?" I say sassily.

Dax chuckles and takes my hand.

"I'm Oaklee. I have a son named Eddie."

Dax shakes my hand. "I'm Dax. I have a lot of trauma from my past, but I'm working on bettering myself."

"Aren't we all?" I smile at him.

He smiles back. "I'd love to take you on a date, Oaklee. Where'd you like to go?"

I bite my lip. "How about New York City? I hear the pizza is amazing, and I'm a sucker for a pizza."

"Seems like an expensive date to fly you all the way to New York City."

I shake my head. "I'll be moving there in about a week. I found a job at a museum and a nice little apartment I can afford. Besides, Eddie's uncle lives there, and I can't imagine him not being in Eddie's life."

"I can't imagine not being in your lives either. I love you, Oaklee."

And then he kisses me. It's a fresh start. It's exactly what we both need—put our pasts behind us and stop pretending. We'll work through our flaws, even if it's a little bumpy along the way. *What's life anyway without a little risk and a chance at happily ever after?*

EPILOGUE

DAX

ONE YEAR Later

"What is this?" Oaklee asks as she walks in the front door of our apartment. We started off living in separate apartments for the first three months but quickly moved back in together. We live in a small, two-bedroom in the city, much smaller than the mansion we had in California, but it's what we can afford, and we're happy.

Neither of us has to worry about Boden anymore. He moved to Australia, and seems to be doing well there living the single life.

Madison finally came clean to her parents. They were upset with her, but they couldn't be too upset when they didn't even recognize the woman claiming to be their daughter wasn't her. They're going to pass the company down to someone who actually cares about fashion, but they let Madison keep her grandmother's heirlooms and some money.

And best of all, our lives are finally our own.

"Pizza!" Eddie says.

"I see that," Oaklee says, kissing me on the cheek before picking up Eddie and spinning him around.

"We're celebrating the one-year anniversary of moving to New York with all our favorite reasons we moved here—pizza and cheesecake," I say.

She smiles. "I can't believe it's been a whole year. I feel like we've been here much longer than that."

I frown as I wrap my arms around them both. "That doesn't seem like a good thing."

She giggles. "No, it's a great thing. I can hardly even remember my life before. It finally feels like this is exactly what life is supposed to be."

"I feel the same way."

"Pizza!" Eddie says again, making us both break out in laughter at his impatience.

I get the pizza set up as Oaklee helps Eddie into his chair. Oaklee frowns at the pizza box on the dining room table.

"Do we really need the box on the table? There's hardly enough space as it is," she says.

I do everything I can to hold back my grin. My plan is going off exactly as I planned.

"Yea, just grab what you want from the box, and then I'll put it back in the kitchen," I say as casually as possible.

Oaklee opens the box. She stares at it a minute and then looks to me. She tries to hide her own smile, but it grows rapidly.

"You are so cheesy," she says.

"Is that a yes?"

"Technically, you haven't asked me. The pizza guy seems to have a crush on me; maybe I'll say yes to him."

I get down on one knee and pull a ring out of my pocket. "Oaklee, I love how sassy you are. I love how you always put me in my place. I love how good of a mother you are. I love how you've encouraged me to be a better person. I love Eddie like my own son. Will you marry me? Will you let me adopt Eddie officially?"

In true Oaklee fashion, she doesn't give me an answer right away. She makes me wait and wait and wait, until she finally explodes.

"Yes, you idiot!" she squeals.

I laugh as she tackles me to the ground while Eddie cheers us on from his high chair. She kisses me deeply and quickly, letting me know what she expects to happen later as soon as we put Eddie to bed. I nip at her lip in response, and her eyes grow heavy.

"Eat!" Eddie squeals, and we both groan. We'll have to wait until later to actually enjoy each other.

Oaklee gets up and helps me to my feet, then we both sit at the table eating our pizza with Eddie. Oaklee is quieter than usual as we eat, which has me a nervous wreck.

Is she second-guessing us already? I want to ask, but I don't. It's a conversation we should have after Eddie goes to sleep.

Of course, getting Eddie down takes us hours tonight when he usually falls asleep in ten minutes.

Oaklee is brushing her teeth in the bathroom, when I finally come back from Eddie's room. I stand in the doorway looking at her, still not sure what she's thinking.

"What's going on? Do you not want to marry me? Do you not want me to legally be Eddie's father? Because if—"

She spits into the sink and then rushes at me. "Jesus, that's what you thought? That I was having doubts?"

I nod, my cheeks flushing.

"No, I was quiet because I was trying to restrain myself."

She launches herself at me, leaping into my arms, and wrapping her legs around me in a hungry kiss.

"Thank god," I moan against her lips as her tongue dips into my mouth.

I grab her ass as her hands dig into my hair wildly and uncontrollably. This last year has been the best year of my life. I did a lot of therapy to deal with my trauma, as did Oaklee. We started learning to trust each other. But every once in a while, the doubt still creeps back in.

Right now, there is no doubt. All I feel is her.

Her kisses.

Her touch.

Her desire.

I have no doubt how much she wants me and how much she plans on having me for the rest of her life.

I lift her onto the counter, not even able to make it to the adjoining bedroom. I need her now. We'll fuck again in the bedroom later.

I kiss down her neck as her hands run down the front of my body. Lower, lower, lower, until she's working on undoing the top of my jeans.

I reach around her back, unhooking her bra before pushing my hands up her shirt to feel her soft mounds.

Her hand pushes inside my jeans, pulling me out and sliding her hand along my hard length.

My hands slip down her sides until I've grabbed her leggings. She lifts her ass as I yank them down to her ankles.

"There's a condom in the drawer to your right," I tell her. "Unless you want to start trying to give Eddie a sibling."

Her eyes darken at the thought. "Get inside me, now."

I grab her hips and plunge inside her wetness. I haven't had her without a condom yet. She doesn't like being on hormonal birth control and likes the ability to start trying for a baby whenever she wants—apparently, like right now.

"Fuck, you feel so good," I groan, sliding in and out of her.

She moans. "I don't ever want to use condoms ever again."

"Fine by me. I want to have dozens of babies with you." I bite her earlobe.

She runs her tongue over her lips and opens her mouth about to say something but then changes her mind.

"What?"

"Make me come first, then I'll tell you."

"You're killing me." I thrust into her faster, needing to know whatever it is she's holding back.

She grips onto the edge of the counter to keep herself grounded as I rock into her again and again with no barrier between us. For the first time in our lives, it feels like there are no secrets between us. No dark pasts, no exes trying to ruin us, no friends asking us for favors—it's just us.

"I love you," I whisper, knowing that saying those words while I'm inside her usually pushes her over the edge. I combine it with my thumb circling her clit.

She responds by screaming my name and pushing me to my own orgasm.

She has a wicked gleam in her eyes, and for a second, I'm too distracted by what we just did to remember to ask what she wanted to tell me.

"We could have just made a baby," I say, still inside her.

She bites her bottom lip. "Actually, we already did."

"What?" my face widens.

"I'm pregnant."

I scoop her off the counter excitedly, slipping my cock out of her. "You're serious?"

She nods furiously. "Are you happy?"

"The happiest. I didn't think I could get any happier, and then you tell me that."

Just then, we hear Eddie cry on the baby monitor.

She laughs as I set her down and prepare to spend the next hour trying to rock Eddie back to sleep.

"Are you sure you're ready for another one?" she asks.

I kiss her once more before I go. "I love being a father. I want tons of babies with you. It's worth all the sleepless nights in the world to have something that is half you. I want as many little yous in the world as possible."

"I feel the same way about you."

And then I go into Eddie's room, pick him up from his crib, and dream about the rest of my life.

No more pretend when it comes to Oaklee—things just got very real. I already have one son, and I'm about to have another child. I can't think of a more perfect way to spend my life making babies with Oaklee and watching them grow.

———

Thank you so much for reading Pretend: The Complete Series! I hope you enjoyed the collection! If you enjoyed Pretend, you should check out my other contemporary romance collection Hate Me or Love Me

ALSO BY ELLA MILES

SINFUL TRUTHS:

Sinful Truth #1

Twisted Vow #2

Reckless Fall #3

Tangled Promise #4

Fallen Love #5

Broken Anchor #6

TRUTH OR LIES:

Taken by Lies #1

Betrayed by Truths #2

Trapped by Lies #3

Stolen by Truths #4

Possessed by Lies #5

Consumed by Truths #6

DIRTY SERIES:

Dirty Beginning

Dirty Obsession

Dirty Addiction

Dirty Revenge

Dirty: The Complete Series

Not Sorry

ABOUT THE AUTHOR

Ella Miles writes steamy romance, including everything from dark suspense romance that will leave you on the edge of your seat to contemporary romance that will leave you laughing out loud or crying. Most importantly, she wants you to feel everything her characters feel as you read.

Ella is currently living her own happily ever after near the Rocky Mountains with her high school sweetheart husband. Her heart is also taken by her goofy five year old black lab who is scared of everything, including her own shadow.

Ella is a USA Today Bestselling Author & Top 50 Bestselling Author.

Stalk Ella at:
www.ellamiles.com
ella@ellamiles.com